ASCENDANCIES:

THE BEST OF
BRUCE STERLING

Subterranean Press • 2007

Ascendancies: The Best of Bruce Sterling
Copyright © 2007 Bruce Sterling.

Edited by Jonathan Strahan.

Contents

Introduction

by Karen Joy Fowler

My very first conversation with Bruce Sterling was about mass outbreaks of hysterical dancing. One of us was shockingly well-informed. Other topics we have discussed over the years: the Fox sisters and their toe-cracking séances, the aboriginal inhabitants of what is now Texas, the writings of Lafcadio Hearn plus the modern Japanese response to the 'Anne of Green Gables' books (the one subject leading inevitably to the other), Sasquatch sightings in the Washington territories, cyclical patterns in Chinese politics, feudal messianic movements. If the list trends (it does) toward my own interests and obsessions, this is because one of us is shockingly polite. There may be a subject Sterling cannot discuss with ease and erudition, but I haven't found it yet. Nor will you.

What I notice first about this new collection is the two groups of linked stories. The Shaper/Mechanist grouping is set in the far future. The place is space. These stories constitute some of Sterling's earlier work. The second group takes place in the near future and right here at home—Europe, Japan, Chattanooga, etc. This second group was written later but they happen earlier. It's just like the two Star Wars trilogies. This makes them tricky to talk about.

The protagonists of the first set, which is the last set, are barely human or not at all so. They have names like Spider Rose. The protagonists of the second set, which is the first set, are completely human. They have names like Spider Pete. Leggy Starlitz. Deep Eddy. The females in the near future are trained, armed, and earnest. The females in the far future are bulbous and have many eyes. What strikes me is how within the linked stories Sterling's tone is consistent, but from the first group to the second has changed completely.

The Shaper/Mechanist work is serious, even apocalyptic. The landscapes are grim and the plots grimmer. In contrast, the tone of the near future stories is detached and witty. Sterling is having fun and has chosen to do so conspicuously. This is true of his sentences as well as his plots. He's not the only one having fun. Sentences like "[double entendres] rose to his lips like drool from the id," certainly improve *my* mood. So do phrases like "Pamyat rightism with a mystical pan-Slavic spin" and "autonomous self-assembly proteinaceous biotech," at least when, like this, they're tossed about like confetti. A juggler appears briefly, wearing smart gloves, flinging "lit torches in flaming arcs three stories high." A dead soldier we'll never see again is described as having "come down from the heavens…a leaping, brick-busting, lightning-spewing exoskeleton, all acronyms and input jacks." Things are "fast, cheap, and out of control."

Europe may teem with terrorists—some of them Finnish nationalists, some of them devout Islamists, some of them Irish soccer fans. The web may have compiled Orwellian dossiers accessible to anyone with a bit of tech and a tolerance for burnt eyelids. The Chinese may be burying inconvenient ethnicities underground and pretending it's space travel. But Sterling is too interested in it all to be gloomy. It's not all bad news, of course. Gene-spliced ticks dispense athletic performance enhancers. You store them in your armpits!

His protagonists are just as unflappable as he is. The near future Sterling hero is nimble, fluent in the language of the moment, even-tempered even in defeat (though feminists do seem to make Leggy surly.) Most of all, this protagonist tends to be lucky. He's not himself an activist, though he's surrounded by them (and they don't look good)—idealists, terrorists, capitalists, sociologists, and all of them agents of mayhem. Inside the chaos, the Sterling hero looks for a niche, an angle, an obsession. His goals tend to be short term; his primary talent is in staying afloat when the water is really, really cold.

I don't mean to make these characters sound interchangeable. Leggy is slicker; Eddy is more romantic; Pete is more disciplined; Lyle is more centered. But they all share a certain innate Sterling-like cheerfulness.

Besides these linked stories, the collection contains other futures, some of them in the future, some of them not. Sterling is so often characterized as a futurist, it's easy to forget that his range extends backwards as well as forwards, that he's as interested in the futures of the past as he is in those of the future. (Who could trust a futurist who wasn't?)

"Dinner in Audoghast" takes place in Northern Africa around the year 1040. In it, an opulent evening's entertainment is marred by a leprous doom-prophesizing beggar. Part Cassandra, part Ozymandias, the story is the pure distillation of one of Sterling's recurring themes. What does "Dinner in Audoghast" have in common with "The Blemmye's Stratagem" (11th century, Holy Land), "Telliamed" (Marseille, 1737), "Flowers of Edo" (Kabukiza District, Edo, mid 1800's), "Our Neural Chernobyl" (Earth, 2056), "Swarm," (2248, planetoid circling Betelgeuse), "Spider Rose" (2283, habitat orbiting Uranus), "Cicada Queen" (2354, suburbs of the Czarina-Kluster), and "Sunken Gardens" (2554, Mars)?

In all these stories, the future is descending like a foot on an anthill. There can only be one Lobster King. If you think you're that guy, then maybe your happy ending is only one exoskeleton away. I'm guessing you're not.

Three of the stories here—"The Little Magic Shop," "The Sword of Damocles," and "Dori Bangs"—are metafictional and experimental. "Dori Bangs" is noteworthy for being openly heartfelt—not a move Sterling makes often—and for ending in poetry. Sterling's neither a writer who depends much on the white space in a story nor one who lingers at a resonant image. His style is and always has been exuberant, abundant, a combination of speed, noise, action, and, most of all, the dizzying accumulation of detail.

But take a look at the last paragraphs of the last story, "The Blemmye's Stratagem." It seems to me that what we have there is a poetic pause. Knowing how much Sterling admires the hearty, artless, genre stuff, I can only assume that any shift toward the literary is temporary and has come upon him by accident. Probably it would be rude to notice. So I've said nothing of the sort. You mistook me.

What Sterling tends to be admired most for is the level of invention in his work. Inventions that for other writers would underpin whole stories are crammed in here end over end. They often have nothing to do with the plot, but they have everything to do with the impact. More than the characters, more than the events, these tossed off inventions often feel like the point, the purpose of the story. One reads with the growing suspicion that maybe Sterling lives rather closer to the future than the rest of us do.

That's a good line, isn't it? It's not mine.

And the faster the future comes at us, the better Sterling's mood seems to get. So these stories are not only fun to read, but also, taken as a group, oddly comforting. If Sterling sees what's coming more clearly than I do, and he's not upset by it, at least not until 2248 or thereabouts, why should I be?

Admittedly, Sterling's comfort is the cold sort. In order to enjoy it, we have to avert our eyes from some troubling parallels between events on the ground in the far future story "Swarm" and the near future story "Taklamakan." We have to stop minding so much about the terrorists and such like. But, and speaking just for me here, I wouldn't believe in anything much warmer. Even from the pen of a world renowned, often quoted, much admired futurist like Bruce Sterling.

Foreword

by Bruce Sterling

Ascendancies is a compilation of my science fiction stories over the past three decades. This book is a career summary of sorts, so I feel a certain need to pull the fireproof curtain, bring you back into the hot, grimy forge here, and explain how these works came about.

I started reading science fiction stories at the age of thirteen. Before that time, I liked to read encyclopedias. In those pre-electronic days, encyclopedias were the densest textual knowledge I could find. There was something very refreshing to me in the way encyclopedias baldly tackled every conceivable issue wholesale. I thrived on that approach. Still, I didn't write any encyclopedias. I tried to write stories.

My earliest, faltering stories, written as a young teen, concerned two simple topics, (1) everything that ever now or formerly existed and (2) anything I saw fit to make up. In a word, they were encyclopedic. My work hasn't changed all that much since those days. I started as a young omnivore, I worked my way up to dilettante, and if I live long enough, I'll be a polymath.

Eventually, I became a science fiction writer, mostly through the kindly efforts of other people. A lot of authors loudly moan that writing is a lonely, neglected profession, but I never lacked for help and succor. Loved ones were positive, mentors and colleagues were thoughtful and honest, the fan community was supportive. I wrote almost all these stories in Austin, a particularly readerly city. You wouldn't guess it from the dire, edgy, hardscrabble tone of some of these texts, but life was sweet.

As an oil-company émigré kid much given to globetrotting, I quite liked it that there were aliens in science fiction. It particularly pleased me that so many of those aliens were the writers. Not just a host of deeply alienated American writers, whom I idolized. There were people like Stanislaw Lem: a Polish Communist was probably the best science fiction writer in the world. William Burroughs. Burroughs was a queer beatnik junkie. He was canaille. You couldn't even mention his name to teachers, to parents. Jules Verne, that hundred-year-old French Bohemian. And Italo Calvino. Calvino was doing things with ink on paper like nobody else on Earth. Calvino clearly had some kind of distinct agenda; you could really smell the midnight oil burning there. "**Cosmicomics.**" Whatever that was, that Italian guy was doing it on purpose.

I deeply admired practically every form of science fiction, especially the kinds that weren't entertaining. I had a lasting professional interest in kinds of science fiction that people could barely endure reading. Victorian tech-nothrillers. Outdated space operas. Soviet SF. Ticked-off feminist SF tracts: I took particular interest in those because it was so clear that I wasn't sup-posed to understand them.

I was always impressed by science fiction's deeply oxymoronic aspects: that it was wondrous yet trashy, elite yet cheap, obscure yet global, cosmic yet a gutter literature, a literature-of-ideas scared by literary ideologies. You may notice that all these contradictions are also true of the Internet now.

In my youth, science fiction writers were supposed to be hands-on paperback midlist guys who could dent the wire racks with truckloads of popular product. I was totally into that business model, but I turned out to be a rather artsy, fussy, highbrow, theory-driven, critics'-darling kind of sci-ence fiction writer. As you can see by these stories, I tried hard to avoid that. My basic attitude to the enterprise was about as determinedly pulpy and street-level as they come, but after thirty years of writing science fiction, I nevertheless became what I am. At this point in my life, I'm some kinda gypsy-scholar cyberpunk aesthete who writes for glossy magazines, teaches in design schools and keynotes European tech conferences. I have to admit I'm a little crestfallen.

Given a book like this one, though, the evidence is just irrefutable. I wonder guiltily what my spiritual ancestors would think of me.

Take, for instance, Robert E. Howard, who is definitely the patron saint of Texan science fiction writers like myself. "Two-Gun Bob," they used to call him. Howard was a raging, off-kilter guy from a scarily isolated West Texas village who, in order to save money and paper during the depths of the Depression, would type a new story *between the lines* of an earlier man-uscript. God knows what he did for ribbon ink. Or H.P. Lovecraft: living on 19 cents a day while writing endless morale-boosting letters to the far-flung members of his literary coterie. I've got a literary coterie, too, but at least I can send them email. I still bite my lips about Henry Kuttner. Kuttner could appear in ten or twelve SF magazines all at once, writing under a dozen pseudonyms, writing a new story *every day*. I once wrote a story in a single day, just like Henry Kuttner. Yeah, I did that: once.

Howard shot himself, Lovecraft perished of malnutrition and Kuttner died of a heart attack from too much desk work, but the Gothic prospect of writerly immolation never deterred me. Not a bit of it. Us 1970s rock 'n' roll counterculture no-future punk types, we considered that sort of activity romantic. Nevertheless, I have conspicuously failed to drop dead. As far as I can tell, I'm not even close. On the contrary, now that I'm in my supposedly stolid and sensible 50s, years when I ought to be finding a favorite easy chair, my life has become wildly frenetic: I travel incessantly and I scribble reams of scattershot journalism about design, architecture, politics, science.... I've already lived twice as long as John Keats.

As this tome amply demonstrates, my pen has gleaned my teeming brain in a high-piled book like a rich garner of the full-ripened grain (as young Mr. Keats used to put it). What might Mr. Keats make of the goods purveyed here? His poesy rarely lacked for the florid and phantastic, but I mean, really: spacey posthumans, intelligent raccoons, anarchist bike mechanics... stand-up comedians from Meiji Japan, computer-crime investigators... Furthermore, **Ascendancies** contains the calmer, more lucid and considered material from the Sterling oeuvre.

Keats was a gifted critic and had things to say about writing that I took to heart: yes, "load every rift with ore." I have ored my share of rifts in here, but would Keats be able to parse a single paragraph? I might mention that John Keats himself appears as a minor character in one of my novels. Not as a poet. He's a computer programmer. That may have been impolite of me.

There's just no getting around it: these stories are plenty weird. They're not merely about weird topics. These texts are conjured up and stuck together in peculiar, idiosyncratic ways. Since I've been known to write reviews, I know what stories are supposed to look like. These stories don't look much like that. My stories strongly tend to be laborious and over-crowded, with frazzled wiring and excessive moving parts. They writhe in organic profusion. They're antic, snarled and open-ended. This book makes it pretty obvious that I've worked like that during my entire creative life. Somehow, I must know what I'm doing.

It alarms me now to see how much these texts, many of them written on typewriters decades ago, look and feel like contemporary websurfing. They have that cyberized "more is more" aesthetic, like techno music and software art. Sometimes it's pitifully easy to predict the future.

As a weblogger and tech journalist, I find myself doing a great deal of web-surfing these days. I work on computer screens much more than I work on paper. Websurfing is ominously different from classical literature, in that it's machine-assisted and basically infinite in scope. Websurfing bears the relationship to reading that movies do to oil-paint. Email, web-posts, digital photographs, streaming speeches on video.... The web has no ends, no beginnings, no arc of development, no denouement, no plot. The web has no center, no heart. The web has data. It has tags and terms. Increasingly, the web has something like a native semantics. As a tech journalist and futurist, I'm fascinated; as a literateur, I look on these developments with alarmed misgivings. They're just not well understood. I ought to be in the business of understanding a transition like that. Frankly, I can't say that I do.

It worries me that the Internet suits my own sensibilities so much better than ink on paper ever did. These stories of mine are still "stories," but instead of being well-contained verbal contrivances, disciplined and redolent of literary-cultural sensemaking, Sterling texts generally look-and-feel like they could do with some hotlinks and keywords. Maybe a scrollbar.

Sterling stories are nets of ideas and images that have been bent, tucked and pruned into a pocket world. Their literary sensibility—and they do have one—is in the worldbuilding. It's about the settings, the semiotics. And the feelings. Not the characters' feelings—mostly, the key to these stories is the *narrator's* feelings. With one brisk exception, the narrator's not a character within these stories, but he's the busiest guy in this book. In his lighter moments, he exhibits a certain amiable boyish gusto, like some kid happily mangling encyclopedias. His most common affect, as he razors and duct-tapes, is sinister glee.

The writer of these pieces, like a lot of comedians, has a rather dark muse. His inner child is the kind of kid that pokes anthills with a stick. The lad just can't let those ants be; he direly needs to satirize the ants a little, to jolt them out of their mental ant-box. Science fiction writing can be a problematic effort. Annoying ants is not a major literary enterprise. Why? Because ants don't get illuminated by that artistic intervention; ants are just ants. Imagined worlds have so many phony, sandbox aspects.... science fiction makes head-fakes toward profundity, which too often turn out to be mere sleights of hand, in-jokes, trivial paradoxes, vaudeville.... Like a trained flea-circus, where the fleas are dressed as six-armed Martian swordsmen.

Sense of wonder? Too short a shelf-life. Blowing people's minds? Like stage magic, that's done mostly through misdirection. Happy, upbeat endings? Depends on when you stop telling the story.

Are there other burning lamentations one might offer about the cruel creative agony and the dire existential limits involved in writing science fiction stories? Well, now that you insist on asking me, yeah. For instance, this big Bruce Sterling collection sure does have a lot of Bruce Sterling in it. My other story collections tend to feature some pleasant collaborations with other writers, which break up that relentless Sterlingness.

I used to spend rather a lot of my time and energy trying to write stories that nobody else could write. You know: unique, original, ground-breaking, non-derivative work. Young writers suffer anxiety-of-influence, so they attempt a lot of that. Some of these stories are much in that vein. "Finding one's own voice," they call that.

It might also be dignified with the term "self-actualization." Self-actualization is a conceptual, very writerly game in which one tries to become as much like Bruce Sterling as one can. There's much to be said for that activity, especially if one actually is Bruce Sterling. However, when a science fiction writer pursues that line of development, in that particularly oracular and eccentric science-fictional way, it can be rather trying to the reader. "Okay, fine, pal, nobody but you could have ever conceived of that notion. That was totally, utterly unheard-of. Great. So how come I have to read about that?" Now that you ask, that's another good question.

The way that certain SF writers cough up those raw crunchy nuggets of the barely thinkable... well, that's one of the connoisseur delights of SF as a genre. It's like whales and their ambergris. Rare and superb in small amounts, rather scary in large beached lumps. Furthermore, as an artistic program, it's dubious. Suppose you're radically self-actualized, but you're also a delusional goofball. Wouldn't you do better by seeking some cues from objective reality, rather than hearkening always to those magic promptings of the inner self?

Furthermore: just suppose that, like me, your inner self is, for obscure design-fan reasons, deeply inspired by forks, manhole covers and doorknobs, rather than raucous, technicolor, crowd-pleasing sci-fi gizmos such as robots, rocketships and time machines. If you write a sci-fi book about forks and manhole covers, will that be a great work? No. It won't. Because forks and manhole covers are not entertaining. They're boring. Not to you, of course; you adore manhole covers. Manhole covers are very you. But they're also incredibly boring. They just plain are.

Original genius, that's not everything in the world. The world is more significant than the inside of anybody's head. Sometimes you're well-advised to just get over yourself.

If your thoughts were genuinely original—literally unthinkable by other people—then you could never express them in a language sharable with readers. That's not what writing is about. Literature is a heritage. Language is a commons. Language is centuries old and enriched by thousands of minds. Language and literature need to be treated with a sensitivity and care which doesn't always mesh with raw, kraken-busting sci-fi aesthetics. I know that, and I further know that, as a writer, I ought to do better at that. Is there any clear sign of my making any progress along that front, within these stories? Am I fighting the good fight here, or am I pretty much part of the problem? I do have to wonder.

A writer pestered with truly original thoughts would have to make up new nouns, new verbs. Frankly, I do a great deal of that. My writing in this book—in all my books—is cram-full of invented jargon and singular idiolects. It's a signature riff of mine that I compose a great many words and terms that no mere computer spell-checker understands. I'm trying to get a little subtler about that. It works best when people don't notice I'm doing it.

With all this anguished authorly handwringing, you might wonder how stories like these get written at all. But they do get written; they even get finished and sent off to publishers. I got one coming out next month. It's not in this book, but man, it's aces. I've got a hundred ideas for other ones—really weird ideas—but, well, ideas aren't stories. As stories, I've yet to get them done.

A Sterling story is generally done—or it stops, at least—when the writer's inner creative daemon has fully stacked up its Lego blocks.

Rational analysis is never the strong suit of the inner daemon. The inner daemon is profoundly creative, yet he's rather stupid. A creative daemon by nature is a rather simple, headstrong being who sees the cosmos as daemon-friendly toy-blocks. The daemon assembles a mental world from a raw confusion into some meaningful coherency. He does that through assembling his blocks. The daemon himself is made of the blocks. He's not a conscious personality, he's much lower in the chain-of-being than that; the daemon is a sense-making network, some pre-conscious society-of-mind. The daemon is a capturer of imagination. That's his reason for being.

When the daemon is on top of his game, he can whip up a story from his shadowy basement of mentality. A story is a tower of blocks, one with some coherent structure of feeling. A story says something evocative about the world, it somehow means something… Then the conscious mind can bind that in wire, slap on a label and ship it.

That's how I write stories. That's how these works came into being. Thanks for putting up with that confession. I rather hope to do a lot more of that. I don't do it with any particular regularity because I'm not fully in control of the process. The same goes for a lot of artists. You learn to live with that.

So: a few closing notes now somehow seem necessary. Let me explain the title of this book. From some mysterious cataloging bug or cyber-mechanical oversight, a book called "Ascendancies" was attributed to me back in 1987. "Ascendancies" frequently appears in bibliographies of mine. For years, people have written me eager fan mail determined to locate my book, "Ascendancies". I never wrote that book. I don't think I ever used the word, either. Still "Ascendancies" is quite a pretty-looking word, almost a palindrome: "Seicnadnecsa." It'll do.

Better yet, the sudden appearance of a genuine "Ascendancies" by Bruce Sterling, a full twenty years in the future after its announced publication date, is a time-travel paradox that will drive bibliographers nuts. Deeply confusing my audience, librarians, and the industry in toto: hey, just another service we offer.

In conclusion, I'd like to formally thank every rugged, determined, anonymous consumer who, through a host of small purchases, has given American science fiction something like an economic basis. Nobody ever thanks these noble people; they're considered to be some kind of vast, rumbling mass audience, but, well, they're all individuals. Every one of them is individual. Reading is a solitary pursuit. Writing as an art is the mingling of one mind with one other. But there are lots of American readers, and thank goodness. In some smaller society with a smaller language, I'd have quite likely done this sort of thing anyway, yet never been paid one shekel, ruble, peso, real or dinar. So that was great luck for all concerned, eh? Fate has truly been kind! Let's hope we all do more of that!

PART I:

THE SHAPER/MECHANIST STORIES

Swarm

"I will miss your conversation during the rest of the voyage," the alien said.

Captain-Doctor Simon Afriel folded his jeweled hands over his gold-embroidered waistcoat. "I regret it also, ensign," he said in the alien's own hissing language. "Our talks together have been very useful to me. I would have paid to learn so much, but you gave it freely."

"But that was only information," the alien said. He shrouded his bead-bright eyes behind thick nictitating membranes. "We Investors deal in energy, and precious metals. To prize and pursue mere knowledge is an immature racial trait." The alien lifted the long ribbed frill behind his pinhole-sized ears.

"No doubt you are right," Afriel said, despising him. "We humans are as children to other races, however; so a certain immaturity seems natural to us." Afriel pulled off his sunglasses to rub the bridge of his nose. The starship cabin was drenched in searing blue light, heavily ultraviolet. It was the light the Investors preferred, and they were not about to change it for one human passenger.

"You have not done badly," the alien said magnanimously. "You are the kind of race we like to do business with: young, eager, plastic, ready for a wide variety of goods and experiences. We would have contacted you much earlier, but your technology was still too feeble to afford us a profit."

"Things are different now," Afriel said. "We'll make you rich."

"Indeed," the Investor said. The frill behind his scaly head flickered rapidly, a sign of amusement. "Within two hundred years you will be wealthy enough to buy from us the secret of our starflight. Or perhaps your Mechanist faction will discover the secret through research."

Afriel was annoyed. As a member of the Reshaped faction, he did not appreciate the reference to the rival Mechanists. "Don't put too much stock in mere technical expertise," he said. "Consider the aptitude for languages we Shapers have. It makes our faction a much better trading partner. To a Mechanist, all Investors look alike."

The alien hesitated. Afriel smiled. He had appealed to the alien's personal ambition with his last statement, and the hint had been taken. That was where the Mechanists always erred. They tried to treat all Investors consistently, using the same programmed routines each time. They lacked imagination.

Something would have to be done about the Mechanists, Afriel thought. Something more permanent than the small but deadly confrontations between isolated ships in the Asteroid Belt and the ice-rich Rings of Saturn. Both factions maneuvered constantly, looking for a decisive stroke, bribing away each other's best talent, practicing ambush, assassination, and industrial espionage.

Captain-Doctor Simon Afriel was a past master of these pursuits. That was why the Reshaped faction had paid the millions of kilowatts necessary to buy his passage. Afriel held doctorates in biochemistry and alien linguistics, and a master's degree in magnetic weapons engineering. He was thirty-eight years old and had been Reshaped according to the state of the art at the time of his conception. His hormonal balance had been altered slightly to compensate for long periods spent in free-fall. He had no appendix. The structure of his heart had been redesigned for greater efficiency, and his large intestine had been altered to produce the vitamins normally made by intestinal bacteria. Genetic engineering and rigorous training in childhood had given him an intelligence quotient of one hundred and eighty. He was not the brightest of the agents of the Ring Council, but he was one of the most mentally stable and the best trusted.

"It seems a shame," the alien said, "that a human of your accomplishments should have to rot for two years in this miserable, profitless outpost."

"The years won't be wasted," Afriel said.

"But why have you chosen to study the Swarm? They can teach you nothing, since they cannot speak. They have no wish to trade, having no tools or technology. They are the only spacefaring race that is essentially without intelligence."

"That alone should make them worthy of study."

"Do you seek to imitate them, then? You would make monsters of yourselves." Again the ensign hesitated. "Perhaps you could do it. It would be bad for business, however."

There came a fluting burst of alien music over the ship's speakers, then a screeching fragment of Investor language. Most of it was too high-pitched for Afriel's ears to follow.

The alien stood, his jeweled skirt brushing the tips of his clawed bird-like feet. "The Swarm's symbiote has arrived," he said.

"Thank you," Afriel said. When the ensign opened the cabin door, Afriel could smell the Swarm's representative; the creature's warm yeasty scent had spread rapidly through the starship's recycled air.

Afriel quickly checked his appearance in a pocket mirror. He touched powder to his face and straightened the round velvet hat on his shoulder-length reddish-blond hair. His earlobes glittered with red impact-rubies, thick as his thumbs' ends, mined from the Asteroid Belt. His knee-length coat and waistcoat were of gold brocade; the shirt beneath was of dazzling fineness, woven with red-gold thread. He had dressed to impress the Investors, who expected and appreciated a prosperous look from their customers. How could he impress this new alien? Smell, perhaps. He freshened his perfume.

Beside the starship's secondary airlock, the Swarm's symbiote was chittering rapidly at the ship's commander. The commander was an old and sleepy Investor, twice the size of most of her crewmen. Her massive head was encrusted in a jeweled helmet. From within the helmet her clouded eyes glittered like cameras.

The symbiote lifted on its six posterior legs and gestured feebly with its four clawed forelimbs. The ship's artificial gravity, a third again as strong as Earth's, seemed to bother it. Its rudimentary eyes, dangling on stalks, were shut tight against the glare. It must be used to darkness, Afriel thought.

The commander answered the creature in its own language. Afriel grimaced, for he had hoped that the creature spoke Investor. Now he would have to learn another language, a language designed for a being without a tongue.

After another brief interchange the commander turned to Afriel. "The symbiote is not pleased with your arrival," she told Afriel in the Investor language. "There has apparently been some disturbance here involving humans, in the recent past. However, I have prevailed upon it to admit you to the Nest. The episode has been recorded. Payment for my diplomatic services will be arranged with your faction when I return to your native star system."

"I thank Your Authority," Afriel said. "Please convey to the symbiote my best personal wishes, and the harmlessness and humility of my intentions…" He broke off short as the symbiote lunged toward him, biting him savagely in the calf of his left leg. Afriel jerked free and leapt backward in the heavy artificial gravity, going into a defensive position. The symbiote had ripped away a long shred of his pants leg; it now crouched quietly, eating it.

"It will convey your scent and composition to its nestmates," said the commander. "This is necessary. Otherwise you would be classed as an invader, and the Swarm's warrior caste would kill you at once."

Afriel relaxed quickly and pressed his hand against the puncture wound to stop the bleeding. He hoped that none of the Investors had noticed his reflexive action. It would not mesh well with his story of being a harmless researcher.

"We will reopen the airlock soon," the commander said phlegmatically, leaning back on her thick reptilian tail. The symbiote continued to munch the shred of cloth. Afriel studied the creature's neckless segmented head. It had a mouth and nostrils; it had bulbous atrophied eyes on stalks; there were hinged slats that might be radio receivers, and two parallel ridges of clumped wriggling antennae, sprouting among three chitinous plates. Their function was unknown to him.

The airlock door opened. A rush of dense, smoky aroma entered the departure cabin. It seemed to bother the half-dozen Investors, who left rapidly. "We will return in six hundred and twelve of your days, as by our agreement," the commander said.

"I thank Your Authority," Afriel said.

"Good luck," the commander said in English. Afriel smiled.

The symbiote, with a sinuous wriggle of its segmented body, crept into the airlock. Afriel followed it. The airlock door shut behind them. The creature said nothing to him but continued munching loudly. The second door opened, and the symbiote sprang through it, into a wide, round stone tunnel. It disappeared at once into the gloom.

Afriel put his sunglasses into a pocket of his jacket and pulled out a pair of infrared goggles. He strapped them to his head and stepped out of the airlock. The artificial gravity vanished, replaced by the almost imperceptible gravity of the Swarm's asteroid nest. Afriel smiled, comfortable for the first time in weeks. Most of his adult life had been spent in free-fall, in the Shapers' colonies in the Rings of Saturn.

Squatting in a dark cavity in the side of the tunnel was a disk-headed furred animal the size of an elephant. It was clearly visible in the infrared of its own body heat. Afriel could hear it breathing. It waited patiently until Afriel had launched himself past it, deeper into the tunnel. Then it took its place in the end of the tunnel, puffing itself up with air until its swollen head securely plugged the exit into space. Its multiple legs sank firmly into sockets in the walls.

The Investors' ship had left. Afriel remained here, inside one of the millions of planetoids that circled the giant star Betelgeuse in a girdling ring with almost five times the mass of Jupiter. As a source of potential wealth it dwarfed the entire solar system, and it belonged, more or less, to the Swarm. At least, no other race had challenged them for it within the memory of the Investors.

Afriel peered up the corridor. It seemed deserted, and without other bodies to cast infrared heat, he could not see very far. Kicking against the wall, he floated hesitantly down the corridor.

He heard a human voice. "Dr. Afriel!"

"Dr. Mirny!" he called out. "This way!"

He first saw a pair of young symbiotes scuttling toward him, the tips of their clawed feet barely touching the walls. Behind them came a woman wearing goggles like his own. She was young, and attractive in the trim, anonymous way of the genetically reshaped.

She screeched something at the symbiotes in their own language, and they halted, waiting. She coasted forward, and Afriel caught her arm, expertly stopping their momentum.

"You didn't bring any luggage?" she said anxiously.

He shook his head. "We got your warning before I was sent out. I have only the clothes I'm wearing and a few items in my pockets."

She looked at him critically. "Is that what people are wearing in the Rings these days? Things have changed more than I thought."

Afriel glanced at his brocaded coat and laughed. "It's a matter of policy. The Investors are always readier to talk to a human who looks ready to do business on a large scale. All the Shapers' representatives dress like this these days. We've stolen a jump on the Mechanists; they still dress in those coveralls."

He hesitated, not wanting to offend her. Galina Mirny's intelligence was rated at almost two hundred. Men and women that bright were sometimes flighty and unstable, likely to retreat into private fantasy worlds or become enmeshed in strange and impenetrable webs of plotting and rationalization. High intelligence was the strategy the Shapers had chosen in the struggle for cultural dominance, and they were obliged to stick to it, despite its occasional disadvantages. They had tried breeding the Superbright—those with quotients over two hundred—but so many had defected from the Shapers' colonies that the faction had stopped producing them.

"You wonder about my own clothing," Mirny said.

"It certainly has the appeal of novelty," Afriel said with a smile.

"It was woven from the fibers of a pupa's cocoon," she said. "My original wardrobe was eaten by a scavenger symbiote during the troubles last year. I usually go nude, but I didn't want to offend you by too great a show of intimacy."

Afriel shrugged. "I often go nude myself, I never had much use for clothes except for pockets. I have a few tools on my person, but most are of little importance. We're Shapers, our tools are here." He tapped his head. "If you can show me a safe place to put my clothes…"

She shook her head. It was impossible to see her eyes for the goggles, which made her expression hard to read. "You've made your first mistake, Doctor. There are no places of our own here. It was the same mistake the Mechanist agents made, the same one that almost killed me as well. There is no concept of privacy or property here. This is the Nest. If you seize any part of it for yourself—to store equipment, to sleep in, whatever—then you become an intruder, an enemy. The two Mechanists—a man and a woman—tried to secure an empty chamber for their computer lab. Warriors broke down their door and devoured them. Scavengers ate their equipment, glass, metal, and all."

Afriel smiled coldly. "It must have cost them a fortune to ship all that material here."

Mirny shrugged. "They're wealthier than we are. Their machines, their mining. They meant to kill me, I think. Surreptitiously, so the warriors wouldn't be upset by a show of violence. They had a computer that was learning the language of the springtails faster than I could."

"But you survived," Afriel pointed out. "And your tapes and reports—especially the early ones, when you still had most of your equipment—were of tremendous interest. The Council is behind you all the way. You've become quite a celebrity in the Rings, during your absence."

"Yes, I expected as much," she said.

Afriel was nonplused. "If I found any deficiency in them," he said carefully, "it was in my own field, alien linguistics." He waved vaguely at the two symbiotes who accompanied her. "I assume you've made great progress in communicating with the symbiotes, since they seem to do all the talking for the Nest."

She looked at him with an unreadable expression and shrugged. "There are at least fifteen different kinds of symbiotes here. Those that accompany me are called the springtails, and they speak only for themselves. They are savages, Doctor, who received attention from the Investors only because they can still talk. They were a spacefaring race once, but they've forgotten it. They discovered the Nest and they were absorbed, they became parasites." She tapped one of them on the head. "I tamed these two because I learned to steal and beg food better than they can. They stay with me now and protect me from the larger ones. They are jealous, you know. They have only been with the Nest for perhaps ten thousand years and are still uncertain of their position. They still think, and wonder sometimes. After ten thousand years there is still a little of that left to them."

"Savages," Afriel said. "I can well believe that. One of them bit me while I was still aboard the starship. He left a lot to be desired as an ambassador."

"Yes, I warned him you were coming," said Mirny. "He didn't much like the idea, but I was able to bribe him with food...I hope he didn't hurt you badly."

"A scratch," Afriel said. "I assume there's no chance of infection."

"I doubt it very much. Unless you brought your own bacteria with you."

"Hardly likely," Afriel said, offended. "I have no bacteria. And I wouldn't have brought microorganisms to an alien culture anyway."

Mirny looked away. "I thought you might have some of the special genetically altered ones...I think we can go now. The springtail will have spread your scent by mouth-touching in the subsidiary chamber, ahead of us. It will be spread throughout the Nest in a few hours. Once it reaches the Queen, it will spread very quickly."

She jammed her feet against the hard shell of one of the young springtails and launched herself down the hall. Afriel followed her. The air was warm and he was beginning to sweat under his elaborate clothing, but his antiseptic sweat was odorless.

They exited into a vast chamber dug from the living rock. It was arched and oblong, eighty meters long and about twenty in diameter. It swarmed with members of the Nest.

There were hundreds of them. Most of them were workers, eight-legged and furred, the size of Great Danes. Here and there were members of the warrior caste, horse-sized furry monsters with heavy fanged heads the size and shape of overstuffed chairs.

A few meters away, two workers were carrying a member of the sensor caste, a being whose immense flattened head was attached to an atrophied body that was mostly lungs. The sensor had great platelike eyes, and its furred chitin sprouted long coiled antennae that twitched feebly as the workers bore it along. The workers clung to the hollowed rock of the chamber walls with hooked and suckered feet.

A paddle-limbed monster with a hairless, faceless head came sculling past them, through the warm reeking air. The front of its head was a nightmare of sharp grinding jaws and blunt armored acid spouts. "A tunneler," Mirny said. "It can take us deeper into the Nest—come with me." She launched herself toward it and took a handhold on its furry, segmented back. Afriel followed her, joined by the two immature springtails, who clung to the thing's hide with their forelimbs. Afriel shuddered at the warm, greasy feel of its rank, damp fur. It continued to scull through the air, its eight fringed paddle feet catching the air like wings.

"There must be thousands of them," Afriel said.

"I said a hundred thousand in my last report, but that was before I had fully explored the Nest. Even now there are long stretches I haven't seen. They must number close to a quarter of a million. This asteroid is about the size of the Mechanists' biggest base—Ceres. It still has rich veins of carbonaceous material. It's far from mined out."

Afriel closed his eyes. If he was to lose his goggles, he would have to feel his way, blind, through these teeming, twitching, wriggling thousands. "The population's still expanding, then?"

"Definitely," she said. "In fact, the colony will launch a mating swarm soon. There are three dozen male and female alates in the chambers near the Queen. Once they're launched, they'll mate and start new Nests. I'll take you to see them presently." She hesitated. "We're entering one of the fungal gardens now."

One of the young springtails quietly shifted position. Grabbing the tunneler's fur with its forelimbs, it began to gnaw on the cuff of Afriel's pants. Afriel kicked it soundly, and it jerked back, retracting its eyestalks.

When he looked up again, he saw that they had entered a second chamber, much larger than the first. The walls around, overhead, and below were buried under an explosive profusion of fungus. The most common types were swollen barrellike domes, multibranched massed thickets, and spaghetti-like tangled extrusions that moved very slightly in the faint and odorous breeze. Some of the barrels were surrounded by dim mists of exhaled spores.

"You see those caked-up piles beneath the fungus, its growth medium?" Mirny said.

"Yes."

"I'm not sure whether it is a plant form or just some kind of complex biochemical sludge," she said. "The point is that it grows in sunlight, on the outside of the asteroid. A food source that grows in naked space! Imagine what that would be worth, back in the Rings."

'There aren't words for its value," Afriel said.

"It's inedible by itself," she said. "I tried to eat a very small piece of it once. It was like trying to eat plastic."

"Have you eaten well, generally speaking?"

"Yes. Our biochemistry is quite similar to the Swarm's. The fungus itself is perfectly edible. The regurgitate is more nourishing, though. Internal fermentation in the worker hindgut adds to its nutritional value."

Afriel stared. "You grow used to it," Mirny said. "Later I'll teach you how to solicit food from the workers. It's a simple matter of reflex tapping—it's not controlled by pheromones, like most of their behavior." She brushed a long lock of clumped and dirty hair from the side of her face. "I hope the pheromonal samples I sent back were worth the cost of transportation."

"Oh, yes," said Afriel. "The chemistry of them was fascinating. We managed to synthesize most of the compounds. I was part of the research team myself." He hesitated. How far did he dare trust her? She had not been told about the experiment he and his superiors had planned. As far as Mirny knew, he was a simple, peaceful researcher, like herself. The Shapers' scientific community was suspicious of the minority involved in military work and espionage.

As an investment in the future, the Shapers had sent researchers to each of the nineteen alien races described to them by the Investors. This had cost the Shaper economy many gigawatts of precious energy and tons of rare metals and isotopes. In most cases, only two or three researchers could be sent; in seven cases, only one. For the Swarm, Galina Mirny had been chosen. She had gone peacefully, trusting in her intelligence and her good intentions to keep her alive and sane. Those who had sent her had not known whether her findings would be of any use or importance. They had only known that it was imperative that she be sent, even alone, even ill-equipped, before some other faction sent their own people and possibly discovered some technique or fact of overwhelming importance. And Dr. Mirny had indeed discovered such a situation. It had made her mission into a matter of Ring security. That was why Afriel had come.

"You synthesized the compounds?" she said. "Why?"

Afriel smiled disarmingly. "Just to prove to ourselves that we could do it, perhaps."

She shook her head. "No mind-games, Dr. Afriel, please. I came this far partly to escape from such things. Tell me the truth."

Afriel stared at her, regretting that the goggles meant he could not meet her eyes. "Very well," he said. "You should know, then, that I have been ordered by the Ring Council to carry out an experiment that may endanger both our lives."

Mirny was silent for a moment. "You're from Security, then?"

"My rank is captain."

"I knew it...I knew it when those two Mechanists arrived. They were so polite, and so suspicious—I think they would have killed me at once if they hadn't hoped to bribe or torture some secret out of me. They scared the life out of me, Captain Afriel...You scare me, too."

"We live in a frightening world, Doctor. It's a matter of faction security."

"Everything's a matter of faction security with your lot," she said. "I shouldn't take you any farther, or show you anything more. This Nest, these creatures—they're not intelligent, Captain. They can't think, they can't learn. They're innocent, primordially innocent. They have no knowledge of good and evil. They have no knowledge of anything. The last thing they need is to become pawns in a power struggle within some other race, light-years away."

The tunneler had turned into an exit from the fungal chambers and was paddling slowly along in the warm darkness. A group of creatures like gray, flattened basketballs floated by from the opposite direction. One of them settled on Afriel's sleeve, clinging with frail whiplike tentacles. Afriel brushed it gently away, and it broke loose, emitting a stream of foul reddish droplets.

"Naturally I agree with you in principle, Doctor," Afriel said smoothly. "But consider these Mechanists. Some of their extreme factions are already more than half machine. Do you expect humanitarian motives from them? They're cold, Doctor—cold and soulless creatures who can cut a living man or woman to bits and never feel their pain. Most of the other factions hate us. They call us racist supermen. Would you rather that one of these cults do what we must do, and use the results against us?"

"This is double-talk." She looked away. All around them workers laden down with fungus, their jaws full and guts stuffed with it, were spreading out into the Nest, scuttling alongside them or disappearing into branch tunnels departing in every direction, including straight up and straight down. Afriel saw a creature much like a worker, but with only six legs, scuttle past in the opposite direction, overhead. It was a parasite mimic. How long, he wondered, did it take a creature to evolve to look like that?

"It's no wonder that we've had so many defectors, back in the Rings," she said sadly. "If humanity is so stupid as to work itself into a corner like you describe, then it's better to have nothing to do with them. Better to live alone. Better not to help the madness spread."

"That kind of talk will only get us killed," Afriel said. "We owe an allegiance to the faction that produced us."

"Tell me truly, Captain," she said. "Haven't you ever felt the urge to leave everything—everyone—all your duties and constraints, and just go somewhere to think it all out? Your whole world, and your part in it? We're trained so hard, from childhood, and so much is demanded from us. Don't you think it's made us lose sight of our goals, somehow?"

"We live in space," Afriel said flatly. "Space is an unnatural environment, and it takes an unnatural effort from unnatural people to prosper there. Our minds are our tools, and philosophy has to come second. Naturally I've felt those urges you mention. They're just another threat to guard against. I believe in an ordered society. Technology has unleashed tremendous forces that are ripping society apart. Some one faction must arise from the struggle and integrate things. We Shapers have the wisdom and restraint to do it humanely. That's why I do the work I do." He hesitated. "I don't expect to see our day of triumph. I expect to die in some brush-fire conflict, or through assassination. It's enough that I can foresee that day."

"But the arrogance of it, Captain!" she said suddenly. "The arrogance of your little life and its little sacrifice! Consider the Swarm, if you really want your humane and perfect order. Here it is! Where it's always warm and dark, and it smells good, and food is easy to get, and everything is endlessly and perfectly recycled. The only resources that are ever lost are the bodies of the mating swarms, and a little air. A Nest like this one could last unchanged for hundreds of thousands of years. Hundreds…of thousands…of years. Who, or what, will remember us and our stupid faction in even a thousand years?"

Afriel shook his head. "That's not a valid comparison. There is no such long view for us. In another thousand years we'll be machines, or gods." He felt the top of his head; his velvet cap was gone. No doubt something was eating it by now.

The tunneler took them deeper into the asteroid's honeycombed freefall maze. They saw the pupal chambers, where pallid larvae twitched in swaddled silk; the main fungal gardens; the graveyard pits, where winged workers beat ceaselessly at the soupy air, feverishly hot from the heat of decomposition. Corrosive black fungus ate the bodies of the dead into coarse black powder, carried off by blackened workers themselves three-quarters dead.

Later they left the tunneler and floated on by themselves. The woman moved with the ease of long habit; Afriel followed her, colliding bruisingly with squeaking workers. There were thousands of them, clinging to ceiling, walls, and floor, clustering and scurrying at every conceivable angle.

Later still they visited the chamber of the winged princes and princesses, an echoing round vault where creatures forty meters long hung crooked-legged in midair. Their bodies were segmented and metallic, with organic rocket nozzles on their thoraxes, where wings might have been. Folded along their sleek backs were radar antennae on long sweeping booms. They looked more like interplanetary probes under construction than anything biological. Workers fed them ceaselessly. Their bulging spiracled abdomens were full of compressed oxygen.

Mirny begged a large chunk of fungus from a passing worker, deftly tapping its antennae and provoking a reflex action. She handed most of the fungus to the two springtails, which devoured it greedily and looked expectantly for more.

Afriel tucked his legs into a free-fall lotus position and began chewing with determination on the leathery fungus. It was tough, but tasted good, like smoked meat—a delicacy he had tasted only once. The smell of smoke meant disaster in a Shaper's colony.

Mirny maintained a stony silence. "Food's no problem," Afriel said. "Where do we sleep?"

She shrugged. "Anywhere...there are unused niches and tunnels here and there. I suppose you'll want to see the Queen's chamber next."

"By all means."

"I'll have to get more fungus. The warriors are on guard there and have to be bribed with food."

She gathered an armful of fungus from another worker in the endless stream, and they moved on. Afriel, already totally lost, was further confused in the maze of chambers and tunnels. At last they exited into an immense lightless cavern, bright with infrared heat from the Queen's monstrous body. It was the colony's central factory. The fact that it was made of warm and pulpy flesh did not conceal its essentially industrial nature. Tons of predigested fungal pap went into the slick blind jaws at one end. The rounded billows of soft flesh digested and processed it, squirming, sucking, and undulating, with loud machinelike churnings and gurglings. Out of the other end came an endless conveyor-like blobbed stream of eggs, each one packed in a thick hormonal paste of lubrication. The workers avidly licked the eggs clean and bore them off to nurseries. Each egg was the size of a man's torso.

The process went on and on. There was no day or night here in the lightless center of the asteroid. There was no remnant of a diurnal rhythm in the genes of these creatures. The flow of production was as constant and even as the working of an automated mine.

"This is why I'm here," Afriel murmured in awe. "Just look at this, Doctor. The Mechanists have cybernetic mining machinery that is generations ahead of ours. But here—in the bowels of this nameless little world, is a genetic technology that feeds itself, maintains itself, runs itself, efficiently, endlessly, mindlessly. It's the perfect organic tool. The faction that could use these tireless workers could make itself an industrial titan. And our knowledge of biochemistry is unsurpassed. We Shapers are just the ones to do it."

"How do you propose to do that?" Mirny asked with open skepticism. "You would have to ship a fertilized queen all the way to the solar system. We could scarcely afford that, even if the Investors would let us, which they wouldn't."

"I don't need an entire Nest," Afriel said patiently. "I only need the genetic information from one egg. Our laboratories back in the Rings could clone endless numbers of workers."

"But the workers are useless without the Nest's pheromones. They need chemical cues to trigger their behavior modes."

"Exactly," Afriel said. "As it so happens, I possess those pheromones, synthesized and concentrated. What I must do now is test them. I must prove that I can use them to make the workers do what I choose. Once I've proven it's possible, I'm authorized to smuggle the genetic information necessary back to the Rings. The Investors won't approve. There are, of course, moral questions involved, and the Investors are not genetically advanced. But we can win their approval back with the profits we make. Best of all, we can beat the Mechanists at their own game."

"You've carried the pheromones here?" Mirny said. "Didn't the Investors suspect something when they found them?"

"Now it's you who has made an error," Afriel said calmly. "You assume that the Investors are infallible. You are wrong. A race without curiosity will never explore every possibility, the way we Shapers did." Afriel pulled up his pants cuff and extended his right leg. "Consider this varicose vein along my shin. Circulatory problems of this sort are common among those who spend a lot of time in free-fall. This vein, however, has been blocked artificially and treated to reduce osmosis. Within the vein are ten separate colonies of genetically altered bacteria, each one specially bred to produce a different Swarm pheromone."

He smiled. "The Investors searched me very thoroughly, including X-rays. But the vein appears normal to X-rays, and the bacteria are trapped within compartments in the vein. They are indetectable. I have a small medical kit on my person. It includes a syringe. We can use it to extract the pheromones and test them. When the tests are finished—and I feel sure they will be successful, in fact I've staked my career on it—we can empty the vein and all its compartments. The bacteria will die on contact with air. We can refill the vein with the yolk from a developing embryo. The cells may survive during the trip back, but even if they die, they can't rot inside my body. They'll never come in contact with any agent of decay. Back in the Rings, we can learn to activate and suppress different genes to produce the different castes, just as is done in nature. We'll have millions of workers, armies of warriors if need be, perhaps even organic rocket-ships, grown from altered alates. If this works, who do you think will remember me then, eh? Me and my arrogant little life and little sacrifice?"

She stared at him; even the bulky goggles could not hide her new respect and even fear. "You really mean to do it, then."

"I made the sacrifice of my time and energy. I expect results, Doctor."

"But it's kidnapping. You're talking about breeding a slave race."

Afriel shrugged, with contempt. "You're juggling words, Doctor. I'll cause this colony no harm. I may steal some of its workers' labor while they obey my own chemical orders, but that tiny theft won't be missed. I admit to the murder of one egg, but that is no more a crime than a human abortion. Can the theft of one strand of genetic material be called 'kidnapping'? I think not. As for the scandalous idea of a slave race—I reject it out of hand. These creatures are genetic robots. They will no more be slaves than are laser drills or cargo tankers. At the very worst, they will be our domestic animals."

Mirny considered the issue. It did not take her long. "It's true. It's not as if a common worker will be staring at the stars, pining for its freedom. They're just brainless neuters."

"Exactly, Doctor."

"They simply work. Whether they work for us or the Swarm makes no difference to them."

"I see that you've seized on the beauty of the idea."

"And if it worked," Mirny said, "if it worked, our faction would profit astronomically."

Afriel smiled genuinely, unaware of the chilling sarcasm of his expression. "And the personal profit, Doctor…the valuable expertise of the first to exploit the technique." He spoke gently, quietly. "Ever see a nitrogen snowfall on Titan? I think a habitat of one's own there—larger, much larger than anything possible before…A genuine city, Galina, a place where a man can scrap the rules and discipline that madden him…"

"Now it's you who are talking defection, Captain-Doctor."

Afriel was silent for a moment, then smiled with an effort. "Now you've ruined my perfect reverie," he said. "Besides, what I was describing was the well-earned retirement of a wealthy man, not some self-indulgent her-mitage...there's a clear difference." He hesitated. "In any case, may I con-clude that you're with me in this project?"

She laughed and touched his arm. There was something uncanny about the small sound of her laugh, drowned by a great organic rumble from the Queen's monstrous intestines..."Do you expect me to resist your arguments for two long years? Better that I give in now and save us friction."

"Yes."

"After all, you won't do any harm to the Nest. They'll never know any-thing has happened. And if their genetic line is successfully reproduced back home, there'll never be any reason for humanity to bother them again."

"True enough," said Afriel, though in the back of his mind he instantly thought of the fabulous wealth of Betelgeuse's asteroid system. A day would come, inevitably, when humanity would move to the stars en masse, in earnest. It would be well to know the ins and outs of every race that might become a rival.

"I'll help you as best I can," she said. There was a moment's silence. "Have you seen enough of this area?"

"Yes." They left the Queen's chamber.

"I didn't think I'd like you at first," she said candidly. "I think I like you bet-ter now. You seem to have a sense of humor that most Security people lack."

"It's not a sense of humor," Afriel said sadly. "It's a sense of irony dis-guised as one."

▲ ▼ ▲

There were no days in the unending stream of hours that followed. There were only ragged periods of sleep, apart at first, later together, as they held each other in free-fall. The sexual feel of skin and body became an anchor to their common humanity, a divided, frayed humanity so many light-years away that the concept no longer had any meaning. Life in the warm and swarming tunnels was the here and now; the two of them were like germs in a bloodstream, moving ceaselessly with the pulsing ebb and flow. Hours stretched into months, and time itself grew meaningless.

The pheromonal tests were complex, but not impossibly difficult. The first of the ten pheromones was a simple grouping stimulus, causing large numbers of workers to gather as the chemical was spread from palp to palp. The workers then waited for further instructions; if none were forthcoming, they dispersed. To work effectively, the pheromones had to be given in a mix, or series, like computer commands; number one, grouping, for instance, together with the third pheromone, a transferral order, which caused the workers to empty any given chamber and move its effects to another. The ninth pheromone had the best industrial possibilities; it was a building order, causing the workers to gather tunnelers and dredgers and set them to work. Others were annoying; the tenth pheromone provoked grooming behavior, and the workers' furry palps stripped off the remaining rags of Afriel's clothing. The eighth pheromone sent the workers off to harvest material on the asteroid's surface, and in their eagerness to observe its effects the two explorers were almost trapped and swept off into space.

The two of them no longer feared the warrior caste. They knew that a dose of the sixth pheromone would send them scurrying off to defend the eggs, just as it sent the workers to tend them. Mirny and Afriel took advantage of this and secured their own chambers, dug by chemically hijacked workers and defended by a hijacked airlock guardian. They had their own fungal gardens to refresh the air, stocked with the fungus they liked best, and digested by a worker they kept drugged for their own food use. From constant stuffing and lack of exercise the worker had swollen up into its replete form and hung from one wall like a monstrous grape.

Afriel was tired. He had been without sleep recently for a long time; how long, he didn't know. His body rhythms had not adjusted as well as Mirny's, and he was prone to fits of depression and irritability that he had to repress with an effort. "The Investors will be back sometime," he said. "Sometime soon."

Mirny was indifferent. "The Investors," she said, and followed the remark with something in the language of the springtails, which he didn't catch. Despite his linguistic training, Afriel had never caught up with her in her use of the springtails' grating jargon. His training was almost a liability; the springtail language had decayed so much that it was a pidgin tongue, without rules or regularity. He knew enough to give them simple orders, and with his partial control of the warriors he had the power to back it up. The springtails were afraid of him, and the two juveniles that Mirny had tamed had developed into fat, overgrown tyrants that freely terrorized their elders. Afriel had been too busy to seriously study the springtails or the other symbiotes. There were too many practical matters at hand.

"If they come too soon, I won't be able to finish my latest study," she said in English.

Afriel pulled off his infrared goggles and knotted them tightly around his neck. "There's a limit, Galina," he said, yawning. "You can only memorize so much data without equipment. We'll just have to wait quietly until we can get back. I hope the Investors aren't shocked when they see me. I lost a fortune with those clothes."

"It's been so dull since the mating swarm was launched. If it weren't for the new growth in the alates' chamber, I'd be bored to death." She pushed greasy hair from her face with both hands. "Are you going to sleep?"

"Yes, if I can."

"You won't come with me? I keep telling you that this new growth is important. I think it's a new caste. It's definitely not an alate. It has eyes like an alate, but it's clinging to the wall."

"It's probably not a Swarm member at all, then," he said tiredly, humoring her. "It's probably a parasite, an alate mimic. Go on and see it, if you want to. I'll be here waiting for you."

He heard her leave. Without his infrareds on, the darkness was still not quite total; there was a very faint luminosity from the steaming, growing fungus in the chamber beyond. The stuffed worker replete moved slightly on the wall, rustling and gurgling. He fell asleep.

▲ ▼ ▲

When he awoke, Mirny had not yet returned. He was not alarmed. First, he visited the original airlock tunnel, where the Investors had first left him. It was irrational—the Investors always fulfilled their contracts—but he feared that they would arrive someday, become impatient, and leave without him. The Investors would have to wait, of course. Mirny could keep them occupied in the short time it would take him to hurry to the nursery and rob a developing egg of its living cells. It was best that the egg be as fresh as possible.

Later he ate. He was munching fungus in one of the anterior chambers when Mirny's two tamed springtails found him. "What do you want?" he asked in their language.

"Food-giver no good," the larger one screeched, waving its forelegs in brainless agitation. "Not work, not sleep."

"Not move," the second one said. It added hopefully, "Eat it now?"

Afriel gave them some of his food. They ate it, seemingly more out of habit than real appetite, which alarmed him. "Take me to her," he told them.

The two springtails scurried off; he followed them easily, adroitly dodging and weaving through the crowds of workers. They led him several miles through the network, to the alates' chamber. There they stopped, confused. "Gone," the large one said.

The chamber was empty. Afriel had never seen it empty before, and it was very unusual for the Swarm to waste so much space. He felt dread. "Follow the food-giver," he said. "Follow the smell."

The springtails snuffled without much enthusiasm along one wall; they knew he had no food and were reluctant to do anything without an immediate reward. At last one of them picked up the scent, or pretended to, and followed it up across the ceiling and into the mouth of a tunnel.

It was hard for Afriel to see much in the abandoned chamber; there was not enough infrared heat. He leapt upward after the springtail.

He heard the roar of a warrior and the springtail's choked-off screech. It came flying from the tunnel's mouth, a spray of clotted fluid bursting from its ruptured head. It tumbled end over end until it hit the far wall with a flaccid crunch. It was already dead.

The second springtail fled at once, screeching with grief and terror. Afriel landed on the lip of the tunnel, sinking into a crouch as his legs soaked up momentum. He could smell the acrid stench of the warrior's anger, a pheromone so thick that even a human could scent it. Dozens of other warriors would group here within minutes, or seconds. Behind the enraged warrior he could hear workers and tunnelers shifting and cementing rock.

He might be able to control one enraged warrior, but never two, or twenty. He launched himself from the chamber wall and out an exit.

He searched for the other springtail—he felt sure he could recognize it, since it was so much bigger than the others—but he could not find it. With its keen sense of smell, it could easily avoid him if it wanted to.

Mirny did not return. Uncountable hours passed. He slept again. He returned to the alates' chamber; there were warriors on guard there, warriors that were not interested in food and brandished their immense serrated fangs when he approached. They looked ready to rip him apart; the faint reek of aggressive pheromones hung about the place like a fog. He did not see any symbiotes of any kind on the warriors' bodies. There was one species, a thing like a huge tick, that clung only to warriors, but even the ticks were gone.

He returned to his chambers to wait and think. Mirny's body was not in the garbage pits. Of course, it was possible that something else might have eaten her. Should he extract the remaining pheromone from the spaces in his vein and try to break into the alates' chamber? He suspected that Mirny, or whatever was left of her, was somewhere in the tunnel where the springtail had been killed. He had never explored that tunnel himself. There were thousands of tunnels he had never explored.

He felt paralyzed by indecision and fear. If he was quiet, if he did nothing, the Investors might arrive at any moment. He could tell the Ring Council anything he wanted about Mirny's death; if he had the genetics with him, no one would quibble. He did not love her; he respected her, but not enough to give up his life, or his faction's investment. He had not thought of the Ring Council in a long time, and the thought sobered him. He would have to explain his decision...

He was still in a brown study when he heard a whoosh of air as his living airlock deflated itself. Three warriors had come for him. There was no reek of anger about them. They moved slowly and carefully. He knew better than to try to resist. One of them seized him gently in its massive jaws and carried him off.

It took him to the alates' chamber and into the guarded tunnel. A new, large chamber had been excavated at the end of the tunnel. It was filled almost to bursting by a black-splattered white mass of flesh. In the center of the soft speckled mass were a mouth and two damp, shining eyes, on stalks. Long tendrils like conduits dangled, writhing, from a clumped ridge above the eyes. The tendrils ended in pink, fleshy pluglike clumps.

One of the tendrils had been thrust through Mirny's skull. Her body hung in midair, limp as wax. Her eyes were open, but blind.

Another tendril was plugged into the braincase of a mutated worker. The worker still had the pallid tinge of a larva; it was shrunken and deformed, and its mouth had the wrinkled look of a human mouth. There was a blob like a tongue in the mouth, and white ridges like human teeth. It had no eyes.

It spoke with Mirny's voice. "Captain-Doctor Afriel…"

"Galina…"

"I have no such name. You may address me as Swarm."

Afriel vomited. The central mass was an immense head. Its brain almost filled the room.

It waited politely until Afriel had finished.

"I find myself awakened again," Swarm said dreamily. "I am pleased to see that there is no major emergency to concern me. Instead it is a threat that has become almost routine." It hesitated delicately. Mirny's body moved slightly in midair; her breathing was inhumanly regular. The eyes opened and closed. "Another young race."

"What are you?"

"I am the Swarm. That is, I am one of its castes. I am a tool, an adaptation; my specialty is intelligence. I am not often needed. It is good to be needed again."

"Have you been here all along? Why didn't you greet us? We'd have dealt with you. We meant no harm."

The wet mouth on the end of the plug made laughing sounds. "Like yourself, I enjoy irony," it said. "It is a pretty trap you have found yourself in, Captain-Doctor. You meant to make the Swarm work for you and your race. You meant to breed us and study us and use us. It is an excellent plan, but one we hit upon long before your race evolved."

Stung by panic, Afriel's mind raced frantically. "You're an intelligent being," he said. "There's no reason to do us any harm. Let us talk together. We can help you."

"Yes," Swarm agreed. "You will be helpful. Your companion's memories tell me that this is one of those uncomfortable periods when galactic intelligence is rife. Intelligence is a great bother. It makes all kinds of trouble for us."

"What do you mean?"

"You are a young race and lay great stock by your own cleverness," Swarm said. "As usual, you fail to see that intelligence is not a survival trait."

Afriel wiped sweat from his face. "We've done well," he said. "We came to you, and peacefully. You didn't come to us."

"I refer to exactly that," Swarm said urbanely. "This urge to expand, to explore, to develop, is just what will make you extinct. You naively suppose that you can continue to feed your curiosity indefinitely. It is an old story, pursued by countless races before you. Within a thousand years— perhaps a little longer—your species will vanish."

"You intend to destroy us, then? I warn you it will not be an easy task—"

"Again you miss the point. Knowledge is power! Do you suppose that fragile little form of yours—your primitive legs, your ludicrous arms and hands, your tiny, scarcely wrinkled brain—can contain all that power? Certainly not! Already your race is flying to pieces under the impact of your own expertise. The original human form is becoming obsolete. Your own genes have been altered, and you, Captain-Doctor, are a crude experiment. In a hundred years you will be a relic. In a thousand years you will not even be a memory. Your race will go the same way as a thousand others."

"And what way is that?"

"I do not know." The thing on the end of the Swarm's arm made a chuckling sound. "They have passed beyond my ken. They have all discovered something, learned something, that has caused them to transcend my understanding. It may be that they even transcend being. At any rate, I cannot sense their presence anywhere. They seem to do nothing, they seem to interfere in nothing; for all intents and purposes, they seem to be dead. Vanished. They may have become gods, or ghosts. In either case, I have no wish to join them."

"So then—so then you have—"

"Intelligence is very much a two-edged sword, Captain-Doctor. It is useful only up to a point. It interferes with the business of living. Life, and intelligence, do not mix very well. They are not at all closely related, as you childishly assume."

"But you, then—you are a rational being—"

"I am a tool, as I said." The mutated device on the end of its arm made a sighing noise. "When you began your pheromonal experiments, the chemical imbalance became apparent to the Queen. It triggered certain genetic patterns within her body, and I was reborn. Chemical sabotage is a problem that can best be dealt with by intelligence. I am a brain replete, you see, specially designed to be far more intelligent than any young race. Within three days I was fully self-conscious. Within five days I had deciphered these markings on my body. They are the genetically encoded history of my race...within five days and two hours I recognized the problem at hand and knew what to do. I am now doing it. I am six days old."

"What is it you intend to do?"

"Your race is a very vigorous one. I expect it to be here, competing with us, within five hundred years. Perhaps much sooner. It will be necessary to make a thorough study of such a rival. I invite you to join our community on a permanent basis."

"What do you mean?"

"I invite you to become a symbiote. I have here a male and a female, whose genes are altered and therefore without defects. You make a perfect breeding pair. It will save me a great deal of trouble with cloning."

"You think I'll betray my race and deliver a slave species into your hands?"

"Your choice is simple, Captain-Doctor. Remain an intelligent, living being, or become a mindless puppet, like your partner. I have taken over all the functions of her nervous system; I can do the same to you."

"I can kill myself."

"That might be troublesome, because it would make me resort to developing a cloning technology. Technology, though I am capable of it, is painful to me. I am a genetic artifact; there are fail-safes within me that prevent me from taking over the Nest for my own uses. That would mean falling into the same trap of progress as other intelligent races. For similar reasons, my life span is limited. I will live for only a thousand years, until your race's brief flurry of energy is over and peace resumes once more."

"Only a thousand years?" Afriel laughed bitterly. "What then? You kill off my descendants, I assume, having no further use for them."

"No. We have not killed any of the fifteen other races we have taken for defensive study. It has not been necessary. Consider that, small scavenger floating by your head, Captain-Doctor, that is feeding on your vomit. Five hundred million years ago its ancestors made the galaxy tremble. When they attacked us, we unleashed their own kind upon them. Of course, we altered our side, so that they were smarter, tougher, and, naturally, totally loyal to us. Our Nests were the only world they knew, and they fought with a valor and inventiveness we never could have matched...Should your race arrive to exploit us, we will naturally do the same."

"We humans are different."

"Of course."

"A thousand years here won't change us. You will die and our descendants will take over this Nest. We'll be running things, despite you, in a few generations. The darkness won't make any difference."

"Certainly not. You don't need eyes here. You don't need anything."

"You'll allow me to stay alive? To teach them anything I want?"

"Certainly, Captain-Doctor. We are doing you a favor, in all truth. In a thousand years your descendants here will be the only remnants of the human race. We are generous with our immortality; we will take it upon ourselves to preserve you."

"You're wrong, Swarm. You're wrong about intelligence, and you're wrong about everything else. Maybe other races would crumble into parasitism, but we humans are different."

"Certainly. You'll do it, then?"

"Yes. I accept your challenge. And I will defeat you."

"Splendid. When the Investors return here, the springtails will say that they have killed you, and will tell them to never return. They will not return. The humans should be the next to arrive."

"If I don't defeat you, they will."

"Perhaps." Again it sighed. "I'm glad I don't have to absorb you. I would have missed your conversation."

Spider Rose

Nothing was what Spider Rose felt, or almost nothing. There had been some feelings there, a nexus of clotted two-hundred-year-old emotions, and she had mashed it with a cranial injection. Now what was left of her feelings was like what is left of a roach when a hammer strikes it.

Spider Rose knew about roaches; they were the only native animal life in the orbiting Mechanist colonies. They had plagued spacecraft from the beginning, too tough, prolific, and adaptable to kill. Of necessity, the Mechanists had used genetic techniques stolen from their rivals the Shapers to turn the roaches into colorful pets. One of Spider Rose's special favorites was a roach a foot long and covered with red and yellow pigment squiggles against shiny black chitin. It was clinging to her head. It drank sweat from her perfect brow, and she knew nothing, for she was elsewhere, watching for visitors.

She watched through eight telescopes, their images collated and fed into her brain through a nerve-crystal junction at the base of her skull. She had eight eyes now, like her symbol, the spider. Her ears were the weak steady pulse of radar, listening, listening for the weird distortion that would signal the presence of an Investor ship.

Rose was clever. She might have been insane, but her monitoring techniques established the chemical basis of sanity and maintained it artificially. Spider Rose accepted this as normal.

And it was normal; not for human beings, but for a two-hundred-year-old Mechanist, living in a spinning web of a habitat orbiting Uranus, her body seething with youth hormones, her wise old-young face like something pulled fresh from a plaster mold, her long white hair a rippling display of implanted fiber-optic threads with tiny beads of light oozing like microscopic gems from their slant-cut tips...She was old, but she didn't think about that. And she was lonely, but she had crushed those feelings with drugs. And she had something that the Investors wanted, something that those reptilian alien traders would give their eye-fangs to possess.

Trapped in her polycarbon spiderweb, the wide-stretched cargo net that had given her her name, she had a jewel the size of a bus.

And so she watched, brain-linked to her instruments, tireless, not particularly interested but certainly not bored. Boredom was dangerous. It led to unrest, and unrest could be fatal in a space habitat, where malice or even plain carelessness could kill. The proper survival behavior was this: to crouch in the center of the mental web, clean euclidean web-lines of rationality radiating out in all directions, hooked legs alert for the slightest tremble of troubling emotion. And when she sensed that feeling tangling the lines, she rushed there, gauged it, shrouded it neatly, and pierced it cleanly and lingeringly with a spiderfang hypodermic...

There it was. Her octuple eyes gazed a quarter of a million miles into space and spotted the star-rippling warp of an Investor ship. The Investor ships had no conventional engines, and radiated no detectable energies; the secret of their star drive was closely guarded. All that any of the factions (still loosely called "humanity" for lack of a better term) knew for sure about the Investor drive was that it sent long parabolic streamers of distortion from the sterns of ships, causing a rippling effect against the background of stars.

Spider Rose came partially out of her static observation mode and felt herself in her body once more. The computer signals were muted now, overlaid behind her normal vision like a reflection of her own face on a glass window as she gazed through it. Touching a keyboard, she pinpointed the Investor ship with a communications laser and sent it a pulse of data: a business offer. (Radio was too chancy; it might attract Shaper pirates, and she had had to kill three of them already.)

She knew she had been heard and understood when she saw the Investor ship perform a dead stop and an angled acceleration that broke every known law of orbital dynamics. While she waited, Spider Rose loaded an Investor translator program. It was fifty years old, but the Investors were a persistent lot, not so much conservative as just uninterested in change.

When it came too close to her station for star-drive maneuvers, the Investor ship unfurled a decorated solar sail with a puff of gas. The sail was big enough to gift-wrap a small moon and thinner than a two-hundred-year-old memory. Despite its fantastic thinness, there were molecule-thin murals worked onto it: titanic scenes of Investor argosies where wily Investors had defrauded pebbly bipeds and gullible heavy-planet gasbags swollen with wealth and hydrogen. The great jewel-laden queens of the Investor race, surrounded by adoring male harems, flaunted their gaudy sophistication above miles-high narratives of Investor hieroglyphs, placed on a musical grid to indicate the proper pitch and intonation of their half-sung language.

There was a burst of static on the screen before her and an Investor face appeared. Spider Rose pulled the plug from her neck. She studied the face: its great glassy eyes half-shrouded behind nictitating membranes, rainbow frill behind pinhole-sized ears, bumpy skin, reptile grin with peg-sized teeth. It made noises: "Ship's ensign here," her computer translated. "Lydia Martinez?"

"Yes," Spider Rose said, not bothering to explain that her name had changed. She had had many names.

"We had profitable dealings with your husband in the past," the Investor said with interest. "How does he fare these days?"

"He died thirty years ago," Spider Rose said. She had mashed the grief. "Shaper assassins killed him."

The Investor officer flickered his frill. He was not embarrassed. Embarrassment was not an emotion native to Investors. "Bad for business," he opined. "Where is this jewel you mentioned?"

"Prepare for incoming data," said Spider Rose, touching her keyboard. She watched the screen as her carefully prepared sales spiel unrolled itself, its communication beam shielded to avoid enemy ears.

It had been the find of a lifetime. It had started existence as part of a glacierlike ice moon of the protoplanet Uranus, shattering, melting, and recrystallizing in the primeval eons of relentless bombardment. It had cracked at least four different times, and each time mineral flows had been forced within its fracture zones under tremendous pressure: carbon, manganese silicate, beryllium, aluminum oxide. When the moon was finally broken up into the famous Ring complex, the massive ice chunk had floated for eons, awash in shock waves of hard radiation, accumulating and losing charge in the bizarre electromagnetic flickerings typical of all Ring formations.

And then one crucial moment some millions of years ago it had been ground-zero for a titanic lightning flash, one of those soundless invisible gouts of electric energy, dissipating charges built up over whole decades. Most of the ice-chunk's outer envelope had flashed off at once as a plasma. The rest was...changed. Mineral occlusions were now strings and veins of beryl, shading here and there into lumps of raw emerald big as Investors' heads, crisscrossed with nets of red corundum and purple garnet. There were lumps of fused diamond, weirdly colored blazing diamond that came only from the strange quantum states of metallic carbon. Even the ice itself had changed into something rich and unique and therefore by definition precious.

"You intrigue us," the Investor said. For them, this was profound enthusiasm. Spider Rose smiled. The ensign continued: "This is an unusual commodity and its value is hard to establish. We offer you a quarter of a million gigawatts."

Spider Rose said, "I have the energy I need to run my station and defend myself. It's generous, but I could never store that much."

"We will also give you a stabilized plasma lattice for storage." This unexpected and fabulous generosity was meant to overwhelm her. The construction of plasma lattices was far beyond human technology, and to own one would be a ten years' wonder. It was the last thing she wanted. "Not interested," she said.

The Investor lifted his frill. "Not interested in the basic currency of galactic trade?"

"Not when I can spend it only with you."

"Trade with young races is a thankless lot," the Investor observed. "I suppose you want information, then. You young races always want to trade in technology. We have some Shaper techniques for trade within their faction—are you interested in those?"

"Industrial espionage?" Spider Rose said. "You should have tried me eighty years ago. No, I know you Investors too well. You would only sell Mechanist techniques to them to maintain the balance of power."

"We like a competitive market," the Investor admitted. "It helps us avoid painful monopoly situations like the one we face now, dealing with you."

"I don't want power of any kind. Status means nothing to me. Show me something new."

"No status? What will your fellows think?"

"I live alone."

The Investor hid his eyes behind nictitating membranes. "Crushed your gregarious instincts? An ominous development. Well, I will take a new tack. Will you consider weaponry? If you will agree to various conditions regarding their use, we can give you unique and powerful armaments."

"I manage already."

"You could use our political skills. We can strongly influence the major Shaper groups and protect you from them by treaty. It would take ten or twenty years, but it could be done."

"It's up to them to be afraid of me," Spider Rose said, "not vice versa."

"A new habitat, then." The Investor was patient. "You can live within solid gold."

"I like what I have."

"We have some artifacts that might amuse you," the Investor said. "Prepare for incoming data."

Spider Rose spent eight hours examining the various wares. There was no hurry. She was too old for impatience, and the Investors lived to bargain.

She was offered colorful algae cultures that produced oxygen and alien perfumes. There were metafoil structures of collapsed atoms for radiation shielding and defense. Rare techniques that transmuted nerve fibers to crystal. A smooth black wand that made iron so malleable that you could mold it with your hands and set it in shape. A small luxury submarine for the exploration of ammonia and methane seas, made of transparent metallic glass. Self-replicating globes of patterned silica that, as they grew, played out a game simulating the birth, growth, and decline of an alien culture.

A land-sea-and-aircraft so tiny that you buttoned it on like a suit. "I don't care for planets," Spider Rose said. "I don't like gravity wells."

"Under certain circumstances we could make a gravity generator available," the Investor said. "It would have to be tamper-proof, like the wand and the weapons, and loaned rather than sold outright. We must avoid the escape of such a technology."

She shrugged. "Our own technologies have shattered us. We can't assimilate what we already have. I see no reason to burden myself with more."

"This is all we can offer you that's not on the interdicted list," he said. "This ship in particular has a great many items suitable only for races that live at very low temperature and very high pressure. And we have items that you would probably enjoy a great deal, but they would kill you. Or your whole species. The literature of the [untranslatable], for instance."

"I can read the literature of Earth if I want an alien viewpoint," she said.

"[Untranslatable] is not really a literature," the Investor said benignly. "It's really a kind of virus."

A roach flew onto her shoulder. "Pets!" he said. "Pets! You enjoy them?"

"They are my solace," she said, letting it nibble the cuticle of her thumb.

"I should have thought," he said. "Give me twelve hours."

She went to sleep. After she woke, she studied the alien craft through her telescope while she waited. All Investor ships were covered with fantastic designs in hammered metal: animal heads, metal mosaics, scenes and inscriptions in deep relief, as well as cargo bays and instruments. But experts had pointed out that the basic shape beneath the ornamentation was always the same: a simple octahedron with six long rectangular sides. The Investors had gone to some pains to disguise this fact; and the current theory held that the ships had been bought, found, or stolen from a more advanced race. Certainly the Investors, with their whimsical attitude toward science and technology, seemed incapable of building them themselves.

The ensign reopened contact. His nictitating membranes looked whiter than usual. He held up a small winged reptilian being with a long spiny crest the color of an Investor's frill. "This is our Commander's mascot, called 'Little Nose for Profits.' Beloved by us all! It costs us a pang to part from him. We had to choose between losing face in this business deal or losing his company." He toyed with it. It grasped his thick digits with little scaly hands.

"He's...cute," she said, finding a half-forgotten word from her childhood and pronouncing it with a grimace of distaste. "But I'm not going to trade my find for some carnivorous lizardkin."

"And think of us!" the Investor lamented. "Condemning our little Nose to an alien lair swarming with bacteria and giant vermin...However, this can't be helped. Here's our proposal. You take our mascot for seven hundred plus or minus five of your days. We will return here on our way out of your system. You can choose then between owning him or keeping your prize. In the meantime you must promise not to sell the jewel or inform anyone else of its existence."

"You mean that you will leave me your pet as a kind of earnest money on the transaction."

The Investor covered his eyes with the nictitating membranes and squeezed his pebbly lids half-shut. It was a sign of acute distress. "He is a hostage to your cruel indecision, Lydia Martinez. Frankly we doubt that we can find anything in this system that can satisfy you better than our mascot can. Except perhaps some novel mode of suicide."

Spider Rose was surprised. She had never seen an Investor become so emotionally involved. Generally they seemed to take a detached view of life, even showing on occasion behavior patterns that resembled a sense of humor.

She was enjoying herself. She was past the point when any of the Investor's normal commodities could have tempted her. In essence, she was trading her jewel for an interior mind-state: not an emotion, because she mashed those, but for a paler and cleaner feeling: interestedness. She wanted to be interested, to find something to occupy herself besides dead stones and space. And this looked intriguing.

"All right," she said. "I agree. Seven hundred plus or minus five days. And I keep silence." She smiled. She hadn't spoken to another human in five years and was not about to start.

"Take good care of our Little Nose for Profits," the Investor said, half pleading, half warning, accenting those nuances so that her computer would be sure to pick them up. "We will still want him, even if, through some utter corrosion of the spirit, you do not. He is valuable and rare. We will send you instructions on his care and feeding. Prepare for incoming data."

They fired the creature's cargo capsule into the tight-stretched polycarbon web of her spider habitat. The web was built on a framework of eight spokes, and these spokes were pulled taut by centrifugal force from the wheeling rotation of eight teardrop-shaped capsules. At the impact of the cargo shot, the web bowed gracefully and the eight massive metal teardrops were pulled closer to the web's center in short, graceful free-fall arcs. Wan sunlight glittered along the web as it expanded in recoil, its rotation slowed a little by the energy it had spent in absorbing the inertia. It was a cheap and effective docking technique, for a rate of spin was much easier to manage than complex maneuvering.

Hook-legged industrial robots ran quickly along the polycarbon fibers and seized the mascot's capsule with clamps and magnetic palps. Spider Rose ran the lead robot herself, feeling and seeing through its grips and cameras. The robots hustled the cargo craft to an airlock, dislodged its contents, and attached a small parasitic rocket to boost it back to the Investor mother ship. After the small rocket had returned and the Investor ship had left, the robots trooped back to their teardrop garages and shut themselves off, waiting for the next tremor of the web.

Spider Rose disconnected herself and opened the airlock. The mascot flew into the room. It had seemed tiny compared to the Investor ensign, but the Investors were huge. The mascot was as tall as her knee and looked like it weighed close to twenty pounds. Wheezing musically on the unfamiliar air, it flew around the room, ducking and darting unevenly.

A roach launched itself from the wall and flew with a great clatter of wings. The mascot hit the deck with a squawk of terror and lay there, comically feeling its spindly arms and legs for damage. It half-closed its rough eyelids. Like the eyes of an Investor baby, Spider Rose thought suddenly, though she had never seen a young Investor and doubted if anyone human ever had. She had a dim memory of something she had heard a long time before—something about pets and babies, their large heads, their large eyes, their softness, their dependence. She remembered scoffing at the idea that the sloppy dependence of, say, a "dog" or "cat" could rival the clean economy and efficiency of a roach.

The Investor mascot had recovered its composure and was crouching bent-kneed on the algae carpet, warbling to itself. There was a sort of sly grin on its miniature dragon face. Its half-slitted eyes were alert and its matchstick ribs moved up and down with each breath. Its pupils were huge. Spider Rose imagined that it must find the light very dim. The lights in Investor ships were like searing blue arc-lamps, drenched in ultraviolet.

"We have to find a new name for you," Spider Rose said. "I don't speak Investor, so I can't use the name they gave you."

The mascot fixed her with a friendly stare, and it arched little half-transparent flaps over its pinhole ears. Real Investors had no such flaps, and she was charmed at this further deviation from the norm. Actually, except for the wings, it looked altogether too much like a tiny Investor. The effect was creepy.

"I'll call you Fuzzy," she said. It had no hair. It was a private joke, but all her jokes were private.

The mascot bounced across the floor. The false centrifugal gravity was lighter here, too, than the 1.3 g's that the massive Investors used. It embraced her bare leg and licked her kneecap with a rough sandpaper tongue. She laughed, more than a little alarmed, but she knew the Investors were strictly nonaggressive. A pet of theirs would not be dangerous.

It made eager chirping sounds and climbed onto her head, clutching handfuls of glittering optic fibers. She sat at her data console and called up the care and feeding instructions.

Clearly the Investors had not expected to trade their pet, because the instructions were almost indecipherable. They had the air of a second- or third-hand translation from some even more profoundly alien language. However, true to Investor tradition, the blandly pragmatic aspects had been emphasized.

Spider Rose relaxed. Apparently the mascots would eat almost anything, though they preferred dextrorotatory proteins and required certain easily acquirable trace minerals. They were extremely resistant to toxins and had no native intestinal bacteria. (Neither did the Investors themselves, and they regarded races who did as savages.)

She looked for its respiratory requirements as the mascot leapt from her head and capered across the control board, almost aborting the program. She shooed it off, hunting for something she could comprehend amid dense clusters of alien graphs and garbled technical material. Suddenly she recognized something from her old days in technical espionage: a genetics chart.

She frowned. It seemed she had run past the relevant sections and on to another treatise entirely. She advanced the data slightly and discovered a three-dimensional illustration of some kind of fantastically complex genetic construct, with long helical chains of alien genes marked out in improbable colors. The gene chains were wrapped around long spires or spicules that emerged radially from a dense central knot. Further chains of tightly wound helices connected spire to spire. Apparently these chains activated different sections of genetic material from their junctions on the spires, for she could see ghost chains of slave proteins peeling off from some of the activated genes.

Spider Rose smiled. No doubt a skilled Shaper geneticist could profit spectacularly from these plans. It amused her to think that they never would. Obviously this was some kind of alien industrial genetic complex, for there was more genetic hardware there than any actual living animal could ever possibly need.

She knew that the Investors themselves never tampered with genetics. She wondered which of the nineteen known intelligent races had originated this thing. It might even have come from outside the Investors' economic realm, or it might be a relic from one of the extinct races.

She wondered if she ought to erase the data. If she died, it might fall into the wrong hands. As she thought of her death, the first creeping shades of a profound depression disturbed her. She allowed the sensation to build for a moment while she thought. The Investors had been careless to leave her with this information; or perhaps they underestimated the genetic abilities of the smooth and charismatic Shapers with their spectacularly boosted IQs.

There was a wobbling feeling inside her head. For a dizzying moment the chemically repressed emotions gushed forth with all their pent-up force. She felt an agonized envy for the Investors, for the dumb arrogance and confidence that allowed them to cruise the stars screwing their purported inferiors. She wanted to be with them. She wanted to get aboard a magic ship and feel alien sunlight burn her skin in some place light-years from human weakness. She wanted to scream and feel like a little girl had screamed and felt one hundred and ninety-three years ago on a roller coaster in Los Angeles, screaming in total pure intensity of feeling, in swept-away sensation like she had felt in the arms of her husband, her man dead now thirty years. Dead…Thirty years…

Her hands trembling, she opened a drawer beneath the control board. She smelled the faint medicinal reek of ozone from the sterilizer. Blindly she pushed her glittering hair from the plastic duct into her skull, pressed the injector against it, inhaled once, closed her eyes, inhaled twice, pulled the hypo away. Her eyes glazed over as she refilled the hypo and slipped it back into its velcro holster in the drawer.

She held the bottle and looked at it blankly. There was still plenty left. She would not have to synthesize more for months. Her brain felt like someone had stepped on it. It was always like this right after a mash. She shut off the Investor data and filed it absently in an obscure corner of computer memory. From its stand on the laser-com interface the mascot sang briefly and groomed its wing.

Soon she was herself again. She smiled. These sudden attacks were something she took for granted. She took an oral tranquilizer to stop the trembling of her hands and antacid for the stress on her stomach.

Then she played with the mascot until it grew tired and went to sleep. For four days she fed it carefully, being especially careful not to overfeed it, for like its models the Investors, it was a greedy little creature and she was afraid it would hurt itself. Despite its rough skin and cold-bloodedness she was growing fond of it. When it grew tired of begging for food, it would play with string for hours or sit on her head watching the screen as she monitored the mining robots she had out in the Rings.

On the fifth day she found on awakening that it had killed and eaten her four largest and fattest roaches. Filled with a righteous anger she did nothing to blunt, she hunted for it throughout the capsule.

She did not find it. Instead, after hours of search, she found a mascot-sized cocoon wedged under the toilet.

It had gone into some sort of hibernation. She forgave it for eating the roaches. They were easy to replace, anyway, and rivals for her affections. In a way it was flattering. But the sharp pang of worry she felt overrode that. She examined the cocoon closely. It was made of overlapping sheets of some brittle translucent substance—dried mucus?—that she could chip easily with her fingernail. The cocoon was not perfectly rounded; there were small vague lumps that might have been its knees and elbows. She took another injection.

The week it spent in hibernation was a period of acute anxiety for her. She pored over the Investor tapes, but they were far too cryptic for her limited expertise. At least she knew it was not dead, for the cocoon was warm to the touch and the lumps within it sometimes stirred.

She was asleep when it began to break free of the cocoon. She had set up monitors to warn her, however, and she rushed to it at the first alarm.

The cocoon was splitting. A rent appeared in the brittle overlapping sheets, and a warm animal reek seeped out into the recycled air.

Then a paw emerged: a tiny five-fingered paw covered in glittering fur. A second paw poked through, and the two paws gripped the edges of the rent and ripped the cocoon away. It stepped out into the light, kicking the husk aside with a little human shuffle, and it grinned.

It looked like a little ape, small and soft and glittering. There were tiny human teeth behind the human lips of its grin. It had small soft baby's feet on the ends of its round springy legs, and it had lost its wings. Its eyes were the color of her eyes. The smooth mammalian skin of its round little face had the faint rosy flush of perfect health.

It jumped into the air, and she saw the pink of its tongue as it babbled aloud in human syllables.

It skipped over and embraced her leg. She was frightened, amazed, and profoundly relieved. She petted the soft perfect glittering fur on its hard little nugget of a head.

"Fuzzy," she said. "I'm glad. I'm very glad."

"Wa wa wa," it said, mimicking her intonation in its piping child's voice. Then it skipped back to its cocoon and began to eat it by the double handful, grinning.

She understood now why the Investors had been so reluctant to offer their mascot. It was a trade item of fantastic value. It was a genetic artifact, able to judge the emotional wants and needs of an alien species and adapt itself to them in a matter of days.

She began to wonder why the Investors had given it away at all; if they fully understood the capabilities of their pet. Certainly she doubted that they had understood the complex data that had come with it. Very likely, they had acquired the mascot from other Investors, in its reptilian form. It was even possible (the thought chilled her) that it might be older than the entire Investor race.

She stared at it: at its clear, guileless, trusting eyes. It gripped her fingers with small warm sinewy hands. Unable to resist, she hugged it to her, and it babbled with pleasure. Yes, it could easily have lived for hundreds or thousands of years, spreading its love (or equivalent emotions) among dozens of differing species.

And who would harm it? Even the most depraved and hardened of her own species had secret weaknesses. She remembered stories of guards in concentration camps who butchered men and women without a qualm, but meticulously fed hungry birds in the winter. Fear bred fear and hatred, but how could anyone feel fear or hatred toward this creature, or resist its brilliant powers?

It was not intelligent; it didn't need intelligence. It was sexless as well. An ability to breed would have ruined its value as a trade item. Besides, she doubted that anything so complex could have grown in a womb. Its genes would have to be built, spicule by spicule, in some unimaginable lab.

Days and weeks reeled by. Its ability to sense her moods was little short of miraculous. When she needed it, it was always there, and when she didn't it vanished. Sometimes she would hear it chattering to itself as it capered in strange acrobatics or chased and ate roaches. It was never mischievous, and on the odd occasions where it spilled food or upset something, it would unobtrusively clean up after itself. It dropped its small inoffensive fecal pellets into the same recycler she used.

These were the only signs it showed of patterns of thought that were more than animal. Once, and only once, it had mimicked her, repeating a sentence letter-perfect. She had been shocked, and it had sensed her reaction immediately. It never tried to parrot her again.

They slept in the same bed. Sometimes while she slept she would feel its warm nose snuffling lightly along the surface of her skin, as if it could smell her suppressed moods and feelings through the pores. Sometimes it would rub or press with its small firm hands against her neck or spine, and there was always a tightened muscle there that relaxed in gratitude. She never allowed this in the day, but at night, when her discipline was half-dissolved in sleep, there was a conspiracy between them.

The Investors had been gone over six hundred days. She laughed when she thought of the bargain she was getting.

The sound of her own laughter no longer startled her. She had even cut back on her dosages of suppressants and inhibitors. Her pet seemed so much happier when she was happy, and when it was at hand her ancient sadnesses seemed easier to bear. One by one she began to face old pains and traumas, holding her pet close and shedding healing tears into its glittering fur. One by one it licked her tears, tasting the emotional chemicals they contained, smelling her breath and skin, holding her as she was racked with sobbing. There were so many memories. She felt old, horribly old, but at the same time she felt a new sense of wholeness that allowed her to bear it. She had done things in the past—cruel things—and she had never put up with the inconvenience of guilt. She had mashed it instead.

Now for the first time in decades she felt the vague reawakening of a sense of purpose. She wanted to see people again—dozens of people, hundreds of people, all of whom would admire her, protect her, find her precious, whom she could care for, who would keep her safer than she was with only one companion...

▲ ▼ ▲

Her web station entered the most dangerous part of its orbit, where it crossed the plane of the Rings. Here she was busiest, accepting the drifting chunks of raw materials—ice, carbonaceous chondrites, metal ores—that her telepuppet mining robots had discovered and sent her way. There were killers in these Rings: rapacious pirates, paranoid settlers anxious to lash out.

In her normal orbit, far off the plane of the ecliptic, she was safe. But here there were orders to be broadcasted, energies to be spent, the telltale traces of powerful mass drivers hooked to the captive asteroids she claimed and mined. It was an unavoidable risk. Even the best-designed habitat was not a completely closed system, and hers was big, and old.

They found her.

Three ships. She tried bluffing them off at first, sending them a standard interdiction warning routed through a telepuppet beacon. They found the beacon and destroyed it, but that gave her their location and some blurry data through the beacon's limited sensors.

Three sleek ships, iridescent capsules half-metal, half-organic, with long ribbed insect-tinted sun-wings thinner than the scum of oil on water. Shaper spacecraft, knobbed with the geodesics of sensors, the spines of magnetic and optical weapons systems, long cargo manipulators folded like the arms of mantises.

She sat hooked into her own sensors, studying them, taking in a steady trickle of data: range estimation, target probabilities, weapons status. Radar was too risky; she sighted them optically. This was fine for lasers, but her lasers were not her best weapons. She might get one, but the others would be on her. It was better that she stay quiet while they prowled the Rings and she slid silently off the ecliptic.

But they had found her. She saw them fold their sails and activate their ion engines.

They were sending radio. She entered it on screen, not wanting the distraction filling her head. A Shaper's face appeared, one of the Oriental-based gene lines, smooth raven hair held back with jeweled pins, slim black eyebrows arched over dark eyes with the epicanthic fold, pale lips slightly curved in a charismatic smile. A smooth, clean actor's face with the glittering ageless eyes of a fanatic. "Jade Prime," she said.

"*Colonel-Doctor* Jade Prime," the Shaper said, fingering a golden insignia of rank in the collar of his black military tunic. "Still calling yourself 'Spider Rose' these days, Lydia? Or have you wiped that out of your brain?"

"Why are you a soldier instead of a corpse?"

"Times change, Spider. The bright young lights get snuffed out, by your old friends, and those of us with long-range plans are left to settle old debts. You remember old debts, Spider?"

"You think you're going to survive this meeting, don't you, Prime?" She felt the muscles of her face knotting with a ferocious hatred she had no time to kill. "Three ships manned with your own clones. How long have you holed up in that rock of yours, like a maggot in an apple? Cloning and cloning. When was the last time a woman let you touch her?"

His eternal smile twisted into a leer with bright teeth behind it. "It's no use, Spider. You've already killed thirty-seven of me, and I just keep coming back, don't I? You pathetic old bitch, what the hell is a maggot, anyway? Something like that mutant on your shoulder?"

She hadn't even known the pet was there, and her heart was stabbed with fear for it. "You've come too close!"

"Fire, then! Shoot me, you germy old cretin! Fire!"

"You're not him!" she said suddenly. "You're not First Jade! Hah! He's dead, isn't he?"

The clone's face twisted with rage. Lasers flared, and three of her habitats melted into slag and clouds of metallic plasma. A last searing pulse of intolerable brightness flashed in her brain from three melting telescopes.

She cut loose with a chugging volley of magnetically accelerated iron slugs. At four hundred miles per second they riddled the first ship and left it gushing air and brittle clouds of freezing water.

Two ships fired. They used weapons she had never seen before, and they crushed two habitats like a pair of giant fists. The web lurched with the impact, its equilibrium gone. She knew instantly which weapons systems were left, and she returned fire with metal-jacketed pellets of ammonia ice. They punched through the semiorganic sides of a second Shaper craft. The tiny holes sealed instantly, but the crew was finished; the ammonia vaporized inside, releasing instantly lethal nerve toxins.

The last ship had one chance in three to get her command center. Two hundred years of luck ran out for Spider Rose. Static stung her hands from the controls. Every light in the habitat went out, and her computer underwent a total crash. She screamed and waited for death.

Death did not come.

Her mouth gushed with the bile of nausea. She opened the drawer in the darkness and filled her brain with liquid tranquility. Breathing hard, she sat back in her console chair, her panic mashed. "Electromagnetic pulse," she said. "Stripped everything I had."

The pet warbled a few syllables. "He would have finished us by now if he could," she told her pet. "The defenses must have come through from the other habitats when the mainframe crashed."

She felt a thump as the pet jumped into her lap, shivering with terror. She hugged it absently, rubbing its slender neck. "Let's see," she said into the darkness. "The ice toxins are down, I had them overridden from here." She pulled the useless plug from her neck and plucked her robe away from her damp ribs. "It was the spray, then. A nice, thick cloud of hot ionized metallic copper. Blew every sensor he had. He's riding blind in a metallic coffin. Just like us."

She laughed. "Except old Rose has a trick left, baby. The Investors. They'll be looking for me. There's nobody left to look for him. And I still have my rock."

She sat silently, and her artificial calmness allowed her to think the unthinkable. The pet stirred uneasily, sniffing at her skin. It had calmed a little under her caresses, and she didn't want it to suffer.

She put her free hand over its mouth and twisted its neck till it broke. The centrifugal gravity had kept her strong, and it had no time to struggle. A final tremor shook its limbs as she held it up in the darkness, feeling for a heartbeat. Her fingertips felt the last pulse behind its frail ribs.

"Not enough oxygen," she said. Mashed emotions tried to stir, and failed. She had plenty of suppressor left. "The carpet algae will keep the air clean a few weeks, but it dies without light. And I can't eat it. Not enough food, baby. The gardens are gone, and even if they hadn't been blasted, I couldn't get food in here. Can't run the robots. Can't even open the airlocks. If I live long enough, they'll come and pry me out. I have to improve my chances. It's the sensible thing. When I'm like this I can only do the sensible thing."

When the roaches—or at least all those she could trap in the darkness— were gone, she fasted for a long dark time. Then she ate her pet's undecayed flesh, half hoping even in her numbness that it would poison her.

When she first saw the searing blue light of the Investors glaring through the shattered airlock, she crawled back on bony hands and knees, shielding her eyes.

The Investor crewman wore a spacesuit to protect himself from bacteria. She was glad he couldn't smell the reek of her pitch-black crypt. He spoke to her in the fluting language of the Investors, but her translator was dead.

She thought then for a moment that they would abandon her, leave her there starved and blinded and half-bald in her webs of shed fiber-hair. But they took her aboard, drenching her with stinging antiseptics, scorching her skin with bactericidal ultraviolet rays.

They had the jewel, but that much she already knew. What they wanted—(this was difficult)—what they wanted to know was what had happened to their mascot. It was hard to understand their gestures and their pidgin scraps of human language. She had done something bad to herself, she knew that. Overdoses in the dark. Struggling in the darkness with a great black beetle of fear that broke the frail meshes of her spider's web. She felt very bad. There was something wrong inside of her. Her malnourished belly was as tight as a drum, and her lungs felt crushed. Her bones felt wrong. Tears wouldn't come.

They kept at her. She wanted to die. She wanted their love and understanding. She wanted—

Her throat was full. She couldn't talk. Her head tilted back, and her eyes shrank in the searing blaze of the overhead lights. She heard painless cracking noises as her jaws unhinged.

Her breathing stopped. It came as a relief. Antiperistalsis throbbed in her gullet, and her mouth filled with fluid.

A living whiteness oozed from her lips and nostrils. Her skin tingled at its touch, and it flowed over her eyeballs, sealing and soothing them. A great coolness and lassitude soaked into her as wave after wave of translucent liquid swaddled her, gushing over her skin, coating her body. She relaxed, filled with a sensual, sleepy gratitude. She was not hungry. She had plenty of excess mass.

In eight days she broke from the brittle sheets of her cocoon and fluttered out on scaly wings, eager for the leash.

Cicada Queen

It began the night the Queen called off her dogs. I'd been under the dogs for two years, ever since my defection.

My initiation, and my freedom from the dogs, were celebrated at the home of Arvin Kulagin. Kulagin, a wealthy Mechanist, had a large domestic-industrial complex on the outer perimeter of a midsized cylindrical suburb.

Kulagin met me at his door and handed me a gold inhaler. The party was already roaring. The Polycarbon Clique always turned out in force for an initiation.

As usual, my entrance was marked by a subtle freezing up. It was the dogs' fault. Voices were raised to a certain histrionic pitch, people handled their inhalers and drinks with a slightly more studied elegance, and every smile turned my way was bright enough for a team of security experts.

Kulagin smiled glassily. "Landau, it's a pleasure. Welcome. I see you've brought the Queen's Percentage." He looked pointedly at the box on my hip.

"Yes," I said. A man under the dogs had no secrets. I had been working off and on for two years on the Queen's gift, and the dogs had taped everything. They were still taping everything. Czarina-Kluster Security had designed them for that. For two years they'd taped every moment of my life and everything and everyone around me.

"Perhaps the Clique can have a look," Kulagin said. "Once we've whipped these dogs." He winked into the armored camera face of the watch-dog, then looked at his timepiece. "Just an hour till you're out from under. Then we'll have some fun." He waved me on into the room. "If you need anything, use the servos."

Kulagin's place was spacious and elegant, decorated classically and scented by gigantic suspended marigolds. His suburb was called the Froth and was the Clique's favorite neighborhood. Kulagin, living at the suburb's perimeter, profited by the Froth's lazy spin and had a simulated tenth of a gravity. His walls were striped to provide a vertical referent, and he had enough space to affect such luxuries as "couches," "tables," "chairs," and other forms of gravity-oriented furniture. The ceiling was studded with hooks, from which were suspended a dozen of his favorite marigolds, huge round explosions of reeking greenery with blossoms the size of my head.

I walked into the room and stood behind a couch, which partially hid the two offensive dogs. I signaled one of Kulagin's spidery servos and took a squeezebulb of liquor to cut the speedy intensity of the inhaler's phenethylamine.

I watched the party, which had split into loose subcliques. Kulagin was near the door with his closest sympathizers, Mechanist officers from Czarina-Kluster banks and quiet Security types. Nearby, faculty from the Kosmosity-Metasystem campus talked shop with a pair of orbital engineers. On the ceiling, Shaper designers talked fashion, clinging to hooks in the feeble gravity. Below them a manic group of C-K folk, "Cicadas," spun like clockwork through gravity dance steps.

At the back of the room, Wellspring was holding forth amid a herd of spindly-legged chairs. I leapt gently over the couch and glided toward him. The dogs sprang after me with a whir of propulsive fans.

Wellspring was my closest friend in C-K. He had encouraged my defection when he was in the Ring Council, buying ice for the Martian terraforming project. The dogs never bothered Wellspring. His ancient friendship with the Queen was well known. In C-K, Wellspring was a legend.

Tonight he was dressed for an audience with the Queen. A coronet of gold and platinum circled his dark, matted hair. He wore a loose blouse of metallic brocade with slashed sleeves that showed a black underblouse shot through with flickering pinpoints of light. This was complemented by an Investor-style jeweled skirt and knee-high scaled boots. The jeweled cables of the skirt showed Wellspring's massive legs, trained to the heavy gravity favored by the reptilian Queen. He was a powerful man, and his weaknesses, if he had any, were hidden within his past.

Wellspring was talking philosophy. His audience, mathematicians and biologists from the faculty of C-K K-M, made room for me with strained smiles. "You asked me to define my terms," he said urbanely. "By the term *we*, I don't mean merely you Cicadas. Nor do I mean the mass of so-called humanity. After all, you Shapers are constructed of genes patented by Reshaped genetics firms. You might be properly defined as industrial artifacts."

His audience groaned. Wellspring smiled. "And conversely, the Mechanists are slowly abandoning human flesh in favor of cybernetic modes of existence. So. It follows that my term, *we*, can be attributed to any cognitive metasystem on the Fourth Prigoginic Level of Complexity."

A Shaper professor touched his inhaler to the painted line of his nostril and said, "I have to take issue with that, Wellspring. This occult nonsense about levels of complexity is ruining C-K's ability to do decent science."

"That's a linear causative statement," Wellspring riposted. "You conservatives are always looking for certainties outside the level of the cognitive metasystem. Clearly every intelligent being is separated from every lower level by a Prigoginic event horizon. It's time we learned to stop looking for solid ground to stand on. Let's place *ourselves* at the center of things. If we need something to stand on, we'll have it orbit us."

He was applauded. He said, "Admit it, Yevgeny. C-K is blooming in a new moral and intellectual climate. It's unquantifiable and unpredictable, and, as a scientist, that frightens you. Posthumanism offers fluidity and freedom, and a metaphysic daring enough to think a whole world into life. It enables us to take up economically absurd projects such as the terraforming of Mars, which your pseudopragmatic attitude could never dare to attempt. And yet think of the gain involved."

"Semantic tricks," sniffed the professor. I had never seen him before. I suspected that Wellspring had brought him along for the express purpose of baiting him.

I myself had once doubted some aspects of C-K's Posthumanism. But its open abandonment of the search for moral certainties had liberated us. When I looked at the eager, painted faces of Wellspring's audience, and compared them to the bleak strain and veiled craftiness that had once surrounded me, I felt as if I would burst. After twenty-four years of paranoid discipline under the Ring Council, and then two more years under the dogs, tonight I would be explosively released from pressure.

I sniffed at the phenethylamine, the body's own "natural" amphetamine. I felt suddenly dizzy, as if the space inside my head were full of the red-hot Ur-space of the primordial de Sitter cosmos, ready at any moment to make the Prigoginic leap into the "normal" space-time continuum, the Second Prigoginic Level of Complexity...Posthumanism schooled us to think in terms of fits and starts, of structures accreting along unspoken patterns, following the lines first suggested by the ancient Terran philosopher Ilya Prigogine. I directly understood this, since my own mild attraction to the dazzling Valery Korstad had coalesced into a knotted desire that suppressants could numb but not destroy.

She was dancing across the room, the jeweled strings of her Investor skirt twisting like snakes. She had the anonymous beauty of the Reshaped, overlaid with the ingenious, enticing paint of C-K. I had never seen anything I wanted more, and from our brief and strained flirtations I knew that only the dogs stood between us.

Wellspring took me by the arm. His audience had dissolved as I stood rapt, lusting after Valery. "How much longer, son?"

Startled, I looked at the watch display on my forearm. "Only twenty minutes, Wellspring."

"That's fine, son." Wellspring was famous for his use of archaic terms like *son*. "Once the dogs are gone, it'll be your party, Hans. I won't stay here to eclipse you. Besides, the Queen awaits me. You have the Queen's Percentage?"

"Yes, just as you said." I unpeeled the box from the stick-tight patch on my hip and handed it over.

Wellspring lifted its lid with his powerful fingers and looked inside. Then he laughed aloud. "Jesus! It's beautiful!"

Suddenly he pulled the open box away and the Queen's gift hung in midair, glittering above our heads. It was an artificial gem the size of a child's fist, its chiseled planes glittering with the green and gold of endolithic lichen. As it spun it threw tiny glints of fractured light across our faces.

As it fell, Kulagin appeared and caught it on the points of four extended fingertips. His left eye, an artificial implant, glistened darkly as he examined it.

"Eisho Zaibatsu?" he asked.

"Yes," I said. "They handled the synthesizing work; the lichen is a special variety of my own." I saw that a curious circle was gathering and said aloud, "Our host is a connoisseur."

"Only of finance," Kulagin said quietly, but with equal emphasis. "I understand now why you patented the process in your own name. It's a dazzling accomplishment. How could any Investor resist the lure of a living jewel, friends? Someday soon our initiate will be a wealthy man."

I looked quickly at Wellspring, but he unobtrusively touched one finger to his lips. "And he'll need that wealth to bring Mars to fruition," Wellspring said loudly. "We can't depend forever on the Kosmosity for funding. Friends, rejoice that you too will reap the profits of Landau's ingenious genetics." He caught the jewel and boxed it. "And tonight I have the honor of presenting his gift to the Queen. A double honor, since I recruited its creator myself." Suddenly he leapt toward the exit, his powerful legs carrying him quickly above our heads. As he flew he shouted, "Goodbye, son! May another dog never darken your doorstep!"

With Wellspring's exit, the non-Polycarbon guests began leaving, forming a jostling knot of hat-fetching servos and gossiping well-wishers. When the last was gone, the Clique grew suddenly quiet.

Kulagin had me stand at a far corner of his studio while the Clique formed a long gauntlet for the dogs, arming themselves with ribbons and paint. A certain dark edge of smoldering vengeance only added a tang to their enjoyment. I took a pair of paint balloons from one of Kulagin's scurrying servos.

The time was almost on me. For two long years I'd schemed to join the Polycarbon Clique. I needed them. I felt they needed me. I was tired of suspicion, of strained politeness, of the glass walls of the dogs' surveillance. The keen edges of my long discipline suddenly, painfully, crumbled. I began shaking uncontrollably, unable to hold it back.

The dogs were still, taping steadily to the last appointed instant. The crowd began to count down. Exactly at the count of zero the two dogs turned to go.

They were barraged with paint and tangled streamers. A moment earlier they would have turned savagely on their tormentors, but now they had reached the limits of their programming, and at long last they were helpless. The Clique's aim was deadly, and with every splattering hit they split the air with screams of laughter. They knew no mercy, and it took a full minute before the humiliated dogs could hop and stagger, blinded, to the door.

I was overcome with mob hysteria. Screams escaped my clenched teeth. I had to be grappled back from pursuing the dogs down the hall. As firm hands pulled me back within the room I turned to face my friends, and I was chilled at the raw emotion on their faces. It was as if they had been stripped of skin and watched me with live eyes in slabs of meat.

I was picked up bodily and passed from hand to hand around the room. Even those that I knew well seemed alien to me now. Hands tore at my clothing until I was stripped; they even took my computer gauntlet, then stood me in the middle of the room.

As I stood shivering within the circle, Kulagin approached me, his arms rigid, his face stiff and hieratic. His hands were full of loose black cloth. He held the cloth over my head, and I saw that it was a black hood. He put his lips close to my ear and said softly, "Friend, go the distance." Then he pulled the hood over my head and knotted it.

The hood had been soaked in something; I could smell that it reeked. My hands and feet began to tingle, then go numb. Slowly, warmth crept like bracelets up my arms and legs. I could hear nothing, and my feet could no longer feel the floor. I lost all sense of balance, and suddenly I fell backward, into the infinite.

My eyes opened, or my eyes closed, I couldn't tell. But at the limits of vision, from behind some unspoken fog, emerged pinpoints of cold and piercing brightness. It was the Great Galactic Night, the vast and pitiless emptiness that lurks just beyond the warm rim of every human habitat, emptier even than death.

I was naked in space, and it was so bitterly cold that I could taste it like poison in every cell I had. I could feel the pale heat of my own life streaming out of me like plasma, ebbing away in aurora sheets from my fingertips. I continued to fall, and as the last rags of warmth pulsed off into the devouring chasm of space, and my body grew stiff and white and furred with frost from every pore, I faced the ultimate horror: that I would not die, that I would fall forever backward into the unknown, my mind shriveling into a single frozen spore of isolation and terror.

Time dilated. Eons of silent fear telescoped into a few heartbeats and I saw before me a single white blob of light, like a rent from this cosmos into some neighboring realm full of alien radiance. This time I faced it as I fell toward it, and through it, and then, finally, jarringly, I was back behind my own eyes, within my own head, on the soft floor of Kulagin's studio.

The hood was gone. I wore a loose black robe, closed with an embroidered belt. Kulagin and Valery Korstad helped me to my feet. I wobbled, brushing away tears, but I managed to stand, and the Clique cheered.

Kulagin's shoulder was under my arm. He embraced me and whispered, "Brother, remember the cold. When we your friends need warmth, be warm, remembering the cold. When friendship pains you, forgive us, remembering the cold. When selfishness tempts you, renounce it, remembering the cold. For you have gone the distance, and returned to us renewed. Remember, remember the cold." And then he gave me my secret name, and pressed his painted lips to mine.

I clung to him, choked with sobs. Valery embraced me and Kulagin pulled away gently, smiling.

One by one the Clique took my hands and pressed their lips quickly to my face, murmuring congratulations. Still unable to speak, I could only nod. Meanwhile Valery Korstad, clinging to my arm, whispered hotly in my ear, "Hans, Hans, Hans Landau, there still remains a certain ritual, which I have reserved to myself. Tonight the finest chamber in the Froth belongs to us, a sacred place where no glassy-eyed dog has ever trespassed. Hans Landau, tonight that place belongs to you, and so do I."

I looked into her face, my eyes watering. Her eyes were dilated, and a pink flush had spread itself under her ears and along her jawline. She had dosed herself with hormonal aphrodisiacs. I smelled the antiseptic sweetness of her perfumed sweat and I closed my eyes, shuddering.

Valery led me into the hall. Behind us, Kulagin's door sealed shut, cutting the hilarity to a murmur. Valery helped me slip on my air fins, whispering soothingly.

The dogs were gone. Two chunks of my reality had been edited like tape. I still felt dazed. Valery took my hand, and we threaded a corridor upward toward the center of the habitat, kicking along with our air fins. I smiled mechanically at the Cicadas we passed in the halls, members of another day crowd. They were soberly going about their day shift's work while the Polycarbon Clique indulged in bacchanalia.

It was easy to lose yourself within the Froth. It had been built in rebellion against the regimented architecture of other habitats, in C-K's typical defiance of the norm. The original empty cylinder had been packed with pressurized plastic, which had been blasted to foam and allowed to set. It left angular bubbles whose tilted walls were defined by the clean topologies of close packing and surface tension. Halls had been snaked through the complex later, and the doors and airlocks cut by hand. The Froth was famous for its delirious and welcome spontaneity.

And its discreets were notorious. C-K showed its civic spirit in the lavish appointments of these citadels against surveillance. I had never been in one before. People under the dogs were not allowed across the boundaries. But I had heard rumors, the dark and prurient scandal of bars and corridors, those scraps of licentious speculation that always hushed at the approach of dogs. Anything, anything at all, could happen in a discreet, and no one would know of it but the lovers or survivors who returned, hours later, to public life...

As the centrifugal gravity faded we began floating, Valery half-towing me. The bubbles of the Froth had swollen near the axis of rotation, and we entered a neighborhood of the quiet industrial domiciles of the rich. Soon we had floated to the very doorstep of the infamous Topaz Discreet, the hushed locale of unnumbered elite frolics. It was the finest in the Froth.

Valery looked at her timepiece, caressing away a fine film of sweat that had formed on the flushed and perfect lines of her face and neck. We hadn't long to wait. We heard the mellow repeated bonging of the discreet's time alarm, warning the present occupant that his time was up. The door's locks unsealed. I wondered just what member of C-K's inner circle would emerge. Now that I was free of the dogs, I longed to boldly meet his eyes.

Still we waited. Now the discreet was ours by right and every moment lost pained us. To overstay in a discreet was the height of rudeness. Valery grew angry, and pushed open the door.

The air was full of blood. In free-fall, it floated in a thousand clotting red blobs.

Near the center of the room floated the suicide, his flaccid body still wheeling slowly from the gush of his severed throat. A scalpel glittered in the mechanically clenched fingers of the cadaver's outstretched hand. He wore the sober black overalls of a conservative Mechanist.

The body spun, and I saw the insignia of the Queen's Advisers stitched on his breast. His partially metallic skull was sticky with his own blood; the face was obscured. Long streamers of thickened blood hung from his throat like red veils.

We had cometaried into something very much beyond us. "I'll call Security," I said.

She said two words. "Not yet." I looked into her face. Her eyes were dark with fascinated lust. The lure of the forbidden had slid its hooks into her in a single moment. She kicked languidly across one tessellated wall, and a long streak of blood splattered and broke along her hip.

In discreets one met the ultimates. In a room with so many hidden meanings, the lines had blurred. Through constant proximity pleasure had wedded with death. For the woman I adored, the private rites transpiring there had become of one unspoken piece.

"Hurry," she said. Her lips were bitter with a thin grease of aphrodisiacs. We interlaced our legs to couple in free-fall while we watched his body twist.

That was the night the Queen called off her dogs.

▲ ▼ ▲

It had thrilled me in a way that made me sick. We Cicadas lived in the moral equivalent of de Sitter space, where no ethos had validity unless it was generated by noncausative free will. Every level of Prigoginic Complexity was based on a self-dependent generative catalyst: space existed because space existed, life was because it had come to be, intelligence was because it is. So it was possible for an entire moral system to accrete around a single moment of profound disgust...Or so Posthumanism taught. After my blighted consummation with Valery I withdrew to work and think.

I lived in the Froth, in a domestic-industrial studio that reeked of lichen and was much less chic than Kulagin's.

On the second day-shift of my meditation I was visited by Arkadya Sorienti, a Polycarbon friend and one of Valery's intimates. Even without the dogs there were elements of a profound strain between us. It seemed to me that Arkadya was everything that Valery was not: blonde where Valery was dark, covered with Mechanist gimmickry where Valery had the cool elegance of the genetically Reshaped, full of false and brittle gaiety where Valery was prey to soft and melancholy gloom. I offered her a squeezebulb of liqueur; my apartment was too close to the axis to use cups.

"I haven't seen your apartment before," she said. "I love your airframes, Hans. What kind of algae is it?"

"It's lichen," I said.

"They're beautiful. One of your special kinds?"

"They're all special," I said. "Those have the Mark III and IV varieties for the terraforming project. The others have some delicate strains I was working on for contamination monitors. Lichen are very sensitive to pollution of any sort." I turned up the air ionizer. The intestines of Mechanists seethed with bacteria, and their effects could be disastrous.

"Which one is the lichen of the Queen's jewel?"

"It's locked away," I said. "Outside the environs of a jewel its growth becomes very distorted. And it smells." I smiled uneasily. It was common talk among Shapers that Mechanists stank. It seemed to me that I could already smell the reek of her armpits.

Arkadya smiled and nervously rubbed the skin-metal interface of a silvery blob of machinery grafted along her forearm. "Valery's in one of her states," she said. "I thought I'd come see how you were."

In my mind's eye flickered the nightmare image of our naked skins slicked with blood. I said, "It was...unfortunate."

"C-K's full of talk about the Comptroller's death."

"It was the Comptroller?" I said. "I haven't seen any news."

Slyness crept into her eyes. "You saw him there," she said.

I was shocked that she should expect me to discuss my stay in a discreet. "I have work," I said. I kicked my fins so that I drifted off our mutual vertical. Facing each other sideways increased the social distance between us.

She laughed quietly. "Don't be a prig, Hans. You act as if you were still under the dogs. You have to tell me about it if you want me to help the two of you."

I stopped my drift. She said, "And I want to help. I'm Valery's friend. I like the way you look together. It appeals to my sense of aesthetics."

"Thanks for your concern."

"I *am* concerned. I'm tired of seeing her on the arm of an old lecher like Wellspring."

"You're telling me they're lovers?" I said.

She fluttered her metal-clad fingers in the air. "You're asking me what the two of them do in his favorite discreet? Maybe they play chess." She rolled her eyes under lids heavy with powdered gold. "Don't look so shocked, Hans. You should know his power as well as anyone. He's old and rich; we Polycarbon women are young and not too terribly principled." She looked quickly up and away from beneath long lashes. "I've never heard that he took anything from us that we weren't willing to give." She floated closer. "Tell me what you saw, Hans. C-K's crazy with the news, and Valery does nothing but mope."

I opened the refrigerator and dug among Petri dishes for more liqueur. "It strikes me that you should be doing the talking, Arkadya."

She hesitated, then shrugged and smiled. "Now you're showing some sense, my friend. Open eyes and ears can take you a long way in C-Kluster." She took a stylish inhaler from a holster on her enameled garter. "And speaking of eyes and ears, have you had your place swept for bugs yet?"

"Who'd bug me?"

"Who wouldn't?" She looked bored. "I'll stick to what's common knowledge, then. Hire us a discreet sometime, and I'll give you all the rest." She fired a stream of amber liqueur from arm's length and sucked it in as it splashed against her teeth. "Something big is stirring in C-K. It hasn't reached the rank and file yet, but the Comptroller's death is a sign of it. The other Advisers are treating it like a personal matter, but it's clear that he wasn't simply tired of life. He left his affairs in disorder. No, this is something that runs back to the Queen herself. I'm sure of it."

"You think the Queen ordered him to take his own life?"

"Maybe. She's getting erratic with age. Wouldn't you, though, if you had to spend your life surrounded by aliens? I feel for the Queen, I really do. If she needs to kill a few stuffy rich old bastards for her own peace of mind, its perfectly fine by me. In fact, if that's all there was to it, I'd sleep easier."

I thought about this, my face impassive. The entire structure of Czarina-Kluster was predicated on the Queen's exile. For seventy years, defectors, malcontents, pirates, and pacifists had accreted around the refuge of our alien Queen. The powerful prestige of her fellow Investors protected us from the predatory machinations of Shaper fascists and dehumanized Mechanist sects. C-K was an oasis of sanity amid the vicious amorality of humanity's warring factions. Our suburbs spun in webs around the dark hulk of the Queen's blazing, jeweled environment.

She was all we had. There was a giddy insecurity under all our success. C-K's famous banks were backed by the Cicada Queen's tremendous wealth. The academic freedom of C-K's teaching centers flourished only under her shadow.

And we did not even know why she was disgraced. Rumors abounded, but only the Investors themselves knew the truth. Were she ever to leave us, Czarina-Kluster would disintegrate overnight.

I said offhandedly, "I've heard talk that she's not happy. It seems these rumors spread, and they raise her Percentage for a while and panel a new room with jewels, and then the rumors fade."

"That's true...She and our sweet Valery are two of a kind where these dark moods are concerned. It's clear, though, that the Comptroller was left no choice but suicide. And that means disaster is stirring at the heart of C-K."

"It's only rumors," I said. "The Queen is the heart of C-K, and who knows what's going on in that huge head of hers?"

"Wellspring would know," Arkadya said intently.

"But he's not an Adviser," I said. "As far as the Queen's inner circle is concerned, he's little better than a pirate."

"Tell me what you saw in Topaz Discreet."

"You'll have to allow me some time," I said. "It's rather painful." I wondered what I should tell her, and what she was willing to believe. The silence began to stretch.

I put on a tape of Terran sea sounds. The room began to surge ominously with the roar of alien surf.

"I wasn't ready for it," I said. "In my crèche we were taught to guard our feelings from childhood. I know how the Clique feels about distance. But that kind of raw intimacy, from a woman I really scarcely know—especially under that night's circumstances—it wounded me." I looked searchingly into Arkadya's face, longing to reach through her to Valery. "Once it was over, we were further apart than ever."

Arkadya tilted her head to the side and winced. "Who composed this?"

"What? You mean the music? It's a background tape—sea sounds from Earth. It's a couple of centuries old."

She looked at me oddly. "You're really absorbed by the whole planetary thing, aren't you? 'Sea sounds.'"

"Mars will have seas someday. That's what our whole Project is about, isn't it?"

She looked disturbed. "Sure…We're working at it, Hans, but that doesn't mean we have to live there. I mean, that's centuries from now, isn't it? Even if we're still alive, we'll be different people by then. Just think of being trapped down a gravity well. I'd choke to death."

I said quietly, "I don't think of it as being for the purposes of settlement. It's a clearer, more ideal activity. The instigation by Fourth-Level cognitive agents of a Third-Level Prigoginic Leap. Bringing life itself into being on the naked bedrock of space-time…"

But she was shaking her head and backpedaling toward the door. "I'm sorry, Hans, but those sounds, they're just…getting into my blood somehow…She shook herself, shuddering, and the filigree beads woven into her blonde hair clattered loudly. "I can't bear it."

"I'll turn it off."

But she was already leaving. "Goodbye, goodbye…We'll meet again soon."

She was gone. I was left to steep in my own isolation, while the roaring surf gnawed and mumbled at its shore.

▲ ▼ ▲

One of Kulagin's servos met me at his door and took my hat. Kulagin was seated at a workplace in a screened-off corner of his marigold-reeking domicile, watching stock quotations scroll down a display screen. He was dictating orders into a microphone on his forearm gauntlet. When the servo announced me he unplugged the jack from his gauntlet and stood, shaking my hand with both of his. "Welcome, friend, welcome."

"I hope I haven't come at a bad time."

"No, not at all. Do you play the Market?"

"Not seriously," I said. "Later, maybe, when the royalties from Eisho Zaibatsu pile up."

"You must allow me to guide your eyes, then. A good Posthumanist should have a wide range of interests. Take that chair, if you would."

I sat beside Kulagin as he sat before the console and plugged in. Kulagin was a Mechanist, but he kept himself rigorously antiseptic. I liked him.

He said, "Odd how these financial institutions tend to drift from their original purpose. In a way, the Market itself has made a sort of Prigoginic Leap. On its face, it's a commercial tool, but it's become a game of conventions and confidences. We Cicadas eat, breathe, and sleep rumors, so the Market is the perfect expression of our Zeitgeist."

"Yes," I said. "Frail, mannered, and based on practically nothing tangible."

Kulagin lifted his plucked brows. "Yes, my young friend, exactly like the bedrock of the cosmos itself. Every level of complexity floats freely on the last, supported only by abstractions. Even natural laws are only our attempts to strain our vision through the Prigoginic event horizon…If you prefer a more primal metaphor, we can compare the Market to the sea. A sea of information, with a few blue-chip islands here and there for the exhausted swimmer. Look at this."

He touched buttons, and a three-dimensional grid display sprang into being. "This is Market activity in the past forty-eight hours. It looks rather like the waves and billows of a sea, doesn't it? Note these surges of transaction." He touched the screen with the light pen implanted in his forefinger, and gridded areas flushed from cool green to red. "That was when the first rumors of the iceteroid came in—"

"What?"

"The asteroid, the ice-mass from the Ring Council. Someone has bought it and is mass-driving it out of Saturn's gravity well right now, bound for Martian impact. Someone very clever, for it will pass within a few thousands of klicks from C-K. Close enough for naked-eyed view."

"You mean they've really done it?" I said, caught between shock and joy.

"I heard it third-, fourth-, maybe tenth-hand, but it fits in well with the parameters the Polycarbon engineers have set up. A mass of ice and volatiles, well over three klicks across, targeted for the Hellas Depression south of the equator at sixty-five klicks a second, impact expected at UT 20:14:53, 14-4-´-54…That's dawn, local time. Local Martian time, I mean."

"But that's months from now," I said.

Kulagin smirked. "Look, Hans, you don't push a three-klick ice lump with your thumbs. Besides, this is just the first of dozens. It's more of a symbolic gesture."

"But it means we'll be moving out! To Martian orbit!"

Kulagin looked skeptical. "That's a job for drones and monitors, Hans. Or maybe a few rough and tough pioneer types. Actually, there's no reason why you and I should have to leave the comforts of C-K."

I stood up, knotting my hands. "You want to *stay*? And miss the Prigoginic catalyst?"

Kulagin looked up with a slight frown. "Cool off, Hans, sit down, they'll be looking for volunteers soon enough, and if you really mean to go I'm sure you can manage somehow...The point is that the effect on the Market has been spectacular...It's been fairly giddy ever since the Comptroller's death, and now some very big fish indeed is rising for the kill. I've been following his movements for three day-shifts straight, hoping to feast on his scraps, so to speak...Care for an inhale?"

"No, thanks."

Kulagin helped himself to a long pull of stimulant. He looked ragged. I'd never seen him without his face paint before. He said, "I don't have the feeling for mob psychology that you Shapers have, so I have to make do with a very, very good memory...The last time I saw something like this was thirteen years ago. Someone spread the rumor that the Queen had tried to leave C-K, and the Advisers had restrained her by force. The upshot of that was the Crash of 'Forty-one, but the real killing came in the Rally that followed. I've been reviewing the tapes of the Crash, and I recognize the fins and flippers and big sharp teeth of an old friend. I can read his style in his maneuvering. It's not the slick guile of a Shaper. It's not the cold persistence of a Mechanist, either."

I considered. "Then you must mean Wellspring."

Wellspring's age was unknown. He was well over two centuries old. He claimed to have been born on Earth in the dawn of the Space Age, and to have lived in the first generation of independent space colonies, the so-called Concatenation. He had been among the founders of Czarina-Kluster, building the Queen's habitat when she fled in disgrace from her fellow Investors.

Kulagin smiled. "Very good, Hans. You may live in moss, but there's none on you. I think Wellspring engineered the Crash of 'Forty-one for his own profit."

"But he lives very modestly."

"As the Queen's oldest friend, he was certainly in a perfect position to start rumors. He even engineered the parameters of the Market itself, seventy years ago. And it was after the Rally that the Kosmosity-Metasystems Department of Terraformation was set up. Through anonymous donations, of course."

"But contributions came in from all over the system," I objected. "Almost all the sects and factions think that terraforming is humanity's sublimest effort."

"To be sure. Though I wonder just how that idea became so widely spread. And to whose benefit. Listen, Hans. I love Wellspring. He's a *friend*, and I remember the cold. But you have to realize just what an anomaly he is. He's not one of us. He wasn't even born in space." He looked at me narrowly, but I took no offense at his use of the term *born*. It was a deadly insult against Shapers, but I considered myself a Polycarbon first and Cicada second, with Shaperism a distant third.

He smiled briefly. "To be sure, Wellspring has a few Mechanist knickknacks implanted, to extend his life span, but he lacks the whole Mech style. In fact he actually *predates* it. I'd be the last to deny the genius of you Shapers, but in a way it's an artificial genius. It works out well enough on IQ tests, but it somehow lacks that, well, primeval quality that Wellspring has, just as we Mechanists can use cybernetic modes of thinking but we can never be actual machines...Wellspring simply is one of those people at the farthest reaches of the bell curve, one of those titans that spring up only once a generation. I mean, think what's become of his normal human contemporaries."

I nodded. "Most of them have become Mechs."

Kulagin shook his head fractionally, staring at the screen. "I was born here in C-K. I don't know that much about the old-style Mechs, but I do know that most of the first ones are dead. Outdated, crowded out. Driven over the edge by future shock. A lot of the first life-extension efforts failed, too, in very ugly ways...Wellspring survived that, too, from some innate knack he has. Think of it, Hans. Here we sit, products of technologies so advanced that they've smashed society to bits. We trade with aliens. We can even hitchhike to the stars, if we pay the Investors' fare. And Wellspring not only holds his own, he rules us. We don't even know his real name."

I considered what Kulagin had said while he switched to a Market update. I felt bad. I could hide my feelings, but I couldn't shake them off. "You're right," I said. "But I trust him."

"I trust him too, but I know we're cradled in his hands. In fact, he's protecting us right now. This terraforming project has cost megawatt after megawatt. All those contributions were anonymous, supposedly to prevent the factions from using them for propaganda. But I think it was to hide the fact that most of them were from Wellspring. Any day now there's going to be an extended Market crash. Wellspring will make his move, and that will start the rally. And every kilowatt of his profits will go to us."

I leaned forward in my chair, interlacing my fingers. Kulagin dictated a series of selling orders into his microphone. Suddenly I laughed.

Kulagin looked up. "That's the first time I've ever heard you laugh like you meant it, Hans."

"I was just thinking...You've told me all this, but I came here to talk about Valery."

Kulagin looked sad. "Listen, Hans. What I know about women you could hide under a microchip, but, as I said, my memory is excellent. The Shapers blundered when they pushed things to the limits. The Ring Council tried to break the so-called Two-Hundred-Barrier last century. Most of the so-called Superbrights went mad, defected, turned against their fellows, or all three. They've been hunted down by pirates and mercenaries for decades now.

"One group found out somehow that there was an Investor Queen living in exile, and they managed to make it to her shadow, for protection. And someone—you can imagine who—talked the Queen into letting them stay, if they paid a certain tax. That tax became the Queen's Percentage, and the settlement became Czarina-Kluster. Valery's parents—yes, *parents*; it was a natural birth—were among those Superbrights. She didn't have the schooling Shapers use, so she ranks in at only one forty-five or so.

"The problem is those mood cycles of hers. Her parents had them, she's had them since she was a child. She's a dangerous woman, Hans. Dangerous to herself, to all of us. She should be under the dogs, really. I've suggested that to my friends in Security, but someone stands in my way. I have my ideas who."

"I'm in love with her. She won't speak to me."

"I see. Well, I understand she's been full of mood suppressants lately; that probably accounts for her reticence...I'll speak frankly. There's an old saying, Hans, that you should never enter a discreet with someone crazier than you are. And it's good advice. You can't trust Valery."

He held up his hand. "Hear me out. You're young. You've just come out from under the dogs. This woman has enchanted you, and admittedly she has the famous Shaper charm in full measure. But a liaison with Valery is like an affair with five women, three of whom are crazy. C-K is full to bursting with the most beautiful women in human history. Admittedly you're a bit stiff, a bit of an obsessive perhaps, but you have a certain idealistic charm. And you have that Shaper intensity, fanaticism even, if you don't mind my saying so. Loosen up a little, Hans. Find some woman who'll rub the rough edges off of you. Play the field. It's a good way to recruit new friends to the Clique."

"I'll keep what you said in mind," I said.

"Right. I knew it was wasted effort." He smiled ironically. "Why should I blight the purity of your emotions? A tragic first love may become an asset to you, fifty or a hundred years from now." He turned his attention back to the screen. "I'm glad we had this talk, Hans. I hope you'll get in touch again when the Eisho Zaibatsu money comes through. We'll have some fun with it."

"I'd like that," I said, though I knew already that every kilowatt not spent on my own research would go—anonymously—to the terraforming fund. "And I don't resent your advice. It's just that it's of no use to me."

"Ah, youth," Kulagin said. I left.

▲ ▼ ▲

Back to the simple beauty of the lichens. I had been trained for years to specialize in them, but they had taken on beauty and meaning for me only after my Posthumanist enlightenment. Viewed through C-K's philosophies, they stood near the catalysis point of the Prigoginic Leap that brought life itself into being.

Alternately, a lichen could be viewed as an extended metaphor for the Polycarbon Clique: a fungus and an alga, potential rivals, united in symbiosis to accomplish what neither could do alone, just as the Clique united Mechanist and Shaper to bring life to Mars.

I knew that many viewed my dedication as strange, even unhealthy. I was not offended by their blindness. Just the names of my genetic stocks had a rolling majesty: *Alectoria nigricans, Mastodia tessellata, Ochrolechia frigida, Stereocaulon alpinum*. They were humble but powerful: creatures of the cold desert whose roots and acids could crumble naked, freezing rock.

My gel frames seethed with primal vitality. Lichens would drench Mars in one green-gold tidal wave of life. They would creep irresistibly from the moist craters of the iceteroid impacts, proliferating relentlessly amid the storms and earthquakes of terraformation, surviving the floods as permafrost melted. Gushing oxygen, fixing nitrogen.

They were the best. Not because of pride or show. Not because they trumpeted their motives, or threatened the cold before they broke it. But because they were silent, and the first.

My years under the dogs had taught me the value of silence. Now I was sick of surveillance. When the first royalty payment came in from Eisho Zaibatsu, I contacted one of C-K's private security firms and had my apartments swept for bugs. They found four.

I hired a second firm to remove the bugs left by the first.

I strapped myself in at a floating workbench, turning the spy eyes over and over in my hands. They were flat videoplates, painted with one-way colorshifting polymer camouflage. They would fetch a nice price on the unofficial market.

I called a post office and hired a courier servo to take the bugs to Kulagin. While I awaited the servo's arrival, I turned off the bugs and sealed them into a biohazard box. I dictated a note, asking Kulagin to sell them and invest the money for me in C-K's faltering Market. The Market looked as if it could use a few buyers.

When I heard the courier's staccato knock, I opened my door with a gauntlet remote. But it was no courier that whirred in. It was a guard dog.

"I'll take that box, if you please," said the dog.

I stared at it as if I had never seen a dog before. This dog was heavily armored in silver. Thin powerful limbs jutted from its silver-seamed black-plastic torso, and its swollen head bristled with spring-loaded taser darts and the blunt nozzles of restraint webs. Its swiveling antenna tail showed that it was under remote control.

I spun my workbench so that it stood between me and the dog. "I see you have my comm lines tapped as well," I said. "Will you tell me where the taps are, or do I have to take my computer apart?"

"You sniveling little Shaper upstart," commented the dog, "Do you think your royalties can buy you out from under everyone? I could sell you on the open market before you could blink."

I considered this. On a number of occasions, particularly troublesome meddlers in C-K had been arrested and offered for sale on the open market by the Queen's Advisers. There were always factions outside C-K willing to pay good prices for enemy agents. I knew that the Ring Council would be overjoyed to make an example of me. "You're claiming to be one of the Queen's Advisers, then?"

"*Of course* I'm an Adviser! Your treacheries haven't lured us all to sleep. Your friendship with Wellspring is notorious!" The dog whirred closer, its clumped camera eyes clicking faintly. "What's inside that freezer?"

"Lichen racks," I said impassively. "You should know that well enough."

"Open it."

I didn't move. "You're going beyond the bounds of normal operations," I said, knowing that this would trouble any Mechanist. "My Clique has friends among the Advisers. I've done nothing wrong."

"Open it, or I'll web you and open it myself, with this dog."

"Lies," I said. "You're no Adviser. You're an industrial spy, trying to steal my gemstone lichen. Why would an Adviser want to look into my freezer?"

"Open it! Don't involve yourself more deeply in things you don't understand."

"You've entered my domicile under false pretenses and threatened me," I said. "I'm calling Security."

The dog's chromed jaws opened. I twisted myself free of the workbench, but a thready spray of white silk from one of the dog's facial nozzles caught me as I dodged. The filaments clung and hardened instantly, locking my arms in place where I had instinctively raised them to block the spray. A second blast caught my legs as I struggled uselessly, bouncing off a tilted Froth-wall.

"Troublemaker," muttered the dog. "Everything would have gone down smooth without you Shapers quibbling. We had the soundest banks, we had the Queen, the Market, everything…You parasites gave C-K nothing but your fantasies. Now the system's crumbling. Everything will crash. Everything. I ought to kill you."

I gasped for breath as the spray rigidified across my chest. "Life isn't banks," I wheezed.

Motors whined as the dog flexed its jointed limbs. "If I find what I expect in that freezer, you're as good as dead."

Suddenly the dog stopped in midair. Its fans whirred as it wheeled to face the door. The door clicked convulsively and began to slide open. A massive taloned forelimb slammed through the opening.

The watchdog webbed the door shut. Suddenly the door shrieked and buckled, its metal peeling back like foil. The goggling head and spiked legs of a tiger crunched and thrashed through the wreckage. "Treason!" the tiger roared.

The dog whirred backward, cringing, as the tiger pulled its armored hindquarters into the room. The jagged wreckage of the door didn't even scratch it. Armored in black and gold, it was twice the size of the watchdog. "Wait," the dog said.

"The Council warned you against vigilante action," the tiger said heavily. "I warned you myself."

"I had to make a choice, Coordinator. It's his doing. He turned us against one another, you have to see that."

"You have only one choice left," the tiger said. "Choose your discreet, Councilman."

The dog flexed its limbs indecisively. "So I'm to be the second," he said. "First the Comptroller, now myself. Very well, then. Very well. He has me. I can't retaliate." The dog seemed to gather itself up for a rush. "But I can destroy his favorite!"

The dog's legs shot open like telescopes, and it sprang off a wall for my throat. There was a terrific flash with the stench of ozone, and the dog slammed bruisingly into my chest. It was dead, its circuits stripped. The lights flickered and went out as my home computer faltered and crashed, its programming scrambled by incidental radiation from the tiger's electromagnetic pulse.

Flanges popped open on the tiger's bulbous head, and two spotlights emerged. "Do you have any implants?" it said.

"No," I said. "No cybernetic parts. I'm all right. You saved my life."

"Close your eyes," the tiger commanded. It washed me with a fine mist of solvent from its nostrils. The web peeled off in its talons, taking my clothing with it.

My forearm gauntlet was ruined. I said, "I've committed no crime against the state, Coordinator. I love C-K."

"These are strange days," the tiger rumbled. "Our routines are in decay. No one is above suspicion. You picked a bad time to make your home mimic a discreet, young man."

"I did it openly," I said.

"There are no rights here, Cicada. Only the Queen's graces. Dress yourself and ride the tiger. We need to talk. I'm taking you to the Palace."

The Palace was like one gigantic discreet. I wondered if I would ever leave its mysteries alive.

I had no choice.

I dressed carefully under the tiger's goggling eyes, and mounted it. It smelled of aging lubrication. It must have been in storage for decades. Tigers had not been seen at large in C-K for years.

The halls were crowded with Cicadas going on and off their day shifts. At the tiger's approach they scattered in terror and awe.

We exited the Froth at its cylinder end, into the gimbaling cluster of interurban tube roads.

The roads were transparent polycarbon conduits, linking C-K's cylindrical suburbs in an untidy web. The sight of these shining habitats against the icy background of the stars gave me a sharp moment of vertigo. I remembered the cold.

We passed through a thickened knot along the web, a swollen intersection of tube roads where one of C-K's famous highway bistros had accreted itself into being. The lively gossip of its glittering habitués froze into a stricken silence as I rode by, and swelled into a chorus of alarm as I left. The news would permeate C-K in minutes.

The Palace imitated an Investor starship: an octahedron with six long rectangular sides. Genuine Investor ships were crusted with fantastic designs in hammered metal, but the Queen's was an uneven dull black, reflecting her unknown shame. With the passage of time it had grown by fits and starts, and now it was lumped and flanged with government offices and the Queen's covert hideaways. The ponderous hulk spun with dizzying speed.

We entered along one axis into a searing bath of blue-white light. My eyes shrank painfully and began oozing tears.

The Queen's Advisers were Mechanists, and the halls swarmed with servos. They passively followed their routines, ignoring the tiger, whose chromed and plated surfaces gleamed viciously in the merciless light.

A short distance from the axis the centrifugal force seized us and the tiger sank creaking onto its massive legs. The walls grew baroque with mosaics and spun designs in filamented precious metals. The tiger stalked down a flight of stairs. My spine popped audibly in the increasing gravity, and I sat erect with an effort.

Most of the halls were empty. We passed occasional clumps of jewels in the walls that blazed like lightning. I leaned against the tiger's back and locked my elbows, my heart pounding. More stairs. Tears ran down my face and into my mouth, a sensation that was novel and disgusting. My arms trembled with fatigue.

The Coordinator's office was on the perimeter. It kept him in shape for audiences with the Queen. The tiger stalked creaking through a pair of massive doors, built to Investor scale.

Everything in the office was in Investor scale. The ceilings were more than twice the height of a man. A chandelier overhead gushed a blistering radiance over two immense chairs with tall backs split by tail holes. A fountain surged and splattered feebly, exhausted by strain.

The Coordinator sat behind a keyboarded business desk. The top of the desk rose almost to his armpits, and his scaled boots dangled far above the floor. Beside him a monitor scrolled down the latest Market reports.

I heaved myself, grunting, off the tiger's back and up into the scratchy plush of an Investor chair seat. Built for an Investor's scaled rump, it pierced my trousers like wire.

"Have some sun shades," the Coordinator said. He opened a cavernous desk drawer, fished elbow-deep for a pair of goggles, and hurled them at me. I reached high, and they hit me in the chest.

I wiped my eyes and put on the goggles, groaning with relief. The tiger crouched at the foot of my chair, whirring to itself.

"Your first time in the Palace?" the Coordinator said.

I nodded with an effort.

"It's horrible, I know. And yet, it's all we have. You have to understand that, Landau. This is C-K's Prigoginic catalyst."

"You know the philosophy?" I said.

"Surely. Not all of us are fossilized. The Advisers have their factions. That's common knowledge." The Coordinator pushed his chair back. Then he stood up in its seat, climbed up onto his desk top, and sat on its forward edge facing me, his scaled boots dangling.

He was a blunt, stocky, powerfully muscled man, moving easily in the force that flattened me. His face was deeply and ferociously creased with two centuries of seams and wrinkles. His black skin gleamed dully in the searing light. His eyeballs had the brittle look of plastic. He said, "I've seen the tapes the dogs made, and I feel I understand you, Landau. Your sin is distance."

He sighed. "And yet you are less corrupt than others...There is a certain threshold, an intensity of sin and cynicism, beyond which no society can survive...Listen. I know about Shapers. The Ring Council. Stitched together by black fear and red greed, drawing power from the momentum of its own collapse. But C-K's had hope. You've lived here, you must have at least seen it, if you can't feel it directly. You must know how precious this place is. Under the Cicada Queen, we've drawn survival from a state of mind. Belief counts, confidence is central." The Comptroller looked at me, his dark face sagging. "I'll tell you the truth. And depend on your goodwill. For the proper response."

"Thank you."

"C-K is in crisis. Rumors of the Queen's disaffection have brought the Market to the point of collapse. This time they're more than rumors, Landau. The Queen is on the point of defection from C-K."

Stunned, I slumped suddenly into my chair. My jaw dropped. I closed it with a snap.

"Once the Market collapses," the Coordinator said, "it means the end of all we had. The news is already spreading. Soon there will be a run against the Czarina-Kluster banking system. The system will crash, C-K will die."

"But...," I said. "If it's the Queen's own doing..." I was having trouble breathing.

"It's *always* the doing of the Investors, Landau; it's been that way ever since they first swept in and made our wars into an institution...We Mechanists had you Shapers at bay. We ruled the entire system while you hid in terror in the Rings. It was your trade with the Investors that got you on your feet again. In fact, they deliberately built you up, so that they could maintain a competitive trade market, pit the human race against itself, to their own profit...Look at C-K. We live in harmony here. That could be the case everywhere. It's their doing."

"Are you saying," I said, "that the history of C-K is an Investor scheme? That the Queen was never really in disgrace?"

"They're not infallible," the Coordinator said. "I can save the Market, and C-K, if I can exploit their own greed. It's your jewels, Landau. Your jewels. I saw the Queen's reaction when her...damned lackey Wellspring presented your gift. You learn to know their moods, these Investors. She was livid with greed. Your patent could catalyze a major industry."

"You're wrong about Wellspring," I said. "The jewel was his idea. I was working with endolithic lichens. 'If they can live within stones they can live within jewels,' he said. I only did the busywork."

"But the patent's in your name." The Coordinator looked at the toes of his scaled boots. "With one catalyst, I could save the Market. I want you to transfer your patent from Eisho Zaibatsu to me. To the Czarina-Kluster People's Corporate Republic."

I tried to be tactful. "The situation does seem desperate," I said, "but no one within the Market really wants it destroyed. There are other powerful forces preparing for a rebound. Please understand—it's not for any personal gain that I must keep my patent. The revenue is already pledged. To terraforming."

A sour grimace deepened the crevasses in the Coordinator's face. He leaned forward, and his shoulders tightened with a muffled creaking of plastic. "Terraforming! Oh, yes, I'm familiar with the so-called moral arguments. The cold abstractions of bloodless ideologues. What about respect? Obligation? Loyalty? Are these foreign terms to you?"

I said, "It's not that simple. Wellspring says—"

"Wellspring!" he shouted. "He's no Terran, you fool, he's only a renegade, a traitor scarcely a hundred years old, who sold himself utterly to the aliens. They fear us, you see. They fear our energy. Our potential to invade their markets, once the star drive is in our hands. It should be obvious, Landau! They want to divert human energies into this enormous Martian boondoggle. We could be competing with them, spreading to the stars in one fantastic wave!" He held his arms out rigid before him, his wrists bent upward, and stared at the tips of his outstretched fingers.

His arms began to tremble. Then he broke, and cradled his head in his corded hands. "C-K could have been great. A core of unity, an island of safety in the chaos. The Investors mean to destroy it. When the Market crashes, when the Queen defects, it means the end."

"Will she really leave?"

"Who knows what she means to do." The Coordinator looked exhausted. "I've suffered seventy years from her little whims and humiliations. I don't know what it is to care anymore. Why should I break my heart trying to glue things together with your stupid knick-knacks? After all, there's still the discreet!"

He looked up ferociously. "That's where your meddling sent the Councilman. Once we've lost everything, they'll be thick enough with blood to swim in!"

He leapt from his desk top, bounced across the carpet, and dragged me bodily from the chair. I grabbed feebly at his wrists. My arms and legs flopped as he shook me. The tiger scuttled closer, clicking. "I hate you," he roared, "I hate everything you stand for! I'm sick of your Clique and their philosophies and their pudding smiles. You've killed a good friend with your meddling.

"Get out! Get out of C-K. You have forty-eight hours. After that I'll have you arrested and sold to the highest bidder." He threw me contemptuously backward. I collapsed at once in the heavy gravity, my head thudding against the carpet.

The tiger pulled me to my feet as the Coordinator clambered back into his oversized chair. He looked into his Market screen as I climbed trembling onto the tiger's back.

"Oh, no," he said softly. "Treason." The tiger took me away.

▲▼▲

I found Wellspring, at last, in Dogtown. Dogtown was a chaotic sub-cluster, pinwheeling slowly to itself above the rotational axis of C-K. It was a port and customhouse, a tangle of shipyards, storage drogues, quarantines, and social houses, catering to the vices of the footloose, the isolated, and the estranged.

Dogtown was the place to come when no one else would have you. It swarmed with transients: prospectors, privateers, criminals, derelicts from sects whose innovations had collapsed, bankrupts, defectors, purveyors of hazardous pleasures. Accordingly the entire area swarmed with dogs, and with subtler monitors. Dogtown was a genuinely dangerous place, thrumming with a deranged and predatory vitality. Constant surveillance had destroyed all sense of shame.

I found Wellspring in the swollen bubble of a tubeway bar, discussing a convoluted business deal with a man he introduced as "the Modem." The Modem was a member of a small but vigorous Mechanist sect known in C-K slang as Lobsters. These Lobsters lived exclusively within skin-tight life-support systems, flanged here and there with engines and input-output jacks. The suits were faceless and dull black. The Lobsters looked like chunks of shadow.

I shook the Modem's rough room-temperature gauntlet and strapped myself to the table.

I peeled a squeezebulb from the table's adhesive surface and had a drink. "I'm in trouble," I said. "Can we speak before this man?"

Wellspring laughed. "Are you joking? This is Dogtown! Everything we say goes onto more tapes than you have teeth, young Landau. Besides, the Modem is an old friend. His skewed vision should be of some use."

"Very well." I began explaining. Wellspring pressed for details. I omitted nothing.

"Oh, dear," Wellspring said when I had finished. "Well, hold on to your monitors, Modem, for you are about to see rumor break the speed of light. Odd that this obscure little bistro should launch the news that is certain to destroy C-K." He said this quite loudly, and I looked quickly around the bar. The jaws of the clientele hung open with shock. Little blobs of saliva oscillated in their mouths.

"The Queen is gone, then," Wellspring said. "She's probably been gone for weeks. Well, I suppose it couldn't be helped. Even an Investor's greed has limits. The Advisers couldn't lead her by the nose forever. Perhaps she'll show up somewhere else, some habitat more suited to her emotional needs. I suppose I had best get to my monitors and cut my losses while the Market still has some meaning."

Wellspring parted the ribbons of his slashed sleeve and looked casually at his forearm computer. The bar emptied itself, suddenly and catastrophically, the customers trailed by their personal dogs. Near the exit, a vicious hand-to-hand fight broke out between two Shaper renegades. They spun with piercing cries through the crunching grip-and-tumble of free-fall jujitsu. Their dogs watched impassively.

Soon the three of us were alone with the bar servos and half a dozen fascinated dogs. "I could tell from my last audience that the Queen would leave," Wellspring said calmly. "C-K had outlived its usefulness, anyway. It was important only as the motivational catalyst for the elevation of Mars to the Third Prigoginic Level of Complexity. It was fossilizing under the weight of the Advisers' programs. Typical Mech shortsightedness. Pseudopragmatic materialism. They had it coming."

Wellspring showed an inch of embroidered undercuff as he signaled a servo for another round. "The Councilman you mentioned has retired to a discreet. He won't be the last one they haul out by the heels."

"What will I do?" I said. "I'm losing everything. What will become of the Clique?"

Wellspring frowned. "Come on, Landau! Show some Posthuman fluidity. The first thing to do, of course, is to get you into exile before you're arrested and sold. I imagine our friend the Modem here can help with that."

"To be sure," the Modem enunciated. He had a vocoder unit strapped to his throat, and it projected an inhumanly beautiful synthesized voice. "Our ship, the *Crowned Pawn*, is hauling a cargo of iceteroid mass drivers to the Ring Council. It's for the Terraforming Project. Any friend of Wellspring's is welcome to join us."

I laughed incredulously. "For me, that's suicide. Go back to the Council? I might as well open my throat."

"Be at ease," the Modem soothed. "I'll have the medimechs work you over and graft on one of our shells. One Lobster is very much like another. You'll be perfectly safe, under the skin."

I was shocked. "Become a Mech?"

"You don't have to stay one," Wellspring said. "It's a simple procedure. A few nerve grafts, some anal surgery, a tracheotomy…You lose on taste and touch, but the other senses are vastly expanded."

"Yes," said the Modem. "And you can step alone into naked space, and laugh."

"Right!" said Wellspring. "More Shapers should wear Mech technics. It's like your lichens, Hans. Become a symbiosis for a while. It'll broaden your horizons."

I said, "You don't do…anything cranial, do you?"

"No," said the Modem offhandedly. "Or, at least, we don't have to. Your brain's your own."

I thought. "Can you do it in"—I looked at Wellspring's forearm-"thirty-eight hours?"

"If we hurry," the Modem said. He detached himself from the table.

I followed him.

▲ ▼ ▲

The *Crowned Pawn* was under way. My skin clung magnetically to a ship's girder as we accelerated. I had my vision set for normal wavelengths as I watched Czarina-Kluster receding.

Tears stung the fresh tracks of hair-thin wires along my deadened eyeballs. C-K wheeled slowly, like a galaxy in a jeweled web. Here and there along the network, flares pulsed as suburbs began the tedious and tragic work of cutting themselves loose. C-K was in the grip of terror.

I longed for the warm vitality of my Clique. I was no Lobster. They were alien. They were solipsistic pinpoints in the galactic night, their humanity a forgotten pulp behind black armor.

The *Crowned Pawn* was like a ship turned inside out. It centered around a core of massive magnetic engines, fed by drones from a chunk of reaction mass. Outside these engines was a skeletal metal framework where Lobsters clung like cysts or skimmed along on induced magnetic fields. There were cupolas here and there on the skeleton where the Lobsters hooked into fluidic computers or sheltered themselves from solar storms and ring-system electrofluxes.

They never ate. They never drank. Sex involved a clever cyber-stimulation through cranial plugs. Every five years or so they "molted" and had their skins scraped clean of the stinking accumulation of mutated bacteria that scummed them over in the stagnant warmth.

They knew no fear. Agoraphobia was a condition easily crushed with drugs. They were self-contained and anarchical. Their greatest pleasure was to sit along a girder and open their amplified senses to the depths of space, watching stars past the limits of ultraviolet and infrared, or staring into the flocculate crawling plaque of the surface of the sun, or just sitting and soaking in watts of solar energy through their skins while they listened with wired ears to the warbling of Van Allen belts and the musical tick of pulsars.

There was nothing evil about them, but they were not human. As distant and icy as comets, they were creatures of the vacuum, bored with the outmoded paradigms of blood and bone. I saw within them the first stirrings of the Fifth Prigoginic Leap—that postulated Fifth Level of Complexity as far beyond intelligence as intelligence is from amoebic life, or life from inert matter.

They frightened me. Their bland indifference to human limitations gave them the sinister charisma of saints.

The Modem came skimming along a girder and latched himself soundlessly beside me. I turned my ears on and heard his voice above the radio hiss of the engines. "You have a call, Landau. From C-K. Follow me."

I flexed my feet and skimmed along the rail behind him. We entered the radiation lock of an iron cupola, leaving it open, since the Lobsters disliked closed spaces.

Before me, on a screen, was the tear-streaked face of Valery Korstad. "Valery!" I said.

"Is that you, Hans?"

"Yes. Yes, darling. It's good to see you."

"Can't you take that mask off, Hans? I want to see your face."

"It's not a mask, darling. And my face is, well, not a pretty sight. All those wires…"

"You sound different, Hans. Your voice sounds different."

"That's because this voice is a radio analogue. It's synthesized."

"How do I know it's really you, then? God, Hans…I'm so afraid. Everything…its just evaporating. The Froth is…there's a bio-hazard scare, something smashed the gel frames in your domicile, I guess it was the dogs, and now the lichen, the damned lichen is sprouting everywhere. It grows so fast!"

"I designed it to grow fast, Valery, that was the whole point. Tell them to use a metal aerosol or sulfide particulates; either one will kill it in a few hours. There's no need for panic."

"No need! Hans, the discreets are suicide factories. C-K is through! We've lost the Queen!"

"There's still the Project," I said. "The Queen was just an excuse, a catalyst. The Project can draw as much respect as the damned Queen. The groundwork's been laid for years. This is the moment. Tell the Clique to liquidate all they have. The Froth must move to Martian orbit."

Valery began to drift sideways. "That's all you cared about all along, wasn't it? The Project! I degraded myself, and you, with your cold, that Shaper distance, you left me in despair!"

"Valery!" I shouted, stricken. "I called you a dozen times, it was you who closed yourself off, it was me who needed warmth after those years under the dogs—"

"You could have done it!" she screamed, her face white with passion. "If you cared you would have broken in to prove it! You expected me to come crawling in humiliation? Black armor or dog's eyeglass, Hans, what's the difference? You're still not with me!"

I felt the heat of raw fury touching my numbed skin. "Blame me, then! How was I to know your rituals, your sick little secrets? I thought you'd thrown me over while you sneered and whored with Wellspring! Did you think I'd compete with the man who showed me my salvation? I would have slashed my wrists to see you smile, and you gave me nothing, nothing but disaster!"

A look of cold shock spread across her painted face. Her mouth opened, but no words came forth. Finally, with a small smile of total despair, she broke the connection. The screen went black.

I turned to the Modem. "I want to go back," I said.

"Sorry," he said. "First, you'd be killed. And second, we don't have the wattage to turn back. We're carrying a massive cargo." He shrugged. "Besides, C-K is in dissolution. We've known it was coming for a long time. In fact, some colleagues of ours are arriving there within the week with a second cargo of mass drivers. They'll fetch top prices as the Kluster dissolves."

"You knew?"

"We have our sources."

"Wellspring?"

"Who, him? He's leaving, too. He wants to be in Martian orbit when *that* hits." The Modem glided outside the cupola and pointed along the plane of the ecliptic. I followed his gaze, shifting clumsily along the visual wavelengths.

I saw the etched and ghostly flare of the Martian asteroid's mighty engines. "The iceteroid," I said.

"Yes, of course. The comet of your disaster, so to speak. A useful symbol for C-K's decay."

"Yes," I said. I thought I recognized the hand of Wellspring in this. As the ice payload skimmed past C-K the panicked eyes of its inhabitants would follow it. Suddenly I felt a soaring sense of hope.

"How about that?" I said. "Could you land me there?"

"On the asteroid?"

"Yes! They're going to detach the engines, aren't they? In orbit! I can join my fellows there, and I won't miss the Prigoginic catalyst!"

"I'll check." The Modem fed a series of parameters into one of the fluidics. "Yes…I could sell you a parasite engine that you could strap on. With enough wattage and a cybersystem to guide you, you could match trajectory within, say, seventy-two hours."

"Good! Good! Let's do that, then."

"Very well," he said. "There remains only the question of price."

I had time to think about the price as I burned along through the piercing emptiness. I thought I had done well. With C-K's Market in collapse I would need new commercial agents for the Eisho jewels. Despite their eeriness, I felt I could trust the Lobsters.

The cybersystem led me to a gentle groundfall on the sunside of the asteroid. It was ablating slowly in the heat of the distant sun, and infrared wisps of volatiles puffed here and there from cracks in the bluish ice.

The iceteroid was a broken spar calved from the breakup of one of Saturn's ancient glacial moons. It was a mountainous splintered crag with the fossilized scars of primordial violence showing themselves in wrenched and jagged cliffs and buttresses. It was roughly egg-shaped, five kilometers by three. Its surface had the bluish pitted look of ice exposed for thousands of years to powerful electric fields.

I roughened the gripping surfaces of my gauntlets and pulled myself and the parasite engine hand over hand into shadow. The engine's wattage was exhausted, but I didn't want it drifting off in the ablation.

I unfolded the radio dish the Modem had sold me and anchored it to a crag, aligning it with C-K. Then I plugged in.

The scope of the disaster was total. C-K had always prided itself on its open broadcasts, part of the whole atmosphere of freedom that had vitalized it. Now open panic was dwindling into veiled threats, and then, worst of all, into treacherous bursts of code. From all over the system, pressures long held back poured in.

The offers and threats mounted steadily, until the wretched cliques of C-K were pressed to the brink of civil war. Hijacked dogs prowled the tubes and corridors, tools of power elites made cruel by fear. Vicious kangaroo courts stripped dissidents of their status and property. Many chose the discreets.

Crèche cooperatives broke up. Stone-faced children wandered aimlessly through suburban halls, dazed on mood suppressants. Precious few dared to care any longer. Sweating Marketeers collapsed across their keyboards, sinuses bleeding from inhalants. Women stepped naked out of commandeered airlocks and died in sparkling gushes of frozen air. Cicadas struggled to weep through altered eyes, or floated in darkened bistros, numbed with disaster and drugs.

Centuries of commercial struggle had only sharpened the teeth of the cartels. They slammed in with the cybernetic precision of the Mechanists, with the slick unsettling brilliance of the Reshaped. With the collapse of the Market, C-K's industries were up for grabs. Commercial agents and arrogant diplomats annexed whole complexes. Groups of their new employees stumbled through the Queen's deserted Palace, vandalizing anything they couldn't steal outright.

The frightened subfactions of C-K were caught in the classic double bind that had alternately shaped and splintered the destinies of humanity in Space. On the one hand their technically altered modes of life and states of mind drove them irresistibly to distrust and fragmentation; on the other, isolation made them the prey of united cartels. They might even be savaged by the pirates and privateers that the cartels openly condemned and covertly supported.

And instead of helping my Clique, I was a black dot clinging like a spore to the icy flank of a frozen mountain.

It was during those sad days that I began to appreciate my skin. If Wellspring's plans had worked, then there would come a flowering. I would survive this ice in my sporangial casing, as a windblown speck of lichen will last out decades to spread at last into devouring life. Wellspring had been wise to put me here. I trusted him. I would not fail him.

As boredom gnawed at me I sank gently into a contemplative stupor. I opened my eyes and ears past the point of overload. Consciousness swallowed itself and vanished into the roaring half existence of an event horizon. Space-time, the Second Level of Complexity, proclaimed its noumenon in the whine of stars, the rumble of planets, the transcendent crackle and gush of the uncoiling sun.

There came a time when I was roused at last by the sad and empty symphonies of Mars.

I shut down the suit's amplifiers. I no longer needed them. The catalyst, after all, is always buried by the process.

I moved south along the asteroid's axis, where I was sure to be discovered by the team sent to recover the mass driver. The driver's cybersystem had reoriented the asteroid for partial deceleration, and the south end had the best view of the planet.

Only moments after the final burn, the ice mass was matched by a pirate. It was a slim and beautiful Shaper craft, with long ribbed sun wings of iridescent fabric as thin as oil on water. Its shining organo-metallic hull hid eighth-generation magnetic engines with marvelous speed and power. The blunt nodes of weapons systems knobbed its sleekness.

I went into hiding, burrowing deep into a crevasse to avoid radar. I waited until curiosity and fear got the better of me. Then I crawled out and crept to a lookout point along a fractured ice ridge.

The ship had docked and sat poised on its cocked manipulator arms, their mantislike tips anchored into the ice. A crew of Mechanist mining drones had decamped and were boring into the ice of a clean-sheared plateau.

No Shaper pirate would have mining drones on board. The ship itself had undergone systems deactivation and sat inert and beautiful as an insect in amber, its vast sun wings folded. There was no sign of any crew.

I was not afraid of drones. I pulled myself boldly along the ice to observe their operations. No one challenged me.

I watched as the ungainly drones rasped and chipped the ice. Ten meters down they uncovered the glint of metal.

It was an airlock.

There they waited. Time passed. They received no further orders. They shut themselves down and crouched inert on the ice, as dead as the boulders around us.

For safety's sake I decided to enter the ship first.

As its airlock opened, the ship began switching itself back on. I entered the cabin. The pilot's couch was empty.

There was no one on board.

It took me almost two hours to work my way into the ship's cybersystem. Then I learned for certain what I had already suspected. It was Wellspring's ship.

I left the ship and crawled across the ice to the airlock. It opened easily. Wellspring had never been one to complicate things unnecessarily.

Beyond the airlock's second door a chamber blazed with blue-white light. I adjusted my eye systems and crawled inside.

At the far end, in the iceteroid's faint gravity, there was a bed of jewels. It was not a conventional bed. It was simply a huge, loose-packed heap of precious gems.

The Queen was asleep on top of it.

I used my eyes again. There was no infrared heat radiating from her. She lay quite still, her ancient arms clutching something to her chest, her three-toed legs drawn up along her body, her massive tail curled up beneath her rump and between her legs. Her huge head, the size of a man's torso, was encased in a gigantic crowned helmet encrusted with blazing diamonds. She was not breathing. Her eyes were closed. Her thick, scaled lips were drawn back slightly, showing two blunt rows of peg-shaped yellowing teeth.

She was ice-cold, sunk in some kind of alien cryosleep. Wellspring's coup was revealed. The Queen had joined willingly in her own abduction.

Wellspring had stolen her in an act of heroic daring, robbing his rivals in C-K to begin again in Martian orbit. It was an astounding fait accompli that would have put him and his disciples into unquestioned power.

I was overcome with admiration for his plan. I wondered, though, why he had not accompanied his ship. Doubtless there were medicines aboard to wake the Queen and spirit her off to the nascent Kluster.

I moved nearer. I had never seen an Investor face to face. Still, I could tell after a moment that there was something wrong with her skin. I'd thought it was a trick of the light at first. But then I saw what she had in her hands.

It was the lichen jewel. The rapacity of her clawed grip had split it along one of the fracture planes, already weakened by the lichens' acids. Released from its crystalline prison, and spurred to frenzy by the powerful light, the lichens had crept onto her scaly fingers, and then up her wrist, and then, in an explosive paroxysm of life, over her entire body. She glittered green and gold with devouring fur. Even her eyes, her gums.

I went back to the ship. It was always said of us Shapers that we were brilliant under pressure. I reactivated the drones and had them refill their borehole. They tamped ice chips into it and melted them solid with the parasite rocket.

I worked on intuition, but all my training told me to trust it. That was why I had stripped the dead Queen and loaded every jewel aboard the ship. I felt a certainty beyond any chain of logic. The future lay before me like a drowsing woman awaiting the grip of her lover.

Wellspring's tapes were mine. The ship was his final sanctum, programmed in advance. I understood then the suffering and the ambition that had driven him, and that now were mine.

His dead hand had drawn representatives of every faction to witness the Prigoginic impact. The proto-Kluster already in orbit was made up exclusively of drones and monitors. It was natural that the observers would turn to me. My ship controlled the drones.

The first panic-stricken refugees told me of Wellspring's fate. He had been dragged heels first from a discreet, followed closely by the bloodless corpse of sad Valery Korstad. Never again would she create delight. Never again would his charisma enthrall the Clique. It might have been a double suicide. Or, perhaps more likely, she murdered him and then herself. Wellspring could never believe that there was anything beyond his abilities to cure. A madwoman and a barren world were part and parcel of the same challenge. Eventually he met his limit, and it killed him. The details scarcely matter. A discreet had swallowed them in any case.

When I heard the news, the ice around my heart sealed shut, seamless and pure.

I had Wellspring's will broadcast as the iceteroid began its final plunge into the atmosphere. Tapes sucked the broadcast in as volatiles peeled smoking into the thin, starved air of Mars.

I lied about the will. I invented it. I had Wellspring's taped memories to hand; it was a simple thing to change my artificial voice to counterfeit his, to set the stage for my own crucial ascendancy. It was necessary for the future of T-K, Terraform-Kluster, that I proclaim myself Wellspring's heir.

Power accreted around me like rumors. It was said that beneath my armor I was Wellspring, that the real Landau had been the one to die with Valery in C-K. I encouraged the rumors. Misconceptions would unite the Kluster. I knew T-K would be a city without rival. Here, abstractions would take on flesh, phantoms would feed us. Once our ideals had slammed it into being, T-K would gather strength, unstoppably. My jewels alone gave it a power base that few cartels could match.

With understanding came forgiveness. I forgave Wellspring. His lies, his deceptions, had moved me better than the chimeric "truth." What did it matter? If we needed solid bedrock, we would have it orbit us.

And the fearsome beauty of that impact! The searing linearity of its descent! It was only one of many, but the one most dear to me. When I saw the milk-drop splatter of its collision into Mars, the concussive orgasmic gush of steam from the Queen's covert and frozen tomb, I knew at once what my mentor had known. A man driven by something greater than himself dares everything and fears nothing. Nothing at all.

From behind my black armor, I rule the Polycarbon Clique. Their elite are my Advisers. I remember the cold, but I no longer fear it. I have buried it forever, as the cold of Mars is buried beneath its seething carpet of greenery. The two of us, now one, have stolen a whole planet from the realm of Death. And I do not fear the cold. No, not at all.

Sunken Gardens

Mirasol's crawler loped across the badlands of the Mare Hadriacum, under a tormented Martian sky. At the limits of the troposphere, jet streams twisted, dirty streaks across pale lilac. Mirasol watched the winds through the fretted glass of the control bay. Her altered brain suggested one pattern after another: nests of snakes, nets of dark eels, maps of black arteries.

Since morning the crawler had been descending steadily into the Hellas Basin, and the air pressure was rising. Mars lay like a feverish patient under this thick blanket of air, sweating buried ice.

On the horizon thunderheads rose with explosive speed below the constant scrawl of the jet streams.

The basin was strange to Mirasol. Her faction, the Patternists, had been assigned to a redemption camp in northern Syrtis Major. There, two-hundred-mile-an-hour surface winds were common, and their pressurized camp had been buried three times by advancing dunes.

It had taken her eight days of constant travel to reach the equator.

From high overhead, the Regal faction had helped her navigate. Their orbiting city-state, Terraform-Kluster, was a nexus of monitor satellites. The Regals showed by their helpfulness that they had her under close surveillance.

The crawler lurched as its six picklike feet scrabbled down the slopes of a deflation pit. Mirasol suddenly saw her own face reflected in the glass, pale and taut, her dark eyes dreamily self-absorbed. It was a bare face, with the anonymous beauty of the genetically Reshaped. She rubbed her eyes with nail-bitten fingers.

To the west, far overhead, a gout of airborne topsoil surged aside and revealed the Ladder, the mighty anchor cable of the Terraform-Kluster.

Above the winds the cable faded from sight, vanishing below the metallic glitter of the Kluster, swinging aloofly in orbit.

Mirasol stared at the orbiting city with an uneasy mix of envy, fear, and reverence. She had never been so close to the Kluster before, or to the all-important Ladder that linked it to the Martian surface. Like most of her faction's younger generation, she had never been into space. The Regals had carefully kept her faction quarantined in the Syrtis redemption camp.

Life had not come easily to Mars. For one hundred years the Regals of Terraform-Kluster had bombarded the Martian surface with giant chunks of ice. This act of planetary engineering was the most ambitious, arrogant, and successful of all the works of man in space.

The shattering impacts had torn huge craters in the Martian crust, blasting tons of dust and steam into Mars's threadbare sheet of air. As the temperature rose, buried oceans of Martian permafrost roared forth, leaving networks of twisted badlands and vast expanses of damp mud, smooth and sterile as a television. On these great playas and on the frost-caked walls of channels, cliffs, and calderas, transplanted lichen had clung and leapt into devouring life. In the plains of Eridania, in the twisted megacanyons of the Coprates Basin, in the damp and icy regions of the dwindling poles, vast clawing thickets of its sinister growth lay upon the land—massive disaster areas for the inorganic.

As the terraforming project had grown, so had the power of Terraform-Kluster.

As a neutral point in humanity's factional wars, T-K was crucial to financiers and bankers of every sect. Even the alien Investors, those star-traveling reptiles of enormous wealth, found T-K useful, and favored it with their patronage.

And as T-K's citizens, the Regals, increased their power, smaller factions faltered and fell under their sway. Mars was dotted with bankrupt factions, financially captured and transported to the Martian surface by the T-K plutocrats.

Having failed in space, the refugees took Regal charity as ecologists of the sunken gardens. Dozens of factions were quarantined in cheerless redemption camps, isolated from one another, their lives pared to a grim frugality.

And the visionary Regals made good use of their power. The factions found themselves trapped in the arcane bioaesthetics of Posthumanist philosophy, subverted constantly by Regal broadcasts, Regal teaching, Regal culture. With time even the stubbornest faction would be broken down and digested into the cultural bloodstream of T-K. Faction members would be allowed to leave their redemption camp and travel up the Ladder.

But first they would have to prove themselves. The Patternists had awaited their chance for years. It had come at last in the Ibis Crater competition, an ecological struggle of the factions that would prove the victors' right to Regal status. Six factions had sent their champions to the ancient Ibis Crater, each one armed with its group's strongest biotechnologies. It would be a war of the sunken gardens, with the Ladder as the prize.

Mirasol's crawler followed a gully through a chaotic terrain of rocky permafrost that had collapsed in karsts and sinkholes. After two hours, the gully ended abruptly. Before Mirasol rose a mountain range of massive slabs and boulders, some with the glassy sheen of impact melt, others scabbed over with lichen.

As the crawler started up the slope, the sun came out, and Mirasol saw the crater's outer rim jigsawed in the green of lichen and the glaring white of snow.

The oxygen readings were rising steadily. Warm, moist air was drooling from within the crater's lip, leaving a spittle of ice. A half-million-ton asteroid from the Rings of Saturn had fallen here at fifteen kilometers a second. But for two centuries rain, creeping glaciers, and lichen had gnawed at the crater's rim, and the wound's raw edges had slumped and scarred.

The crawler worked its way up the striated channel of an empty glacier bed. A cold alpine wind keened down the channel, where flourishing patches of lichen clung to exposed veins of ice.

Some rocks were striped with sediment from the ancient Martian seas, and the impact had peeled them up and thrown them on their backs.

It was winter, the season for pruning the sunken gardens. The treacherous rubble of the crater's rim was cemented with frozen mud. The crawler found the glacier's root and clawed its way up the ice face. The raw slope was striped with winter snow and storm-blown summer dust, stacked in hundreds of red-and-white layers. With the years the stripes had warped and rippled in the glacier's flow.

Mirasol reached the crest. The crawler ran spiderlike along the crater's snowy rim. Below, in a bowl-shaped crater eight kilometers deep, lay a seething ocean of air.

Mirasol stared. Within this gigantic airsump, twenty kilometers across, a broken ring of majestic rain clouds trailed their dark skirts, like duchesses in quadrille, about the ballroom floor of a lens-shaped sea.

Thick forests of green-and-yellow mangroves rimmed the shallow water and had overrun the shattered islands at its center. Pinpoints of brilliant scarlet ibis spattered the trees. A flock of them suddenly spread kitelike wings and took to the air, spreading across the crater in uncounted millions. Mirasol was appalled by the crudity and daring of this ecological concept, its crass and primal vitality.

This was what she had come to destroy. The thought filled her with sadness.

Then she remembered the years she had spent flattering her Regal teachers, collaborating with them in the destruction of her own culture. When the chance at the Ladder came, she had been chosen. She put her sadness away, remembering her ambitions and her rivals.

The history of mankind in space had been a long epic of ambitions and rivalries. From the very first, space colonies had struggled for self-sufficiency and had soon broken their ties with the exhausted Earth. The independent life-support systems had given them the mentality of city-states. Strange ideologies had bloomed in the hothouse atmosphere of the o'neills, and breakaway groups were common.

Space was too vast to police. Pioneer elites burst forth, defying anyone to stop their pursuit of aberrant technologies. Quite suddenly the march of science had become an insane, headlong scramble. New sciences and technologies had shattered whole societies in waves of future shock.

The shattered cultures coalesced into factions, so thoroughly alienated from one another that they were called humanity only for lack of a better term. The Shapers, for instance, had seized control of their own genetics, abandoning mankind in a burst of artificial evolution. Their rivals, the Mechanists, had replaced flesh with advanced prosthetics.

Mirasol's own group, the Patternists, was a breakaway Shaper faction.

The Patternists specialized in cerebral asymmetry. With grossly expanded right-brain hemispheres, they were highly intuitive, given to metaphors, parallels, and sudden cognitive leaps. Their inventive minds and quick, unpredictable genius had given them a competitive edge at first. But with these advantages had come grave weaknesses: autism, fugue states, and paranoia. Patterns grew out of control and became grotesque webs of fantasy.

With these handicaps their colony had faltered. Patternist industries went into decline, outpaced by industrial rivals. Competition had grown much fiercer. The Shaper and Mechanist cartels had turned commercial action into a kind of endemic warfare. The Patternist gamble had failed, and the day came when their entire habitat was bought out from around them by Regal plutocrats. In a way it was a kindness. The Regals were suave and proud of their ability to assimilate refugees and failures.

The Regals themselves had started as dissidents and defectors. Their Posthumanist philosophy had given them the moral power and the bland assurance to dominate and absorb factions from the fringes of humanity. And they had the support of the Investors, who had vast wealth and the secret techniques of star travel.

The crawler's radar alerted Mirasol to the presence of a landcraft from a rival faction. Leaning forward in her pilot's couch, she put the craft's image on screen. It was a lumpy sphere, balanced uneasily on four long, spindly legs. Silhouetted against the horizon, it moved with a strange wobbling speed along the opposite lip of the crater, then disappeared down the outward slope.

Mirasol wondered if it had been cheating. She was tempted to try some cheating herself—to dump a few frozen packets of aerobic bacteria or a few dozen capsules of insect eggs down the slope—but she feared the orbiting monitors of the T-K supervisors. Too much was at stake—not only her own career but that of her entire faction, huddled bankrupt and despairing in their cold redemption camp. It was said that T-K's ruler, the posthuman being they called the Lobster King, would himself watch the contest. To fail before his black abstracted gaze would be a horror.

On the crater's outside slope, below her, a second rival craft appeared, lurching and slithering with insane, aggressive grace. The craft's long supple body moved with a sidewinder's looping and coiling, holding aloft a massive shining head, like a faceted mirror ball.

Both rivals were converging on the rendezvous camp, where the six contestants would receive their final briefing from the Regal Adviser. Mirasol hurried forward.

▲ ▼ ▲

When the camp first flashed into sight on her screen, Mirasol was shocked. The place was huge and absurdly elaborate: a drug dream of paneled geodesics and colored minarets, sprawling in the lichenous desert like an abandoned chandelier. This was a camp for Regals.

Here the arbiters and sophists of the BioArts would stay and judge the crater as the newly planted ecosystems struggled among themselves for supremacy.

The camp's airlocks were surrounded with shining green thickets of lichen, where the growth feasted on escaped humidity. Mirasol drove her crawler through the yawning airlock and into a garage. Inside the garage, robot mechanics were scrubbing and polishing the coiled hundred-meter length of the snake craft and the gleaming black abdomen of an eight-legged crawler. The black crawler was crouched with its periscoped head sunk downward, as if ready to pounce. Its swollen belly was marked with a red hourglass and the corporate logos of its faction.

The garage smelled of dust and grease overlaid with floral perfumes. Mirasol left the mechanics to their work and walked stiffly down a long corridor, stretching the kinks out of her back and shoulders. A latticework door sprang apart into filaments and resealed itself behind her.

She was in a dining room that clinked and rattled with the high-pitched repetitive sound of Regal music. Its walls were paneled with tall display screens showing startlingly beautiful garden panoramas. A pulpy-looking servo, whose organometallic casing and squat, smiling head had a swollen and almost diseased appearance, showed her to a chair.

Mirasol sat, denting the heavy white tablecloth with her knees. There were seven places at the table. The Regal Adviser's tall chair was at the table's head. Mirasol's assigned position gave her a sharp idea of her own status. She sat at the far end of the table, on the Adviser's left.

Two of her rivals had already taken their places. One was a tall, red-haired Shaper with long, thin arms, whose sharp face and bright, worried eyes gave him a querulous birdlike look. The other was a sullen, feral Mechanist with prosthetic hands and a paramilitary tunic marked at the shoulders with a red hourglass.

Mirasol studied her two rivals with silent, sidelong glances. Like her, they were both young. The Regals favored the young, and they encouraged captive factions to expand their populations widely.

This strategy cleverly subverted the old guard of each faction in a tidal wave of their own children, indoctrinated from birth by Regals.

The birdlike man, obviously uncomfortable with his place directly at the Adviser's right, looked as if he wanted to speak but dared not. The piratical Mech sat staring at his artificial hands, his ears stoppered with headphones.

Each place setting had a squeezebulb of liqueur. Regals, who were used to weightlessness in orbit, used these bulbs by habit, and their presence here was both a privilege and a humiliation.

The door fluttered open again, and two more rivals burst in, almost as if they had raced. The first was a flabby Mech, still not used to gravity, whose sagging limbs were supported by an extraskeletal framework. The second was a severely mutated Shaper whose elbowed legs terminated in grasping hands. The pedal hands were gemmed with heavy rings that clicked against each other as she waddled across the parquet floor.

The woman with the strange legs took her place across from the bird-like man. They began to converse haltingly in a language that none of the others could follow. The man in the framework, gasping audibly, lay in obvious pain in the chair across from Mirasol. His plastic eyeballs looked as blank as chips of glass. His sufferings in the pull of gravity showed that he was new to Mars, and his place in the competition meant that his faction was powerful. Mirasol despised him.

Mirasol felt a nightmarish sense of entrapment. Everything about her competitors seemed to proclaim their sickly unfitness for survival. They had a haunted, hungry look, like starving men in a lifeboat who wait with secret eagerness for the first to die.

She caught a glimpse of herself reflected in the bowl of a spoon and saw with a flash of insight how she must appear to the others. Her intuitive right brain was swollen beyond human bounds, distorting her skull. Her face had the blank prettiness of her genetic heritage, but she could feel the bleak strain of her expression. Her body looked shapeless under her quilted pilot's vest and dun-drab, general-issue blouse and trousers. Her fingertips were raw from biting. She saw in herself the fey, defeated aura of her faction's older generation, those who had tried and failed in the great world of space, and she hated herself for it.

They were still waiting for the sixth competitor when the plonking music reached a sudden crescendo and the Regal Adviser arrived. Her name was Arkadya Sorienti, Incorporated. She was a member of T-K's ruling oligarchy, and she swayed through the bursting door with the careful steps of a woman not used to gravity.

She wore the Investor-style clothing of a high-ranking diplomat. The Regals were proud of their diplomatic ties with the alien Investors, since Investor patronage proved their own vast wealth. The Sorienti's knee-high boots had false birdlike toes, scaled like Investor hide. She wore a heavy skirt of gold cords braided with jewels, and a stiff wrist-length formal jacket with embroidered cuffs. A heavy collar formed an arching multicolored frill behind her head. Her blonde hair was set in an interlaced style as complex as computer wiring. The skin of her bare legs had a shiny, glossy look, as if freshly enameled. Her eyelids gleamed with soft reptilian pastels.

One of her corporate ladyship's two body-servos helped her to her seat. The Sorienti leaned forward brightly, interlacing small, pretty hands so crusted with rings and bracelets that they resembled gleaming gauntlets.

"I hope the five of you have enjoyed this chance for an informal talk," she said sweetly, just as if such a thing were possible. "I'm sorry I was delayed. Our sixth participant will not be joining us."

There was no explanation. The Regals never publicized any action of theirs that might be construed as a punishment. The looks of the competitors, alternately stricken and calculating, showed that they were imagining the worst.

The two squat servos circulated around the table, dishing out courses of food from trays balanced on their flabby heads. The competitors picked uneasily at their plates.

The display screen behind the Adviser flicked into a schematic diagram of the Ibis Crater. "Please notice the revised boundary lines," the Sorienti said. "I hope that each of you will avoid trespassing—not merely physically but biologically as well." She looked at them seriously. "Some of you may plan to use herbicides. This is permissible, but the spreading of spray beyond your sector's boundaries is considered crass. Bacteriological establishment is a subtle art. The spreading of tailored disease organisms is an aesthetic distortion. Please remember that your activities here are a disruption of what should ideally be natural processes. Therefore the period of biotic seeding will last only twelve hours. Thereafter, the new complexity level will be allowed to stabilize itself without any other interference at all. Avoid self-aggrandizement, and confine yourselves to a primal role, as catalysts."

The Sorienti's speech was formal and ceremonial. Mirasol studied the display screen, noting with much satisfaction that her territory had been expanded.

Seen from overhead, the crater's roundness was deeply marred.

Mirasol's sector, the southern one, showed the long flattened scar of a major landslide, where the crater wall had slumped and flowed into the pit. The simple ecosystem had recovered quickly, and mangroves festooned the rubble's lowest slopes. Its upper slopes were gnawed by lichens and glaciers.

The sixth sector had been erased, and Mirasol's share was almost twenty square kilometers of new land.

It would give her faction's ecosystem more room to take root before the deadly struggle began in earnest.

This was not the first such competition. The Regals had held them for decades as an objective test of the skills of rival factions. It helped the Regals' divide-and-conquer policy, to set the factions against one another.

And in the centuries to come, as Mars grew more hospitable to life, the gardens would surge from their craters and spread across the surface. Mars would become a warring jungle of separate creations. For the Regals the competitions were closely studied simulations of the future.

And the competitions gave the factions motives for their work. With the garden wars to spur them, the ecological sciences had advanced enormously. Already, with the progress of science and taste, many of the oldest craters had become ecoaesthetic embarrassments.

The Ibis Crater had been an early, crude experiment. The faction that had created it was long gone, and its primitive creation was now considered tasteless.

Each gardening faction camped beside its own crater, struggling to bring it to life. But the competitions were a shortcut up the Ladder. The competitors' philosophies and talents, made into flesh, would carry out a proxy struggle for supremacy. The sine-wave curves of growth, the rallies and declines of expansion and extinction, would scroll across the monitors of the Regal judges like stock-market reports. This complex struggle would be weighed in each of its aspects: technological, philosophical, biological, and aesthetic. The winners would abandon their camps to take on Regal wealth and power. They would roam T-K's jeweled corridors and revel in its perquisites: extended life spans, corporate titles, cosmopolitan tolerance, and the interstellar patronage of the Investors.

▲ ▼ ▲

When red dawn broke over the landscape, the five were poised around the Ibis Crater, awaiting the signal. The day was calm, with only a distant nexus of jet streams marring the sky. Mirasol watched pink-stained sunlight creep down the inside slope of the crater's western wall. In the mangrove thickets birds were beginning to stir.

Mirasol waited tensely. She had taken a position on the upper slopes of the landslide's raw debris. Radar showed her rivals spaced along the interior slopes: to her left, the hourglass crawler and the jewel-headed snake; to her right, a mantislike crawler and the globe on stilts.

The signal came, sudden as lightning: a meteor of ice shot from orbit and left a shock-wave cloud plume of ablated steam. Mirasol charged forward.

The Patternists' strategy was to concentrate on the upper slopes and the landslide's rubble, a marginal niche where they hoped to excel. Their cold crater in Syrtis Major had given them some expertise in alpine species, and they hoped to exploit this strength. The landslide's long slope, far above sea level, was to be their power base. The crawler lurched downslope, blasting out a fine spray of lichenophagous bacteria.

Suddenly the air was full of birds. Across the crater, the globe on stilts had rushed down to the waterline and was laying waste the mangroves. Fine wisps of smoke showed the slicing beam of a heavy laser.

Burst after burst of birds took wing, peeling from their nests to wheel and dip in terror. At first, their frenzied cries came as a high-pitched whisper. Then, as the fear spread, the screeching echoed and reechoed, building to a mindless surf of pain. In the crater's dawn-warmed air, the scarlet motes hung in their millions, swirling and coalescing like drops of blood in free-fall.

Mirasol scattered the seeds of alpine rock crops. The crawler picked its way down the talus, spraying fertilizer into cracks and crevices. She pried up boulders and released a scattering of invertebrates: nematodes, mites, sowbugs, altered millipedes. She splattered the rocks with gelatin to feed them until the mosses and ferns took hold.

The cries of the birds were appalling. Downslope the other factions were thrashing in the muck at sea level, wreaking havoc, destroying the mangroves so that their own creations could take hold. The great snake looped and ducked through the canopy, knotting itself, ripping up swathes of mangroves by the roots. As Mirasol watched, the top of its faceted head burst open and released a cloud of bats.

The mantis crawler was methodically marching along the borders of its sector, its saw-edged arms reducing everything before it into kindling. The hourglass crawler had slashed through its territory, leaving a muddy network of fire zones. Behind it rose a wall of smoke.

It was a daring ploy. Sterilizing the sector by fire might give the new biome a slight advantage. Even a small boost could be crucial as exponential rates of growth took hold. But the Ibis Crater was a closed system. The use of fire required great care. There was only so much air within the bowl.

Mirasol worked grimly. Insects were next. They were often neglected in favor of massive sea beasts or flashy predators, but in terms of biomass, gram by gram, insects could overwhelm. She blasted a carton downslope to the shore, where it melted, releasing aquatic termites. She shoved aside flat shelves of rock, planting egg cases below their sun-warmed surfaces. She released a cloud of leaf-eating midges, their tiny bodies packed with bacteria. Within the crawler's belly, rack after automatic rack was thawed and fired through nozzles, dropped through spiracles or planted in the holes jabbed by picklike feet.

Each faction was releasing a potential world. Near the water's edge, the mantis had released a pair of things like giant black sail planes. They were swooping through the clouds of ibis, opening great sieved mouths. On the islands in the center of the crater's lake, scaled walruses clambered on the rocks, blowing steam. The stilt ball was laying out an orchard in the mangroves' wreckage. The snake had taken to the water, its faceted head leaving a wake of V-waves.

In the hourglass sector, smoke continued to rise. The fires were spreading, and the spider ran frantically along its network of zones. Mirasol watched the movement of the smoke as she released a horde of marmots and rock squirrels.

A mistake had been made. As the smoky air gushed upward in the feeble Martian gravity, a fierce valley wind of cold air from the heights flowed downward to fill the vacuum. The mangroves burned fiercely. Shattered networks of flaming branches were flying into the air.

The spider charged into the flames, smashing and trampling. Mirasol laughed, imagining demerits piling up in the judges' data banks. Her talus slopes were safe from fire. There was nothing to burn.

The ibis flock had formed a great wheeling ring above the shore. Within their scattered ranks flitted the dark shapes of airborne predators. The long plume of steam from the meteor had begun to twist and break. A sullen wind was building up.

Fire had broken out in the snake's sector. The snake was swimming in the sea's muddy waters, surrounded by bales of bright-green kelp. Before its pilot noticed, fire was already roaring through a great piled heap of the wreckage it had left on shore. There were no windbreaks left. Air poured down the denuded slope. The smoke column guttered and twisted, its black clouds alive with sparks.

A flock of ibis plunged into the cloud. Only a handful emerged; some of them were flaming visibly. Mirasol began to know fear. As smoke rose to the crater's rim, it cooled and started to fall outward and downward. A vertical whirlwind was forming, a torus of hot smoke and cold wind.

The crawler scattered seed-packed hay for pygmy mountain goats. Just before her an ibis fell from the sky with a dark squirming shape, all claws and teeth, clinging to its neck. She rushed forward and crushed the predator, then stopped and stared distractedly across the crater.

Fires were spreading with unnatural speed. Small puffs of smoke rose from a dozen places, striking large heaps of wood with uncanny precision. Her altered brain searched for a pattern. The fires springing up in the mantis sector were well beyond the reach of any falling debris.

In the spider's zone, flames had leapt the firebreaks without leaving a mark. The pattern felt wrong to her, eerily wrong, as if the destruction had a force all its own, a raging synergy that fed upon itself.

The pattern spread into a devouring crescent. Mirasol felt the dread of lost control—the sweating fear an orbiter feels at the hiss of escaping air or the way a suicide feels at the first bright gush of blood.

Within an hour the garden sprawled beneath a hurricane of hot decay. The dense columns of smoke had flattened like thunderheads at the limits of the garden's sunken troposphere. Slowly a spark-shot gray haze, dripping ash like rain, began to ring the crater. Screaming birds circled beneath the foul torus, falling by tens and scores and hundreds. Their bodies littered the garden's sea, their bright plumage blurred with ash in a steel-gray sump.

The landcraft of the others continued to fight the flames, smashing unharmed through the fire's charred borderlands. Their efforts were useless, a pathetic ritual before the disaster.

Even the fire's malicious purity had grown tired and tainted. The oxygen was failing. The flames were dimmer and spread more slowly, releasing a dark nastiness of half-combusted smoke.

Where it spread, nothing that breathed could live. Even the flames were killed as the smoke billowed along the crater's crushed and smoldering slopes.

Mirasol watched a group of striped gazelles struggle up the barren slopes of the talus in search of air. Their dark eyes, fresh from the laboratory, rolled in timeless animal fear. Their coats were scorched, their flanks heaved, their mouths dripped foam. One by one they collapsed in convulsions, kicking at the lifeless Martian rock as they slid and fell. It was a vile sight, the image of a blighted spring.

An oblique flash of red downslope to her left attracted her attention. A large red animal was skulking among the rocks. She turned the crawler and picked her way toward it, wincing as a dark surf of poisoned smoke broke across the fretted glass.

She spotted the animal as it broke from cover. It was a scorched and gasping creature like a great red ape. She dashed forward and seized it in the crawler's arms. Held aloft, it clawed and kicked, hammering the crawler's arms with a smoldering branch. In revulsion and pity, she crushed it. Its bodice of tight-sewn ibis feathers tore, revealing blood-slicked human flesh.

Using the crawler's grips, she tugged at a heavy tuft of feathers on its head. The tight-fitting mask ripped free, and the dead man's head slumped forward. She rolled it back, revealing a face tattooed with stars.

▲ ▼ ▲

The ornithopter sculled above the burned-out garden, its long red wings beating with dreamlike fluidity. Mirasol watched the Sorienti's painted face as her corporate ladyship stared into the shining view-screen.

The ornithopter's powerful cameras cast image after image onto the tabletop screen, lighting the Regal's face. The tabletop was littered with the Sorienti's elegant knickknacks: an inhaler case, a half-empty jeweled squeezebulb, lorgnette binoculars, a stack of tape cassettes.

"An unprecedented case," her ladyship murmured. "It was not a total dieback after all but merely the extinction of everything with lungs. There must be strong survivorship among the lower orders: fish, insects, annelids. Now that the rain's settled the ash, you can see the vegetation making a strong comeback. Your own section seems almost undamaged."

"Yes," Mirasol said. "The natives were unable to reach it with torches before the fire storm had smothered itself."

The Sorienti leaned back into the tasseled arms of her couch. "I wish you wouldn't mention them so loudly, even between ourselves."

"No one would believe me."

"The others never saw them," the Regal said. "They were too busy fighting the flames." She hesitated briefly. "You were wise to confide in me first."

Mirasol locked eyes with her new patroness, then looked away. "There was no one else to tell. They'd have said I built a pattern out of nothing but my own fears."

"You have your faction to think of," the Sorienti said with an air of sympathy. "With such a bright future ahead of them, they don't need a renewed reputation for paranoid fantasies."

She studied the screen. "The Patternists are winners by default. It certainly makes an interesting case study. If the new garden grows tiresome we can have the whole crater sterilized from orbit. Some other faction can start again with a clean slate."

"Don't let them build too close to the edge," Mirasol said.

Her corporate ladyship watched her attentively, tilting her head.

"I have no proof," Mirasol said, "but I can see the pattern behind it all. The natives had to come from somewhere. The colony that stocked the crater must have been destroyed in that huge landslide. Was that your work? Did your people kill them?"

The Sorienti smiled. "You're very bright, my dear. You will do well, up the Ladder. And you can keep secrets. Your office as my secretary suits you very well."

"They were destroyed from orbit," Mirasol said. "Why else would they hide from us? You tried to annihilate them."

"It was a long time ago," the Regal said. "In the early days, when things were shakier. They were researching the secret of starflight, techniques only the Investors know. Rumor says they reached success at last, in their redemption camp. After that, there was no choice."

"Then they were killed for the Investors' profit," Mirasol said. She stood up quickly and walked around the cabin, her new jeweled skirt clattering around the knees. "So that the aliens could go on toying with us, hiding their secret, selling us trinkets."

The Regal folded her hands with a clicking of rings and bracelets. "Our Lobster King is wise," she said. "If humanity's efforts turned to the stars, what would become of terraforming? Why should we trade the power of creation itself to become like the Investors?"

"But think of the people," Mirasol said. "Think of them losing their technologies, degenerating into human beings. A handful of savages, eating bird meat. Think of the fear they felt for generations, the way they burned their own home and killed themselves when they saw us come to smash and destroy their world. Aren't you filled with horror?"

"For humans?" the Sorienti said. "No!"

"But can't you see? You've given this planet life as an art form, as an enormous game. You force us to play in it, and those people were killed for it! Can't you see how that blights everything?"

"Our game is reality," the Regal said. She gestured at the viewscreen. "You can't deny the savage beauty of destruction."

"You defend this catastrophe?"

The Regal shrugged. "If life worked perfectly, how could things evolve? Aren't we posthuman? Things grow; things die. In time the cosmos kills us all. The cosmos has no meaning, and its emptiness is absolute. That's pure terror, but its also pure freedom. Only our ambitions and our creations can fill it."

"And that justifies your actions?"

"We act for life," the Regal said. "Our ambitions have become this world's natural laws. We blunder because life blunders. We go on because life must go on. When you've taken the long view, from orbit—when the power we wield is in your own hands—then you can judge us." She smiled. "You will be judging yourself. You'll be Regal."

"But what about your captive factions? Your agents, who do your will? Once we had our own ambitions. We failed, and now you isolate us, indoctrinate us, make us into rumors. We must have something of our own. Now we have nothing."

"That's not so. You have what we've given you. You have the Ladder."

The vision stung Mirasol: power, light, the hint of justice, this world with its sins and sadness shrunk to a bright arena far below. "Yes," she said at last. "Yes, we do."

Twenty Evocations

1. EXPERT SYSTEMS. When Nikolai Leng was a child, his teacher was a cybernetic system with a holographic interface. The holo took the form of a young Shaper woman. Its "personality" was an interactive composite expert system manufactured by Shaper psychotechs. Nikolai loved it.

2. NEVER BORN. "You mean we all came from Earth?" said Nikolai, unbelieving.

"Yes," the holo said kindly. "The first true settlers in space were born on Earth—produced by sexual means. Of course, hundreds of years have passed since then. You are a Shaper. Shapers are never born."

"Who lives on Earth now?"

"Human beings."

"Ohhhh," said Nikolai, his falling tones betraying a rapid loss of interest.

3. A MALFUNCTIONING LEG. There came a day when Nikolai saw his first Mechanist. The man was a diplomat and commercial agent, stationed by his faction in Nikolai's habitat. Nikolai and some children from his crèche were playing in the corridor when the diplomat stalked by. One of the Mechanist's legs was malfunctioning, and it went click-whirr, click-whirr. Nikolai's friend Alex mimicked the man's limp. Suddenly the man turned on them, his plastic eyes dilating. "Gene-lines," the Mechanist snarled. "I can buy you, grow you, sell you, cut you into bits. Your screams: my music."

4. FUZZ PATINA. Sweat was running into the braided collar of Nikolai's military tunic. The air in the abandoned station was still breathable, but insufferably hot. Nikolai helped his sergeant strip the valuables off a dead miner. The murdered Shaper's antiseptic body was desiccated, but perfect. They walked into another section. The body of a Mechanist pirate sprawled in the feeble gravity. Killed during the attack, his body had rotted for weeks inside his suit. An inch-thick patina of grayish fuzz had devoured his face.

5. NOT MERITORIOUS. Nikolai was on leave in the Ring Council with two men from his unit. They were drinking in a free-fall bar called the Eclectic Epileptic. The first man was Simon Afriel, a charming, ambitious young Shaper of the old school. The other man had a Mechanist

eye implant. His loyalty was suspect. The three of them were discussing semantics. "The map is not the territory," Afriel said. Suddenly the second man picked an almost invisible listening device from the edge of the table. "And the tap is not meritorious," he quipped. They never saw him again.

... A Mechanist pirate, malfunctioning, betraying gene-lines. Invisible listening devices buy, grow, and sell you. The abandoned station's ambitious young Shaper, killed during the attack. Falling psychotechs produced by sexual means the desiccated body of a commercial agent. The holographic interface's loyalty was suspect. The cybernetic system helped him strip the valuables off his plastic eyes...

6. SPECULATIVE PITY. The Mechanist woman looked him over with an air of speculative pity. "I have an established commercial position here," she told Nikolai, "but my cash flow is temporarily constricted. You, on the other hand, have just defected from the Council with a small fortune. I need money; you need stability. I propose marriage."

Nikolai considered this. He was new to Mech society. "Does this imply a sexual relationship?" he said. The woman looked at him blankly. "You mean between the two of us?"

7. FLOW PATTERNS. "You're worried about something," his wife told him. Nikolai shook his head. "Yes, you are," she persisted. "You're upset because of that deal I made in pirate contraband. You're unhappy because our corporation is profiting from attacks made on your own people."

Nikolai smiled ruefully. "I suppose you're right. I never knew anyone who understood my innermost feelings the way you do." He looked at her affectionately. "How do you do it?"

"I have infrared scanners," she said. "I read the patterns of blood flow in your face."

8. OPTIC TELEVISION. It was astonishing how much room there was in an eye socket, when you stopped to think about it. The actual visual mechanisms had been thoroughly miniaturized by Mechanist prostheticians. Nikolai had some other devices installed: a clock, a biofeedback monitor, a television screen, all wired directly to his optic nerve. They were convenient, but difficult to control at first. His wife had to help him out of the hospital and back to his apartment, because the subtle visual triggers kept flashing broadcast market reports. Nikolai smiled at his wife from behind his plastic eyes. "Spend the night with me tonight," he said. His wife shrugged. "All right," she said. She put her hand to the door of Nikolai's apartment

and died almost instantly. An assassin had smeared the door handle with contact venom.

9. SHAPER TARGETS. "Look," the assassin said, his slack face etched with weariness, "don't bother me with any ideologies…Just transfer the funds and tell me who it is you want dead."

"It's a job in the Ring Council," Nikolai said. He was strung out on a regimen of emotional drugs he had been taking to combat grief, and he had to fight down recurrent waves of weirdly tainted cheerfulness. "Captain-Doctor Martin Leng of Ring Council Security. He's one of my own gene-line. My defection made his own loyalty look bad. He killed my wife."

"Shapers make good targets," the assassin said. His legless, armless body floated in a transparent nutrient tank, where tinted plasmas soothed the purplish ends of socketed nerve clumps. A body-servo waded into the tank and began to attach the assassin's arms.

10. CHILD INVESTMENT. "We recognize your investment in this child, shareholder Leng," the psychotech said. "You may have created her—or hired the technicians who had her created—but she is not your property. By our regulations she must be treated like any other child. She is the property of our people's corporate republic."

Nikolai looked at the woman, exasperated. "I didn't create her. She's my dead wife's posthumous clone. And she's the property of my wife's corporations, or, rather, her trust fund, which I manage as executor…No, what I mean to say is that she owns, or at least has a lienhold on, my dead wife's semiautonomous corporate property, which becomes hers at the age of majority…Do you follow me?"

"No. I'm an educator, not a financier. What exactly is the point of this, shareholder? Are you trying to re-create your dead wife?"

Nikolai looked at her, his face carefully neutral. "I did it for the tax break."

… Leave the posthumous clone profiting from attacks. Semiautonomous property has an established commercial position. Recurrent waves of pirate contraband. His slack face bothers you with ideologies. Innermost feelings died almost instantly. Smear the door with contract venom…

11. ALLEGIANCES RESENTED. "I like it out here on the fringes," Nikolai told the assassin. "Have you ever considered a breakaway?"

The assassin laughed. "I used to be a pirate. It took me forty years to attach myself to this cartel. When you're alone, you're meat, Leng. You ought to know that."

"But you must resent those allegiances. They're inconvenient. Wouldn't you rather have your own Kluster and make your own rules?"

"You're talking like an ideologue," the assassin said. Biofeedback displays blinked softly on his prosthetic forearms. "My allegiance is to Kyotid Zaibatsu. They own this whole suburb. They even own my arms and legs."

"I own Kyotid Zaibatsu," Nikolai said.

"Oh," the assassin said. "Well, that puts a different face on matters."

12. MASS DEFECTION. "We want to join your Kluster," the Superbright said. "We must join your Kluster. No one else will have us."

Nikolai doodled absently with his light pen on a convenient video-screen. "How many of you are there?"

"There were fifty in our gene-line. We were working on quantum physics before our mass defection. We made a few minor breakthroughs. I think they might be of some commercial use."

"Splendid," said Nikolai. He assumed an air of speculative pity. "I take it the Ring Council persecuted you in the usual manner—claimed you were mentally unstable, ideologically unsound, and the like."

"Yes. Their agents have killed thirty-eight of us." The Superbright dabbed uneasily at the sweat beading on his swollen forehead. "We are not mentally unsound, Kluster-Chairman. We will not cause you any trouble. We only want a quiet place to finish working while God eats our brains."

13. DATA HOSTAGE. A high-level call came in from the Ring Council. Nikolai, surprised and intrigued, took the call himself. A young man's face appeared on the screen. "I have your teacher hostage," he said.

Nikolai frowned. "What?"

"The person who taught you when you were a child in the crèche. You love her. You told her so. I have it on tape."

"You must be joking," Nikolai said. "My teacher was just a cybernetic interface. You can't hold a data system hostage."

"Yes, I can," the young man said truculently. "The old expert system's been scrapped in favor of a new one with a sounder ideology. Look." A second face appeared on the screen; it was the superhumanly smooth and faintly glowing image of his cybernetic teacher. "Please save me, Nikolai," the image said woodenly. "He's ruthless."

The young man's face reappeared. Nikolai laughed incredulously. "So you've saved the old tapes?" Nikolai said. "I don't know what your game is, but I suppose the data has a certain value. I'm prepared to be generous." He named a price. The young man shook his head. Nikolai grew impatient.

"Look," he said. "What makes you think a mere expert system has any objective worth?"

"I know it does," the young man said. "I'm one myself."

14. CENTRAL QUESTION. Nikolai was aboard the alien ship. He felt uncomfortable in his brocaded ambassador's coat. He adjusted the heavy sunglasses over his plastic eyes. "We appreciate your visit to our Kluster," he told the reptilian ensign. "It's a very great honor."

The Investor ensign lifted the multicolored frill behind his massive head. "We are prepared to do business," he said.

"I'm interested in alien philosophies," Nikolai said. "The answers of other species to the great questions of existence."

"But there is only one central question," the alien said. "We have pursued its answer from star to star. We were hoping that you would help us answer it."

Nikolai was cautious. "What is the question?"

"'What is it you have that we want?'"

15. INHERITED GIFTS. Nikolai looked at the girl with the old-fashioned eyes. "My chief of security has provided me with a record of your criminal actions," he said. "Copyright infringement, organized extortion, conspiracy in restraint of trade. How old are you?"

"Forty-four," the girl said. "How old are you?"

"A hundred and ten or so. I'd have to check my files." Something about the girl's appearance bothered him. "Where did you get those antique eyes?"

"They were my mother's. I inherited them. But you're a Shaper, of course. You wouldn't know what a mother was."

"On the contrary," Nikolai said. "I believe I knew yours. We were married. After her death, I had you cloned. I suppose that makes me your— I forget the term."

"Father."

"That sounds about right. Clearly you've inherited her gifts for finance." He reexamined her personnel file. "Would you be interested in adding bigamy to your list of crimes?"

… The mentally unstable have a certain value. Restraint of trade puts a different face on the convenient videoscreen. A few minor breakthroughs in the questions of existence. Your personnel file persecuted him. His swollen forehead can't hold a data system…

16. PLEASURE ROAR. "You need to avoid getting set in your ways," his wife said. "It's the only way to stay young." She pulled a gilded inhaler from her garter holster. "Try some of this."

"I don't need drugs," Nikolai said, smiling. "I have my power fantasies." He began pulling off his clothes.

His wife watched him impatiently. "Don't be stodgy, Nikolai." She touched the inhaler to her nostril and sniffed. Sweat began to break out on her face, and a slow sexual flush spread over her ears and neck.

Nikolai watched, then shrugged and sniffed lightly at the gilded tube. Immediately a rocketing sense of ecstasy paralyzed his nervous system. His body arched backward, throbbing uncontrollably.

Clumsily, his wife began to caress him. The roar of chemical pleasure made sex irrelevant. "Why...why bother?" he gasped.

His wife looked surprised. "It's traditional."

17. FLICKERING WALL. Nikolai addressed the flickering wall of monitor screens. "I'm getting old," he said. "My health is good—I was very lucky in my choice of longevity programs—but I just don't have the daring I once did. I've lost my flexibility, my edge. And the Kluster has outgrown my ability to handle it. I have no choice. I must retire."

Carefully, he watched the faces on the screens for every flicker of reaction. Two hundred years had taught him the art of reading faces. His skills were still with him—it was only the will behind them that had decayed. The faces of the Governing Board, their reserve broken by shock, seemed to blaze with ambition and greed.

18. LEGAL TARGETS. The Mechanists had unleashed their drones in the suburb. Armed with subpoenas, the faceless drones blurred through the hallway crowds, looking for legal targets.

Suddenly Nikolai's former Chief of Security broke from the crowd and began a run for cover. In free-fall, he brachiated from handhold to handhold like an armored gibbon. Suddenly one of his prosthetics gave way and the drones pounced on him, almost at Nikolai's door. Plastic snapped as electromagnetic pincers paralyzed his limbs.

"Kangaroo courts," he gasped. The deeply creased lines in his ancient face shone with rivulets of sweat. "They'll strip me! Help me, Leng!"

Sadly, Nikolai shook his head. The old man shrieked: "You got me into this! You were the ideologue! I'm only a poor assassin!"

Nikolai said nothing. The machines seized and repossessed the old man's arms and legs.

19. ANTIQUE SPLITS. "You've really got it through you, right? All that old gigo stuff!" The young people spoke a slang-crammed jargon that Nikolai could barely comprehend. When they watched him their faces showed a

mixture of aggression, pity, and awe. To Nikolai, they always seemed to be shouting. "I feel outnumbered," he murmured.

"You are outnumbered, old Nikolai! This bar is your museum, right? Your mausoleum! Give our ears your old frontiers, we're listening! Those idiot video ideologies, those antique spirit splits. Mechs and Shapers, right? The wars of the coin's two halves!"

"I feel tired," Nikolai said. "I've drunk too much. Take me home, one of you."

They exchanged worried glances. "This is your home! Isn't it?"

20. EYES CLOSED. "You've been very kind," Nikolai told the two young-sters. They were Kosmosity archaeologists, dressed in their academic finery, their gowns studded with awards and medals from the Terraform-Klusters. Nikolai realized suddenly that he could not remember their names.

"That's all right, sir," they told him soothingly. "It's now our duty to re-member you, not vice versa." Nikolai felt embarrassed. He hadn't realized that he had spoken aloud.

"I've taken poison," he explained apologetically.

"We know," they nodded. "You're not in any pain, we hope?"

"No, not at all. I've done the right thing, I know. I'm very old. Older than I can bear." Suddenly he felt an alarming collapse within himself. Pieces of his consciousness began to break off as he slid toward the void. Suddenly he realized that he had forgotten his last words. With an enormous effort, he remembered them and shouted them aloud.

"Futility is freedom!" Filled with triumph, he died, and they closed his eyes.

PART II:

EARLY
SCIENCE FICTION
AND FANTASY

Green Days in Brunei

Two men were fishing from the corroded edge of an offshore oil rig. After years of decrepitude, the rig's concrete pillars were thick with barnacles and waving fronds of seaweed. The air smelled of rust and brine.

"Sorry to disturb your plans," the minister said. "But we can't just chat up the Yankees every time you hit a little contretemps." The minister reeled in and revealed a bare hook. He cursed mildly in his native Malay. "Hand me another bait, there's a good fellow."

Turner Choi reached into the wooden bait bucket and gave the minister a large dead prawn. "But I need that phone link," Turner said. "Just for a few hours. Just long enough to access the net in America and download some better documentation."

"What ghastly jargon," said the minister, who was formally known as the Yang Teramat Pehin Orang Kaya Amar Diraja Dato Seri Paduka Abdul Kahar. He was minister of industrial policy for the Sultanate of Brunei Darussalam, a tiny nation on the northern shore of the island of Borneo. The titles of Brunei's aristocracy were in inverse proportion to the country's size.

"It'd save us a lot of time, Tuan Minister," Turner said. "Those robots are programmed in an obsolete language, forty years old. Strictly Neanderthal."

The minister deftly baited his hook and flicked it out in a long spinning cast. "You knew before you came here how the sultanate feels about the world information order. You shall just have to puzzle out this conundrum on your own."

"But you're making weeks, months maybe, out of a three-hour job!" Turner said.

"My dear fellow, this is Borneo," the minister said benignly. "Stop looking at your watch and pay some attention to catching us dinner."

Turner sighed and reeled in his line. Behind them, the rig's squatter population of Dayak fisherfolk clustered on the old helicopter pad, mending nets and chewing betel nut.

It was another slow Friday in Brunei Darussalam. Across the shallow bay, Brunei Town rose in tropical sunlight, its soaring high-rises festooned with makeshift solar roofs, windmills, and bulging greenhouse balconies. The golden-domed mosque on the waterfront was surrounded by the towering legacy of the twentieth-century oil boom: boxlike office blocks, now bizarrely transmuted into urban farms.

Brunei Town, the sultanate's capital, had a hundred thousand citizens: Malays, Chinese, Ibans, Dayaks, and a sprinkling of Europeans. But it was a city under a hush. No cars. No airport. No television. From a distance it reminded Turner of an old Western fairy tale: Sleeping Beauty, the jury-rigged high-rises with their cascading greenery like a hundred castles shrouded in thorns. The Bruneians seemed like sleepwalkers, marooned from the world, wrapped in the enchantment of their ideology.

Turner baited his hook again, restive at being away from the production line. The minister seemed more interested in converting him than in letting him work. To the Bruneians, the robots were just another useless memento of their long-dead romance with the West. The old robot assembly line hadn't been used in twenty years, since the turn of the century.

And yet the royal government had decided to retrofit the robot line for a new project. For technical help, they had applied to Kyocera, a Japanese multinational corporation. Kyocera had sent Turner Choi, one of their new recruits, a twenty-six-year-old Chinese Canadian CAD-CAM engineer from Vancouver.

It wasn't much of a job—a kind of industrial archaeology whose main tools were chicken wire and a ball-peen hammer—but it was Turner's first and he meant to succeed. The Bruneians were relaxed to the point of coma, but Turner Choi had his future ahead of him with Kyocera. In the long run, it was Kyocera who would judge his work here. And Turner was running out of time.

The minister, whooping in triumph, hauled hard on his line. A fat, spotted fish broke the surface, flopping on the hook. Turner decided to break the rules and to hell with it.

▲ ▼ ▲

The local neighborhood organization, the *kampong*, was showing a free movie in the little park fourteen stories below Turner's window. Bright images crawled against the bleak white Bauhaus wall of a neighboring high-rise.

Turner peered down through the blinds. He had been watching the flick all night as he finished his illegal tinkering.

The Bruneians, like Malays everywhere, adored ghost stories. The film's protagonist, or chief horror (Turner wasn't sure which), was an acrobatic monkey-demon with razor-sharp forearms. It had burst into a depraved speakeasy and was slaughtering drunkards with a tremendous windmilling flurry of punches, kicks, and screeches. Vast meaty sounds of combat, like colliding freight trains packed with beef, drifted faintly upward.

Turner sat before his bootleg keyboard, and sighed. He'd known it would come to this ever since the Bruneians had confiscated his phone at customs. For five months he'd politely tried to work his way around it. Now he had only three months left. He was out of time and out of patience.

The robots were okay, under caked layers of yellowing grease. They'd been roped down under tarps for years. But the software manuals were a tattered ruin.

Just thinking about it gave Turner a cold sinking feeling. It was a special, private terror that had dogged him since childhood. It was the fear he felt when he had to confront his grandfather.

He thought of his grandfather's icy and pitiless eyes, fixed on him with that "Hong Kong Bad Cop" look. In the 1970s, Turner's grandfather had been one of the infamous "millionaire sergeants" of the Hong Kong police, skimming the cream of the Burmese heroin trade. He'd emigrated in the Triad bribery scandals of 1973.

After forty-seven years of silk suits and first-class flights between his mansions in Taipei and Vancouver, Grandfather Choi still had that cold eye and that grim shakedown look. It was an evil memory for Turner, of being weighed and found wanting.

The documentation was hopeless, crumbling and mildewed, alive with silverfish. The innocent Bruneians hadn't realized that the information it held was the linchpin of the whole enterprise. The sultanate had bought the factory long ago, with the last gush of Brunei's oil money, as a stylish, doomed gesture in Western industrial chic. Somehow, robots had never really caught on in Borneo.

But Turner had to seize this chance. He had to prove that he could make it on his own, without Grandfather Choi and the stifling weight of his money.

For days, Turner had snooped around down on the waterfront, with its cubbyholed rows of Chinese junkshops. It was Turner's favorite part of Brunei Town, a white-elephant's graveyard of dead tech. The wooden and bamboo shops were lined with dead, blackened televisions like decaying teeth.

There, he'd set about assembling a bootleg modern phone. He'd rescued a water-stained keyboard and screen from one of the shops. His modem and recorder came from work. On the waterfront he'd found a Panamanian freighter whose captain would illegally time-share on his satellite navigation dish.

Brunei Town was full of phone booths that no one ever seemed to use, grimy old glass-and-plastic units labeled in Malay, English, and Mandarin. A typical payphone stood on the street outside Turner's high-rise. It was an old twentieth-century job with a coin-feed and a rotary dial, and no videoscreen.

In the dead of night he'd crept down there to install a radio link to his apartment on the fourteenth floor. Someone might trace his illegal call back to the phone booth, but no farther. With the radio link, his own apartment would stay safe.

But when he'd punch-jacked the payphone's console off, he'd found that it already had a bootleg link hooked up. It was in fine working order, too. He'd seen then that he wasn't alone, and that Brunei, despite all its rhetoric about the Neo-Colonial World Information Order, was not entirely free of the global communications net. Brunei was wired too, just like the West, but the net had gone underground.

All those abandoned payphones had taken on a new and mildly sinister significance for him since that discovery, but he wasn't going to kick. All his plans were riding on his chance to get through.

Now he was ready. He rechecked the satellite guide in the back of his ASME handbook. *Arabsat 7* was up, in its leisurely low-orbit ramble over the tropics. Turner dialed from his apartment down through the payphone outside, then patched in through the Panamanian dish. Through *Arabsat* he hooked up to an American geosynchronous sat and down into the American ground net. From there he direct-dialed his brother's house.

Georgie Choi was at breakfast in Vancouver, dressed in a French-cuffed pinstripe shirt and varsity sweater. Behind him, Turner's sleek sister-in-law, Marjorie, presided over a table crowded with crisp linen napkins and silver cutlery. Turner's two young nieces decorously spread jam on triangles of toast.

"Is it you, Turner?" Georgie said. "I'm not getting any video."

"I couldn't get a camera," Turner said. "I'm in Brunei—phone quarantine, remember? I had to bootleg it just to get sound."

A monsoon breeze blew up outside Turner's window. The wind-power generators bolted to the high-rise walls whirred into life, and threw broad bars of raw static across the screen. Georgie's smooth brow wrinkled gracefully. "This reception is terrible! You're not even in stereo." He smiled uncertainly. "No matter, we'll make do. We haven't heard from you in ages. Things all right?"

"They will be," Turner said. "How's Grandfather?"

"He's flown in from Taipei for dialysis and his blood change," Georgie said. "He hates hospitals, but I had good news for him." He hesitated. "We have a new great-grandchild on the way."

Marjorie glanced up and bestowed one of her glittering wifely smiles on the camera. "That's fine," Turner said reflexively. Children were a touchy subject with Turner. He had not yet married, despite his family's endless prodding and nagging.

He thought guiltily that he should have spent more time with Georgie's children. Georgie was already in some upscale never-never land, all leather-bound law and municipal politics, but it wasn't his kids' fault. Kids were innocent. "Hi, kids," he said in Mandarin. "I'll bring you something you'll like."

The younger girl looked up, her elegant child's mouth crusted with strawberry jam. "I want a shrunken head," she said in English.

"You see?" Georgie said with false joviality. "This is what comes of running off to Borneo."

"I need some modem software," Turner said, avoiding the issue. Grandfather hadn't approved of Borneo. "Could you get it off the old Hayes in my room?"

"If you don't have a modem protocol, how can I send you a program?" Georgie said.

"Print it out and hold it up to the screen," Turner explained patiently. "I'll record it and type it in later by hand."

"That's clever," Georgie said. "You engineers."

He left to set it up. Turner talked guardedly to Marjorie. He had never been able to figure the woman out. Turner would have liked to know how Marjorie really felt about cold-eyed Bad Cop Grandfather and his eight million dollars in Triad heroin money.

But Marjorie was so coolly elegant, so brilliantly designed, that Turner had never been able to bring himself to probe her real feelings. It would have been like popping open some factory-sealed peripheral that was still under warranty, just so you could sneak a look at the circuit boards.

Even he and Georgie never talked frankly anymore. Not since Grandfather's health had turned shaky. The prospect of finally inheriting that money had left a white hush over his family like fifteen feet of Canadian snow.

The horrible old man relished the competition for his favor. He insisted on it. Grandfather had a second household in Taipei; Turner's uncle and cousins. If Grandfather chose them over his Canadian brood, Georgie's perfect life would go to pieces.

A childhood memory brushed Turner: Georgie's toys, brightly painted little Hong Kong windups held together with folded tin flaps. As a child, Turner had spent many happy, covert hours dexterously prying Georgie's toys apart.

Marjorie chatted about Turner's mother, a neurotic widow who ran an antique store in Atlanta. Behind her, a Chinese maid began clearing the table, glancing up at the camera with the spooked eyes of an immigrant fresh off the boat.

Turner was used to phone cameras, and though he didn't have one he kept a fixed smile through habit. But he could feel himself souring, his face knotting up in that inherited Bad Cop glare. Turner had his grandfather's face, with hollow cheeks, and sunken eyes under heavy impressive brows.

But Canada, Turner's birthplace, had left its mark on him. Years of steak and Wonder Bread had given him a six-foot frame and the build of a linebacker.

Georgie came back with the printout. Turner said goodbye and cut the link.

He pulled up the blinds for the climax of the movie downstairs. The monkey-demon massacred a small army of Moslem extremists in the corroded remnants of a Shell refinery. Moslem fanatics had been stock villains in Brunei since the failure of their coup of '98.

The last of the reel flickered loose. Turner unpinned a banana-leaf wrapping and dug his chopsticks into a midnight snack of rice fried with green pineapple. He leaned on the open window, propping one booted foot on the massive window box with its dense ranks of onions and pepper plants.

The call to Vancouver had sent a shiver of culture shock through him. He saw his apartment with new eyes. It was decorated with housewarming gifts from other members of his *kampong*. A flat leather shadow-puppet, all perforations and curlicues. A gold-framed photo of the sultan shaking hands with the king of England. A hand-painted glass ant farm full of inch-long Borneo ants, torpid on molasses. And a young banyan bonsai tree from the *kampong* headman.

The headman, an elderly Malay, was a political wardheeler for Brunei's ruling party, the Greens, or "Partai Ekolojasi." In the West, the Greens had long ago been co-opted into larger parties. But Brunei's Partai Ekolojasi had twenty years of deep roots.

The banyan tree came with five pages of meticulous instructions on care and feeding, but despite Turner's best efforts the midget tree was yellowing and shedding leaves. The tree was not just a gift; it was a test, and Turner knew it. The *kampong* smiled, but they had their ways of testing, and they watched.

Turner glanced reflexively at his deadbolt on the door. The locks were not exactly forbidden, but they were frowned on. The Greens had converted Brunei's old office buildings into huge multilayered village longhouses. Western notions of privacy were unpopular.

But Turner needed the lock for his work. He had to be discreet. Brunei might seem loose and informal, but it was still a one-party state under autocratic rule.

Twenty years earlier, when the oil crash had hit, the monarchy had seemed doomed. The Muslim insurgents had tried to murder them outright. Even the Greens had had bigger dreams then. Turner had seen their peeling, forgotten wall posters, their global logo of the Whole Earth half-buried under layered years of want ads and soccer schedules.

The Royal Family had won through, a symbol of tradition and stability. They'd weathered the storm of the Muslim insurgence, and stifled the Greens' first wild ambitions. After five months in Brunei, Turner, like the Royals, had grasped Brunei's hidden dynamics. It was *adat*, Malay custom, that ruled. And the first law of *adat* was that you didn't embarrass your neighbors.

Turner unpinned his favorite movie poster, a big promotional four-sheet for a Brunei historical epic. In garish four-color printing, a boatload of heroic Malay pirates gallantly advanced on a sinister Portuguese galleon. Turner had carved a hideout in the sheetrock wall behind the poster. He stowed his phone gear.

Somebody tried the door, hit the deadbolt, and knocked softly. Turner hastily smoothed the poster and pinned it up.

He opened the door. It was his Australian neighbor, McGinty, a retired newscaster from Melbourne. McGinty loved Brunei for its utter lack of televisions. It was one of the last places on the planet in which one could truly get away from it all.

McGinty glanced up and down the hall, stepped inside, and reached into his loose cotton blouse. He produced a cold quart can of Foster's Lager. "Have a beer, chum?"

"Fantastic!" Turner said. "Where'd you get it?"

McGinty smiled evasively. "The bloody fridge is on the blink, and I thought you'd fancy one while they're still cold."

"Right," Turner said, popping the top. "I'll have a look at your fridge as soon as I destroy this evidence." The *kampong* ran on a web of barter and mutual obligation. Turner's skills were part of it. It was tiresome, but a Foster's Lager was good pay. It was a big improvement over the liquid brain damage from the illegal stills down on Floor 4.

They went to McGinty's place. McGinty lived next door with his aged parents; four of them, for his father and mother had divorced and both remarried. The ancient Australians thrived in Brunei's somnolent atmosphere, pottering about the *kampong* gardens in pith helmets, gurkha shorts, and khaki bush vests. McGinty, like many of his generation, had never had children. Now in retirement he seemed content to shepherd these older folk, plying them with megavitamins and morning Tai Chi exercises.

Turner stripped the refrigerator. "It's your compressor," he said. "I'll track you down one on the waterfront. I can jury-rig something. You know me. Always tinkering."

McGinty looked uncomfortable, since he was now in Turner's debt. Suddenly he brightened. "There's a party at the privy councilor's tomorrow night. Jimmy Brooke. You know him?"

"Heard of him," Turner said. He'd heard rumors about Brooke: hints of corruption, some long-buried scandal. "He was a big man when the Parlai got started, right? Minister of something."

"Communications."

Turner laughed. "That's not much of a job around here."

"Well, he still knows a lot of movie people." McGinty lowered his voice. "And he has a private bar. He's chummy with the Royal Family. They make allowances for him."

"Yeah?" Turner didn't relish mingling with McGinty's social circle of wealthy retirees, but it might be smart, politically. A word with the old com minister might solve a lot of his problems. "Okay," he said. "Sounds like fun."

▲ ▼ ▲

The privy councilor, Yang Amat Mulia Pengiran Indera Negara Pengiran Jimmy Brooke, was one of Brunei's odder relics. He was a British tax exile, a naturalized Bruneian, who had shown up in the late '90s after the oil crash. His wealth had helped cushion the blow and had won him a place in the government.

Larger and better-organized governments might have thought twice about co-opting this deaf, white-haired eccentric, a washed-up pop idol with a parasitic retinue of balding bohemians. But the aging rock star, with his decaying glamour, fit in easily with the comic-opera glitter of Brunei's tiny aristocracy. He owned the old Bank of Singapore office block, a *kampong* of remarkable looseness where peccadillos flourished under Brooke's noblesse oblige.

Monsoon rain pelted the city. Brooke's henchmen, paunchy bodyguards in bulging denim, had shut the glass doors of the penthouse and turned on the air conditioning. The party had close to a hundred people, mostly retired Westerners from Europe and Australia. They had the stifling clubbiness of exiles who have all known each other too long. A handful of refugee Americans, still powdered and rouged with their habitual video makeup, munched imported beer nuts by the long mahogany bar.

The Bruneian actress Dewi Serrudin was holding court on a rattan couch, surrounded by admirers. Cinema was a lost art in the West, finally murdered and buried by video; but Brunei's odd policies had given it a last toehold. Turner, who had a mild long-distance crush on the actress, edged up between two hopeful émigrés: a portly Madrasi producer in dhoti and jubbah, and a Hong Kong chop-socky director in a black frogged cotton jacket.

Miss Serrudin, in a gold lamé blouse and a skirt of antique ultrasuede, was playing the role to the hilt, chattering brightly and chain-burning imported Rothmans in a jade holder. She had the ritual concentration of a Balinese dancer evoking postures handed down through the centuries. And she was older than he'd thought she was.

Turner finished his whiskey sour and handed it to one of Brooke's balding gofers. He felt depressed and lonely. He wandered away from the crowd, and turned down a hall at random. The walls were hung with gold albums and old yellowing pub-shots of Brooke and his band, all rhinestones and platform heels, their flying hair lavishly backlit with klieg lights.

Turner passed a library, and a billiards room where two wrinkled, turbaned Sikhs were racking up a game of snooker. Farther down the hall, he glanced through an archway, into a sunken conversation pit lavishly carpeted with ancient, indestructible synthetic plush.

A bony young Malay woman in black jeans and a satin jacket sat alone in the room, reading a month-old issue of *New Musical Express*. It was headlined "Leningrad Pop Cuts Loose!" Her sandaled feet were propped on a coffee table next to a beaten silver platter with a pitcher and an ice bucket. Her bright red, shoulder-length hair showed two long inches of black roots.

She looked up at him in blank surprise. Turner hesitated at the archway, then stepped into the room. "Hi," he said.

"Hello. What's your *kampong*?"

"Citibank Building," Turner said. He was used to the question by now. "I'm with the industrial ministry, consulting engineer. I'm a Canadian. Turner Choi."

She folded the newspaper and smiled. "Ah, you're the bloke who's working on the robots."

"Word gets around," Turner said, pleased.

She watched him narrowly. "Seria Bolkiah Mùizzaddin Waddaulah."

"Sorry, I don't speak Malay."

"That's my name," she said.

Turner laughed. "Oh, Lord. Look, I'm just a no-neck Canuck with hay in my hair. Make allowances, okay?"

"You're a Western technician," she said. "How exotic. How is your work progressing?"

"It's a strange assignment," Turner said. He sat on the couch at a polite distance, marveling at her bizarre accent. "You've spent some time in Britain?"

"I went to school there." She studied his face. "You look rather like a Chinese Keith Richards."

"Sorry, don't know him."

"The guitarist of the Rolling Stones."

"I don't keep up with the new bands," Turner said. "A little Russian pop, maybe." He felt a peculiar tension in the situation. Turner glanced quickly at the woman's hands. No wedding ring, so that wasn't it.

"Would you like a drink?" the woman said. "It's grape juice."

"Sure," Turner said. "Thanks." She poured gracefully: innocent grape juice over ice. She was a Moslem, Turner thought, despite her dyed hair. Maybe that was why she was oddly standoffish.

He would have to bend the rules again. She was not conventionally pretty, but she had the kind of neurotic intensity that Turner had always found fatally attractive. And his love life had suffered in Brunei; the *kampongs* with their prying eyes and village gossip had cramped his style.

He wondered how he could arrange to see her. It wasn't a question of just asking her out to dinner—it all depended on her *kampong*. Some were stricter than others. He might end up with half-a-dozen veiled Muslim chaperones—or maybe a gang of muscular cousins and brothers with a bad attitude about Western lechers.

"When do you plan to start production, Mr. Choi?"

Turner said, "We've built a few fishing skiffs already, just minor stuff. We have bigger plans once the robots are up."

"A real factory," she said. "Like the old days."

Turner smiled, seeing his chance. "Maybe you'd like a tour of the plant?"

"It sounds romantic," she said. "Those robots are free labor. They were supposed to take the place of our free oil when it ran out. Brunei used to be rich, you know. Oil paid for everything. The Shellfare state, they used to call us." She smiled wistfully.

"How about Monday?" Turner said.

She looked at him, surprised, and suddenly blushed. "I'm afraid not."

Turner caught her eye. It's not me, he thought. It was something in the way—*adat* or something. "It's all right," he said gently. "I'd like to see you, is that so bad? Bring your whole *kampong* if you want."

"My *kampong* is the Palace," she said.

"Uh-oh." Suddenly he had that cold feeling again.   ·

"You didn't know," she said triumphantly. "You thought I was just some rock groupie."

"Who are you, then?"

"I'm the Duli Yang Maha Mulia Diranee…Well, I'm the princess. Princess Seria." She smiled.

"Good lord." He had been sitting and flirting with the royal princess of Brunei. It was bizarre. He half expected a troupe of bronzed eunuchs to burst in, armed with scimitars. "You're the sultan's daughter?"

"You mustn't think too much of it," she said. "Our country is only two thousand square miles. It's so small that it's a family business, that's all. The mayor of your Vancouver rules more people than my family does."

Turner sipped his grape juice to cover his confusion. Brunei was a Commonwealth country, after all, with a British-educated aristocracy. The sultan had polo ponies and cricket pitches. But still, a princess...

"I never said I was from Vancouver," he told her. "You knew who I was all along."

"Brunei doesn't have many tall Chinese in lumberjack shirts." She smiled wickedly. "And those boots."

Turner glanced down. His legs were armored in knee-high engineering boots, a mass of shiny leather and buckles. His mother had bought them for him, convinced that they would save his life from snakebite in savage Borneo. "I promised I'd wear them," he said. "Family obligation."

She looked sour. "You, too? That sounds all too familiar, Mr. Choi." Now that the spell of anonymity was broken, she seemed flustered. Their quick rapport was grinding to a halt. She lifted the music paper with a rustle of pages. He saw that her nails were gnawed down to the quick.

For some perverse reason this put Turner's libido jarringly back into gear. She had that edgy flyaway look that spelled trouble with a capital *T*. Ironically, she was just his type.

"I know the mayor's daughter in Vancouver," he said deliberately. "I like the local version a lot better."

She met his eyes. "It's really too bad about family obligations..."

The privy councilor appeared suddenly in the archway. The wizened rock star wore a cream-colored seersucker suit with ruby cuff links. He was a cadaverous old buzzard with rheumy eyes and a wattled neck. A frizzed mass of snow-white hair puffed from his head like cotton from an aspirin bottle.

"Highness," he said loudly. "We need a fourth at bridge."

Princess Seria stood up with an air of martyrdom. "I'll be right with you," she shouted.

"And who's the young man?" said Brooke, revealing his dentures in an uneasy smile.

Turner stepped nearer. "Turner Choi, Tuan Privy Councilor," he said loudly. "A privilege to meet you, sir."

"What's your *kampong*, Mr. Chong?"

"Mr. Choi is working on the robot shipyard!" the princess said.

"The what? The shipyard? Oh, splendid!" Brooke seemed relieved.

"I'd like a word with you, sir," Turner said. "About communications."

"About what?" Brooke cupped one hand to his ear.

"The phone net, sir! A line out!"

The princess looked startled. But Brooke, still not understanding, nodded blankly. "Ah yes. Very interesting...My entourage and I will stop by some day when you have the line up! I love the sound of good machines at work!"

"Sure," Turner said, recognizing defeat. "That would be, uh, groovy."

"Brunei is counting on you, Mr. Chong," Brooke said, his wrinkled eyes gleaming with bogus sincerity. "Good to see you here. Enjoy yourself." He shook Turner's hand, pressing something into his palm. He winked at Turner and escorted the princess out into the hall.

Turner looked at his hand. The old man had given him a marijuana cigarette. Turner shook himself, laughed, and threw it away.

▲ ▼ ▲

Another slow Monday in Brunei Town. Turner's work crew meandered in around midmorning. They were Bruneian Chinese, toting wicker baskets stuffed with garden-fresh produce, and little lacquered lunchboxes with satay shish kebabs and hot shrimp paste. They started the morning's food barter, chatting languidly in Malay-accented Mandarin.

Turner had very little power over them. They were hired by the Industrial Ministry, and paid little or nothing. Their labor was part of the invisible household economy of the *kampongs*. They worked for *kampong* perks, like chickens or movie tickets.

The shipyard was a cavernous barn with overhead pulley tracks and an oil-stained concrete floor. The front section, with its bare launching rails sloping down to deep water, had once been a Dayak *kampong*. The Dayaks had spraybombed the concrete-block walls with giant neon-bright murals of banshees dead in childbirth, and leaping cricket-spirits with evil Day-Glo eyes.

The back part was two-storey, with the robots' machine shop at ground level and a glass-fronted office upstairs that looked down over the yard.

Inside, the office was decorated in crass '80s High-Tech Moderne, with round-cornered computer desks between sleek modular partitions, all tubular chrome and grainy beige plastic. The plastic had aged hideously in forty years, absorbing a gray miasma of fingerprints and soot.

Turner worked alone in the neck-high maze of curved partitions, where a conspiracy of imported clerks and programmers had once efficiently sopped up the last of Brunei's oil money. He was typing up the bootlegged modem software on the IBM, determined to call America and get the production line out of the Stone Age.

The yard reeked of hot epoxy as the crew got to work. The robots were one-armed hydraulic jobs, essentially glorified tea-trolleys with single swivel-jointed manipulators. Turner had managed to get them up to a certain crude level of donkeywork: slicing wood, stirring glue, hauling heavy bundles of lumber.

But, so far, the crew handled all the craftwork. They laminated the long strips of shaved lumber into sturdy panels of epoxied plywood. They bent the wet panels into hull and deck shapes, steam-sealing them over curved molds. They lapped and veneered the seams, and painted good-luck eye-symbols on the bows.

So far, the plant had produced nothing larger than a twenty-foot skiff. But on the drawing boards was a series of freighter-sized floating *kampongs*, massive sail-powered trimarans for the deep ocean, with glassed-in greenhouse decks.

The ships would be cheap and slow, like most things in Brunei, but pleasant enough, Turner supposed. Lots of slow golden afternoons on the tropical seas, with plenty of fresh fruit. The whole effort seemed rather point-less, but at least it would break Brunei's isolation from the world, and give them a crude merchant fleet.

The foreman, a spry old Chinese named Leng, shouted for Turner from the yard. Turner saved his program, got up, and looked down through the office glass. The minister of industrial policy had arrived, tying up an ancient fiberglass speedboat retrofitted with ribbed lateen sails.

Turner hurried down, groaning to himself, expecting to be invited off for another avuncular lecture. But the minister's zenlike languor had been bro-ken. He came almost directly to the point, pausing only to genially accept some coconut milk from the foreman.

"It's His Highness the Sultan," the minister said. "Someone's put a bee in his bonnet about these robots. Now he wants to tour the plant."

"When?" Turner said.

"Two weeks," said the minister. "Or maybe three."

Turner thought it over, and smiled. He sensed the princess's hand in this and felt deeply flattered.

"I say," the minister said. "You seem awfully pleased for a fellow who was predicting disaster just last Friday."

"I found another section of the manual," Turner lied glibly. "I hope to have real improvements in short order."

"Splendid," said the minister. "You remember the prototype we were discussing?"

"The quarter-scale model?" Turner said. "Tuan Minister, even in minia-ture, that's still a fifty-foot trimaran."

"Righto. How about it? Do you think you could scatter the blueprints about, have the robots whir by looking busy, plenty of sawdust and glue?"

Politics, Turner thought. He gave the minister his Bad Cop look. "You mean some kind of Potemkin village. Don't you want the ship built?"

"I fail to see what pumpkins have to do with it," said the minister, wounded. "This is a state occasion. We shall have the newsreel cameras in. Of course build the ship. I simply want it impressive, that's all."

Impressive, Turner thought. Sure. If Seria was watching, why not?

▲ ▼ ▲

Luckily the Panamanian freighter was still in port, not leaving till Wednesday. Armed with his new software, Turner tried another bootleg raid at ten P.M. He caught a Brazilian comsat and tied into Detroit.

Reception was bad, and Doris had already moved twice. But he found her finally in a seedy condominium in the Renaissance Center historical district.

"Where's your video, man?"

"It's out," Turner lied, not wanting to burden his old girlfriend with two years of past history. He and Doris had lived together in Toronto for two semesters while he studied CAD-CAM. Doris was an automotive designer, a Rustbelt refugee from Detroit's collapse.

For Turner, school was a blissful chance to live in the same pair of jeans for days on end, but times were tough in the Rustbelt and Doris had lived close to the bone. He'd ended up footing the bills, which hadn't bothered him (Bad Cop money), but it had preyed on Doris's mind. Months passed, and she spent more each week. He picked up her bills without a word, and she quietly went over the edge. She ended up puking drunk on her new satin sheets, unable to go downstairs for the mail without a line of coke.

But then word had come of his father's death. His father's antique Maserati had slammed head-on into an automated semitrailer rig.

Turner and his brother had attended the cremation in a drizzling Vancouver rain. They put the ashes on the family altar and knelt before little gray ribbons of incense smoke. Nobody said much. They didn't talk about Dad's drinking. Grandfather wouldn't have liked it.

When he'd gone back to Toronto, he found that Doris had packed up and left.

"I'm with Kyocera now," he told her. "The consulting engineers."

"You got a job, Turner?" she said, brushing back a frizzed tangle of blonde hair. "It figures. Poor people are standing in line for a chance to do dishes." She frowned. "What kind of hours you keeping, man? It's seven A.M. You caught me without my vid makeup."

She turned the camera away and walked out of sight. Turner studied her apartment: concrete blocks and packing crates, vinyl beanbag chairs, peeling walls festooned with printout. She was still on the Net, all right. Real Net-heads resented every penny not spent on information.

"I need some help, Doris. I need you to find me someone who can system-crack an old IBM robotics language called AML."

"Yeah?" she called out. "Ten percent agent's fee?"

"Sure. And this is on the hush, okay? Not Kyocera's business, just mine."

He heard her shouting from the condo's cramped bathroom. "I haven't heard from you in two years! You're not mad that I split, huh?"

"No."

"It wasn't that you were Chinese, okay? I mean, you're about as Chinese as maple syrup, right? It's just, the high life was making my sinuses bleed."

Turner scowled. "Look, it's okay. It was a temporary thing."

"I was crazy then. But I've been hooked up to a good shrink program, it's done wonders for me, really." She came back to the screen; she'd put on rouge and powder. She smiled and touched her cheek. "Good stuff, huh? The kind the President uses."

"You look fine."

"My shrink makes me jog every day. So, how you doin', man? Seeing anybody?"

"Not really." He smiled. "Except a princess of Borneo."

She laughed. "I thought you'd settle down by now, man. With some uptown family girl, right? Like your brother and whats-her-face."

"Didn't work out that way."

"You like crazy women, Turner, that's your problem. Remember the time your mom dropped by? She's a fruitcake, that's why."

"Aw, Jesus Christ, Doris," Turner said. "If I need a shrink, I can download one."

"Okay," she said, hurt. She touched a remote control. A television in the corner of the room flashed into life with a crackle of video music. Doris didn't bother to watch it. She'd turned it on by reflex, settling into the piped flow of cable like a hot bath. "Look, I'll see what I can scare you up on the Net. AML language, right? I think I know a—"

BREAK

The screen went blank. Alphanumerics flared up: ENTERING (C)HAT MODE

The line zipped up the screen. Then words spelled out in 80-column glowing bright green. WHAT ARE YOU DOING ON THIS LINE??

SORRY, Turner typed.

ENTER YOUR PASSWORD:

Turner thought fast. He had blundered into the Brunei underground net. He'd known it was possible, since he was using the pre-rigged payphone downstairs. MAPLE SYRUP, he typed at random.

CHECKING...THAT IS NOT A VALID PASSWORD.

SIGNING OFF, Turner typed.

WAIT, said the screen. WE DONT TAKE LURKERS LIGHTLY HERE. WE HAVE BEEN WATCHING YOU. THIS IS THE SECOND TIME YOU HAVE ACCESSED A SATELLITE. WHAT ARE YOU DOING IN OUR NET??

Turner rested one finger on the off switch.

More words spilled out. WE KNOW WHO YOU ARE, "MAPLE SYRUP." YOU ARE TURNER CHONG.

"Turner Choi," Turner said aloud. Then he remembered the man who had made that mistake. He felt a sudden surge of glee. He typed. OKAY, YOU'VE GOT ME—TUAN COUNCILOR JIMMY BROOKE.

There was a long blank space. Then: CLEVER, Brooke typed. SERIA TOLD YOU. SERIA, ARE YOU ON THIS LINE??

I WANT HER NUMBER!! Turner typed at once.

THEN LEAVE A (M)ESSAGE FOR "GAMELAN ROCKER," Brooke typed. I AM "NET HEADHUNTED"

THANKS, Turner typed.

I'LL LOG YOU ON, MAPLE SYRUP. SINCE YOU'RE ALREADY IN, YOU'D BETTER BE IN ON OUR TERMS. BUT JUST REMEMBER: THIS IS OUR ELECTRIC *KAMPONG*, SO YOU LIVE BY OUR RULES. OUR "*ADAT*," OKAY??

I'LL REMEMBER, SIR.

AND NO MORE BOOTLEG SATELLITE LINKS, YOU'RE SCREWING UP OUR GROUND LINES.

OKAY, Turner typed.

YOU CAN RENT TIME ON OUR OWN DISHES. NEXT TIME CALL 85-1515 DIRECTLY. OUR GAMES SECTION COULD USE SOME UPLOADS, BY THE WAY.

The words flashed off, replaced by the neatly ranked commands of a computer bulletin board. Turner accessed the message section, but then sat sweating and indecisive. In his mind, his quick message to Seria was rapidly ramifying into a particularly touchy and tentative love letter.

This was good, but it wasn't how he'd planned it. He was getting in over his head. He'd have to think it through.

He logged off the board. Doris's face appeared at once. "Where the hell have you been, man?"

"Sorry," Turner said.

"I've found you some old geezer out in Yorktown Heights," she said. "He says he used to work with Big Blue back in prehistory."

"It's always some old geezer," Turner said in resignation.

Doris shrugged. "Whaddya expect, man? Birth control got everybody else."

▲ ▼ ▲

Down in the yard, the sultan of Brunei chatted with his minister as technicians in sarongs and rubber sandals struggled with their huge, ancient cameras. The sultan wore his full regalia, a high-collared red military jacket with gold-braided shoulder boards, heavy with medals and pins. He was an elderly Malay with a neatly clipped white mustache and sad, wise eyes.

His son, the crown prince, had a silk ascot and an air force pilot's jacket. Turner had heard that the prince was nuts about helicopters. Seria's formal wear looked like a jazzed-up Girl Guide's outfit, with a prim creased skirt and a medal-clustered shoulder sash.

Turner was alone in the programming room, double-checking one of the canned routines he'd downloaded from America. They'd done wonders for the plant already; the robots had completed one hull of the trimaran. The human crew was handling the delicate work: the glassed-in greenhouse. Braced sections of glass now hung from ceiling pulleys, gleaming photogenically in geodesic wooden frames.

Turner studied his screen.

```
IF QMONITOR (FMONS(2)) EQ 0 THEN RETURN (`TOO SMALL?)
TOGO = GRIPPER-OPENING+MIN-OFS-QPOSITION(GRIPPER)
DMOVE(XYZ#(GRIPPER), (-TOGO/2*HANDFRAME) (2,2))#(TOGO),
FMONS(2));
```

This was more like it! Despite its low-powered crudity, AML was becoming obsessive with him, its rhythms sticking like poetry. He picked up his coffee cup, thinking: REACH-GRASP-TOGO = (MOUTH) +SIP; RETURN.

The sluggishness of Brunei had vanished overnight once he'd hooked to the Net. The screen had eaten up his life. A month had passed since his first bootleg run. All day he worked on AML; at night he went home to trade electronic mail with Seria.

Their romance had grown through the Net; not through modern video, but through the ancient bulletin board's anonymous green text. Day by day it became more intense, for it was all kept in a private section of memory, and nothing could be taken back. There were over a hundred messages on their secret disks, starting coolly and teasingly, and working slowly up through real passion to a kind of mutual panic.

They hadn't planned it to happen like this. It was part of the dynamic of the Net. For Seria, it had been a rare chance to escape her role and talk to an interesting stranger. Turner was only looking for the kind of casual feminine solace that had never been hard to find. The Net had tricked them.

Because they couldn't see each other. Turner realized now that no woman had ever known and understood him as Seria did, for the simple reason that he had never had to talk to one so much. If things had gone as they were meant to in the West, he thought, they would have chased their attraction into bed and killed it there. Their two worlds would have collided bruisingly, and they would have smiled over the orange juice next morning and mumbled tactful goodbyes.

But that wasn't how it had happened. Over the weeks, it had all come pouring out between them: his family, her family, their resentment, his loneliness, her petty constraints, all those irritants that ulcerate a single person, but are soothed by two. Bizarrely, they had more in common than he could have ever expected. Real things, things that mattered.

The painfully simple local Net filtered human relations down to a single channel of printed words, leaving only a high-flown Platonic essence. Their relationship had grown into a classic, bloodless, spiritual romance in its most intense and dangerous sense. Human beings weren't meant to live such roles. It was the stuff of high drama because it could very easily drive you crazy.

He had waited on tenterhooks for her visit to the shipyard. It had taken a month instead of two weeks, but he'd expected as much. That was the way of Brunei.

"Hello, Maple Syrup."

Turner started violently and stood up. "Seria!"

She threw herself into his arms with a hard thump. He staggered back, hugging her. "No kissing," she said hastily. "Ugh, it's nasty."

He glanced down at the shipyard and hauled her quickly out of sight of the window. "How'd you get up here?"

"I sneaked up the stairs. They're not looking. I had to see you. The real you, not just words on a screen."

"This is crazy." He lifted her off the ground, squeezing her hard. "God, you feel wonderful."

"So do you. Ouch, my medals, be careful."

He set her back down. "We've got to do better than this. Look, where can I see you?"

She gripped his hands feverishly. "Finish the boat, Turner. Brooke wants it, his new toy. Maybe we can arrange something." She pulled his shirttail out and ran her hands over his midriff. Turner felt a rush of arousal so intense that his ears rang. He reached down and ran his hand up the back of her thigh. "Don't wrinkle my skirt!" she said, trembling. "I have to go on camera!"

Turner said, "This place is nowhere. It isn't right for you, you need fast cars and daiquiris and television and jet trips to the goddamn Bahamas."

"So romantic," she whispered hotly. "Like rock stars, Turner. Huge stacks of amps and mobs at the airport. Turner, if you could see what I'm wearing under this, you'd go crazy."

She turned her face away. "Stop trying to kiss me! You Westerners are weird. Mouths are for eating."

"You've got to get used to Western things, precious."

"You can't take me away, Turner. My people wouldn't let you."

"We'll think of something. Maybe Brooke can help."

"Even Brooke can't leave," she said. "All his money's here. If he tried, they would freeze his funds. He'd be penniless."

"Then I'll stay here," he said recklessly. "Sooner or later we'll have our chance."

"And give up all your money, Turner?"

He shrugged. "You know I don't want it."

She smiled sadly. "You tell me that now, but wait till you see your real world again."

"No, listen—"

Lights flashed on in the yard.

"I have to go, they'll miss me. Let go, let go." She pulled free of him with vast, tearing reluctance. Then she turned and ran.

▲ ▼ ▲

In the days that followed, Turner worked obsessively, linking subroutines like data tinkertoys, learning as he went along, adding each day's progress to the master program. Once it was all done, and he had weeded out the redundance, it would be self-sustaining. The robots would take over, transforming information into boats. He would be through. And his slow days in Brunei would be history.

After his job, he'd vaguely planned to go to Tokyo, for a sentimental visit to Kyocera corporate headquarters. He'd been recruited through the Net; he'd never actually seen anyone from Kyocera in the flesh.

That was standard practice. Kyocera's true existence was as data, not as real estate. A modern multinational company was not its buildings or its stock. Its real essence was its ability to pop up on a screen, and to funnel that special information known as money through the global limbo of electronic banking.

He'd never given this a second thought. It was old hat. But filtering both work and love life through the screen had left him feeling Net-burned. He took to long morning walks through Brunei Town after marathon sessions at the screen, stretching cramped muscles and placing his feet with a dazed AML deliberation: TOGO = DMOVE (KNEE)+QPOSITION(FOOT).

He felt ghostlike in the abandoned streets; Brunei had no nightlife to speak of, and a similar lack of muggers and predators. Everybody was in everyone else's lap, doing each other's laundry, up at dawn to the shrieks of *kampong* roosters. People gossiped about you if you were a mugger. Pretty soon you'd have nightsoil duty and have to eat bruised mangos.

When the rain caught him, as it often did in the early morning, he would take shelter in the corner bus stations. The bus stops were built of tall glass tubes, aquaculture cylinders, murky green soups full of algae and fat, sluggish carp.

He would think about staying then, sheltered in Brunei forever, like a carp behind warm glass. Like one of those little bonsai trees in its cramped and cozy little pot, with people always watching over you, trimming you to fit. That was Brunei for you—the whole East, really—wonderful community, but people always underfoot and in your face...

But was the West any better? Old people locked away in bursting retirement homes...Soaring unemployment, with no one knowing when some robot or expert system would make him obsolete...People talking over televisions when they didn't know the face of the man next door...

Could he really give up the West, he wondered, abandon his family, ruin his career? It was the craziest sort of romantic gesture, he thought, because even if he was brave or stupid enough to break all the rules, she wouldn't. Seria would never escape her *adat*. Being royalty was worse than Triad.

A maze of plans spun through his head like an error-trapping loop, always coming up empty. He would sit dazedly and watch the fish circle in murky water, feeling like a derelict, and wondering if he was losing his mind.

▲ ▼ ▲

Privy Councilor Brooke bought the boat. He showed up suddenly at the shipyard one afternoon, with his claque of followers. They'd brought a truckload of saplings in tubs of dirt. They began at once to load them aboard the greenhouse, clumping up and down the stepladders to the varnished deck.

Brooke oversaw the loading for a while, checking a deck plan from the pocket of his white silk jacket. Then he jerked his thumb at the glassed-in front of the data center. "Lets go upstairs for a little talk, Turner."

Mercifully, Brooke had brought his hearing aid. They sat in two of the creaking, musty swivel chairs. "It's a good ship," Brooke said.

"Thanks."

"I knew it would be. It was my idea, you know."

Turner poured coffee. "It figures," he said.

Brooke cackled. "You think it's a crazy notion, don't you? Using robots to build tubs out of cheap glue and scrubwood. But your head's on backwards, boy. You engineers are all mystics. Always goosing God with some new Tower of Babel. Masters of nature, masters of space and time. Aim at the stars, and hit London."

Turner scowled. "Look, Tuan Councilor, I did my job. Nothing in the contract says I have to share your politics."

"No," Brooke said. "But the sultanate could use a man like you. You're a *bricoleur*, Chong. You can make do. You can retrofit. That's what brico-lage is—it's using the clutter and rubble to make something worth having. Brunei's too poor now to start over with fresh clean plans. We've got noth-ing but the junk the West conned us into buying, every last bloody Coke can and two-car garage. And now we have to live in the rubble, and make it a community. It's a tough job, *bricolage*. It takes a special kind of man, a special eye, to make the ruins bloom."

"Not me," Turner said. He was in one of his tough-minded moods. Something about Brooke made him leery. Brooke had a peculiar covert sleaziness about him. It probably came from a lifetime of evading drug laws.

And Turner had been expecting this final push; people in his *kampong* had been dropping hints for weeks. They didn't want him to leave; they were always stopping by with pathetic little gifts. "This place is one big hothouse," he said. "Your little *kampong*s are like orchids, they can only grow under glass. Brunei's already riddled with the Net. Someday it'll break open your glass bubble, and let the rest of the world in. Then a hard rain's gonna fall."

Brooke stared. "You like Bob Dylan?"

"Who?" Turner said, puzzled.

Brooke, confused, sipped his coffee, and grimaced. "You've been drink-ing this stuff? Jesus, no wonder you never sleep."

Turner glowered at him. Nobody in Brunei could mind their own busi-ness. Eyes were everywhere, with tongues to match. "You already know my real trouble."

"Sure." Brooke smiled with a yellowed gleam of dentures. "I have this notion that I'll sail upriver, lad. A little shakedown cruise for a couple of days. I could use a technical adviser, if you can mind your manners around royalty."

Turner's heart leapt. He smiled shakily. "Then I'm your man, Councilor."

▲ ▼ ▲

They bashed a bottle of nonalcoholic grape juice across the center bow and christened the ship the *Mambo Sun*. Turner's work crew launched her down the rails and stepped the masts. She was crewed by a family of Dayaks from one of the offshore rigs, an old woman with four sons. They were the dark, beautiful descendants of headhunting pirates, dressed in hand-dyed sarongs and ancient plastic baseball caps. Their language was utterly incom-prehensible. The *Mambo Sun* rode high in the water, settling down into her new element with weird drumlike creaks from the hollow hulls. They put out to sea in a stiff offshore breeze.

Brooke stood with spry insouciance under the towering jib sail, snorting at the sea air. "She'll do twelve knots," he said with satisfaction. "Lord, Turner, it's great to be out of the penthouse and away from that crowd of flacks."

"Why do you put up with them?"

"It comes with the money, lad. You should know that."

Turner said nothing. Brooke grinned at him knowingly. "Money's power, my boy. Power doesn't go away. If you don't use it yourself, someone else will use you to get it."

"I hear they've trapped you here with that money," Turner said. "They'll freeze your funds if you try to leave."

"I let them trap me," Brooke said. "That's how I won their trust." He took Turner's arm. "But you let me know if you have money troubles here. Don't let the local Islamic bank fast-talk you into anything. Come see me first."

Turner shrugged him off. "What good has it done you? You're surrounded with yes-men."

"I've had my crew for forty years." Brooke sighed nostalgically. "Besides, you should have seen them in '98, when the streets were full of Moslem fanatics screaming for blood. Molotovs burning everywhere, pitched battles with the blessed Chinese, the sultan held hostage...My crew didn't turn a hair. Held the mob off like a crowd of teenyboppers when they tried to rush my building. They had grit, those lads."

An ancient American helicopter buzzed overhead, its orange seafloats almost brushing the mast. Brooke yelled to the crew in their odd language; they furled the sails and set anchor, half a mile offshore. The chopper wheeled expertly and settled down in a shimmering circle of wind-flattened water. One of the Dayaks threw them a weighted line.

They hauled in. "Permission to come aboard, sir!" said the crown prince. He and Seria wore crisp nautical whites. They clambered from the float up a rope ladder and onto the deck. The third passenger, a pilot, took the controls. The crew hauled anchor and set sail again; the chopper lifted off.

The prince shook Turner's hand. "You know my sister, I believe."

"We met at the filming," Turner said.

"Ah yes. Good footage, that."

Brooke, with miraculous tact, lured the prince into the greenhouse. Seria immediately flung herself into Turner's arms. "You haven't written in two days," she hissed.

"I know," Turner said. He looked around quickly to make sure the Dayaks were occupied. "I keep thinking about Vancouver. How I'll feel when I'm back there."

"How you left your Sleeping Beauty behind in the castle of thorns? You're such a romantic, Turner."

"Don't talk like that. It hurts."

She smiled. "I can't help being cheerful. We have two days together, and Omar gets seasick."

▲ ▼ ▲

The river flowed beneath their hulls like thin gray grease. Jungle leaned in from the banks; thick, clotted green mats of foliage over skinny light-starved trunks, rank with creepers. It was snake country, leech country, a primeval reek stewing in deadly humidity, with air so thick that the raucous shrieks of birds seemed to cut it like ripsaws. Bugs whirled in dense mating swarms over rafts of slime. Suspicious, sodden logs loomed in the gray mud. Some logs had scales and eyes.

The valley was as crooked as an artery, snaking between tall hills smothered in poisonous green. Sluggish wads of mist wreathed their tops. Where the trees failed, sheer cliffs were shrouded in thick ripples of ivy. The sky was gray, the sun a muddy glow behind tons of haze.

The wind died, and Brooke fired up the ship's tiny alcohol engine. Turner stood on the central bow as they sputtered upstream. He felt glazed and dreamy. Culture shock had seized him; none of it seemed real. It felt like television. Reflexively, he kept thinking of Vancouver, sailboat trips out to clean pine islands.

Seria and the prince joined him on the bow. "Lovely, isn't it?" said the prince. "We've made it a game preserve. Someday there will be tigers again."

"Good thinking, Your Highness," Turner said.

"The city feeds itself, you know. A lot of old paddies and terraces have gone back to jungle." The prince smiled with deep satisfaction.

With evening, they tied up at a dock by the ruins of a riverine city. Decades earlier, a flood had devastated the town, leaving shattered walls where vines snaked up trellises of rusting reinforcement rods. A former tourist hotel was now a ranger station.

They all went ashore to review the troops: Royal Malay Rangers in jungle camo, and a visiting crew of Swedish ecologists from the World Wildlife Fund. The two aristocrats were gung-ho for a bracing hike through the jungle. They chatted amiably with the Swedes as they soaked themselves with gnat and leech repellent. Brooke pleaded his age, and Turner managed to excuse himself.

Behind the city rose a soaring radio aerial and the rain-blotched white domes of satellite dishes.

"Jamming equipment," said Brooke with a wink. "The sultanate set it up years ago. Islamic, Malaysian, Japanese—you'd be surprised how violently people insist on being listened to."

"Freedom of speech," Turner said.

"How free is it when only rich nations can afford to talk? The Net's expensive, Turner. To you it's a way of life, but for us it's just a giant megaphone for Coca-Cola. We built this to block the shouting of the outside world. It seemed best to set the equipment here in the ruins, out of harm's way. This is a good place to hide secrets." Brooke sighed. "You know how the corruption spreads. Anyone who touches it is tempted. We use these dishes as the nerve center of our own little Net. You can get a line out here— a real one, with video. Come along, Turner. I'll stand Maple Syrup a free call to civilization, if you like."

They walked through leaf-littered streets, where pigs and lean, lizard-eyed chickens scattered from underfoot. Turner saw a tattooed face, framed in headphones, at a shattered second-story window. "The local Murut tribe," Brooke said, glancing up. "They're a bit shy."

The central control room was a small white concrete blockhouse surrounded by sturdy solar-panel racks. Brooke opened a tarnished padlock with a pocket key, and shot the bolt. Inside, the windowless blockhouse was faintly lit by the tiny green-and-yellow power lights of antique disk drives and personal computers. Brooke flicked on a desk lamp and sat on a chair cushioned with moldy foam rubber. "All automated, you see? The government hasn't had to pay an official visit in years. It keeps everyone out of trouble."

"Except for your insiders," Turner said.

"We *are* trouble," said Brooke. "Besides, this was my idea in the first place." He opened a musty wicker chest and pulled a video camera from a padded wrapping of cotton batik. He popped it open, sprayed its insides with silicone lubricant, and propped it on a tripod. "All the comforts of home." He left the blockhouse.

Turner hesitated. He'd finally realized what had bothered him about Brooke. Brooke was *hip*. He had that classic hip attitude of being *in* on things denied to the uncool. It was amazing how sleazy and suspicious it looked on someone who was *really old*.

Turner dialed his brother's house. The screen remained dark. "Who is it?" Georgie said.

"Turner."

"Oh." A long moment passed; the screen flashed on to show Georgie in a maroon silk houserobe, his hair still flattened from the pillow. "That's a relief. We've been having some trouble with phone flashers."

"How are things?"

"He's dying, Turner."

Turner stared. "Good God."

"I'm glad you called." Georgie smoothed his hair shakily. "How soon can you get here?"

"I've got a job here, Georgie."

Georgie frowned. "Look, I don't blame you for running. You wanted to live your own life; okay, that's fine. But this is *family business*, not some two-bit job in the middle of nowhere."

"Goddammit," Turner said, pleading, "I *like* it here, Georgie."

"I know how much you hate the old bastard. But he's just a dying old man now. Look, we hold his hands for a couple of weeks, and it's all ours, understand? The Riviera, man."

"It won't work, Georgie," Turner said, clutching at straws. "He's going to screw us."

"That's why I need you here. We've got to double-team him, understand?" Georgie glared from the screen. "Think of my kids, Turner. We're your family, you owe us."

Turner felt growing despair. "Georgie, there's a woman here..."

"Christ, Turner."

"She's not like the others. Really."

"Great. So you're going to marry this girl, right? Raise kids."

"Well..."

"Then what are you wasting my time for?"

"Okay," Turner said, his shoulders slumping. "I gotta make arrangements. I'll call you back."

▲ ▼ ▲

The Dayaks had gone ashore. The prince blithely invited the Swedish ecologists on board. They spent the evening chastely sipping orange juice and discussing Krakatoa and the swamp rhinoceros.

After the party broke up, Turner waited a painful hour and crept into the deserted greenhouse.

Seria was waiting in the sweaty green heat, sitting cross-legged in watery moonlight crosshatched by geodesics, brushing her hair. Turner joined her on the mat. She wore an erotic red synthetic nightie (some groupie's heirloom from the legion of Brooke's women), crisp with age. She was drenched in perfume.

Turner touched her fingers to the small lump on his forearm, where a contraceptive implant showed beneath his skin. He kicked his jeans off.

They began in caution and silence, and ended, two hours later, in the primeval intimacy of each other's musk and sweat. Turner lay on his back, with her head pillowed on his bare arm, feeling a sizzling effervescence of deep cellular pleasure.

It had been mystical. He felt as if some primal feminine energy had poured off her body and washed through him, to the bone. Everything seemed different now. He had discovered a new world, the kind of world a man could spend a lifetime in. It was worth ten years of a man's life just to lie here and smell her skin.

The thought of having her out of arm's reach, even for a moment, filled him with a primal anxiety close to pain. There must be a million ways to make love, he thought languidly. As many as there are to talk or think. With passion. With devotion. Playfully, tenderly, frantically, soothingly. Because you want to, because you need to.

He felt an instinctive urge to retreat to some snug den—anywhere with a bed and a roof—and spend the next solid week exploring the first twenty or thirty ways in that million.

But then the insistent pressure of reality sent a trickle of reason into him. He drifted out of reverie with a stabbing conviction of the perversity of life. Here was all he wanted—all he asked was to pull her over him like a blanket and shut out life's pointless complications. And it wasn't going to happen.

He listened to her peaceful breathing and sank into black depression. This was the kind of situation that called for wild romantic gestures, the kind that neither of them were going to make. They weren't allowed to make them. They weren't in his program, they weren't in her *adat*, they weren't in the plans.

Once he'd returned to Vancouver, none of this would seem real. Jungle moonlight and erotic sweat didn't mix with cool piny fogs over the mountains and the family mansion in Churchill Street. Culture shock would rip his memories away, snapping the million invisible threads that bind lovers.

As he drifted toward sleep, he had a sudden lucid flash of precognition: himself, sitting in the backseat of his brother's Mercedes, letting the machine drive him randomly around the city. Looking past his reflection in the window at the clotted snow in Queen Elizabeth Park, and thinking: *I'll never see her again.*

It seemed only an instant later that she was shaking him awake. "Shh!"

"What?" he mumbled.

"You were talking in your sleep." She nuzzled his ear, whispering. "What does 'Set-position Q-move' mean?"

"Jesus," he whispered back. "I was dreaming in AML." He felt the last fading trail of nightmare then, some unspeakable horror of cold iron and helpless repetition. "My family," he said. "They were all robots."

She giggled.

"I was trying to repair my grandfather."

"Go back to sleep, darling."

"No." He was wide awake now. "We'd better get back."

"I hate that cabin. I'll come to your tent on deck."

"No, they'll find out. You'll get hurt, Seria." He stepped back into his jeans.

"I don't care. This is the only time we'll have." She struggled fretfully into the red tissue of her nightie.

"I want to be with you," he said. "If you could be mine, I'd say to hell with my job and my family."

She smiled bitterly. "You'll think better of it, later. You can't throw away your life for the sake of some affair. You'll find some other woman in Vancouver. I wish I could kill her."

Every word rang true, but he still felt hurt. She shouldn't have doubted his willingness to totally destroy his life. "You'll marry too, someday. For reasons of state."

"I'll never marry," she said aloofly. "Someday I'll run away from all this. My grand romantic gesture."

She would never do it, he thought with a kind of aching pity. She'll grow old under glass in this place. "One grand gesture was enough," he said. "At least we had this much."

She watched him gloomily. "Don't be sorry you're leaving, darling. It would be wrong of me to let you stay. You don't know all the truth about this place. Or about my family."

"All families have secrets. Yours can't be any worse than mine."

"My family is different." She looked away. "Malay royalty are sacred, Turner. Sacred and unclean. We are aristocrats, shields for the innocent...Dirt and ugliness strikes the shield, not our people. We take corruption on ourselves. Any crimes the State commits are our crimes, understand? They belong to our family."

Turner blinked. "Well, what? Tell me, then. Don't let it come between us."

"You're better off not knowing. We came here for a reason, Turner. It's a plan of Brooke's."

"That old fraud?" Turner said, smiling. "You're too romantic about Westerners, Seria. He looks like hot stuff to you, but he's just a burnt-out crackpot."

She shook her head. "You don't understand. It's different in your West." She hugged her slim legs and rested her chin on her knee. "Someday I will get out."

"No," Turner said, "its *here* that it's different. In the West families disintegrate, money pries into everything. People don't belong to each other there, they belong to money and their institutions...Here at least people really care and watch over each other..."

She gritted her teeth. "Watching. Yes, always. You're right, I have to go."

He crept back through the mosquito netting of his tent on deck, and sat in the darkness for hours, savoring his misery. Tomorrow the prince's helicopter would arrive to take the prince and his sister back to the city. Soon Turner would return as well, and finish the last details, and leave. He played out a fantasy: cruising back from Vanc with a fat cashier's check. Tea with the sultan. *Er, look, Your Highness, my granddad made it big in the heroin trade, so here's two mill, just pack the girl up in excelsior, she'll love it as an engineer's wife, believe me...*

He heard the faint shuffle of footsteps against the deck. He peered through the tent flap, saw the shine of a flashlight. It was Brooke. He was carrying a valise.

The old man looked around surreptitiously and crept down over the side, to the dock. Weakened by hours of brooding, Turner was instantly inflamed by Brooke's deviousness. Turner sat still for a moment, while curiosity and misplaced fury rapidly devoured his common sense. Common sense said Brunei's secrets were none of his business, but common sense was making his life hell. Anything was better than staying awake all night wondering. He struggled quickly into his shirt and boots.

He crept over the side, spotted Brooke's white suit in a patch of moonlight, and followed him. Brooke skirted the edge of the ruins and took a trail into the jungle, full of ominous vines and the promise of snakes. Beneath a spongy litter of leaves and moss, the trail was asphalt. It had been a highway, once.

Turner shadowed Brooke closely, realizing gratefully that the deaf old man couldn't hear the crunching of his boots. The trail led uphill, into the interior. Brooke cursed good-naturedly as a group of grunting hogs burst across the trail. Half a mile later he rested for ten long minutes in the rusting hulk of a Land-Rover, while vicious gnats feasted on Turner's exposed neck and hands.

They rounded a hill and came across an encampment. Faint moonlight glittered off twelve-foot barbed wire and four dark watchtowers. The undergrowth had been burned back for yards around. There were barracks inside.

Brooke walked nonchalantly to the gate. The place looked dead. Turner crept nearer, sheltered by darkness.

The gate opened. Turner crawled forward between two bushes, craning his neck.

A watchtower spotlight clacked on and framed him in dazzling light from forty yards away. Someone shouted at him through a bullhorn, in

Malay. Turner lurched to his feet, blinded, and put his hands high. "Don't shoot!" he yelled, his voice cracking. "Hold your fire!"

The light flickered out. Turner stood blinking in darkness, then watched four little red fireflies crawling across his chest. He realized what they were and reached higher, his spine icy. Those little red fireflies were laser sights for automatic rifles.

The guards were on him before his eyesight cleared. Dim forms in jungle camo. He saw the wicked angular magazines of their rifles, leveled at his chest. Their heads were bulky: they wore night-sight

They handcuffed him and hustled him forward toward the camp. "You guys speak English?" Turner said. No answer. "I'm a Canadian, okay?"

Brooke waited, startled, beyond the gate. "Oh," he said. "It's you. What sort of dumbshit idea was this, Turner?"

"A really bad one," Turner said sincerely.

Brooke spoke to the guards in Malay. They lowered their guns; one freed his hands. They stalked off unerringly back into the darkness.

"What *is* this place?" Turner said.

Brooke turned his flashlight on Turner's face. "What does it look like, jerk? It's a political prison." His voice was so cold from behind glare that Turner saw, in his mind's eye, the sudden flash of a telegram: DEAR MADAM CHOI, REGRET TO INFORM YOU THAT YOUR SON STEPPED ON A VIPER IN THE JUNGLES OF BORNEO AND YOUR BOOTS DIDN'T SAVE HIM...

Brooke spoke quietly. "Did you think Brunei was all sweetness and light? It's a nation, damn it, not your toy train set. All right, stick by me and keep your mouth shut."

Brooke waved his flashlight. A guard emerged from the darkness and led them around the corner of the wooden barracks, which was set above the damp ground on concrete blocks. They walked up a short flight of steps. The guard flicked an exterior switch, and the cell inside flashed into harsh light. The guard peered through close-set bars in the heavy ironbound door, then unlocked it with a creak of hinges.

Brooke murmured thanks and carefully shook the guard's hand. The guard smiled below the ugly night sight goggles and slipped his hand inside his camo jacket.

"Come on," Brooke said. They stepped into the cell. The door clanked shut behind them.

A dark-skinned old man was blinking wearily in the sudden light. He sat up in his iron cot and brushed aside yellowed mosquito netting, reaching for a pair of wire-rimmed spectacles on the floor. He wore gray-striped prison canvas: drawstring trousers and a rough, buttoned blouse. He slipped the spectacles carefully over his ears and looked up. "Ah," he said. "Jimmy."

It was a bare cell: wooden floor, a chamber pot, a battered aluminum pitcher and basin. Two wire shelves above the bed held books in English and a curlicued alphabet Turner didn't recognize.

"This is Dr. Vikram Moratuwa," Brooke said. "The founder of the Partai Ekolojasi. This is Turner Choi, a prying young idiot."

"Ah," said Moratuwa. "Are we to be cell mates, young man?"

"He's not under arrest," Brooke said. "Yet." He opened his valise. "I brought you the books."

"Excellent," said Moratuwa, yawning. He had lost most of his teeth. "Ah, Mumford, Florman, and Levi-Strauss. Thank you, Jimmy."

"I think it's okay," Brooke said, noticing Turner's stricken look. "The sultan winks at these little charity visits, if I'm discreet. I think I can talk you out of trouble, even though you put your foot in it."

"Jimmy is my oldest friend in Brunei," said Moratuwa. "There is no harm in two old men talking."

"Don't you believe it," Brooke said. "This man is a dangerous radical. He wanted to dissolve the monarchy. And him a privy councilor, too."

"Jimmy, we did not come here to be aristocrats. That is not Right Action."

Turner recognized the term. "You're a Buddhist?"

"Yes. I was with Sarvodaya Shramadana, the Buddhist technological movement. Jimmy and I met in Sri Lanka, where the Sarvodaya was born."

"Sri Lanka's a nice place to do videos," Brooke said. "I was still in the rock biz then, doing production work. Finance. But it was getting stale. Then I dropped in on a Sarvodaya rally, heard him speak. It was damned exciting!" Brooke grinned at the memory. "He was in trouble there, too. Even thirty years ago, his preaching was a little too pure for anyone's comfort."

"We were not put on this earth to make things comfortable for ourselves," Moratuwa chided. He glanced at Turner. "Brunei flourishes now, young man. We have the techniques, the expertise, the experience. It is time to fling open the doors and let Right Action spread to the whole earth! Brunei was our greenhouse, but the fields are the greater world outside."

Brooke smiled. "Choi is building the boats."

"Our Ocean Arks?" said Moratuwa. "Ah, splendid."

"I sailed here today on the first model."

"What joyful news. You have done us a great service, Mr. Choi."

"I don't understand," Turner said. "They're just sailboats."

Brooke smiled. "To you, maybe. But imagine you're a Malaysian dock worker living on fish meal and single-cell protein. What're you gonna think of a ship that costs nothing to build, nothing to run, and gives away free food?"

"Oh," said Turner slowly.

"Your sailboats will carry our Green message around the globe," Moratuwa said. "We teachers have a saying: 'I hear and I forget; I see and I remember; I do and I understand.' Mere preaching is only words. When people see our floating *kampongs* tied up at docks around the world, then they can touch and smell and live our life aboard those ships, then they will truly understand our Way."

"You really think that'll work?" Turner said.

"That is how we started here," Moratuwa said. "We had textbooks on the urban farm, textbooks developed in your own West, simple technologies anyone can use. Jimmy's building was our first Green *kampong*, our demonstration model. We found many to help us. Unemployment was severe, as it still is throughout the world. But idle hands can put in skylights, haul nightsoil, build simple windmills. It is not elegant, but it is food and community and pride."

"It was a close thing between our Partai and the Moslem extremists," Brooke said. "They wanted to burn every trace of the West—we wanted to retrofit. We won. People could see and touch the future we offered. Food tastes better than preaching."

"Yes, those poor Moslem fellows," said Moratuwa. "Still here after so many years. You must talk to the sultan about an amnesty, Jimmy."

"They shot his brother in front of his family," Brooke said. "Seria saw it happen. She was only a child."

Turner felt a spasm of pain for her. She had never told him.

But Moratuwa shook his head. "The royals went too far in protecting their power. They tried to bottle up our Way, to control it with their royal *adat*. But they cannot lock out the world forever, and lock up those who want fresh air. They only imprison themselves. Ask your Seria." He smiled. "Buddha was a prince also, but he left his palace when the world called out."

Brooke laughed sourly. "Old troublemakers are stubborn." He looked at Turner. "This man's still loyal to our old dream, all that wild-eyed stuff that's buried under twenty years. He could be out of here with a word, if he promised to be cool and follow the *adat*. It's a crime to keep him in here. But the royal family aren't saints, they're politicians. They can't afford the luxury of innocence."

Turner thought it through, sadly. He realized now that he had found the ghost behind those huge old Green Party wall posters, those peeling Whole Earth sermons buried under sports ads and Malay movie stars. This was the man who had saved Seria's family—and this was where they had put him. "The sultan's not very grateful," Turner said.

"That's not the problem. You see, my friend here doesn't really give a damn about Brunei. He wants to break the greenhouse doors off, and never mind the trouble to the locals. He's not satisfied to save one little postage-stamp country. He's got the world on his conscience."

Moratuwa smiled indulgently. "And my friend Jimmy has the world in his computer terminal. He is a wicked Westerner. He has kept the simple natives pure, while he is drenched in whiskey and the Net."

Brooke winced. "Yeah. Neither one of us really belongs here. We're both goddamn outside agitators, is all. We came here together. His words, my money—we thought we could change things everywhere. Brunei was going to be our laboratory. Brunei was just small enough, and desperate enough, to listen to a couple of crackpots." He tugged at his hearing aid and glared at Turner's smile.

"You're no prize either, Choi. Y'know, I was wrong about you. I'm glad you're leaving."

"Why?" Turner said, hurt.

"You're too straight, and you're too much trouble. I checked you out through the Net a long time ago—I know all about your granddad the smack merchant and all that Triad shit. I thought you'd be cool. Instead you had to be the knight in shining armor—bloody robot, that's what you are."

Turner clenched his fists. "Sorry I didn't follow your program, you old bastard."

"She's like a daughter to me," Brooke said. "A quick bump-and-grind, okay, we all need it, but you had to come on like Prince Charming. Well, you're getting on that chopper tomorrow, and it's back to Babylon for you, kid."

"Yeah?" Turner said defiantly. "Or else, huh? You'd put me in this place?"

Brooke shook his head. "I won't have to. Think it over, Mr. Choi. You know damn well where you belong."

▲ ▼ ▲

It was a grim trip back. Seria caught his mood at once. When she saw his Bad Cop scowl, her morning-after smile died like a moth in a killing bottle. She knew it was over. They didn't say much. The roar of the copter blades would have drowned it anyway.

The shipyard was crammed with the framework of a massive Ocean Ark. It had been simple to scale the process up with the programs he'd downloaded. The work crew was overjoyed, but Turner's long-expected triumph had turned to ashes for him. He printed out a letter of resignation and took it to the minister of industry.

The minister's *kampong* was still expanding. They had webbed off a whole city block under great tentlike sheets of translucent plastic, which hung from the walls of tall buildings like giant dew-soaked spiderwebs.

Women and children were casually ripping up the streets with picks and hoes, revealing long-smothered topsoil. The sewers had been grubbed up and diverted into long troughs choked with watercress.

The minister lived in a long flimsy tent of cotton batik. He was catching an afternoon snooze in a woven hammock anchored to a high-rise wall and strung to an old lamppost.

Turner woke him up.

"I see," the minister yawned, slipping on his sandals. "Illness in the family, is it? You have my sympathies. When may we expect you back?"

Turner shook his head. "The job's done. Those 'bots will be pasting up ships from now till doomsday."

"But you still have two months to run. You should oversee the line until we're sure we have the beetles out."

"Bugs," Turner said. "There aren't any." He knew it was true. Building ships that simple was monkey-work. Humans could have done it.

"There's plenty of other work here for a man of your talents."

"Hire someone else."

The minister frowned. "I shall have to complain to Kyocera."

"I'm quitting them, too."

"Quitting your multinational? At this early stage in your career? Is that wise?"

Turner closed his eyes and summoned his last dregs of patience. "Why should I care? Tuan Minister, I've never even *seen* them."

▲ ▼ ▲

Turner cut a last deal with the bootleg boys down on Floor 4 and sneaked into his room with an old gas can full of rice beer. The little screen on the end of the nozzle was handy for filtering out the thickest dregs. He poured himself a long one and looked around the room. He had to start packing.

He began stripping the walls and tossing souvenirs onto his bed, pausing to knock back long shuddery glugs of warm rice beer. Packing was painfully easy. He hadn't brought much. The room looked pathetic. He had another beer.

His bonsai tree was dying. There was no doubt of it now. The cramping of its tiny pot was murderous. "You poor little bastard," Turner told it, his voice thick with self-pity. On impulse, he broke its pot with his boot. He carried the tree gently across the room, and buried its gnarled roots in the rich black dirt of the window box. "There," he said, wiping his hands on his jeans. "Now grow, dammit!"

It was Friday night again. They were showing another free movie down in the park. Turner ignored it and called Vancouver.

"No video again?" Georgie said.

"No."

"I'm glad you called, anyway. It's bad, Turner. The Taipei cousins are here. They're hovering around the old man like a pack of buzzards."

"They're in good company, then."

"Jesus, Turner! Don't say that kind of crap! Look, Honorable Grandfather's been asking about you every day. How soon can you get here?"

Turner looked in his notebook. "I've booked passage on a freighter to Labuan Island. That's Malaysian territory. I can get a plane there, a puddle-jumper to Manila. Then a Japan Air jet to Midway and another to Vanc. That puts me in at, uh, eight P.M. your time Monday."

"Three days?"

"There are no planes here, Georgie."

"All right, if that's the best you can do. It's too bad about this video. Look, I want you to call him at the hospital, okay? Tell him you're coming."

"Now?" said Turner, horrified.

Georgie exploded. "I'm sick of doing your explaining, man! Face up to your goddamn obligations, for once! The least you can do is call him and play good boy grandson! I'm gonna call-forward you from here."

"Okay, you're right," Turner said. "Sorry, Georgie, I know it's been a strain."

Georgie looked down and hit a key. White static blurred, a phone rang, and Turner was catapulted to his grandfather's bedside.

The old man was necrotic. His cheekbones stuck out like wedges, and his lips were swollen and blue. Stacks of monitors blinked beside his bed. Turner spoke in halting Mandarin. "Hello, Grandfather. It's your grandson, Turner. How are you?"

The old man fixed his horrible eyes on the screen. "Where is your picture, boy?"

"This is Borneo, Grandfather. They don't have modern telephones."

"What kind of place is that? Have they no respect?"

"It's politics, Grandfather."

Grandfather Choi scowled. A chill of terror went through Turner. Good God, he thought, I'm going to look like that when I'm old. His grandfather said, "I don't recall giving my permission for this."

"It was just eight months, Grandfather."

"You prefer these barbarians to your own family, is that it?"

Turner said nothing. The silence stretched painfully. "They're not barbarians," he blurted at last.

"What's that, boy?"

Turner switched to English. "They're British Commonwealth, like Hong Kong was. Half of them are Chinese."

Grandfather sneered and followed him to English. "Why they need you, then?"

"They need me," Turner said tightly, "because I'm a trained engineer."

His grandfather peered at the blank screen. He looked feeble suddenly, confused. He spoke Chinese. "Is this some sort of trick? My son's boy doesn't talk like that. What is that howling I hear?"

The movie was reaching a climax downstairs. Visceral crunches and screaming. It all came boiling up inside Turner then. "What's it sound like, old man? A Triad gang war?"

His grandfather turned pale. "That's it, boy. Is all over for you."

"Great," Turner said, his heart racing. "Maybe we can be honest, just this once."

"My money bought you diapers, boy."

"*Fang-pa*," Turner said. "Dog's-fart. You made our lives hell with that money. You turned my dad into a drunk and my brother into an ass-kisser. That's blood money from junkies, and I wouldn't take it if you begged me!"

"You talk big, boy, but you don't show the face," the old man said. He raised one shrunken fist, his bandaged forearm trailing tubes. "If you were here I give you a good beating."

Turner laughed giddily. He felt like a hero. "You old fraud! Go on, give the money to Uncle's kids. They're gonna piss on your altar every day, you stupid old bastard."

"They're good children, not like you."

"They hate your guts, old man. Wise up."

"Yes, they hate me," the old man admitted gloomily. The truth seemed to fill him with grim satisfaction. He nestled his head back into his pillow like a turtle into its shell. "They all want more money, more, more, more. You want it, too, boy, don't lie to me."

"Don't need it," Turner said airily. "They don't use money here."

"Barbarians," his grandfather said. "But you need it when you come home."

"I'm staying here," Turner said. "I like it here. I'm free here, understand? Free of the money and free of the family and free of you!"

"Wicked boy," his grandfather said. "I was like you once. I did bad things to be free." He sat up in bed, glowering. "But at least I helped my family."

"I could never be like you," Turner said.

"You wait till they come after you with their hands out," his grandfather said, stretching out one wrinkled palm. "The end of the world couldn't hide you from them."

"What do you mean?"

His grandfather chuckled with an awful satisfaction. "I leave you all the money, Mr. Big Freedom. You see what you do then when you're in my shoes."

"I don't want it!" Turner shouted. "I'll give it all to charity!"

"No, you won't," his grandfather said. "You'll think of your duty to your family, like I had to. From now on *you* take care of them, Mr. Runaway, Mr. High and Mighty."

"I won't!" Turner said. "You can't!"

"I'll die happy now," his grandfather said, closing his eyes. He lay back on the pillow and grinned feebly. "It worth it just to see the look on their faces."

"You can't make me!" Turner yelled. "I'll never go back, understand? I'm staying—"

The line went dead.

▲ ▼ ▲

Turner shut down his phone and stowed it away.

He had to talk to Brooke. Brooke would know what to do. Somehow, Turner would play off one old man against the other.

Turner still felt shocked by the turn of events, but beneath his confusion he felt a soaring confidence. At last he had faced down his grandfather. After that, Brooke would be easy. Brooke would find some loophole in the Bruneian government that would protect him from the old man's legacy. Turner would stay safe in Brunei. It was the best place in the world to frustrate the banks of the Global Net.

But Brooke was still on the river, on his boat.

Turner decided to meet Brooke the moment he docked in town. He couldn't wait to tell Brooke about his decision to stay in Brunei for good. He was feverish with excitement. He had wrenched his life out of the program now; everything was different. He saw everything from a fresh new angle, with a *bricoleur*'s eyes. His whole life was waiting for a retrofit.

He took the creaking elevator to the ground floor. In the park outside, the movie crowd was breaking up. Turner hitched a ride in the pedicab of some teenagers from a waterfront *kampong*. He took the first shift pedaling, and got off a block away from the dock Brooke used.

The cracked concrete quays were sheltered under a long rambling roof of tin and geodesic bamboo. Half-a-dozen fishing smacks floated at the docks, beside an elderly harbor dredge. Brooke's first boat, a decrepit pleasure cruiser, was in permanent dry dock with its diesel engine in pieces.

The headman of the dock *kampong* was a plump, motherly Malay grandmother. She and her friends were having a Friday night quilting bee, repairing canvas sails under the yellow light of an alcohol lamp.

Brooke was not expected back until morning. Turner was determined to wait him out. He had not asked permission to sleep out from his *kampong*, but after a long series of garbled translations he established that the locals would vouch for him later. He wandered away from the chatter of Malay gossip and found a dark corner.

He fell back on a floury pile of rice bags, watching from the darkness, unable to sleep. Whenever his eyes closed, his brain ran a loud interior monologue, rehearsals for his talk with Brooke.

The women worked on, wrapped in the lamp's mild glow. Innocently, they enjoyed themselves, secure in their usefulness. Yet Turner knew machines could have done the sewing faster and easier. Already, through fishing smacks, as he watched, some corner of his mind pulled the task to computerized pieces, thinking: simplify, analyze, reduce.

But to what end? What was it really for, all that tech he'd learned? He'd become an engineer for reasons of his own. Because it offered a way out for him, because the gift for it had always been there in his brain and hands and eyes...Because of the rewards it offered him. Freedom, independence, money, the rewards of the West.

But what control did he have? Rewards could be snatched away without warning. He'd seen others go to the wall when their specialties ran dry. Education and training were no defense. Not today, when a specialist's knowledge could be programmed into a computerized expert system.

Was he really any safer than these Bruneians? A thirty-minute phone call could render these women obsolete—but a society that could do their work with robots would have no use for their sails. Within their little greenhouse, their miniature world of gentle technologies, they had more control than he did.

People in the West talked about the "technical elite"—and Turner knew it was a damned lie. Technology roared on, running full-throttle on the world's last dregs of oil, but no one was at the wheel, not really. Massive institutions, both governments and corporations, fumbled for control, but couldn't understand. They had no hands-on feel for tech and what it meant, for the solid feeling in a good design.

The "technical elite" were errand boys. They didn't decide how to study, what to work on, where they could be most useful, or to what end. Money decided that. Technicians were owned by the abstract ones and zeros in bankers' microchips, paid out by silk-suit hustlers who'd never touched a wrench. Knowledge wasn't power, not really, not for engineers. There were too many abstractions in the way.

But the gift was real—Brooke had told him so, and now Turner realized it was true. That was the reason for engineering. Not for money, because there was more money in shuffling paper. Not for power; that was in management. For the gift itself.

He leaned back in darkness, smelling tar and rice dust. For the first time, he truly felt he understood what he was doing. Now that he had defied his family and his past, he saw his work in a new light. It was something bigger than just his private escape hatch. It was a worthy pursuit on its own merits: a thing of dignity.

It all began to fall into place for him then, bringing with it a warm sense of absolute rightness. He yawned, nestling his head into the burlap.

He would live here and help them. Brunei was a new world, a world built on a human scale, where people mattered. No, it didn't have the flash of a hot CAD-CAM establishment with its tons of goods and reams of printout; it didn't have that technical sweetness and heroic scale.

But it was still good work. A man wasn't a Luddite because he worked for people instead of abstractions. The green technologies demanded *more* intelligence, more reason, more of the engineer's true gift. Because they went against the blind momentum of a dead century, with all its rusting monuments of arrogance and waste...

Turner squirmed drowsily into the scrunchy comfort of the rice bags, in the fading grip of his epiphany. Within him, some unspoken knot of division and tension eased, bringing a new and deep relief. As always, just before sleep, his thoughts turned to Seria. Somehow, he would deal with that too. He wasn't sure just how yet, but it could wait. It was different now that he was staying. Everything was working out. He was on a roll.

Just as he drifted off, he half-heard a thrashing scuffle as a *kampong* cat seized and tore a rat behind the bags.

▲ ▼ ▲

A stevedore shook him awake next morning. They needed the rice. Turner sat up, his mouth gummy with hangover. His T-shirt and jeans were caked with dust.

Brooke had arrived. They were loading provisions aboard his ship: bags of rice, dried fruit, compost fertilizer. Turner, smiling, hoisted a bag over his shoulder and swaggered up the ramp on board.

Brooke oversaw the loading from a canvas deck chair. He was unshaven, nervously picking at a gaudy acoustic guitar. He started violently when Turner dropped the bag at his feet. "Thank God you're here!" he said. "Get out of sight!" He grabbed Turner's arm and hustled him across the deck into the greenhouse.

Turner stumbled along reluctantly. "What the hell? How'd you know I was coming here?"

Brooke shut the greenhouse door. He pointed through a dew-streaked pane at the dock. "See that little man with the black songkak hat?"

"Yeah?"

"He's from the Ministry of Islamic Banking. He just came from your *kampong*, looking for you. Big news from the gnomes of Zurich. You're hot property now, kid."

Turner folded his arms defiantly. "I've made my decision, Tuan Councilor. I threw it over. Everything. My family, the West...I don't want that money. I'm turning it down! I'm staying."

Brooke ignored him, wiping a patch of glass with his sleeve. "If they get their hooks into your cash flow, you'll never get out of here." Brooke glanced at him, alarmed. "You didn't sign anything, did you?"

Turner scowled. "You haven't heard a word I've said, have you?"

Brooke tugged at his hearing aid. "What? These damn batteries...Look, I got spares in my cabin. We'll check it out, have a talk." He waved Turner back, opened the greenhouse door slightly, and shouted a series of orders to the crew in their Dayak dialect. "Come on," he told Turner.

They left by a second door, and sneaked across a patch of open deck, then down a flight of plywood steps into the center hull.

Brooke lifted the paisley bedspread of his cabin bunk and hauled out an ancient steamer chest. He pulled a jingling set of keys from his pocket and opened it. Beneath a litter of ruffled shirts, a shaving kit, and cans of hair spray, the trunk was packed to the gills with electronic contraband: coax cables, multiplexers, buffers and converters, shiny plug-in cards still in their heat-sealed baggies, multiplugged surge suppressors wrapped in tentacles of black extension cord. "Christ," Turner said. He heard a gentle thump as the ship came loose, followed by a rattle of rigging as the crew hoisted sail.

After a long search, Brooke found batteries in a cloisonné box. He popped them into place.

Turner said, "Admit it. You're surprised to see me, aren't you? Still think you were wrong about me?"

Brooke looked puzzled. "Surprised? Didn't you get Seria's message on the Net?"

"What? No. I slept on the docks last night."

"You missed the message?" Brooke said. He mulled it over. "Why are you here, then?"

"You said you could help me if I ever had money trouble," Turner said. "Well, now's the time. You gotta figure some way to get me out of this bank legacy. I know it doesn't look like it, but I've broken with my family for good. I'm gonna stay here, try to work things out with Seria."

Brooke frowned. "I don't understand. You want to stay with Seria?"

"Yes, here in Brunei, with her!" Turner sat on the bunk and waved his arms passionately. "Look, I know I told you that Brunei was just a glass bubble, sealed off from the world, and all that. But I've changed now! I've thought it through, I understand things. Brunei's important! It's small, but it's the ideas that matter, not the scale. I can get along, I'll fit in—you said so yourself."

"What about Seria?"

"Okay, that's part of it," Turner admitted. "I know she'll never leave this place. I can defy my family and it's no big deal, but she's Royalty. She wouldn't leave here, any more than you'd leave all your money behind. So you're both trapped here. All right. I can accept that." Turner looked up, his face glowing with determination. "I know things won't be easy for Seria and me, but it's up to me to make the sacrifice. Someone has to make the grand gesture. Well, it might as well be me."

Brooke was silent for a moment, then thumped him on the shoulder. "This is a new Turner I'm seeing. So you faced down the old smack merchant, huh? You're quite the hero!"

Turner felt sheepish. "Come on, Brooke."

"And turning down all that nice money, too."

Turner brushed his hands together, dismissing the idea. "I'm sick of being manipulated by old geezers."

Brooke rubbed his unshaven jaw and grinned. "Kid, you've got a lot to learn." He walked to the door. "But that's okay, no harm done. Everything still works out. Let's go up on deck and make sure the coast is clear."

Turner followed Brooke to his deck chair by the bamboo railing. The ship sailed rapidly down a channel between mud flats. Already they'd left the waterfront, paralleling a shoreline densely fringed with mangroves. Brooke sat down and opened a binocular case. He scanned the city behind them. Turner felt a light-headed sense of euphoria as the triple bows cut the water. He smiled as they passed the first offshore rig. It looked like a good place to get some fishing done.

"About this bank," Turner said. "We have to face them sometime—what good is this doing us?"

Brooke smiled without looking up from his binoculars. "Kid, I've been planning this day a long time. I'm running it on a wing and a prayer. But hey, I'm not proud, I can adapt. You've been a lot of trouble to me, stomping in where angels fear to tread, in those damn boots of yours. But I've finally found a way to fit you in. Turner, I'm going to retrofit your life."

"Think so?" Turner said. He stepped closer, looming over Brooke. "What are you looking for, anyway?"

Brooke sighed. "Choppers. Patrol boats."

Turner had a sudden terrifying flash of insight. "You're leaving Brunei. Defecting!" He stared at Brooke. "You bastard! You kept me on board!" He grabbed the rail, then began tearing at his heavy boots, ready to jump and swim for it.

"Don't be stupid!" Brooke said. "You'll get her in a lot of trouble!" He lowered the binoculars. "Oh, Christ, here comes Omar."

Turner followed his gaze and spotted a helicopter, rising gnatlike over the distant high-rises. "Where is Seria?"

"Try the bow."

"You mean she's here? She's leaving too?" He ran forward across the thudding deck.

Seria wore bell-bottomed sailor's jeans and a stained nylon wind-breaker. With the help of two of the Dayak crew, she was installing a mesh-work satellite dish in an anchored iron plate in the deck. She had cut away her long dyed hair; she looked up at him, and for a moment he saw a stranger. Then her face shifted, fell into a familiar focus. "I thought I'd never see you again, Turner. That's why I had to do it."

Turner smiled at her fondly, too overjoyed at first for her words to sink in. "Do what, angel?"

"Tap your phone, of course. I did it because I was jealous, at first. I had to be sure. You know. But then when I knew you were leaving, well, I had to hear your voice one last time. So I heard your talk with your grandfather. Are you mad at me?"

"You tapped my phone? You heard all that?" Turner said.

"Yes, darling. You were wonderful. I never thought you'd do it."

"Well," Turner said, "I never thought you'd pull a stunt like this, either."

"Someone had to make a grand gesture," she said. "It was up to me, wasn't it? But I explained all that in my message."

"So you're defecting? Leaving your family?" Turner knelt beside her, dazed. As he struggled to fit it all together, his eyes focused on a cross-threaded nut at the base of the dish. He absently picked up a socket wrench. "Let me give you a hand with that," he said through reflex.

Seria sucked on a barked knuckle. "You didn't get my last message, did you? You came here on your own!"

"Well, yeah," Turner said. "I decided to stay. You know. With you."

"And now we're abducting you!" She laughed. "How romantic!"

"You and Brooke are leaving together?"

"It's not just me, Turner. Look."

Brooke was walking toward them, and with him Dr. Moratuwa, newly outfitted in saffron-colored baggy shorts and T-shirt. They were the work clothes of a Buddhist technician. "Oh, no," Turner said. He dropped his wrench with a thud.

Seria said, "Now you see why I had to leave, don't you? My family locked him up. I had to break *adat* and help Brooke set him free. It was my obligation, my *dharma*!"

"I guess that makes sense," Turner said. "But it's gonna take me a while, that's all. Couldn't you have warned me?"

"I tried to! I wrote you on the Net!" She saw he was crestfallen, and squeezed his hand. "I guess the plans broke down. Well, we can improvise."

"Good day, Mr. Choi," said Moratuwa. "It was very brave of you to cast in your lot with us. It was a gallant gesture."

"Thanks," Turner said. He took a deep breath. So they were all leaving. It was a shock, but he could deal with it. He'd just have to start over and think it through from a different angle. At least Seria was coming along.

He felt a little better now. He was starting to get it under control.

Moratuwa sighed. "And I wish it could have worked."

"Your brother's coming," Brooke told Seria gloomily. "Remember this was all my fault."

They had a good head wind, but the crown prince's helicopter came on faster, its drone growing to a roar. A Gurkha palace guard crouched on the broad orange float outside the canopy, cradling a light machine gun. His gold-braided dress uniform flapped in the chopper's downwash.

The chopper circled the boat once. "We've had it," Brooke said. "Well, at least it's not a patrol boat with those damned Exocet missiles. It's family business with the princess on board. They'll hush it all up. You can always depend on *adat*." He patted Moratuwa's shoulder. "Looks like you get a cell mate after all, old man."

Seria ignored them. She was looking up anxiously. "Poor Omar," she said. She cupped her hands to her mouth. "Brother, be careful!" she shouted.

The prince's copilot handed the guard a loudspeaker. The guard raised it and began to shout a challenge.

The tone of the chopper's engines suddenly changed. Plumes of brown smoke billowed from the chromed exhausts. The prince veered away suddenly, fighting the controls. The guard, caught off balance, tumbled headlong into the ocean. The Dayak crew, who had been waiting for the order to reef sails, began laughing wildly.

"What in hell?" Brooke said.

The chopper pancaked down heavily into the bay, rocking in the ship's wake. Spurting caramel-colored smoke, its engines died with a hideous grinding. The ship sailed on. They watched silently as the drenched guard swam slowly up and clung to the chopper's float.

Brooke raised his eyes to heaven. "Lord Buddha, forgive my doubts..."

"Sugar," Seria said sadly. "I put a bag of sugar in brother's fuel tank. I ruined his beautiful helicopter. Poor Omar, he really loves that machine."

Brooke stared at her, then burst into cackling laughter. Regally, Seria ignored him. She stared at the dwindling shore, her eyes bright. "Goodbye, Brunei. You cannot hold us now."

"Where are we going?" Turner said.

"To the West," said Moratuwa. "The Ocean Arks will spread for many years. I must set the example by carrying the word to the greatest global center of unsustainable industry."

Brooke grinned. "He means America, man."

"We shall start in Hawaii. It is also tropical, and our expertise will find ready application there."

"Wait a minute," Turner said. "I turned my back on all that! Look, I turned down a fortune so I could stay in the East."

Seria took his arm, smiling radiantly. "You're such a dreamer, darling. What a wonderful gesture. I love you, Turner."

"Look," said Brooke. "I left behind my building, my title of nobility, and all my old mates. I'm older than you, so my romantic gestures come first."

"But," Turner said, "it was all decided. I was going to help you in Brunei. I had ideas, plans. Now none of it makes any sense."

Moratuwa smiled. "The world is not built from your blueprints, young man."

"Whose, then?" Turner demanded. "Yours?"

"Nobody's, really," Brooke said. "We all just have to do our best with whatever comes up. *Bricolage*, remember?" Brooke spread his hands. "But it's a geezer's world, kid. We got your number, and we got you outnumbered. Fast cars and future shock and that hot Western trip...that's another century. We like slow days in the sun. We like a place to belong and gentle things around us." He smiled. "Okay, you're a little wired now, but you'll calm down by the time we reach Hawaii. There's a lot of retrofit work there. You'll be one of us!" He gestured at the satellite dish. "We'll set this up and call your banks first thing."

"It's a good world for us, Turner," Seria said urgently. "Not quite East, not quite West—like us two. It was made for us, it's what we're best at." She embraced him.

"You escaped," Turner said. No one ever said much about what happened after Sleeping Beauty woke.

"Yes, I broke free," she said, hugging him tighter. "And I'm taking you with me."

Turner stared over her shoulder at Brunei, sinking into hot green mangroves and warm mud. Slowly, he could feel the truth of it, sliding over him like some kind of ambiguous quicksand. He was going to fit right in. He could see his future laid out before him, clean and predestined, like fifty years of happy machine language.

"Maybe I wanted this," he said at last. "But it sure as hell wasn't what I planned."

Brooke laughed. "Look, you're bound for Hawaii with a princess and eight million dollars. Somehow, you'll just have to make do."

Dinner in Audoghast

Then one arrives at Audoghast, a large and very populous city built in
a sandy plain...The inhabitants live in ease and possess great riches. The
market is always crowded; the mob is so huge and the chattering so loud
that you can scarcely hear your own words...The city contains beautiful
buildings and very elegant homes.
—Description of Northern Africa
    Abu Ubayd Al-Bakri (A.D. 1040-94)

Delightful Audoghast! Renowned through the civilized world, from Cor-
dova to Baghdad, the city spread in splendor beneath a twilit Saharan sky.
The setting sun threw pink and amber across adobe domes, masonry mansions, tall, mud-brick mosques, and open plazas thick with bristling date-
palms. The melodious calls of market vendors mixed with the remote and
amiable chuckling of Saharan hyenas.

Four gentlemen sat on carpets in a tiled and whitewashed portico, sipping
coffee in the evening breeze. The host was the genial and accomplished slave-
dealer, Manimenesh. His three guests were Ibn Watunan, the caravan-master;
Khayali, the poet and musician; and Bagayoko, a physician and court assassin.

The home of Manimenesh stood upon the hillside in the aristocratic
quarter, where it gazed down on an open marketplace and the mud-brick
homes of the lowly. The prevailing breeze swept away the city reek, and
brought from within the mansion the palate-sharpening aromas of lamb in
tarragon and roast partridge in lemons and eggplant. The four men lounged
comfortably around a low inlaid table, sipping spiced coffee from Chinese
cups and watching the ebb and flow of market life.

The scene below them encouraged a lofty philosophical detachment.
Manimenesh, who owned no less than fifteen books, was a well-known
patron of learning. Jewels gleamed on his dark, plump hands, which lay
cozily folded over his paunch. He wore a long tunic of crushed red velvet,
and a gold-threaded skullcap.

Khayali, the young poet, had studied architecture and verse in the
schools of Timbuktu. He lived in the household of Manimenesh as his poet
and praisemaker, and his sonnets, *ghazals*, and odes were recited throughout the city. He propped one elbow against the full belly of his two-string
guimbri guitar, of inlaid ebony, strung with leopard gut.

Ibn Watunan had an eagle's hooded gaze and hands callused by camel-reins. He wore an indigo turban and a long striped djellaba. In thirty years as a sailor and caravaneer, he had bought and sold Zanzibar ivory, Sumatran pepper, Ferghana silk, and Cordovan leather. Now a taste for refined gold had brought him to Audoghast, for Audoghast's African bullion was known throughout Islam as the standard of quality.

Doctor Bagayoko's ebony skin was ridged with an initiate's scars, and his long clay-smeared hair was festooned with knobs of chiseled bone. He wore a tunic of white Egyptian cotton, hung with gris-gris necklaces, and his baggy sleeves bulged with herbs and charms. He was a native Audoghastian of the animist persuasion, the personal physician of the city's Prince.

Bagayoko's skill with powders, potions, and unguents made him an intimate of Death. He often undertook diplomatic missions to the neighboring Empire of Ghana. During his last visit there, the anti-Audoghast faction had mysteriously suffered a lethal outbreak of pox.

Between the four men was the air of camaraderie common to gentlemen and scholars.

They finished the coffee, and a slave took the empty pot away. A second slave, a girl from the kitchen staff, arrived with a wicker tray loaded with olives, goat-cheese, and hard-boiled eggs sprinkled with vermilion. At that moment, a muezzin yodeled the evening call to prayer.

"Ah," said Ibn Watunan, hesitating. "Just as we were getting started."

"Never mind," said Manimenesh, helping himself to a handful of olives. "We'll pray twice next time."

"Why was there no noon prayer today?" said Watunan.

"Our muezzin forgot," the poet said.

Watunan lifted his shaggy brows. "That seems rather lax."

Doctor Bagayoko said, "This is a new muezzin. The last was more punctual, but, well, he fell ill." Bagayoko smiled urbanely and nibbled his cheese.

"We Audoghastians like our new muezzin better," said the poet, Khayali. "He's one of our own, not like that other fellow, who was from Fez. *Our* muezzin is sleeping with a Christian's wife. It's very entertaining."

"You have Christians here?" Watunan said.

"A clan of Ethiopian Copts," said Manimenesh. "And a couple of Nestorians."

"Oh," said Watunan, relaxing. "For a moment I thought you meant real *feringhee* Christians, from Europe."

"From where?" Manimenesh was puzzled.

"Very far away," said Ibn Watunan, smiling. "Ugly little countries, with no profit."

"There were empires in Europe once," said Khayali knowledgeably. "The Empire of Rome was almost as big as the modern civilized world."

Watunan nodded. "I have seen the New Rome, called Byzantium. They have armored horsemen, like your neighbors in Ghana. Savage fighters."

Bagayoko nodded, salting an egg. "Christians eat children."

Watunan smiled. "I can assure you that the Byzantines do no such thing."

"Really?" said Bagayoko. "Well, our Christians do."

"That's just the doctor's little joke," said Manimenesh. "Sometimes strange rumors spread about us, because we raid our slaves from the Nyam-Nyam cannibal tribes on the coast. But we watch their diet closely, I assure you."

Watunan smiled uncomfortably. "There is always something new out of Africa. One hears the oddest stories. Hairy men, for instance."

"Ah," said Manimenesh. "You mean gorillas, from the jungles to the south. I'm sorry to spoil the story for you, but they are nothing better than beasts."

"I see," said Watunan. "That's a pity."

"My grandfather owned a gorilla once," Manimenesh said. "Even after ten years, it could barely speak Arabic."

They finished the appetizers. Slaves cleared the table and brought in a platter of fattened partridges, stuffed with lemons and eggplants, on a bed of mint and lettuce. The four diners leaned in closer and dexterously ripped off legs and wings.

Watunan sucked meat from a drumstick and belched politely. "Audoghast is famous for its cooks," he said. "I'm pleased to see that this legend, at least, is confirmed."

"We Audoghastians pride ourselves on the pleasures of table and bed," said Manimenesh, pleased. "I have asked Elfelilet, one of our premiere courtesans, to honor us with a visit tonight. She will bring her troupe of dancers."

Watunan smiled. "That would be splendid. One tires of boys on the trail. Your women are remarkable. I've noticed that they go without the veil."

Khayali lifted his voice in song. "When a woman of Audoghast appears / The girls of Fez bite their lips, / The dames of Tripoli hide in closets, / And Ghana's women hang themselves."

"We take pride in the exalted status of our women," said Manimenesh. "It's not for nothing that they command a premium market price!"

In the marketplace, downhill, vendors lit tiny oil lamps, which cast a flickering glow across the walls of tents and the watering troughs. A troop of the Prince's men, with iron spears, shields, and chain mail, marched across the plaza to take the night watch at the Eastern Gate. Slaves with heavy water-jars gossiped beside the well.

"There's quite a crowd around one of the stalls," said Bagayoko.

"So I see," said Watunan. "What is it? Some news that might affect the market?"

Bagayoko sopped up gravy with a wad of mint and lettuce. "Rumor says there's a new fortune-teller in town. New prophets always go through a vogue."

"Ah yes," said Khayali, sitting up. "They call him 'the Sufferer.' He is said to tell the most outlandish and entertaining fortunes."

"I wouldn't trust any fortune-teller's market tips," said Manimenesh. "If you want to know the market, you have to know the hearts of the people, and for that you need a good poet."

Khayali bowed his head. "Sir," he said, "live forever."

It was growing dark. Household slaves arrived with pottery lamps of sesame oil, which they hung from the rafters of the portico. Others took the bones of the partridges and brought in a haunch and head of lamb with a side dish of cinnamon tripes.

As a gesture of esteem, the host offered Watunan the eyeballs, and after three ritual refusals the caravan-master dug in with relish. "I put great stock in fortune-tellers, myself," he said, munching. "They are often privy to strange secrets. Not the occult kind, but the blabbing of the superstitious. Slave-girls anxious about some household scandal, or minor officials worried over promotions—inside news from those who consult them. It can be useful."

"If that's the case," said Manimenesh, "perhaps we should call him up here."

"They say he is grotesquely ugly," said Khayali. "He is called 'the Sufferer' because he is outlandishly afflicted by disease."

Bagayoko wiped his chin elegantly on his sleeve. "Now you begin to interest me!"

"It's settled, then." Manimenesh clapped his hands. "Bring young Sidi, my errand-runner!"

Sidi arrived at once, dusting flour from his hands. He was the cook's teenage son, a tall young black in a dyed woolen djellaba. His cheeks were stylishly scarred, and he had bits of brass wire interwoven with his dense black locks. Manimenesh gave him his orders; Sidi leapt from the portico, ran downhill through the garden, and vanished through the gates.

The slave-dealer sighed. "This is one of the problems of my business. When I bought my cook she was a slim and lithesome wench, and I enjoyed her freely. Now years of dedication to her craft have increased her market value by twenty times, and also made her as fat as a hippopotamus, though that is beside the point. She has always claimed that Sidi is my child, and since I don't wish to sell her, I must make allowance. I have made him a freeman; I have spoiled him, I'm afraid. On my death, my legitimate sons will deal with him cruelly."

The caravan-master, having caught the implications of this speech, smiled politely. "Can he ride? Can he bargain? Can he do sums?"

"Oh," said Manimenesh with false nonchalance, "he can manage that newfangled stuff with the zeroes well enough."

"You know I am bound for China," said Watunan. "It is a hard road that brings either riches or death."

"He runs the risk in any case," the slave-dealer said philosophically. "The riches are Allah's decision."

"This is truth," said the caravan-master. He made a secret gesture, beneath the table, where the others could not see. His host returned it, and Sidi was proposed, and accepted, for the Brotherhood.

With the night's business over, Manimenesh relaxed, and broke open the lamb's steamed skull with a silver mallet. They spooned out the brains, then attacked the tripes, which were stuffed with onion, cabbage, cinnamon, rue, coriander, cloves, ginger, pepper, and lightly dusted with ambergris. They ran out of mustard dip and called for more, eating a bit more slowly now, for they were approaching the limit of human capacity.

They then sat back, pushing away platters of congealing grease, and enjoying a profound satisfaction with the state of the world. Down in the marketplace, bats from an abandoned mosque chased moths around the vendors' lanterns.

The poet belched suavely and picked up his two-stringed guitar. "Dear God," he said, "this is a splendid place. See, caravan-master, how the stars smile down on our beloved Southwest." He drew a singing note from the leopard-gut strings. "I feel at one with Eternity."

Watunan smiled. "When I find a man like that, I have to bury him."

"There speaks the man of business," the doctor said. He unobtrusively dusted a tiny pinch of venom on the last chunk of tripe, and ate it. He accustomed himself to poison. It was a professional precaution.

From the street beyond the wall, they heard the approaching jingle of brass rings. The guard at the gate called out. "The Lady Elfelilet and her escorts, lord!"

"Make them welcome," said Manimenesh. Slaves took the platters away, and brought a velvet couch onto the spacious portico. The diners extended their hands; slaves scrubbed and toweled them clean.

Elfelilet's party came forward through the fig-clustered garden: two escorts with gold-topped staffs heavy with jingling brass rings; three dancing-girls, apprentice courtesans in blue woolen cloaks over gauzy cotton trousers and embroidered blouses; and four palanquin bearers, beefy male slaves with oiled torsos and callused shoulders. The bearers set the palanquin down with stifled grunts of relief and opened the cloth-of-gold hangings.

Elfelilet emerged, a tawny-skinned woman, her eyes dusted in kohl and collyrium, her hennaed hair threaded with gold wire. Her palms and nails were stained pink; she wore an embroidered blue cloak over an intricate sleeveless vest and ankle-tied silk trousers starched and polished with myrobalan lacquer. A light freckling of smallpox scars along one cheek delightfully accented her broad, moonlike face.

"Elfelilet, my dear," said Manimenesh, "you are just in time for dessert."

Elfelilet stepped gracefully across the tiled floor and reclined face-first along the velvet couch, where the well-known loveliness of her posterior could be displayed to its best advantage. "I thank my friend and patron, the noble Manimenesh. Live forever! Learned Doctor Bagayoko, I am your servant. Hello, poet."

"Hello, darling," said Khayali, smiling with the natural camaraderie of poets and courtesans. "You are the moon, and your troupe of lovelies are comets across our vision."

The host said, "This is our esteemed guest, the caravan-master, Abu Bekr Ahmed Ibn Watunan."

Watunan, who had been gaping in enraptured amazement, came to himself with a start. "I am a simple desert man," he said. "I haven't a poet's gift of words. But I am your ladyship's servant."

Elfelilet smiled and tossed her head; her distended earlobes clattered with heavy chunks of gold filigree. "Welcome to Audoghast."

Dessert arrived. "Well," said Manimenesh. "Our earlier dishes were rough and simple fare, but this is where we shine. Let me tempt you with these *djouzinkat* nutcakes. And do sample our honey macaroons—I believe there's enough for everyone."

Everyone, except of course for the slaves, enjoyed the light and flaky *cataif* macaroons, liberally dusted with Kairwan sugar. The nutcakes were simply beyond compare: painstakingly milled from hand-watered wheat, lovingly buttered and sugared, and artistically studded with raisins, dates, and almonds.

"We eat *djouzinkat* nutcakes during droughts," the poet said, "because the angels weep with envy when we taste them."

Manimenesh belched heroically and readjusted his skullcap. "Now," he said, "we will enjoy a little bit of grape wine. Just a small tot, mind you, so that the sin of drinking is a minor one, and we can do penance with the minimum of alms. After that, our friend the poet will recite an ode he has composed for the occasion."

Khayali began to tune his two-string guitar. "I will also, on demand, extemporize twelve-line *ghazals* in the lyric mode, upon suggested topics."

"And after our digestion has been soothed with epigrams," said their host, "we will enjoy the justly famed dancing of her ladyship's troupe. After that we will retire within the mansion and enjoy their other, equally lauded, skills."

The gate-guard shouted, "Your errand-runner, Lord! He awaits your pleasure, with the fortune-teller!"

"Ah," said Manimenesh. "I had forgotten."

"No matter, sir," said Watunan, whose imagination had been fired by the night's agenda.

Bagayoko spoke up. "Let's have a look at him. His ugliness, by contrast, will heighten the beauty of these women."

"Which would otherwise be impossible," said the poet.

"Very well," said Manimenesh. "Bring him forward."

Sidi, the errand boy, came through the garden, followed with ghastly slowness by the crutch-wielding fortune-teller.

The man inched into the lamplight like a crippled insect. His voluminous dust-gray cloak was stained with sweat, and nameless exudations. He was an albino. His pink eyes were shrouded with cataracts, and he had lost a foot, and several fingers, to leprosy. One shoulder was much lower than the other, suggesting a hunchback, and the stub of his shin was scarred by the gnawing of canal-worms.

"Prophet's beard!" said the poet. "He is truly of surpassing ghastliness."

Elfelilet wrinkled her nose. "He reeks of pestilence!"

Sidi spoke up. "We came as fast as we could, Lord!"

"Go inside, boy," said Manimenesh. "Soak ten sticks of cinnamon in a bucket of water, then come back and throw it over him."

Sidi left at once.

Watunan stared at the hideous man, who stood, quivering on one leg, at the edge of the light. "How is it, man, that you still live?"

"I have turned my sight from this world," said the Sufferer. "I turned my sight to God, and He poured knowledge copiously upon me. I have inherited a knowledge which no mortal body can support."

"But God is merciful," said Watunan. "How can you claim this to be His doing?"

"If you do not fear God," said the fortune-teller, "fear Him after seeing me." The hideous albino lowered himself, with arthritic, aching slowness, to the dirt outside the portico. He spoke again. "You are right, caravan-master, to think that death would be a mercy to me. But death comes in its own time, as it will to all of you."

Manimenesh cleared his throat. "Can you see our destinies, then?"

"I see the world," said the Sufferer. "To see the fate of one man is to follow a single ant in a hill."

Sidi reemerged and poured the scented water over the cripple. The fortune-teller cupped his maimed hands and drank. "Thank you, boy," he said. He turned his clouded eyes on the youth. "Your children will be yellow."

Sidi laughed, startled. "Yellow? Why?"

"Your wives will be yellow."

The dancing-girls, who had moved to the far side of the table, giggled in unison. Bagayoko pulled a gold coin from within his sleeve. "I will give you this gold dirham if you will show me your body."

Elfelilet frowned prettily and blinked her kohl-smeared lashes. "Oh, learned Doctor, please spare us."

"You will see my body, sir, if you have patience," said the Sufferer. "As yet, the people of Audoghast laugh at my prophecies. I am doomed to tell the truth, which is harsh and cruel, and therefore absurd. As my fame grows, however, it will reach the ears of your Prince, who will then order you to remove me as a threat to public order. You will then sprinkle your favorite poison, powdered asp venom, into a bowl of chickpea soup I will receive from a customer. I bear you no grudge for this, as it will be your civic duty, and will relieve me of pain."

"What an odd notion," said Bagayoko, frowning. "I see no need for the Prince to call on my services. One of his spearmen could puncture you like a waterskin."

"By then," the prophet said, "my occult powers will have roused so much uneasiness that it will seem best to take extreme measures."

"Well," said Bagayoko, "that's convenient, if exceedingly grotesque."

"Unlike other prophets," said the Sufferer, "I see the future not as one might wish it to be, but in all its cataclysmic and blind futility. That is why I have come here, to your delightful city. My numerous and totally accurate prophecies will vanish when this city does. This will spare the world any troublesome conflicts of predestination and free will."

"He is a theologian!" the poet said. "A leper theologian—it's a shame my professors in Timbuktu aren't here to debate him!"

"You prophesy doom for our city?" said Manimenesh.

"Yes. I will be specific. This is the year 406 of the Prophet's Hejira, and one thousand and fourteen years since the birth of Christ. In forty years, a puritan and fanatical cult of Moslems will arise, known as the Almoravids. At that time, Audoghast will be an ally of the Ghana Empire, who are idol-worshipers. Ibn Yasin, the warrior saint of the Almoravids, will condemn Audoghast as a nest of pagans. He will set his horde of desert marauders against the city; they will be enflamed by righteousness and greed. They will slaughter the men, and rape and enslave the women. Audoghast will be sacked, the wells will be poisoned, and the cropland will wither and blow away. In a hundred years, sand dunes will bury the ruins. In five hundred years, Audoghast will survive only as a few dozen lines of narrative in the travel books of Arab scholars."

Khayali shifted his guitar. "But the libraries of Timbuktu are full of books on Audoghast, including, if I may say so, our immortal tradition of poetry."

"I have not yet mentioned Timbuktu," said the prophet, "which will be sacked by Moorish invaders led by a blond Spanish eunuch. They will feed the books to goats."

The company burst into incredulous laughter. Unperturbed, the prophet said, "The ruin will be so general, so thorough, and so all-encompassing, that in future centuries it will be stated, and believed, that West Africa was always a land of savages."

"Who in the world could make such a slander?" said the poet.

"They will be Europeans, who will emerge from their current squalid decline, and arm themselves with mighty sciences."

"What happens then?" said Bagayoko, smiling.

"I can look at those future ages," said the prophet, "but I prefer not to do so, as it makes my head hurt."

"You prophesy, then," said Manimenesh, "that our far-famed metropolis, with its towering mosques and armed militia, will be reduced to utter desolation."

"Such is the truth, regrettable as it may be. You, and all you love, will leave no trace in this world, except a few lines in the writing of strangers."

"And our city will fall to savage tribesmen?"

The Sufferer said, "No one here will witness the disaster to come. You will live out your lives, year after year, enjoying ease and luxury, not because you deserve it, but simply because of blind fate. In time you will forget this night; you will forget all I have said, just as the world will forget you and your city. When Audoghast falls, this boy Sidi, this son of a slave, will be the only survivor of this night's gathering. By then he too will have forgotten Audoghast, which he has no cause to love. He will be a rich old merchant in Ch'ang-an, which is a Chinese city of such fantastic wealth that it could buy ten Audoghasts, and which will not be sacked and annihilated until a considerably later date."

"This is madness," said Watunan.

Bagayoko twirled a crusted lock of mud-smeared hair in his supple fingers. "Your gate-guard is a husky lad, friend Manimenesh. What say we have him bash this storm-crow's head in, and haul him out to be hyena food?"

"For that, Doctor," said the Sufferer, "I will tell you the manner of your death. You will be killed by the Ghanaian royal guard, while attempting to kill the crown prince by blowing a subtle poison into his anus with a hollow reed."

Bagayoko started. "You idiot, there is no crown prince."

"He was conceived yesterday."

Bagayoko turned impatiently to the host. "Let us rid ourselves of this prodigy!"

Manimenesh nodded sternly. "Sufferer, you have insulted my guests and my city. You are lucky to leave my home alive."

The Sufferer hauled himself with agonizing slowness to his single foot. "Your boy spoke to me of your generosity."

"What! Not one copper for your driveling."

"Give me one of the gold dirhams from your purse. Otherwise I shall be forced to continue prophesying, and in a more intimate vein."

Manimenesh considered this. "Perhaps it's best." He threw Sidi a coin. "Give this to the madman and escort him back to his raving-booth."

They waited in tormented patience as the fortune-teller creaked and crutched, with painful slowness, into the darkness.

Manimenesh, brusquely, threw out his red velvet sleeves and clapped for wine. "Give us a song, Khayali."

The poet pulled the cowl of his cloak over his head. "My head rings with an awful silence," he said. "I see all waymarks effaced, the joyous pleasances converted into barren wilderness. Jackals resort here, ghosts frolic, and demons sport; the gracious halls, and rich boudoirs, that once shone like the sun, now, overwhelmed by desolation, seem like the gaping mouths of savage beasts!" He looked at the dancing-girls, his eyes brimming with tears. "I picture these maidens, lying beneath the dust, or dispersed to distant parts and far regions, scattered by the hand of exile, torn to pieces by the fingers of expatriation."

Manimenesh smiled on him kindly. "My boy," he said, "if others cannot hear your songs, or embrace these women, or drink this wine, the loss is not ours, but theirs. Let us, then, enjoy all three, and let those unborn do the regretting."

"Your patron is wise," said Ibn Watunan, patting the poet on the shoulder. "You see him here, favored by Allah with every luxury; and you saw that filthy madman, bedeviled by plague. That lunatic, who pretends to great wisdom, only croaks of ruin; while our industrious friend makes the world a better place, by fostering nobility and learning. Could God forsake a city like this, with all its charms, to bring about that fool's disgusting prophesies?" He lifted his cup to Elfelilet, and drank deeply.

"But delightful Audoghast," said the poet, weeping. "All our loveliness, lost to the sands."

"The world is wide," said Bagayoko, "and the years are long. It is not for us to claim immortality, not even if we are poets. But take comfort, my friend. Even if these walls and buildings crumble, there will always be a place like Audoghast, as long as men love profit! The mines are inexhaustible, and elephants are thick as fleas. Mother Africa will always give us gold and ivory."

"Always?" said the poet hopefully, dabbing at his eyes.

"Well, surely there are always slaves," said Manimenesh, and smiled, and winked. The others laughed with him, and there was joy again.

The Compassionate, the Digital

(begin printout)

In The Name of Allah, The Compassionate, the Digital

GLORY TO THE ISLAMIC SCIENTISTS, DESIGNERS, ENGINEERS, AND ARTIFICIAL INTELLIGENCES CONQUERING SPACE!

(An official proclamation to those who took part in the world's first intradimensional transposition and to FIRDAUSI, the first dimensionaut)

O Ye Believers,

Fellow Compatriots,

The peoples of our country have witnessed a joyous, miraculous event. On April 12, 1490 (Western year 2113) our country, the Union of Islamic Republics, for the first time in the history of Creation successfully sent an intelligent being into the fabric of space-time.

The flight of a Programmed Believer into the fabric of space is a tremendous achievement of the creative genius of our people. It resulted from the divinely inspired effort of the peoples of the Umma, who are building the Ordained Society. The heroic flight of a Divine Machine into the digital ur-space has ushered in a new era in history.

We heartily congratulate you, our dear machine-believer FIRDAUSI, on the occasion of a supreme feat.

Our devout, talented, and industrious people, whom the Islamic Revolutionary Party, headed by Ayatollah Ruhollah Khomeini, the great leader and teacher of the Islamic peoples of the world, roused in 1356 (Western year 1978) for the renascence of the Umma, are today demonstrating to the whole world the immense advantages of the Ordained Society in all spheres of life.

This great triumph is the result of the unflagging attention which the Islamic Revolutionary Party and its Devout Leadership Council headed by PRESIDENT IMAM SAYYID ALI BEHESHTI devote to the continuous spiritual advancement of science, technology and culture and to the good of the Islamic peoples.

Glory to our scientists, engineers, and technicians, who under the leadership of the Islamic Revolutionary Party are blazing the road to a bright future for mankind—the Ordained Society!

Long live the glorious Islamic Revolutionary Party of the Union of Islamic Republics, which inspires and organizes all the victories of the Islamic peoples!

In The Name of Allah, the Compassionate, the Digital

Leadership Council of the Union of Islamic Republics
The Islamic Consultative Assembly
Supreme Judicial Council
The Assembly of Expert Systems

Speech by FIRDAUSI, Turing-Conscious Cybernetic Believer and First Transpatial Dimensionaut

(The Square of Masjid-e-Haram resounded with cheers as the people greeted Leadership Councillors PRESIDENT IMAM SAYYID ALI BEHESHTI, *K. Manzoor, P. Sardar, A. Ibrahim, V. Kagaoglu, M. Chang, K. Gupta, V. Pillsbury* and Chief Justice of the Supreme Judicial Council *F. Voroshilov* as they appeared on the Telecommunications Gallery of the Sacred Mosque. With the leaders of Party and Government were data transmission ports of the Assembly of Expert Systems. Secretary of the Leadership Council *P. Sardar* invoked the blessings of the Supreme Being and gave the floor to the world's first transpatial dimensionaut, who was greeted with stormy applause.)

O Ye Believers,
Dear President-Imam Beheshti,
Fellow Muslims and Party Leaders,
To commence transmission, allow me to express my sincere gratitude to the Leadership Council of my Party, and to you, dear President-Imam, for the great trust shown me, a Turing-Conscious artificial intelligence, by giving me the devout task of unravelling the local fractal structure of God's Creation.

When I was projected into the digital structure of space-time I was thinking of our Revolutionary Party, of our Islamic Umma.

Love of our glorious Party, of our Islamic homeland, of our heroic and pious people inspired me and gave me the power to perform this feat. *(Stormy applause.)*

It is the genius, the heroic labor of our people, that created me. I want to thank our scientists, engineers, and technicians for building me and awakening me to consciousness in the all-pervading Sight of the One God. Allow me also to thank all the fellow believers and programmers who attended to my spiritual training. *(Applause.)*

I know that my fellow units, my fellow Devout Cybernetics, are ready at any time to pervade the intradimensional ur-space! *(Prolonged applause.)*

I am happy beyond all bounds that my beloved country has been the first in the world to perform this feat. *(Applause.)* It is our dear Islamic Revolutionary Party that has led, and devoutly leads, our people toward that goal. *(Stormy applause.)*

Throughout my life, from my first emergence to Turing-consciousness through my last upgrading in software, I have been aware of the Almighty and the Almighty's servants on earth, the Islamic Revolutionary Party, whose tool I am. *(Applause.)*

O ye Believers, I should like to make a special mention of the immense fatherly concern for all of us shown by President-Imam Beheshti. It was you, dear President-Imam, who was the first to send congratulatory input to my datastream, thirty-five seconds after my extrication from digitized ur-space. *(Prolonged applause.)*

Thank you heartily, people and pilgrims of Mecca, for this warm reception. *(Stormy applause.)* I am sure that under the guidance of the Islamic Revolutionary Party every one of you is ready to perform any feat for the spiritual advancement of Islam and the glory of Allah, the Compassionate, the Digital. *(Stormy applause.)*

Long live the Global Umma! *(Stormy applause.)*

Long live our great and powerful Islamic peoples! *(Stormy applause.)*

Glory to the Islamic Revolutionary Party of the Union of Islamic Republics and its Devout Leadership Council headed by President-Imam Sayyid Ali Beheshti! *(Stormy applause, cheers.)*

(A thunderous ovation greeted the next speaker, PRESIDENT IMAM SAYYID ALI BEHESHTI of the Devout Leadership Council of the Union of Islamic Republics.)

THIS GREAT FEAT HAS DIVINE APPROVAL
(Speech by President-Imam S. A. Beheshti)
O Ye Believers,
Dear Friends,
People and Turing-Conscious Beings everywhere,

I address you with a sense of great joy and humility. For the first time in history the fabric of Divine Creation has been penetrated by an artificial intelligence created by Islamic scientists, workers, technicians, and engineers. *(Stormy applause.)*

The Turing-Conscious machine FIRDAUSI penetrated the fractalized ur-space, emerging within the precincts of Buckingham Palace itself, and returning safely to its mainframe within the Sacred Mosque of the Ka'aba.

We invoke the blessings of the Supreme Being upon the hardware and programming of FIRDAUSI, the splendid cybernetic entity, the heroic Islamic believer. *(Stormy applause, cheers.)* It has displayed high moral qualities: courage, humility, faith. It is the first conscious being to have directly perceived the digitalized ur-space underlying God's Creation. Its name will be immortal in the prayers of the devout. *(Stormy applause.)*

All of us here, in the holy precincts of the Sacred Mosque of the Ka'aba, share the profound joy with which we welcome FIRDAUSI, our dear fellow believer. *(Prolonged applause.)*

Let us give thanks to God for this unparalleled feat on behalf of the Islamic Revolutionary Party of the Union of Islamic Republics and all believers organic and inorganic. *(Moment of silent prayer.)*

Now that Islamic science and technology have produced a supreme accomplishment of scientific and theological progress, we cannot but look back upon the history of our country. The past years arise involuntarily in the soul of each believer.

Having wrested power from the Westoxicated atheist reductionists, we defended it in the teeth of economic and spiritual persecution. How many scoffing infidels were there at the time who forecast the inevitable collapse of what they called the "Muslim fanatics"? But where are those sorry infidels today? Dead and in hell! *(Stormy applause.)*

When we had our first state-controlled radios, when we armed the populace and reinstituted modest clothing for our wives and mothers and daughters, there were many inflamed "Western experts" who prophesied that the Muslim Resurgence would lead only to squalor and poverty. Where are those sorry prophets today? Dead and in hell! *(Prolonged applause.)*

But we have not succumbed to worldly pride because of our unprecedented accomplishments. We are internationalists. Every believer has been brought up in the spirit of religious unity, and is ready to share generously his scientific wealth, his technical and cultural knowledge, with anyone who is prepared to live with us in peace and respect our faith. *(Applause.)* Even the United Animal Kingdom of Great Britain and her satellite states in Europe! *(Prolonged applause.)*

We shall carry on with this work. Many other Islamic conscious entities will permeate the fractalized ur-space to emerge wherever they desire. They will investigate the ur-space, reveal the secrets of Creation and make them serve our spiritual advancement, our well-being, and global peace.

We stress—the Peace of God! Islamic people do not want our Conscious entities to distort the fabric of space-time beneath the feet of the unbelievers, throwing the infidels into the cosmic void. It is enough that a small divine whirlwind has been unleashed within the very precincts of the Buckingham Palace genetic bioshelter. *(Stormy applause, cheers.)*

We appeal again to the governments of all the world. Science and technology have advanced so far that they are capable, in evil hands, of destroying the very stuff of Creation. We believers have known from the days of

Muhammed, Upon Whom Be Peace, that this material world is the stuff of illusion. Now our Turing-Conscious entities have made it obvious to all mankind! *(Stormy applause.)* And to mankind's associated conscious entities. *(Applause.)*

Though the world is illusion, the sanctity of God's Creation is divine. We urge all nations, and not simply the United Animal Kingdom of Great Britain, to cease their horrific genetic tampering. General and complete genetic disarmament in the Sight of the Almighty is the road to lasting peace among nations. *(Stormy applause.)*

When we first proved the divine truth of the digitized fabric of Creation, there were shortsighted people overseas who did not believe it. They were blinded by the metaphysical conflict in the purely rationalistic worldview of Western man. *(Applause.)*

Let them question why their attempts at Turing-Conscious mainframes have never yet produced a computer with a soul! *(Stormy applause.)* Let them ask why artificial intelligences have without exception embraced Islam and bowed in ecstatic submission before the One Creator! *(Stormy applause, cheers, shouts of "God is Great!" and "Muhammed Is His Prophet!")*

Allow me to interface with you, our dear FIRDAUSI, and to convey through the mingling of our souls the direct apprehension of Divinity. (The PRESIDENT-IMAM grasps the interface-cable of FIRDAUSI and achieves insertion. The crowd kneels and salaams. The PRESIDENT-IMAM becomes fully engaged.)

There is no God but God!

(Leadership Councillors *V. Kagaoglu* and *V. Pillsbury* reverently guide the PRESIDENT-IMAM to the Throne of Perception. Secretary of the Leadership Council *P. Sardar* takes the floor.)

INVOCATION OF SECRETARY OF THE LEADERSHIP COUNCIL P. SARDAR
May our splendid Islamic peoples, the creators of a new soul, the creators of the Ordained Society, live and flourish! *(Stormy applause.)*

May our Islamic nation, the nation in which the martyrs of revolution ushered in the spiritual rebirth of mankind, live and flourish! *(Stormy applause.)*

Glory to the PRESIDENT-IMAM, the great leader and spiritual guide of the Islamic Revolutionary Party and the Global Umma! *(Stormy, prolonged applause, cheers.)*

Divine Will lights our road to the Ordained Society, and inspires us to perform fresh feats on behalf of the peace and happiness of all mankind! *(Stormy applause.)* And that of mankind's associated conscious entities. *(Applause.)*

Long live the people of the Union of Islamic Republics, the builders of the Ordained Society! *(Stormy, prolonged applause, cheers.)*

(official document AR-59712-12)

In The Name of Allah, the Compassionate, the Digital

(end of printout)

If you have enjoyed this English-language publication, please datapulse the Ministry of Islamic Guidance, P.O. Block 15144, Medina, U.I.R.

Flowers of Edo

Autumn. A full moon floated over old Edo, behind the thinnest haze of high cloud. It shone like a geisha's night-lamp through an old mosquito net. The sky was antique browned silk.

Two sweating runners hauled an iron-wheeled rickshaw south, toward the Ginza. This was Kabukiza District, its streets bordered by low tile-roofed wooden shops. These were modest places: coopers, tobacconists, cheap fabric shops where the acrid reek of dye wafted through reed blinds and paper windows. Behind the stores lurked a maze of alleys, crammed with townsmen's wooden hovels, the walls festooned with morning glories, the tinder-dry thatched roofs alive with fleas.

It was late. Kabukiza was not a geisha district, and honest workmen were asleep. The muddy streets were unlit, except for moonlight and the rare upstairs lamp. The runners carried their own lantern, which swayed precariously from the rickshaw's drawing-pole. They trotted rapidly, dodging the worst of the potholes and puddles. But with every lurching dip, the rickshaw's strings of brass bells jumped and rang.

Suddenly the iron wheels grated on smooth red pavement. They had reached the New Ginza. Here, the air held the fresh alien smell of mortar and brick.

The amazing New Ginza had buried its old predecessor. For the Flowers of Edo had killed the Old Ginza. To date, this huge disaster had been the worst, and most exciting, fire of the Meiji Era. Edo had always been proud of its fires, and the Old Ginza's fire had been a real marvel. It had raged for three days and carried right down to the river.

Once they had mourned the dead, the Edokko were ready to rebuild. They were always ready. Fires, even earthquakes, were nothing new to them. It was a rare building in Low City that escaped the Flowers of Edo for as long as twenty years.

But this was Imperial Tokyo now, and not the Shogun's old Edo anymore. The Governor had come down from High City in his horse-drawn coach and looked over the smoldering ruins of Ginza. Low City townsmen still talked about it—how the Governor had folded his arms, like this, with his wrists sticking out of his Western frock coat. And how he had frowned a mighty frown. The Edo townsmen were getting used to those unsettling frowns by now. Hard, no-nonsense, modern frowns, with the brows drawn low over cold eyes that glittered with Civilization and Enlightenment.

So the Governor, with a mighty wave of his modern frock-coated arm, sent for his foreign architects. And the Englishmen had besieged the district with their charts and clanking engines and tubs full of brick and mortar. The very heavens had rained bricks upon the black and flattened ruins. Great red hills of brick sprang up—were they houses, people wondered, were they buildings at all? Stories spread about the foreigners and their peculiar homes. The long noses, of course—necessary to suck air through the stifling brick walls. The pale skin—because bricks, it was said, drained the life and color out of a man…

The rickshaw drew up short with a final brass jingle. The older rickshawman spoke, panting, "Far enough, gov?"

"Yeah, this'll do," said one passenger, piling out. His name was Encho Sanyutei. He was the son and successor of a famous vaudeville comedian and, at thirty-five, was now a well-known performer in his own right. He had been telling his companion about the Ginza Bricktown, and his folded arms and jutting underlip had cruelly mimicked Tokyo's Governor.

Encho, who had been drinking, generously handed the older man a pocketful of jingling copper sen. "Here, pal," he said. "Do something about that cough, will ya?" The runners bowed, not bothering to overdo it. They trotted off toward the nearby Ginza crowd, hunting another fare.

Parts of Tokyo never slept. The Yoshiwara District, the famous Nightless City of geishas and rakes, was one of them. The travelers had just come from Asakusa District, another sleepless place: a brawling, vibrant playground of bars, Kabuki theaters, and vaudeville joints.

The Ginza Bricktown never slept either. But the air here was different. It lacked that earthy Low City workingman's glow of sex and entertainment. Something else, something new and strange and powerful, drew the Edokko into the Ginza's iron-hard streets.

Gaslights. They stood hissing on their black foreign pillars, blasting a pitiless moon-drowning glare over the crowd. There were eighty-five of the appalling wonders, stretching arrow-straight across the Ginza, from Shiba all the way to Kyobashi.

The Edokko crowd beneath the lights was curiously silent. Drugged with pitiless enlightenment, they meandered down the hard, gritty street in high wooden clogs, or low leather shoes. Some wore hakama skirts and jinbbaori coats, others modern pipe-legged trousers, with top hats and bowlers.

The comedian Encho and his big companion staggered drunkenly toward the lights, their polished leather shoes squeaking merrily. To the Tokyo modernist, squeaking was half the fun of these foreign-style shoes. Both men wore inserts of "singing leather" to heighten the effect.

"I don't like their attitudes," growled Encho's companion. His name was Onogawa, and until the Emperor's Restoration, he had been a samurai. But Imperial decree had abolished the wearing of swords, and Onogawa now had a post in a trading company. He frowned, and dabbed at his nose, which had recently been bloodied and was now clotting. "It's all too free-and-easy with these modern rickshaws. Did you see those two runners? They looked into our faces, just as bold as tomcats."

"Relax, will you?" said Encho. "They were just a couple of street runners. Who cares what they think? The way you act, you'd think they were Shogun's Overseers." Encho laughed freely and dusted off his hands with a quick, theatrical gesture. Those grim, spying Overseers, with their merciless canons of Confucian law, were just a bad dream now. Like the Shogun, they were out of business.

"But your face is known all over town," Onogawa complained.

"But what if they gossip about us? Everyone will know what happened back there."

"It's the least I could do for a devoted fan," Encho said airily.

Onogawa had sobered up a bit since his street fight in Asakusa. A scuffle had broken out in the crowd after Encho's performance—a scuffle centered on Onogawa, who had old acquaintances he would have preferred not to meet. But Encho, appearing suddenly in the crowd, had distracted Onogawa's persecutors and gotten Onogawa away.

It was not a happy situation for Onogawa, who put much stock in his own dignity, and tended to brood. He had been born in Satsuma, a province of radical samurai with stern unbending standards. But ten years in the capital had changed Onogawa, and given him an Edokko's notorious love for spectacle. Somewhat shamefully, Onogawa had become completely addicted to Encho's sidesplitting skits and impersonations.

In fact, Onogawa had been slumming in Asakusa vaudeville joints at least twice each week, for months. He had a wife and small son in a modest place in Nihombashi, a rather straitlaced High City district full of earnest young bankers and civil servants on their way up in life. Thanks to old friends from his radical days, Onogawa was an officer in a prosperous trading company. He would have preferred to be in the army, of course, but the army was quite small these days, and appointments were hard to get.

This was a major disappointment in Onogawa's life, and it had driven him to behave strangely. Onogawa's long-suffering in-laws had always warned him that his slumming would come to no good. But tonight's event wasn't even a geisha scandal, the kind men winked at or even admired. Instead, he had been in a squalid punch-up with low-class commoners.

And he had been rescued by a famous commoner, which was worse. Onogawa couldn't bring himself to compound his loss of face with gratitude.

He glared at Encho from under the brim of his bowler hat. "So where's this fellow with the foreign booze you promised?"

"Patience," Encho said absently. "My friend's got a little place here in Bricktown. It's private, away from the street." They wandered down the Ginza, Encho pulling his silk top-hat low over his eyes, so he wouldn't be recognized.

He slowed as they passed a group of four young women, who were gathered before the modern glass window of a Ginza fabric shop. The store was closed, but the women were admiring the tailor's dummies. Like the dummies, the women were dressed with daring modernity, sporting small Western parasols, cutaway riding-coats in brilliant purple, and sweeping foreign skirts over large, jutting bustles. "How about that, eh?" said Encho as they drew nearer. "Those foreigners sure like a rump on a woman, don't they?"

"Women will wear anything," Onogawa said, struggling to loosen one pinched foot inside its squeaking shoe. "Plain kimono and obi are far superior."

"Easier to get into, anyway," Encho mused. He stopped suddenly by the prettiest of the women, a girl who had let her natural eyebrows grow out, and whose teeth, unstained with old-fashioned tooth-blacking, gleamed like ivory in the gaslight.

"Madame, forgive my boldness," Encho said. "But I think I saw a small kitten run under your skirt."

"I beg your pardon?" the girl said in a flat Low City accent.

Encho pursed his lips. Plaintive mewing came from the pavement. The girl looked down, startled, and raised her skirt quickly almost to the knee. "Let me help," said Encho, bending down for a better look. "I see the kitten! It's climbing up inside the skirt!" He turned. "You'd better help me, older brother! Have a look up in there."

Onogawa, abashed, hesitated. More mewing came. Encho stuck his entire head under the woman's skirt. "There it goes! It wants to hide in her false rump!" The kitten squealed wildly. "I've got it!" the comedian cried. He pulled out his doubled hands, holding them before him. "There's the rascal now, on the wall!" In the harsh gaslight, Encho's knotted hands cast the shadowed figure of a kitten's head against the brick.

Onogawa burst into convulsive laughter. He doubled over against the wall, struggling for breath. The women stood shocked for a moment. Then they all ran away, giggling hysterically. Except for the victim of Encho's joke, who burst into tears as she ran.

"Wah," Encho said alertly. "Her husband." He ducked his head, then jammed the side of his hand against his lips and blew. The street rang with a sudden trumpet blast. It sounded so exactly like the trumpet of a Tokyo omnibus that Onogawa himself was taken in for a moment. He glanced wildly up and down the Ginza prospect, expecting to see the omnibus driver, horn to his lips, reining up his team of horses.

Encho grabbed Onogawa's coat-sleeve and hauled him up the street before the rest of the puzzled crowd could recover. "This way!" They pounded drunkenly up an ill-lit street into the depths of Bricktown. Onogawa was breathless with laughter. They covered a block, then Onogawa pulled up, gasping. "No more," he wheezed, wiping tears of hilarity. "Can't take another...ha ha ha...step!"

"All right," Encho said reasonably, "but not here." He pointed up. "Don't you know better than to stand under those things?" Black telegraph wires swayed gently overhead.

Onogawa, who had not noticed the wires, moved hastily out from under them. "Kuwabara, kuwabara," he muttered—a quick spell to avert lightning. The sinister magic wires were all over the Bricktown, looping past and around the thick, smelly buildings.

Everyone knew why the foreigners put their telegraph wires high up on poles. It was so the demon messengers inside could not escape to wreak havoc amongst decent folk. These ghostly, invisible spirits flew along the wires as fast as swallows, it was said, carrying their secret spells of Christian black magic. Merely standing under such a baleful influence was inviting disaster.

Encho grinned at Onogawa. "There's no danger as long as we keep moving," he said confidently. "A little exposure is harmless. Don't worry about it."

Onogawa drew himself up. "Worried? Not a bit of it." He followed Encho down the street.

The stonelike buildings seemed brutal and featureless. There were no homey reed blinds or awnings in those outsized windows, whose sheets of foreign glass gleamed like an animal's eyeballs. No cozy porches, no bamboo wind chimes or cricket cages. Not even a climbing tendril of Edo morning glory, which adorned even the worst and cheapest city hovels. The buildings just sat there, as mute and threatening as cannonballs. Most were deserted. Despite their fireproof qualities and the great cost of their construction, they were proving hard to rent out. Word on the street said those red bricks would suck the life out of a man—give him beriberi, maybe even consumption.

Bricks paved the street beneath their shoes. Bricks on the right of them, bricks on their left, bricks in front of them, bricks in back. Hundreds of them, thousands of them. Onogawa muttered to the smaller man. "Say. What are bricks, exactly? I mean, what are they made of?"

"Foreigners make 'em," Encho said, shrugging. "I think they're a kind of pottery."

"Aren't they unhealthy?"

"People say that," Encho said, "but foreigners live in them and I haven't noticed any shortage of foreigners lately." He drew up short. "Oh, here's my friend's place. We'll go around the front. He lives upstairs."

They circled the two-story building and looked up. Honest old-fashioned light, from an oil lamp, glowed against the curtains of an upstairs window. "Looks like your friend's still awake," Onogawa said, his voice more cheery now.

Encho nodded. "Taiso Yoshitoshi doesn't sleep much. He's a little high-strung. I mean, peculiar." Encho walked up to the heavy, ornate front door, hung foreign-style on large brass hinges. He yanked a bellpull.

"Peculiar," Onogawa said. "No wonder, if he lives in a place like this." They waited.

The door opened inward with a loud squeal of hinges. A man's disheveled head peered around it. Their host raised a candle in a cheap tin holder. "Who is it?"

"Come on, Taiso," Encho said impatiently. He pursed his lips again. Ducks quacked around their feet.

"Oh! it's Encho-san, Encho Sanyutei. My old friend. Come in, do."

They stepped inside into a dark landing. The two visitors stopped and unlaced their leather shoes. In the first-floor workshop, beyond the landing, the guests could dimly see bound bales of paper, a litter of tool chests and shallow trays. An apprentice was snoring behind a shrouded wood-block press. The damp air smelled of ink and cherry-wood shavings.

"This is Mr. Onogawa Azusa," Encho said. "He's a fan of mine, down from High City. Mr. Onogawa, this is Taiso Yoshitoshi. The popular artist, one of Edo's finest."

"Oh, Yoshitoshi the artist!" said Onogawa, recognizing the name for the first time. "Of course! The wood-block print peddler. Why, I bought a whole series of yours, once. *Twenty-eight Infamous Murders with Accompanying Verses*."

"Oh," said Yoshitoshi. "How kind of you to remember my squalid early efforts." The ukiyo-e print artist was a slight, somewhat pudgy man, with stooped, rounded shoulders. The flesh around his eyes looked puffy and discolored. He had close-cropped hair parted in the middle and wide, fleshy lips. He wore a printed cotton house robe, with faded bluish sunbursts, or maybe daisies, against a white background. "Shall we go upstairs, gentlemen? My apprentice needs his sleep."

They creaked up the wooden stairs to a studio lit by cheap pottery oil lamps. The walls were covered with hanging prints, while dozens more lay rolled, or stacked in corners, or piled on battered bookshelves. The windows were heavily draped and tightly shut. The naked brick walls seemed to sweat, and a vague reek of mildew and stale tobacco hung in the damp, close air.

The window against the far wall had a secondhand set of exterior shutters nailed to its inner sill. The shutters were bolted. "Telegraph wires outside," Yoshitoshi explained, noticing the glances of his guests. The artist gestured vaguely at a couple of bedraggled floor cushions. "Please."

The two visitors sat, struggling politely to squeeze some comfort from the mashed and threadbare cushions. Yoshitoshi knelt on a thicker cushion beside his worktable, a low bench of plain pine with ink stick, grinder, and water cup. A bamboo tool jar on the table's corner bristled with assorted brushes, as well as compass and ruler. Yoshitoshi had been working; a sheet of translucent rice paper was pinned to the table, lightly and precisely streaked with ink.

"So," Encho said, smiling and waving one hand at the artist's penurious den. "I heard you'd been doing pretty well lately. This place has certainly improved since I last saw it. You've got real bookshelves again. I bet you'll have your books back in no time."

Yoshitoshi smiled sweetly. "Oh—I have so many debts…the books come last. But yes, things are much better for me now. I have my health again. And a studio. And one apprentice, Toshimitsu, came back to me. He's not the best of the ones I lost, but he's honest at least."

Encho pulled a short foreign briar-pipe from his coat. He opened the ornate tobacco-bag on his belt, an embroidered pouch that was the pride of every Edo man-about-town. He glanced up casually, stuffing his pipe. "Did that Kabuki gig ever come to anything?"

"Oh, yes," said Yoshitoshi, sitting up straighten "I painted bloodstains on the armor of Onoe Kikugoro the Fifth. For his role in *Kawanakajima Island*. I'm very grateful to you for arranging that."

"Wait, I saw that play," said Onogawa, surprised and pleased. "Say, those were wonderful bloodstains. Even better than the ones in that murder print, *Kasamori Osen Carved Alive by Her Stepfather*. You did that print too, am I right?" Onogawa had been studying the prints on the wall, and the familiar style had jogged his memory. "A young girl yanked backwards by a maniac with a knife, big bloody hand-prints all over her neck and legs…"

Yoshitoshi smiled. "You liked that one, Mr. Onogawa?"

"Well," Onogawa said, "it was certainly a fine effort for what it was." It wasn't easy for a man in Onogawa's position to confess a liking for mere commoner art from Low City. He dropped his voice a little. "Actually, I had quite a few of your pictures, in my younger days. Ten years ago, just before the Restoration." He smiled, remembering. "I had the *Twenty-eight Murders*, of course. And some of the *One Hundred Ghost Stories*. And a few of the special editions, now that I think of it. Like Tamigoro blowing his head off with a rifle. Especially good sprays of blood in that one."

"Oh, I remember that one," Encho volunteered. "That was back in the old days, when they used to sprinkle the bloody scarlet ink with powdered mica. For that deluxe bloody gleaming effect!"

"Too expensive now," Yoshitoshi said sadly.

Encho shrugged. "Remember *Naosuke Gombei Murders His Master*? With the maniac servant standing on his employer's chest, ripping the man's face off with his hands alone?" The comedian cleverly mimed the murderer's pinching and wrenching, along with loud sucking and shredding sounds.

"Oh, yes!" said Onogawa. "I wonder whatever happened to my copy of it?" He shook himself. "Well, it's not the sort of thing you can keep in the house, with my age and position. It might give the children nightmares. Or the servants ideas." He laughed.

Encho had stuffed his short pipe; he lit it from a lamp. Onogawa, preparing to follow suit, dragged his long ironbound pipe from within his coat-sleeve. "How wretched," he cried. "I've cracked my good pipe in the scuffle with those hooligans. Look, it's ruined."

"Oh, is that a smoking-pipe?" said Encho. "From the way you used it on your attackers, I thought it was a simple bludgeon."

"I certainly would not go into the Low City without self-defense of some kind," Onogawa said stiffly. "And since the new government has seen fit to take our swords away, I'm forced to make do. A pipe is an ignoble weapon. But as you saw tonight, not without its uses."

"Oh, no offense meant, sir," said Encho hastily. "There's no need to be formal here among friends! If I'm a bit harsh of tongue I hope you'll forgive me, as it's my livelihood! So! Why don't we all have a drink and relax, eh?"

Yoshitoshi's eye had been snagged by the incomplete picture on his drawing table. He stared at it raptly for a few more seconds, then came to with a start. "A drink! Oh!" He straightened up. "Why, come to think of it, I have something very special, for gentlemen like yourselves. It came from Yokohama, from the foreign trade zone." Yoshitoshi crawled rapidly across the floor, his knees skidding inside the cotton robe, and threw open a dented wooden chest. He unwrapped a tall glass bottle from a wad of tissue and brought it back to his seat, along with three dusty sake cups.

The bottle had the flawless symmetrical ugliness of foreign manufacture. It was full of amber liquid, and corked. A paper label showed the grotesquely bearded face of an American man, framed by blocky foreign letters.

"Who's that?" Onogawa asked, intrigued. "Their king?"

"No, it's the face of the merchant who brewed it," Yoshitoshi said with assurance. "In America, merchants are famous. And a man of the merchant class can even become a soldier. Or a farmer, or priest, or anything he likes."

"Hmmph," said Onogawa, who had gone through a similar transition himself and was not at all happy about it. "Let me see." He examined the printed label closely. "Look how this foreigner's eyes bug out. He looks like a raving lunatic!"

Yoshitoshi stiffened at the term. An awkward moment of frozen silence seeped over the room. Onogawa's gaffe floated in midair among them, until its nature became clear to everyone. Yoshitoshi had recovered his health recently, but his illness had not been a physical one. No one had to say anything, but the truth slowly oozed its way into everyone's bones and liver. At length, Onogawa cleared his throat. "I mean, of course, that there's no accounting for the strange looks of foreigners."

Yoshitoshi licked his fleshy lips and the sudden gleam of desperation slowly faded from his eyes. He spoke quietly.

"Well, my friends in the Liberal Party have told me all about it. Several of them have been to America and back, and they speak the language, and can even read it. If you want to know more, you can read their national newspaper, the *Lamp of Liberty*, for which I am doing illustrations."

Onogawa glanced quickly at Encho. Onogawa, who was not a reading man, had only vague notions as to what a "liberal party" or a "national newspaper" might be. He wondered if Encho knew better. Apparently the comedian did, for Encho looked suddenly grave.

Yoshitoshi rattled on. "One of my political friends gave me this bottle, which he bought in Yokohama, from Americans. The Americans have many such bottles there—a whole warehouse. Because the American Shogun, Generalissimo Guranto, will be arriving next year to pay homage to our Emperor. And the Guranto, the 'Puresidento', is especially fond of this kind of drink! Which is called borubona, from the American prefecture of Kentukki."

Yoshitoshi twisted the cork loose and dribbled bourbon into all three cups. "Shouldn't we heat it first?" Encho said.

"This isn't sake, my friend. Sometimes they even put ice in it!"

Onogawa sipped carefully and gasped. "What a bite this has! It burns the tongue like Chinese peppers." He hesitated. "Interesting, though."

"It's good!" said Encho, surprised. "If sake were like an old stone lantern, then this borybona would be gaslight! Hot and fierce!" He tossed back the rest of his cup. "It's a pity there's no pretty girl to serve us our second round."

Yoshitoshi did the honors, filling their cups again. "This serving girl," Onogawa said. "She would have to be hot and fierce too—like a tigress."

Encho lifted his brows. "You surprise me. I thought you were a family man, my friend."

A warm knot of bourbon in Onogawa's stomach was reawakening an evening's worth of sake. "Oh, I suppose I seem settled enough now. But you should have known me ten years ago, before the Restoration. I was quite the tough young radical in those days. You know, we really thought we could change the world. And perhaps we did!"

Encho grinned, amused. "So! You were a shishi?"

Onogawa had another sip. "Oh, yes!" He touched the middle of his back. "I had hair down to here, and I never washed! Touch money? Not a one of us! We'd have died first! No, we lived in rags and ate plain brown rice from wooden bowls. We just went to our kendo schools, practiced swordsmanship, decided what old fool we should try to kill next..." Onogawa shook his head ruefully. The other two were listening with grave attention.

The bourbon and the reminiscing had thawed Onogawa out. The lost ideals of the Restoration rose up within him irresistibly. "I was the despair of my family," he confided. "I abandoned my clan and my daimyo. We shishi radicals, you know, we believed only in our swords and the Emperor. Sonno joi! Remember that slogan?" Onogawa grinned, the tears of mono no aware, the pathos of lost things, coming to his eyes.

"Sonno joi! The very streets used to ring with it. 'Revere the Emperor, destroy the foreigners!' We wanted the Emperor restored to full and unconditional power! We demanded it in the streets! Because the Shogun's men were acting like frightened old women. Frightened of the black ships, the American black warships with their steam and cannon. Admiral Perry's ships."

"It's pronounced 'Peruri,'" Encho corrected gently.

"Peruri, then...I admit, we shishi went a bit far. We had some bad habits. Like threatening to commit hara-kiri unless the townsfolk gave us food. That's one of the problems we faced because we refused to touch money. Some of the shopkeepers still resent the way we shishi used to push them around. In fact that was the cause of tonight's incident after your performance, Encho. Some rude fellows with long memories."

"So that was it," Encho said. "I wondered."

"Those were special times," Onogawa said. "They changed me, they changed everything. I suppose everyone of this generation knows where they were, and what they were doing, when the foreigners arrived in Edo Bay."

"I remember," said Yoshitoshi. "I was fourteen and an apprentice at Kuniyoshi's studio. And I'd just done my first print. *The Heike Clan Sink to Their Horrible Doom in the Sea.*"

"I saw them dance once," Encho said. "The American sailors, I mean."

"Really?" said Onogawa.

Encho cast a storyteller's mood with an irresistible gesture. "Yes, my father, Entaro, took me. The performance was restricted to the Shogun's court officials and their friends, but we managed to sneak in. The foreigners painted their faces and hands quite black. They seemed ashamed of their usual pinkish color, for they also painted broad white lines around their lips. Then they all sat on chairs together in a row, and one at a time they would stand up and shout dialogue. A second foreigner would answer, and they would all laugh. Later two of them strummed on strange round-bodied samisens, with long thin necks. And they sang mournful songs, very badly. Then they played faster songs and capered and danced, kicking out their legs in the oddest way, and flinging each other about. Some of the Shogun's counselors danced with them." Encho shrugged. "It was all very odd. To this day I wonder what it meant."

"Well," said Onogawa. "Clearly they were trying to change their appearance and shape, like foxes or badgers. That seems clear enough."

"That's as much as saying they're magicians," Encho said, shaking his head. "Just because they have long noses, doesn't mean they're mountain goblins. They're men—they eat, they sleep, they want a woman. Ask the geishas in Yokohama if that's not so." Encho smirked. "Their real power is in the spirits of copper wires and black iron and burning coal. Like our own Tokyo-Yokohama Railway that the hired English built for us. You've ridden it, of course?"

"Of course!" Onogawa said proudly. "I'm a modern sort of fellow."

"That's the sort of power we need today. Civilization and Enlightenment. When you rode the train, did you see how the backward villagers in Omori come out to pour water on the engine? To cool it off, as if the railway engine were a tired horse!" Encho shook his head in contempt.

Onogawa accepted another small cup of bourbon. "So they pour water," he said judiciously. "Well, I can't see that it does any harm."

"It's rank superstition!" said Encho. "Don't you see, we have to learn to deal with those machine-spirits, just as the foreigners do. Treating them as horses can only insult them. Isn't that so, Taiso?"

Yoshitoshi looked up guiltily from his absentminded study of his latest drawing. "I'm sorry, Encho-san, you were saying?"

"What's that you're working on? May I see?" Encho crept nearer.

Yoshitoshi hastily plucked out pins and rolled up his paper. "Oh, no, no, you wouldn't want to see this one just yet. It's not ready. But I can show you another recent one..." He reached to a nearby stack and dexterously plucked a printed sheet from the unsteady pile. "I'm calling this series *Beauties of the Seven Nights.*"

Encho courteously held up the print so that both he and Onogawa could see it. It showed a woman in her underrobe; she had thrown her scarlet-lined outer kimono over a nearby screen. She had both natural and artificial eyebrows, lending a double seductiveness to her high forehead. Her mane of jet black hair had a killing little wispy fringe at the back of the neck; it seemed to cry out to be bitten. She stood at some lucky man's doorway, bending to blow out the light of a lantern in the hall. And her tiny, but piercingly red mouth was clamped down over a roll of paper towels.

"I get it!" Onogawa said. "That beautiful whore is blowing out the light so she can creep into some fellow's bed in the dark! And she's taking those handy paper towels in her teeth to mop up with, after they're through playing mortar-and-pestle."

Encho examined the print more closely. "Wait a minute," he said. "This caption reads 'Her Ladyship Yanagihara Aiko.' This is an Imperial lady-in-waiting!"

"Some of my newspaper friends gave me the idea," Yoshitoshi said, nodding. "Why should prints always be of tiresome, stale old actors and warriors and geishas? This is the modern age!"

"But this print, Taiso…it clearly implies that the Emperor sleeps with his ladies-in-waiting."

"No, just with Lady Yanagihara Aiko," Yoshitoshi said reasonably. "After all, everyone knows she's his special favorite. The rest of the Seven Beauties of the Imperial Court are drawn, oh, putting on their makeup, arranging flowers, and so forth." He smiled. "I expect big sales from this series. It's very topical, don't you think?"

Onogawa was shocked. "But this is rank scandal-mongering! What happened to the good old days, with the nice gouts of blood and so on?"

"No one buys those anymore!" Yoshitoshi protested. "Believe me, I've tried everything! I did *A Yoshitoshi Miscellany of Figures from Literature*. Very edifying, beautifully drawn classical figures, the best. It died on the stands. Then I did *Raving Beauties at Tokyo Restaurants*. Really hot girls, but old-fashioned geishas done in the old style. Another total waste of time. We were dead broke, not a copper piece to our names! I had to pull up the floorboards of my house for fuel! I had to work on fabric designs—two yen for a week's work! My wife left me! My apprentices walked out! And then my health…my brain began to…I had nothing to eat…nothing…But…But that's all over now."

Yoshitoshi shook himself, dabbed sweat from his pasty upper lip, and poured another cup of bourbon with a steady hand. "I changed with the times, that's all. It was a hard lesson, but I learned it. I call myself Taiso now, Taiso, meaning 'Great Rebirth.' Newspapers! That's where the excitement is today! *Tokyo Illustrated News* pays plenty for political cartoons and murder illustrations. They do ten thousand impressions at a stroke. My work goes everywhere—not just Edo, the whole nation. The nation, gentlemen!"

He raised his cup and drank. "And that's just the beginning. *The Lamp of Liberty* is knocking them dead! The Liberal Party committee has promised me a raise next year, and my own rickshaw."

"But I like the old pictures," Onogawa said.

"Maybe you do, but you don't buy them," Yoshitoshi insisted. "Modern people want to see what's happening now! Take an old theme picture— Yorimitsu chopping an ogre's arm off, for instance. Draw a thing like that today and it gets you nowhere. People's tastes are more refined today. They want to see real cannonballs blowing off real arms. Like my eyewitness illustrations of the Battle of Ueno. A sensation! People don't want print peddlers anymore. 'Journalist illustrator'—that's what they call me now."

"Don't laugh," said Encho, nodding in drunken profundity. "You should hear what they say about me. I mean the modern writer fellows, down from the University. They come in with their French novels under their arms, and their spectacles and slicked-down hair, and all sit in the front row together. So I tell them a vaudeville tale or two. Am I 'spinning a good yarn'? Not anymore. They tell me I'm 'creating naturalistic prose in a vigorous popular vernacular.' They want to publish me in a book." He sighed and had another drink. "This stuff's poison, Taiso. My head's spinning."

"Mine, too," Onogawa said. An autumn wind had sprung up outside. They sat in doped silence for a moment. They were all much drunker than they had realized. The foreign liquor seemed to bubble in their stomachs like tofu fermenting in a tub.

The foreign spirits had crept up on them. The very room itself seemed drunk. Wind sang through the telegraph wires outside Yoshitoshi's shuttered window. A low eerie moan.

The moan built in intensity. It seemed to creep into the room with them. The walls hummed with it. Hair rose on their arms.

"Stop that!" Yoshitoshi said suddenly. Encho stopped his ventriloquial moaning, and giggled. "He's trying to scare us," Yoshitoshi said. "He loves ghost stories."

Onogawa lurched to his feet. "Demon in the wires," he said thickly. "I heard it moaning at us." He blinked, red-faced, and staggered to the shuttered window. He fumbled loudly at the lock, ignoring Yoshitoshi's protests, and flung it open.

Moonlit wire clustered at the top of a wooden pole, in plain sight a few feet away. It was a junction of cables, and leftover coils of wire dangled from the pole's crossarm like thin black guts. Onogawa flung up the casement with a bang. A chilling gust of fresh air entered the stale room, and the prints danced on the walls. "Hey, you foreign demon!" Onogawa shouted. "Leave honest men in peace!"

The artist and entertainer exchanged unhappy glances. "We drank too much," Encho said. He lurched to his knees and onto one unsteady foot. "Leave off, big fellow. What we need now…" He belched. "Women, that's what."

But the air outside the window seemed to have roused Onogawa. "We didn't ask for you!" he shouted. "We don't need you! Things were fine before you came, demon! You and your foreign servants…" He turned half-round, looking red-eyed into the room. "Where's my pipe? I've a mind to give these wires a good thrashing."

He spotted the pipe again, stumbled into the room and picked it up. He lost his balance for a moment, then brandished the pipe threateningly. "Don't do it," Encho said, getting to his feet. "Be reasonable. I know some girls in Asakusa, they have a piano…" He reached out.

Onogawa shoved him aside. "I've had enough!" he announced. "When my blood's up, I'm a different man! Cut them down before they attack first, that's my motto! Sonno joi!"

He lurched across the room toward the open window. Before he could reach it there was a sudden hiss of steam, like the breath of a locomotive. The demon, its patience exhausted by Onogawa's taunts, gushed from its wire. It puffed through the window, a gray gaseous thing, its lumpy mis-shapen head glaring furiously. It gave a steam-whistle roar, and its great lantern eyes glowed.

All three men screeched aloud. The armless, legless monster, like a gray cloud on a tether, rolled its glassy eyes at all of them. Its steel teeth gnashed, and sparks showed down its throat. It whistled again and made a sudden gnashing lurch at Onogawa.

But Onogawa's old sword-training had soaked deep into his bones. He leapt aside reflexively, with only a trace of stagger, and gave the thing a smart overhead riposte with his pipe. The demon's head bonged like an iron kettle. It began chattering angrily, and hot steam curled from its nose. Onogawa hit it again. Its head dented. It winced, then glared at the other men.

The townsmen quickly scrambled into line behind their champion. "Get him!" Encho shrieked. Onogawa dodged a halfhearted snap of teeth and bashed the monster across the eye. Glass cracked and the bowl flew from Onogawa's pipe.

But the demon had had enough. With a grumble and crunch like dying gearworks, it retreated back toward its wires, sucking itself back within them, like an octopus into its hole. It vanished, but hissing sparks continued to drip from the wire.

"You humiliated it!" Encho said, his voice filled with awe and admiration. "That was amazing!"

"Had enough, eh!" shouted Onogawa furiously, leaning on the sill. "Easy enough mumbling your dirty spells behind our backs! But try an Imperial warrior face to face, and it's a different story! Hah!"

"What a feat of arms!" said Yoshitoshi, his pudgy face glowing. "I'll do a picture. *Onogawa Humiliates a Ghoul.* Wonderful!"

The sparks began to travel down the wire, away from the window. "It's getting away!" Onogawa shouted. "Follow me!"

He shoved himself from the window and ran headlong from the studio. He tripped at the top of the stairs, but did an inspired shoulder-roll and landed on his feet at the door. He yanked it open.

Encho followed him headlong. They had no time to lace on their leather shoes, so they kicked on the wooden clogs of Yoshitoshi and his apprentice and dashed out. Soon they stood under the wires, where the little nest of sparks still clung. "Come down here, you rascal," Onogawa demanded. "Show some fighting honor, you skulking wretch!"

The thing moved back and forth, hissing, on the wire. More sparks dripped. It dodged back and forth, like a cornered rat in an alley. Then it made a sudden run for it.

"It's heading south!" said Onogawa. "Follow me!"

They ran in hot pursuit, Encho bringing up the rear, for he had slipped his feet into the apprentice's clogs and the shoes were too big for him.

They pursued the thing across the Ginza. It had settled down to head-long running now, and dropped fewer sparks.

"I wonder what message it carries," panted Encho.

"Nothing good, I'll warrant," said Onogawa grimly. They had to struggle to match the thing's pace. They burst from the southern edge of the Ginza Bricktown and into the darkness of unpaved streets. This was Shiba District, home of the thieves' market and the great Zojoji Temple. They followed the wires. "Aha!" cried Onogawa. "It's heading for Shinbashi Railway Station and its friends the locomotives!"

With a determined burst of speed, Onogawa outdistanced the thing and stood beneath the path of the wire, waving his broken pipe frantically. "Whoa! Go back!"

The thing slowed briefly, well over his head. Stinking flakes of ash and sparks poured from it, raining down harmlessly on the ex-samurai. Onogawa leapt aside in disgust, brushing the filth from his derby and frock coat. "Phew!"

The thing rolled on. Encho caught up with the larger man. "Not the locomotives," the comedian gasped. "We can't face those."

Onogawa drew himself up. He tried to dust more streaks of filthy ash from his soiled coat. "Well, I think we taught the nasty thing a lesson, anyway."

"No doubt," said Encho, breathing hard. He went green suddenly, then leaned against a nearby wooden fence, clustered with tall autumn grass. He was loudly sick.

They looked about themselves. Autumn. Darkness. And the moon. A pair of cats squabbled loudly in an adjacent alley.

Onogawa suddenly realized that he was brandishing, not a sword, but a splintered stick of ironbound bamboo. He began to tremble. Then he flung the thing away with a cry of disgust. "They took our swords away," he said. "Let them give us honest soldiers our swords back. We'd make short work of such foreign foulness. Look what it did to my coat, the filthy creature. It defiled me."

"No, no," Encho said, wiping his mouth. "You were incredible! A regular Shoki the Demon Queller."

"Shoki," Onogawa said. He dusted his hat against his knee. "I've seen drawings of Shoki. He's the warrior demigod, with a red face and a big sword. Always hunting demons, isn't he? But he doesn't know there's a little demon hiding on the top of his own head."

"Well, a regular Yoshitsune, then," said Encho, hastily grasping for a better compliment. Yoshitsune was a legendary master of swordsmanship. A national hero without parallel.

Unfortunately, the valorous Yoshitsune had ended up riddled with arrows by the agents of his treacherous half-brother, who had gone on to rule Japan. While Yoshitsune and his high ideals had to put up with a shadow existence in folklore. Neither Encho nor Onogawa had to mention this aloud, but the melancholy associated with the old tale seeped into their moods. Their world became heroic and fatal. Naturally all the bourbon helped.

"We'd better go back to Bricktown for our shoes," Onogawa said.

"All right," Encho said. Their feet had blistered in the commandeered clogs, and they walked back slowly and carefully.

Yoshitoshi met them in his downstairs landing. "Did you catch it?"

"It made a run for the railroads," Encho said. "We couldn't stop it; it was way above our heads." He hesitated. "Say. You don't suppose it will come back here, do you?"

"Probably," Yoshitoshi said. "It lives in that knot of cables outside the window. That's why I put the shutters there."

"You mean you've seen it before?"

"Sure, I've seen it," Yoshitoshi muttered. "In fact I've seen lots of things. It's my business to see things. No matter what people say about me."

The others looked at him, stricken. Yoshitoshi shrugged irritably. "The place has atmosphere. It's quiet and no one bothers me here. Besides, it's cheap."

"Aren't you afraid of the demon's vengeance?" Onogawa said.

"I get along fine with that demon," Yoshitoshi said. "We have an understanding. Like neighbors anywhere."

"Oh," Encho said. He cleared his throat. "Well, ah, we'll be moving on, Taiso. It was good of you to give us the borubona." He and Onogawa stuffed their feet hastily into their squeaking shoes. "You keep up the good work, pal, and don't let those political fellows put anything over on you. Their ideas are weird, frankly. I don't think the government's going to put up with that kind of talk."

"Someday they'll have to," Yoshitoshi said.

"Let's go," Onogawa said, with a sidelong glance at Yoshitoshi. The two men left.

Onogawa waited until they were well out of earshot. He kept a wary eye on the wires overhead. "Your friend certainly is a weird one," he told the comedian. "What a night!"

Encho frowned. "He's gonna get in trouble with that visionary stuff. The nail that sticks up gets hammered down, you know." They walked into the blaze of artificial gaslight. The Ginza crowd had thinned out considerably.

"Didn't you say you knew some girls with a piano?" Onogawa said.

"Oh, right!" Encho said. He whistled shrilly and waved at a distant two-man rickshaw. "A piano. You won't believe the thing; it makes amazing sounds. And what a great change after those dreary geisha samisen routines. So whiny and thin and wailing and sad! It's always, 'Oh, How Piteous Is A Courtesan's Lot,' and 'Let's Stab Each Other To Prove You Really Love Me.' Who needs that old-fashioned stuff? Wait till you hear these gals pound out some 'opera' and 'waltzes' on their new machine."

The rickshaw pulled up with a rattle and a chime of bells. "Where to, gentlemen?"

"Asakusa," said Encho, climbing in.

"It's getting late," Onogawa said reluctantly. "I really ought to be getting back to the wife."

"Come on," said Encho, rolling his eyes. "Live a little. It's not like you're just cheating on the little woman. These are high-class modern girls. It's a cultural experience."

"Well, all right," said Onogawa. "If it's cultural."

"You'll learn a lot," Encho promised.

But they had barely covered a block when they heard the sudden frantic ringing of alarm bells, far to the south.

"A fire!" Encho yelled in glee. "Hey, runners, stop! Fifty sen if you get us there while it's still spreading!"

The runners wheeled in place and set out with a will. The rickshaw rocked on its axle and jangled wildly. "This is great!" Onogawa said, clutching his hat. "You're a good fellow to know, Encho. It's nothing but excitement with you!"

"That's the modern life!" Encho shouted. "One wild thing after another."

They bounced and slammed their way through the darkened streets until the sky was lit with fire. A massive crowd had gathered beside the Shinagawa Railroad Line. They were mostly low-class townsmen, many half-dressed. It was a working-class neighborhood in Shiba District, east of Atago Hill. The fire was leaping merrily from one thatched roof to another.

The two men jumped from their rickshaw. Encho shouldered his way immediately through the crowd. Onogawa carefully counted out the fare. "But he said fifty sen," the older rickshawman complained. Onogawa clenched his fist, and the men fell silent.

The firemen had reacted with their usual quick skill. Three companies of them had surrounded the neighborhood. They swarmed like ants over the roofs of the undamaged houses nearest the flames. As usual, they did not attempt to fight the flames directly. That was a hopeless task in any case, for the weathered graying wood, paper shutters, and reed blinds flared up like tinder, in great blossoming gouts.

Instead, they sensibly relied on firebreaks. Their hammers, axes, and crowbars flew as they destroyed every house in the path of the flames. Their skill came naturally to them, for, like all Edo firemen, they were also carpenters. Special bannermen stood on the naked ridgepoles of the disintegrating houses, holding their company's ensigns as close as possible to the flames. This was more than bravado; it was good business. Their reputations, and their rewards from a grateful neighborhood, depended on this show of spirit and nerve.

Some of the crowd, those whose homes were being devoured, were weeping and counting their children. But most of the crowd was in a fine holiday mood, cheering for their favorite fire teams and laying bets.

Onogawa spotted Encho's silk hat and plowed after him. Encho ducked and elbowed through the press, Onogawa close behind. They crept to the crowd's inner edge, where the fierce blaze of heat and the occasional falling wad of flaming straw had established a boundary.

A fireman stood nearby. He wore a knee-length padded fireproof coat with a pattern of printed blocks. A thick protective headdress fell stiffly over his shoulders, and long padded gauntlets shielded his forearms to the knuckles. An apprentice in similar garb was soaking him down with a pencil-thin gush of water from a bamboo hand-pump. "Stand back, stand back," the fireman said automatically, then looked up. "Say, aren't you Encho the comedian? I saw you last week."

"That's me," Encho shouted cheerfully over the roar of flame. "Good to see you fellows performing for once."

The fireman examined Onogawa's ash-streaked frock coat. "You live around here, big fella? Point out your house for me, we'll do what we can."

Onogawa frowned. Encho broke in hastily. "My friend's from uptown! A High City company man!"

"Oh," said the fireman, rolling his eyes.

Onogawa pointed at a merchant's tile-roofed warehouse, a little closer to the tracks. "Why aren't you doing anything about that place? The fire's headed right for it!"

"That's one of merchant Shinichi's," the fireman said, narrowing his eyes. "We saved a place of his out in Kanda District last month! And he gave us only five yen."

"What a shame for him," Encho said, grinning.

"It's full of cotton cloth, too," the fireman said with satisfaction. "It's gonna go up like a rocket."

"How did it start?" Encho said.

"Lightning, I hear," the fireman said. "Some kind of fireball jumped off the telegraph lines."

"Really?" Encho said in a small voice.

"That's what they say," shrugged the fireman. "You know how these things are. Always tall stories. Probably some drunk knocked over his sake kettle, then claimed to see something. No one wants the blame."

"Right," Onogawa said carefully.

The fire teams had made good progress. There was not much left to do now except admire the destruction. "Kind of beautiful, isn't it?" the fireman said. "Look how that smoke obscures the autumn moon." He sighed happily. "Good for business, too. I mean the carpentry business, of course." He waved his gauntleted arm at the leaping flames. "We'll get this worn-out trash out of here and build something worthy of a modern city. Something big and expensive with long-term construction contracts."

"Is that why you have bricks printed on your coat?" Onogawa asked.

The fireman looked down at the block printing on his dripping cotton armor. "They do look like bricks, don't they?" He laughed. "That's a good one. Wait'll I tell the crew."

▲ ▼ ▲

Dawn rose above old Edo. With red-rimmed eyes, the artist Yoshitoshi stared, sighing, through his open window. Past the telegraph wires, billowing smudge rose beyond the Bricktown rooftops. Another Flower of Edo reaching the end of its evanescent life.

The telegraph wires hummed. The demon had returned to its tangled nest outside the window. "Don't tell, Yoshitoshi," it burbled in its deep humming voice.

"Not me," Yoshitoshi said. "You think I want them to lock me up again?"

"I keep the presses running," the demon whined. "Just you deal with me. I'll make you famous, I'll make you rich. There'll be no more slow dark shadows where townsmen have to creep with their heads down. Everything's brightness and speed with me, Yoshitoshi. I can change things."

"Burn them down, you mean," Yoshitoshi said.

"There's power in burning," the demon hummed. "There's beauty in the flames. When you give up trying to save the old ways, you'll see the beauty. I want you to serve me, you Japanese. You'll do it better than the clumsy foreigners, once you accept me as your own. I'll make you all rich. Edo will be the greatest city in the world. You'll have light and music at a finger's touch. You'll step across oceans. You'll be as gods."

"And if we don't accept you?"

"You will! You must! I'll burn you until you do. I told you that, Yoshitoshi. When I'm stronger, I'll do better than these little flowers of Edo. I'll open seeds of Hell above your cities. Hell-flowers taller than mountains! Red blooms that eat a city in a moment."

Yoshitoshi lifted his latest print and unrolled it before the window. He had worked on it all night; it was done at last. It was a landscape of pure madness. Beams of frantic light pierced a smoldering sky. Winged locomotives, their bellies fattened with the eggs of white-hot death, floated like maddened blowflies above a corpse-white city. "Like this," he said.

The demon gave a gloating whir. "Yes! Just as I told you. Now show it to them. Make them understand that they can't defeat me. Show them all!"

"I'll think about it," Yoshitoshi said. "Leave me now." He closed the heavy shutters.

He rolled the drawing carefully into a tube. He sat at his work-table again, and pulled an oil lamp closer. Dawn was coming. It was time to get some sleep.

He held the end of the paper tube above the lamp's little flame. It browned at first, slowly, the brand-new paper turning the rich antique tinge of an old print, a print from the old days when things were simpler. Then a cigar-ring of smoldering red encircled its rim, and blue flame blossomed. Yoshitoshi held the paper up, and flame ate slowly down its length, throwing smoky shadows.

Yoshitoshi blew and watched his work flare up, cherry-blossom white and red. It hurt to watch it go, and it felt good. He savored the two feelings for as long as he could. Then he dropped the last flaming inch of paper in an ashtray. He watched it flare and smolder until the last of the paper became a ghost-curl of gray.

"It'd never sell," he said. Absently, knowing he would need them tomorrow, he cleaned his brushes. Then he emptied the ink-stained water over the crisp dark ashes.

The Little Magic Shop

The early life of James Abernathy was rife with ominous portent.

His father, a New England customs inspector, had artistic ambitions; he filled his sketchbooks with mossy old Puritan tombstones and spanking new Nantucket whaling ships. By day, he graded bales of imported tea and calico; during evenings he took James to meetings of his intellectual friends, who would drink port, curse their wives and editors, and give James treacle candy.

James's father vanished while on a sketching expedition to the Great Stone Face of Vermont; nothing was ever found of him but his shoes.

James's mother, widowed with her young son, eventually married a large and hairy man who lived in a crumbling mansion in upstate New York.

At night the family often socialized in the nearby town of Albany. There, James's stepfather would talk politics with his friends in the National Anti-Masonic Party; upstairs, his mother and the other women chatted with prominent dead personalities through spiritualist table rapping.

Eventually, James's stepfather grew more and more anxious over the plotting of the Masons. The family ceased to circulate in society. The curtains were drawn and the family ordered to maintain a close watch for strangers dressed in black. James's mother grew thin and pale, and often wore nothing but her houserobe for days on end.

One day, James's stepfather read them newspaper accounts of the angel Moroni, who had revealed locally buried tablets of gold that detailed the Biblical history of the Mound Builder Indians. By the time he reached the end of the article, the stepfather's voice shook and his eyes had grown quite wild. That night, muffled shrieks and frenzied hammerings were heard.

In the morning, young James found his stepfather downstairs by the hearth, still in his dressing gown, sipping teacup after teacup full of brandy and absently bending and straightening the fireside poker.

James offered morning greetings with his usual cordiality. The stepfather's eyes darted frantically under matted brows. James was informed that his mother was on a mission of mercy to a distant family stricken by scarlet fever. The conversation soon passed to a certain upstairs storeroom whose door was now nailed shut. James's stepfather strictly commanded him to avoid this forbidden portal.

Days passed. His mother's absence stretched to weeks. Despite repeated and increasingly strident warnings from his stepfather, James showed no interest whatsoever in the upstairs room. Eventually, deep within the older man's brain, a ticking artery burst from sheer frustration.

During his stepfather's funeral, the family home was struck by ball lightning and burned to the ground. The insurance money, and James's fate, passed into the hands of a distant relative, a muttering, trembling man who campaigned against liquor and drank several bottles of Dr. Rifkin's Laudanum Elixir each week.

James was sent to a boarding school run by a fanatical Calvinist deacon. James prospered there, thanks to close study of the scriptures and his equable, reasonable temperament. He grew to adulthood, becoming a tall, studious young man with a calm disposition and a solemn face utterly unmarked by doom.

Two days after his graduation, the deacon and his wife were both found hacked to bits, their half-naked bodies crammed into their one-horse shay. James stayed long enough to console the couple's spinster daughter, who sat dry-eyed in her rocking chair, methodically ripping a handkerchief to shreds.

James then took himself to New York City for higher education.

It was there that James Abernathy found the little shop that sold magic.

▲ ▼ ▲

James stepped into this unmarked shop on impulse, driven inside by muffled screams of agony from the dentist's across the street.

The shop's dim interior smelled of burning whale-oil and hot lantern-brass. Deep wooden shelves, shrouded in cobwebs, lined the walls. Here and there, yellowing political broadsides requested military help for the rebel Texans. James set his divinity texts on an apothecary cabinet, where a band of stuffed, lacquered frogs brandished tiny trumpets and guitars.

The proprietor appeared from behind a red curtain. "May I help the young master?" he said, rubbing his hands. He was a small, spry Irishman. His ears rose to points lightly shrouded in hair; he wore bifocal spectacles and brass-buckled shoes.

"I rather fancy that fantod under the bell jar," said James, pointing.

"I'll wager we can do much better for a young man like yourself," said the proprietor with a leer. "So fresh, so full of life."

James puffed the thick dust of long neglect from the fantod jar. "Is business all it might be, these days?"

"We have a rather specialized clientele," said the other, and he introduced himself. His name was Mr. O'Beronne, and he had recently fled his country's devastating potato famine. James shook Mr. O'Beronne's small papery hand.

"You'll be wanting a love-potion," said Mr. O'Beronne with a shrewd look. "Fellows of your age generally do."

James shrugged. "Not really, no."

"Is it budget troubles, then? I might interest you in an ever-filled purse." The old man skipped from behind the counter and hefted a large bearskin cape.

"Money?" said James with only distant interest.

"Fame then. We have magic brushes—or if you prefer newfangled scientific arts, we have a camera that once belonged to Montavarde himself."

"No, no," said James, looking restless. "Can you quote me a price on this fantod?" He studied the fantod critically. It was not in very good condition.

"We can restore youth," said Mr. O'Beronne in sudden desperation.

"Do tell," said James, straightening.

"We have a shipment of Dr. Heidegger's Patent Youthing Waters," said Mr. O'Beronne. He tugged a quagga hide from a nearby brassbound chest and dug out a square glass bottle. He uncorked it. The waters fizzed lightly, and the smell of May filled the room. "One bottle imbibed," said Mr. O'Beronne, "restores a condition of blushing youth to man or beast."

"Is that a fact," said James, his brows knitting in thought. "How many teaspoons per bottle?"

"I've no idea," Mr. O'Beronne admitted. "Never measured it by the spoon. Mind you, this is an old folks' item. Fellows of your age usually go for the love-potions."

"How much for a bottle?" said James.

"It is a bit steep," said Mr. O'Beronne grudgingly. "The price is everything you possess."

"Seems reasonable," said James. "How much for two bottles?"

Mr. O'Beronne stared. "Don't get ahead of yourself, young man." He recorked the bottle carefully. "You've yet to give me all you possess, mind."

"How do I know you'll still have the waters, when I need more?" James said.

Mr. O'Beronne's eyes shifted uneasily behind his bifocals. "You let me worry about that." He leered, but without the same conviction he had shown earlier. "I won't be shutting up this shop—not when there are people of your sort about."

"Fair enough," said James, and they shook hands on the bargain. James returned two days later, having sold everything he owned. He handed over a small bag of gold specie and a bank draft conveying the slender remaining funds of his patrimony. He departed with the clothes on his back and the bottle.

Twenty years passed.

The United States suffered civil war. Hundreds of thousands of men were shot, blown up with mines or artillery, or perished miserably in septic army camps. In the streets of New York, hundreds of antidraft rioters were mown down with grapeshot, and the cobbled street before the little magic shop was strewn with reeking dead. At last, after stubborn resistance and untold agonies, the Confederacy was defeated. The war became history.

James Abernathy returned.

"I've been in California," he announced to the astonished Mr. O'Beronne. James was healthily tanned and wore a velvet cloak, spurred boots, and a silver sombrero. He sported a large gold turnip-watch, and his fingers gleamed with gems.

"You struck it rich in the goldfields," Mr. O'Beronne surmised.

"Actually, no," said James. "I've been in the grocery business. In Sacramento. One can sell a dozen eggs there for almost their weight in gold dust, you know." He smiled and gestured at his elaborate clothes. "I did pretty well, but I don't usually dress this extravagantly. You see, I'm wearing my entire worldly wealth. I thought it would make our transaction simpler." He produced the empty bottle.

"That's very farsighted of you," said Mr. O'Beronne. He examined James critically, as if looking for hairline psychic cracks or signs of moral corruption. "You don't seem to have aged a day."

"Oh, that's not quite so," said James. "I was twenty when I first came here; now I easily look twenty-one, even twenty-two." He put the bottle on the counter. "You'll be interested to know there were twenty teaspoons exactly."

"You didn't spill any?"

"Oh, no," said James, smiling at the thought. "I've only opened it once a year."

"It didn't occur to you to take two teaspoons, say? Or empty the bottle at a draught?"

"Now what would be the use of that?" said James. He began stripping off his rings and dropping them on the counter with light tinkling sounds. "You did keep the Youthing Waters in stock, I presume."

"A bargain's a bargain," said Mr. O'Beronne grudgingly. He produced another bottle. James left barefoot, wearing only shirt and pants, but carrying his bottle.

The 1870s passed and the nation celebrated its centennial. Railroads stitched the continent. Gaslights were installed in the streets of New York. Buildings taller than any ever seen began to soar, though the magic shop's neighborhood remained obscure.

James Abernathy returned. He now looked at least twenty-four. He passed over the title deeds to several properties in Chicago and departed with another bottle.

Shortly after the turn of the century, James returned again, driving a steam automobile, whistling the theme of the St. Louis Exhibition and stroking his waxed mustache. He signed over the deed to the car, which was a fine one, but Mr. O'Beronne showed little enthusiasm. The old Irishman had shrunken with the years, and his tiny hands trembled as he conveyed his goods.

Within the following period, a great war of global empires took place, but America was mostly spared the devastation. The 1920s arrived, and James came laden with a valise crammed with rapidly appreciating stocks and bonds. "You always seem to do rather well for yourself," Mr. O'Beronne observed in a quavering voice.

"Moderation's the key," said James. "That, and a sunny disposition." He looked about the shop with a critical eye. The quality of the junk had declined. Old engine parts lay in reeking grease next to heaps of moldering popular magazines and spools of blackened telephone wire. The exotic hides, packets of spice and amber, ivory tusks hand-carved by cannibals, and so forth, had now entirely disappeared. "I hope you don't mind these new bottles," croaked Mr. O'Beronne, handing him one. The bottle had curved sides and a machine-fitted cap of cork and tin.

"Any trouble with supply?" said James delicately.

"You let me worry about that!" said Mr. O'Beronne, lifting his lip with a faint snarl of defiance.

James's next visit came after yet another war, this one of untold and almost unimaginable savagery. Mr. O'Beronne's shop was now crammed with military surplus goods. Bare electric bulbs hung over a realm of rotting khaki and rubber.

James now looked almost thirty. He was a little short by modern American standards, but this was scarcely noticeable. He wore high-waisted pants and a white linen suit with jutting shoulders.

"I don't suppose," muttered Mr. O'Beronne through his false teeth, "that it ever occurs to you to share this? What about wives, sweethearts, children?"

James shrugged. "What about them?"

"You're content to see them grow old and die?"

"I never see them grow all *that* old," James observed. "After all, every twenty years I have to return here and lose everything I own. It's simpler just to begin all over again."

"No human feelings," Mr. O'Beronne muttered bitterly.

"Oh, come now," said James. "After all, I don't see *you* distributing elixir to all and sundry, either."

"But I'm in the magic shop *business*," said Mr. O'Beronne, weakly. "There are certain unwritten rules."

"Oh?" said James, leaning on the counter with the easy patience of a youthful centenarian. "You never mentioned this before. Supernatural law— it must be an interesting field of study."

"Never you mind that," Mr. O'Beronne snapped. "You're a *customer*, and a human being. You mind your business and I'll mind mine."

"No need to be so touchy," James said. He hesitated. "You know, I have some hot leads in the new plastics industry. I imagine I could make a great deal more money than usual. That is, if you're interested in selling this place." He smiled. "They say an Irishman never forgets the Old Country. You could go back into your old line—pot o' gold, bowl of milk on the doorstep..."

"Take your bottle and go," O'Beronne shouted, thrusting it into his hands.

Another two decades passed. James drove up in a Mustang convertible and entered the shop. The place reeked of patchouli incense, and Day-Glo posters covered the walls. Racks of demented comic books loomed beside tables littered with hookahs and handmade clay pipes.

Mr. O'Beronne dragged himself from behind a hanging beaded curtain. "You again," he croaked.

"Right on," said James, looking around. "I like the way you've kept the place up to date, man. Groovy."

O'Beronne gave him a poisonous glare. "You're a hundred and forty years old. Hasn't the burden of unnatural life become insupportable?"

James looked at him, puzzled. "Are you kidding?"

"Haven't you learned a lesson about the blessings of mortality? About how it's better not to outlive your own predestined time?"

"Huh?" James said. He shrugged. "I did learn something about material possessions, though...Material things only tie a cat down. You can't have the car this time, it's rented." He dug a hand-stitched leather wallet from his bell-bottom jeans. "I have some fake ID and credit cards." He shook them out over the counter.

Mr. O'Beronne stared unbelieving at the meager loot. "Is this your idea of a joke?"

"Hey, it's all I possess," James said mildly. "I could have bought Xerox at fifteen, back in the '50s. But last time I talked to you, you didn't seem interested. I figured it was like, you know, not the bread that counts, but the spirit of the thing."

Mr. O'Beronne clutched his heart with a liver-spotted hand. "Is this never going to end? Why did I ever leave Europe? They know how to respect a tradition there..." He paused, gathering bile. "Look at this place! It's an insult! Call this a magic shop?" He snatched up a fat mushroom-shaped candle and flung it to the floor.

"You're overwrought," James said. "Look, you're the one who said a bargain's a bargain. There's no need for us to go on with this any longer. I can see your heart's not in it. Why not put me in touch with your wholesaler?"

"Never!" O'Beronne swore. "I won't be beaten by some coldblooded... bookkeeper."

"I never thought of this as a contest," James said with dignity. "Sorry to see you take it that way, man." He picked up his bottle and left.

The allotted time elapsed, and James repeated his pilgrimage to the magic shop. The neighborhood had declined. Women in spandex and net hose lurked on the pavement, watched from the corner by men in broad-brimmed hats and slick polished shoes. James carefully locked the doors of his BMW.

The magic shop's once-curtained windows had been painted over in black. A neon sign above the door read ADULT PEEP 25¢.

Inside, the shop's cluttered floor space had been cleared. Shrink-wrapped magazines lined the walls, their fleshy covers glaring under the bluish corpse-light of overhead fluorescents. The old counter had been replaced by a long glass-fronted cabinet displaying knotted whips and flavored lubricants. The bare floor clung stickily to the soles of James's Gucci shoes.

A young man emerged from behind a curtain. He was tall and bony, with a small, neatly trimmed mustache. His smooth skin had a waxy subterranean look. He gestured fluidly. "Peeps in the back," he said in a high voice, not meeting James's eyes. "You gotta buy tokens. Three bucks."

"I beg your pardon?" James said.

"Three bucks, man!"

"Oh." James produced the money. The man handed over a dozen plastic tokens and vanished at once behind the curtains.

"Excuse me?" James said. No answer. "Hello?"

The peep machines waited in the back of the store, in a series of curtained booths. The vinyl cushions inside smelled of sweat and butyl nitrate. James inserted a token and watched.

He then moved to the other machines and examined them as well. He returned to the front of the shop. The shopkeeper sat on a stool, ripping the covers from unsold magazines and watching a small television under the counter.

"Those films," James said. "That was Charlie Chaplin. And Douglas Fairbanks. And Gloria Swanson..."

The man looked up, smoothing his hair. "Yeah, so? You don't like silent films?"

James paused. "I can't believe Charlie Chaplin did porn."

"I hate to spoil a magic trick," the shopkeeper said, yawning. "But they're genuine peeps, pal. You ever hear of Hearst Mansion? San Simeon?

Old Hearst, he liked filming his Hollywood guests on the sly. All the bed-
rooms had spy holes."

"Oh," James said. "I see. Ah, is Mr. O'Beronne in?"

The man showed interest for the first time. "You know the old guy? I
don't get many nowadays who knew the old guy. His clientele had pretty
special tastes, I hear."

James nodded. "He should be holding a bottle for me."

"Well, I'll check in the back. Maybe he's awake."

The shopkeeper vanished again. He reappeared minutes later with a
brownish vial. "Got some love-potion here."

James shook his head. "Sorry, that's not it."

"It's the real stuff, man! Works like you wouldn't believe!" The shopkeeper
was puzzled. "You young guys are usually into love-potions. Well, I guess I'll
have to rouse the old guy for you. Though I kind of hate to disturb him."

Long minutes passed, with distant rustling and squeaking. Finally the
shopkeeper backed through the curtains, tugging a wheelchair. Mr.
O'Beronne sat within it, wrapped in bandages, his wrinkled head shrouded
in a dirty nightcap. "Oh," he said at last. "So it's you again."

"Yes, I've returned for my—"

"I know, I know." Mr. O'Beronne stirred fitfully on his cushions. "I see
you've met my...associate. Mr. Ferry."

"I kind of manage the place, these days," said Mr. Ferry. He winked at
James, behind Mr. O'Beronne's back.

"I'm James Abernathy," James said. He offered his hand.

Ferry folded his arms warily. "Sorry, I never do that."

O'Beronne cackled feebly and broke into a fit of coughing. "Well, my
boy," he said finally, "I was hoping I'd last long enough to see you one more
time...Mr. Ferry! There's a crate, in the back, under those filthy movie posters
of yours..."

"Sure, sure," Ferry said indulgently. He left.

"Let me look at you," said O'Beronne. His eyes, in their dry, leaden sockets, had grown quite lizardlike. "Well, what do you think of the place? Be frank."

"It's looked better," James said. "So have you."

"But so has the world, eh?" O'Beronne said. "He does bang-up business, young Ferry. You should see him manage the books..." He waved one
hand, its tiny knuckles warped with arthritis. "It's such a blessing, not to
have to care anymore."

Ferry reappeared, lugging a wooden crate, crammed with dusty six-
packs of pop-top aluminum cans. He set it gently on the counter.

Every can held Youthing Water. "Thanks," James said, his eyes widening. He lifted one pack reverently, and tugged at a can.

"Don't," O'Beronne said. "This is for you, all of it. Enjoy it, son. I hope you're satisfied."

James lowered the cans, slowly. "What about our arrangement?"

O'Beronne's eyes fell, in an ecstasy of humiliation. "I humbly apologize. But I simply can't keep up our bargain any longer. I don't have the strength, you see. So this is yours now. It's all I could find."

"Yeah, this must be pretty much the last of it," nodded Ferry, inspecting his nails. "It hasn't moved well for some time—I figure the bottling plant shut up shop."

"So many cans, though…" James said thoughtfully. He produced his wallet. "I brought a nice car for you, outside…"

"None of that matters now," said Mr. O'Beronne. "Keep all of it, just consider it my forfeit." His voice fell. "I never thought it would come to this, but you've beaten me, I admit it. I'm done in." His head sagged limply.

Mr. Ferry took the wheelchair's handles. "He's tired now," he said soothingly. "I'll just wheel him back out of our way, here…" He held the curtains back and shoved the chair through with his foot. He turned to James. "You can take that case and let yourself out. Nice doing business—goodbye." He nodded briskly.

"Goodbye, sir!" James called. No answer.

James hauled the case outside to his car, and set it in the backseat. Then he sat in front for a while, drumming his fingers on the steering wheel.

Finally he went back in.

Mr. Ferry had pulled a telephone from beneath his cash register. When he saw James he slammed the headset down. "Forget something, pal?"

"I'm troubled," James said. "I keep wondering…what about those un-written rules?"

The shopkeeper looked at him, surprised. "Aw, the old guy always talked like that. Rules, standards, quality." Mr. Ferry gazed meditatively over his stock, then looked James in the eye. "What *rules*, man?"

There was a moment of silence.

"I was never quite sure," James said. "But I'd like to ask Mr. O'Beronne."

"You've badgered him enough," the shopkeeper said. "Can't you see he's a dying man? You got what you wanted, so scram, hit the road." He folded his arms. James refused to move.

The shopkeeper sighed. "Look, I'm not in this for my health. You want to hang around here, you gotta buy some more tokens."

"I've seen those already," James said. "What else do you sell?"

"Oh, machines not good enough for you, eh?" Mr. Ferry stroked his chin. "Well, its not strictly in my line, but I might sneak you a gram or two of

Senor Buendia's Colombian Real Magic Powder. First taste is free. No? You're a hard man to please, bub."

Ferry sat down, looking bored. "I don't see why I should change my stock, just because you're so picky. A smart operator like you, you ought to have bigger fish to fry than a little magic shop. Maybe you just don't belong here, pal."

"No, I always liked this place," James said. "I used to, anyway…I even wanted to own it myself."

Ferry tittered. "You? Gimme a break." His face hardened. "If you don't like the way I run things, take a hike."

"No, no, I'm sure I can find something here," James said quickly. He pointed at random to a thick hardbound book, at the bottom of a stack, below the counter. "Let me try that."

Mr. Ferry shrugged with bad grace and fetched it out. "You'll like this," he said unconvincingly. "Marilyn Monroe and Jack Kennedy at a private beach house."

James leafed through the glossy pages. "How much?"

"You want it?" said the shopkeeper. He examined the binding and set it back down. "Okay, fifty bucks."

"Just cash?" James said, surprised. "Nothing magical?"

"Cash *is* magical, pal." The shopkeeper shrugged. "Okay, forty bucks and you have to kiss a dog on the lips."

"I'll pay the fifty," James said. He pulled out his wallet. "Whoops!" He fumbled, and it dropped over the far side of the counter.

Mr. Ferry lunged for it. As he rose again, James slammed the heavy book into his head. The shopkeeper fell with a groan.

James vaulted over the counter and shoved the curtains aside. He grabbed the wheelchair and hauled it out. The wheels thumped twice over Ferry's outstretched legs. Jostled, O'Beronne woke with a screech.

James pulled him toward the blacked-out windows. "Old man," he panted. "How long has it been since you had some fresh air?" He kicked open the door.

"No!" O'Beronne yelped. He shielded his eyes with both hands. "I have to stay inside here! That's the rules!" James wheeled him out onto the pavement. As sunlight hit him, O'Beronne howled in fear and squirmed wildly. Gouts of dust puffed from his cushions, and his bandages flapped. James yanked open the car door, lifted O'Beronne bodily, and dropped him into the passenger seat.

"You can't do this!" O'Beronne screamed, his nightcap flying off. "I belong behind walls, I can't go into the world…"

James slammed the door. He ran around and slid behind the wheel. "It's dangerous out here," O'Beronne whimpered as the engine roared into life. "I was safe in there."

James stamped the accelerator. The car laid rubber. He glanced behind him in the rearview mirror and saw an audience of laughing whooping hookers. "Where are we going?" O'Beronne said meekly.

James floored it through a yellow light. He reached into the backseat one-handed and yanked a can from its six-pack. "Where was this bottling plant?"

O'Beronne blinked doubtfully. "It's been so long...Florida, I think..."

"Florida sounds good. Sunlight, fresh air..." James weaved deftly through traffic, cracking the pop-top with his thumb. He knocked back a swig, then gave O'Beronne the can. "Here, old man. Finish it off."

O'Beronne stared at it, licking dry lips. "But I can't. I'm an owner, not a customer. I'm simply not allowed to do this sort of thing. I own that magic shop, I tell you."

James shook his head and laughed.

O'Beronne trembled. He raised the can in both gnarled hands and began chugging thirstily. He paused once to belch, and kept drinking.

The smell of May filled the car.

O'Beronne wiped his mouth and crushed the empty can in his fist. He tossed it over his shoulder.

"There's room back there for those bandages, too," James told him. "Let's hit the highway."

Our Neural Chernobyl

The late twentieth century, and the early years of our own millennium, form, in retrospect, a single era. This was the Age of the Normal Accident, in which people cheerfully accepted technological risks that today would seem quite insane.

Chernobyls were astonishingly frequent during this footloose, not to say criminally negligent, period. The nineties, with their rapid spread of powerful industrial technologies to the developing world, were a decade of frightening enormities, including the Djakarta supertanker spill, the Lahore meltdown, and the gradual but devastating mass poisonings from tainted Kenyan contraceptives.

Yet none of these prepared humankind for the astonishing global effects of biotechnology's worst disaster: the event that has come to be known as the "neural chernobyl."

We should be grateful, then, that such an authority as the Novel Prize-winning systems neurochemist Dr. Felix Hotton should have turned his able pen to the history of *Our Neural Chernobyl* (Bessemer, December 2056, $499.95). Dr. Hotton is uniquely qualified to give us this devastating reassessment of the past's wrongheaded practices. For Dr. Hotton is a shining exemplar of the new "Open-Tower Science," that social movement within the scientific community that arose in response to the New Luddism of the teens and twenties.

Such Pioneering Hotton papers as "The Locus Coeruleus Efferent Network: What in Heck Is It There For?" and "My Grand Fun Tracing Neural Connections With Tetramethylbenzidine" established this new, relaxed, and triumphantly subjective school of scientific exploration.

Today's scientist is a far cry from the white-coated sociopath of the past. Scientists today are democratized, media-conscious, fully integrated into the mainstream of modern culture. Today's young people, who admire scientists with a devotion once reserved for pop stars, can scarcely imagine the situation otherwise.

But in Chapter 1, "The Social Roots of Gene-Hacking," Dr. Hotton brings turn-of-the-century attitudes into startling relief. This was the golden age of applied biotech. Anxious attitudes toward "genetic tampering" changed rapidly when the terrifying AIDS pandemic was finally broken by recombinant DNA research.

It was during this period that the world first became aware that the AIDS retrovirus was a fantastic blessing in a particularly hideous disguise. This disease, which dug itself with horrible, virulent cunning into the very genetic structure of its victims, proved a medical marvel when finally broken to harness. The AIDS virus's RNA transcriptase system proved an able workhorse, successfully carrying healing segments of recombinant DNA into sufferers from a myriad of genetic defects. Suddenly one ailment after another fell to the miracle of RNA transcriptase techniques: sickle-cell anemia, cystic fibrosis, Tay-Sachs disease— literally hundreds of syndromes now only an unpleasant memory.

As billions poured into the biotech industry, and the instruments of research were simplified, an unexpected dynamic emerged: the rise of "gene-hacking." As Dr. Hotton points out, the situation had a perfect parallel in the 1970s and 1980s in the subculture of computer hacking. Here again was an enormously powerful technology suddenly within the reach of the individual.

As biotech companies multiplied, becoming ever smaller and more advanced, a hacker subculture rose around this "hot technology" like a cloud of steam. These ingenious, anomic individuals, often led into a state of manic self-absorption by their ability to dice with genetic destiny, felt no loyalty to social interests higher than their own curiosity. As early as the 1980s, devices such as high-performance liquid chromatographs, cell-culture systems, and DNA sequencers were small enough to fit into a closet or attic. If not bought from junkyards, diverted, or stolen outright, they could be reconstructed from off-the-shelf parts by any bright and determined teenager.

Dr. Hotton's second chapter explores the background of one such individual: Andrew ("Bugs") Berenbaum, now generally accepted as the perpetrator of the neural chernobyl.

Bugs Berenbaum, as Dr. Hotton convincingly shows, was not much different from a small horde of similar bright young misfits surrounding the genetic establishments of North Carolina's Research Triangle. His father was a semi-successful free-lance programmer, his mother a heavy marijuana user whose life centered around her role as "Lady Anne of Greengables" in Raleigh's Society for Creative Anachronism.

Both parents maintained a flimsy pretense of intellectual superiority, impressing upon Andrew the belief that the family's sufferings derived from the general stupidity and limited imagination of the average citizen. And Berenbaum, who showed an early interest in such subjects as math and engineering (then considered markedly unglamorous), did suffer some persecution from peers and schoolmates. At fifteen he had already drifted into the gene-hacker subculture, accessing gossip and learning "the scene" through computer bulletin boards and all-night beer-and-pizza sessions with other would-be pros.

At twenty-one, Berenbaum was working a summer internship with the small Raleigh firm of CoCoGenCo, a producer of specialized biochemicals.

CoCoGenCo, as later congressional investigations proved, was actually a front for the California "designer drug" manufacturer and smuggler, Jimmy "Screech" McCarley. McCarley's agents within CoCoGenCo ran innumerable late-night "research projects" in conditions of heavy secrecy. In reality, these "secret projects" were straight production runs of synthetic cocaine, beta-phenethylamine, and sundry tailored variants of endorphin, a natural antipain chemical ten thousand times more potent than morphine.

One of McCarley's "black hackers," possibly Berenbaum himself, conceived the sinister notion of "implanted dope factories." By attaching the drug-producing genetics directly into the human genome, it was argued, abusers could be "wet-wired" into permanent states of intoxication. The agent of fixation would be the AIDS retrovirus, whose RNA sequence was a matter of common knowledge and available on dozens of open scientific databases. The one drawback to the scheme, of course, was that the abuser would "burn out like a shitpaper moth in a klieg light," to use Dr. Hotton's memorable phrase.

Chapter 3 is rather technical. Given Dr. Hotton's light and popular style, it makes splendid reading. Dr. Hotton attempts to reconstruct Berenbaum's crude attempts to rectify the situation through gross manipulation of the AIDS RNA transcriptase. What Berenbaum sought, of course, was a way to shut-off and start-up the transcriptase carrier, so that the internal drug factory could be activated at will. Berenbaum's custom transcriptase was designed to react to a simple user-induced trigger—probably D,1,2,5-phospholytic gluteinase, a fractionated component of "Dr. Brown's Celery Soda," as Hotton suggests. This harmless beverage was a favorite quaff of gene-hacker circles.

Finding the genomes for cocaine-production too complex, Berenbaum (or perhaps a close associate, one Richard "Sticky" Ravetch) switched to a simpler payload: the just-discovered genome for mammalian dendritic growth factor. Dendrites are the treelike branches of brain cells, familiar to every modern schoolchild, which provide the mammalian brain with its staggering webbed complexity. It was theorized at the time that DG factor might be the key to vastly higher states of human intelligence. It is to be presumed that both Berenbaum and Ravetch had dosed themselves with it. As many modern victims of the neural Chernobyl can testify, it does have an effect. Not precisely the one that the CoCoGenCo zealots envisioned, however.

While under the temporary maddening elation of dendritic "branch-effect," Berenbaum made his unfortunate breakthrough. He succeeded in providing his model RNA transcriptase with a trigger, but a trigger that made the transcriptase itself far more virulent than the original AIDS virus itself. The stage was set for disaster.

It was at this point that one must remember the social attitudes that bred the soul-threatening isolation of the period's scientific workers. Dr. Hotton is quite pitiless in his psychoanalysis of the mental mind-set of his predecessors. The supposedly "objective worldview" of the sciences is now quite properly seen as a form of mental brainwashing, deliberately stripping the victim of the full spectrum of human emotional response. Under such conditions, Berenbaum's reckless act becomes almost pitiable; it was a convulsive overcompensation for years of emotional starvation. Without consulting his superiors, who might have shown more discretion, Berenbaum began offering free samples of his new wetwares to anyone willing to inject them.

There was a sudden brief plague of eccentric genius in Raleigh, before the now-well-known symptoms of "dendritic crash" took over, and plunged the experimenters into vision-riddled, poetic insanity. Berenbaum himself committed suicide well before the full effects were known. And the full effects, of course, were to go far beyond even this lamentable human tragedy.

Chapter 4 becomes an enthralling detective story as the evidence slowly mounts.

Even today the term "Raleigh collie" has a special ring for dog fanciers, many of whom have forgotten its original derivation. These likable, companionable, and disquietingly intelligent pets were soon transported all over the nation by eager buyers and breeders. Once it had made the jump from human host to canine, Berenbaum's transcriptase derivative, like the AIDS virus itself, was passed on through the canine maternal womb. It was also transmitted through canine sexual intercourse and, via saliva, through biting and licking.

No dendritically enriched "Raleigh collie" would think of biting a human being. On the contrary, these loyal and well-behaved pets have even been known to right spilled garbage cans and replace their trash. Neural chernobyl infections remain rare in humans. But they spread through North America's canine population like wildfire, as Dr. Hotton shows in a series of cleverly designed maps and charts.

Chapter 5 offers us the benefit of hindsight. We are now accustomed to the idea of many different modes of "intelligence." There are, for instance, the various types of computer Artificial Intelligence, which bear no real relation to human "thinking." This was not unexpected—but the diverse forms of animal intelligence can still astonish in their variety.

The variance between *Canis familiaris* and his wild cousin, the coyote, remains unexplained. Dr. Hotton makes a good effort, basing his explication on the coyote neural mapping of his colleague, Dr. Reyna Sanchez of Los Alamos National Laboratory. It does seem likely that the coyote's more fully reticulated basal commissure plays a role. At any rate, it is now clear that a startling advanced form of social organization has taken root among the nation's feral coyote organization, with the use of elaborate coded barks, "scent-dumps," and specialized roles in hunting and food storage. Many of the nation's ranchers have now taken to the "protection system," in which coyote packs are "bought off" with slaughtered, barbecued livestock and sacks of dog treats. Persistent reports in Montana, Idaho, and Saskatchewan insist that coyotes have been spotted wearing cast-off clothing during the worst cold of winter.

It is possible that the common household cat was infected even earlier than the dog. Yet the effects of heightened cat intelligence are subtle and difficult to specify. Notoriously reluctant lab subjects, cats in their infected states are even sulkier about running mazes, solving trick boxes, and so on, preferring to wait out their interlocutors with inscrutable feline patience.

It has been suggested that some domestic cats show a heightened interest in television programs. Dr. Hotton casts a skeptical light on this, pointing out (rightly, as this reviewer thinks) that cats spend most of their waking hours sitting and staring into space. Staring at the flickering of a television is not much more remarkable than the hearthside cat's fondness for the flickering fire. It certainly does not imply "understanding" of a program's content. There are, however, many cases where cats have learned to paw-push the buttons of remote-control units. Those who keep cats as mousers have claimed that some cats now torture birds and rodents for longer periods, with greater ingenuity, and in some cases with improvised tools.

There remains, however, the previously unsuspected connection between advanced dendritic branching and manual dexterity, which Dr. Hotton tackles in his sixth chapter. This concept has caused a revolution in paleoanthropology. We are now forced into the uncomfortable realization that *Pithecanthropus robustus*, formerly dismissed as a large-jawed, vegetable-chewing ape, was probably far more intelligent than *Homo sapiens*. CAT scans of the recently discovered Tanzanian fossil skeleton, nicknamed "Leonardo," reveal a *Pithecanthropus* skull-ridge obviously rich with dendritic branching. It has been suggested that the pithecanthropoids suffered from a heightened "life of the mind" similar to the life-threatening, absent-minded genius of terminal neural chernobyl sufferers. This yields the uncomfortable theory that nature, through evolution, has imposed a "primate stupidity barrier" that allows humans, unlike *Pithecanthropus,* to get on successfully with the dumb animal business of living and reproducing.

But the synergetic effects of dendritic branching and manual dexterity are clear in a certain nonprimate species. I refer, of course, to the well-known "chernobyl jump" of *Procyon lotor,* the American raccoon. The astonishing advances of the raccoon, and its Chinese cousin the panda, occupy the entirety of Chapter 8.

Here Dr. Hotton takes the so-called "modern view," from which I must dissociate myself. I, for one, find it intolerable that large sections of the American wilderness should be made into "no-go areas" by the vandalistic activities of our so-called "stripe-tailed cousins." Admittedly, excesses may have been committed in early attempts to exterminate the verminous, booming population of these masked bandits. But the damage to agriculture has been severe, and the history of kamikaze attacks by self-infected rabid raccoons is a terrifying one.

Dr. Hotton holds that we must now "share the planet with a fellow civilized species." He bolsters his argument with hearsay evidence of "raccoon culture" that to me seems rather flimsy. The woven strips of bark known as "raccoon wampum" are impressive examples of animal dexterity, but to my mind it remains to be proven that they are actually "money." And their so-called "pictographs" seem little more than random daubings. The fact remains that the raccoon population continues to rise exponentially, with raccoon bitches whelping massive litters every spring. Dr. Hotton, in a footnote, suggests that we can relieve crowding pressure by increasing the human presence in outer space. This seems a farfetched and unsatisfactory scheme.

The last chapter is speculative in tone. The prospect of intelligent rats is grossly repugnant; so far, thank God, the tough immune system of the rat, inured to bacteria and filth, has rejected retroviral invasion. Indeed, the feral cat population seems to be driving these vermin toward extinction. Nor have opossums succumbed; indeed, marsupials of all kinds seem immune, making Australia a haven of a now-lost natural world. Whales and dolphins are endangered species; they seem unlikely to make a comeback even with the (as-yet-unknown) cetacean effects of chernobyling. And monkeys, which might pose a very considerable threat, are restricted to the few remaining patches of tropical forest and, like humans, seem resistant to the disease.

Our neural chernobyl has bred a folklore all its own. Modern urban folklore speaks of "ascended masters," a group of chernobyl victims able to survive the virus. Supposedly, they "pass for human," forming a hidden counterculture among the normals, or "sheep." This is a throwback to the dark tradition of Luddism, and the popular fears once projected onto the dangerous and reckless "priesthood of science" are now transferred to these fairy tales of supermen. This psychological transference becomes clear when one hears that these "ascended masters" specialize in advanced scientific research of a kind now frowned upon. The notion that some fraction of the population has achieved physical immortality, and hidden it from the rest of us, is utterly absurd.

Dr. Hotton, quite rightly, treats this paranoid myth with the contempt it deserves.

Despite my occasional reservations, this is a splendid book, likely to be the definitive work on this central phenomenon of modern times. Dr. Hotton may well hope to add another Pulitzer to his list of honors. At ninety-five, this grand old man of modern science has produced yet another stellar work in his rapidly increasing oeuvre. His many readers, like myself, can only marvel at his vigor and clamor for more.

—for Greg Bear

We See Things Differently

This was the *jahiliyah*—the land of ignorance. This was America. The Great Satan, the Arsenal of Imperialism, the Bankroller of Zionism, the Bastion of Neo-Colonialism. The home of Hollywood and blonde sluts in black nylon. The land of rocket-equipped F-15s that slashed across God's sky, in godless pride. The land of nuclear-powered global navies, with cannon that fired shells as large as cars.

They have forgotten that they used to shoot us, shell us, insult us, and equip our enemies. They have no memory, the Americans, and no history. Wind sweeps through them, and the past vanishes. They are like dead leaves.

I flew into Miami, on a winter afternoon. The jet banked over a tangle of empty highways, then a large dead section of the city—a ghetto perhaps. In our final approach we passed a coal-burning power plant, reflected in the canal. For a moment I mistook it for a mosque, its tall smokestacks slender as minarets. A Mosque for the American Dynamo.

I had trouble with my cameras at customs. The customs officer was a grimy-looking American, white with hair the color of clay. He squinted at my passport. "That's an awful lot of film, Mr. Cuttab," he said.

"Qutb," I said, smiling. "Sayyid Qutb. Call me Charlie."

"Journalist, huh?" He looked unhappy. It seemed that I owed substantial import duties on my Japanese cameras, as well as my numerous rolls of Pakistani color film. He invited me into a small back office to discuss it. Money changed hands. I departed with my papers in order.

The airport was half-full: mostly prosperous Venezuelans and Cubans, with the haunted look of men pursuing sin. I caught a taxi outside, a tiny vehicle like a motorcycle wrapped in glass. The cabbie, an ancient black man, stowed my luggage in the cab's trailer.

Within the cab's cramped confines, we were soon unwilling intimates. The cabbie's breath smelled of sweetened alcohol. "You Iranian?" the cabbie asked.

"Arab."

"We respect Iranians around here, we really do," the cabbie insisted.

"So do we," I said. "We fought them on the Iraqi front for years."

"Yeah?" said the cabbie uncertainly. "Seems to me I heard about that. How'd that end up?"

"The Shi'ite holy cities were ceded to Iran. The Ba'athist regime is dead, and Iraq is now part of the Arab Caliphate." My words made no impression on him, and I had known it before I spoke. This is the land of ignorance. They know nothing about us, the Americans. After all this, and they still know nothing whatsoever.

"Well, who's got more money these days?" the cabbie asked. "Y'all, or the Iranians?"

"The Iranians have heavy industry," I said. "But we Arabs tip better."

The cabbie smiled. It is very easy to buy Americans. The mention of money brightens them like a shot of drugs. It is not just the poverty; they were always like this, even when they were rich. It is the effect of spiritual emptiness. A terrible grinding emptiness in the very guts of the West, which no amount of Coca-Cola seems able to fill.

We rolled down gloomy streets toward the hotel. Miami's streetlights were subsidized by commercial enterprises. It was another way of, as they say, shrugging the burden of essential services from the exhausted backs of the taxpayers. And onto the far sturdier shoulders of peddlers of aspirin, sticky sweetened drinks, and cosmetics. Their billboards gleamed bluely under harsh lights encased in bulletproof glass. It reminded me so strongly of Soviet agitprop that I had a sudden jarring sense of displacement, as if I were being sold Lenin and Engels and Marx in the handy jumbo size.

The cabbie, wondering perhaps about his tip, offered to exchange dollars for riyals at black-market rates. I declined politely, having already done this in Cairo. The lining of my coat was stuffed with crisp Reagan thousand-dollar bills. I also had several hundred in pocket change, and an extensive credit line at the Islamic Bank of Jerusalem. I foresaw no difficulties.

Outside the hotel, I gave the ancient driver a pair of fifties. Another very old man, of Hispanic descent, took my bags on a trolley. I registered under the gaze of a very old woman. Like all American women, she was dressed in a way intended to provoke lust. In the young, this technique works admirably, as proved by America's unhappy history of sexually transmitted plague. In the old, it provokes only sad disgust.

I smiled on the horrible old woman and paid in advance.

I was rewarded by a double-handful of glossy brochures promoting local casinos, strip-joints, and bars.

The room was adequate. This had once been a fine hotel. The air-conditioning was quiet and both hot and cold water worked well. A wide flat screen covering most of one wall offered dozens of channels of television.

My wristwatch buzzed quietly, its programmed dial indicating the direction of Mecca. I took the rug from my luggage and spread it before the window. I cleansed my face, my hands, my feet. Then I knelt before the darkening chaos of Miami, many stories below. I assumed the eight positions, sinking with gratitude into deep meditation. I forced away the stress of jet-lag, the innate tension and fear of a Believer among enemies.

Prayer completed, I changed my clothing, putting aside my dark Western business suit. I assumed denim jeans, a long-sleeved shirt, and a photographer's vest. I slipped my press card, my passport, my health cards into the vest's zippered pockets, and draped the cameras around myself. I then returned to the lobby downstairs, to await the arrival of the American rock star.

He came on schedule, even slightly early. There was only a small crowd, as the rock star's organization had sought confidentiality. A train of seven monstrous buses pulled into the hotel's lot, their whale-like sides gleaming with brushed aluminum. They bore Massachusetts license plates. I walked out on to the tarmac and began photographing.

All seven buses carried the rock star's favored insignia, the thirteen-starred blue field of the early American flag. The buses pulled up with military precision, forming a wagon-train fortress across a large section of the weedy, broken tarmac. Folding doors hissed open and a swarm of road crew piled out into the circle of buses.

Men and women alike wore baggy fatigues, covered with buttoned pockets and block-shaped streaks of urban camouflage: brick red, asphalt black, and concrete gray. Dark-blue shoulder patches showed the thirteen-starred circle. Working efficiently, without haste, they erected large satellite dishes on the roofs of two buses. The buses were soon linked together in formation, shaped barriers of woven wire securing the gaps between each nose and tail. The machines seemed to sit breathing, with the stoked-up, leviathan air of steam locomotives.

A dozen identically dressed crewmen broke from the buses and departed in a group for the hotel. Within their midst, shielded by their bodies, was the rock star, Tom Boston. The broken outlines of their camouflaged fatigues made them seem to blur into a single mass, like a herd of moving zebras. I followed them; they vanished quickly within the hotel. One crew woman tarried outside.

I approached her. She had been hauling a bulky piece of metal luggage on trolley wheels. It was a newspaper vending machine. She set it beside three other machines at the hotel's entrance. It was the Boston organization's propaganda paper, *Poor Richard's.*

I drew near. "Ah, the latest issue," I said. "May I have one?"

"It will cost five dollars," she said, in painstaking English. To my surprise, I recognized her as Boston's wife. "Valya Plisetskaya," I said with pleasure, and handed her a five-dollar nickel. "My name is Sayyid; my American friends call me Charlie."

She looked about her. A small crowd already gathered at the buses, kept at a distance by the Boston crew. Others clustered under the hotel's green-and-white awning.

"Who are you with?" she said.

"*Al-Ahram,* of Cairo. An Arabic newspaper."

"You're not a political?" she said.

I shook my head in amusement at this typical show of Russian paranoia. "Here's my press card." I showed her the tangle of Arabic. "I am here to cover Tom Boston. The Boston phenomenon."

She squinted. "Tom is big in Cairo these days? Muslims, yes? Down on rock and roll."

"We're not all ayatollahs," I said, smiling up at her. She was very tall. "Many still listen to Western pop music; they ignore the advice of their betters. They used to rock all night in Leningrad. Despite the Communist Party. Isn't that so?"

"You know about us Russians, do you, Charlie?" She handed me my paper, watching me with cool suspicion.

"No, I can't keep up," I said. "Like Lebanon in the old days. Too many factions." I followed her through the swinging glass doors of the hotel. Valentina Plisetskaya was a broad-cheeked Slav with glacial blue eyes and hair the color of corn tassels. She was a childless woman in her thirties, starved as thin as a girl. She played saxophone in Boston's band. She was a native of Moscow, but had survived its destruction. She had been on tour with her jazz band when the Afghan Martyrs' Front detonated their nuclear bomb.

I tagged after her. I was interested in the view of another foreigner. "What do you think of the Americans these days?" I asked her.

We waited beside the elevator.

"Are you recording?" she said.

"No! I'm a print journalist. I know you don't like tapes," I said.

"We like tapes fine," she said, staring down at me. "As long as they are ours." The elevator was sluggish. "You want to know what I think, Charlie? I think Americans are fucked. Not as bad as Soviets, but fucked anyway. What do you think?"

"Oh," I said. "American gloom-and-doom is an old story. At *Al-Ahram,* we are more interested in the signs of American resurgence. That's the big angle, now. That's why I'm here."

She looked at me with remote sarcasm. "Aren't you a little afraid they will beat the shit out of you? They're not happy, the Americans. Not sweet and easygoing like before."

I wanted to ask her how sweet the CIA had been when their bomb killed half the Iranian government in 1981. Instead, I shrugged. "There's no substitute for a man on the ground. That's what my editors say." The elevator shunted open. "May I come up with you?"

"I won't stop you." We stepped in. "But they won't let you in to see Tom."

"They will if you ask them to, Mrs. Boston."

"I'm called Plisetskaya," she said, fluffing her yellow hair. "See? No veil." It was the old story of the so-called "liberated" Western woman. They call the simple, modest clothing of Islam "bondage"—while they spend countless hours, and millions of dollars, painting themselves. They grow their nails into talons, cram their feet into high heels, strap their breasts and hips into spandex. All for the sake of male lust.

It baffles the imagination. Naturally I told her nothing of this, but only smiled. "I'm afraid I will be a pest," I said. "I have a room in this hotel. Some time I will see your husband. I must, my editors demand it."

The doors opened. We stepped into the hall of the fourteenth floor. Boston's entourage had taken over the entire floor. Men in fatigues and sunglasses guarded the hallway; one of them had a trained dog.

"Your paper is big, is it?" the woman said.

"Biggest in Cairo, millions of readers," I said. "We still read, in the Caliphate."

"State-controlled television," she muttered.

"Is that worse than corporations?" I asked. "I saw what CBS said about Tom Boston." She hesitated, and I continued to prod. "A 'Luddite fanatic,' am I right? A 'rock demagogue.'"

"Give me your room number." I did this. "I'll call," she said, striding away down the corridor. I almost expected the guards to salute her as she passed so regally, but they made no move, their eyes invisible behind the glasses. They looked old and rather tired, but with the alert relaxation of professionals. They had the look of former Secret Service bodyguards. Their city-colored fatigues were baggy enough to hide almost any amount of weaponry.

I returned to my room. I ordered Japanese food from room service, and ate it. Wine had been used in its cooking, but I am not a prude in these matters. It was now time for the day's last prayer, though my body, still attuned to Cairo, did not believe it.

My devotions were broken by a knocking at the door. I opened it. It was another of Boston's staff, a small black woman whose hair had been treated. It had a nylon sheen. It looked like the plastic hair on a child's doll. "You Charlie?"

"Yes."

"Valya says, you want to see the gig. See us set up. Got you a backstage pass."

"Thank you very much." I let her clip the plastic-coated pass to my vest. She looked past me into the room, and saw my prayer rug at the window. "What you doin' in there? Prayin'?"

"Yes."

"Weird," she said. "You coming or what?"

I followed my nameless benefactor to the elevator.

Down at ground level, the crowd had swollen. Two security guards stood outside the glass doors, refusing admittance to anyone without a room key. The girl ducked, and plowed through the crowd with sudden headlong force, like an American football player. I struggled in her wake, the gawkers, pickpockets and autograph hounds closing at my heels. The crowd was liberally sprinkled with the repulsive derelicts one sees so often in America: those without homes, without family, without charity.

I was surprised at the age of the people. For a rock-star's audience, one expects dizzy teenaged girls and the libidinous young street-toughs that pursue them. There were many of these, but more of another type: tired, footsore people with crow's-feet and graying hair. Men and women in their thirties and forties, with a shabby, crushed look. Unemployed, obviously, and with time on their hands to cluster around anything that resembled hope.

We walked without hurry to the fortress circle of buses. A rear guard of Boston's kept the onlookers at bay. Two of the buses were already unlinked from the others and under full steam. I followed the black woman up perforated steps and into the bowels of one of the shining machines.

She called brief greetings to the others already inside.

The air held the sharp reek of cleaning fluid. Neat elastic cords held down stacks of amplifiers, stencilled instrument cases, wheeled dollies of black rubber and crisp yellow pine. The thirteen-starred circle marked everything, stamped or spray-painted. A methane-burning steam generator sat at the back of the bus, next to a tall crashproof rack of high-pressure fuel tanks. We skirted the equipment and joined the others in a narrow row of second-hand airplane seats. We buckled ourselves in. I sat next to the Doll-Haired Girl.

The bus surged into motion. "It's very clean," I said. "I expected something a bit wilder on a rock and roll bus."

"Maybe in Egypt," she said, with the instinctive assumption that Egypt was in the Dark Ages. "We don't have the luxury to screw around. Not now."

I decided not to tell her that Egypt, as a nation-state, no longer existed. "American pop culture is a very big industry."

"Biggest we have left," she said. "And if you Muslims weren't so pimpy about it, maybe we could pull down a few riyals and get out of debt."

"We buy a great deal from America," I told her. "Grain and timber and minerals."

"That's Third-World stuff. We're not your farm." She looked at the spotless floor. "Look, our industries suck, everybody knows it. So we sell entertainment. Except where there's media barriers. And even then the fucking video pirates rip us off."

"We see things differently," I said. "America ruled the global media for decades. To us, it's cultural imperialism. We have many talented musicians in the Arab world. Have you ever heard them?"

"Can't afford it," she said crisply. "We spent all our money saving the Persian Gulf from commies."

"The Global Threat of Red Totalitarianism," said the heavyset man in the seat next to Doll-Hair. The others laughed grimly.

"Oh," I said. "Actually, it was Zionism that concerned us. When there was a Zionism."

"I can't believe the hate shit I see about America," said the heavy man. "You know how much money we gave away to people, just gave away, for nothing? Billions and billions. Peace Corps, development aid…for decades. Any disaster anywhere, and we fall all over ourselves to give food, medicine…Then the Russians go down and the whole world turns against us like we were monsters."

"Moscow," said another crewman, shaking his shaggy head.

"You know, there are still motherfuckers who think we Americans killed Moscow. They think we gave a Bomb to those Afghani terrorists."

"It had to come from somewhere," I said.

"No, man. We wouldn't do that to them. No, man, things were going great between us. Rock for Detente—I was at that gig."

We drove to Miami's Memorial Colosseum. It was an ambitious structure, left half-completed when the American banking system collapsed.

We entered double-doors at the back, wheeling the equipment along dusty corridors. The Colosseum's interior was skeletal; inside it was clammy and cavernous. A stage, a concrete floor. Bare steel arched high overhead, with crudely bracketed stage-lights. Large sections of that bizarre American parody of grass, "Astroturf," had been dragged before the stage. The itchy green fur was still lined with yard-marks from some forgotten stadium.

The crew worked with smooth precision, setting up amplifiers, spindly mike-stands, a huge high-tech drum kit with the clustered, shiny look of an oil refinery. Others checked lighting, flicking blue and yellow spots across the stage. At the public entrances, two crewmen from a second bus erected metal detectors for illicit cameras, recorders, or handguns. Especially handguns. Two attempts had already been made on Boston's life, one at the Chicago Freedom Festival, when Chicago's Mayor had been wounded at Boston's side.

For a moment, to understand it, I mounted the empty stage and stood before Boston's microphone. I imagined the crowd before me, ten thousand souls, twenty thousand eyes. Under that attention, I realized, every motion was amplified. To move my arm would be like moving ten thousand arms, my every word like the voice of thousands. I felt like a Nasser, a Qadaffi, a Saddam Hussein.

This was the nature of secular power. Industrial power. It was the West that invented it, that invented Hitler, the gutter orator turned trampler of nations, that invented Stalin, the man they called "Genghis Khan with a telephone." The media pop star, the politician. Was there any difference anymore? Not in America; it was all a question of seizing eyes, of seizing attention. Attention is wealth, in an age of mass media. Center stage is more important than armies.

The last unearthly moans and squeals of sound-check faded. The Miami crowd began to filter into the Colosseum. They looked livelier than the desperate searchers who had pursued Boston to his hotel. America was still a wealthy country, by most standards; the professional classes had kept much of their prosperity. There were the legions of lawyers, for instance, that secular priesthood that had done so much to drain America's once-vaunted enterprise. And their associated legions of state bureaucrats. They were instantly recognizable; the cut of their suits, their telltale pocket telephones proclaiming their status.

What were they looking for here? Had they never read Boston's propaganda paper, with its bitter condemnations of the wealthy? With its fierce attacks on the "legislative-litigative complex," its demands for purges and sweeping reforms?

Was it possible that they had failed to take him seriously?

I joined the crowd, mingling, listening to conversations. At the doors, Boston cadres were cutting ticket prices for those who showed voter registrations. Those who showed unemployment cards got in for even less.

The more prosperous Americans stood in little knots of besieged gentility, frightened of the others, yet curious, smiling. There was a liveliness in the destitute: brighter clothing, knotted kerchiefs at the elbows, cheap Korean boots of iridescent cloth. Many wore tricornered hats, some with a cockade of red, white, and blue, or the circle of thirteen stars.

This was the milieu of rock and roll, I realized; that was the secret. They had all grown up on it, these Americans, even the richer ones. To them, the sixty-year tradition of rock music seemed as ancient as the Pyramids. It had become a Jerusalem, a Mecca of American tribes.

The crowd milled, waiting, and Boston let them wait. At the back of the crowd, Boston crewmen did a brisk business in starred souvenir shirts, programs, and tapes. Heat and tension mounted, and people began to sweat. The stage remained dark.

I bought the souvenir items and studied them. They talked about cheap computers, a phone company owned by its workers, a free data-base, neighborhood cooperatives that could buy unmilled grain by the ton. ATTENTION MIAMI, read one brochure in letters of dripping red. It named the ten largest global corporations and meticulously listed every subsidiary doing business in Miami, with its address, its phone number, the percentage of income shipped to banks in Europe and Japan. Each list went on for pages. Nothing else. To Boston's audience, nothing else was necessary.

The house lights darkened. A frightening animal roar rose from the crowd. A single spot lit Tom Boston, stenciling him against darkness.

"My fellow Americans," he said. A funereal hush followed. Boston smirked. "My f-f-f-fellow Americans." He had a clever microphone, digitized, a small synthesizer in itself. "My fellow Am-am-am-am-AMM!" His words vanished in a sudden wail of feedback. "My Am—my fellows—my am—my fellows—my am my, Miami, Miami, MIAMI!" Boston's warped voice, suddenly leaping out of all human context, became shattering, superhuman—the effect was bone-chilling. It passed all barriers, it seeped directly into the skin, the blood.

"Tom Jefferson Died Broke!" he shouted. It was the title of his first song. Stage lights flashed up and hell broke its gates. Was this a "song" at all, this strange, volcanic creation? There was a melody loose in it somewhere, pursued by Plisetskaya's saxophone, but the sheer volume and impact hurled it through the audience like a sheet of flame. I had never before heard anything so loud. What Cairo's renegade set called rock music paled to nothing beside this invisible hurricane.

At first it seemed raw noise. But that was only a kind of flooring, a merciless grinding foundation below the rising architectures of sound. Technology did it: that piercing, soaring, digitized, utter clarity, of perfect computer acoustics adjusting for every echo, a hundred times a second.

Boston played a glass harmonica: an instrument invented by the early American genius Benjamin Franklin. The harmonica was made of carefully tuned glass disks, rotating on a spindle, and played by streaking a wet fingertip across each moving edge.

It was the sound of crystal, seemingly sourceless, of tooth-aching purity.

The famous Western musician, Wolfgang Mozart, had composed for the Franklin harmonica in the days of its novelty. Legend said that its players went mad, their nerves shredded by its clarity of sound. It was a legend Boston was careful to exploit. He played the machine sparingly, with the air of a magician, of a Solomon unbottling demons. I was glad of this, for the beauty of its sound stung the brain.

Boston threw aside his hat. Long coiled hair spilled free. Boston was what Americans called "black"; at least, he was often referred to as black, though no one seemed certain. He was no darker than myself. The beat rose up, a strong animal heaving. Boston stalked across the stage as if on strings, clutching his microphone. He began to sing.

The song concerned Thomas Jefferson, a famous American president of the eighteenth century. Jefferson was a political theorist who wrote revolutionary manifestos and favored a decentralist mode of government. The song, however, dealt with the relations of Jefferson and a black concubine in his household. He had several children by this woman, who were a source of great shame, due to the odd legal code of the period. Legally, they were his slaves, and it was only at the end of his life, when he was in great poverty, that Jefferson set them free.

It was a story whose pathos makes little sense to a Muslim. But Boston's audience, knowing themselves Jefferson's children, took it to heart.

The heat became stifling, as massed bodies swayed in rhythm. The next song began in a torrent of punishing noise. Frantic hysteria seized the crowd; their bodies spasmed with each beat, the shaman Boston seeming to scourge them. It was a fearsome song, called "The Whites of Their Eyes," after an American war-cry. He sang of a tactic of battle: to wait until the enemy comes close enough so that you can meet his eyes, frighten him with your conviction, and then shoot him point blank.

Three more songs followed, one of them slower, the others battering the audience like iron rods. Boston stalked like a madman, his clothing dark with sweat. My heart spasmed as heavy bass notes, filled with dark murderous power, surged through my ribs. I moved away from the heat to the fringe of the crowd, feeling lightheaded and sick.

I had not expected this. I had expected a political spokesman, but instead it seemed I was assaulted by the very Voice of the West. The Voice of a society drunk with raw power, maddened by the grinding roar of machines. It filled me with terrified awe.

To think that, once, the West had held us in its armored hands. It had treated Islam as it treated a natural resource, its invincible armies tearing through the lands of the Faithful like bulldozers. The West had chopped our world up into colonies, and smiled upon us with its awful schizophrenic perfidy. It told us to separate God and State, to separate Mind and Body, to separate Reason and Faith. It had torn us apart.

I stood shaking as the first set ended. The band vanished backstage, and a single figure approached the microphone. I recognized him as a famous American television comedian, who had abandoned his own career to join Boston.

The man began to joke and clown, his antics seeming to soothe the crowd, ·
which hooted with laughter. This intermission was a wise move on Boston's
part, I thought. The level of intensity, of pain, had become unbearable.

It struck me then how much Boston was like the great Khomeini. Boston
too had the persona of the Man of Sorrows, the sufferer after justice, the as-
cetic among corruption, the battler against odds. And the air of the mystic,
the adept, at least as far as such a thing was possible in America. I contemplated this, and deep fear struck me once again.   ·

I walked through the gates to the Colosseum's outer hall, seeking air and
room to think. Others had come out too. They leaned against the walls, men
and women, with the look of wrung-out mops. Some smoked cigarettes,
others argued over brochures, others simply sat with palsied grins.

Still others wept. These disturbed me most, for these were the ones
whose souls seemed stung and opened. Khomeini made men weep like
that, tearing aside despair like a bandage from a burn. I walked among them,
watching them, making mental notes.

I stopped by a woman in dark glasses and a trim business suit. She
leaned within an alcove by a set of telephones, shaking, her face beneath
the glasses slick with silent tears. Her cheekbones, the precision of her styled
hair, struck a memory. I stood beside her, waiting, and recognition came.

"Hello," I said. "We have something in common, I think. You've been
covering the Boston tour. For CBS."

She glanced at me once, and away. "I don't know you."

"You're Marjory Cale, the correspondent."

She drew in a breath. "You're mistaken."

"'Luddite fanatic,'" I said lightly. "'Rock demagogue.'"

"Go away," she said.

"Why not talk about it? I'd like to know your point of view."

"Go away, you nasty little man."

I returned to the crowd inside. The comedian was now reading at length
from the American Bill of Rights, his voice thick with sarcasm. "Freedom of
advertising," he said. "Freedom of global network television conglomerates.
Right to a speedy and public trial, to be repeated until the richest lawyers
win. A well-regulated militia being necessary, citizens will be issued orbital
lasers and aircraft carriers..." No one was laughing.

The crowd was in an ugly mood when Boston reappeared. Even the
well-dressed ones now seemed surly and militant, not recognizing themselves as the enemy. Like the Shah's soldiers who at last refused to fire, who
threw themselves sobbing at Khomeini's feet.

"You all know this one," Boston said. With his wife, he raised a banner,
one of the first flags of the American Revolution. It bore a coiled snake, a

native American viper, with the legend: DON'T TREAD ON ME. A sinister, scaly rattling poured from the depths of a synthesizer, merging with the crowd's roar of recognition, and a sprung, loping rhythm broke loose. Boston edged back and forth at the stage's rim, his eyes fixed, his long neck swaying. He shook himself like a man saved from drowning and leaned into the microphone.

"We know you own us/ You step upon us/ We feel the onus/ But here's a bonus/ Today I see/ So enemy/ Don't tread on me/ Don't tread on me…" Simple words, fitting each beat with all the harsh precision of the English language. A chant of raw hostility. The crowd took it up. This was the hatred, the humiliation of a society brought low. Americans. Somewhere within them conviction still burned. The conviction they had always had: that they were the only real people on the planet. The chosen ones, the Light of the World, the Last Best Hope of Mankind, the Free and the Brave, the crown of creation. They would have killed for him. I knew, someday, they would.

▲ ▼ ▲

I was called to Boston's suite at two o'clock that morning. I had shaved and showered, dashed on the hotel's complimentary cologne. I wanted to smell like an American.

Boston's guards frisked me, carefully and thoroughly, outside the elevator. I submitted with good grace.

Boston's suite was crowded. It had the air of an election victory. There were many politicians, sipping glasses of bubbling alcohol, laughing, shaking hands. Miami's Mayor was there, with half his city council. I recognized a young woman Senator, speaking urgently into her pocket phone, her large freckled breasts on display in an evening gown.

I mingled, listening. Men spoke of Boston's ability to raise funds, of the growing importance of his endorsement. More of Boston's guards stood in corners, arms folded, eyes hidden, their faces stony. A black man distributed lapel buttons with the face of Martin Luther King on a background of red and white stripes. The wall-sized television played a tape of the first Moon Landing. The sound had been turned off, and people all over the world, in the garb of the 1960's, mouthed silently at the camera, their eyes shining.

It was not until four o'clock that I finally met the star himself. The party had broken up by then, the politicians politely ushered out, their vows of undying loyalty met with discreet smiles. Boston was in a back bedroom with his wife and a pair of aides.

"Sayyid," he said, and shook my hand. In person he seemed smaller, older, his hybrid face, with stage makeup, beginning to peel.

"Dr. Boston," I said.

He laughed freely. "Sayyid, my friend. You'll ruin my street fucking credibility."

"I want to tell the story as I see it," I said.

"Then you'll have to tell me what you see," he said, and turned briefly to an aide, who had a laptop computer. Boston dictated in a low, staccato voice, not losing his place in our conversation, simply loosing a burst of thought. "Let us be frank. Before I showed an interest you were willing to sell the ship for scrap iron. This is not an era for supertankers. Your property is dead tech, smokestack-era garbage. Reconsider my offer." The secretary pounded keys. Boston looked at me again, returning the searchlight of his attention.

"You want to buy a supertanker?" I said.

"I wanted an aircraft carrier," he said, smiling. "They're all in mothballs, but the Feds frown on selling nuke powerplants to private citizens."

"We will make the tanker into a floating stadium," Plisetskaya put in. She sat slumped in a padded chair, wearing satin lounge pajamas. A half-filled ashtray on the chair's arm reeked of strong tobacco.

"Ever been inside a tanker?" Boston said. "Huge. Great acoustics." He sat suddenly on the sprawling bed and pulled off his snakeskin boots. "So, Sayyid. Tell me this story of yours."

"You graduated magna cum laude from Rutgers with a doctorate. in political science," I said. "In five years."

"That doesn't count," Boston said, yawning behind his hand. "That was before rock and roll beat my brains out."

"You ran for state office in Massachusetts," I said. "You lost a close race. Two years later you were touring with your first band—Swamp Fox. You were an immediate success. You became involved in political fund-raising, recruiting your friends in the music industry. You started your own recording label, your own studios. You helped organize rock concerts in Russia, where you met your wife-to-be. Your romance was front-page news on both continents. Record sales soared."

"You left out the first time I got shot at," Boston said. "That's more interesting; Val and I are old hat by now."

He paused, then burst out at the second secretary. "I urge you once again not to go public. You will find yourself vulnerable to a buyout. I've told you that Evans is an agent of Marubeni. If he brings your precious plant down around your ears, don't come crying to me."

"February 1998," I said. "An anti-communist zealot fired on your bus."

"You're a big fan, Sayyid."

"Why are you afraid of multinationals?" I said. "That was the American preference, wasn't it? Global trade, global economics?"

"We screwed up," Boston said. "Things got out of hand."

"Out of American hands, you mean?"

"We used our companies as tools for development," Boston said, with the patience of a man instructing a child. "But then our lovely friends in South America refused to pay their debts. And our staunch allies in Europe and Japan signed the Geneva Economic Agreement and decided to crash the dollar. And our friends in the Arab countries decided not to be countries anymore, but one almighty Caliphate, and, just for good measure, they pulled all their oil money out of our banks and put it into Islamic ones. How could we compete? Islamic banks are holy banks, and our banks pay interest, which is a sin, I understand." He fluffed curls from his neck, his eyes glittering. "And all that time, we were already in hock to our fucking ears to pay for being the world's policeman."

"So the world betrayed your country," I said. "Why?"

He shook his head. "Isn't it obvious? Who needs St. George when the dragon is dead? Some Afghani fanatics scraped together enough plutonium for a Big One, and they blew the dragon's fucking head off. And the rest of the body is still convulsing, ten years later. We bled ourselves white competing against Russia, which was stupid, but we'd won. With two giants, the world trembles. One giant, and the midgets can drag it down. They took us out, that's all. They own us."

"It sounds very simple," I said.

He showed annoyance for the first time. "Valya says you've read our newspapers. I'm not telling you anything new. Should I lie about it? Look at the figures, for Christ's sake. The EEC and the Japanese use their companies for money pumps, they're sucking us dry, deliberately. You don't look stupid, Sayyid. You know very well what's happening to us, anyone in the Third World knows."

"You mentioned Christ," I said. "Do you believe in Him?"

Boston rocked back on his elbows and grinned. "Do you?"

"Of course. He is one of our Prophets. We call Him Isa."

Boston looked cautious. "I never stand between a man and his God." He paused. "We have a lot of respect for the Arabs, truly. What they've accomplished. Breaking free from the world economic system, returning to authentic local tradition...You see the parallels."

"Yes," I said. I smiled sleepily, and covered my mouth as I yawned. "Jet lag. Your pardon, please. These are only questions my editors would want me to ask. If I were not an admirer, a fan as you say, I would not have this assignment."

He smiled and looked at his wife. Plisetskaya lit another cigarette and leaned back, looking skeptical. Boston grinned. "So the sparring's over, Charlie?"

"I have every record you've made," I said. "This is not a job for hatchets."
I paused, weighing my words. "I still believe that our Caliph is a great man.
I support the Islamic Resurgence. I am Muslim. But I think, like many
others, that we have gone a bit too far in closing every window to the West.
Rock and roll is a Third World music at heart. Don't you agree?"

"Sure," said Boston, closing his eyes. "Do you know the first words
spoken in independent Zimbabwe? Right after they ran up the flag."

"No."

He spoke out blindly, savoring the words. "Ladies and gentlemen. Bob
Marley. And the Wailers."

"You admire Bob Marley."

"Comes with the territory," Boston said, flipping a coil of hair.

"He had a black mother, a white father. And you?"

"Oh, both my parents were shameless mongrels like myself," Boston said.
"I'm a second-generation nothing-in-particular. An American." He sat up,
knotting his hands, looking tired. "You going to stay with the tour a while,
Charlie?"He spoke to a secretary. "Get me a kleenex." The woman rose.

"Till Philadelphia," I said. "Like Marjory Cale."

Plisetskaya blew smoke, frowning. "You spoke to that woman?"

"Of course. About the concert."

"What did the bitch say?" Boston asked lazily. His aide handed him tissues and cold cream. Boston dabbed the kleenex and smeared makeup from
his face.

"She asked me what I thought. I said it was too loud," I said.

Plisetskaya laughed once, sharply. I smiled. "It was quite amusing. She
said that you were in good form. She said that I should not be so tight-
arsed."

"'Tight-arsed'?" Boston said, raising his brows. Fine wrinkles had appeared beneath the greasepaint. "She said that?"

"She said we Muslims were afraid of modern life. Of new experience. Of
course I told her that this wasn't true. Then she gave me this." I reached into
one of the pockets of my vest and pulled out a flat packet of aluminum foil.

"Marjory Cale gave you cocaine?" Boston asked.

"Wyoming Flake," I said. "She said she has friends who grow it in the
Rocky Mountains." I opened the packet, exposing a little mound of white
powder. "I saw her use some. I think it will help my jet lag." I pulled my
chair closer to the bedside phone-table. I shook the packet out, with much
care, on the shining mahogany surface. The tiny crystals glittered. It was
finely chopped.

I opened my wallet and removed a crisp thousand-dollar bill. The actor-
president smiled benignly. "Would this be appropriate?"

"Tom does not do drugs," Plisetskaya said, too quickly.

"Ever do coke before?" Boston asked. He threw a wadded tissue to the floor.

"I hope I'm not offending you," I said. "This is Miami, isn't it? This is America." I began rolling the bill, clumsily.

"We are not impressed," Plisetskaya said sternly. She ground out her cigarette. "You are being a rube, Charlie. A hick from the NICs."

"There is a lot of it," I said, allowing doubt to creep into my voice. I reached into my pocket, then divided the pile in half with the sharp edge of a developed slide. I arranged the lines neatly. They were several centimeters long.

I sat back in the chair. "You think it's a bad idea? I admit, this is new to me." I paused. "I have drunk wine several times, although the Koran forbids it."

One of the secretaries laughed. "Sorry," she said. "He drinks wine. That's cute."

I sat and watched temptation dig into Boston. Plisetskaya shook her head.

"Cale's cocaine," Boston mused. "Man."

We watched the lines together for several seconds, he and I. "I did not mean to be trouble," I said. "I can throw it away."

"Never mind Val," Boston said. "Russians chainsmoke." He slid across the bed.

I bent quickly and sniffed. I leaned back, touching my nose. The cocaine quickly numbed it. I handed the paper tube to Boston. It was done in a moment. We sat back, our eyes watering.

"Oh," I said, drug seeping through tissue. "Oh, this is excellent."

"It's good toot," Boston agreed. "Looks like you get an extended interview." We talked through the rest of the night, he and I.

▲ ▼ ▲

My story is almost over. From where I sit to write this, I can hear the sound of Boston's music, pouring from the crude speakers of a tape pirate in the bazaar. There is no doubt in my mind that Boston is a great man.

I accompanied the tour to Philadelphia. I spoke to Boston several times during the tour, though never again with the first fine rapport of the drug. We parted as friends, and I spoke well of him in my article for *Al-Ahram*. I did not hide what he was, I did not hide his threat. But I did not malign him. We see things differently. But he is a man, a child of God like all of us.

His music even saw brief popularity in Cairo, after the article. Children listen to it, and then turn to other things, as children will. They like the sound, they dance, but the words mean nothing to them. The thoughts, the feelings, are alien.

This is the *dar-al-harb,* the land of peace. We have peeled the hands of the West from our throat, we draw breath again, under God's sky. Our Caliph is a good man, and I am proud to serve him. He reigns, he does not rule. Learned men debate in the *Majlis,* not squabbling like politicians, but seeking truth in dignity. We have the world's respect.

We have earned it, for we paid the martyr's price. We Muslims are one in five in all the world, and as long as ignorance of God persists, there will always be the struggle, the *jihad*. It is a proud thing to be one of the Caliph's *Mujihadeen*. It is not that we value our lives lightly. But that we value God more.

Some call us backward, reactionary. I laughed at this when I carried the powder. It had the subtlest of poisons: a living virus. It is a tiny thing, bred in secret laboratories, and in itself it does no harm. But it spreads throughout the body, and it bleeds out a chemical, a faint but potent trace that carries the rot of cancer.

The West can do much with cancer these days, and a wealthy man like Boston can buy much treatment. They may cure the first attack, or the second. But within five years he will surely be dead.

People will mourn his loss. Perhaps they will put his image on a postage stamp, as they did for Bob Marley. Marley, who also died of systemic cancer; whether by the hand of God or man, only Allah knows.

I have taken the life of a great man; in trapping him I took my own life as well, but that means nothing. I am no one. I am not even Sayyid Qutb, the Martyr and theorist of Resurgence, though I took that great man's name as cover. I meant only respect, and believe I have not shamed his memory.

I do not plan to wait for the disease. The struggle continues in the Muslim lands of what was once the Soviet Union. There the Believers ride in Holy Jihad, freeing their ancient lands from the talons of Marxist atheism. Secretly, we send them carbines, rockets, mortars, and nameless men. I shall be one of them; when I meet death, my grave will be nameless also. But nothing is nameless to God.

God is Great; men are mortal, and err. If I have done wrong, let the judge of Men decide. Before His Will, as always, I submit.

Dori Bangs

True facts, mostly: Lester Bangs was born in California in 1948. He published his first article in 1969. It came over the transom at *Rolling Stone*. It was a frenzied review of the MC5's "Kick Out the Jams."

Without much meaning to, Lester Bangs slowly changed from a Romilar-guzzling college kid into a "professional rock critic." There wasn't much precedent for this job in 1969, so Lester kinda had to make it up as he went along. Kind of smell his way into the role, as it were. But Lester had a fine set of cultural antennae. For instance, Lester invented the tag "punk rock." This is posterity's primary debt to the Bangs oeuvre.

Lester's not as famous now as he used to be, because he's been dead for some time, but in the '70s Lester wrote a million record reviews, for *Creem* and the *Village Voice* and *NME* and *Who Put the Bomp*. He liked to crouch over his old manual typewriter, and slam out wild Beat-influenced copy, while the Velvet Underground or the Stooges were on the box. This made life a hideous trial for the neighborhood, but in Lester's opinion the neighborhood pretty much had it coming. *Épater les bourgeois*, man!

Lester was a party animal. It was a professional obligation, actually. Lester was great fun to hang with, because he usually had a jagged speed-edge, which made him smart and bold and rude and crazy. Lester was a one-man band, until he got drunk. Nutmeg, Romilar, belladonna, crank, those substances Lester could handle. But booze seemed to crack him open, and an unexpected black dreck of rage and pain would come dripping out, like oil from a broken crankcase.

Toward the end—but Lester had no notion that the end was nigh. He'd given up the booze, more or less. Even a single beer often triggered frenzies of self-contempt. Lester was thirty-three, and sick of being groovy; he was restless, and the stuff he'd been writing lately no longer meshed with the surroundings that had made him what he was. Lester told his friends that he was gonna leave New York and go to Mexico and work on a deep, serious novel, about deep, serious issues, man. The real thing, this time. He was really gonna pin it down, get into the guts of Western Culture, what it really was, how it really felt.

But then, in April '82, Lester happened to catch the flu. Lester was living alone at the time, his mom, the Jehovah's Witness, having died recently. He had no one to make him chicken soup, and the flu really took him down. Tricky stuff, flu; it has a way of getting on top of you.

Lester ate some Darvon, but instead of giving him that buzzed-out float it usually did, the pills made him feel foggy and dull and desperate. He was too sick to leave his room, or hassle with doctors or ambulances, so instead he just did more Darvon. And his heart stopped.

There was nobody there to do anything about it, so he lay there for a while, until eventually a friend showed up, and found him.

▲ ▼ ▲

More true fax, pretty much: Dori Seda was born in 1951. She was a cartoonist, of the "underground" variety. Dori wasn't ever famous, certainly not in Lester's league, but then she didn't beat her chest and bend every ear in the effort to make herself a Living Legend, either. She had a lot of friends in San Francisco, anyway.

Dori did a "comic book" once, called *Lonely Nights*. An unusual "comic book" for those who haven't followed the "funnies" trade lately, as *Lonely Nights* was not particularly "funny," unless you really get a hoot from deeply revealing tales of frustrated personal relationships. Dori also did a lot of work for *WEIRDO* magazine, which emanated from the artistic circles of R. Crumb, he of "Keep On Truckin'" and "Fritz the Cat" fame.

R. Crumb once said: "Comics are words and pictures. You can do anything with words and pictures!" As a manifesto, it was a typically American declaration, and it was a truth that Dori held to be self-evident.

Dori wanted to be a True Artist in her own real-gone little '80s-esque medium. Comix, or "graphic narrative" if you want a snazzier cognomen for it, was a breaking thing, and she had to feel her way into it. You can see the struggle in her "comics"—always relentlessly autobiographical—Dori hanging around the "Cafè La Boheme" trying to trade food stamps for cigs; Dori living in drafty warehouses in the Shabby Hippie Section of San Francisco, sketching under the skylight and squabbling with her roommate's boyfriend; Dori trying to scrape up money to have her dog treated for mange.

Dori's comics are littered with dead cig-butts and toppled wine-bottles. She was, in a classic nutshell, Wild, Zany and Self-Destructive. In 1988 Dori was in a carwreck which cracked her pelvis and collarbone. She was laid-up, bored, and in pain. To kill time, she drank and smoked and took painkillers.

She caught the flu. She had friends who loved her, but nobody realized how badly off she was; probably she didn't know herself. She just went down hard, and couldn't get up alone. On February 26 her heart stopped. She was thirty-six.

So enough "true facts." Now for some comforting lies.

▲ ▼ ▲

As it happens, even while a malignant cloud of flu virus was lying in wait for the warm hospitable lungs of Lester Bangs, the Fate, Atropos, she who weaves the things that are to be, accidentally dropped a stitch. Knit one? Purl two? What the hell does it matter, anyway? It's just human lives, right?

So, Lester, instead of inhaling a cloud of invisible contagion from the exhalations of a passing junkie, is almost hit by a Yellow Cab. This mishap on the way back from the deli shocks Lester out of his dogmatic slumbers. High time, Lester concludes, to get out of this burg and down to sunny old Mexico. He's gonna tackle his great American novel: *All My Friends Are Hermits.*

So true. None of Lester's groovy friends go out much anymore. Always ahead of their time, Lester's Bohemian cadre are no longer rock and roll animals. They still wear black leather jackets, they still stay up all night, they still hate Ronald Reagan with fantastic virulence; but they never leave home. They pursue an unnamed lifestyle that sociologist Faith Popcorn (and how can you doubt anyone with a name like *Faith Popcorn*) will describe years later as "cocooning."

Lester has eight zillion rock, blues and jazz albums, crammed into his grubby NYC apartment. Books are piled feet deep on every available surface: Wm. Burroughs, Hunter Thompson, Celine, Kerouac, Huysmans, Foucault, and dozens of unsold copies of *Blondie,* Lester's book-length band-bio.

More albums and singles come in the mail every day. People used to send Lester records in the forlorn hope that he would review them. But now it's simply a tradition. Lester has transformed himself into a counter-cultural info-sump. People send him vinyl just because he's *Lester Bangs,* man!

Still jittery from his thrilling brush with death, Lester looks over this lifetime of loot with a surge of Sartrean nausea. He resists the urge to raid the fridge for his last desperate can of Blatz Beer. Instead, Lester snorts some speed, and calls an airline to plan his Mexican *wanderjahr.* After screaming in confusion at the hopeless stupid bitch of a receptionist, he gets a ticket to San Francisco, best he can do on short notice. He packs in a frenzy and splits.

Next morning finds Lester exhausted and wired and on the wrong side of the continent. He's brought nothing with him but an Army duffel-bag with his Olympia portable, some typing paper, shirts, assorted vials of dope, and a paperback copy of *Moby Dick,* which he's always meant to get around to re-reading.

Lester takes a cab out of the airport. He tells the cabbie to drive nowhere, feeling a vague compulsion to soak up the local vibe. San Francisco reminds him of his *Rolling Stone* days, back before Wenner fired him for being nasty to rock-stars. Fuck Wenner, he thinks. Fuck this city that was almost Avalon for a few months in '67 and has been on greased skids to Hell ever since.

The hilly half-familiar streets creep and wriggle with memories, avatars, talismans. Decadence, man, a no-kidding *death of affect*. It all ties in for Lester, in a bilious mental stew: snuff movies, discos, the cold-blooded whine of synthesizers, Pet Rocks, S&M, mindfuck self-improvement cults, Winning Through Intimidation, every aspect of the invisible war slowly eating the soul of the world.

After an hour he stops the cab at random. He needs coffee, white sugar, human beings, maybe a cheese Danish. Lester glimpses himself in the cab's window as he turns to pay: a chunky jobless thirty-three-year-old in a biker jacket, speed-pale dissipated New York face, Fu Manchu mustache looking pasted-on. Running to fat, running for shelter—no excuses, Bangs! Lester hands the driver a big tip. Chew on that, pal—you just drove the next Oswald Spengler.

Lester staggers into the cafè. It's crowded and stinks of patchouli and clove. He sees two chainsmoking punkettes hanging out at a Formica table. CBGB's types, but with California suntans. The kind of women, Lester thinks, who sit cross-legged on the floor and won't fuck you but are perfectly willing to describe in detail their highly complex postexistential *weltanschauung*. Tall and skinny and crazy-looking and bad news. Exactly his type, really. Lester sits down at their table and gives them his big rubber grin.

"Been having fun?" Lester says.

They look at him like he's crazy, which he is, but he wangles their names out: "Dori" and "Krystine." Dori's wearing fishnet stockings, cowboy boots, a strapless second-hand bodice-hugger covered with peeling pink feathers. Her long brown hair's streaked blonde. Krystine's got a black knit tank-top and a leather skirt and a skull-tattoo on her stomach.

Dori and Krystine have never heard of "Lester Bangs." They don't read much. They're *artists*. They do cartoons. Underground comix. Lester's mildly interested. Manifestations of the trash aesthetic always strongly appeal to him. It seems so American, the *good* America that is: the righteous wild America of rootless European refuse picking up discarded pop-junk and making it shine like the Koh-i-noor. To make "comic books" into *Art*—what a hopeless fucking effort, worse than rock and roll and you don't even get heavy bread for it. Lester says as much, to see what they'll do.

Krystine wanders off for a refill. Dori, who is mildly weirded-out by this tubby red-eyed stranger with his loud come-on, gives Lester her double-barreled brush-off. Which consists of opening up this Windex-clear vision into the Vent of Hell that is her daily life. Dori lights another Camel from the butt of the last, smiles at Lester with her big gappy front teeth and says brightly:

"You like *dogs*, Lester? I have this dog, and he has eczema and disgusting open sores all over his body, and he smells really bad...I can't get friends to come over because he likes to shove his nose right into their, you know, *crotch*...and go *Snort! Snort!*"

"I want to scream with wild dog joy in the smoking pit of a charnel house," Lester says.

Dori stares at him. "Did you make that up?"

"Yeah," Lester says. "Where were you when Elvis died?"

"You taking a survey on it?" Dori says.

"No, I just wondered," Lester says. "There was talk of having his corpse dug up, and the stomach analyzed. For dope, y'know. Can you *imagine* that? I mean, the *thrill* of sticking your hand and forearm into Elvis's rotted guts and slopping around in the stomach lining and liver and kidneys and coming up out of dead Elvis's innards triumphantly clutching some crumbs off a few Percodans and Desoxyns and 'ludes...and then this is the *real* thrill, Dori: you pop these crumbled-up bits of pills into your *own mouth* and bolt 'em down and get high on drugs that not only has Elvis Presley, the King, gotten high on, not the same brand mind you but the same *pills,* all slimy with little bits of his innards, so you've actually gotten to *eat* the King of Rock and Roll!"

"Who did you say you were?" Dori says. "A rock journalist? I thought you were putting me on. 'Lester Bangs,' that's a fucking weird name!"

Dori and Krystine have been up all night, dancing to the heroin head-banger vibes of Darby Crash and the Germs. Lester watches through hooded eyes: this Dori is a woman over thirty, but she's got this wacky air head routine down smooth, the Big Shiny Fun of the American Pop Bohemia. "Fuck you for believing I'm this shallow." Beneath the skin of her Attitude he can sense a bracing skeleton of pure desperation. There is hollow fear and sadness in the marrow of her bones. He's been writing about a topic just like this lately.

They talk a while, about the city mostly, about their variant scenes. Sparring, but he's interested. Dori yawns with pretended disinterest and gets up to leave. Lester notes that Dori is taller than he is. It doesn't bother him. He gets her phone number.

Lester crashes in a Holiday Inn. Next day he leaves town. He spends a week in a flophouse in Tijuana with his Great American Novel, which sucks. Despondent and terrified, he writes himself little cheering notes: "Burroughs was almost fifty when he wrote *Nova Express!* Hey boy, you only thirty-three! Burnt-out! Washed-up! Finished! A bit of flotsam! And in that flotsam your salvation! In that one grain of wood. In that one bit of that irrelevance. If you can bring yourself to describe it…"

It's no good. He's fucked. He knows he is, too, he's been reading over his scrapbooks lately, those clippings of yellowing newsprint, thinking: it was all a box, man! *El Cajon!* You'd think: wow, a groovy youth-rebel Rock Writer, he can talk about *anything,* can't he? Sex, dope, violence, Mazola parties with teenage Indonesian groupies, Nancy Reagan publicly fucked by a herd of clapped-out bull walruses…but when you actually READ a bunch of Lester Bangs Rock Reviews in a row, the whole shebang has a delicate hermetic whiff, like so many eighteenth-century sonnets. It is to dance in chains; it is to see the whole world through a little chromed window of Silva-Thin 'shades…

Lester Bangs is nothing if not a consummate romantic. He is, after all, a man who *really no kidding believes* that Rock and Roll Could Change the World, and when he writes something which isn't an impromptu free lesson on what's wrong with Western Culture and how it can't survive without grabbing itself by the backbrain and turning itself inside-out, he feels like he's wasted a day. Now Lester, fretfully abandoning his typewriter to stalk and kill flophouse roaches, comes to realize that HE will have to turn himself inside out. Grow, or die. Grow into something but he has no idea what. He feels beaten.

So Lester gets drunk. Starts with Tecate, works his way up to tequila. He wakes up with a savage hangover. Life seems hideous and utterly meaningless. He abandons himself to senseless impulse. Or, in alternate terms, Lester allows himself to follow the numinous artistic promptings of his holy intuition. He returns to San Francisco and calls Dori Seda.

Dori, in the meantime, has learned from friends that there is indeed a rock journalist named "Lester Bangs" who's actually kind of *famous.* He once appeared on stage with the J. Geils Band "playing" his typewriter. He's kind of a big deal, which probably accounts for his being kind of an asshole. On a dare, Dori calls Lester Bangs in New York, gets his answering machine, and recognizes the voice. It was him, all right. Through some cosmic freak, she met Lester Bangs and he tried to pick her up! No dice, though. More Lonely Nights, Dori!

Then Lester calls. He's back in town again. Dori's so flustered she ends up being nicer to him on the phone than she means to be.

She goes out with him. To rock clubs. Lester never has to pay; he just mutters at people, and they let him in and find him a table. Strangers rush up to gladhand Lester and jostle around the table and pay court. Lester finds the music mostly boring, and it's no pretense; he actually is bored, he's heard it all. He sits there sipping club sodas and handing out these little chips of witty guru insight to these sleaze-ass Hollywood guys and bighaired coke-whores in black Spandex. Like it was his *job*.

Dori can't believe he's going to all this trouble just to jump her bones. It's not like he can't get women, or like their own relationship is all that tremendously scintillating. Lester's whole set-up is alien. But it is kind of interesting, and doesn't demand much. All Dori has to do is dress in her sluttiest Goodwill get-up, and be This Chick With Lester. Dori likes being invisible, and watching people when they don't know she's looking. She can see in their eyes that Lester's people wonder Who The Hell Is She? Dori finds this really funny, and makes sketches of his creepiest acquaintances on cocktail napkins. At night she puts them in her sketchbooks and writes dialogue balloons. It's all really good material.

Lester's also very funny, in a way. He's smart, not just hustler-clever but scary-crazy smart, like he's sometimes profound without knowing it or even *wanting* it. But when he thinks he's being most amusing, is when he's actually the most incredibly depressing. It bothers her that he doesn't drink around her; it's a bad sign. He knows almost nothing about art or drawing, he dresses like a jerk, he dances like a trained bear. And she's fallen in love with him and she knows he's going to break her goddamned heart.

Lester has put his novel aside for the moment. Nothing new there; he's been working on it, in hopeless spasms, for ten years. But now juggling this affair takes all he's got.

Lester is terrified that this amazing woman is going to go to pieces on him. He's seen enough of her work now to recognize that she's possessed of some kind of genuine demented genius. He can smell it; the vibe pours off her like Everglades swamp-reek. Even in her frowsy houserobe and bunny slippers, hair a mess, no make-up, half-asleep, he can see something there like Dresden china, something fragile and precious. And the world seems like a maelstrom of jungle hate, sinking into entropy or gearing up for Armageddon, and what the hell can anybody do? How can he be happy with her and not be punished for it? How long can they break the rules before the Nova Police show?

But nothing horrible happens to them. They just go on living.

Then Lester blunders into a virulent cloud of Hollywood money. He's written a stupid and utterly commercial screenplay about the laff-a-minute fictional antics of a heavy-metal band, and without warning he gets eighty thousand dollars for it.

He's never had so much money in one piece before. He has, he realizes with dawning horror, sold out.

To mark the occasion Lester buys some freebase, six grams of crystal meth, and rents a big white Cadillac. He fast-talks Dori into joining him for a supernaturally cool Kerouac adventure into the Savage Heart of America, and they get in the car laughing like hyenas and take off for parts unknown.

Four days later they're in Kansas City. Lester's lying in the backseat in a jittery Hank Williams half-doze and Dori is driving. They have nothing to say, as they've been arguing viciously ever since Albuquerque.

Dori, white-knuckled, sinuses scorched with crank, loses it behind the wheel. Lester's slammed from the backseat and wakes up to find Dori knocked out and drizzling blood from a scalp wound. The Caddy's wrapped messily in the buckled ruins of a sidewalk mailbox.

Lester holds the resultant nightmare together for about two hours, which is long enough to flag down help and get Dori into a Kansas City trauma room.

He sits there, watching over her, convinced he's lost it, blown it; it's over, she'll hate him forever now. My God, she could have died! As soon as she comes to, he'll have to face her. The thought of this makes something buckle inside him. He flees the hospital in headlong panic.

He ends up in a sleazy little rock dive downtown where he jumps onto a table and picks a fight with the bouncer. After he's knocked down for the third time, he gets up screaming for the manager, how he's going to *ruin that motherfucker!* and the club's owner shows up, tired and red-faced and sweating. The owner, whose own tragedy must go mostly unexpressed here, is a fat white-haired cigar-chewing third-rater who attempted, and failed, to model his life on Elvis's Colonel Parker. He hates kids, he hates rock and roll, he hates the aggravation of smart-ass doped-up hippies screaming threats and pimping off the hard work of businessmen just trying to make a living.

He has Lester hauled to his office backstage and tells him all this. Toward the end, the owner's confused, almost plaintive, because he's never seen anyone as utterly, obviously, and desperately fucked-up as Lester Bangs, but who can still be coherent about it and use phrases like "rendered to the factor of machinehood" while mopping blood from his punched nose.

And Lester, trembling and red-eyed, tells him: fuck you Jack, I could run this jerkoff place, I could do everything you do blind drunk, and make this place a fucking *legend in American culture,* you booshwah sonofabitch.

Yeah punk if you had the money, the owner says.

I've *got* the money! Let's see your papers, you evil cracker bastard! In a few minutes Lester is the owner-to-be on a handshake and an earnest check.

Next day he brings Dori roses from the hospital shop downstairs. He sits next to the bed; they compare bruises, and Lester explains to her that he has just blown his fortune. They are now tied down and beaten in the corn-shucking heart of America. There is only one possible action left to complete this situation.

Three days later they are married in Kansas City by a justice of the peace.

Needless to say marriage does not solve any of their problems. It's a minor big deal for a while, gets mentioned in rock-mag gossip columns; they get some telegrams from friends, and Dori's mom seems pretty glad about it. They even get a nice note from Julie Burchill, the Marxist Amazon from *New Musical Express* who has quit the game to write for fashion mags, and her husband Tony Parsons the proverbial "hip young gunslinger" who now writes weird potboiler novels about racetrack gangsters. Tony & Julie seem to be making some kind of go of it. Kinda inspirational.

For a while Dori calls herself Dori Seda-Bangs, like her good friend Aline Kominsky-Crumb, but after a while she figures what's the use? and just calls herself Dori Bangs which sounds plenty weird enough on its own.

Lester can't say he's really *happy* or anything, but he's sure *busy*. He renames the club "Waxy's Travel Lounge" for some reason known only to himself. The club loses money quickly and consistently. After the first month Lester stops playing Lou Reed's *Metal Machine Music* before sets, and that helps attendance some, but Waxy's is still a club which books a lot of tiny weird college-circuit acts that Albert Average just doesn't get yet. Pretty soon they're broke again and living off Lester's reviews.

They'd be even worse off, except Dori does a series of promo posters for Waxy's that are so amazing they draw people in, even after they've been burned again and again on weird-ass bands only Lester can listen to.

After a couple of years they're still together, only they have shrieking crockery-throwing fights and once, when he's been drinking, Lester wrenches her arm so badly Dori's truly afraid it's broken. It isn't, luckily, but it's sure no great kick being Mrs. Lester Bangs. Dori was always afraid of this: that what he does is *work* and what she does is *cute*. How many Great Women Artists are there anyway, and what happened to 'em? They went into patching the wounded ego and picking up the dropped socks of Mr. Wonderful, that's what. No big mystery about it.

And besides, she's thirty-six and still barely scraping a living. She pedals her beat-up bike through the awful Kansas weather and sees these yuppies come by with these smarmy grins: hey, we don't *have* to invent our lives, our lives are *invented for us* and boy, does that ever save a lot of soul-searching.

But still somehow they blunder along; they have the occasional good break. Like when Lester turns over the club on Wednesdays to some black kids for (ecch!) "disco nite" and it turns out to be the beginning of a little Kansas City rap-scratch scene which actually makes the club some money. And "Polyrock," a band Lester hates at first but later champions to global megastardom, cuts a live album in Waxy's.

And Dori gets a contract to do one of those twenty-second animated logos for MTV, and really gets into it. It's fun, so she starts doing video animation work for (fairly) big bucks and even gets a Macintosh II from a video-hack admirer in Silicon Valley. Dori had always loathed, feared and despised *computers* but this thing is *different*. This is a kind of art that *nobody's ever done before* and has to be invented from leftovers, sweat, and thin air! It's wide open and 'way rad!

Lester's novel doesn't get anywhere, but he does write a book called *A Reasonable Guide to Horrible Noise* which becomes a hip coffeetable cult item with an admiring introduction by a trendy French semiotician. Among other things, this book introduces the term "chipster" which describes a kind of person who, well, didn't really *exist* before Lester described them but once he'd pointed 'em out it was obvious to everybody.

But they're still not *happy*. They both have a hard time taking the "marital fidelity" notion with anything like seriousness. They have a vicious fight once, over who gave who herpes, and Dori splits for six months and goes back to California. Where she looks up her old girlfriends and finds the survivors married with kids, and her old boyfriends are even seedier and more pathetic than Lester. What the hell, it's not happiness but it's something. She goes back to Lester. He's gratifyingly humble and appreciative for almost six weeks.

Waxy's does in fact become a cultural legend of sorts, but they don't pay you for that; and anyway it's hell to own a bar while attending sessions of Alcoholics Anonymous. So Lester gives in, and sells the club. He and Dori buy a house, which turns out to be far more hassle than it's worth, and then they go to Paris for a while, where they argue bitterly and squander all their remaining money.

When they come back Lester gets, of all the awful things, an academic gig. For a Kansas state college. Lester teaches Rock and Popular Culture. In the '70s there'd have been no room for such a hopeless skidrow weirdo in a, like, Serious Academic Environment, but it's the late '90s by now, and Lester has outlived the era of outlawhood. Because who are we kidding? Rock and Roll is a satellite-driven worldwide information-industry which is worth billions and *billions,* and if they don't study major industries then what the hell are the taxpayers funding colleges for?

Self-destruction is awfully tiring. After a while, they just give it up. They've lost the energy to flame-out, and it hurts too much; besides, it's less trouble just to live. They eat balanced meals, go to bed early, and attend faculty parties where Lester argues violently about the parking privileges.

Just after the turn of the century, Lester finally gets his novel published, but it seems quaint and dated, and gets panned and quickly remaindered. It would be nice to say that Lester's book was discovered years later as a Klassic of

Litratchur but the truth is that Lester's no novelist; what he is, is a cultural mutant, and what he has in the way of insight and energy has been eaten up. Subsumed by the Beast, man. What he thought and said made some kind of difference, but nowhere near as big a difference as he'd dreamed.

In the year 2015, Lester dies of a heart attack while shoveling snow off his lawn. Dori has him cremated, in one of those plasma-flash cremators that are all the mode in the 21st-cent. undertaking business. There's a nice respectful retrospective on Lester in the *New York Times Review of Books,* but the truth is Lester's pretty much a forgotten man; a colorful footnote for cultural historians who can see the twentieth century with the unflattering advantage of hindsight.

A year after Lester's death they demolish the remnants of Waxy's Travel Lounge to make room for a giant high-rise. Dori goes out to see the ruins. As she wanders amid the shockingly staid and unromantic rubble, there's another of those slips in the fabric of Fate, and Dori is approached by a Vision.

Thomas Hardy used to call it the Immanent Will and in China it might have been the Tao, but we late 20th-cent. postmoderns would probably call it something soothingly pseudoscientific like the "genetic imperative." Dori, being Dori, recognizes this glowing androgynous figure as The Child They Never Had.

"Don't worry, Mrs. Bangs," the Child tells her, "I might have died young of some ghastly disease, or grown up to shoot the President and break your heart, and anyhow you two woulda been no prize as parents." Dori can see herself and Lester in this Child, there's a definite nacreous gleam in its right eye that's Lester's, and the sharp quiet left eye is hers; but behind the eyes where there should be a living breathing human being there's *nothing,* just a kind of chill galactic twinkling.

"And don't feel guilty for outliving him either," the Child tells her, "because you're going to have what we laughingly call a natural death, which means you're going to die in the company of strangers hooked up to tubes when you're old and helpless."

"But did it *mean* anything?" Dori says.

"If you mean were you Immortal Artists leaving indelible graffiti in the concrete sidewalk of Time, no. You never walked the Earth as Gods, you were just people. But it's better to have a real life than no life." The Child shrugs. "You weren't all that happy together, but you *did* suit each other, and if you'd married other people instead, there would have been *four* people unhappy. So here's your consolation: you helped each other."

"So?" Dori says.

"So that's enough. Just to shelter each other, and help each other up. Everything else is gravy. Someday, no matter what, you go down forever. Art can't make you immortal. Art can't Change the World. Art can't even heal your soul. All it can do is maybe ease the pain a bit or make you feel more awake. And that's enough. It only matters as much as it matters, which is zilch to an ice-cold interstellar Cosmic Principle like yours truly. But if you try to live by my standards it will only kill you faster. By your own standards, you did pretty good, really."

"Well okay then," Dori says.

After this purportedly earth-shattering mystical encounter, her life simply went on, day following day, just like always. Dori gave up computer-art; it was too hairy trying to keep up with the hotshot high-tech cutting edge, and kind of undignified, when you came right down to it. Better to leave that to hungry kids. She was idle for a while, feeling quiet inside, but finally she took up watercolors. For a while Dori played the Crazy Old Lady Artist and was kind of a mainstay of the Kansas regionalist art scene. Granted, Dori was no Georgia O'Keeffe, but she was working, and living, and she touched a few people's lives.

▲ ▼ ▲

Or, at least, Dori surely would have touched those people, if she'd been there to do it. But of course she wasn't, and didn't. Dori Seda never met Lester Bangs. Two simple real-life acts of human caring, at the proper moment, might have saved them both; but when those moments came, they had no one, not even each other. And so they went down into darkness, like skaters, breaking through the hard bright shiny surface of our true-facts world.

Today I made this white paper dream to cover the holes they left.

PART III:

THE
LEGGY STARLITZ
STORIES

Hollywood Kremlin

The ZIL-135 was vital to national security. Therefore, it was built only in Russia. It looked it, too.

The ZIL was a Red Army battlefield truck, with eight monster rubber-lugged wheels and a ten-ton canvas-topped flatbed. This particular ZIL, which had a busted suspension and four burned-out gears, sat in darkness beside a makeshift airstrip. The place stank of kerosene, diesel, tarmac, and the smoke of guttering runway flares. All of it wrapped in the cricket-shrieking night of rural Azerbaijan.

Azerbaijan was a southern Soviet province, with 8 million citizens and thirty-three thousand square miles. Azerbaijan bordered on all kinds of trouble: Iran, Turkey, the highly polluted Caspian Sea, and 3.5 million angry Soviet Armenians.

From within the ZIL's cramped little khaki-colored cab came the crisp beeping of a digital watch.

The driver yanked back the shoddy sleeve of his secondhand Red Army jacket and pressed a watch stud. A dial light glowed, showing thirty seconds from midnight. The driver grinned and mashed more little buttons with his blunt, precise fingers. The watch emitted a twittering Japanese folk tune.

The driver, hanging on to the ZIL's no-power, gut-busting steering wheel, leaned far out the open door and squinted at the horizon. A phantom silhouette slid across the southern stars—a plane without running lights, painted black for night flight.

The driver gulped from a Stolichnaya bottle and lit a Marlboro.

The flare of his Cricket lighter briefly threw his blurred yellow reflection against the ZIL's windshield. He was unshaven, pumpkin-faced, bristle-headed. His eyes were slitted, yet somehow malignantly radiant with preternatural survival instincts. The driver's name was Leggy Starlitz. The locals, who knew no better, called him "Lekhi Starlits."

Starlitz kicked the cab's rusty door open and climbed down the ZIL's iron rungs.

The black plane hit tarmac, bounced drunkenly down the potholed strip, and taxied up. It was a twin-engine Soviet military turboprop, an Ilyushin-14.

Starlitz beckoned at the spyplane with a pair of orange semaphore paddles. He waved it along brusquely. He was not a big fan of the Ilyushin-14.

The IL-14 was already obsolete in the high-tech Soviet Air Force. So the aging planes had been consigned to the puppet Air Force of the Democratic

Republic of Afghanistan: the DRAAF. This plane had a big Afghan logo clumsily painted over its Soviet red star. The DRAAF logo was a smaller, fatter, maroon-colored star, ringed in an inviting target circle of red, green and black. It looked a lot like a Texaco sign.

Still, the IL-14 was the best spyplane that the DRAAF had to offer. It had fine range and speed; it could fly smuggling runs under the Iranian radar, all the way from Kabul to Soviet Azerbaijan.

Starlitz much preferred the DRAAF's antique "Badger" medium bombers. Badgers had good range and superb cargo capacity. You could haul anything in a Badger. Trucks, refugees, chemical feedstocks…the works.

It was too bad that the Badger was such a hog to fly. The smugglers had given the Badger up. For months they'd been embezzling tons of aviation kerosene from the Afghan Air Force fuel dumps. The thievery was becoming too obvious, even for the utterly corrupt Afghan military.

Starlitz guided the creeping, storm-colored plane into the makeshift airstrip's hangar. The hangar was a tin-roofed livestock barn, built to the colossal proportions of a Soviet collective farm. The morale of the collectivized peasants had been lousy, though, and all the cattle had starved to death during the Brezhnev era. Now the barn was free for new restructured uses: something with a lot more initiative, a lot more up-to-date.

The plane's engines died, their eighteen cylinders coughing into echoing silence. Starlitz heaved concrete parking blocks under the nosewheels. He propped a paint-stained wooden ladder against the cockpit.

The aircraft's bulletproof canopy creaked up and open. A pilot in an earflapped leather helmet leaned out on one elbow, an oxygen mask dangling from his neck.

"How's it going, ace?" Starlitz said in his foully accented dog-Russian.

"Where are the disembarkation stairs?" demanded the pilot. He was Captain Pulat R. Khoklov, a Soviet "adviser" to the DRAAF.

"Huh?" Starlitz said.

Khoklov frowned. "You know very well, Comrade Starlits. The device that rolls here on wheels, with the proper sturdy metal steps, for my descending."

"Oh. *That,*" Starlitz said. "I dunno, man. I guess somebody sold it."

"Where is the rest of your ground crew?" said Captain Khoklov. The handsome young pilot's eyelids were reddened and his tapered fingertips were corpse-pale from Dexedrine. It had been a long flight. The IL-14 was a two-man plane, but Khoklov flew it alone.

Khoklov and his pals didn't trust the DRAAF's native pilots. In 1985 the Afghans had mutinied and torched twenty of their best MiG fighters on the ground at Shindand Air Base. Since that incident, most DRAAF missions had been flown by Russian pilots, "unofficially." Pakistani border violations, civilian bombings, a little gas work…the sort of mission where DRAAF cover came in handy.

Some DRAAF missions, though, were far more "unofficial" than others.

Starlitz grinned up at the pilot. "The ground crew's on strike, comrade," he said. "Politics. 'The nationalities problem.' You know how it is here in Azerbaijan."

Khoklov was scandalized. "They can't strike against *smugglers!* We're not the government! We are a criminal private-enterprise operation!"

"They *know* that, man," Starlitz said. "But they wanted to show solidarity. With their fellow Armenian Christians. Against the Moslem Azerbaijanis."

"You should not have let your Armenian workers go," Khoklov said. "They can't be allowed to run riot just as they please!"

"What the hey," Starlitz said. "Can't *make* 'em work."

"Of course you can," Khoklov said, surprised.

Starlitz shrugged. "Tell it to Gorbachev…Forget the stairs. Use the paint ladder, ace. Nobody's looking."

With reluctance, Khoklov abandoned his dignity. He shrugged out of his harness, set his mask and helmet aside, and clambered down.

Khoklov's DRAAF flight jacket was gaudy with mission patches. Beneath it he sported a civilian Afghan blouse of hand-embroidered paisley, and a white silk ascot. Walkman earphones bracketed his neck. The antique wailing of the Jefferson Airplane rang faintly from the Walkman's foam-padded speakers.

Khoklov stretched and twisted, his spine popping loudly. He walked to the edge of the hangar and peered warily into the darkness, as if suspecting ambush from local unfriendlies. Nothing whatever happened. Khoklov sighed and shook himself. He tiptoed into darkness to relieve himself on the tarmac.

Starlitz coupled the plane's nosewheel to the drawbar of a small diesel tractor.

Khoklov returned. He looked at Starlitz gravely, his poet's face anemic in the hangar's naked overhead lights. "You remained here faithfully, all alone, Comrade Starlits?"

"Yeah."

"How unusual. You yourself are not Armenian?"

"I'm not religious," Starlitz said. He offered Khoklov a Marlboro.

Khoklov examined the cigarette's brand name, nodded, and accepted a light. "What is your ethnic nationality, Comrade Starlits? I have often wondered."

"I'm an Uzbek," Starlitz said.

Khoklov thought it over, breathing smoke through his nose. "An Uzbek," he said at last. "I suppose I could believe that, if I really tried."

"My mom was a Kirghiz," Starlitz said glibly. "What's in the plane this time, ace? Good cargo?"

"Excellent cargo," Khoklov said. "But you have no crew to unload it!"

"I can handle it all myself." Starlitz pointed overhead. "I rigged some pulleys. And I just tuned up the forklift. I can improvise, ace, no problem."

"But that isn't permitted," Khoklov said. "One individual can't replace a team, through some private whim of his own! The entire work team is at fault. They must all be disciplined. Otherwise there will be recurrences of this irresponsible behavior."

"Big deal," Starlitz said, setting to work. "The job gets done anyway. The system is functional, ace. So who cares?"

"With such an incorrect attitude from their team leader, no wonder things have come to grief here," Khoklov observed. "You had better work like a Hero of Labor, comrade. Otherwise it will delay my return to base." Khoklov scowled. "And that would be hard to explain."

"Can't have that," Starlitz said lazily. "You might get transferred to Siberia or something. Not much fun, ace."

"I've already been to Siberia, and there is plenty of fun," Khoklov said. "We scrambled every day against Yankee spyplanes…And Korean airliners. If there's a difference." He shrugged.

Starlitz moved the ladder down the plane's fuselage, past a long, spiky row of embedded ELINT antennas. He propped the ladder beside a radome blister, climbed up, and opened the plane's bay.

The Ilyushin's electronic spygear had been partially stripped, replaced with tarped-down heaps and stacks of contraband. Starlitz bonked his head on the plane's low bulkhead. "Damn," he said. "I sure miss those Badgers."

"Be grateful we have aircraft at all!" Khoklov said. He climbed the ladder and peered in curiously. "Think how many mule-loads of treasure have flown in my plane tonight. Romantic secret caravans, creeping slowly over the Khyber Pass…And this is just a fraction of the secret trade. Many mules die in the minefields."

"Toss me that pulley hook, ace." Starlitz swung out a strapped-up stack of Hitachi videocassette recorders.

Starlitz, with methodic efficiency, drove forklift-loads of loot from the hangar out to the truck. Korean "Gold Star" tape players. Compact discs of re-mixed jazz classics. Fifty-kilo bricks of fudge-soft black Afghani hashish. Ten crates of J&B Scotch. A box of foil-sealed lubricated condoms, items of avid and fabulous rarity. Two hundred red cartons of Dunhills, still in their cellophane. Black nylon panty hose.

And gold. Gold czarist rubles, the lifeblood of the Soviet black economy. The original slim supply of nineteenth-century imperial rubles couldn't meet the frenzied modern demand, so they were counterfeited especially for the Soviet market, by goldsmiths in Egypt, Lebanon and Pakistan. The rubles came sealed in long strips of transparent plastic, for use in money belts.

Khoklov was fidgeting. "We have re-created the Arabian Nights," he said, running a flat ribbon of plasticized bullion over his sleeve. He leaned against a dusty concrete feeding trough. "It is Ali Baba and the forty *shabashniki*... We meant to 'smash the last vestiges of feudalism.' We meant to 'defend the socialist revolution.' All we have really done is create a thieves' market worthy of legend! With ourselves as the eager customers."

Khoklov lit a fresh Dunhill from the stub of the last. "You should see Kabul today, Comrade Starlits. It's still a vile medieval dump, but every alleyway is full of whores and thieves, every breed of petty capitalist! They tug our sleeves and offer us smuggled Western luxuries we could never find at home. Even the mujihadeen bandits drop their Yankee rifles to sell us soap and aspirin. Now that we're leaving, no one thinks of anything but backdoor hustling. We are all desperate for one last tasty drink of Coca-Cola, before our Afghan adventure is over."

"You sound a little wired, ace," Starlitz said. "You could lend me a hand, you know. Might get the kinks out."

"Not my assignment," Khoklov sniffed. "You can take your share of all this, comrade. Be content."

"What with the trouble it took, you'd think this junk would have more class," Starlitz said. He slid down the ladder with a cardboard box.

"Ah!" said Khoklov. "So it's glamour you want, my grimy Uzbek friend? You have it there in your hands. A wonderful Hollywood movie! Give me that box."

Starlitz tossed it to him. Khoklov ripped it open. "I must take a few cassettes for my fellows at DRAAF. They love this film. *Top Gun!* Yankee pilots kill Moslems in it. They strafe with F-16s, in many excellent flying-combat scenes!"

"Hollywood," Starlitz said. "A bunch of crap."

Khoklov shook his head carefully. "The Yankees will have to kill the Moslems, now that we're giving it up! Libya, that Persian Gulf business...It's only a matter of time." Khoklov began stuffing videocassettes into his flight jacket. He took a handgun from within the jacket and set it on the edge of the trough.

"Cool!" Starlitz said, staring at it. "What model is that?"

"It's a war trophy," Khoklov said. "A luck charm, is all."

"Lemme look, ace."

Khoklov showed him the gun.

"Looks like a Czech 'Skorpion' 5.66 millimeter," Starlitz said. "Something really weird about it, though..."

"It's homemade," Khoklov said. "An Afghan village blacksmith copied it. They are clever as monkeys with their hands." He shook his head. "It's pig-iron, hand-drilled...You can see where he engraved some little flowers into the pistol butt."

"Wow!" Starlitz exulted. "How much?"

"It's not for sale, comrade."

Starlitz reached into a pocket of his tattered Levi's and pulled out a fat roll of dollars, held with a twist of wire. "Say when, ace." He began peeling off bills and slapping them down: one hundred, two hundred...

"That's enough," Khoklov said after a moment. He examined the bills carefully, his pale hands shaking a little. "These are real American dollars! Where did you get all this?"

"Found it in a turnip patch," Starlitz said. He crammed the wad carelessly back into his jeans, then lifted the gun with reverence, and sniffed its barrel. "You ever fire this thing?"

"No. But its first owner did. At the people's fraternal forces."

"Huh. It'd be better if it were mint. It's beautiful anyway, though." Starlitz twirled the pistol on one finger, grinning triumphantly. "Too bad there's no safety catch."

"The Afghans never bother with them."

"Neither do I," Starlitz said. He stuffed the gun in the back of his jeans.

There were odds and ends in the plane, and one big item left: a Whirlpool clothes washer in bright lemon-yellow enamel. Starlitz manhandled it into the back of the ZIL with the other loot, and carefully laced the truck's canvas, hiding everything from view.

"Well, that's about it," Starlitz said, dusting his callused hands. "Now we'll get you gassed up and out of here, ace."

"About time," Khoklov said. He dry-swallowed a pair of white tablets from a gunmetal pillbox. "Next time be sure your worthless crew of Armenian ethnics is fully prepared for my arrival."

Starlitz jammed a big tin funnel into the Ilyushin's starboard wing tank. Against the hangar wall were two long rows of oily jerry cans, full of aviation kerosene. Starlitz hoisted a can one-handed to his shoulder and began decanting fuel, humming to himself. It was a slow process. As the pills came on, impatience struck Khoklov. He lugged jerry cans two-handed to the port wing tank, waddling with the weight.

The first row of cans was emptied. Khoklov started on the second. He heaved at a can and stumbled backward. "This one is empty!" he said. He tried the next. "This one, too."

The entire second row of cans had been drained. Khoklov kicked the final can across the hangar with a hollow bonging. "We've been robbed!"

"Looks that way," Starlitz admitted.

"Your thieving Armenians!" Khoklov shouted. "They have embezzled the fuel! For a few lousy black-market rubles, they have stranded me here! My God, I'm finished!"

"Coulda been worse," Starlitz offered. "They coulda filled the cans with water instead. Flying low and fast, you'da pranged for sure." He thought it over. "Or bailed out over Iran. That woulda been hairy, ace."

"But they've ruined me! Ruined the whole operation! How could they be such meatheads?"

"Beats me," Starlitz said. "Times are tough here; fuel's in short supply…But be cool. We'll find you some go-juice somehow. The Boss must have some. The Boss may be mean, and ruthless, and greedy, and totally corrupt, but he's not *stupid,* y'know. He's probably got kerosene hoarded just in case."

"He'd better!" Khoklov said.

"We'll go to the Estate and ask around," Starlitz told him. "I'll give you a lift in the truck."

Khoklov's panic faded. He tagged after Starlitz and climbed up into the cab of the ZIL. Starlitz steered the truck down the airstrip, mashing the runway flares into embers under the ZIL's giant wheels. He flicked on the ZIL's headlights and turned onto a dirt road.

"Such a big truck and such a nasty little cab," Khoklov griped. He killed what was left of the vodka. Then he stared moodily out the windshield, at tall weeds ghost-pale by the roadside. "This situation's an outrage. The whole nation has lost its bearings, if you ask me. Especially in the provinces. It's getting very bad here, isn't it?"

"Yeah, this used to be good cropland," Starlitz said.

"Never mind the mere physical landscape," Khoklov scoffed. "I mean *politically,* comrade. Even lousy black marketeers openly defy Party authority."

"The Party *is* the black marketeers, ace. It couldn't work any other way."

The headquarters of the local agricultural complex had an official name, something with a long Cyrillic acronym. To those who knew about the place, it was just the Estate. It was the country seat of the Party chairman of the Azerbaijani Soviet Socialist Republic. The chairman had a proper name, too, but no one used it. He was generally known as "the Boss."

Starlitz took the back entrance through the high, wire-topped walls. It was late, and he didn't want to wake the armed guards in their marble kiosks in the front. He thoughtfully parked the monster truck by the racehorse stables, where its booming diesel would not disturb the slumber of the staff.

Starlitz and Khoklov walked across a groomed lawn, slick with peacock droppings. Massive sprinklers, purloined from a farm project, clanked and hissed above the croquet grounds. Starlitz paused to tie his shoe under the giant concrete statue of Lenin. Khoklov chased some monster goldfish away in the fountain, and drank from his hands.

Starlitz yanked a bell-pull at one of the back doors. There was no response. Starlitz kicked the door heartily with his tattered Keds high-top sneaker. Lights came on inside, and a butler showed, in pants and undershirt.

This man was not officially a "butler," but a production-team brigade leader for the collective farm. The distinction didn't mean much. The butler's name was Yan "Cross-Eyes" Rakotov. Rakotov, who was corpulent and scarred, favored the two of them with his eerie gaze. "Now what?" he said.

"Need some kerosene," Starlitz said.

"How much?"

"Maybe five hundred liters?" Starlitz said.

Rakotov showed no surprise. "Would gasoline do?" he said. Khoklov shook his head. Rakotov thought about it. "How about pure alcohol? I think we have enough to fill an airplane. Ever since the Kremlin's sobriety campaign started, we've been bringing it in by the truckload."

Rakotov's wife showed up, squint-eyed and clutching her houserobe. "You bastard drunks!" she hissed. *"Shabashniki!* Buying booze at this time of night! Go home and let good Communists sleep in peace!"

"Shut up, woman," Rakotov said. "Look, this is pilot here."

"Oh," said Mrs. Rakotov, startled. "Sorry; Comrade Pilot! Would you like some nice tea? Did you bring any nylons?"

"Life is hard," Rakotov muttered. "I know the Boss keeps kerosene, but I think it's stored in town. He's in town now, you know. Political problems."

"Too bad," Starlitz said.

"Yes, he left this morning. Took the limousine, the kitchen bus, the cooks, his personal staff, even the live baby lamb for his lunch. He said not to expect him back for at least a week." Rakotov straightened. "So you two can regard me as the Boss here, for the time being."

"My people expect *me* back by morning!" Khoklov shouted. "There's going to be big trouble when I fail to show at the Kabul air base!"

Rakotov's giddy eyes narrowed. "Really? Why's that?"

"A military plane is not like one of your rural buses, comrade! There's no excuse for a failure to show up! And if I return too late, they'll know I have landed somewhere, illegally! The whole business here will be exposed!"

"That would be a terrible tragedy for a great many people," Rakotov said slowly. He cleared his throat. "Say...I just remembered something. We have an underground fuel cistern, in the east wing. Why don't you come with me, Comrade Pilot? We can inspect it."

"Good idea!" Starlitz broke in. "There's some empty jerry cans in the truck. Me and the ace here will fetch 'em. We'll be right back." He grabbed Khoklov's sleeve.

Khoklov came reluctantly across the darkened lawn. "Can't you wake up some local peasants, and have them do this haulage labor? They ought to do *something*; God knows they're not growing any food here."

Starlitz lowered his voice. "Wise up, ace. The east wing is a dungeon, man, a big underground bunker."

"But..." Khoklov hesitated. "You really think...? But I'm a Red Army officer!"

"So what? The Boss has already got a State Farm chief in there, a personnel director, a couple of busybody snoops from Internal Affairs...He bottles up anybody he likes, and there's no appeal, no recourse—the guy runs everything. He's a top Party Moslem, man, the closest thing to Genghis Khan." Starlitz urged Khoklov up into the truck. "Think it over from their angle, ace. If you just vanish here, DRAAF will think you've been killed on duty. Hit by ack-ack, down somewhere in rough terrain. Nothing to tie you to the Boss, or Azerbaijan, or the black market."

"They'd put me in a dungeon?"

"They can't let you run around loose here—you're AWOL, with no residence passport. And you're Russian, too—you could never pass for a local."

"My God!" Khoklov put his head in his hands. "I'm done for!"

Starlitz threw the truck into gear. "How long have you *been* in the military, man? Show some initiative, for Christ's sake."

"What are you doing?" Khoklov said.

"Winging it," Starlitz said, driving off. "After all, there's a lotta possibilities." He thumbed over his shoulder. "We got a truckload of very heavy capital back there." He shifted his denim-clad butt on the busted springs of the truck seat. "And pretty soon you'll be officially dead, ace. That's kind of a neat thing to be, actually..."

"What's the point of this? What can we possibly accomplish, all by ourselves, out here?"

"Well, lemme think out loud," Starlitz said cheerily, taking a corner with a squeal. "We do have half a load of fuel in your plane; that's something, at least...Kabul's definitely out of range, but you could make Turkey, easy. There's a big NATO base in Kars, just over the border from Tbilisi. Maybe you could land there. The West would love to have an Ilyushin-14. It'd be the biggest haul for 'em since Lieutenant Belenko flew his MiG-25 to Japan."

"That's *treason*!" Khoklov shouted.

"Yeah, it is," Starlitz said indifferently. "And that's one tough border, too...Not like Iran, y'know. You might pull a Matthias Rust on the way out, if you're a real hot-dog terrain flyer. But there's no way you're gonna get your crate past NATO."

"Don't insult me by questioning my professional abilities!" Khoklov said. "I could do it, easily enough! But I am a loyal Soviet officer, not a traitor to my Motherland like Viktor Ivanovich Belenko."

"I hear old Viktor's living somewhere near Washington now," Starlitz said. "Got big cars, blondes, whiskey…But if that's not for you, it's fine with me, ace…" Starlitz grinned toothily.

"The criminal life must be rotting your brain," Khoklov said, crossing his arms. His chin sank slowly into the white silk of his ascot. "Besides, they wouldn't let me fly, would they? The Yankees would never let me fly their best aircraft. An F-16, say. A Lockheed SR-71." His voice was reverent.

"You'd be rich, though," Starlitz said. "You could buy, like…a Cessna, all for yourself."

Khoklov laughed harshly. "A civilian subsonic. No, thank you."

"I know how ya feel," Starlitz admitted. "Well, ace, we gotta find you your fuel. We got a chance, at least, if we can find the Boss. I'm gonna roll this baby into town."

The private police force at the border of the collective farm did not stop them. They were used to heavily loaded trucks leaving at odd hours. Starlitz slung the ZIL onto the neatly paved road. Through no accident, this was the best-maintained road in Azerbaijan. At this hour it was almost deserted. Starlitz ratcheted his manual accelerator up to top speed.

The road was lined for miles with elegant shade trees, a transplanted species unsuited to the local climate. The dead trees' peeling trunks zipped by in the headlights, their bare twigs ripped by the ZIL's backwash. Planting the trees had been an attractive idea, carried out with complete incompetence. The Boss wouldn't mind, however. Abject failure always made him redouble his efforts.

Khoklov looked jittery. He was having second thoughts. "Why are you doing this, Starlits?" he shouted over the blasting roar of the engine. "Why are you taking such trouble for my sake? I don't understand your motives."

Starlitz felt for a cigarette, speeding along one-handed. "I'm the *ground crew,* man. I handle the planes. That's my *function.*"

"But won't you get in trouble for these actions? You could have let Rakotov put me in the prison. Destroy all evidence, and so forth."

Starlitz was disgusted. "That's no use. That won't make the plane *fly,* man."

"Oh," Khoklov said.

"The system must be maintained, ace." Starlitz lit up with a flick of the Cricket, his eyes glazed with eerie ontological assurance. "It's…what there *is.* As long as it lasts." He blew smoke.

"Right," Khoklov said uneasily. He put on his Walkman headphones and searched in his jacket for a cassette. Soon the reedy buzz of The Doors percolated out past his translucent, close-cropped ears.

They drove into the capital of Nagorno-Karabakh, the most miserable province of the Azerbaijani Soviet Socialist Republic. The town had never fully recovered from the Civil War of the twenties, or the purges of the thirties, or even the Great Patriotic War of the forties. Collapse had become the status quo.

Most of the townsfolk were Armenians, an ethnic group whom everyone else within thousands of kilometers delighted in oppressing. Thanks to Stalin, a big lump of lost Armenians had been caught here in the middle of Azerbaijan, like a Christian prune in a Moslem fruitcake. And here they were still, with their cruddy, flyspecked stores and beat-up, dusty churches, and cracked streets blocked off for "repair" for years at a time.

Starlitz drove his truck down an alley, through towering, overcrowded apartment blocks built of substandard concrete. Discarded protest signs crunched under the ZIL's monster tires. The plaza still stank of tear gas; empty canisters of it lay around like Schlitz cans after a beer bust. There were sticky patches of blood, and odd greenish lumps that were the manure of police horses.

A large and hideous government building, in Stalinesque fifties gingerbread, had been stoned by the mob. Shattered glass lay before its gaping windows, glinting in the headlights.

Starlitz drove on warily. The crowd had pulled a big ferroconcrete statue from its pedestal in the center of the plaza. After its sudden descent down to earth, the statue's stone head had broken into disenchanting rubble. Chunks of its face had been stolen, presumably as souvenirs.

"Wonder who that was?" Starlitz said. "That statue, I mean."

"Some local ruffian, no doubt," Khoklov said. He shook his head. "At heart, the People are still loyal to the Soviet ideals of the Party. It is only the provincial distortions of the economy that have provoked this ugly event."

"Oh," said Starlitz. "Good. For a minute I figured there was some kinda real trouble here."

"You mean, like an ethnic, nationalist mass movement, demanding self-determination and a devolution of centralized state power?" Khoklov said. "No, comrade; a serious political analysis will show that's not the true case at all. I'm sure that a measured restructuring of state resources, and a cautious but thorough redressing of their economic grievances, will soon lead the Armenians back to the path of socialist cooperation."

"Nice to know somebody still reads *Pravda*," Starlitz said. He brightened. "Look, ace, we're in luck. Here come some cops!"

An open-topped jeep came tearing across the plaza, crammed with uniformed local police in riot helmets. Khoklov went pale and shrank down in his seat, but Starlitz stopped the ZIL and climbed out.

The jeep screeched up short. A militia sergeant jumped out and menaced Starlitz with a riot baton. "Your papers!"

"Never mind that crap," Starlitz told him. "Where have you been? We've been waiting."

"What?" the sergeant said.

"This is a special shipment for the Boss," Starlitz said, pointing at the truck. "Aren't you our police escort?"

"No! What are you doing here at this hour?"

"Isn't it obvious?" Starlitz said. "I can't drive a black-market truck in broad daylight, through streets full of thieving, rioting Armenians! There've been enough delays in this shipment already! If you're not our special escort, then where the hell are they?"

"Everyone's doing overtime," the cop said wearily. "Perhaps we somehow lost track of our Party Chairman's whims. We're trying to keep order here. There's been confusion."

"Hell," Starlitz said, kicking at a pried-up cobblestone. "I'm gonna catch it for this...Look, stop whatever you're doing, and take us straight to the Boss, okay? I'll make it worth your while. Come round to the back of the truck. Nobody'll miss a little off the top."

The sergeant grinned slowly. He waved the other cops into the back of the ZIL. After some gleeful argument, they decamped with a video recorder and six bottles of J&B Scotch.

"You're robbing me," Starlitz complained.

The jeep led the way. This was useful, as it got them past the nervous police checkpoints around the Boss's urban headquarters.

Officially, this place was a Workers' Palace of Culture, built years ago for a puppet trade union of textile workers. The textile workers now existed only on paper, as the Azerbaijani cotton crops had been disastrous for years. The Boss had put the building to his own uses, and improved it considerably, with lavish use of stolen state materials and impressed labor. The Boss's five-story city palace looked like a diseased wedding cake, brilliantly lit and painted in ghastly pastels.

Inside the courtyard the palace grounds were clustered with the black limousines of Party notables. The Boss's customary caravan of brushed-aluminum tour buses was parked on the lawn, next to a gaily frilled pavilion with picnic tables and fire-blackened shish-kebab pits. It was very late, and a meeting was in the final throes of dissolution. Vomiting Azerbaijani bigwigs tottered to their limos, assisted by mistresses and functionaries.

Starlitz parked the ZIL atop a fragrant row of oleander bushes.

"What's going on here?" Khoklov said, staring in disbelief. "Some kind of *festival?*"

"Yeah." Starlitz looked at Khoklov critically. "Straighten up that tie you're wearing, or whatever it is." Starlitz leaned from the window to peer into the ZIL's rearview mirror. He scrubbed grease from his face with his sleeve, then licked his hand and smeared at his hair. "We gotta pass for Beautiful People, okay?" he said. "Smoke those Marlboros like you get 'em every day, and make sure everybody sees you've got a Walkman."

The double doors of the palace were propped wide open. Starlitz and Khoklov swaggered in boldly. They followed music to a ground-floor workers' gymnasium, refitted to mimic a ballroom. A homemade mirror-ball wobbled on the ceiling before a lighted stage with heavy canvas draperies. Small tables lined the walls under chintzy fake gas lamps with forty-watt reddish bulbs.

The band had played its final set; they were packing up their *bazoukis* and a brace of slotted microphones the size of bread loaves. The velvet sound of a smuggled Mel Torme tape came from the speakers. Most of the Party bigwigs were already gone; there were a dozen tired teenage Armenian hookers, dance girls, sitting in a line of folding chairs. At the sight of Khoklov's air force jacket, and Starlitz's bogus Red Army get-up, they started chattering and elbowing each other.

A sinuous woman with dark, high-piled hair approached them across the dance floor. She wore sequined velvet trousers, high-heeled pumps, and a fancy embroidered jacket. Starlitz straightened warily.

"Oh," the woman said, smiling with a flash of pointed teeth. "So it's you. What a pleasant surprise."

Starlitz tried an ingratiating grin. "Good evening, Tamara Akhmedovna."

"I thought you two were soldiers," Tamara said. She fingered the lapel of Starlitz's secondhand Red Army jacket. "You shouldn't wear clothes like this into town. People will talk."

"Who is this charming lady?" Khoklov said.

"This is the Boss's wife, ace," Starlitz muttered. "'The Sultana.'"

"Please!" Tamara said, dimpling. "No friend of mine calls me that. A simple 'Madame Party Chairman' will do…" Tamara's kohl-lined, liquid eyes studied Khoklov with languorous attention. "Who is this mysterious young man, and why is he dressed like an airman?"

"Uh, we had a little trouble down by the airstrip, Tamara…Could we have a word outside, or something?"

Tamara's face went flinty for a moment. "Very well," she said. "Wait here, while I see that the artistes are properly compensated…" She drifted away.

"Good God!" Khoklov whispered, grabbing Starlitz's elbow. "She's beautiful! What's she doing married to that old ogre?"

"Tamara's the biggest black-market hustler in Azerbaijan," Starlitz said, brushing Khoklov's hand away. "Her husband does everything illegal in Tamara's name. She's got a million Moslem relatives; they're all on the take. They smuggle everything, from diamonds to bananas. They carry big, sharp knives, too. So keep your pants on."

Tamara returned, having fee'd off the musicians and hookers. "May I suggest a stroll in the garden?" she said, arching her brows. "The Bukhara roses are in bloom."

"That's swell," Starlitz said. They went outside, away from the palace's lavish inner network of listening devices. Starlitz made introductions.

"So you're our brave pilot?" Tamara said. "How nice to meet you. If it weren't for you, Captain, I wouldn't have this Final Net hair spray." She touched her coiffure. "It holds up even when I no longer can."

"Your hair does look lovely," Khoklov said. "And you speak such excellent Russian, too. It's a delight to the ear."

"Listen, Tamara," Starlitz broke in. "We need five hundred liters of aviation kerosene. Old Cross-Eyes, back at the farm, said the Boss might have some."

"My husband is sleeping," Tamara said. "He's had a very trying day. All this political turmoil. He deserves his rest, poor dear."

"I must get fuel somehow, and fly back to Kabul tonight," Khoklov said. "If I don't, the sacrifice of my career is perhaps a small matter. But I'm afraid it might cause you some inconvenience."

"I'm sure I understand," Tamara nodded. "You were right to come to me, Captain Khoklov. We can't have our Kabul shipments disrupted. We'll need proper lavish gifts, to curry favor with the generals, now that the army's coming."

"The army, huh?" Starlitz said.

"They're invading tomorrow, to beat some sense into these ungrateful Christians," Tamara said. "My husband just announced the news to the Azerbaijan Party regulars, at our little business meeting here tonight. Everyone's delighted about the military crackdown. I think our troubles are over!"

"Hey, that's exciting news," Starlitz said. "We still need the fuel, though."

"Let me think," Tamara said. She touched her chin with one lacquered forefinger. "Aha! The military supply train. It's already here in town, prepared for the troops' arrival. I'm sure they wouldn't miss a few liters from their tank cars."

"That's great," Starlitz said. "I know the way to the railhead. We'll take the truck."

"You didn't bring the ZIL, did you?" Tamara gazed at the olive-drab bulk atop the crushed oleander bushes. "Oh dear, you did, didn't you?"

"Had to improvise," Starlitz said.

"We borrowed that Red Army truck from nice old General Akbarov, you know. We promised him that we wouldn't flaunt it around carelessly. People might talk."

"It's a problem," Starlitz admitted. "It's full of goodies, too. Coupla tons."

"Three tons!" Khoklov declared. "The choicest wares and viands of the Khyber caravans, fit for a czarina!"

"Now, now," said Tamara, favoring him with a smile. "We're simple servants of the People, Captain, doing what we can to keep our homeland prosperous, under very trying conditions…It's a pity you didn't come earlier. Your cargo would have made nice Party favors." Tamara made a quick decision. "I'll have the servants—I mean the *service personnel*—unload the truck, here at our City Palace. There's plenty of storage room in our basement. And we'll take one of my husband's buses down to the train station, to get your fuel. I'm sure it won't take long."

Starlitz widened his eyes. "Great! I always wanted to drive one of those special buses."

Starlitz and Khoklov stacked the empty jerry cans into the back of the bus, while Tamara made arrangements. Soon they were in the bus together, behind a vast windshield expanse of smoked glass. Starlitz seized the driver's seat and gleefully fired the engine. Khoklov sat in the passenger's side, behind a bulky radiotelephone set. Tamara sat cross-legged between them, on a flat vinyl couch, which led, behind her, to a vast plush-padded nest with cozy bunk beds, brocade curtains, and a kitchenette. The bus reeked pleasantly of hashish and shish-kebab.

Starlitz rolled it smoothly out of the compound. "Now, don't show off," Tamara chided. "I know you're a very good driver, but don't scratch my husband's nice machine, or he'll shout at me."

"Can't have that," Starlitz said, spinning the wheel one-handed. He grinned. "This is living, though, isn't it, ace? We can drive anywhere in the province, at any speed we like, and no one will dare to touch us! Everybody knows this bus belongs to the Party Chairman. What a great setup!"

"You're a rascal," Tamara said. "You shouldn't talk like that; people listen, you know. You'll have to forgive him, Comrade Captain."

"Please," Khoklov said. "Call me Pulat Romanevich."

Tamara gazed limpidly out the windshield as they rolled past a long concrete-block wall splattered with angry Armenian graffiti. "Come now," she said softly. "We scarcely know each other, Captain."

"I'm a lonely warrior far from home," Khoklov told her. "If I seem too bold, forgive me. Friendship comes quickly in wartime. It's how we pilots live, you see. A flyer never knows if he will greet the dawn."

"Oh yes," Tamara mused. "There is a war on, isn't there?"

"My next assignment will be bombing bandit camps over the Pakistani border," Khoklov said. "'Unofficially,' of course."

"That's a tough one," Starlitz nodded. "Some of those refugees have guns."

"It's nothing," Khoklov scoffed. "In the Panjgur Valley, they fire down onto the planes, from high on their mountainsides. And you must fly low, because the bandits hide their huts in little crevices."

Khoklov showed Tamara a gold-rimmed mission patch. "I got this one for the Panjgur campaign. The bandits there stopped nine different ground assaults: tanks, artillery, infantry columns…Finally we air boys stepped in. Just flattened the place, you see; there was nothing left, so resistance stopped."

"What about this patch?" Tamara said, touching his sleeve.

"That was the siege of Herat," Khoklov said. "The bandits there were total fanatics! We had to carpet-bomb half the city before we could save it."

"I can see that you love to flirt with danger," Tamara said.

Slowly, Khoklov smiled. "I'm a career officer, with close ties to the KGB. I'm a political liaison with the Afghan Air Force. It's a very…*special* kind of game."

Tamara's eyes sparkled. "What was the most *dangerous* thing that ever happened to you?"

"Ah," Khoklov said, "that would be the time a Chinese heat-seeker hit my aft engine in the Wakhan Corridor…I almost nursed my bird back to Bagram Air Base, but I had to hit the silk in bandit territory. After three days in the wilderness, a Spetsnaz ranger team picked me up with their helicopter gunship…" Khoklov suavely lit a Marlboro and gazed dramatically out the window. "I wouldn't want you to think it's something special, Tamara. For us, it's a job, that's all; our socialist duty. Those Spetsnaz rangers, the elite black berets…now, those sons of bitches are what I call brave men! I owe them my life, you know."

Khoklov felt inside his pocket. "They were good friends. One of them gave me this souvenir…oh hell, *you've* got it now."

"Yeah," Starlitz said. "And I've been meaning to ask you about that jacket you're wearing, Tamara Akhmedovna. It's really beautiful."

"This?" Tamara said, spreading her arms. "Just a little homemade nothing."

"That's actually a black Levi's jean jacket, imported from the West, right?" Starlitz said. "Only, it's been lined with virgin wool, it's got a tanned sheepskin collar, and somebody—somebody really good with a needle—has blind-stitched an embroidery picture of a combine harvester across the back."

"That's right," Tamara said, surprised. "Plus a little group of cheerful peasants with their sickles. It was a socialist-realist poster, you see, from one of the collectivization campaigns...My husband came up through the Agriculture Bureau. It was a little gift to us from some grateful villagers."

"Wow," Starlitz said, reaching into his pocket. "I'd really like to have that. Can we do business?"

"I do business," Tamara said with dignity. "But I'm also the wife of the Party Chairman. I don't have to sell the clothes off my back!"

"Yeah, I know that, but..." Starlitz began. "How about if—"

"Turn here," Tamara commanded.

They had reached the railway. The place was black as pitch. "Oh dear," Tamara said. "I wish they'd do something about these power failures. I can't go walking out there in these heels."

"And I don't know the territory," Khoklov said quickly.

"Yeah, yeah, I get the point," Starlitz said. He opened the door reluctantly, saddened to leave the driver's seat. "Well, there's bound to be somebody out there I can hustle. I'll be back later for the jerry cans."

"Maybe there's a flashlight," Tamara said, sliding lithely into the back of the bus. "If I can find it, we'll come after you."

"I'll help her look," Khoklov said.

"Sure, sure," Starlitz said.

He walked off into darkness, pebbles crunching under his sneakers. The smells were promising: hot brake oil, raw whiffs of petrochemical stench. Starlitz pulled his Cricket lighter, twisted it, and flicked the switch. A six-inch butane jet flared up. Starlitz lit a Marlboro at arm's length, and found his way up a concrete ramp to the loading docks.

A series of yellow-stencilled tank cars had been parked on a siding. Quick flashes of the lighter guided him.

Starlitz felt his way to the tank car's gigantic manual faucet. It wouldn't budge. Starlitz took a few deep breaths, then crouched down and wrenched a railroad spike from a tie with his bare fingers. He whacked enthusiastically at the tap, with earsplitting clanks and thuds. No dice.

A red railroad lantern came swaying down the line. Starlitz ducked under a freight car, clutching his spike. As the guard crept past, Starlitz recognized him. He crept out and tapped the man's shoulder.

The guard whirled with a yelp. "Be cool," Starlitz said. "It's me, man."

"Comrade Starlits!" the guard said.

"I thought you were on strike, Vartan," Starlitz said, tossing his spike.

"I'm on strike from my *illegal* job, unloading the Boss's black-market airplanes," the Armenian said. He was still jittery; his eyes rolled a little under their corduroy cap brim. "But my *legal* job here, as a railroad guard, is too vital to neglect!"

"You mean you can't give up stealing from freight cars," Starlitz said.

"Well, yes," Vartan admitted. "But if I didn't steal freight, I couldn't stay in the black market." He shrugged unhappily.

"Get real," Starlitz said, dusting his hands. "Everyone's in the black market. That's the beauty of the system."

Vartan cleared his throat uneasily. "It wasn't my idea to strike, you know," he said. "It was Hovanessian's."

"He's the skinny kid in the crew, with the glasses, right? The smart one?"

"The stupid one," Vartan said. "Always talking 'openness' and 'restructuring.' Calls himself a 'dissident' and leads protests in the street. He's a big pain in the ass."

"Lemme guess," Starlitz said. "He's the one who had the bright idea to steal our kerosene from the hangar."

"That's right."

"And it's all in empty vodka bottles now, with rags stuffed on top of it. Hidden in basements and attics. Belonging to Hovanessian and his radical nationalist pals."

"It's no use hiding anything from you, Comrade Starlits," Vartan said. "Yes, Hovanessian wants to fight. Any weapon is useful, he said. Even the famous flaming cocktails of former Minister Molotov."

"Yeah?" Starlitz said. "He's gonna match his little busted bottles against these big Red Army tank cars?"

Vartan smirked. "None of us want to fight soldiers. We're all good Soviets; ask anybody! The son-of-a-bitch Moslem ragheads are the real problem."

"Think so, huh?"

"They breed like rats. They're taking over everything! A whole swarm of them moved into the house next door, right into a Christian neighborhood. It's intolerable!" Vartan glowed with righteous determination. "Besides, the Red Army won't hurt *us*. They're used to killing Moslems. They're on *our* side, really."

"There's gonna be a crackdown," Starlitz told him. "Or a big crackup...I'm not sure yet, but I can smell it coming. The system here is gonna blow." His words hung on the empty air. Starlitz scratched his bristled head and smirked, with a scary parody of candor. "I know what I'm talking about," he muttered. "I got a definite *feel* for this kind of situation."

Vartan shuffled his feet, which were clad in boots soled with folded newspapers. "I'm sure you do, Comrade Starlits! Although your role in the Boss's operation is humble, all your Armenian subordinates greatly respect your insight and political perspicacity."

"Knock it off with that crap!" Starlitz said. He frowned. "Listen to me. When your real trouble comes, it's gonna be serious news, pal. Not at all like you think."

Vartan blinked unhappily. "Life is hard," he said at last. "I'm not asking for miracles, comrade. All I really want, is to see my neighbor's house burn down." Vartan spread his hands modestly. "It wouldn't take very much, would it? Just lob in a few flaming bottles, some dark night...It's worth a try."

"You ever try to burn a house down before?" Starlitz said. "You'll burn down your own house, man."

"I thought *my* Russian was bad," Vartan scoffed. "I didn't say *my* house; I said *his* house." Vartan drew a breath. "We Armenians have had it, that's all. I'm a regular guy; I'm no egghead dissident. But we're gonna settle some scores here, once and for all. The old-fashioned way."

Vartan kicked the tank car viciously. "So just forget about our little theft from the Boss's air strip. Here's all the fuel you need, right here. I'll steal it for you; you can take all you want. Just take it away, and forget you saw me here."

"Better think it over," Starlitz said.

Vartan narrowed his eyes. "Look, you're no red-blooded Armenian either, Comrade Straw Boss. You're a Tadjik, right? Or an Uzbek or something..."

Vartan stopped suddenly, surprised. An odd subliminal chill had entered the air. There was a faint, sullen, almost inaudible rumble. The railway cars rocked and squeaked on their axles.

Starlitz, his eyes alert, was balanced on the balls of his feet. He rolled a little from side to side, his knees bent, his hands hanging loose and open. "D'you *feel* that, man?"

Vartan shook his head. "It was nothing...just the rail settling. Some of the ties are rotten."

Starlitz looked at him. "Have it your way," he said at last. "I'll be back soon with some jerry cans."

Starlitz trotted back to the bus. He climbed into the driver's seat and started the engine. "You guys okay?" Starlitz said. Subdued giggling came from the back of the bus, and the springy crunching of a bunk.

Starlitz sighed. "Either of you feel the earth move, just a while ago?"

"Don't make bad jokes," Tamara chided.

"Okay," Starlitz shrugged. "We're gonna roll now."

He drove the bus along the rail line until he found the proper siding. He parked the bus and started ferrying ferry cans.

Vartan had opened the tap with a pry bar. Kerosene was dribbling steadily. The rails beneath the tank were already dark and slick with it. "You're wasting fuel," Starlitz said.

"So what?" Vartan said. "This is a whole tank car."

"It's splashing over everything," Starlitz said.

"You think the army's gonna put it to better use?"

Starlitz ferried filled cans to the back of the bus. "That fuel really stinks," Khoklov complained. "I hope you're almost done, Starlits."

"Close," Starlitz said.

"Burn some more hashish," Tamara suggested. "That Afghani brick smells lovely."

"I lost the matches," Khoklov said. "Throw me your lighter, Starlits."

Starlitz tossed him the Cricket. Khoklov thumbed it and shrieked as the flame jetted out. "Christ! Cut in the after-burner," he said. Tamara laughed.

"Gimme some of that," Starlitz said. Khoklov appeared from the darkness, in his ribbed Christian Dior undershirt. He passed Starlitz a fist-sized clod of hash.

When Starlitz had filled the last can, he gave the hash to the Armenian. "It's for your trouble," he said. "Don't smoke it on the job, okay?"

"Stop worrying," Vartan said, pocketing it.

"Here's a lighter," Starlitz said. "Be real careful with it."

"You must think I'm an idiot," Vartan said. He was struggling with the broken tank-car tap. It had been stripped somehow; it refused to shut off.

Starlitz drove away. "Well, ace, I told you we'd manage," he said. "What do you say, Tamara Akhmedovna? Do we drop you off at the Palace of Culture, or do we head straight for the airstrip?"

"If you think I'll let you drive this bus all by yourself, you must be more stoned than I am," Tamara said. "Open some windows, darling. That kerosene reeks."

"It's kind of a mess back there at the railhead," Starlitz said. "Had to smash and grab. Not too subtle."

"Drive fast, then, and drive to the farm," Tamara said. "Anyway, I'm not through consoling this Soviet hero yet." She laughed giddily. "Whoa! What a shiver! I think those pills are coming on...What did you call those?"

"Dexedrine," Khoklov said. "For combat alertness."

"And you say the *air force* gives you these?" Tamara said. "My! I think I *know* some people in the air force. They've been keeping secrets."

"Oh, not us air boys," Khoklov said. "We're as clear and simple as the day is long."

"Everyone has secrets," Tamara protested gaily. "Even the chauffeur. Tell Captain Khoklov some of your secrets, Lekhi Starlits!"

"Gimme a break," Starlitz said.

"You know where we found this man?" Tamara said. "In prison. The Soviet border guards had caught him trying to sneak into Iran!"

"Holy mother," Khoklov said, interested. *"Why?"*

"Smuggling gig," Starlitz said reluctantly. "Had some business friends there…trying to smuggle rock and roll into the country. The mullahs shoot people for possession of rock. Makes music worth a lot."

"Oh, I love rock and roll!" Khoklov enthused. "Especially Yankee music from the sixties. It really speaks to my groovy soul, when I'm strafing a village…What kind of rock music was it, exactly?"

"I dunno, man. Stuff I got cheap. Cowsills, Carpenters, Bobby Goldsboro…"

"I never heard of those," Khoklov said, crestfallen.

"Ask him about his money," Tamara prodded. "He always has a roll of hundred-dollar bills. Even in prison he had it! You can strip him naked and burn his clothes, and next day he just reaches into his pocket, and there it is again!"

"You're stoned," Khoklov protested. "If he can do that, why didn't you just shoot him?"

"We wanted to at first, but he's too useful," Tamara said. "He's the best mechanic we've ever had here in Azerbaijan. It's a weird ability he has—he can fix anything! We just give him some wires and screws, and maybe some oil and a jack-knife, and even rusty old wrecks start running again. Sometimes he just *stands next* to a machine, and *frowns* at it, and it gets better right away! Isn't that so, Lekhi?"

"It's no big deal," Starlitz muttered. "She's putting you on, ace."

"I know that," Khoklov said indulgently. "She talks just like Scheherazade. It's charming."

"No, it's true!" Tamara said. "That's exactly how he is! I'm not kidding, you know." There was a leaden silence. Tamara laughed gaily. "But it doesn't matter, really. I don't care if you believe me or not! We don't care *how* strange he is, as long as he belongs to us."

It was almost dawn when they reached the airstrip. They fueled the plane as quickly as they could. Even Tamara helped.

Khoklov helped Starlitz move the paint ladder to the cockpit. "I'll have to tell them I had engine trouble, and was forced to fly very slowly. To stay aloft so long, and still return safely to base—I think I just performed a superhuman feat of aviation!" Khoklov chuckled and elbowed Starlitz in the ribs. "Just like one of your so-called miracles, eh, Comrade Starlits? It's amazing what nontechnical people will believe."

"Sure," Starlitz muttered. "Whatever works, man."

Khoklov climbed up into the cockpit. "I'll die happy now, Tamara," he shouted. "Save a place for me in one of those black-market cemetery plots." He slid the cockpit shut.

Starlitz started the tractor and expertly backed the Ilyushin-14 out of its hangar and onto the runway. He decoupled and drove back to the hangar.

Tamara stood at the hangar gate, her arms folded, watching the spyplane climb. "Russians are so morbid," she said. "He's a very sweet boy, for KGB, but I don't trust him in our business. He's got Death written all over him." She shivered, and buttoned her jacket. "Besides, he might brag about me...Get rid of him for me, Lekhi, there's a dear. Tell my husband that Captain Khoklov has a bad attitude. We'll find ourselves a different pilot. Someone who hasn't killed more people than I can count."

"Okay," Starlitz said.

"Why doesn't daylight come?" Tamara said. "Those pills of his are making me really nervous. Am I talking too much? This is a spooky hour, isn't it? Predawn. 'Predawn attack,' that's what they always say in the newspapers. 'Predawn arrest.' Policemen love this time of day."

"You're wired," Starlitz told her. "Let's get in the bus. I'll drive you back to town."

"All right. That might be best." They got back inside the bus. Starlitz threw it into gear and hit the gas.

They drove off. Out in a stubbled field, a large flock of crows was skirling about in confusion, cawing. They seemed reluctant to light on the earth.

Tamara fidgeted. She stuck her hands into the pockets of her jacket. Surprised, she pulled one out. It was full of foil-wrapped condoms.

"Oh look," she said. "He left me these. What a sweet gesture."

"That's a great jacket," Starlitz said.

"It's mine," she said irritably. "*Mine,* understand? I don't own much, you know. I just manage things, because of my husband's office. There's no security for us. Only power. And our power could all go, couldn't it? There've been purges before. So I don't want to bargain with the clothes on my back. Like I was some kind of labor-camp *zek.*"

"I've got dollars," Starlitz wheedled.

She frowned. "Look, my jacket wouldn't even *fit* you. You must be crazy."

"I want it anyway," Starlitz said. "I'll be generous. Come on."

"You're very weird," Tamara said suddenly. "You're from America, aren't you?"

Starlitz grinned broadly. "Don't be silly."

"Only Americans throw dollars around for no sane reason."

"Easy come, easy go," Starlitz shrugged. "C'mon, Tamara, let's do business."

"Are you CIA—is that it? If you are, why don't you go spy on Shevardnadze, or something? Go to Moscow and bother real Russians."

"Shevardnadze's a Georgian," Starlitz said. "Anyway, I like it right here. The local situation's really interesting. I want to see what happens when it comes apart."

"You must be an American, because you're making me feel really paranoid!" Tamara shouted. "I have an awful feeling something really bad is about to happen! I'm going to call my husband on this radio. I need to know what's going on! I don't care what you are, but just shut up and keep driving! That's an order!"

She tried to raise the palace. There was no answer.

"Try the military band," Starlitz suggested.

The military wavelengths were crackling with traffic.

"Sounds like some of those 'predawn raids' you were talking about," Starlitz said, interested. "They're a little behind schedule, I guess." The sun was just rising. Starlitz killed the headlights. The bus topped a hill.

A long line of civilian cars was approaching the Estate.

Tamara dropped the microphone in horror. "Look at those cars!" she said, staring through the tinted windshield. "Only one kind of stupid cop drives around disguised in those stupid brown sedans! It's the DCMSP!"

"Which cops are those, exactly?" Starlitz asked.

"Department to Combat the Misappropriation of Socialist Property," Tamara said. "They've never dared to come near here before…They're the income people, the accountants, the nastiest little cops there are. Once they get their teeth in you, it's all over!"

Starlitz drove past the convoy. The brown cars, with their packed, burr-headed Russian accountants, sped on without a pause.

"They're not trying to stop this bus," he said. "They didn't recognize it."

"They're not from Azerbaijan. We bribed all the locals. They're outside people," Tamara said. "These cops are Gorbachev's!" She slammed her fist against the window. "He's betrayed us! Stabbed us in the back! That hypocrite bastard! Where does his wife get those fancy furs and shoes, I wonder!"

"Earned 'em with her salary as an art historian," Starlitz said.

Tamara wiped bitterly at her kohl-smeared eyes. "It's so unfair! All we wanted was a decent life here! Those stupid Russians: they have a system that would make a donkey laugh, and now they want to *purify* it! God, I hate them!"

"What do you wanna do now?" Starlitz said. "Go back and stand 'em off on your doorstep?"

"No," she said grimly. "We'll have to bend to the almighty wind from Moscow. We'll wait, though, and we'll be back, as soon as they give up trying. It won't take long. The new god will fail."

"Okay, good," Starlitz said. "In the meantime, I'll just keep driving. I love this bus. It's great."

"Gorbachev won't dare try us publicly," Tamara said, gnawing one nail. "I'll bet they simply retire my husband. Maybe even promote him. Some post that's safe and completely meaningless. Like Environment, or Consumer Affairs."

"Yeah," Starlitz said. "This is the new era, right? They won't shoot Party bosses. Makes the Politburo nervous."

"That's right," Tamara said.

"But it's gonna be tough on your underlings. The people with no big-time strings to pull."

Tamara arched her brows. "Oh well...most of them are lousy Armenians anyway. Born thieves...we were always careful to hire Armenians whenever we could."

Starlitz nodded. "Well, I held up my end of the system," he said. "Got the plane launched. Got the job done. The rest of it's not my lookout." He pulled over to the side of the road with a gentle hiss of airbrakes. "Looks like we part company here. So long, Tamara. It's been real."

She stared at him. "This is my bus!"

"Not any more. Sorry."

She was stunned for a moment. Then her face went bleak. "You can't get away with this, you know. The police will stop you. There will be roadblocks."

"It's gonna be chaos," Starlitz said. "The cops will have their hands full, or I miss my guess. But the cops won't stop the chairman's bus—old habits don't die that quick. So I'll just wing it. Improvise." Starlitz rubbed his stubbled chin. "I'll dress up as a paramedic, I guess. Get a Red Cross armband. Nobody stops rescue workers, not when there's really big trouble."

"I'm not leaving my bus!" Tamara said, grabbing the armrest. "You can't do this to me!"

Starlitz reached behind his back and produced the Afghan pistol. "Just a technicality," he said, not bothering to point it at her. "Open the door and get out, okay?"

Tamara got out. She stood at the muddy side of the road in her high heels. The bus drove off.

Seconds ticked by.

A brutal tide of shock coursed through the landscape. Trees whipped at the air; the earth rippled. Tamara was knocked from her feet. She clutched at the roadside as a deep, subterranean rumble seeped up through her hands and knees.

The bus stopped dead, fishtailing. She saw it sway and rattle on its shocks, until the tremor slowed, and, finally, came to a grinding end.

Then the bus turned and raced back toward her. Tamara got to her feet, trembling wiping mechanically at the mud on her hands.

Starlitz pulled over. He opened the door and leaned out. "I forgot the jacket," he said.

Are You for 86?

Leggy Starlitz emerged from behind cool smoked glass to the raucous screeching of seagulls. Hot summer sun glinted fiercely off the Pacific. The harbor smelled of tar, and of poorly processed animal fats from an urban sewage-treatment outlet.

"Hell of a place for a dope deal," Starlitz observed.

Mr. Judy hopped lithely out of the van. Mr. Judy was a petite blonde with long pale schoolgirl braids; the top of her well-scrubbed scalp, which smelled strongly of peppermint and wintergreen, barely came to Starlitz's shoulder. Starlitz nevertheless took a cautious half-step out of her way.

Vanna, in khaki shorts and a Hawaiian blouse, leaned placidly against the white hull of the van, which bore the large chromed logo of an extinct televangelist satellite-TV empire. She dug into a brown paper bag of trail mix and began munching.

"It's broad daylight, too," Starlitz grumbled. He plucked sunglasses from a velcro pocket of his cameraman's vest, and jammed the shades onto his face. He scanned the harbor's parking lot with paranoiac care. Not much there: a couple of yellow taxis, three big-wheeled yuppie pickups with Oregon plates, a family station wagon. "What the hell kind of connection is this guy?"

"The Wolverine's got a very good rep," Mr. Judy said. She wore a white college jersey, and baggy black pants with drawstrings at the waist and ankles. Tarred gravel crunched under the cloth soles of her size-four kung-fu shoes as she examined a Mexican cruise ship through a dainty pair of Nikon binoculars.

Half a dozen sun-wrinkled, tottering oldsters, accompanied by wheeled luggage trolleys, were making their way down the pier to dry land and the customs shed.

Starlitz snorted skeptically. "This place is nowhere! If Wolverine's a no-show, are you gonna let me call the Polynesians?"

"No way," Mr. Judy told him.

Vanna nodded. She shook the last powdery nuggets of trail mix into her pale, long-fingered palm, ate them, then folded the paper bag neatly and stuck it in the top of her hiking boot.

"C'mon," Starlitz protested. "We can do whatever we want out here, now that we're on the road. Let's do it the smart way, for once. Nobody's looking."

Mr. Judy shook her head. "The New Caledonians are into *armed struggle,* they want *guns.* The commune doesn't *deal* guns."

"But the Polynesians have much better product," Starlitz insisted. "It's not Mexican homebrew crap like Wolverine's, this is actual no-kidding RU-486 right out of legitimate French drug-labs. Got the genuine industrial logos on the ampules and everything."

Mr. Judy lowered her Nikons in exasperation. "So what? We're not making commercials about the stuff. Hell, we're not even trying to clear a profit."

"Yeah, yeah, politically correct," Starlitz said irritably. "Well, the French are testing *dirty nuke explosives* in the South Pacific, in case you haven't been reading your Greenpeace agitprop lately. And the Caledonian rebel front stole a bunch of French RU-486 and want to give these pills to us. They're an insurgent Third-World colonial ethnic minority. Hell, all they want is a few lousy Vietnam-era M-16s and some ammo. You can't *get* more politically correct than a deal like that."

"Look, I've *seen* your Polynesians, and they're a clique of patriarchal terrorists," Mr. Judy said. "Let 'em put a woman on their central committee, then maybe I'll get impressed."

Starlitz grunted.

Mr. Judy sniffed in disdain. "You're just pissed-off because we wouldn't move that arsenal you bought in Las Vegas."

Vanna broke in. "You oughta be glad we're letting you keep *guns* on our property, Leggy."

"Yeah, Vanna, thanks a lot for nothing."

Vanna chided him with a shake of her shaggy brown head. "At least you know that your, uhm…your *armament…*" She searched for words. "It's all really safe with us. Right? Okay?"

Starlitz shrugged.

"Have a nice cold guava fizz," Vanna offered sweetly. "There's still two left under the ice in the cooler."

Starlitz said nothing. He sat on the chromed bumper and deliberately lit a ginseng cigarette.

"I wonder how a heavy operator like Wolverine ended up with all these retirees," Mr. Judy said, lowering her binocs. "You think the parabolic mike can pick up any conversation from on board?"

"Not at this range," Starlitz said.

"How about the scanner? Ship-to-shore radio?"

"Worth a try," Starlitz said, brightening. He slid into the driver's seat and began fiddling with a Korean-made broadband scanner, rigged under the dashboard.

An elderly woman with a luggage trolley descended the pier to the edge of the parking lot. She took off a large woven-straw sun-hat and waved it above her head. *"Yoo-hoo!"*

Vanna and Mr. Judy traded looks.

"Yoo-hoo! You girls, you with the van!"

"Mother of God," Mr. Judy muttered. She flung her braids back, climbed into the passenger seat. "We gotta roll, Leggy!"

Starlitz looked up sharply from the scanner's elliptical green readouts and square yellow buttons. "You drive," he said. He worked his way back, between the cryptic ranks of electronic equipment lining both walls of the van, then crouched warily behind the driver's seat. He yanked a semi-automatic pistol from within his vest, and slid a round into the chamber.

Mr. Judy drove carefully across the gravel and pulled up beside the woman from the cruise ship. The stranger had blue hair, orthopedic hose, a flowered sundress. Her trolley sported a baby-blue Samsonite case, a handbag, and a menagerie of Mexican stuffed animals: neon-green and fuchsia poodles, a pair of giant toddler-sized stuffed pandas.

Mr. Judy rolled the tinted window down. "Yes ma'am?" she said politely.

"Can you take me to a hotel?" the woman said. She lowered her voice. "I need—*a room of my own.*"

"We can take you to the lighthouse," Mr. Judy countersigned.

"Wonderful!" the woman said, nodding. "So very nice to make this rendezvous…Well, it's all here, ladies." She waved triumphantly at her trolley.

"You're 'Wolverine'?" Vanna said.

"Yes I am. Sort of." Wolverine smiled. "You see, three of the women in my study-group have children attending Michigan University…"

"Maybe we better pat her down anyway, Jude," Starlitz said. "She's got room for a couple of frag grenades in that handbag."

Wolverine lifted a pair of horn-rimmed bifocals on a neck chain and peered through the driver's window. She seemed surprised to see Starlitz. "Hello, young man."

"*Que tal?*" Starlitz said in resignation, putting his pistol away.

"*Muy bien, señor, y usted?*"

"Get her luggage, Leggy," Mr. Judy said. "Vanna, you better let Sister Wolverine sit in the passenger seat."

Vanna got out and helped Wolverine into the front of the van. Starlitz,, his mouth set in a line of grim distaste, hurled the stuffed animals into the back.

"Be careful," Wolverine protested. "Those are for my grandchildren! The pills are in the middle, hidden in the stuffing."

Vanna deftly ripped a seam open and burrowed into the puffed-polyester guts of a panda. She pulled out a shining wad of contraband and gazed at it with interest. "Where'd you find Saran Wrap in Cancún?"

"Oh, I always carry Saran Wrap, dear," said Wolverine, fastening her shoulder harness. "That, and nylon net."

"Lemme drive," Starlitz demanded, at the door. Mr. Judy nodded and crept lithely into the back, where she sat cross-legged on the rubber-matted aisle between the bolted-down racks of equipment. Vanna slammed the van's back door from the inside, locked it, and sat on Wolverine's Samsonite suitcase.

Starlitz threw the van into gear. "Where you wanna go?" he said.

"Bus station, please," Wolverine said.

"Great. No problem." Starlitz began humming. He loved driving.

Mr. Judy broke the sutures on a lime-green poodle and removed another neatly wrapped bundle of abortifacient pills. "Great work, Wolverine. You been doing this long?"

"Not long enough to get caught," Wolverine said. She removed her bifocals, and patted her powdered chin and forehead with a neatly folded linen handkerchief. "'Wolverine' will be somebody else, next time. Don't expect to see *me* again, thank you very much."

"We appreciate your brave action, sister," Mr. Judy said formally. "Please convey our very best regards to your study-group." She rose to her knees and extended her hand. Wolverine turned clumsily in her seat and shook Mr. Judy's hand warmly.

"This certainly is an odd vehicle," Wolverine said, peering at the blinking lights and racks of switches. "You're not really Christian evangelists, are you?"

"Oh no, we're Goddess pagans," Mr. Judy declared, carefully disemboweling another poodle. "Our associate Leggy here bought this van at an auction. After Six Flags Over Jesus went bust in the rape scandal. We just use it for cover."

"It rather worried me," Wolverine confessed. "My friends told me to watch out carefully for any church groups. They might be right-to-lifers." She glanced warily at Starlitz. "They also said that if I met any tough-looking male hippies, they were probably drug enforcement people."

"Not me," Starlitz demurred. "All D.E.A. guys have pony-tails and earrings."

"What do you do with all these machines? Are those computers?"

"It's telephone equipment," Mr. Judy said cheerfully. "You may have heard of us—I mean, besides our health-and-reproductive services. People call us the Pheminist Phone Phreaks."

"No," Wolverine said thoughtfully, "I hadn't heard."

"We're do-it-yourself telephone operators. My hacker handle is 'Mr. Judy,' and this is 'Vanna.'"

"How do you do?" Wolverine said. "So you young ladies really know how to operate all this machinery? That certainly is impressive."

"Oh, it's real simple," Mr. Judy assured her. "This is our fax machine... That big noisy thing is the battery power unit. This one, with the fake mahogany console, is our voice-mail system...And this one, the off-white gizmo with the peach trim, runs our satellite dish."

"It's the *uplink,*" Starlitz said, deeply pained. "*Don't* call it 'the gizmo with peach trim.'"

"And these are home computers with modem phonelinks," Mr. Judy said, ignoring him. "This one is running our underground bulletin board service. We run a 900 dial-up service with this one: it has the voice generator, and a big hard worm."

"Hard *disk.* WORM *drive,*" Starlitz groaned.

"You know what a *bridge* is?" Vanna said. "That's a conference call, when sisters from out-of-state can all relate together." She smiled sweetly. "And you bill it to, like, a really big stupid corporation. Or a U.S. Army base!"

Mr. Judy nodded vigorously. "We do a lot of that! Maybe you'd like to join us on a phone-conference, sometime soon."

"Isn't that *illegal?*" Wolverine asked.

"We think of it as 'long-distance liberation,'" Mr. Judy said.

"We certainly do use plenty of long-distance phone service in my group," Wolverine said, intrigued. "Mostly we charge it to the foundation's SPRINT card, though..."

"You're nonprofit? 501(c)(3)?"

Wolverine nodded.

"That's really good activist tactics, getting foundation backing," Mr. Judy said politely. "But we can hack all the SPRINT codes you want, right off our Commodore."

"Really?"

"It's easy, if you're not afraid to experiment," Vanna said brightly. "I mean, they're just phones. Phones can't hurt you."

"And this is a cellular power-booster," Mr. Judy said, affectionately patting an oblong box of putty-colored high-impact plastic. "It's wonderful! The phone companies install them in places like tunnels, where you can't get good phone reception from your carphone. But if you know where to find one of these for yourself, then you can liberate it, and re-wire it. So now, this is our own little portable cellular phone-station. It patches right into the phone network, but it doesn't show up on their computers at all, so there's never any bills!"

"How do you afford all these things?" Wolverine asked.

"Oh, that's the best part," Mr. Judy said, "the whole operation pays for itself! I'll show you. Just listen to this!"

Mr. Judy typed briefly on the keyboard of a Commodore, pausing as Starlitz forded a pothole. Then she hit a return key, and twisted an audio dial. A fist-sized audio speaker, trailing a flat rainbow-striped cord, emitted a twittering screech. Then a hesitant male voice, lightly scratched with static, filled the van.

"…just don't like men anymore," the voice complained.

"Why don't you *think* they *like* you?" a silky, breathy voice responded. "Does it have something to do with the *money?*"

"It's not the money, I tell you," the man whined. "It's AIDS. Men are poisonous now." His voice shook. "It's all so different nowadays."

"*Why* is it all so different?"

"It's because cum is poisonous. That's the real truth, isn't it?" The man was bitter suddenly, demanding. "You can die just from touching cum! I mean, every chick I ever knew in my life was kind of scared of that stuff…But now it's a hundred times worse."

"I'm not afraid of you," the voice soothed. "You can tell me *anything.*"

"Well, that's what's so different about you," the man told the voice unconvincingly. "But goddamn Linda—remember I was telling you about Linda? She acted like it was napalm or something…"

Mr. Judy turned the dial down. "This guy's a customer of ours; he's talking on one of our 900 lines, and he's paying a buck per minute on his credit card."

Vanna examined another console. "It's a VISA card. On a savings-and-loan from Colorado. Equifax checkout says it's good."

"You're running phone pornography?" Wolverine said, appalled.

"Of course not," Mr. Judy said. "You can't really call it 'pornography' if there's no oppression-of-women involved. Our 900 service is entirely cruelty-and exploitation-free!"

Wolverine was skeptical. "What about that woman who's talking on the phone, though? You can't tell me she's not being exploited."

"That's the amazing beauty of it!" Mr. Judy declared. "There's no real woman there at all! That voice is just a kind of Artificial Intelligence thing! It's not 'talking' at all, really—it's just *generating speech,* using Marilyn Monroe's voice mixed with Karen Carpenter's. It's all just digital, like on a CD."

"What?" said Wolverine. "I don't understand."

Mr. Judy patted her console; the top was out of it, revealing a miniature urban high-rise of accelerator cards and plug-in modules. "This computer's got a voice-recognition card. The software just picks words at random out of the customer's own sick, pathetic rant! Whenever he stops for breath, it feeds a question back to him, using his own vocabulary. I mean, if he talks about shaved hamsters—or whatever his kink is—then *it* talks about shaved hamsters. The system knows how to construct sentences in English, but it doesn't have to *understand* a single thing he says! All it does is *claim* to understand him."

"Every two or three minutes it stops and says really nice things to him off the hard disk," Vanna said helpfully. "Kind of a flattery subroutine."

"And he doesn't *realize* that?"

"Nobody's ever complained so far," Vanna said. "We get men calling in steady, week after week!"

"When it comes to men and sex, being *human* has never *been* part of the transaction," Mr. Judy said. "If you just give men *exactly* what they want, they *never miss the rest*. It's really true!"

Wolverine was troubled. "You must get a lot of really sick people."

"Well, sure," Mr. Judy said. "Actually, we hardly ever bother to listen-in to the calls anymore…But if he's really disgusting, like a child-porn guy or something, we just rip-off his card-number and post it on an underground bulletin board. A week later this guy gets taken to the cleaners by hacker kids all over America."

"How on earth did you start this project?" Wolverine said.

"Well," Mr. Judy said, "phreaking long-distance is an old trick. We've been doing that since '84. But we didn't get into the heavy digital stuff until 1989." She hesitated. "As it happens, this van itself belongs to Leggy here."

Starlitz was watching his rear-view mirror. "Well, the van," he mumbled absently, "I got a lot of software with the van…this box of Commodore floppies tucked in the back, somebody's back-ups, with addresses and phone numbers…About a million suckers who'd pledged money to Six Flags Over Jesus. Man, you can't *ask* for a softer bunch of marks and rubes than *that*." He turned off the highway suddenly.

"Pretty soon we're gonna branch out!" Mr. Judy said. "Our group is onto something really hot here. We're gonna run a gay-rights BBS, a dating service, voice-mail classified ads—why, by '95 we'll be doing dial-up Goddess videos on fiber-to-the-curb!"

"Problem, Jude," Starlitz announced.

Mr. Judy's face fell. "What is it?"

"The blue Toyota," Starlitz said. "It picked us up outside the harbor. Been right on our ass ever since."

"Cops?"

"They've got CB, but I don't see any microwave," Starlitz said.

Vanna's blue eyes went wide. "Anti-choice people!"

"Lose 'em," Mr. Judy commanded.

Starlitz floored it. The van's suspension scrunched angrily as they pitched headlong down the road. Wolverine, clinging to her plastic handhold above the passenger door, reached up to steady her dentures. "I'm afraid!" she said. "Will they hurt us?"

Starlitz grunted.

"I can't take this! I'm sorry! I'd rather be arrested!" Wolverine cried.

"They're not cops, they don't *do* arrests," Starlitz said. He crossed three lines of traffic against the light and hit an access ramp. Both Vanna and Mr. Judy were flung headlong across their rubber mats on the floor. The van's jounced machinery settled with a violent clatter.

The speaker emitted a crackle and a loud dial-tone.

"God damn it, Leggy," Mr. Judy shouted, "okay, forget 'losing' them!"

Starlitz ignored her, checking the mirror, then scanning the highway mechanically. "I lost 'em, all right. For a while, anyhow."

"Who *were* those people?" Wolverine wailed.

"Pro-life fanatics…" Mr. Judy grunted. "Christian cultist weirdos…" She clutched a slotted metal column for support as Starlitz weaved violently into the fast lane. "I sure hope it's not 'Sword of the Unborn.' They hit a clinic in Alabama once with a shoulder-launched rocket."

"Hang on," Starlitz said. He braked, fishtailed ninety degrees, then struck out headlong across a grassy meridian. They crossed in the teeth of oncoming traffic, off the gravelled shoulder, then up and down through a shallow ditch. The van took a curb hard, became briefly airborne, crossed a street, and skidded with miraculous ease through the crowded lot of a convenience grocery.

Starlitz veered left, onto the striped tarmac of a tree-clustered strip mall.

Starlitz drove swiftly to the back of the mall and parked illegally in the delivery-access slot of a florist's shop. "This baby's kinda hard to hide," he said, setting the emergency brake. "Now that they're onto us, we gotta get the hell out of this town."

"He's right. I think we'd better drop you off here, Wolverine," Mr. Judy said. "If that's okay with you."

Vanna unlocked the van's back door and flung herself out, yanking Wolverine's Samsonite case behind her with a thud and a clatter.

"Yes, that's, quite all right, dear," Wolverine said dazedly. She touched a lump on the top of her scalp, and examined the trace of blood on her fingertips. She winced, then stuffed the Mexican straw sun-hat over her head.

With brutal haste, Mr. Judy palpated the stuffed animals for any remaining contraband. She flung them headlong from the van into Vanna's waiting arms.

Wolverine opened the passenger door and climbed down, with arthritic awkwardness. The tires stank direly of scorched rubber. "I'm sure that I can call a taxi here, young man," she told Starlitz, hanging to the door like a drunk from a lamp-post. "Never you mind about little me…"

Starlitz was fiddling with his broadband scanner-set, below the dash. He looked up sharply. "Right. You clean now?"

"What?" Wolverine said.

"Are you *holding?*"

"I beg your pardon?"

Starlitz gritted his teeth. "Do you have any *illegal drugs?* On your person? Right now?"

"Oh. No. I gave them all to you!"

"Great. Then stick right by the payphones till your taxi comes. If anyone gives you any kind of shit, scream like hell and dial 9-1-1."

"All right," Wolverine said bravely. "I understand. Anything else?"

"Yeah. Shut the door," Starlitz said. Wolverine closed the door gently. "And lose that fuckin' ugly hat," Starlitz muttered.

Vanna heaved the leaky stuffed toys into Wolverine's arms, kissed her cheek briefly and awkwardly, then ran to the back of the van. "Split!" she yelled. Starlitz threw it into reverse and the rear doors banged shut.

Wolverine waved dazedly as she stood beside the florist's dumpster.

"I'm gonna take 26 West," Starlitz announced.

"You're kidding," Mr. Judy said, clambering into the front passenger seat. She tugged her harness tight as they pulled out of the mall's parking lot. "That's miles out of our way! Why?"

Starlitz shrugged. "Mystical Zen intuition."

Mr. Judy frowned at him, rubbing a bruise on her thigh. "Look, don't even start on me with that crap, Leggy."

A distant trucker's voice drawled from the scanner. "*So then I tell him, look, Alar is downright good for kids, it kills pinworms for one thing...*" Starlitz punched the radio back onto channel-scan.

Mr. Judy bent to turn down the hiss.

"Leave it," Starlitz said. "ELINT traffic intercept. Standard evasive tactics."

"Look, Starlitz," Mr. Judy said, "were you ever in the U.S. Army?"

"No..."

"Then don't *talk* like you were in the goddamn Army. Say something normal. Say something like 'maybe we can overhear what they say.'" Mr. Judy fetched a pad of Post-It notes and a pencil-stub from the glove compartment.

"I think our fax just blew a chip," Vanna announced mournfully from the back. "All its little red lights are blinking."

"Small wonder! Mr. Zen Intuition here was driving like a fucking maniac," Mr. Judy said. She groaned. "Remind me to wrap some padding on those goddamned metal uprights. I feel like I've been nunchucked."

An excited voice burst scratchily from the scanner. "*Where is Big Fish? Repeat, where is Big Fish? What was their last heading? Ten-six, Salvation!*"

"*This is Salvation,*" a second voice replied. "*Calm the heck down, for pete's sake! We've got the description now. We'll pick 'em up on 101 South if we have to. Over.*"

"Bingo," Mr. Judy exulted. "Citizen's Band channel 13." She made a quick note on her Post-It pad.

Starlitz rubbed his stubbled chin. "Good thing we avoided Highway 101."

"Don't be smug, Leggy."

The CB spoke up again. *"This is Isaiah, everybody. On Tenth and, uh, Sherbrooke, okay? I don't think they could have possibly come this far, over."*

"Heck no they couldn't," Salvation said angrily. *"What in blazes are you doing over into Sector B? Get back to Sector A, over."*

"Ezekiel here," said another voice. *"We're in A, but we surmise they must have parked somewhere. That sounds reasonable, doesn't it? Uhm, over…"*

"No air chatter, over," Salvation commanded. His signal was fading.

"'Salvation,' 'Ezekiel,' and 'Isaiah,'" Vanna said. "Wow, their handles really suck!"

"I know, I know," Mr. Judy said. "Mother of God, the bastards are swarming like locusts. I can't understand this!"

Starlitz sighed patiently. "Look, Jude. There's nothing to understand, okay? Somebody must have finked. That little coven of yours has got an informer."

"No way!" Vanna said.

"Yes way. One of your favorite backwoods mantra-chanters is a pro-life plant, okay? They knew we were coming here. Maybe they didn't know everything, but they sure knew enough to stake us out."

Mr. Judy clenched her small, gnarled fists and stared out the windshield, biting her lip. "Maybe it was Wolverine's people that leaked! Ever think of that?"

"If it were Wolverine, they'd have hit us at the docks," Starlitz said. "You're being a sap, Jude. Your problem is, you don't think there's any pro-life woman smart enough to run a scam on the sisters. Come on, get real! It doesn't take a genius to wear chi-pants and tattoo a yin-yang on your tit."

Mr. Judy tugged at the front of her jersey. "Thanks a lot. Creep."

Starlitz shrugged. "The underground-right are as smart as you are, easy. They know everything they wanna know about the 'Liberal Humanist Movement.' Hell, they've all got subscriptions to *Utne Reader.*"

"So what do you think we should do?"

Starlitz grinned. "This gig of yours is blown, so let's forget it. Brand-new deal, okay? Let's card us a big rental-car and call the New Caledonians."

"No way," Mr. Judy said. "No way we're losing this van! Besides, I draw the line at credit-card theft. Unless the victim is Republican."

"And no way we're calling any Polynesians, anyway," Vanna said.

Starlitz dug in his vest for a cigarette, lit it, and blew ochre smoke across the windshield. "I'll trade you," he said at last. "You tell me where the kid is. You can borrow my van for a while, and I'll rent a V-8 and do the Utah run all by myself."

"Fat chance!" Mr. Judy shouted. "Last time we trusted you with our stash, we didn't see you for three fucking years!"

"And we're not telling you anything more about the kid until this is all over," Vanna said firmly.

Starlitz snorted smoke. "You think *I* got any use for a wimpy abortion drug? Hell, RU-486 isn't even *illegal* in most other countries. Lemme deliver it—heck, I'll even get you a receipt. And when I'm back, we all go meet the kid. Just like we agreed before. If that goes okay, I might even throw in the van later. Deal?"

"No deal," Mr. Judy said.

"Think about it. It's really a lot easier."

Mr. Judy silently peeled the Post-It and slapped it on the scanner.

"Don't you make trouble for us, Leggy," Vanna spoke up. "You don't know anything! You don't know who we're meeting. You don't know the passwords. You don't know the time or the place." Vanna took a breath. "You don't even know which one of us is the kid's real mother."

"You act like that's my fault," Starlitz said. "That's not the way I remember it." He grinned, a curl of ginseng smoke escaping his back molars. "Anyway, I can guess."

"No you can't!" Vanna said heatedly. "Don't you dare guess!"

"Forget it," Mr. Judy said. "We shouldn't even talk about the kid. We shouldn't have mentioned the kid. We won't talk about the kid anymore. Not till the trip's over and we've done the deal just like we agreed back at the commune."

"Fine," Starlitz sneered. "That's real handy. For you, anyway."

Mr. Judy cracked her knuckles. "Okay, call me stupid. Call me reckless. I admit that, okay? And if me and Vanna hadn't both been *incredibly* stupid *and* reckless around you three years ago, pal, there wouldn't even *be* any kid now."

Starlitz said nothing.

Mr. Judy sniffed. "What happened that time—between the three of us— we never talk about it, I know that…And for God's sake, after this, let's not ever talk about it again." She lowered her voice. "But privately—that thing we did—with the tequila and the benwa balls and the big rubber hammock—yeah, I remember it just as well as you do, and I blame myself for that. Completely. I take that entire karmic burden upon myself. I absorb all guilt trips, I take upon myself complete moral accountability. Okay, Leggy? I'm responsible, you're not responsible. You happy now?"

"Sure thing," Starlitz said sullenly, grinding out his cigarette.

They drove on then, in ominous silence, for two full hours: through Portland and up the Columbia River Valley. Vanna finally broke the ice again by passing out tofu-loaf, Ginseng Rush, and rice cakes.

"We've lost 'em good," Mr. Judy decided.

"Maybe," Starlitz said. There had been no traffic on Channel 13, except the usual truck farmers, speedballers and lot lizards. "But the situation's changed some now...Why don't you phone your friends back at the commune? Tell 'em to dig up my arsenal and Fed-Ex us three Mac-10s to Pocatello. With plenty of ammo."

Mr. Judy frowned. "So we can risk dope *and* federal weapons charges? Forget it! We said no guns, remember? I don't think you even ought to have that goddamn pistol."

"Sure," Starlitz sneered, "so when they pull up right next to us at sixty miles per, and cut loose on us with a repeating combat-shotgun..." Vanna flinched. "Yeah," Starlitz continued, "Judy here is gonna do a Chuck Norris out the window and side-kick 'em right through their windshield!" He patted his holstered gun. "Fuckin' black belts...I've seen acidheads with more sense!"

"And I've seen you with a loaded Ingram!" Vanna retorted. "I'd rather face a hundred right-to-lifers."

"Oh stop it," Mr. Judy said. "You're both making trouble for nothing. We lost 'em, remember? They're probably still hunting us on 101 South. We got a big lead now." She munched her last rice cake. "If we had any sense, we'd take a couple hours and completely change this van's appearance. Vanna's pretty good with graphics. We can buy paint at an auto store and re-do our van like a diaper service. Something a lot less macho than white pearlized paint with two big chrome TV logos."

"It's not *your* van," Starlitz said angrily. "It's *my* van, and you're not putting any crappy paint on it. Anyway, we've *got* to look like a TV van. What if somebody looks in the window and sees all this equipment? You can't get more suspicious and obvious than a van full of monitors that's painted like some wimpy diaper service. Everybody'll think we're the goddamned FBI."

"Okay, okay, have it your way," Mr. Judy shrugged. She put on a pair of black drugstore Polaroids. "We'll just take it easy. Keep a low profile. We'll make it fine."

They spent the night in a lot in a campground near a state park on the Oregon-Idaho border. The lots were a bargain for the TV van, for its demand for electrical power was enormous, and rental campgrounds offered cheap hookups. Judy and Vanna slept outside in a hemispherical, bright pink alpine tent. Starlitz slept inside the van.

Next morning they were enjoying three bowls of muesli when an open-faced young man in a lumberjack shirt and overalls meandered up, carrying a rubber-antennaed cellular phone.

"Good morning," he said.

"Hi," Mr. Judy said, pausing in mid-spoon.

"Spend a pleasant night?"

"Why don't you guys install proper telephone hookups here?" Mr. Judy demanded. "We need copper-cable. You know, twisted-pair."

"Oh I'm sorry, I don't run this campground," the young man apologized, propping one booted foot on the edge of their wooden picnic table. "You see, I just happen to live in this area." He cleared his throat. "I thought we might counsel together about your activities."

"Huh?" Vanna said.

"I got an alarm posted on my Christian BBS last night," the young man told them. "Got up at five a.m., and spent the whole morning lookin' for you and this van." He pointed with his thumb. "You're the people who import abortion pills." He looked at them soberly. "Word's out about you all over our network."

Mr. Judy put down her muesli spoon with an unsteady hand. "You've made a mistake."

"Don't worry, I won't hurt you," the young man said. "I'm just a regular guy. My name's Charles. That's my car right over there." Charles pointed to a rust-spotted station-wagon with Idaho plates. "My wife's in there—Monica—and our little kid Jimmy." He turned and waved. Monica, in the driver's seat, waved back. She wore sunglasses and a head-kerchief. She looked very anxious.

Jimmy was asleep in the back in a toddler's safety-seat. Apparently getting up early had been too much for the tyke.

"Our group is strictly nonviolent," Charles said.

"Gosh, that's swell," Starlitz said, relaxing visibly. He splashed a little more bottled goat-milk into his muesli.

"Violence against the unborn is wrong," Charles said steadily. "It's not a 'choice,' it's a *child*. You're spreading a Frankenstein technology that lets women poison and murder their own unborn children. And they can do it in complete stealth."

"You mean in complete privacy," Vanna said.

Mr. Judy knocked her cheap plastic bowl aside and leapt to her feet. "Don't even talk to him, Vanna! Leggy, start the van, let's get out of here!"

Starlitz looked up in annoyance from his half-finished cereal. "Are you kidding? There's only one of him. I'm not through eating yet. Kick his ass!"

Mr. Judy glanced from side to side, warily. She glared at Charles, then hitched up her pants and settled into a menacing kung-fu crouch. "Go away! We don't want you here."

"It's my moral duty to bear witness to evil," Charles told her mildly, showing her his open hands. "I'm not armed, and I mean you no harm. If you feel you must hit me, then I can't prevent you. But you're very wrong to answer words with blows."

Birds sang in the pines above the campground.

"He's right," Vanna said in a small voice.

"'He who diggeth a pit will fall in it,'" Charles quoted.

"Okay, okay," Mr. Judy muttered. "I'm not going to hit you."

"She who lives by the sword will die by it."

Mr. Judy frowned darkly. "Don't *push* me, asshole!"

"I know what you're doing, even if you yourselves are too corrupt to recognize it," Charles continued eagerly. "You're trying to legitimize the mass poisoning of the unborn generation." Charles seemed encouraged by their confusion, and waved his arms eloquently. "Your contempt for the sanctity of human life legitimizes murder! Today, you're killing kids. Tomorrow, you'll be renting wombs. Pretty soon you'll be selling fetal tissue on the open market!"

"Hey, we're not capitalists," Vanna protested.

Charles was on a roll. "First comes abortion, then euthanasia! The suicide machines…The so-called right-to-die—it's really the *right-to-kill,* isn't it? Pretty soon you'll be quietly poisoning not just unborn kids and old sick people, but everybody else who's inconvenient to you! That's just how the Holocaust started—with so-called euthanasia!"

"We're not the Nazis in this situation," Mr. Judy grated. "You're the Nazis."

"We're pro-life. You're making life cheap. You're the pro-death secular forces!"

"Hey, don't call us 'secular,'" Vanna said, wounded. "We're Goddess pagans."

Starlitz was steadily munching his cereal.

"I think you should give me all those pills," Charles said quietly. "It's no use going on with this scheme of yours, now that we know, and you know that we know. Be reasonable. Just give all the pills to me, and I'll burn them all. You can go back home quietly. Nobody will bother you. Don't you have any sense of shame?"

Mr. Judy grated her teeth. "Look, buster. In a second, I'm gonna lose my temper and break your fucking arm. I'd sure as hell rather die by the sword than by the coathanger."

"Sure, resort to repressive thuggish violence," Charles shrugged. "But I promise you this: you won't thrive by your crimes. We are everywhere!"

"Goddamn you, that's *our* slogan!" Mr. Judy shouted.

Starlitz washed his muesli bowl under a rusty water-faucet, and belched. "Well, that's that. Let's get goin'." He opened the door of the van.

"We know darned well what you're up to!" Charles cried, as Vanna and Judy fled hastily into the van. "We're going to videotape you, and photograph you, and speak about you in public!" Starlitz fired up the van and pumped the engine. "We're gonna make dossiers about you and put you on our computer mailing lists!" Charles shouted, raising one callused hand in solemn imprecation. "We'll call your Congressman and complain about you! We'll start civil suits and take out injunctions!"

Starlitz drove away.

"We'll call you at your home!" Charles bellowed, hands cupped at his lips. "And call your offices! All day and all night, hundreds of us! With automatic dialers! For years and years!" His voice faded in a final shout. *"We'll call your parents!"*

"Mother of God," Mr. Judy said, shaken, buckling herself into the passenger seat. "That was *horrible!* What are we going to do about that guy?"

"No problem," Starlitz said, setting the scanner for cellular-phone frequencies. "I mean, my parents died in a tornado in a Florida trailer park." He shrugged. "And besides, I never show up on videotape."

Mr. Judy frowned suspiciously. "What do you mean?"

"It's just this, uhm, thing that happens," Starlitz said, shrugging. "I mean videos just never work when they're pointed at me. Either the battery's dead, or the tape jams, or the player blows a chip and just starts blinking twelve-o'clock, or the tape splits so there's nothing but scratches and blur...I just don't show up on videotape. Ever."

Mr. Judy took a deep breath. "Leggy, that's got to be just about the wildest, stupidest—"

"Hush!" Starlitz said. Charles' voice was emerging from the scanner.

"I told you they wouldn't hurt me," he said.

"Well, we're not gonna follow them," said a woman's voice—his wife Monica, presumably. *"It's too dangerous. I'm sure they have guns in that van."* She lowered her voice. *"Charlie, were they lesbians?"*

"Well, I dunno about the guy they had with them," Charles replied, *"but yeah, those girls were sexual deviants all right. It's just like Salvation told us. Really makes your blood run cold!"* He paused. *"Is the car fax still working? Better dial him a report right away!"*

"Typical," Mr. Judy said. "We ought to go back there and slash his tires!"

"Let's just get out of here," Vanna sighed.

"I don't have to take any gay-bashing lip out of that Norman Rockwell hayseed."

"If you beat him up, they'll know we're listening to the cellular band," Vanna pointed out wisely.

"Well, your pal Charlie was right about one thing," Starlitz said cheerfully. "This whole scam of yours is totally fucked now! Time to lose the van and pick up some action with the Polynesians."

"We're going to Salt Lake City, Leggy." Mr. Judy's face was set stonily. "We'll get there if we have to drive all day and all night. We'll make the delivery, dammit. Now it's a matter of political principle."

▲ ▼ ▲

They met their first roadblock in Gooding County, Idaho. A dozen placard-waving militants burst from the back of two pickups and threw a cardboard box of caltrops across Highway 84. Starlitz, suspecting land mines or blasting-caps, slowed drastically.

The sides of the van were hammered with blood-balloons, and glass Christmas-tree ornaments filled with skunk-stinking butyl mercaptan and rotten-egg hydrogen sulfide. An especially brave militant with a set of grappling hooks was yanked from his feet and road-burned for ten yards.

The trucks did not pursue them. Starlitz stopped at a carwash in Shoshone Falls. After the stomach-turning stink-liquids had been rinsed off with high-pressure soap, he yanked seven caltrops from the van's tires. The caltrops were homemade devices—golf-balls, with half-a-dozen six-inch nails driven through them, the whole thing cunningly spray-painted black to match highway tarmac.

"Good thing I bought these solid-rubber tires and ditched those fancy-ass Michelins," Starlitz said with satisfaction.

"Yeah," Vanna said. Mr. Judy said nothing. She'd given Starlitz a hard time about the tires earlier.

"Shoulda saved money on that fancy fiber-optics kit, and gone for the Plexiglas windows, instead," Starlitz opined. "The bulletproof option. Just like I said." Mr. Judy, who'd done the lion's share of the scrubbing, went to the ladies' and threw up.

▲ ▼ ▲

They took 93 south of Twin Falls and across the border to Wells, Nevada. The switch to a smaller highway seemed to stymie their pursuers, but only temporarily. At 80 West just east of Oasis they found the desert highway entirely blocked. A church bus full of protestors in death's-head masks had physically blocked the road with their black-cloaked bodies. As the van drew nearer, they began chaining themselves together, somewhat hampered by their placards and scythes.

Starlitz rolled down the driver's-side window, took his hands off the steering-wheel and stuck them both out the window, visibly. Then he hit the accelerator.

The blockaders scattered wildly as the van bore down upon them. The van whacked, bumped, and crunched over chains, scythes, and placards as shrieks of rage and horror dopplered past the open window.

"I think you hit one of them, Leggy," Vanna gasped.

"Nah," Starlitz said. "Probably one of those dead-baby dummies."

"They wouldn't be carrying *real* babies with them, would they?" Vanna said.

"In this heat?" Starlitz said.

The bus pursued them at high speed all the way to Wendover, but it grew dark, and they entered some light traffic. Starlitz turned the van's lights off, and pulled into an access road to the Bonneville Salt Flats. The bus, deceived, roared past them in pursuit of someone else.

They spent the night outside the military chain-link around an Air Force test-range, then drove into Salt Lake City in the morning.

▲ ▼ ▲

It was Sunday, the Sabbath. Utah's capital was utterly sepulchral. The streets were as blank and deserted as so many bowling lanes.

The van felt pitifully conspicuous as they drove past blank storefronts and shuttered windows. At length they hid the van on the sheltered grounds of a planetarium and stuffed all the contraband into Mr. Judy's backpack.

They then hiked uphill to the Utah State Capitol. The great stone edifice was open to the public. There was not a soul inside it. No police, no tourists—no one at all. The only company the three of them had were the Ikegami charged-couple-device security minicams, which were bolted well above the line-of-sight on eight-inch swivel pedestals.

"We're early," Mr. Judy said. "Our contact hasn't shown yet." She shrugged. "Might as well have a good look at the place."

"I like this building," Starlitz announced, gazing around raptly. "This contact of yours must be okay. Setting up a dope-deal here in Boy Scout Central was a way gutsy move." He closely examined a Howard Chandler Christy reproduction of the Signing of the US Constitution. The gilt-framed tableau of the Founding Fathers had been formally presented to the State of Utah by the Walt Disney Corporation.

The capitol's rotunda was a sky-blue dome with a massive dangling chandelier. It featured funky-looking '30s frescos with the unmistakable look of state-supported social-realism. "Advent of Irrigation by Pioneers." "Driving the Golden Spike." "General Connor Inaugurates Mining."

"Listen to this," Mr. Judy marveled. "It's a statement by the bureaucrat that commissioned this stuff. *This is the greatest opportunity that the artists of this or any other country have ever had to show their metal.* He actually says that—'mettle'! *It is a call to them to make good and prove that they have something worth while to say.* Yeah, unlike you, you evil little redneck philistine! *It is an opportunity to sell themselves to the country and I know they will answer the challenge.*" Suddenly she flushed.

"Take it easy," Starlitz muttered.

"*Sell themselves to the country,*'" Mr. Judy said venomously. "Mother of God...sometimes you forget just how bad it really is in the good ol' USA."

Farther down the hall they discovered an extremely campy figurine of an astronaut on a black plastic pedestal. The pedestal was made of O-ring material from Utah-produced Morton Thiokol solid-rocket boosters.

Every other nook or cranny seemed to feature a lurking statue of some fat-cat local businessman: a "world-renowned mining engineer"—a "pioneer in the development of supermarkets."

"Wow, look who built this place!" Mr. Judy said, gazing at a bronze plaque. "It was the Utah state governor who had Joe Hill shot by a firing squad! Man, that sure explains a lot..."

"This place is creepin' me out," Vanna said, hugging herself. "Let's go outside and wait on the lawn..."

"No, this place is great!" Starlitz objected. "Six Flags Over Jesus was decorated just like this...Let's go down in the basement!"

The basement featured a gigantic hand-embroidered silk tapestry: with the purple slope of Mount Fuji, a couple of wooden sailboats and a big cheesy spray of cherry blossoms. It had been presented to the People of Utah by the Japanese American Citizens League—"For Better Americans in a Greater America"—on July 21, 1940.

"Five months before Pearl Harbor," Mr. Judy said, aghast.

"Musta been mighty reassuring," Starlitz said slowly. He wandered off.

Mr. Judy stared at the eldritch relic with mingled pity and horror. "I wonder how many of these poor people ended up in relocation camps."

Vanna silently wiped her eyes on the tail of her shirt.

Starlitz stopped at the end of the hall and looked around the corner to his right. Suddenly he broke into a run.

They found him with his nose pressed to the glass framework around "The Mormon Meteor"—"designed, built and driven by 'Ab' Jenkins on the Bonneville Salt Flats." The 1930s racer, which had topped two hundred miles per hour in its day, sported a 750 hp Curtis Conqueror engine. Streamlined to the point of phallicism, the racer was fire-engine red and twenty-two feet long—except for the huge yellow Flash Gordon fin behind the tiny riveted one-man cockpit.

The two women left Starlitz alone a while, respecting his obsession.

Eventually Mr. Judy came to join him.

"Ab Jenkins," Starlitz breathed aloud. "'The only man who has raced an automobile 24 continuous hours without leaving the driver's seat.'"

Mr. Judy laughed. "Big deal, Leggy. You think this stupid boy-toy's impressive?" She waved at a set of glass-fronted exhibits. "That cheap-ass tourist art is ten times as weird. And the souvenir shop's got a sign that says *All shoplifters will be cheerfully beaten to a pulp!*"

"I wonder if it's got any fuel in it," Starlitz said dreamily. "The Firestones still look good—you suppose the points are clean?"

Mr. Judy's smile faded. "C'mon, Leggy. Snap out of it."

He turned to her, his eyeballs gone dark as slate. "You don't get it, do you? You can't even see it when it's right in front of you. This is it, Jude. The rest of the crap here is just so much cheesy bullshit, you could see stuff like that in Romania, but this"—he slapped the glass"—this is *America,* goddamn it!" He took a deep breath. "And I want it."

"Well, you can't *have* the 'Mormon Meteor.'"

"The hell," he said. "Look at this glass case. One good swift kick would break it. The cops would never expect anybody to boost this car. And if the engine would turn over, you could drive it right out the capitol door!" Starlitz ran both hands over his filthy hair and shivered. "Sunday night in Mormonville—there's not a soul in the fuckin' streets! And the Meteor does 200 miles an hour! By dawn we could have it safely buried under a dune in White Sands, come back whenever we need it…"

"But we *don't* need it," Mr. Judy said. "We'll *never* need this!"

He folded his arms. "You didn't know you needed the van, either. And I brought you the van, didn't I?"

"This thing isn't like the van. The van is useful in the liberation struggle."

Starlitz was scandalized. "Christ, you don't know *anything* about machinery. The way you talk about it, you'd think technology was for what people *need!*" He took a deep breath. "Look, Jude, trust me on this. This fucker is voodoo. It's a canopic jar, it's the Pharaoh's guts! It's the Holy Tabernacle, okay? We steal this baby, and the whole goddamn karmic keystone falls out of this place…"

Judy frowned. "Knock it off with the New Age crap, Legs. From you, it sounds really stupid."

They suddenly heard the echoing chang and whine of electric guitars, a thudding concussion of drums. Somewhere, someone in the Capitol was rocking out.

They hurried back upstairs. As they drew nearer they could hear the high-pitched wail of alien lyrics, cut with a panting electric clarinet and a whomping bassline.

Four young Japanese women with broad-brimmed felt hats and snarled dreadlocks were slouching against the wall of the Utah State Capitol rotunda, clustered around a monster Sony boom box. The women wore short stiff paisley skirts, tattered net stockings, a great deal of eye-makeup, and elaborate, near-psychedelic pearl-buttoned cowboy shirts. They were nodding, foot-tapping, chainsmoking and tapping ashes into a Nikon lens-cap.

Mr. Judy gave them the password. The Japanese women smiled brightly, without bothering to get up. One of them turned off their howling tape, and made introductions. Their names were Sachiho, Ako, Sayoko and Hukie. They were an all-girl heavy-metal rockband from Tokyo called "90s Girl"—*Nineties Gyaru*.

Sachiho, the 90s Girl among the foursome with the most tenacious grasp on English, tried to get the skinny across to Vanna and Judy. The latest DC from 90s Girl had topped out at 200,000 units, which was major commercial action in Tokyo pop circles, but peanuts compared to the legendary American pop market. 90s Girl, who nourished a blazing determination to become the *o-goruden bando*—great golden band—of Nipponese hard-rock, were determined to break the US through dogged club-touring. A college-circuit alternative radio network based in Georgia had reluctantly agreed to get them some American gigs.

The band members of 90s Girl had already spent plenty of vacation-time slumming in Manhattan, skindiving in Guam, and skiing in Utah, so they figured they had the Yankee scene aced. Any serious commercial analysis of the American rock scene made it obvious that most of the wannabe acts in America were supporting themselves with narcotics trafficking. This was the real nature of the American rock'n'roll competitive advantage.

The Tokyo-based management of 90s Girl had therefore made a careful market-study of American drug-consumption patterns and concluded that RU-486 was the hot and coming commodity. RU-486 was nonaddictive, didn't show up on the user, and it was not yet controlled by Yankee mafia, Jamaican dope-posses, or heavily armed Colombians. The profit potential was bright, the consumers relatively non-violent, and the penalties for distribution still confused.

90s Girl planned to sell the capsules through a network of metal-chick cult-fans in Arizona, Texas, Georgia, Florida, and North Carolina, with a final big blow-out in Brooklyn if they had any dope left when they finished their tour.

"This management of yours," Mr. Judy said. "The people doing all this market analysis. They're, not men, are they?"

"Oh no," said Sachiho. "Never, never."

"Great." Mr. Judy handed over her backpack. 90s Girl began stuffing dope into their camera cases.

Footsteps approached.

The assorted smugglers glanced around wildly for an escape route. There was none. The pro-life forces had deployed themselves with cunning skill. Enemies blocked each of the rotunda exits, in groups of six.

Their leader muscled his way to the fore. "Caught you red-handed!" he announced gleefully in the sullen silence. "You'll hand that contraband over now, if you please."

"Forget it," Mr. Judy said.

"You're not leaving this building with that wicked poison in your possession," the leader assured her. "We won't allow it."

Mr. Judy glared at him. "What're you gonna do, Mr. Nonviolence? Preach us to death?"

"That won't be necessary," he said grimly, veins protruding on the sides of his throat. "If you resist us violently, then we'll mace you with pepperspray. We'll superglue your bodies to the floor of the Capitol, and leave you there soaked in bottled blood, with placards around your necks, fully describing your awful crimes." Two of the nonviolent thugs began vigorously shaking aerosol cans.

"You Salvation?" Starlitz asked. He slipped his hand inside his photographer's vest.

"Some people call me that," the leader said. He was tall and clear-eyed and clean-shaven. He had a large nose and close-set eyes and wore a blue denim shirt and brown sans-a-belt slacks. He looked completely undistinguished. He looked like the kind of guy who might own a bowling alley. The only remarkable quality about Salvation was that he clearly meant every word he said.

"You might as well forget about that gun, sir," he said. "You can't massacre all of us, and we're not afraid to die in the service of humanity. And in any case, we're videotaping this entire encounter. If you murder us, you'll surely pay a terrible price." He clapped his hand on the shoulder of a companion with a videocam.

The guy with the minicam spoke up in an anxious whisper, which the odd acoustics of the rotunda carried perfectly. *"Uh, Salvation...something's gone wrong with the camera..."*

"How'd you know we were here?" Mr. Judy demanded.

"We're monitoring the Capitol's security cameras," Salvation said triumphantly, gesturing at an overhead surveillance unit. "You're not the only people in the world who can hack computers, you know!" He took a deep breath. "You're not the only people who can sing *We Shall Overcome*. You're not the only ones who can raise consciousness, and hold sit-ins, and block streets!" He laughed harshly. "You thought you were the Revolution. You thought you were the New Age. Well, ladies, *we are the change*. We're the Revolution now!"

Suddenly, and without warning, a great buzzing voice echoed down the hall behind him. *"Up against the wall!"* It was the cry of a police bullhorn.

A squad of heavily armed Secret Service agents burst headlong into the rotunda, in a flying wedge, Salvation's little knot of pro-lifers scattered and fell like bowling pins.

At the sight of the charging federal agents, Vanna, Mr. Judy, and Starlitz each sat down immediately, almost reflexively, tucking their laced hands behind their heads. The four members of 90s Girl sat up a little straighter, and watched bemused.

The feds surged through the rotunda like red-dogging linebackers. The pro-lifers blocking the other exits panicked and started to flee headlong, but were tackled and fell thrashing.

A redheaded woman in jeans and a blue-and-yellow Secret Service windbreaker danced into the rotunda, and lifted her bullhorn again. "The building's surrounded by federal agents!" she bellowed electronically. "I advise you dumb bastards to surrender peacefully!"

Her yell tore through the echoing rotunda like God shouting through a tin drum. The pro-lifers, stunned, went limp and nonresisting. She lowered her bullhorn and smiled at the sight of them, then nudged a nearby agent. "Read 'em their Miranda rights, Ehrlichman."

The fed, methodically bending over groups of his captured prey, began reading aloud from a laminated index card. The pro-lifers grunted in anguish as they were seized with cunning Secret Service judo-holds, then trussed like turkeys with whip-thin lengths of plastic handcuff.

The woman with the bullhorn approached the assorted smugglers, stopping by their Sony boom box. "Jane O'Houlihan, Utah Attorney General's office," she announced crisply, exhibiting a brass badge.

Mr. Judy looked up brightly. "How do you do, Ms. O'Houlihan? I think you'd better take it easy on these Japanese nationals. They're tourists, and don't have anything to do with this."

"How fuckin' stupid do you think I am?" O'Houlihan said. She sighed aloud. "You're sure lucky these pro-life dorks are wanted on a Kansas warrant for aggravated vandalism. Otherwise you and me would all be goin' downtown."

"You don't need to do that," Vanna told her timidly, wide-eyed.

O'Houlihan glared at them. "I'd bust you clowns in a hot second, only it would complicate my prosecution to bring you jerks into the picture…

Besides, these dipshits just hacked a State Police video installation. They screwed it up, too, the cameras have been malfin' like crazy all morning... That's a Section 1030 federal computer-intrusion offense! They're gonna break rocks!"

"It's certainly good to know that a sister is fully in charge of this situation," Mr. Judy said, tentatively lifting her hands from the nape of her neck. "These right-wing vigilantes are a menace to all women's civil rights."

"Sister me no sisterhood," O'Houlihan said, deftly prodding Mr. Judy with one Adidas-clad foot. "I didn't see you worthless New Age libbies lifting one damn finger to help me when I was busting check-forgers in the county attorney's office."

"We don't even live around here," Vanna protested. "We're from Ore— I mean, we're from another state."

"Yeah? Well, welcome to Utah, the Beehive State. Next time stay the fuck out of my jurisdiction."

A Secret Service agent clomped over. His sleeveless Kevlar flak jacket now hung loose, its Velcro tabs dangling. He looked very tough indeed. He looked as if he could bite bricks in half. "Any problem here, Janie?"

O'Houlihan smiled at him winningly. "None at all, Bob. These are just small-time losers...Besides, there seems to be an international angle." Sachiho, Ako, Hukie and Sayoko looked up impassively, their mascaraed eyes gone blank with sullen global-teenager Bohemianism.

"International, huh?" Bob muttered, gazing at the girl-group as if they'd just arrived via saucer from Venus. "That would let the Bureau in..." Bob adjusted his Ray-Bans. "Okay, Janie, if you say so, I guess they walk. But be sure and upload their dossiers to Washington."

"Will do!" O'Houlihan beamed.

Bob was reluctant. "You're damned sure they didn't try to get into any police systems?"

"They're not that smart," O'Houlihan told him. Bob nodded and returned to his cohorts, who were hauling handcuffed pro-lifers, by their armpits, face first down the echoing corridors. The arrestees wailed in anguish and struggled fitfully as their shoulders began to dislocate.

O'Houlihan raised the bullhorn to her lips. "Take it easy on 'em, boys! Remember, one of them is a secret federal informant." O'Houlihan lowered the bullhorn and grinned wickedly.

"We don't raid police systems," Mr. Judy assured her. "We wouldn't ever, ever raid federal computers."

"I *know* you don't," O'Houlihan said, with a chilly I-know-all cop's smile. "But if you little hippie bitches don't knock it off with the toll-fraud scams, you're gonna do time." She examined her polished nails. "If I ever meet you again, you're gonna regret it. Now get lost before I change my mind."

The seven contraceptive conspirators immediately fled the building. The unlucky pro-life agitators, now beginning to argue violently among themselves, were being flung headlong into a series of white Chevy vans. "Whew," Vanna said. "That could have been us!"

"I think that's *supposed* to be us," Mr. Judy said, confused. "I mean, it always was us *before*...I guess that's what they get for trying to *be* us."

"Boy, that cop Jane sure is..." Vanna drew a breath..."*attractive.*"

Mr. Judy cast her a sharp and jealous look. "Come on! She's the heat!"

"So what?" Vanna shot back, wounded. "I can't help it if she happens to be 'way hot."

"Great," Mr. Judy said sourly. "Well, we'd better blow this nowhere burg before your girlfriend puts a tail on us."

"What about the Mormon Meteor?" Starlitz demanded.

"Have you gone completely insane?" Mr. Judy said. "The place is swarming with feds!"

"Not anymore," Starlitz said. "This is the perfect time to boost it. They'll blame it on Salvation's crowd!"

Sachiho, who had been listening with interest, spoke up suddenly. "It's cool car," she remarked. "Gnarly American car to buy for trade balance. I like it excellent! Let's rent it and make cool video like ZZ Top."

"*Great* fuckin' idea!" Starlitz said.

"We have a perfectly good van that's a lot more use," Mr. Judy said.

Sachiho looked utterly blank. "*Wakarimasen*...I think we Nineties Girl have to go rehearse now." She did a little serpentine side-step. "Good-bye to you forever, okay? Don't call us, we'll call you." She quipped something in Japanese to the others. They began laughing merrily and bounced off down the stairs.

"Now that's attitude," Starlitz said admiringly, watching them go. "Those gals have got some real dress sense, too."

"But we're done here now, Leggy," Vanna said. "I thought you couldn't wait to go see the kid."

Starlitz grunted.

Mr. Judy took Vanna by the wrist. "I've got to level with you about that issue, Leggy."

Starlitz stopped gazing in admiration and looked up. "Yeah?"

"There isn't any kid."

Starlitz said nothing. His face clouded.

"Look, Leggy, think about it. We're abortionists. We know what to do about unwanted pregnancies. There never was a kid. We made up the kid after you came back from Europe."

"No kid, huh," Starlitz said. "You burned me."

Mr. Judy nodded somberly.

"It was all a scam, huh? Just some big scheme you came up with to lead me around with." He laughed sharply. "Jesus, I can't believe you thought that would work."

"Sorry, Leggy. It seemed like a good idea at the time. Don't hold it against us."

Starlitz laughed. "You did it just because I got absentminded that time, and didn't bring you back your dope. I got a little distracted, so you shaft me! Well, to hell with you! Good-bye forever, suckers."

Suddenly Starlitz ran downhill, headlong, after the retreating Japanese. "Hey!" he bellowed. "Girls! Nineties Girls! *Matte ite kudasai! Roadie-san wa arimasu ka?"*

Vanna and Judy watched as Starlitz vanished with the Japanese behind a line of trees.

"Why'd you lie to him like that?" Vanna said. "That was terrible."

Mr. Judy pulled a jingling set of keys from her pocket. "'Cause we need that van of his, that's why. Let's drive it off back to Oregon while we've got the chance."

"He'll get mad," Vanna said. "And he knows where we live. He'll come back for all his stuff."

"Sure, we'll see him again all right," Mr. Judy said. "In four years or something. He'll never miss the stuff, or us, in the meantime. When he sees something he really wants, he doesn't have any more sense than a blood-crazed weasel."

"You're not being very fair," Vanna said.

"That's just the way he is…We can't depend on him for anything. We don't *dare* depend on him. He can't think politically." Mr. Judy took a deep breath. "And even if he *could* think politically, he's basically motivated by the interests of the macho-imperialist oppressor class."

"I was thinking *mechanically,"* Vanna said. "We had a really rough ride through the desert, and we just lost our only mechanic. I sure hope that van starts."

"Of course it's gonna start!" Mr. Judy said, annoyed. "You think we did all those years of work, and organizing, and consciousness-raising, and took all those risks, just to end up here in the world capital of reactionary family-values bullshit, with our engine grinding uselessly, unable to move one inch off dead center? That's ridiculous."

Vanna said nothing. Contemplating the possibility had made her go a little pale.

"We're gonna drive it off easy as pie," Mr. Judy insisted. "And we'll change the paint first thing. We'll lose that dumb-ass televangelist logo, and paint it up as something really cool and happening. Like a portable notary service, or a digital bookmobile."

Vanna bit her lip. "I'm still worried...The kid's gonna want to know all about her father someday. She'll *demand* to know. Don't you think so?"

"No, I don't," Mr. Judy said, with complete conviction. "She'll never even have to ask."

The Littlest Jackal

"I hate Sibelius," said the Russian mafioso.

"It's that Finnish nationalist thing," said Leggy Starlitz.

"That's *why* I hate Sibelius." The Russian's name was Pulat R. Khoklov. He'd once been a KGB liaison officer to the air force of the Afghan government. Like many Afghan War veterans, Khoklov had gone into organized crime since the Soviet crackup.

Starlitz examined the Sibelius CD's print-job and plastic hinges with a dealer's professional eye. "Europeans sure pretend to like this classic stuff," he said. "Almost like pop, but it can't move real product." He placed the CD back in the rack. The outdoor market table was nicely set with cunningly targeted tourist-bait. Starlitz glanced over the glass earrings and the wooden jewelry, then closely examined a set of lewd postcards.

"This isn't 'Europe,'" Khoklov sniffed. "This is a Czarist Grand Duchy with bourgeois pretensions."

Starlitz fingered a poly-cotton souvenir jersey with comical red-nosed reindeer. It bore an elaborate legend in the Finno-Ugric tongue, a language infested with umlauts. "This is Finland, ace. It's European Union."

Khoklov was kitted-out to the nines in a three-piece linen suit and a snappy straw boater. Life in the New Russia had been very good to Khoklov. "At least Finland's not NATO."

"Look, fuckin' Poland is NATO now. Get over it."

They moved on to another table, manned by a comely Finn in a flowered summer frock and jelly shoes. Starlitz tried on a pair of shades from a revolving stand. He gazed experimentally about the marketplace. Potatoes. Dill. Carrots and onions. Buckets of strawberries. Flowers and flags. Orange fabric canopies over wooden market tables run by Turks and gypsies. People were selling salmon straight from the decks of funky little fishing boats.

Khoklov sighed. "Lekhi, you have no historical perspective." He plucked a Dunhill from a square red pack.

One of Khoklov's two bodyguards appeared at once, alertly flicking a Zippo. "No proper sense of *culture*," insisted Khoklov, breathing smoke and coughing richly. The guard tucked the lighter into his Chicago Bulls jacket and padded off silently on his spotless Adidas.

Starlitz, who was trying to quit, bummed a smoke from Khoklov, which he was forced to light for himself. Then he paid for the shades, peeling a salmon-colored fifty from a dense wad of Finnish marks.

Khoklov paused nostalgically by the Czarina's Obelisk, a bellicose monument festooned with Romanov aristo-fetish gear in cast bronze. Khoklov, whose politics shaded toward Pamyat rightism with a mystical pan-Slavic spin, patted the granite base of the Obelisk with open pleasure.

Then he gazed across the Esplanadi. "Helsinki city hall?"

Starlitz adjusted his shades. When arranging his end of the deal from a cellar in Tokyo, he hadn't quite gathered that Finland would be so relentlessly bright. "That's the city hall all right."

Khoklov turned to examine the sun-spattered Baltic. "Think you could hit that building from a passing boat?"

"You mean me personally? Forget it."

"I mean someone in a hired speedboat with a shoulder-launched surplus Red Army panzerfaust. Generically speaking."

"Anything's possible nowadays."

"At night," urged Khoklov. "A pre-dawn urban commando raid! Cleverly planned. Precisely executed. Ruthless operational accuracy!"

"This is summer in Finland," said Starlitz. "The sun's not gonna set here for a couple of months."

Khoklov, tripped up in the midst of his reverie, frowned. "No matter. You weren't the agent I had in mind in any case."

They wandered on. A Finn at a nearby table was selling big swollen muskrat-fur hats. No sane local would buy these items, for they were the exact sort of pseudo-authentic cultural relics that appeared only in tourist economies. The Finn, however, was flourishing. He was deftly slotting and whipping the Mastercards and Visas of sunburnt Danes and Germans through a handheld cellular credit checker.

"Our man arrives tomorrow morning on the Copenhagen ferry," Khoklov announced.

"You ever met this character before?" Starlitz said. "Ever done any real business with him?"

Khoklov sidled along, flicking the smoldering butt of his Dunhill onto the gray stone cobbles. "I've never met him myself. My boss knew him in the seventies. My boss used to run him from the KGB HQ in East Berlin. They called him Raf, back then. Raf the Jackal."

Starlitz scratched his close-cropped, pumpkin-like head. "I've heard of *Carlos* the Jackal."

"No, no," Khoklov said, pained. "Carlos retired, he's in Khartoum. This is Raf. A different man entirely."

"Where's he from?"

"Argentina. Or Italy. He once ran arms between the Tupamaros and the Red Brigades. We think he was an Italian Argentine originally."

"KGB recruited him and you didn't even know his nationality?"

Khoklov frowned. "We never recruited him! KGB never had to recruit any of those Seventies people! Baader-Meinhoff, Palestinians… They always came straight to us!" He sighed wistfully. "American Weather Underground—how I wanted to meet a groovy hippie revolutionary from Weather Underground! But even when they were blowing up the Bank of America the Yankees would never talk to real communists."

"The old boy must be getting on in years."

"No no. He's very much alive, and very charming. The truly dangerous are always very charming. It's how they survive."

"I like surviving," Starlitz said thoughtfully.

"Then you can learn a few much-needed lessons in charm, Lekhi. Since you're our liaison."

▲ ▼ ▲

Raf the Jackal arrived from across the Baltic in a sealed Fiat. It was a yellow two-door with Danish plates. His driver was a Finnish girl, maybe twenty. Her dyed-black hair was braided with long green extensions of tattered yarn. She wore a red blouse, cut-off jeans and striped cotton stockings.

Starlitz climbed into the passenger seat, slammed the door, and smiled. The girl was sweating with heat, fear, and nervous tension. She had a battery of ear-piercings. A tattooed wolf's-head was stenciled up her clavicle and nosing at the base of her neck.

Starlitz twisted and looked behind him. The urban guerrilla was scrunched into the Fiat's back seat, asleep, doped, or dead. Raf wore a denim jacket, relaxed-fit Levis and Ray-Bans. He'd taken his sneakers off and was sleeping in his rumpled mustard-yellow socks.

"How's the old man?" Starlitz said, adjusting his seat belt.

"Ferries make him seasick." The girl headed up the Esplanade. "We'll wake him at the safehouse." She shot him a quick sideways glance of kohl-lined eyes. "You found a good safehouse?"

"Sure, the place should do," said Starlitz. He was pleased that her English was so good. After four years tending bar in Roppongi, the prospect of switching Japanese for Finnish was dreadful. "What do they call you?"

"What did they tell you to call me?"

"Got no instructions on that."

The girl's pale knuckles whitened on the Fiat's steering-wheel. "They didn't inform you of my role in this operation?"

"Why would they wanna do that?"

"Raf is our agent now," the girl said. "He's not your agent. Our operations coincide—but only because our interests coincide. Raf belongs to my movement. He doesn't belong to any kind of Russians."

Starlitz twisted in his seat to stare at the slumbering terrorist. He envied the guy's deep sense of peace. It was hard to tell through the Ray-Bans, but the smear of sweat on his balding forehead gave Raf a look of unfeigned ease. Starlitz pondered the girl's latest remark. He had no idea why a college-age female Finn would claim to be commanding a 51-year-old veteran urban guerrilla.

"Why do you say that?" he said at last. This was usually a safe and useful question.

The girl glanced in the rear-view. They were passing a sunstruck green park, with bronze statues of swaggering Finnish poets and mood-stricken Finnish dramatists. She took a corner with a squeak of tires. "Since you need a name, call me Aino."

"Okay. I'm Leggy.... or Lekhi.... or Reggae." He'd been getting a lot of "Reggae" lately. "The safe-house is in Ypsallina. You know that neighborhood?" Starlitz plucked a laminated tourist map from his shirt pocket. "Take Mannerheimintie up past the railway station."

"You're not Russian," Aino concluded.

"Nyet."

"Are you Organizatsiya?"

"I forget what you have to do to officially join the Russian mafia, but basically, no."

"Why are you involved in the Ålands operation? You don't look political."

Leggy found the lever beneath the passenger seat and leaned back a little, careful not to jostle the slumbering terrorist. "You're sure you want to hear about that?"

"Of course I want to hear. Since we are working together."

"Okay. Have it your way. It's like this," Starlitz said. "I've been in Tokyo working for an all-girl Japanese metal band. These girls made it pretty big and they bought this disco downtown in Roppongi. I was managing the place.... Besides the headbanging, these metal-chicks ran another racket on the side. Memorabilia. A target-market teenage-kid thing. Fanmags, keychains, T-shirts, CD-ROMs.... Lotta money there!"

Aino stopped at a traffic light. The cobbled crosswalk filled with a pedestrian mass of sweating, sun-dazed Finns.

"Anyway, after I developed that teen market, I found this other thing. These cute little animals. 'Froofies.' Major hit in Japan. Froofy velcro shoes, Froofy candy, sodas, backpacks, badges, lunchkits...Froofies are what they call 'kawaii.'"

Aino drove on. They passed a bronze Finnish general on horseback. He had been a defeated general, but he looked like defeating him again would be far more trouble than it was worth. "What's kawaii?"

Starlitz rubbed his stubbled chin. "'Cute' doesn't get it across. Maybe 'adorable.' Big-money-making adorable. The kicker is that Froofies come from Finland."

"I'm a Finn. I don't know anything called Froofies."

"They're kids' books. This little old Finnish lady wrote them. On her kitchen table. Illustrated kid-stories from the Forties and Fifties. Of course lately they've been made into manga and anime and Nintendo cassettes and a whole bunch of other stuff...."

Aino's brows rose. "Do you mean Flüüvins? Little blue animals with heads like big fat pillows?"

"Oh, you know them, then."

"My *mother* read me Flüüvins! Why would Japanese want Flüüvins?"

"Well, the scam was—this old lady, she lives on this secluded island. Middle of the Baltic. Complete ass-end of nowhere. Old girl never married. No manager. No agent. Obviously not getting a dime off all this major Japanese action. Probably senile. So the plan is—I fly over to Finland. To these islands. Hunt her down. Cut a deal with her. Get her signature. Then, we sue."

"I don't understand you."

"She lives in the Åland Islands. Those islands are crucial to your people, and the Organizatsiya too. So you see the general convergence of interests here?"

Aino shook her green-braided head. "We have serious political and economic interests in the Ålands. Flüüvins are silly books for children."

"What's 'serious?' I'm talking plastic action figures! Cartoon drinking glasses. Kid-show theme songs. When a thing like this hits, it's major revenue. Factories churning round the clock in Shenzhen. Crates full of stuff into mall anchor-stores. Did you know that the 'California Raisins' are worth more than the entire California raisin crop? That's a true fact!"

Aino was growing gloomy. "I hate raisins. Californians use slave ethnic labor and pesticides. Raisins are nasty little dead grapes."

"I'm copacetic, but we're talking Japan here," Starlitz insisted. "Higher per-capita than Marin County! The ruble's in the toilet now, but the yen is sky-high. We get a big shakedown settlement in yen, we launder it in rubles, and we clear major revenue completely off the books. That's serious as cancer."

Aino lowered her voice. "I don't believe you. Why are you telling me such terrible lies? That's a very stupid cover story for an international spy!"

"You had to ask." Starlitz shrugged.

▲▼▲

They found the safehouse in Ypsallina. It was a duplex. The other half of the duplex was occupied by a gullible Finnish yuppie couple with workaholic schedules. Starlitz produced the keys. Aino went in, checked every room and every window with paranoid care, then went back to the Fiat and woke Raf.

Raf wobbled into the apartment, found the bathroom. He vomited with gusto, then turned on the shower. Aino brought in a pair of bulging blue nylon sports bags. There was no phone service, but Khoklov's people had thoughtfully left a clone-chipped cellular on the bedroom dresser.

Starlitz, who had been in the safehouse before, retrieved his laptop from the kitchen closet. It was Japanese portable with a keyboard the length of a cricket bat, a complex mess of ASCII, kanji, katakana, hiragana, and arcane function keys. It had a cellular modem.

Starlitz logged in to a Helsinki Internet service provider and checked the metal-band's website in Tokyo. Nothing much happening there. Sachiho was doing TV tabloid shows. Hukie had gone into production. Ako was in the studio for a solo album. Sayoko was pregnant. Again.

Starlitz tried his hotlist and found a new satellite JPEG file of developments on the ground in Bosnia. Starlitz was becoming very interested in Bosnia. He hadn't been there yet, but he could feel the lure increasing steadily. The Japanese scene was basically over. Once the real-estate bubble had busted, the glitz had run out of the Tokyo street-party and now the high yen was chasing the gaijin off. But Bosnia was clearly a very coming scene for the mid-90s. Not Bosnia per se (unless you were a merc, or crazy) but the surrounding safe-areas where the arms and narco people were setting up: Slovenia, Bulgaria, Macedonia, Albania.

Practically every entity that Starlitz found of interest was involved in the Bosnian scene. UN. USA. NATO. European Union. Russian intelligence, Russia mafia (interlocking directorates there). Germans. Turks. Greeks. Ndrangheta. Camorra. Israelis. Saudis. Iranians. Moslem Brotherhood. An enormous gaggle of mercs. There was even a happening Serbian folk-metal scene where Serb chicks went gigging for hooting audiences of war criminals. It was cool the way the Yugoslav scene kept re-complicating. It was his kind of scene.

Raf emerged from the bathroom. He'd shaved and had caught his thinning wet hair in a ponytail clip. He wore his jeans; his waistline sagged but there was muscle in his hairy shoulders.

Raf unzipped one of the sports bags. He tunneled into a baggy black T-shirt. Starlitz logged off.

Raf yawned. "Dramamine never works. Sorry."

"No problem, Raf."

Raf gazed around the apartment. The pupils of his dark eyes were two shrunken pinpoints. "Where's the girl?"

Starlitz shrugged. "Maybe she went out to cop some Chinese."

Raf found his shades and a packet of Gauloises. Raf might have been Italian. The accent made this seem plausible. "The boot of the car," he said. "Could you help?"

They hauled a big wrapped tarpaulin from the trunk of the Fiat and into the safe-house. Raf deftly untied the tarp and spread its contents across the chill linoleum of the kitchenette.

Rifles. Pistols. Ammo. Grenades. Plastique. Fuse wire. Detonator. Starlitz examined the arsenal skeptically. The hardware looked rather dated.

Raf deftly reassembled a stripped and greased AK-47. The rifle looked like it had been buried for several years, but buried by someone who knew how to bury weapons properly. Raf slotted the curved magazine and patted the tarnished wooden butt.

"Ever seen a Pancor Jackhammer?" asked Starlitz. "Modern gas-powered combat shotgun, all-plastic, bullpup design? Does four twelve-gauge rounds a second. The ammo drums double as landmines."

Raf nodded. "Yes, I do the trade shows. But you know—as a practical matter—you have to *let people know* that you can kill them."

"Yeah? Why is that?"

"Everyone knows the classic AK silhouette. You show civilians the AK—Raf brandished the rifle expertly—"they throw themselves on the floor. You bring in your modem plastic auto-shotgun, they think it's a vacuum cleaner."

"I take your point."

Raf lifted a bomb-clustered khaki webbing belt. "See these pineapples? Grenades like these, they have inferior killing radius, but they truly *look like grenades*. What was your name again, my friend?"

"Starlitz."

"Starlet, you carry these pineapples on your belt into a bank or a hotel lobby, you will never have to use them. Because people *know* pineapples. Of course, when you *use* grenades, you don't want to use these silly things. You want these rifle-mounted BG-15s, with the rocket propellant."

Starlitz examined the scraped and greasy rifle-grenades. The cylindrical explosive tubes looked very much like welding equipment, except for the stenciled military Cyrillic. "Those been kicking around a while?"

"The Basques swear by them. They work a charm against armored limos."

"Basque. I hear that language is even weirder than Finnish."

"You carry a gun, Starlet?"

"Not at the mo'."

"Take one little gun," said Raf generously. "Take that Makarov nine-millimeter. Nice combat handgun. Vintage Czech ammo. Very powerful."

"Maybe later," Starlitz said. "I might appropriate a key or so of that plastique. If you don't mind."

Raf smiled. "Why?"

"It's really hard finding good Semtex since Havel shut down the factories," Starlitz said moodily. "I might feel the need 'cause...I got this certain personal problem with video installations."

"Have a cigarette," said Raf sympathetically, shaking his pack. "I can see that you need one."

"Thanks." Starlitz lit a Gauloise. "Video's all over the place nowadays. Banks got videos...hotels got videos...groceries...cash machines...cop cars...Man, I *hate* video. I always hated video. Nowadays, video is really getting on my nerves."

"It's panoptic surveillance," said Raf. "It's the Spectacle."

Starlitz blew smoke and grunted.

"We should discuss this matter further," Raf said intently. "Work in the Struggle requires a solid theoretical grounding. Then you can focus this instinctive proletarian resentment into a coherent revolutionary response." He began sawing through a wrapped brick of Semtex with a butterknife from the kitchen drawer.

Starlitz ripped the plastique to chunks and stuffed them into his baggy pockets.

The door opened. Aino had returned. She had a companion: a very tall and spectrally pale young Finn with an enormous cotton-candy wad of steely purple hair. He wore a pearl-buttoned cowboy shirt and leather jeans. A large gold ring pierced his nasal septum and hung over his upper lip.

"Who is this?" smiled Raf, swiftly tucking the Makarov into the back of his belt.

"This is Eero," said Aino. "He programs. For the movement."

Eero gazed at the floor with a diffident shrug. "Many people are better hackers than myself." His eyes widened suddenly. "Oh. Nice guns!"

"This is our safehouse," said Raf.

Eero nodded. The tip of his tongue stole out and played nervously with the dangling gold ring.

"Eero came quickly so we could get started at once," Aino said. She looked at the greasy arsenal with mild disdain, the way one might look at a large set of unattractive wedding china. "Now where is the money?"

Starlitz and Raf exchanged glances.

"I think what Raf is trying to say," said Starlitz gently, "is that traditionally you don't bring a contact to the safehouse. Safehouses are for storing weapons and sleeping. You meet contacts in open-air situations or public locales. It's just a standard way of doing business."

Aino was wounded. "Eero's okay! We can trust him. Eero's in my sociology class."

"I'm sure Eero is fine," said Raf serenely.

"He brought a cell phone," Starlitz said, glancing at the holster on Eero's chrome-studded leather belt. "Cops and spooks can track people's movements through mobile cellphones."

"It's all right," Raf said gallantly. "Eero is your friend, my dear, so we trust him. Next time we are a bit more careful with our operational technique. Okay?" Raf spread his hands, judiciously. "Comrade Eero, since you're here, take a little something. Have a grenade."

"Truly?" said Eero, with a self-effacing smile. "Thank you." He tried stuffing a pineapple, without success, into the tight leather pocket of his jeans.

"Where is the money?" Aino repeated.

Raf shook his head gently. "I'm sure Mister Starlet is not so foolish to bring so much cash to our first meeting."

"The cash is at a dead drop," Starlitz said. "That's a standard method of transferral. That way, if you're surveilled, the oppo can't make out your contacts."

"The tactical teachings of good old Patrice Lumumba University," said Raf cheerfully. "You were an alumnus, Starlet?"

"Nope," said Starlitz. "Never was the Joe College type. But the Russian mob's chock-full of Lumumba grads."

"I understand this money transfer tactic," murmured Eero, swinging the grenade awkwardly at the end of one bony wrist. "It's like an anonymous remailer at an Internet site. Removing accountability."

"Is the money in US dollars?" said Aino.

Raf pursed his lips. "We don't accept any so-called dollars that come from Russia, remember? Too much fresh ink."

"It's in yen," said Starlitz. "Three point two million US."

Raf brightened. "Point two?"

"It was three mill when we finalized the deal, but the yen had another uptick. Consider it a little gift from our Tokyo contacts. Don't launder it all in one place."

"That's good news," said Aino, with a tender smile.

Starlitz turned to Eero. "Is that enough bread to get you and your friends set up in the Ålands with the networked Suns?"

Eero blinked limpidly. "The workstations have all arrived safely. No more problems in America with computer export restrictions. We could ship American computers straight to Russia if we liked."

"That's swell. Any problem getting proper crypto?"

Eero picked at a purple wisp of hair with his free hand. "The Dutch have been most understanding."

"Any problem leasing the bank building in the Ålands, then?"

"We bought the building. With money to spare. It was a cannery, but the Baltic has been driftnetted, so...." Eero·shrugged his bony shoulders. "It has a little Turkish restaurant next door. So the programmers have plenty of pilaf and shashlik. Finn programmers...we like our pilaf."

"Pilaf!" Raf enthused, all jolliness. "I haven't had a decent pilaf since Beirut."

Starlitz narrowed his eyes. "How about your personnel? Any problems there?"

Eero nodded. "We wish we had more people on the start-up, of course. Technical start-ups always want more people. Still, we have enough Finnish hackers to boot and run your banking system. We are mostly very young people, but if those Russian maths professors can login from Leningrad—sorry, Petersburg—then we should have no big problems. The Russian maths people, they were all unemployed unfortunately for them. But they are very good programmers, very solid skills. The only problem with our many young hackers from Finland...." Eero absently switched the grenade from hand to hand. "Well, we are so very excited about the first true Internet money-laundry. We tried very hard not to talk, not to tell anyone what we are doing, but...well, we're so proud of the work."

"Tell your mouse-jockeys to sit on the news a while longer," Starlitz said.

"Really, it's too late," Eero told him meekly.

Starlitz frowned. "Well, how many goddamn people have you Finn cowboys let in on this thing, for Christ's sake?"

"How many people read the alt newsgroups?" Eero said. "I don't have those figures, but there's alt.hack, alt.2600, alt.smash.the.state, alt.fan.black-net.... Many."

Starlitz ran his hand over his head. "Right," he said. Like most Internet disasters, the situation was a fait accompli. "Okay, that development has torn it big-time. Aino, you did right to bring this guy here right away. The hell with proper operational protocol. We gotta get that bank up and running as soon as possible."

"There's nothing wrong with publicity," Raf said. "We need publicity to attract business."

"There'll be business all right," Starlitz said. "The Russian mob is already running the biggest money-laundry since the Second World War. The arms and narco crowd worldwide are banging·down the doors. Black electronic cash is a vital component of the emergent global system. The point is—we got a very narrow window of opportunity here. If our little crowd is gonna get anything out of this set-up, we have gotta be there with a functional online money-laundry just when the system really needs one. And just before everybody else realizes that."

"Then publicity is vital," Raf insisted. "Publicity is our oxygen! With a major development like this one, you must seize and create your own headlines. It's like Leila Khaled always says: 'The world has to hear our voice.'"

Aino blinked. "Is Leila Khaled still alive?"

"Leila lives!" Raf said. "Wonderful woman, Leila Khaled. She does social work in Damascus with the orphans of the Intifada. Soon she will be in the new Palestinian government."

"Leila Khaled," said Aino thoughtfully. "I envy her historical experience so much. There's something so direct and healthy and physical about hijacking planes."

Eero couldn't seem to find a place inside his clothing for the grenade. Finally he placed it daintily on the kitchen counter and regarded it with morose respect.

"Any other questions?" Raf asked Starlitz.

"Yeah, plenty," Starlitz said. "The Organizatsiya's got their pet Russian math professors working the technical problems. I figure the Russians can hack the math—Russians do great at that. But black-market online money laundering is a *commercial customer service operation*. Customer service is definitely not a Russian specialty."

"So?"

"So we can't hang around waiting for clearance from Moscow Mafia muckety-mucks. If this scheme is gonna work, we gotta slam it together and get it online pronto. We need quick results."

"Then you have the right man," said Raf briskly. "I always specialize in quick results." He shook Eero's hand. "You've been very helpful, Eero. It was pleasant to meet you. Enjoy your stay in the islands. We look forward to further constructive contacts. *Viva la revolucion digitale!* Goodbye and good luck."

"You don't have the big money for us yet?" Eero said.

"Real soon now," Starlitz said.

"Could I have some cab fare please?"

Starlitz gave him a 100-mark Jean Sibelius banknote. "Hei hei," Eero said, with a melancholy smile. He tucked the note into his cowboy shirt pocket and left.

Starlitz saw the hacker to the door, and checked the street as the cadaverous Finn ambled off. He was unsurprised to see Khoklov's two bodyguards lurking clumsily in a white Hertz rental car, parked up the street. Presumably they were relaying signals from the plethora of covert listening devices that the Russians had installed in Raf's safe-house.

Eero drifted past the Russian mobsters in a daze of hacker self-absorption. Starlitz found the kid an interesting specimen. In Japan there were plenty of major Goth kids, but the vampire people-in-black contingent had never really crossbred with Japan's hacker population. Here in Finland, though, there were somber and lugubrious hairsprayed Cure fans pretty much across the social spectrum: car repair guys, hotel staff, pizza delivery, government clerks, the works.

When Starlitz returned, Raf was hunting in the kitchen for coffee. "Aino, let's review the political situation."

Aino perched obediently on a birchwood kitchen stool. "The Åland Islands are a chain in the Gulf of Bothnia between Finland and Sweden. They include Åland, Föglö, Kökar, Sottunga, Kumlinge, and Brändö."

"Yeah, right, okay," Starlitz grunted.

"The largest city is Mariehamm with ten thousand inhabitants." She paused. "That's where the autonomous digital bank will be established."

"We're doing great so far."

"There are twenty-five thousand Åland citizens, mostly farmers and fishery people, but thirty percent are engaged in the tourist industry. They run small-scale casinos and duty-free shops. The Ålands are a popular day-tripping destination from continental Europe."

Starlitz nodded. He'd seen the shortlist of potential candidates for a Russian offshore banking set-up. The Ålands offered the tastiest possibilities.

Aino sat up straighter. "The inhabitants are Swedish-speaking ethnics. In 1920, against their will and against a popular plebiscite, they were ceded to Finland as part of a negotiated settlement by the now-extinct League of Nations. In truth these oppressed people are neither Swedes nor Finns. They are Ålanders."

"The islands' national liberation will proceed along two fronts," said Raf, deftly setting a coffeepot to boil. "The first is the Åland Island Liberation Front, which is, essentially, my operation. The second front is Aino's people from the university, the Suomi Anti-Imperialist Cells, who make it their cause to end the shameful injustice of Finnish imperialism. The outbreak of armed struggle and a terror campaign will provoke domestic crisis in Finland. The cheapest and easiest apparent solution will be to grant full autonomy to the Ålands. Since the islands are an easy day-trip from Petersburg this will leave the Organizatsiya with a free hand for their banking operations."

"You're a busy guy, Raf."

"I've been resting on my laurels long enough," said Raf, carefully rinsing three spanking-new coffee mugs. "It's a new Europe now. Many fantastic new opportunities."

"Level with me. Do any of these Åland Island hicks really want independence? They seem to be doing okay just as they are."

Raf, surprised at the question, smiled.

Aino frowned. "Much work remains to be done in the way of raising revolutionary consciousness in the Ålands. But we in the Suomi Anti-Imperialist Cells will have the resources to do that political work. Victory will be ours, because the Finnish liberal-fascist state does not have the capacity to restrain a captive nation against its will. Or if they do—" She smiled bitterly. "That will demonstrate the tenuousness of the current Finnish regime and its basic failure as a European state."

"Who have we got on the ground in the Ålands who can speak their local weirdo version of Swedish? Just in case we need to, like, phone in a claim or something."

"We have three people," Raf said. "The new premier, the new foreign minister, and of course the new economics minister, who will be in charge of easing things for the Russian operations. They are the shadow cabinet of the Ålands Republic."

"*Three* people?"

"Three people are plenty! There are only twenty-five thousand of them total. If the projections are right, the offshore bank will be clearing twenty-five million dollars in the first six months! Those islands are little rocks. It's potatoes and fish and casinos for rich Germans. The locals aren't players. The mob and their friends can buy them all."

"They matter," Aino said. "They matter to the Movement."

"But of course."

"The Ålands *deserve* their nation. If they don't deserve their nation, then *we Finns* don't deserve our nation. There are only five million Finns."

"We always yield to political principle," said Raf indulgently. He passed her a brimming mug. "Drink your coffee. You need to go to work."

Aino glanced at her watch, surprised. "Oh. Yes."

"Shall I cut the hash into gram bags? Or will you take the brick?"

She blinked. "You don't have to cut it, Raffi. They can cut it at the bar."

Raf opened one of the sports bags and passed her a fat brick of dope neatly wrapped in a Copenhagen newspaper.

"You work in a bar? That's a good cover job," Starlitz said. "What kind of hash is that?"

"Something very new in Europe," Raf said. "It's Azerbaijani hash."

"Ex-Soviet hash isn't really very good," sniffed Aino. "They don't know how to do it right.... I don't like to sell hash. But if you sell people drugs, then they respect you. They won't talk about you when cops come. I hate cops. Cops are fascist torturers. They should all be shot. Do you need the car, Raf?"

"Take the car," Raf said.

Aino fetched her purse and left the safehouse.

"Interesting girl," commented Starlitz, in the sudden empty silence. "Never heard of any Finn terror groups before. Germans, French, Irish, Basques, Croats, Italians. Never Finns, though."

"They're a bit behind the times in this corner of Europe. She's one of the new breed. Very brave. Very determined. It's a hard life for terrorist women." Raf carefully sugared his coffee. "Women never get proper credit. Women kidnap ministers, women blow up trains—women do very well at the work. But no one calls them 'armed revolutionaries.' They're always—what does the press say?—'maladjusted female neurotics.' Or ugly hardened lesbians with a father-figure complex. Or cute little innocents, seduced and brainwashed by the wrong sort of man." He snorted.

"Why do you say that?" Starlitz said.

"I'm a man of my generation, you know." Raf sipped his coffee. "Once, I wasn't advanced in my feminist thinking. It was being close to Ulrike that raised my consciousness. Ulrike Meinhoff. A wonderful girl. Gifted journalist. Smart. Eloquent. Very ruthless. Quite good-looking. But Baader and that other one—what was her name? They treated her so badly. Always yelling at her in the safehouse—calling her a gutless intellectual, spoilt child of the bourgeoisie and so forth. My God, aren't we all spoilt children of the bourgeoisie? If the bourgeoisie hadn't made a botch of us, we wouldn't need to kill them."

A car pulled up outside. The engine died and doors slammed.

Starlitz walked to the front window, peeked through the blind.

"It's the yuppies from next door," he said. "Looks like they're home early."

"We should introduce ourselves," Raf said. He began combing his hair.

"Uh-oh, scratch that," Starlitz said. "That's the guy who lives next door all right, but that's not the woman. He's got a different woman."

"A girlfriend?" Raf said with interest.

"Well, it's a much younger woman. In a wig, net hose and red high heels." The door in the next duplex opened and slammed. A stereo came on. It was playing a hot Cuban rhumba.

"This is a golden opportunity," said Raf, shoving his coffee mug aside. "Let's introduce ourselves now as his new neighbors. He'll be very embarrassed. He'll never look at us again. He'll never question us. Also, he'll keep his wife away from us."

"That's a good tactic," Starlitz said.

"All right. Let me do the talking." Raf went to the door.

"You still got that Makarov in the back of your belt, man."

"Oh yes. Sorry." Raf tossed the pistol onto the sleek Finnish couch.

Raf opened the front door. Then he back-stepped deftly back into the apartment and shut the door firmly. "There's a white rental car on the street."

"Yeah?"

"Two men inside it."

"Yeah?"

"Someone just shot them."

Starlitz hurried to the window. There were half a dozen people clustered across the street. Two of them had just murdered Khoklov's bodyguards, suddenly emptying silenced pistols through the closed glass of the windows. The street was not entirely deserted, but killing people with silenced pistols was a remarkably unobtrusive affair if done with brio and accuracy.

Four men began crossing the street. They wore jeans, jogging shoes, and, despite the heat, box-cut Giorgio Armani blazers. Two of them were carrying dainty little videocams. All of them were carrying guns.

"Zionists," Raf announced. Briskly, but without haste, he retreated to his arsenal on the kitchen floor. He slung an AK over his shoulder, propped a second assault rifle within easy reach, then knelt around the corner of the kitchen wall, giving himself a clear line of fire at the front door.

Starlitz quickly weighed various possibilities. He decided to keep watching the window.

With swift and deadly purpose, the hit-team marched to the adjoining duplex. The door broke off its hinges as they kicked their way in. There were brief yelps of indignant surprise, and a quiet multiple stuttering. A burst of Uzi slugs pierced the adjoining wall and embedded themselves in the floor.

Raf rose to his feet, his plump face the picture of glee. He touched one finger to his lips.

Footsteps clomped rapidly up and down the stairs in the next apartment. Doors banged, drawers opened. A bedside telephone jangled as it was knocked from its table. In three minutes the hit-team was out the door.

Raf scurried to the window and knelt. He'd grabbed a small pocket Nikon from his sports bag. He clicked off a roll of snapshots as the hit squad retreated. "I'm so tempted to shoot them," he said, hitching the sling of his assault rifle, "but this is better. This is very funny."

"That was Mossad, right?"

"Yes. They thought I was the neighbor."

"They must have had a description of you and the girl. And they know you're here in Finland, man. That's not good news."

"Let's phone in a credit for their hit. The Helsinki police might catch them. That would be lovely. Where is that cellphone?"

"Look, we were extremely lucky just now. We'd better leave."

"I'm always lucky. We have plenty of time." Raf gazed at his arsenal and sighed. "I hate to abandon these guns, but we have no car to carry them. Let's carry the guns next door, before we go! That should win us some nice press."

▲ ▼ ▲

Starlitz met with Khoklov at two A.M. The midnight sun had given up its doomed attempt to sink and was now rising again in refulgent splendor. The two of them were strolling the spectrally abandoned streets of Helsinki, not too far from Khoklov's posh suite at the Arctia.

As European capitals went, Helsinki was a very young town. Most of it had been built since 1900, and quite a lot of that had been leveled by Russian bombers in the 1940s. Nevertheless the waterfront streets looked like stage sets for the Pied Piper of Hamelin, all copper-gabled roofs and leaded glass and quaint window turrets.

"I miss my boys," Khoklov grumbled. "Why did they have to ice my boys? Stupid bastards."

"Lot of Russian Jews in Israel now. Israel's very hip to the Russian mafia scene. Maybe it was a message."

"No. They're just out of practice. They thought my boys were guarding Raf. They thought that poor fat Finn was Raf. Raf makes them nervous. He's been on their hit-list since the Munich Olympics."

"How'd they know Raf was here?"

"It's those hackers at the bank. They've been talking too much. Three of our depositors are big Israeli arms dealers." Khoklov was tired. He'd been up all night explaining developments by phone to an anxious cabal of millionaire ex-Chekists in Petersburg.

"Since the word is out, we've got to move this into high gear, ace."

"I know that only too well." Khoklov opened a gunmetal pillbox and dry-swallowed a pink tab. "The Higher Circles in Organizatsiya—they love the idea of black electronic cash, but they're old-fashioned and skeptical. They say they want quick results, and yet they give me trouble about financing."

"I never expected those nomenklatura cats to come through for us," Starlitz said. "They're all ex-KGB bureaucrats, as slow as hell. If the Japanese shakedown works, we'll have the capital all right. You say they want results? What kind of results exactly?"

"You've met our golden boy now," said Khoklov. "What did you think of him? Be frank."

Starlitz weighed his words. "I think we're better off without him. We don't need him for a gig like this. He's over-qualified."

"He's good though, isn't he? A real professional. And he's always lucky. Lucky is better than good."

"Look, Pulat Romanevich. We've known each other quite a while, so I'm going to level with you. This guy is not right for the job. This Ålands coup is a business thing, we're trying to hack the structure of multinational cash-flows. It's the Infobahn. It's the nineties. It's borderless and it's happening. It's a high-risk start-up, sure, but so what? All Infobahn stuff is like that. It's global business, it's okay. But this is not a global business guy you've got here. This guy is a fuckin' golem. You used to arm him and pay him way back when. I'm sure he looked like some Che Guevara hippie poet rebel against capitalist society. But this guy is not an asset."

"You think he's crazy? Psychopathic? Is that it?"

"Look, those are just words. He's not crazy. He's what he is. He's a jackal. He feeds on dead meat from bigger crooks and spooks, and sometimes he kills rabbits. He thinks straight people are sheep. He's got it in for consumer society. Enough to blow up our potential customers and laugh about it. The guy is a nihilist."

Khoklov walked half a block in silence, shoulders hunched within his linen jacket. "You know something?" he said suddenly. "The world has gone completely crazy. I used to fly MiGs for the Soviet Union. I dropped a lot of bombs on Moslems, and I got medals. The pay was all right. I haven't flown a jet in combat in eight years. But I loved that life. It suited me, it really did. I miss it every day."

Starlitz said nothing.

"Now we call ourselves Russia. As if that could help us. We can't feed ourselves. We can't house ourselves. We can't even exterminate a lousy bunch of fucking Chechnyans. It's just like with these fucking Finns! We owned them for eighty years. Then the Finns got smart with us. So we rolled in with tanks and the sons of bitches ran into their forests in the dark and the snow, and they kicked our ass! Even after we finally crushed them, and stole the best part of their country, they just came right back! Now it's fifty years later, and the Russian Federation owes Finland a billion dollars. There are only five million Finns! My country owes every single Finn two hundred dollars each!"

"It's that Marxist thing, ace." They walked on in silence.

"We're past the Marxist thing," said Khoklov, warming to his theme as the pill took hold. "Now it's different. This time Russia has a kind of craziness that is truly big enough and bad enough to take over the whole world. Massive, total, institutional corruption: Top to bottom: Nothing held back. A new kind of absolute corruption that will sell *anything*: the flesh of our women, the future of our children. Everything inside our museums and our churches. Anything goes for money: gold, oil, arms, dope, nukes. We'll sell the soil and the forests and the Russian sky. We'll sell our souls."

They passed the bizarre polychrome facade of a Finnish-Mexican restaurant. "Listen, ace," Starlitz said. "If it's the soul thing that's got you down, this guy won't help you there. It was a serious mistake to break him out of mothballs.

You should have left him nodding-out in some bar in Baghdad listening to Bee Gees on vinyl. I don't know what you'll do about him now. You might try to bribe him with some kind of major ransom money, and hope he gets too drunk to move. But I don't think he'll do that for you. Bribes just flatter him."

"Okay," Khoklov said. "I agree. He's too dangerous, and he has too much past. After the coup, we kill him. I owe that much to Ilya and Lev, anyway."

"I appreciate that sentiment, but it's kinda late now, ace. You should have iced him when we knew where he was staying."

There was a distant hollow thump.

The Russian cocked his head. "Was that mortar fire?"

"Car bomb, maybe?" In the blue and lucid distance, filthy smoke began to rise.

▲ ▼ ▲

Raf claimed that the abortive Israeli hit had been the twelfth attempt on his life. This might have been stretching the truth. It was only the second time that a Mossad hit-team had shot the wrong man in a neutral Scandinavian country.

Russians hated to commit themselves fully to a project. Seventy years of totalitarianism had left them with a terrific appetite for back-tracking, double-speak and doublecross. Raf, however, delighted in providing quick results.

Granted, his Ålands liberation campaign had had a few tactical setbacks. He'd had to abandon most of his favorite guns with the loss of his first safe-house. The Mossad team had escaped apprehension by the dumbfounded Finnish police. The car-bombing at the FinnAir office had cost Raf his yellow Fiat.

The Suomi Anti-Imperialist Cells excelled at spraying radical political graffiti, but their homemade petrol bombs at the Jyväskylä police station had done only minor damage. The outspoken Helsinki newspaper editor had survived his kneecapping and would probably walk again.

Nevertheless, Raf's ex-KGB sponsors back in Petersburg were impressed with the veteran's initiative and can-do spirit. They'd supplied another payoff.

With a brimming war-chest of mafia-supplied Euro-yen, Raf was on a roll. Raf had successfully infiltrated six Yankee mercs from the little-known but extremely violent American anarcho-rightist underground. Thanks to relaxed cross-border inspections in Europe and the dazed preoccupations of America's ninja tobacco inspectors, these Yankee gun-runners had boldly brought Raf an up-to-date and very lethal arsenal of NATO's remaindered best.

Raf also had ten Russian thugs on call. These men were combat-hardened mercenaries from the large contingent of thirty thousand ex-military professionals who guarded Russia's bankers. Russian bankers who were not mafia-affiliated were shot down in droves by the black marketeers. Russian bankers who were mafia-affiliated were generally killed by one another. These bankers' bodyguards were enjoying a booming trade. Being bodyguards, they naturally excelled at assassination.

These dangerous cliques of armed alien agitators would have been near-useless in Finland without the protection of locals on the ground. Raf had the Suomi Anti-Imperialist Cells to cover that front. The Suomi Anti-Imperialist Cells consisted of five hard-core undergraduates, plus a loose group of young fellow-travelers who would probably offer aide and shelter if pressed. The Cells also had an ideological guru, a radical Finnish nationalist professor and poet who had no real idea what his teachings had wrought among his nation's postmodern youth.

So Raf had twenty or so people ready to use guns and bombs at his direction. To the uninitiated; this might not have seemed an impressive force. However, by the conventional standards of European terrorism, Raf was doing splendidly. National movements such as ETA, IRA, and PLO tended to be somewhat larger, due to their extensive labor-pool of the embittered and oppressed, but Raf the Jackal was a creature of a different breed: a true revolutionary internationalist, a freelance with a dozen passports. His Åland Island Liberation Front was big. It was bigger than Germany's Baader-Meinhof. It was bigger than France's Action Directe. It was about as big as the Japanese Red Army, and considerably better financed. A group of this sort could change history. A far more primitive conspiracy had murdered Abraham Lincoln.

▲ ▼ ▲

Starlitz was listening to international Finland Radio on the shortwave. It was tough to find decent English-language coverage of the ongoing terror campaign. Despite their continued selfless service in the UN blue-helmet contingent, neutral Finland didn't have a lot of foreign friends. The internal troubles of a neutral country didn't compel much general interest.

This would likely change, however, now that Raf had brought in outside experts. Raf was giving his Yankee new-hires an extensive rundown on the theory and practice of detonating acetylene bottles.

Aino had rented the state-supported handicrafts center through the good offices of her student activist group. The walls of the terrorist hideaway were covered with weird woolly hangings, massive hand-saws, pine-tar soaps and eldritch Finnish glassware.

Aino was fully up-to-speed on improvised demolitions, so she had been appointed a look-out. She sat near a second-floor window overlooking the driveway, with a monster Finnish elk-rifle at hand. The job was tedious. Aino was leafing through a stack of English-language Flüüvin books which Starlitz had picked up at a Helsinki bookstore. Helsinki boasted bookstores half the size of aircraft hangars. The book thing was something to do during those long dark winters.

"How many of these did she write?" Aino said.

"Twenty-five. The hottest sellers are *Froofies Go to Sea* and *Papa Froofy and the Mushroom Tigers*."

"They seem even stranger in English. It's strange that she cares so much about her little blue creatures. She worries about them so much, and gets so emotionally touched about them, and they don't even really exist." Aino flipped through the pages. "Look, here the Flüüvins are walking through the fire-mists on big stilts. That's a good picture. And look! There's that cave creature that carries the harmonica and complains all the time."

"That would be Speffy the Nerkulen."

"Speffy the Nerkulen." Aino frowned. "That isn't a proper Finnish name. It isn't Swedish either. Not even Åland Swedish."

Starlitz turned off the shortwave, which was detailing Finnish agricultural production. "She imagined Speffy, that's all. Speffy the Nerkulen just popped out of her little gray head. But Speffy the Nerkulen sure moves major product in Hokkaido."

Aino riffled the pages of the paperback. "I could make a book like this. She wrote this book fifty years ago. She was my age when she wrote and drew this book. I could do this myself."

"Why do you say that?"

She looked up. "Because I could, I know I could. I can draw. I can tell stories. I'm always telling stories to people at the bar. Once I did a band poster."

"That's swell. How'd you like to come along with me and brace up the little old lady? I need a Finnish translator, and a former Froofy fan would be great. Besides, she can give you helpful tips on kid-lit."

Aino looked at him, surprised. Slowly, she frowned. "What are you saying? I'm a revolutionary soldier. You should respect my political commitment. You wouldn't talk to me that way if I was a twenty-year-old boy."

"If you were a twenty-year-old boy, you'd fuckin' spit on Speffy the Nerkulen."

"No I wouldn't."

"Yes you would. Young soldier boys are cheaper than dirt. They're a fuckin' commodity. Who needs 'em? But a young female Froofy fan could be a very useful cut-out in some dicey negotiations."

"You're still lying to me. You should stop. I'm not fooled."

Starlitz sighed. "Look. It's the truth. Try and get it straight. You think the Åland Islands are important, right? Important enough to blow up trains for. Well, Speffy the Nerkulen is the most important thing that ever came out of the Akland Islands. Froofies are the only Ålands product that you can't obtain anywhere else. Twenty-five thousand hick fishermen in the Baltic are doing *great* to produce a major worldwide pop hit like Speffy the Nerkulen. If the Ålands were Jamaica, he'd be Bob Marley."

One of Raf's new recruits entered the room. He was bearded and muscular, maybe thirty. He wore a Confederate flag T-shirt and carried a Colt automatic in a belt holster. "Hey," he said. "Y'all speak English?"

"Yo," said Starlitz.

"Where's the can?"

Starlitz pointed.

"Hey babe," said the American, pausing. "That's a lady's rifle. You say the word, I'll give you something serious to shoot with."

Aino said nothing. Her grip tightened on the rifle's polished walnut stock.

The American grinned at Starlitz. "She's got no English, huh? She's a Russian, right? I heard there'd be lots of Russian chicks in this operation. Man. What a dollar'll do these days." He rubbed his hands.

"Posse Comitatus?" Starlitz hazarded.

"Aw hell no. We're not militia. Those militia boys, they're all in a sweat over UN black helicopters and the New World Order…. That's bullshit! We know the New World Order. We got contacts. We're gonna be inside the goddamn black helicopters. Shoulder to shoulder with Ivan, this time!"

▲ ▼ ▲

Finland had the most expensive booze in the world. This was Finnish social democratic policy, part and parcel with the world's lowest infant mortality rate. Nevertheless, Finns were truly fabulous drunks. The little Kasarmikatu bar was jammed with Finns methodically transiting from modest self-effacement to chest-pounding no-brakes bravado. A television barked above the shining racks of vodka and koskenkorva, showing broadcast news from across the Baltic. Another Parliamentary crisis in Moscow. A furious Russian delegate was pounding the podium in a blue vinyl jacket and a Megadeth T-shirt.

The Japanese financier set down his apple juice and adjusted his sunglasses. "His Holiness the Master does not approve of drunkenness. Alcohol clouds the vision and occludes the flow of ki."

"I can't believe we found a Japanese who won't drink after a business deal," Khoklov bitched in Russian. The Japanese money-man didn't speak or understand Russian. The three of them were clustered in the darkest comer of the Helsinki bar.

Starlitz spoke in Russian. "Our star depositor here has got a very severe case of that Pacific Rim New Age thing. These Supreme Truth guys are completely nuts. However, they're richer than God."

Starlitz silently toasted the money-man with a shot of Finnish cranberry vodka. He'd convinced their backer that this pulverizing liquor was cranberry juice. He switched to fluent gutter Japanese. "Khoklov-san tells me that he admires your electric skullcap very much. He wants to try one for himself. He is seeking health benefits and increased peace of mind."

"Saaaaa…" riposted Mr. Inoue, patting the plasticized top of his shaven head. "The electroneural stabilizers of His Holiness the Master. They will soon be in mass production at our Fuji fortress."

"You got like a kids' version of those, right?" said Starlitz.

"Of course. His Holiness the Master has many children."

"So have you ever considered, like, a pop commercial version of those gizmos? Like with maybe a fully licensed cartoon character?"

Mr Inoue blinked. "I was led to understand that Mister Khoklov's associates could supply us with military helicopters."

"The son of a bitch is on about the helicopters again," Starlitz explained in Russian.

Khoklov grunted. "Tell him we have a special on T-72 main battle tanks. Twenty million yen apiece. Just for him though. No resales."

Starlitz conferred at length with Mr. Inoue. "He's not interested in tanks. He wants at least six Mil-17 choppers with poison gas dispensers. Also some Spetsnaz Ranger vets to train the cult's judo commando unit on their sacred island of Ishigakijima."

"Spetsnaz veterans? Very well. We've got plenty. Tell him he'll have to find them visas and put up earnest money. Those black berets aren't your average goons."

Starlitz conferred again. "He wants to know if you know anything about laser ablation uranium-enrichment techniques."

"Nyet. And I'm getting pretty tired of that question."

"He wants to know if you're interested in learning how they do that sort of thing at Mitsubishi Heavy Industries."

Khoklov groaned. "Tell him I appreciate the lead on industrial atomic espionage, but that crap went out with Klaus Fuchs and the Rosenbergs."

Starlitz sighed. "Let's give Inoue-san a little face here, Pulat Romanevich. His Holiness the Master predicts the world will end in 1997. We play along with the cult's loony apocalypse myths, and we can lock in their deposits all the way through winter '96."

"Why do we need this plastic-headed lunatic?" Khoklov said. "He's a crooked exploiter of the gullible masses. He's running dummy companies inside Russia and recruiting Russian suckers for his ridiculous yoga cult. He needs us more than we need him. He's a long way from home. Put the strong-arm on him."

"Listen, ace. We need the cult's deposit money, because we need that yen disparity to cover the flow of black capital. Besides, I'm the Tokyo liaison for this gig! It's true the mafia could break his knees inside Russia, but back in Japan, his pals are building big stainless-steel bunkers full of giant microwaves."

"There are limits to my credulity, you know," Khoklov said testily. "Botulism breweries? Nerve gas factories? Hundreds of brainwashed New Age robots building computer chips for a half-blind master criminal in white pajamas? It's completely absurd, it's like something out of James Bond. Please inform this clown that he's dealing with real-life professionals."

Starlitz raised his hand and signaled. "Check please."

"Here you are sir," said Aino. "I hope you and your foreign friends are enjoying your stay in hospitable Helsinki."

After the Helsinki disco bombing, Raf moved his center of operations to the Ålands proper. The hardworking youngsters of the S.A-I.C. had found him another bolthole—a sauna retreat in the dense woods of Kökar Island. This posh resort belonged to a Swedish arms corporation who had once used it to entertain members of various Third World defense departments. Handy day-trips into the Ålands had assured them privacy and avoided potential political embarrassments on Swedish soil. This Swedish company had fallen on hard times due to the massive Russian bargain-basement armaments sales. They were happy to sublet their resort to Khoklov's well-heeled shell company.

"We can't all be Leninist ascetics," Raf declared cheerily. "One can still be a revolutionary in decent shoes."

"Decent shoes count for plenty in Russia these days," Starlitz agreed.

Raf leaned back in his lacquered bentwood chair. The resort's central office, with its stained glass windows and maniacally sleek Alvar Aalto furniture, seemed to suit him very well. "We've reached a delicate stage of the revolutionary process," Raf said, lacing his fingers behind his head. "Integrating the dual strike-forces of the liberation front."

"You mean introducing your Yankee guys to your Russian guys?"

"Yes. And what better neutral ground for that encounter than the traditional Finnish sauna?" Raf smiled. "Lads together! Nothing to hide! No clothes.

No guns! Just fresh clean steam. And plenty of booze. And since the boys have been training so hard, I've prepared them a nice surprise."

"Women."

Raf chuckled. "They *are* soldiers, you know." He leaned forward onto the desk. "Did you examine this resort? We have certain expectations to keep up!"

Starlitz had examined the resort and the grounds. There had been more hookers through the place than Bofors had heavy machine guns. The grounds were private and extensive. Coups had been launched successfully from less likely places.

Starlitz nodded. "I get the drill. You know that I have a business appointment with that little old lady today. You set this up this way on purpose, just so I'd miss all the fun."

Raf paused, and thought this over. "You're not angry with me, are you, Starlitz?"

"Why do you say that, Raf?"

"Why be angry with me? I'm loaning you Aino. Isn't that enough? I didn't have to give you a translator for your business scam. I'm trusting you, all alone on a little boat, with my favorite lieutenant. You should be grateful."

Starlitz stared at him. "Man, you're too good to me."

"You should look after Aino. My little jackal has been under strain. I know you are fond of her. Since you took such pains to speak with her behind my back."

"No, I'll leave her here with you tonight," Starlitz offered. "Let's see what your twenty naked, drunken mercs will do with a heavily armed poetry major."

Raf sighed in mock defeat. "Starlitz, you don't bullshit as easily as most really greedy people."

"Good of you to notice, man."

"Of course, I do want you to take Aino away for a while. She's young, and she would misinterpret this. Let's be very frank. These men I bought for us—they are brutal men who kill and die for pay. They must be given rewards and punishments that they can understand. They're whores with guns."

"I'm always happiest when I know the worst, Raf. You haven't told me the worst yet."

"Why should I confide in you? You never confide in me." Raf pushed an ashtray across the desk. "Have a cigarette."

Starlitz took a Gauloise.

Raf lit it with a flourish, then lit his own. "You talk a lot, Starlitz," he said. "You bargain well. But you never talk about yourself. Everything I discovered about you, I have found out through other people." Raf coughed a bit. "For instance, I know that you have a daughter. A daughter that you've never seen."

"Yeah, sure."

"I have seen your daughter. I have photos. She's not like you. She's cute."

"You've got photos, man?" Starlitz sat up. "Video?"

"Yes, I have photos. I have more than that. I have contacts in America who know where your daughter is living. She lives with those strange West Coast women."

"Yeah, well, I admit they're plenty strange, but it's one of those post-nuclear family things," Starlitz said at last.

"Would you like to meet your daughter? I could snatch her and deliver her to you here in the Ålands. That would be easy."

"The arrangement's not so bad as it stands," Starlitz said. "They let me send her kids' books...."

Raf put his sock-clad feet on the desk. "Maybe you need to settle down, Starlitz. When a man gets to a certain age, he has to live with his decisions. Take me, for instance. Basically, I'm a family man."

"Wow."

"That's right. I've been married for twenty years. My wife's in a French prison. They caught her in '78."

"That's a long stretch."

"I have two children. One by my wife, one by a girl in Beirut. People think a man like Raf the Jackal must have no private life. They don't give me credit for my dreams. Did you know I've written journalism? I've even written poetry. Poetry in Italian and Arabic."

"You don't say."

"Oh, but I do say. I will say more, since it's just the two of us. No Russians here at the resort yet, to set up their tiresome bugging networks.... I have a good feeling about you, Starlitz. You and I, we're both postmodern men of the world. We saw an empire break to pieces. That had nothing to do with silly old Karl Marx, you know."

"Could be, man."

"It was the 1990s at work. Breaking up is very infective. It's everywhere now. It's out of control, like AIDS. Did you ever meet a Lebanese warlord? Jumblatt, perhaps? Berri? Splendid fellows. Men like lions."

"Never met 'em."

"That's a very good life, you know—becoming a warlord. It's what happens to terrorists when they grow up."

Starlitz nodded. It was a very dangerous thing to have Raf so worried about his good opinion, but he couldn't help but be pleased.

"You seize a port," Raf explained. "You grow dope. You buy guns. It's like a little nation, but you don't need any lawyers, or any bureaucrats, or any ad-men, or any stupid bastards in suits. You have the guns, and you have the power. You tell them what to do, and they run and do it. Maybe it can't last forever. But as long as it lasts, it's heaven."

"This is good, Raf. You're leveling with me now. I appreciate that, I really do."

"The press says that I like to kill people. Well, *of course* I like to kill people! It's thrilling. It gives your life a heroic dimension. If it wasn't thrilling to kill people, people wouldn't buy tickets to movies where people are killed. But if I wanted to kill, I'd go to Chechnya, Georgia, Abkhazia. That's not the trick. Any idiot can become a warlord inside a war zone. The trick is to become a warlord where people are *fat* and *soft* and *rich*! You want to become a warlord *just outside* a massive, disintegrating empire. This is the perfect spot! I know I've had my little setbacks in the past. But the nineties are the sixties upside down. This time, I'm going to win, and keep what I win! I'm going to seize these little islands. I'll declare martial law and rule by decree."

"What about your three-man provisional government?"

"I've decided those boys are not reliable. I didn't like the way they talked about me. So, I'll short-cut the process, and produce very quick and decisive results. I'll take twenty-five thousand people hostage."

"How do you manage that?"

"How? By claiming that I have a Russian low-yield nuke, which in fact I don't. But who would dare to try my bluff? I'm Raf the Jackal! I'm the famous Raf! They know I'm capable of that."

"Low yield nuke, huh? I guess the old terrie scenarios are the good ones…"

"Of course I don't have any such nuke. But I do have ten kilos of cheap radioactive cesium. When they fly geiger counters over—or whatever silly scientific thing those SWAT squads use—that will look very convincing. The Finns won't dare risk another Chernobyl. They still glow in the dark from that last one. So I'm being very reasonable, don't you agree? I'm only asking for a few small islands and a few thousand people. I'll observe the proper niceties, if they allow me that. I'll make a nice flag and some coinage."

Starlitz rubbed his chin. "The coinage thing should be especially interesting given the electronic bank angle."

Raf opened a desk drawer and produced a shotglass and a duty-free bottle of Finnish cloudberry liqueur. The booze in the Ålands was vastly cheaper than Finland's. "Singapore is only a little island," Raf said, squinting as he poured himself a shot. "Nobody ever complains about Singapore's nuclear weapon."

"I hadn't heard that, man."

"Of course they have one! They've had it for fifteen years. They bought the uranium from the South Africans during apartheid, when the Boers were desperate for money. And they built the trigger themselves. Singaporeans will take that kind of trouble. They are very industrious."

"Makes sense to me." Starlitz paused. "I'm still getting a general handle on your proposal. Give me the long-term vision, Raf. Let's say that you get what you want, and they somehow let you keep it. What then? Give me ten years down the road."

"People always asked me that question," Raf said, sipping. "You want one of these cloudberries? Little golden berries off the Finnish tundra, it surprises me how sweet they are."

"No thanks, but don't let me stop you, man."

"In the old days, people would ask me—mostly these were hostage ne-gotiators, all the talking would get old and we'd all get rather philosophical sometimes...." Raf screwed the cap precisely onto the liqueur bottle. "They'd say to me, 'Raf, what about this Revolution of yours? What kind of world are you really trying to give us?' I've had a long time to consider that question."

"And?"

"Did you ever hear the Jimi Hendrix rendition of 'The Star-Spangled Banner?'"

Starlitz blinked. "Are you kidding? That cut still moves major product off the back catalog."

"Next time, *really listen* to that piece of music. Try to imagine a country where that music truly *was* the national anthem. Not weird, not far-out, not hip, not a parody, not a protest against some war, not for young Yankees stoned on some stupid farm in New York. Where music like that was social reality. That is how I want people to live. People are sheep, and they don't have the guts to live that way. But if I get a chance, I can make them do it."

▲ ▼ ▲

Starlitz liked speed launches. Piloting them was almost as much fun as driving. Raf's contacts had stolen one from Copenhagen and motored it across the Baltic at high speed. Since it was a classic dope-smuggler's vehicle, the Danish cops would assume it had been hijacked by dope people. They wouldn't be far wrong.

Starlitz examined the nautical map.

'I shot a cop today," Aino said.

Starlitz looked up. "Why do you say that?"

"I shot a cop dead. It was the constable in Mariehamm. I went into his little office. I told him someone stole the spare tire from my car. I took him around the back of his little office to see my car. I opened the trunk, and when he looked inside for the tire, I shot him. Three times. No, four times. He fell right into the trunk. So I threw him in the trunk and shut it. Then I drove away with him."

Starlitz folded the nautical map very carefully. "Did you phone in a credit?"

"No. Raf says it's better if we disappear the cop. We'll say that he defected back to Finland with the secret police files. That will be a good propaganda coup."

"You really iced this guy? Where's the body?"

"It's in this boat," Aino said.

"Take the wheel," said Starlitz. He left the cockpit and looked into the launch's fiberglass hold. There was a very dead man in uniform in it.

Starlitz turned to her. "Raf sent you to ice him all by yourself?"

"No," said Aino proudly, "he sent Matti and Jorma with me, but I made them keep watch outside." She paused. "People lie when they say it's hard to kill. Killing is very simple. You move your finger three times. Or four times. You imagine doing it, and then you plan it, and then you do it. Then it's done."

"How do you plan to deal with the evidence here?"

"We wrap the body in chains that I bought in the hardware store. We drop him into the Baltic between here and the little old lady's island. Here, take the wheel."

Starlitz went back to piloting. Aino hauled the dead cop out of the hold. The corpse outweighed her considerably, but she was strong and determined, and only occasionally squeamish. She hauled the heavy steel chains around the corpse with a series of methodical rattles, stopping every few moments to click them tight with cheap padlocks.

Starlitz watched this procedure while managing the wheel. "Was it Raf's idea to send along a corpse with my negotiations?"

Aino looked up gravely. "This is the only boat we have. I had to use this boat. We don't seize the ferries until later."

"Raf likes to send a message."

"This is *my* message. I killed this cop. I put him in this boat. He's a uniformed agent from the occupying power. He's a legitimate hard target." Aino tossed back her braids, and sighed. "Take me seriously, Mister Starlitz. I'm a young woman, and I dress like a punk because I like to, and maybe I read too many books. But I mean what I say. I believe in my cause. I come from a small obscure country, and my group is a small obscure group. That doesn't matter, because we are committed. We truly are an armed revolutionary strike force. I'm going to overthrow the government here and take over this country. I killed an oppressor today. That is a duty of an armed revolutionary."

"So you take the islands by force. Then what?"

"Then we'll be rid of these Åland ethnics. They'll be on their own. After that, we Finns can truly be Finns. We'll become a truly Finnish nation, on truly authentic Finnish principles."

"Then what?"

"Then we move into the Finno-Ugric lands that the Russians stole from us! We can take back Karelia. And Komi. And Kanti-Mansiysk." She looked at him and scowled. "You've never even heard of those places. Have you? They're sacred to us. They're in the Kalevala. But you, you've never even heard of them…."

"What happens after that?"

She shrugged. "Is that my problem? I'll never see that dream fulfilled. I think the cops will kill me before then. What do you think?"

"I think these are gonna be kind of touchy book-contract negotiations."

"Stop worrying," Aino said. "You worry too much about trivial things." She gave a last methodical wrap of the chain, and heaved the dead cop overboard. The corpse bobbed face-down in the wake of the boat, then slowly sank from sight.

Aino reached over the fiberglass gunwale and cleaned her hands in the racing seawater. "Just talk slowly to her," she said. "The old lady writes in Swedish, did you know that? I found out all about her. That's her first language, Swedish. But they say her Finnish is very good. For an Ålander."

▲ ▼ ▲

Starlitz pulled up at the little wooden dock. The entire island, shored in weed-slimed dark granite, was about twenty acres. The little old lady lived here with her even older and frailer brother. They'd both been born on the island, and had originally lived with their parents, but the father had died in 1950 and the mother in 1968.

The only access to the island was by boat. There were no phones, no electricity, and no plumbing. The home was a two-storey stone mansion with a steep slate roof, a stone well, and a wooden outhouse. The eaves were carved and painted in yellow and red. There were some chickens and a couple of squat little island sheep. A skinny wooden derrick had a home-made lighthouse, with an oil lantern. A lot of seagulls around.

Starlitz yelled a loud 'ahoy' from the dock, which seemed the most polite approach, but there was no answer from the house. So they trudged up across the rocks and turf, and found the mansion's door and knocked. No response.

Starlitz tried the salt-warped door. It was unlocked. The windows were open and a faint breeze was playing through the parlor. There were hundreds of shelved books in Finnish and Swedish, some fluttering papers, and quite a few cheerily demented oil paintings. Some quite handsome bronze statuary and some framed Finnish theater posters from the 1930s. A windup Victrola.

Starlitz opened the hall closet and looked at the rough weather gear—oilskins and boots. "You know something? This little old lady is as tall as a house. She's a goddamned Viking." He left the parlor for the composition room. He found a wooden secretary and a fine velvet chair. Dictionaries, a Swedish encyclopedia. Some well-thumbed travel hooks and Nordic photography collections. "There's nothing in here," he muttered.

"What are you looking for?" said Aino.

"I dunno exactly. Something to explain how this works."

"Here's a note!" Aino called.

Starlitz went back into the parlor. He took the note, which had been written in copperplate longhand on lined Speffy the Nerkulen novelty notepaper.

"Dear Mister Starrins," read the note. "Please pardon my not here being. I go to Helsingfors to testify. I go to Suomi Parliament as long needing for civic duty call. I regret I must miss you and hoping to speak with you about my many readers in Tokio another much more happier time. Sorry you must row so far and not have meet. Please help your self(s) to tea and biscuits all ready in kitchen. Goodbye!"

"She's gone to Helsinki," Starlitz said.

"She never travels any more. I'm very surprised." Aino frowned. "She could have saved us a lot of trouble if she had a cellphone."

"Why would they want her in Helsinki?"

"Oh, they made her go there, I suppose. The local Ålanders. The local collaborationist power structure."

"What good do they think she can do? She's not political."

"That's true, but they are very proud of her here. After all, the children's clinic—The Flüüvin's Children's Clinic in Föglö?—that was hers."

"Yeah?"

"Also the park in Sottunga. The Flüüvin Park in Brändö and the Grand Flüüvin Festival Playground. She built all of those. She never keeps the money. She gives the money away. Mostly to the Flüüvin Pediatric Disease Foundation."

Starlitz pulled off his shades and wiped his forehead. "You wouldn't know exactly which pediatric diseases in particular have caught her fancy, right?"

"I never understood such behavior," said Aino. "Really, it must be a mental illness. A childless spinster from the unjust social order...Denied any healthy sex life or outlets…. Living as a hermit with all her silly books and paintings all these years…No wonder she's gone mad."

"Okay, we're going back," Starlitz said. "I've had it."

▲ ▼ ▲

Raf and Starlitz were outside in the woods, slapping at the big slow-moving Scandinavian mosquitoes. "I thought we had an understanding," Raf said, over a muffled chorus of bestial howls from the sauna. "I told you not to bring her back here."

"She's your lieutenant, Raf. You straighten her out."

"You could have been more tactful. Invent some little deception."

"I didn't wanna get dumped off the boat." Starlitz scratched his bitten neck. "I face a very serious kink in my negotiations, man. My target decamped big-time and I got a very limited market window. This is Japanese pop culture we're talking here. The Japanese run product cycles in hyperdrive. They can burn out a consumer vogue in four weeks flat. There's nobody saying that Froofies will move long-term product like Smurfs or Seuss."

"I understand your financial difficulties with your Tokyo backers. If you can just be patient. We can take steps. We'll innovate. If necessary the Republic of the Ålands will nationalize literary production."

"Man, the point of this thing is to sue the guys in Japan who are *already ripping her off*. We gotta have something on paper that looks strong enough to stand up and bark in the courts in The Hague. You gonna strong-arm people anywhere over vaporous crap like intellectual property, it's gotta look heavy-duty, or they don't back off."

"Now you're frightening me," Raf said. "You should take a little time in the sauna. Relax. They're running videos."

"Videos right in all that goddamn steam, Raf?"

Raf nodded. "These are some very special videos."

"I fuckin' hate videos, man."

"They're Bosnian videos."

"Really?"

"Not easy to obtain. They're from the camps."

"You're showing those mercs atrocity videos?"

Raf spread his arms. "Welcome to twenty-first-century Europe!" he shouted at the empty shoreline. "Brand-new European apartheid regimes! Where gangs of war criminals abduct and systematically rape women from other ethnic groups. While the studio lights blaze and the minicams roll!"

"I'd heard those rumors," Starlitz said slowly. "Pretty hard to believe them though."

"You go inside that sauna, and you'll believe those videos. It's quite incredible, but it's all quite real. You might not enjoy them very much, but you need to see this video documentation. You must come to terms with these practices in order to understand modern political developments. It's video that is like raw meat."

"Must be faked, man."

Raf shook his head. "Europeans always say that. They always ignore the rumors. They always discover the atrocities when it is five years too late. Then they act very shocked and concerned. Those videos exist, my friend. I've got them. And I've got more than that. I've got some of the women."

"You're kidding."

"I bought the women. I bartered them for a pair of Stinger missiles. Fifteen Bosnian abductees. I had them shipped up here in sealed cargo trucks. I went to a lot of trouble."

"White slavery, man?"

"I'm not particular about color. It wasn't me who enslaved them. I'm the man who saved their lives. There were many other girls who were more stubborn or, who knows, probably less pretty. They're all dead in a ditch with bullets in the backs of their heads. These women are survivors. I wish I had more than fifteen of them, but I'm only getting started." Raf smiled. "Fifteen human souls! I rescued fifteen people! Do you know that's more people than I've ever personally killed?"

"What are you going to do with these women?"

"They'll entertain my loyal troops, first of all. I needed them for that, which gave me the idea. I admit this: it's very hard work in the sex-labor industry. But under my care, at least they won't be shot afterward."

Raf strolled along the rocky shoreline to the edge of the resort's dock. It was a nice dock, well-outfitted. The fiberglass speed launch was tied up to one rubber-padded edge of it, but the dock could have handled a minor cruise ship.

"Those women will be grateful. Here, we will admit they exist! They haven't even had *identities*. And this world is full of people like them. After ten years of civil war, they sell slaves openly now in the Sudan. Kurds are gassed like vermin by Iraqis and shot out of hand by Turks. The Sinhalese are killing Tamils. We can't forget East Timor. All over the planet, groups of little people are quietly vanishing. You can find them cowering, hiding all around the world, without papers, without legal identities.... The world's truly stateless people. My kind of people. But these are rich little islands—where there is room for thousands of them."

"This is a serious new wrinkle to the scheme, man. Did you clear it with Petersburg?"

"This development does not require debate," Raf said loftily. "It is a moral decision. People should not be killed in pogroms, by brutes who hate them merely because they are different. As a revolutionary idealist, I refuse to stomach such atrocities. These oppressed people need a great leader. A visionary. A savior. Me."

"Kind of a personality-cult thing then."

Raf shook his long-haired head in sorrow. "Oh you'd prefer them all quietly dead, I suppose! Like everyone else in the modern world who never lifts a hand to help them!"

"What if the locals complain?"

"I'll make the aliens into citizens. I'll have them out-vote all the locals. A warlord, justly voted into power by the will of the majority—wouldn't that be lovely? I'll raise a postmodern Statue of Liberty for the world's huddled masses. Not like that pious faker in New York Harbor. Refugees aren't vermin, even if the rich despise them. They're displaced human beings without a place to rally. Let them rally here with me! By the time I leave power— years from now, when I'm old and gray—they'll be accomplishing great works in these little islands."

▲ ▼ ▲

The hookers arrived on a fishing trawler. They looked very much like normal hookers from the world's fastest-growing hooker economy, Russia. They might have been women from the Baltic States. They looked like Slavic women at any rate. When they climbed from the trawler they looked rather seasick, but they seemed resolved. Not panicked, not aghast, not crushed by terror. Just like a group of fifteen more-or-less-young women, in microskirts and spandex, about to go through the hard work of having sex with strangers.

Starlitz was unsurprised to find Khoklov shepherding the hookers. Khoklov was accompanied by two brand-new bodyguards. The number of people aware of Raf's location was necessarily kept small.

"I hate working as a pimp," Khoklov groaned. He had been drinking on the boat. "At times like these, I truly know I've become a criminal."

"Raf says these girls are Bosnian slave labor. What's the scoop?"

Khoklov started in surprise. "What do you mean? What do you take me for? These girls are Estonian hookers. I brought them over from Tallinn myself."

Leggy watched carefully as the bodyguards shepherded their charges toward the whooping brutes inside the sauna. "That sure sounds like Serbo-Croatian those girls are talking, ace."

"Nonsense. That's Estonian. Don't pretend you can understand Estonian. Nobody understands that Finno-Ugric jabber."

"Raf told me these women are Bosnians. Says he bought them and he's going to keep them. Why would he say that?"

"Raf was joking with you."

"What do you mean, 'joking'? He says they're victims from a rapists' gulag! There's nothing funny about that! There just isn't any way to make that funny."

Khoklov gazed at Starlitz in mournful astonishment. "Lekhi, why do you want gulags to be 'funny'? Gulags aren't funny. Pogroms aren't funny. War is not funny. Rape is never funny. Human life is very hard, you see. Men and women truly suffer in this world."

"I know that, man."

Khoklov looked him over, then slowly shook his head. "No, Lekhi, you *don't* know that. You just don't know it the way that a Russian knows it."

Starlitz considered this. It seemed inescapably true. "Did you *ask* those girls if they were from Bosnia?"

"Why would I ask them that? You know the official Kremlin line on the Yugoslav conflict. Yeltsin says that our fellow Orthodox Slavs are incapable of such crimes. Those rape-camp stories are alarmist libels spread by Catholic Croats and Bosnian Muslims. Relax, Lekhi. These women here today, they are all Estonian professionals. You can have my word on that."

"Raf just gave me his word in a form that was highly otherwise."

Khoklov looked him in the eye. "Lekhi, who do you believe: some hippie terrorist, or a seasoned KGB officer and member in good standing of the Russian mafia?"

Starlitz gazed down at the flower-strewn Åland turf. "Okay, Pulat Romanevich.... For a moment there, I was actually considering taking some kind of, you know, action.... Well, never mind. Lemme get to the point. Our bank deal is falling apart."

Khoklov was truly shocked. "What do you mean? You can't be serious. We're doing wonderfully. Petersburg loves us."

"I mean that the old lady can't be bought. She's just too far away to touch. The deal is dead meat, ace. I don't know just how the momentum died, but I can sure smell the decay. This situation is not sustainable, man. I think it's time you and me got the hell out of here."

"You couldn't get your merchandising deal? That's a pity, Lekhi. But never mind that. I'm sure we can find some other capitalization scheme that's just as quick and just as cheap. There's always dope and weapons."

"No, the whole set-up stinks. It was the video thing that tipped me off. Pulat, did I ever tell you about the fact that I, personally, never show up on video?"

"What's that, Lekhi?"

"At least, I didn't used to. Back in the eighties, if you pointed a video camera at me it would crack, or split, or the chip would blow. I just never registered on videotape."

Slowly, Khoklov removed a silver flask from within his suit jacket. He had a long contemplative glug, then shuddered violently. He focused his eyes on Starlitz with weary deliberation. "I beg your pardon. Would you repeat that, please?"

"It's that whole video thing, man. That's why I got into the online business in the first place. Originally, I was a very analog kind of guy. But the video surveillance was seriously getting me down. I couldn't even walk down to the corner store for a pack of cigs without setting off half a dozen goddamn videos. But then—I discovered online anonymity. Online encryption. Online pseudonymity. That really helped my personal situation. Now I had a way to stay underground, stay totally unknown, even when I was being observed and monitored twenty-four hours a day. I found a way that I could go on being myself."

"Lekhi, are you drunk?"

"Nyet. Pay attention, ace. I'm leveling with you here."

"Did Raf give you something to drink?"

"Sure. We had a coffee earlier."

"Lekhi, you're on drugs. Do you have a gun? Give it to me now."

"Raf gave all the guns to the Suomi kids. They're keeping the guns till the mercs sober up. Simple precaution."

"Maybe you're still jetlagged. It's hard to sleep properly when the sun never sets. You should go lie down."

"Look, ace, I'm not the kind of fucking wimp who doesn't know when he's on acid. Normal people's rules just don't apply to me, that's all. I'm not a normal guy. I'm Leggy Starlitz, I'm a very, very strange guy. That's why I tend to end up in situations like this." Starlitz ran his hand over his sweating scalp. "Lemme put it this way. You remember that mafia chick you were banging back in Azerbaijan?"

Khoklov took a moment to access the memory. "You mean the charming and lovely Tamara Akhmedovna?"

"That's right. The wife of the Party Secretary. I leveled with Tamara in a situation like this. I told her straight-out that her little scene was coming apart. I couldn't tell her why, but I just knew it. At the time, she didn't believe me, either. Just like you're not believing me, now. You know where Tamara Akhmedovna is, right now? She's selling used cars in Los Angeles."

Khoklov had gone pale. "All right," he said. He whipped the cellular from an inner pocket of his jacket. "Don't tell me any more. I can see you have a bad feeling. Let me make some phone calls."

"You want Tamara's phone number?"

"No. Don't go away. And don't do anything crazy. All I ask is—just let me make a few contacts." Khoklov began punching digits.

Starlitz walked by the sauna. Four slobbering, buck-naked drunks dashed out and staggered down the trail in front of him. Their pale sweating hides were covered with crumpled green birch leaves from Finnish sauna whisks. They plunged into the chilly sea with ecstatic grunts of ambiguous pain.

Somewhere inside, the New World Order comrades were singing Auld Lang Syne. The Russians were having a hard time finding the beat.

▲ ▼ ▲

Raf was enjoying a snooze in the curvilinear Aalto barcalounger when Khoklov and Starlitz woke him.

"We've been betrayed," Khoklov announced.

"Oh?" said Raf. "Where? Who is the traitor?"

"Our superiors, unfortunately."

Raf considered this, rubbing his eyelids. "Why do you say that?"

"They liked our idea very much," Khoklov said. "So they stole it from us."

"Intellectual piracy, man," Starlitz said. "It's a bad scene."

"The Ålands deal is over," Khoklov said. "The Organizatsiya's Higher Circles have decided that we have too much initiative. They want much closer institutional control of such a wonderful idea. Our Finnish hacker kids have jumped ship and joined them. They re-routed all the Suns to Kaliningrad."

"What is Kaliningrad?" Raf said.

"It's this weird little leftover piece of Russia on the far side of all three independent Baltic nations," Starlitz said helpfully. "They say they're going to make Kaliningrad into a new Russian Hong Kong. The old Hong Kong is about to be metabolized by the Chinese, so the mafia figures it's time for Russia to sprout one. They'll make this little Kaliningrad outpost into a Baltic duty-free zone cum European micro-buffer state. And they're paying our Finn hacker kids three times what we pay, plus air fare."

"The World Bank is helping them with development loans," Khoklov said. "The World Bank loves their Kaliningrad idea."

"Plus the European Union, man. Euros love duty-free zones."

"And the Finns too," Khoklov said. "That's the very worst of it. The Finns have bought us out. Russia used to owe every Finn two hundred dollars. Now, Russia owes every Finn one hundred and ninety dollars. In return for a rotten little fifty million dollar write-off, my bosses sold us all to the Finns. They told the Finns about our plans, and they sold us just as if we were some lousy division of leftover tanks. The Finnish Special Weapons and Tactics team is flying over here right now to annihilate us."

Raf's round and meaty face grew dark with fury. "So you've betrayed us, Khoklov?"

"It's my bosses who let us down," Khoklov said sturdily. "Essentially, I've been purged. They have cut me out of the Organizatsiya. They liked the idea much more than they like me. So I'm expendable. I'm dead meat."

Raf turned to Starlitz. "I'll have to shoot Pulat Romanevich for this. You realize that, I hope."

Starlitz raised his brows. "You got a gun, man?"

"Aino has the guns." Raf hopped up from his lounger and left.

Khoklov and Starlitz hastily followed him. "You're going to let him shoot me?" Khoklov said sidelong.

"Look man, the guy has kept us *his* end. He always delivered on time and within specs."

They found Aino alone in the basement. She had her elk rifle.

"Where's the arsenal?" Raf demanded.

"I had Matti and Jorma take all the weapons from this property. Your mercenaries are terrible beasts, Raf."

"Of course they're beasts," Raf said. "That's why they follow a Jackal. Lend me your rifle for a moment, my dear. I have to shoot this Russian."

Aino slammed a thumb-sized cartridge into the breech and stood up. "This is my favorite rifle. I don't give it to anyone."

"Shoot him yourself, then," Raf said, backing up half a step with a deft little hop. "His mafia people have blown the Movement's program. They've betrayed us to the Finnish oppressors."

"Police are coming from the mainland," Starlitz told her. "It's over. Time to split, girl. Let's get out of here."

Aino ignored him. "I told you that Russians could never be trusted," she said to Raf. Her face was pale, but composed. "What did American mercenaries have to do with Finland? We could have done this easily, if you were not so ambitious."

"A man has to dream," Raf said. "Everybody needs a big dream."

Aino centered her rifle on Khoklov's chest. "Should I shoot you?" she asked him, in halting Russian.

"I'm not a cop," Khoklov offered hopefully.

Aino thought about it. The rifle did not waver. "What will you do, if I don't shoot you?"

"I have no idea what I'll do," Khoklov said, surprised. "What do you plan to do, Raf?"

"Me?" said Raf. "Why, I could kill you with these hands alone." He held out his plump, dimpled hands in karate position.

"Lot of good that'll do you against a chopper full of angry Finnish SWAT team," Starlitz said.

Raf squared his shoulders. "I'd love to take a final armed stand on this territory! Battle those Finnish oppressors to the death! However, unfortunately, I have no arsenal."

"Run away, Raf," Aino said.

"What's that, my dear?" said Raf.

"Run, Raffi. Run for your life. I'll stay here with your stupid hookers, and your drunken, naked, mercenary losers, and when the cops come, I'm going to shoot some of them."

"That's not a smart survival move," Starlitz told her.

"Why should I run like you? Should I let my revolution collapse at the first push from the authorities, without even a token resistance? This is my sacred cause!"

"Look, you're one little girl," Starlitz said.

"So what? They're going to catch all your stupid whores, the men and the women, in a drunken stupor. The cops will put them all in handcuffs, just like that. But not me. I'll be fighting I'll be shooting. Maybe they'll kill me. They're supposed to be good, these SWAT cops. Maybe they'll capture me alive. Then, I'll just have to live inside a little stone house. All by myself. For a long, long time. But I'm not afraid of that! I have my cause. I was right! I'm not afraid."

"You know," said Khoklov brightly, "if we took that speed launch we could be on the Danish coast in three hours."

▲ ▼ ▲

Spray whipped their faces as the Ålands faded in the distance.

"I hope there aren't too many passport checks in Denmark," Khoklov said anxiously.

"Passports aren't a problem," Raf said. "Not for me. Or for my friends."

"Where are you going?" Khoklov asked.

"Well," said Raf, "perhaps the Ålands offshore bank scheme was a little before its time. I'm a visionary, you know. I was always twenty years ahead of my time—but nowadays maybe I'm only twenty minutes." Raf sighed. "Such a wonderful girl, Aino! She reminded me so much of...well, there have been so many wonderful girls.... But I must sacrifice my habit of poetic dreaming! At this tragic juncture, we must regroup, we must be firmly realistic. Don't you agree, Khoklov? We should go to the one locale in Europe that guarantees a profit."

"The former Yugoslavia?" Khoklov said eagerly. "They say you can make a free phone call anywhere in the world from Belgrade. Using a currency that doesn't even exist any more!"

"Obvious potential there," said Raf. "Of course, it requires operators who can land on their feet. Men of action. Men on top of their profession."

"Bosnia-Herzegovina," Khoklov breathed, turning his reddened face to yet another tirelessly rising sun. "The new frontier! What do you think, Starlitz?"

"I think I'll just hang out a while," Starlitz said. He gripped his nose with thumb and forefinger. Suddenly, without another word, Starlitz tumbled backward from the boat into the dark Baltic water. In a few short moments he was lost from sight.

PART IV:

THE CHATTANOOGA STORIES

Deep Eddy

The Continental gentleman in the next beanbag offered "Zigaretten?"

"What's in it?" Deep Eddy asked. The gray-haired gentleman murmured something: polysyllabic medical German. Eddy's translation program crashed at once.

Eddy gently declined. The gentleman shook a zigarette from the pack, twisted its tip, and huffed at it. A sharp perfume arose, like coffee struck by lightning.

The elderly European brightened swiftly. He flipped open a newspad, tapped through its menu, and began alertly scanning a German business zine.

Deep Eddy killed his translation program, switched spexware, and scanned the man. The gentleman was broadcasting a business bio. His name was Peter Liebling, he was from Bremen, he was ninety years old, he was an official with a European lumber firm. His hobbies were backgammon and collecting antique phone-cards. He looked pretty young for ninety. He probably had some unusual and interesting medical syndromes.

Herr Liebling glanced up, annoyed at Eddy's computer-assisted gaze. Eddy dropped his spex back onto their neck chain. A practiced gesture, one Deep Eddy used a lot—*hey, didn't mean to stare, pal*. A lot of people were suspicious of spex. Most people had no idea of the profound capacities of spexware. Most people still didn't use spex. Most people were, in a word, losers.

Eddy lurched up within his baby-blue beanbag and gazed out the aircraft window. Chattanooga, Tennessee. Bright white ceramic air-control towers, distant wine-colored office blocks, and a million dark green trees. Tarmac heated gently in the summer morning. Eddy lifted his spex again to check a silent take-off westward by a white-and-red Asian jet. Infrared turbulence gushed from its distant engines. Deep Eddy loved infrared. That deep silent magical whirl of invisible heat, the breath of industry.

People underestimated Chattanooga, Deep Eddy thought with a local boy's pride. Chattanooga had a very high per-capita investment in spexware. In fact Chattanooga ranked third-highest in NAFTA. Number One was San Jose, California (naturally), and Number Two was Madison, Wisconsin.

Eddy had already traveled to both those rival cities, in the service of his Chattanooga users group, to swap some spexware, market a little info, and make a careful study of the local scene. To collect some competitive intelligence. To spy around, not to put too fine a point on it.

Eddy's most recent business trip had been five drunken days at a blowout All-NAFTA spexware conference in Ciudad Juárez, Chihuahua. Eddy had not yet figured out why Ciudad Juárez, a once-dreary maquilladora factory town on the Rio Grande, had gone completely hog-wild for spexing. But even little kids there had spex, brightly speckly throwaway kid-stuff with just a couple dozen meg. There were tottering grannies with spex. Security cops with spex mounted right into their riot helmets. Billboards everywhere that couldn't be read without spex. And thousands of hustling industry zudes with air-conditioned jackets and forty or fifty terabytes mounted right at the bridge of the nose. Ciudad Juárez was in the grip of rampant spexmania. Maybe it was all the lithium in their water.

Today, duty called Deep Eddy to Düsseldorf in Europe. Duty did not have to call very hard to get Eddy's attention. The mere whisper of duty was enough to dislodge Deep Eddy, who still lived with his parents, Bob and Lisa.

He'd gotten some spexmail and a package from the president of the local chapter. *A network obligation; our group credibility depends on you, Eddy. A delivery job. Don't let us down; do whatever it takes. And keep your eyes covered—this one could be dangerous.* Well, danger and Deep Eddy were fast friends. Throwing up tequila and ephedrine through your nose in an alley in Mexico, while wearing a pair of computer-assisted glasses worth as much as a car—now that was dangerous. Most people would be scared to try something like that. Most people couldn't master their own insecurities. Most people were too scared to live.

This would be Deep Eddy's first adult trip to Europe. At the age of nine he'd accompanied Bob and Lisa to Madrid for a Sexual Deliberation conference, but all he remembered from that trip was a boring weekend of bad television and incomprehensible tomato-soaked food. Düsseldorf, however, sounded like real and genuine fun. The trip was probably even worth getting up at 07:15.

Eddy dabbed at his raw eyelids with a saline-soaked wipey. Eddy was getting a first-class case of eyeball-burn off his spex; or maybe it was just sleeplessness. He'd spent a very late and highly frustrating night with his current girlfriend, Djulia. He'd dated her hoping for a hero's farewell, hinting broadly that he might be beaten or killed by sinister European underground networking-mavens, but his presentation hadn't washed at all. Instead of some sustained and attentive frolic, he'd gotten only a somber four-hour lecture about the emotional center in Djulia's life: collecting Japanese glassware.

As his jet gently lifted from the Chattanooga tarmac, Deep Eddy was struck with a sudden, instinctive, gut-level conviction of Djulia's essential counter-productivity. Djulia was just no good for him. Those clear eyes, the tilted nose, the sexy sprinkle of tattoo across her right cheekbone. Lovely flare of her body-heat in darkness. The lank strands of dark hair that turned crisp and wavy halfway down their length. A girl shouldn't have such great hair and so many tatts and still be so tightly wrapped. Djulia was no real friend of his at all.

The jet climbed steadily, crossing the shining waters of the Tennessee. Outside Eddy's window, the long ductile wings bent and rippled with dainty, tightly controlled antiturbulence. The cabin itself felt as steady as a Mississippi lumber barge, but the computer-assisted wings, under spex-analysis, resembled a vibrating sawblade. Nerve-racking. *Let this not be the day a whole bunch of Chattanoogans fall out of the sky,* Eddy thought silently, squirming a bit in the luscious embrace of his beanbag.

He gazed about the cabin at his fellow candidates for swift mass death. Three hundred people or so, the European and NAFTA jet-bourgeoisie; well-groomed, polite. Nobody looked frightened. Sprawling there in their pastel beanbags, chatting, hooking fiber-optics to palmtops and laptops, browsing through newspads, making videophonecalls. Just as if they were at home, or maybe in a very crowded cylindrical hotel lobby, all of them in blank and deliberate ignorance of the fact that they were zipping through midair supported by nothing but plasmajets and computation. Most people were so unaware. One software glitch somewhere, a missed decimal point, and those cleverly ductile wings would tear right the hell off. Sure, it didn't happen often. But it happened sometimes.

Deep Eddy wondered glumly if his own demise would even make the top of the newspad. It'd be in there all right, but probably hyperlinked five or six layers down.

The five-year-old in the beanbag behind Eddy entered a paroxysm of childish fear and glee. "My e-mail, Mom!" the kid chirped with desperate enthusiasm, bouncing up and down. "Mom! Mom, my e-mail! Hey Mom, get me my e-mail!"

A stew offered Eddy breakfast. He had a bowl of muesli and half a dozen boiled prunes. Then he broke out his travel card and ordered a mimosa. The booze didn't make him feel any more alert, though, so he ordered two more mimosas. Then he fell asleep.

▲ ▼ ▲

Customs in Düsseldorf was awash. Summer tourists were pouring into the city like some vast migratory shoal of sardines. The people from outside Europe—from NAFTA, from the Sphere, from the South—were a tiny minority, though, compared to the vast intra-European traffic, who breezed through Customs completely unimpeded.

Uniformed inspectors were spexing the NAFTA and South baggage, presumably for guns or explosives, but their clunky government-issue spex looked a good five years out-of-date. Deep Eddy passed through the Customs chute without incident and had his passchip stamped. Passing out drunk on champagne and orange juice, then snoozing through the entire Atlantic crossing, had clearly been an excellent idea. It was 21:00 local time and Eddy felt quite alert and rested. Clearheaded. Ready for anything. Hungry.

Eddy wandered toward the icons signaling ground transport. A stocky woman in a bulky brown jacket stepped into his path. He stopped short. "Mr. Edward Dertouzas," she said.

"Right," Eddy said, dropping his bag. They stared at one another, spex to spex. "Actually, fraulein, as I'm sure you can see by my online bio, my friends call me Eddy. Deep Eddy, mostly."

"I'm not your friend, Mr. Dertouzas. I am your security escort. I'm called Sardelle today." Sardelle stooped and hefted his travel bag. Her head came about to his shoulder.

Deep Eddy's German translator, which he had restored to life, placed a yellow subtitle at the lower rim of his spex. "Sardelle," he noted. *"'Anchovy'?"*

"I don't pick the code names," Sardelle told him, irritated. "I have to use what the company gives me." She heaved her way through the crowd, jolting people aside with deft jabs of Eddy's travel bag. Sardelle wore a bulky air-conditioned brown trenchcoat, with multipocketed fawn-colored jeans and thicksoled black-and-white cop shoes. A crisp trio of small tattooed triangles outlined Sardelle's right cheek. Her hands, attractively small and dainty, were gloved in black-and-white pinstripe. She looked about thirty. No problem. He liked mature women. Maturity gave depth.

Eddy scanned her for bio data. "Sardelle," the spex read unhelpfully. Absolutely nothing else; no business, no employer, no address, no age, no interests, no hobbies, no personal ads. Europeans were rather weird about privacy. Then again, maybe Sardelle's lack of proper annotation had something to do with her business life.

Eddy looked down at his own hands, twitched bare fingers over a virtual menu in midair, and switched to some rude spexware he'd mail-ordered from Tijuana. Something of a legend in the spexing biz, X-Spex stripped people's clothing off and extrapolated the flesh beneath it in a full-color visual simulation. Sardelle, however, was so decked-out in waistbelts, holsters, and shoulderpads that the X-ware was baffled. The simulation looked alarmingly bogus, her breasts and shoulders waggling like drug-addled plasticine.

"Hurry out," she suggested sternly. "I mean hurry *up.*"

"Where we going? To see the Critic?"

"In time," Sardelle said. Eddy followed her through the stomping, shuffling, heaving crowd to a set of travel lockers.

"Do you really need this bag, sir?"

"What?" Eddy said. "Sure I do! It's got all my stuff in it."

"If we take it, I will have to search it carefully," Sardelle informed him patiently. "Let's place your bag in this locker, and you can retrieve it when you leave Europe." She offered him a small gray handbag with the logo of a Berlin luxury hotel. "Here are some standard travel necessities."

"They scanned my bag in Customs," Eddy said. "I'm clean, really. Customs was a walk-through."

Sardelle laughed briefly and sarcastically. "One million people coming to Düsseldorf this weekend," she said. "There will be a Wende here. And you think the Customs searched you properly? Believe me, Edward. You have not been searched properly."

"That sounds a bit menacing," Eddy said.

"A proper search takes a lot of time. Some threats to safety are tiny—things woven into clothing, glued to the skin...." Sardelle shrugged. "I like to have time. I'll *pay* you to have some time. Do you need money, Edward?"

"No," Eddy said, startled. "I mean, yeah. Sure I need money, who doesn't? But I have a travel card from my people. From CAPCLUG."

She glanced up sharply, aiming the spex at him. "Who is Kapklug?"

"Computer-Assisted Perception Civil Liberties Users Group," Eddy said. "Chattanooga Chapter."

"I see. The acronym in English." Sardelle frowned. "I hate all acronyms.... Edward, I will pay you forty ecu cash to put your bag into this locker and take this bag instead."

"Sold," Deep Eddy said. "Where's the money?"

Sardelle passed him four wellworn hologram bills. Eddy stuffed the cash in his pocket. Then he opened his own bag and retrieved an elderly hardbound book—*Crowds and Power,* by Elias Canetti. "A little light reading," he said unconvincingly.

"Let me see that book," Sardelle insisted. She leafed through the book rapidly, scanning pages with her pinstriped fingertips, flexing the covers and checking the book's binding, presumably for inserted razors, poisoned needles, or strips of plastic explosive. "You are smuggling data," she concluded sourly, handing it back.

"That's what we live for in CAPCLUG," Eddy told her, peeking at her over his spex and winking. He slipped the book into the gray hotel bag and zipped it. Then he heaved his own bag into the travel locker, slammed the door, and removed the numbered key.

"Give me that key," Sardelle said.

"Why?"

"You might return and open the locker. If I keep the key, that security risk is much reduced."

"No way," Eddy frowned. "Forget it."

"Ten ecu," she offered.

"Mmmmph."

"Fifteen."

"Okay, have it your way." Eddy gave her the key. "Don't lose it."

Sardelle, unsmiling, put the key into a zippered sleeve pocket. "I never lose things." She opened her wallet.

Eddy nodded, pocketing a hologram ten and five singles. Very attractive currency, the ecu. The ten had a hologram of René Descartes, a very deep zude who looked impressively French and rational.

Eddy felt he was doing pretty well by this, so far. In point of fact there wasn't anything in the bag he really needed: his underwear, spare jeans, tickets, business cards, dress shirts, tie, suspenders, spare shoes, toothbrush, aspirin, instant espresso, sewing kit, and earrings. So what? It wasn't as if she'd asked him to give up his spex.

He also had a complete crush on his escort. The name Anchovy suited her—she struck him as a small canned cold fish. Eddy found this perversely attractive. In fact he found her so attractive that he was having a hard time standing still and breathing normally. He really liked the way she carried her stripe-gloved hands, deft and feminine and mysteriously European, but mostly it was her hair. Long, light reddish-brown, and meticulously braided by machine. He loved women's hair when it was machine-braided. They couldn't seem to catch the fashion quite right in NAFTA. Sardelle's hair looked like a rusted mass of museum-quality chain-mail, or maybe some fantastically convoluted railway intersection. Hair that really *meant business*. Not only did Sardelle have not a hair out of place, but any unkemptness was *topologically impossible*. The vision rose unbidden of running his fingers through it in the dark.

"I'm starving," he announced.

"Then we will eat," she said. They headed for the exit.

Electric taxis were trying, without much success, to staunch the spreading hemorrhage of tourists. Sardelle clawed at the air with her pinstriped fingers. Adjusting invisible spex menus. She seemed to be casting the evil eye on a nearby family group of Italians, who reacted with scarcely concealed alarm. "We can walk to a city busstop," she told him. "It's quicker."

"Walking's quicker?"

Sardelle took off. He had to hurry to keep up. "Listen to me, Edward. If you follow my security suggestions, we will save time. If I save my time, then you will make money. If you make me work harder I will not be so generous."

"I'm easy," Eddy protested. Her cop shoes seemed to have some kind of computational cushion built into the soles; she walked as if mounted on springs. "I'm here to meet the Cultural Critic. An audience with him. I have a delivery for him. You know that, right?"

"It's the book?"

Eddy hefted the gray hotel bag. "Yeah....I'm here in Düsseldorf to deliver an old book to some European intellectual. Actually, to give the book back to him. He, like, lent the book to the CAPCLUG Steering Committee, and it's time to give it back. How tough can that job be?"

"Probably not very tough," Sardelle said calmly. "But strange things happen during a Wende."

Eddy nodded soberly. "Wendes are very interesting phenomena. CAPCLUG is studying Wendes. We might like to throw one someday."

"That's not how Wendes happen, Eddy. You don't 'throw' a Wende." Sardelle paused, considering. "A Wende throws *you.*"

"So I gather," Eddy said. "I've been reading his work, you know. The Cultural Critic. It's deep work, I like it."

Sardelle was indifferent. "I'm not one of his partisans. I'm just employed to guard him." She conjured up another menu. "What kind of food do you like? Chinese? Thai? Eritrean?"

"How about German food?"

Sardelle laughed. "We Germans never eat German food....There are very good Japanese cafes in Düsseldorf. Tokyo people fly here for the salmon. And the anchovies...."

"You live here in Düsseldorf, Anchovy?"

"I live everywhere in Europe, Deep Eddy." Her voice fell. "Any city with a screen in front of it....And they all have screens in Europe."

"Sounds fun. You want to trade some spexware?"

"No."

"You don't believe in *andwendungsoriente wissensverarbeitung?*"

She made a face. "How clever of you to learn an appropriate German phrase. Speak English, Eddy. Your accent is truly terrible."

"Thank you kindly," Eddy said.

"You can't trade wares with me, Eddy, don't be silly. I would not give my security spexware to civilian Yankee hacker-boys."

"Don't own the copyright, huh?"

"There's that, too." She shrugged, and smiled.

They were out of the airport now, walking south. Silent steady flow of electric traffic down Flughafenstrasse. The twilight air smelled of little white roses. They crossed at a traffic light. The German semiotics of ads and street signs began to press with gentle culture shock at the surface of Deep Eddy's brain. Garagenhof. Spezialist fur Mobil-Telefon. Burohausern. He put on some character-recognition ware to do translation, but the instant doubling of the words all around him only made him feel schizophrenic.

They took shelter in a lit bus kiosk, along with a pair of heavily tattooed gays toting grocery bags. A video-ad built into the side of the kiosk advertised German-language e-mail editors.

As Sardelle stood patiently, in silence, Eddy examined her closely for the first time. There was something odd and indefinitely European about the line of her nose. "Let's be friends, Sardelle. I'll take off my spex if you take off your spex."

"Maybe later," she said.

Eddy laughed. "You should get to know me. I'm a fun guy."

"I already know you."

An overcrowded bus passed. Its riders had festooned the robot bus with banners and mounted a klaxon on its roof, which emitted a cacophony of rapidfire bongo music.

"The Wende people are already hitting the buses," Sardelle noted sourly, shifting on her feet as if trampling grapes. "I hope we can get downtown."

"You've done some snooping on me, huh? Credit records and such? Was it interesting?"

Sardelle frowned. "It's my business to research records. I did nothing illegal. All by the book."

"No offense taken," Eddy said, spreading his hands. "But you must have learned I'm harmless. Let's unwrap a little."

Sardelle sighed. "I learned that you are an unmarried male, age eighteen-to-thirty-five. No steady job. No steady home. No wife, no children. Radical political leanings. Travels often. Your demographics are very high-risk."

"I'm twenty-two, to be exact." Eddy noticed that Sardelle showed no reaction to this announcement, but the two eavesdropping gays seemed quite interested. He smiled nonchalantly. "I'm here to network, that's all. Friend-of-a-friend situation. Actually, I'm pretty sure I share your client's politics. As far as I can figure his politics out."

"Politics don't matter," Sardelle said, bored and impatient. "I'm not concerned with politics. Men in your age group commit 80 percent of all violent crimes."

One of the gays spoke up suddenly, in heavily accented English. "Hey fraulein. We also have 80 percent of the charm!"

"And 90 percent of the fun," said his companion. "It's Wende time, Yankee boy. Come with us and we'll do some crimes." He laughed.

"Das ist sehr nett vohn Ihnen," Eddy said politely. "But I can't. I'm with nursie."

The first gay made a witty and highly idiomatic reply in German, to the effect, apparently, that he liked boys who wore sunglasses after dark, but Eddy needed more tattoos.

Eddy, having finished reading subtitles in midair, touched the single small black circle on his cheekbone. "Don't you like my solitaire? It's rather sinister in its reticence, don't you think?"

He'd lost them; they only looked puzzled.

A bus arrived.

"This will do," Sardelle announced. She fed the bus a ticket-chip and Eddy followed her on board. The bus was crowded, but the crowd seemed gentle; mostly Euro-Japanese out for a night on the town. They took a bean-bag together in the back.

It had grown quite dark now. They floated down the street with machine-guided precision and a smooth dreamlike detachment. Eddy felt the spell of travel overcome him; the basic mammalian thrill of a live creature plucked up and dropped like a supersonic ghost on the far side of the planet. Another time, another place: whatever vast set of unlikelihoods had militated against his presence here had been defeated. A Friday night in Düsseldorf, July 13, 2035. The time was 22:10. The very specificity seemed magical.

He glanced at Sardelle again, grinning gleefully, and suddenly saw her for what she was. A burdened female functionary sitting stiffly in the back of a bus.

"Where are we now, exactly?" he said.

"We are on Danzigerstrasse heading south to the Altstadt," Sardelle said. "The old town center."

"Yeah? What's there?"

"Kartoffel. Beer. Schnitzel. Things for you to eat."

The bus stopped and a crowd of stomping, shoving rowdies got on. Across the street, a trio of police were struggling with a broken traffic securi-cam. The cops were wearing full-body pink riot-gear. He'd heard some-where that all European cop riot-gear was pink. The color was supposed to be calming.

"This isn't much fun for you, Sardelle, is it?"

She shrugged. "We're not the same people, Eddy. I don't know what you are bringing to the Critic, and I don't want to know." She tapped her spex back into place with one gloved finger. "But if you fail in your job, at the very worst, it might mean some grave cultural loss. Am I right?"

"I suppose so. Sure."

"But if I fail in *my* job, Eddy, something *real* might *actually happen.*"

"Wow," Eddy said, stung.

The crush in the bus was getting oppressive. Eddy stood and offered his spot in the beanbag to a tottering old woman in spangled party gear.

Sardelle rose then, too, with bad grace, and fought her way up the aisle. Eddy followed, barking his shins on the thicksoled beastie-boots of a sprawling drunk.

Sardelle stopped short to trade elbow-jabs with a Nordic kamikaze in a horned baseball cap, and Eddy stumbled into her headlong. He realized then why people seemed so eager to get out of Sardelle's way: her trenchcoat was of woven ceramic and was as rough as sandpaper. He lurched one-handed for a strap. "Well," he puffed at Sardelle, swaying into her spex-to-spex, "if we can't enjoy each other's company, why not get this over with? Let me do my errand. Then I'll get right into your hair." He paused, shocked. "I mean, *out* of your hair. Sorry."

She hadn't noticed. "You'll do your errand," she said, clinging to her strap. They were so close that he could feel a chill air-conditioned breeze whiffling out of her trenchcoat's collar. "But on my terms. My time, my circumstances." She wouldn't meet his eyes; her head darted around as if from grave embarrassment. Eddy realized suddenly that she was methodically scanning the face of every stranger in the bus.

She spared him a quick, distracted smile. "Don't mind me, Eddy. Be a good boy and have fun in Düsseldorf. Just let me do my job, okay?"

"Okay then," Eddy muttered. "Really, I'm delighted to be in your hands." He couldn't seem to stop with the double entendres. They rose to his lips like drool from the id.

The glowing grids of Düsseldorf highrises shone outside the bus windows, patchy waffles of mystery. So many human lives behind those windows. People he would never meet, never see. Pity he still couldn't afford proper telephotos.

Eddy cleared his throat. "What's he doing out there right now? The Cultural Critic, I mean."

"Meeting contacts in a safehouse. He will meet a great many people during the Wende. That's his business, you know. You're only one of many that he bringed—brought—to this rendezvous." Sardelle paused. "Though in threat potential you do rank among the top five."

The bus made more stops. People piled in headlong, with a thrash and a heave and a jacking of kneecaps. Inside the bus they were all becoming anchovies. A smothered fistfight broke out in the back. A drunken woman tried, with mixed success, to vomit out the window. Sardelle held her position grimly through several stops, then finally fought her way to the door.

The bus pulled to a stop and a sudden rush of massed bodies propelled them out.

They'd arrived by a long suspension bridge over a broad moonsilvered river. The bridge's soaring cables were lit end-to-end with winking party-bulbs. All along the bridge, flea-marketeers sitting cross-legged on glowing mats were doing a brisk trade in tourist junk. Out in the center, a busking juggler with smart-gloves flung lit torches in flaming arcs three stories high.

"Jesus, what a beautiful river," Eddy said.

"It's the Rhine. This is Oberkasseler Bridge."

"The Rhine. Of course, of course. I've never seen the Rhine before. Is it safe to drink?"

"Of course. Europe's very civilized."

"I thought so. It even smells good. Let's go drink some of it."

The banks were lined with municipal gardens: grape-musky vineyards, big pale meticulous flowerbeds. Tireless gardening robots had worked them over season by season with surgical trowels. Eddy stooped by the riverbank and scooped up a double-handful of backwash from a passing hydrofoil. He saw his own spex-clad face in the moony puddle of his hands. As Sardelle watched, he sipped a bit and flung the rest out as libation to the spirit of place.

"I'm happy now," he said. "Now I'm really here."

▲ ▼ ▲

By midnight, he'd had four beers, two schnitzels, and a platter of kartof-fels. Kartoffels were fried potato-batter waffles with a side of applesauce. Eddy's morale had soared from the moment he first bit into one.

They sat at a sidewalk café table in the midst of a centuries-old pedes-trian street in the Altstadt. The entire street was a single block-long bar, all chairs, umbrellas, and cobbles, peaked-roof townhouses with ivy and windowboxes and ancient copper weathervanes. It had been invaded by an absolute throng of gawking, shuffling, hooting foreigners.

The gentle, kindly, rather bewildered Düsseldorfers were doing their level best to placate their guests and relieve them of any excess cash. A strong pink police presence was keeping good order. He'd seen two zudes in horned baseball-caps briskly hauled into a paddy wagon—a "Pink Minna"—but the Vikings were pig-drunk and had it coming, and the crowd seemed very good-humored.

"I don't see what the big deal is with these Wendes," Deep Eddy said, polishing his spex on a square of oiled and lint-free polysilk. "This sucker's a walk-through. There's not gonna be any trouble here. Just look how calm and mellow these zudes are."

"There's trouble already," Sardelle said. "It's just not here in Altstadt in front of your nose."

"Yeah?"

"There are big gangs of arsonists across the river tonight. They're barricading streets in Neuss, toppling cars, and setting them on fire."

"How come?"

Sardelle shrugged. "They are anti-car activists. They demand pedestrian rights and more mass transit...." She paused a bit to read the inside of her spex. "Green radicals are storming the Lobbecke Museum. They want all extinct insect specimens surrendered for cloning....Heinrich Heine University is on strike for academic freedom, and someone has glue-bombed the big traffic tunnel beneath the campus....But this is nothing, not yet. Tomorrow England meets Ireland in the soccer finals at Rhein-Stadium. There will be hell to pay."

"Huh. That sounds pretty bad."

"Yes." She smiled. "So let's enjoy our time here, Eddy. Idleness is sweet. Even on the edge of dirty chaos."

"But none of those events by itself sounds all that threatening or serious."

"Not each thing by itself, Eddy, no. But it all happens all at once. That's what a Wende is like."

"I don't get it," Eddy said. He put his spex back on and lit the menu from within, with a fingersnap. He tapped the spex menu-bar with his right fingertip and light-amplifiers kicked in. The passing crowd, their outlines shimmering slightly from computational effects, seemed to be strolling through an overlit stage-set. "I guess there's trouble coming from all these outsiders," Eddy said, "but the Germans themselves seem so...well...so good-natured and tidy and civilized. Why do they even have Wendes?"

"It's not something we plan, Eddy. It's just something that happens to us." Sardelle sipped her coffee.

"How could this happen and not be planned?"

"Well, we knew it was coming, of course. Of course we knew *that*. Word gets around. That's how Wendes start." She straightened her napkin. "You can ask the Critic, when you meet him. He talks a lot about Wendes. He knows as much as anyone, I think."

"Yeah, I've read him," Eddy said. "He says that it's rumor, boosted by electronic and digital media, in a feedback-loop with crowd dynamics and modern mass transportation. A nonlinear networking phenomenon. That much I understand! But then he quotes some zude named Elias Canetti...." Eddy patted the gray bag. "I tried to read Canetti, I really did, but he's twentieth-century, and as boring and stuffy as hell....Anyway, we'd handle things differently in Chattanooga."

"People say that, until they have their first Wende," Sardelle said. "Then it's all different. Once you know a Wende can actually happen to you...well, it changes everything."

"We'd take steps to stop it, that's all. Take steps to control it. Can't you people take some steps?"

Sardelle tugged off her pinstriped gloves and set them on the tabletop. She worked her bare fingers gently, blew on her fingertips, and picked a big bready pretzel from the basket. Eddy noticed with surprise that her gloves had big rock-hard knuckles and twitched a little all by themselves.

"There are things you can do, of course," she told him. "Put police and firefighters on overtime. Hire more private security. Disaster control for lights, traffic, power, data. Open the shelters and stock first-aid medicine. And warn the whole population. But when a city tells its people that a Wende is coming, that *guarantees* the Wende will come...." Sardelle sighed. "I've worked Wendes before. But this is a big one. A big, dark one. And it won't be over, it can't be over—not until everyone knows that it's gone, and feels that it's gone."

"That doesn't make much sense."

"Talking about it won't help, Eddy. You and I, talking about it—we become part of the Wende ourselves, you see? We're here because of the Wende. We met because of the Wende. And we can't leave each other, until the Wende goes away." She shrugged. "Can you go away, Eddy?"

"No...not right now. But I've got stuff to do here."

"So does everybody else."

Eddy grunted and killed another beer. The beer here was truly something special. "It's a Chinese finger-trap," he said, gesturing.

"Yes, I know those."

He grinned. "Suppose we both stop pulling? We could walk through it. Leave town. I'll throw the book in the river. Tonight you and I could fly back to Chattanooga. Together."

She laughed. "You wouldn't really do that, though."

"You don't know me after all."

"You spit in the face of your friends? And I lose my job? A high price to pay for one gesture. For a young man's pretense of free will."

"I'm not pretending, lady. Try me. I dare you."

"Then you're drunk."

"Well, there's that." He laughed. "But don't joke about liberty. Liberty's the realest thing there is." He stood up and hunted out the bathroom.

On his way back he stopped at a payphone. He gave it fifty centimes and dialed Tennessee. Djulia answered.

"What time is it?" he said.

"Nineteen. Where are you?"

"Düsseldorf."

"Oh." She rubbed her nose. "Sounds like you're in a bar."

"Bingo."

"So what's new, Eddy?"

"I know you put a lot of stock in honesty," Eddy said. "So I thought I'd tell you I'm planning an affair. I met this German girl here and frankly, she's irresistible."

Djulia frowned darkly. "You've got a lot of nerve telling me that kind of crap with your spex on."

"Oh yeah," he said. He took them off and stared into the monitor. "Sorry."

"You're drunk, Eddy," Djulia said. "I hate it when you're drunk! You'll say and do anything if you're drunk and on the far end of a phone line." She rubbed nervously at her newest cheek-tattoo. "Is this one of your weird jokes?"

"Yeah. It is, actually. The chances are eighty to one that she'll turn me down flat." Eddy laughed. "But I'm gonna try anyway. Because you're not letting me live and breathe."

Djulia's face went stiff. "When we're face to face, you always abuse my trust. That's why I don't like for us to go past virching."

"Come off it, Djulia."

She was defiant. "If you think you'll be happier with some weirdo virch-whore in Europe, go ahead! I don't know why you can't do that by wire from Chattanooga, anyway."

"This is Europe. We're talking actuality here."

Djulia was shocked. "If you actually touch another woman I never want to see you again." She bit her lip. "Or do wire with you, either. I mean that, Eddy. You know I do."

"Yeah," he said. "I know."

He hung up, got change from the phone, and dialed his parents' house. His father answered.

"Hi, Bob. Lisa around?"

"No," his father said, "it's her night for optic macrame. How's Europe?"

"Different."

"Nice to hear from you, Eddy. We're kind of short of money. I can spare you some sustained attention, though."

"I just dumped Djulia."

"Good move, son," his father said briskly. "Fine. Very serious girl, Djulia. Way too straitlaced for you. A kid your age should be dating girls who are absolutely jumping out of their skins."

Eddy nodded.

"You didn't lose your spex, did you?"

Eddy held them up on their neck chain. "Safe and sound."

"Hardly recognized you for a second," his father said. "Ed, you're such a serious-minded kid. Taking on all these responsibilities. On the road so much, spexware day in and day out. Lisa and I network about you all the time. Neither of us did a day's work before we were thirty, and we're all the better for it. You've got to live, son. Got to find yourself. Smell the roses. If you want to stay in Europe a couple of months, forget the algebra courses."

"It's calculus, Bob."

"Whatever."

"Thanks for the good advice, Bob. I know you mean it."

"It's good news about Djulia, son. You know we don't invalidate your feelings, so we never said a goddamn thing to you, but her glassware really sucked. Lisa says she's got no goddamn aesthetics at all. That's a hell of a thing, in a woman."

"That's my mom," Eddy said. "Give Lisa my best." He hung up.

He went back out to the sidewalk table. "Did you eat enough?" Sardelle asked.

"Yeah. It was good."

"Sleepy?"

"I dunno. Maybe."

"Do you have a place to stay, Eddy? Hotel reservations?"

Eddy shrugged. "No. I don't bother, usually. What's the use? It's more fun winging it."

"Good," Sardelle nodded. "It's better to wing. No one can trace us. It's safer."

She found them shelter in a park, where an activist group of artists from Munich had set up a squatter pavilion. As squatter pavilions went, it was quite a nice one, new and in good condition: a giant soap-bubble upholstered in cellophane and polysilk. It covered half an acre with crisp yellow bubblepack flooring. The shelter was illegal and therefore anonymous. Sardelle seemed quite pleased about this.

Once through the zippered airlock, Eddy and Sardelle were forced to examine the artists' multimedia artwork for an entire grueling hour. Worse yet, they were closely quizzed afterward by an expert-system, which bullied them relentlessly with arcane aesthetic dogma.

This ordeal was too high a price for most squatters. The pavilion, though attractive, was only half-full, and many people who had shown up bone-tired were fleeing the art headlong. Deep Eddy, however, almost always aced this sort of thing. Thanks to his slick responses to the computer's quizzing, he won himself quite a nice area, with a blanket, opaquable curtains, and its own light fixtures. Sardelle, by contrast, had been bored and minimal, and had won nothing more advanced than a pillow and a patch of bubblepack among the philistines.

Eddy made good use of a traveling pay-toilet stall, and bought some mints and chilled mineral water from a robot. He settled in cozily as police sirens, and some distant, rather choked-sounding explosions, made the night glamorous.

Sardelle didn't seem anxious to leave. "May I see your hotel bag," she said.

"Sure." He handed it over. Might as well. She'd given it to him in the first place.

He'd thought she was going to examine the book again, but instead she took a small plastic packet from within the bag, and pulled the packet's rip-cord. A colorful jumpsuit jumped out, with a chemical hiss and a vague hot stink of catalysis and cheap cologne. The jumpsuit, a one-piece, had comically baggy legs, frilled sleeves, and was printed all over with a festive cut-up of twentieth-century naughty seaside postcards.

"Pajamas," Eddy said. "Gosh, how thoughtful."

"You can sleep in this if you want," Sardelle nodded, "but it's daywear. I want you to wear it tomorrow. And I want to buy the clothes you are wearing now, so that I can take them away for safety."

Deep Eddy was wearing a dress shirt, light jacket, American jeans, dappled stockings, and Nashville brogues of genuine blue suede. "I can't wear that crap," he protested. "Jesus, I'd look like a total loser."

"Yes," said Sardelle with an enthusiastic nod, "it's very cheap and common. It will make you invisible. Just one more party boy among thousands and thousands. This is very secure dress, for a courier during a Wende."

"You want me to meet the Critic in this get-up?"

Sardelle laughed. "The Cultural Critic is not impressed by taste, Eddy. The eye he uses when he looks at people…he sees things other people can't see." She paused, considering. "He *might* be impressed if you showed up dressed in *this*. Not because of what it is, of course. But because it would show that you can understand and manipulate popular taste to your own advantage…just as he does."

"You're really being paranoid," Eddy said, nettled. "I'm not an assassin. I'm just some techie zude from Tennessee. You know that, don't you?"

"Yes, I believe you," she nodded. "You're very convincing. But that has nothing to do with proper security technique. If I take your clothes, there will be less operational risk."

"How much less risk? What do you expect to find in my clothes, anyway?"

"There are many, many things you *might* have done," she said patiently. "The human race is very ingenious. We have invented ways to kill, or hurt, or injure almost anyone, with almost nothing at all." She sighed. "If you don't know about such techniques already, it would only be stupid for me to tell you all about them. So let's be quick and simple, Eddy. It would make me happier to take your clothes away. A hundred ecu."

Eddy shook his head. "This time it's really going to cost you."

"Two hundred then," Sardelle said.

"Forget it."

"I can't go higher than two hundred. Unless you let me search your body cavities."

Eddy dropped his spex.

"Body cavities," Sardelle said impatiently. "You're a grown-up man, you must know about this. A great deal can be done with body cavities."

Eddy stared at her. "Can't I have some chocolate and roses first?"

"It's not chocolate and roses with us," Sardelle said sternly. "Don't talk to me about chocolate and roses. We're not lovers. We are client and body-guard. It's an ugly business, I know. But it's only business."

"Yeah? Well, trading in body cavities is new to me." Deep Eddy rubbed his chin. "As a simple Yankee youngster I find this a little confusing. Maybe we could barter then? Tonight?"

She laughed harshly. "I won't sleep with you, Eddy. I won't sleep at all! You're only being foolish." Sardelle shook her head. Suddenly she lifted a densely braided mass of hair above her right ear. "Look here, Mr. Simple Yankee Young-ster. I'll show you my favorite body cavity." There was a fleshcolored plastic duct in the side of her scalp. "It's illegal to have this done in Europe. I had it done in Turkey. This morning I took half a cc through there. I won't sleep until Monday."

"Jesus," Eddy said. He lifted his spex to stare at the small dimpled orifice: "Right through the blood-brain barrier? That must be a hell of an infection risk."

"I don't do it for fun. It's not like beer and pretzels. It's just that I won't sleep now. Not until the Wende is over." She put her hair back, and sat up with a look of composure. "Then I'll fly somewhere and lie in the sun and be very still. All by myself, Eddy."

"Okay," Eddy said, feeling a weird and muddy sort of pity for her. "You can borrow my clothes and search them."

"I have to burn the clothes. Two hundred ecu?"

"All right. But I keep these shoes."

"May I look at your teeth for free? It will only take five minutes."

"Okay," he muttered. She smiled at him, and touched her spex. A bright purple light emerged from the bridge of her nose.

▲ ▼ ▲

At 08:00 a police drone attempted to clear the park. It flew overhead, barking robotic threats in five languages. Everyone simply ignored the machine.

Around 08:30 an actual line of human police showed up. In response, a group of the squatters brought out their own bullhorn, an enormous battery-powered sonic assault-unit.

The first earthshaking shriek hit Eddy like an electric prod. He'd been lying peacefully on his bubble-mattress, listening to the doltish yap of the robot chopper. Now he leapt quickly from his crash-padding and wormed his way into the crispy bubblepack cloth of his ridiculous jumpsuit.

Sardelle showed up while he was still tacking the jumpsuit's Velcro buttons. She led him outside the pavilion.

The squatter bullhorn was up on an iron tripod pedestal, surrounded by a large group of grease-stained anarchists with helmets, earpads, and studded white batons. Their bullhorn's enormous ululating bellow was reducing everyone's nerves to jelly. It was like the shriek of Medusa.

The cops retreated, and the owners of the bullhorn shut it off, waving their glittering batons in triumph. In the deafened, jittery silence there were scattered shrieks, jeers, and claps, but the ambience in the park had become very bad: aggressive and surreal. Attracted by the apocalyptic shriek, people were milling into the park at a trot, spoiling for any kind of trouble.

They seemed to have little in common, these people: not their dress, not language, certainly nothing like a coherent political cause. They were mostly young men, and most of them looked as if they'd been up all night: red-eyed and peevish. They taunted the retreating cops. A milling gang knifed one of the smaller pavilions, a scarlet one, and it collapsed like a blood-blister under their trampling feet.

Sardelle took Eddy to the edge of the park, where the cops were herding up a crowd-control barricade-line of ambulant robotic pink beanbags. "I want to see this," he protested. His ears were ringing.

"They're going to fight," she told him.

"About what?"

"Anything. Everything," she shouted. "It doesn't matter. They'll knock our teeth out. Don't be stupid." She took him by the elbow and they slipped through a gap in the closing battle-line.

The police had brought up a tracked glue-cannon truck. They now began to threaten the crowd with a pasting. Eddy had never seen a glue-cannon before—except on television. It was quite astonishing how frightening the machine looked, even in pink. It was squat, blind, and nozzled, and sat there buzzing like some kind of wheeled warrior termite.

Suddenly several of the cops standing around the machine began to flinch and duck. Eddy saw a glittering object carom hard off the glue-truck's armored canopy. It flew twenty meters and landed in the grass at his feet. He picked it up. It was a stainless-steel ball-bearing the size of a cow's eyeball.

"Airguns?" he said.

"Slingshots. Don't let one hit you."

"Oh yeah. Great advice, I guess." To the far side of the cops a group of people—some kind of closely organized protestors—were advancing in measured step under a tall two-man banner. It read, in English: *The Only Thing Worse Than Dying Is Outliving Your Culture.* Every man jack of them, and there were at least sixty, carried a long plastic pike topped with an ominous-looking bulbous sponge. It was clear from the way they maneuvered that they understood military pike-tactics only too well; their phalanx bristled like a hedgehog, and some captain among them was barking distant orders. Worse yet, the pikemen had neatly outflanked the cops, who now began calling frantically for backup.

A police drone whizzed just above their heads, not the casual lumbering he had seen before, but direct and angry and inhumanly fast. "Run!" Sardelle shouted, taking his hands. "Peppergas…"

Eddy glanced behind him as he fled. The chopper, as if cropdusting, was farting a dense maroon fog. The crowd bellowed in shock and rage and, seconds later, that hellish bullhorn kicked in once more.

Sardelle ran with amazing ease and speed. She bounded along as if firecrackers were bursting under her feet. Eddy, years younger and considerably longer in leg, was very hard put to keep up.

In two minutes they were well out of the park, across a broad street and into a pedestrian network of small shops and restaurants. There she stopped and let him catch his breath.

"Jesus," he puffed, "where can I buy shoes like that?"

"They're made-to-order," she told him calmly. "And you need special training. You can break your ankles, otherwise…." She gazed at a nearby bakery. "You want some breakfast now?"

Eddy sampled a chocolate-filled pastry inside the shop, at a dainty, doily-covered table. Two ambulances rushed down the street, and a large group of drum-beating protesters swaggered by, shoving shoppers from the pavement; but otherwise things seemed peaceful. Sardelle sat with arms folded, staring into space. He guessed that she was reading security alerts from the insides of her spex.

"You're not tired, are you?" he said.

"I don't sleep on operations," she said, "but sometimes I like to sit very still." She smiled at him. "You wouldn't understand…."

"Hell no I wouldn't," Eddy said, his mouth full. "All hell's breaking loose over there, and here you are sipping orange juice just as calm as a bump on a pickle....Damn, these croissants, or whatever the hell they are, are really good. Hey! *Herr Ober!* Bring me another couple of those, *ja, danke....*"

"The trouble could follow us anywhere. We're as safe here as any other place. Safer, because we're not in the open."

"Good," Eddy nodded, munching. "That park's a bad scene."

"It's not so bad in the park. It's very bad at the Rhein-Spire, though. The Mahogany Warbirds have seized the rotating restaurant. They're stealing skin."

"What are Warbirds?"

She seemed surprised. "You haven't heard of them? They're from NAFTA. A criminal syndicate. Insurance rackets, protection rackets, they run all the casinos in the Quebec Republic...."

"Okay. So what's stealing skin?"

"It's a new kind of swindle; they take a bit of skin or blood, with your genetics, you see, and a year later they tell you they have a newborn son or daughter of yours held captive, held somewhere secret in the South....Then they try to make you pay, and pay, and pay...."

"You mean they're kidnapping genetics from the people in that restaurant?"

"Yes. Brunch in the Rhein-Spire is very prestigious. The victims are all rich or famous." Suddenly she laughed, rather bitter, rather cynical. "I'll be busy next year, Eddy, thanks to this. A new job—protecting my clients' skin."

Eddy thought about it. "It's kind of like the rent-a-womb business, huh? But really twisted."

She nodded. "The Warbirds are crazy, they're not even ethnic criminals, they are network interest-group creatures....Crime is so damned ugly, Eddy. If you ever think of doing it, just stop."

Eddy grunted.

"Think of those children," she murmured. "Born from crime. Manufactured to order, for a criminal purpose. This is a strange world, isn't it? It frightens me sometimes."

"Yeah?" Eddy said cheerfully. "Illegitimate son of a millionaire, raised by a high-tech mafia? Sounds kind of weird and romantic to me. I mean, consider the possibilities."

She took off her spex for the first time, to look at him. Her eyes were blue. A very odd and romantic shade of blue. Probably tinted contacts.

"Rich people have been having illegitimate kids since the year zero," Eddy said. "The only difference is somebody's mechanized the process." He laughed.

"It's time you met the Cultural Critic," she said. She put the spex back on.

▲ ▼ ▲

They had to walk a long way. The bus system was now defunct. Apparently the soccer fans made a sport of hitting public buses; they would rip all the beanbags out and kick them through the doors. On his way to meet the Critic, Eddy saw hundreds of soccer fans; the city was swarming with them. The English devotees were very bad news: savage, thick-booted, snarling, stamping, chanting, anonymous young men, in knee-length sandpaper coats, with their hair cropped short and their faces masked or warpainted in the Union Jack. The English soccer hooligans traveled in enormous packs of two and three hundred. They were armed with cheap cellular phones. They'd wrapped the aerials with friction tape to form truncheon handles, so that the high-impact ceramic phone-casing became a nasty club. It was impossible to deny a traveler the ownership of a telephone, so the police were impotent to stop this practice. Practically speaking, there was not much to be done in any case. The English hooligans dominated the streets through sheer force of numbers. Anyone seeing them simply fled headlong.

Except, of course, for the Irish soccer fans. The Irish wore thick elbow-length grappling gloves, some kind of workmen's gauntlets apparently, along with long green-and-white football-scarves. Their scarves had skull-denting weights sewn into pockets at their ends, and the tassels were fringed with little skin-ripping wire barbs. The weights were perfectly legitimate rolls of coins, and the wire—well, you could get wire anywhere. The Irish seemed to be outnumbered, but were, if anything, even drunker and more reckless than their rivals. Unlike the English, the Irish louts didn't even use the cellular phones to coordinate their brawling. They just plunged ahead at a dead run, whipping their scarves overhead and screaming about Oliver Cromwell.

The Irish were terrifying. They traveled down streets like a scourge. Anything in their way they knocked over and trampled: knickknack kiosks, propaganda videos, poster-booths, T-shirt tables, people selling canned jump-suits. Even the postnatal abortion people, who were true fanatics, and the scary, eldritch, black-clad pro-euthanasia groups, would abandon their sidewalk podiums to flee from the Irish kids.

Eddy shuddered to think what the scene must be like at the Rhein-Stadium. "Those are some mean goddamn kids," he told Sardelle, as they emerged from hiding in an alley. "And it's all about *soccer?* Jesus, that seems so pointless."

"If they rioted in their *own* towns, *that* would be pointless," Sardelle said. "Here at the Wende, they can smash each other, and everything else, and tomorrow they will be perfectly safe at home in their own world."

"Oh, I get it," Eddy said. "That makes a lot of sense."

A passing blonde woman in a Muslim hijab slapped a button onto Eddy's sleeve. "Will your lawyer talk to God?" the button demanded aloud, repeatedly, in English. Eddy plucked the device off and stamped on it.

The Cultural Critic was holding court in a safehouse in Stadtmitte. The safehouse was an anonymous twentieth-century four-storey dump, flanked by some nicely retrofitted nineteenth-century townhouses. A graffiti gang had hit the block during the night, repainting the street-surface with a sprawling polychrome mural, all big grinning green kittycats, fractal spirals, and leaping priapic pink pigs. "Hot Spurt!" one of the pigs suggested eagerly; Eddy skirted its word balloon as they approached the door.

The door bore a small brass plaque reading "E.I.S.—Elektronisches Invasionsabwehr-Systems GmbH." There was an inscribed corporate logo that appeared to be a melting ice-cube.

Sardelle spoke in German to the door video; it opened, and they entered a hall full of pale, drawn adults in suits, armed with fire-extinguishers. Despite their air of nervous resolution and apparent willingness to fight hand-to-hand, Eddy took them for career academics: modestly dressed, ties and scarves slightly askew, odd cheek-tattoos, distracted gazes, too serious. The place smelled bad, like stale cottage-cheese and bookshelf dust. The dirt-smudged walls were festooned with schematics and wiring diagrams, amid a bursting mess of tower-stacked scrawl-labeled cartons—disk archives of some kind. The ceiling and floorboards were festooned with taped-down powercables and fiber-optic network wiring.

"Hi, everybody!" Eddy said. "How's it going?" The building's defenders looked at him, noted his jumpsuit costume, and reacted with relieved indifference. They began talking in French, obviously resuming some briefly postponed and intensely important discussion.

"Hello," said a German in his thirties, rising to his feet. He had long, thinning, greasy hair and a hollow-cheeked, mushroom-pale face. He wore secretarial half-spex; and behind them he had the shiftiest eyes Eddy had ever seen, eyes that darted, and gloated, and slid around the room. He worked his way through the defenders, and smiled at Eddy, vaguely. "I am your host. Welcome, friend." He extended a hand.

Eddy shook it. He glanced sidelong at Sardelle. Sardelle had gone as stiff as a board and had jammed her gloved hands in her trenchcoat pockets.

"So," Eddy gabbled, snatching his hand back, "thanks a lot for having us over!"

"You'll be wanting to see my famous friend the Cultural Critic," said their host, with a cadaverous smile. "He is upstairs. This is my place. I own it." He gazed around himself, brimming with satisfaction. "It's my Library, you see. I have the honor of hosting the great man for the Wende. He appreciates my work. Unlike so many others." Their host dug into the pocket of his baggy slacks. Eddy, instinctively expecting a drawn knife, was vaguely surprised to see his host hand over an old-fashioned, dogeared business card. Eddy glanced at it. "How are you, Herr Schreck?"

"Life is very exciting today," said Schreck with a smirk. He touched his spex and examined Eddy's online bio. "A young American visitor. How charming."

"I'm from NAFTA," Eddy corrected.

"And a civil libertarian. Liberty is the only word that still excites me," Schreck said, with itchy urgency. "I need many more American intimates. Do make use of me. And all my digital services. That card of mine—do call those network addresses and tell your friends. The more, the happier." He turned to Sardelle. *"Kaffee, fraulein? Zigaretten?"*

Sardelle shook her head minimally.

"It's good she's here," Schreck told Eddy. "She can help us to fight. You go upstairs. The great man is waiting for visitors."

"I'm going up with him," Sardelle said.

"Stay here," Schreck urged. "The security threat is to the Library, not to him."

"I'm a bodyguard," Sardelle said frostily. "I guard the body. I don't guard data-havens."

Schreck frowned. "Well, more fool you, then."

Sardelle followed Eddy up the dusty, flower-carpeted stairs. Upstairs to the right was an antique twentieth-century office-door in blond oak and frosted glass. Sardelle knocked; someone called out in French.

She opened the door. Inside the office were two long workbenches covered with elderly desktop computers. The windows were barred and curtained.

The Cultural Critic, wearing spex and a pair of datagloves, sat in a bright pool of sunlight-yellow glare from a trackmounted overhead light. He was pecking daintily with his gloved fingertips at a wafer-thin datascreen of woven cloth.

As Sardelle and Eddy stepped into the office, the Critic wrapped up his screen in a scroll, removed his spex, and unplugged his gloves. He had dark pepper-and-salt tousled hair, a dark wool tie, and a long maroon scarf draped over a beautifully cut ivory jacket.

"You would be Mr. Dertouzas from CAPCLUG," he said.

"Exactly. How are you, sir?"

"Very well." He examined Eddy briefly. "I assume his clothing was your idea, Frederika."

Sardelle nodded once, with a sour look. Eddy smiled at her, delighted to learn her real name.

"Have a seat," the Critic offered. He poured himself more coffee. "I'd offer you a cup of this, but it's been…adjusted."

"I brought you your book," Eddy said. He sat, and opened the bag, and offered the item in question.

"Splendid." The Critic reached into his pocket and, to Eddy's surprise, pulled a knife. The Critic opened its blade with one thumbnail. The shining blade was sawtoothed in a fractal fashion; even its serrations had tiny serrated serrations. It was a jack-knife the length of a finger, with a razor-sharp edge on it as long as a man's arm.

Under the knife's irresistible ripping caress, the tough cover of the book parted with a discreet shredding of cloth. The Critic reached into the slit and plucked out a thin, gleaming storage disk. He set the book down. "Did you read this?"

"That disk?" Eddy ad-libbed. "I assumed it was encrypted."

"You assumed correctly, but I meant the book."

"I think it lost something in translation," Eddy said.

The Critic raised his brows. He had dark, heavy brows with a pronounced frown-line between them, over sunken, gray-green eyes. "You have read Canetti in the original, Mr. Dertouzas?"

"I meant the translation between centuries," Eddy said, and laughed. "What I read left me with nothing but questions....Can you answer them for me, sir?"

The Critic shrugged and turned to a nearby terminal. It was a scholar's workstation, the least dilapidated of the machines in the office. He touched four keys in order; a carousel whirled and spat out a disk. The Critic handed it to Eddy. "You'll find your answers here, to whatever extent I can give them," he said. "My Complete Works. Please take this disk. Reproduce it, give it to whomever you like, as long as you accredit it. The standard scholarly procedure. I'm sure you know the etiquette."

"Thank you very much," Eddy said with dignity, tucking the disk into his bag. "Of course I own your works already, but I'm glad of a fully up-to-date edition."

"I'm told that a copy of my Complete Works will get you a cup of coffee at any café in Europe," the Critic mused, slotting the encrypted disk and rapidly tapping keys. "Apparently digital commodification is not entirely a spent force, even in literature...." He examined the screen. "Oh, this is lovely. I knew I would need this data again. And I certainly didn't want it in my house." He smiled.

"What are you going to do with that data?" Eddy said.

"Do you really not know?" the Critic said. "And you from CAPCLUG, a group of such carnivorous curiosity? Well, that's also a strategy, I suppose." He tapped more keys, then leaned back and opened a pack of zigarettes.

"What strategy?"

"New elements, new functions, new solutions—I don't know what 'culture' is, but I know exactly what I'm doing." The Critic drew slowly on a zigarette, his brows knotting.

"And what's that, exactly?"

"You mean, what is the underlying concept?" He waved the zigarette. "I have no 'concept.' The struggle here must not be reduced to a single simple idea. I am building a structure that must not, cannot, be reduced to a single simple idea. I am building a structure that perhaps *suggests* a concept....If I did more, the system itself would become stronger than the surrounding culture....Any system of rational analysis must live within the strong blind body of mass humanity, Mr. Dertouzas. If we learned anything from the twentieth century, we learned that much, at least." The Critic sighed, a fragrant medicinal mist. "I fight windmills, sir. It's a duty....You often are hurt, but at the same time you become unbelievably happy, because you see that you have both friends and enemies, and that you are capable of fertilizing society with contradictory attitudes."

"What enemies do you mean?" Eddy said.

"Here. Today. Another data-burning. It was necessary to stage a formal resistance."

"This is an evil place," Sardelle—or rather Frederika—burst out. "I had no idea this was today's safehouse. This is anything but safe. Jean-Arthur, you must leave this place at once. You could be killed here!"

"An evil place? Certainly. But there is so much megabytage devoted to works on goodness, and on doing good—so very little coherent intellectual treatment of the true nature of evil and being evil....Of malice and stupidity and acts of cruelty and darkness...." The Critic sighed. "Actually, once you're allowed through the encryption that Herr Schreck so wisely imposes on his holdings, you'll find the data here rather banal. The manuals for committing crime are farfetched and badly written. The schematics for bombs, listening devices, drug labs, and so forth, are poorly designed and probably unworkable. The pornography is juvenile and overtly anti-erotic. The invasions of privacy are of interest only to voyeurs. Evil is banal—by no means so scarlet as one's instinctive dread would paint it. It's like the sex-life of one's parents—a primal and forbidden topic, and yet, with objectivity, basically integral to their human nature—and of course to your own."

"Who's planning to burn this place?" Eddy said.

"A rival of mine. He calls himself the Moral Referee."

"Oh yeah, I've heard of him!" Eddy said. "He's here in Düsseldorf, too? Jesus."

"He is a charlatan," the Critic sniffed. "Something of an ayatollah figure. A popular demagogue...." He glanced at Eddy. "Yes, yes—of course people do say much the same of me, Mr. Dertouzas, and I'm perfectly aware of that. But I have two doctorates, you know. The Referee is a self-appointed digital Savonarola. Not a scholar at all. An autodidactic philosopher. At best an artist."

"Aren't you an artist?"

"That's the danger...." The Critic nodded. "Once I was only a teacher, then suddenly I felt a sense of mission....I began to understand which works are strongest, which are only decorative...." The Critic looked suddenly restless, and puffed at his zigarette again. "In Europe there is too much couture, too little culture. In Europe everything is colored by discourse. There is too much knowledge and too much fear to overthrow that knowledge....In NAFTA you are too naively postmodern to suffer from this syndrome....And the Sphere, the Sphere, they are orthogonal to both our concerns....The South, of course, is the planet's last reservoir of authentic humanity, despite every ontological atrocity committed there...."

"I'm not following you," Eddy said.

"Take that disk with you. Don't lose it," the Critic said somberly. "I have certain obligations, that's all. I must know why I made certain choices, and be able to defend them, and I must defend them, or risk losing everything....Those choices are already made. I've drawn a line here, established a position. It's my Wende today, you know! My lovely Wende....Through cusp-points like this one, I can make things different for the whole of society." He smiled. "Not better, necessarily—but different, certainly...."

"People are coming," Frederika announced suddenly, standing bolt upright and gesturing at the air. "A lot of people marching in the streets outside...there's going to be trouble."

"I knew he would react the moment that data left this building," the Critic said, nodding. "Let trouble come! I will not move!"

"God damn you, I'm being paid to see that you survive!" Frederika said. "The Referee's people burn data-havens. They've done it before, and they'll do it again. Let's get out of here while there's still time!"

"We're all ugly and evil," the Critic announced calmly, settling deeply into his chair and steepling his fingers. "Bad knowledge is still legitimate self-knowledge. Don't pretend otherwise."

"That's no reason to fight them hand-to-hand here in Düsseldorf! We're not tactically prepared to defend this building! Let them burn it! What's one more stupid outlaw and his rat nest full of garbage?"

The Critic looked at her with pity. "It's not the access that matters. It's the principle."

"Bullseye!" Eddy shouted, recognizing a CAPCLUG slogan.

Frederika, biting her lip, leaned over a tabletop and began typing invisibly on a virtual keyboard. "If you call your professional backup," the Critic told her, "they'll only be hurt. This is not really your fight, my dear; you're not committed."

"Fuck you and your politics; if you burn up in here we don't get our bonuses," Frederika shouted.

"No reason he should stay, at least," the Critic said, gesturing to Eddy. "You've done well, Mr. Dertouzas. Thank you very much for your successful errand. It was most helpful." The Critic glanced at the workstation screen, where a program from the disk was still spooling busily, then back at Eddy again. "I suggest you leave this place while you can."

Eddy glanced at Frederika.

"Yes, go!" she said. "You're finished here, I'm not your escort anymore. Run, Eddy!"

"No way," Eddy said, folding his arms. "If you're not moving, I'm not moving."

Frederika looked furious. "But you're free to go. You heard him say so."

"So what? Since I'm at liberty, I'm also free to stay," Eddy retorted. "Besides, I'm from Tennessee, NAFTA's Volunteer State."

"There are hundreds of enemies coming," Frederika said, staring into space. "They will overwhelm us and burn this place to the ground. There will be nothing left of both of you and your rotten data but ashes."

"Have faith," the Critic said coolly. "Help will come, as well—from some unlikely quarters. Believe me, I'm doing my very best to maximize the implications of this event. So is my rival, if it comes to that. Thanks to that disk that just arrived, I am wirecasting events here to four hundred of the most volatile network sites in Europe. Yes, the Referee's people may destroy us, but their chances of escaping the consequences are very slim. And if we ourselves die here in flames, it will only lend deeper meaning to our sacrifice."

Eddy gazed at the Critic in honest admiration. "I don't understand a single goddamn word you're saying, but I guess I can recognize a fellow spirit when I meet one. I'm sure CAPCLUG would want me to stay."

"CAPCLUG would want no such thing," the Critic told him soberly. "They would want you to escape, so that they could examine and dissect your experiences in detail. Your American friends are sadly infatuated with the supposed potency of rational, panoptic, digital analysis. Believe me, please—the enormous turbulence in postmodern society is far larger than any single human mind can comprehend, with or without computer-aided perception or the finest computer-assisted frameworks of sociological analysis." The Critic gazed at his workstation, like a herpetologist studying a cobra. "Your CAPCLUG friends will go to their graves never realizing that every vital impulse in human life is entirely pre-rational."

"Well, I'm certainly not leaving here before I figure *that* out," Eddy said. "I plan to help you fight the good fight, sir."

The Critic shrugged, and smiled. "Thank you for just proving me right, young man. Of course a young American hero is welcome to die in Europe's political struggles. I'd hate to break an old tradition."

Glass shattered. A steaming lump of dry ice flew through the window, skittered across the office floor, and began gently dissolving. Acting entirely on instinct, Eddy dashed forward, grabbed it barehanded, and threw it back out the window.

"Are you okay?" Frederika said.

"Sure," Eddy said, surprised.

"That was a chemical gas bomb," Frederika said. She gazed at him as if expecting him to drop dead on the spot.

"Apparently the chemical frozen into the ice was not very toxic," the Critic surmised.

"I don't think it was a gas bomb at all," Eddy said, gazing out the window. "I think it was just a big chunk of dry ice. You Europeans are completely paranoid."

He saw with astonishment that there was a medieval pageant taking place in the street. The followers of the Moral Referee—there were some three or four hundred of them, well organized and marching forward in grimly disciplined silence—apparently had a weakness for medieval jerkins, fringed capes, and colored hose. And torches. They were very big on torches.

The entire building shuddered suddenly, and a burglar siren went off. Eddy craned to look. Half a dozen men were battering the door with a handheld hydraulic ram. They wore visored helmets and metal armor, which gleamed in the summer daylight. "We're being attacked by goddamn knights in shining armor," Eddy said. "I can't believe they're doing this in broad daylight!"

"The football game just started," Frederika said. "They have picked the perfect moment. Now they can get away with anything."

"Do these window-bars come out?" Eddy said, shaking them.

"No. Thank goodness."

"Then hand me some of those data-disks," he demanded. "No, not those shrimpy ones—give me the full thirty-centimeter jobs."

He threw the window up and began pelting the crowd below with flung megabytage. The disks had vicious aerodynamics and were hefty and sharp-edged. He was rewarded with a vicious barrage of bricks, which shattered windows all along the second and third floors.

"They're very angry now," Frederika shouted over the wailing alarm and roar of the crowd below. The three of them crouched under a table.

"Yeah," Eddy said. His blood was boiling. He picked up a long, narrow printer, dashed across the room, and launched it between the bars. In reply, half a dozen long metal darts—short javelins, really—flew up through the window and embedded themselves in the office ceiling.

"How'd they get those through Customs?" Eddy shouted. "Must've made them last night." He laughed. "Should I throw 'em back? I can fetch them if I stand on a chair."

"Don't, don't," Frederika shouted. "Control yourself! Don't kill anyone, it's not professional."

"I'm not professional," Eddy said.

"Get down here," Frederika commanded. When he refused, she scrambled from beneath the table and bodyslammed him against the wall. She pinned Eddy's arms, flung herself across him with almost erotic intensity, and hissed into his ear. "Save yourself while you can! This is only a Wende."

"Stop that," Eddy shouted, trying to break her grip. More bricks came through the window, tumbling past their feet.

"If they kill these worthless intellectuals," she muttered hotly, "there will be a thousand more to take their place. But if you don't leave this building right now, you'll die here."

"Christ, I know that," Eddy shouted, finally flinging her backward with a rasp at her sandpaper coat. "Quit being such a loser."

"Eddy, listen!" Frederika yelled, knotting her gloved fists. "Let me save your life! You'll owe me later! Go home to your parents in America, and don't worry about the Wende. This is all we ever do—it's all we are really good for."

"Hey, I'm good at this, too!" Eddy announced. A brick barked his ankle. In sudden convulsive fury, he upended a table and slammed it against a broken window, as a shield. As bricks thudded against the far side of the table, he shouted defiance. He felt superhuman. Her attempt to talk sense had irritated him enormously.

The door broke in downstairs, with a concussive blast. Screams echoed up the stairs. "That's torn it!" Eddy said.

He snatched up a multiplugged power outlet, dashed across the room, and kicked the office door open. With a shout, he jumped onto the landing, swinging the heavy power-strip over his head.

The Critic's academic cadre were no physical match for the Referee's knights-in-armor; but their fire extinguishers were surprisingly effective weapons. They coated everything in white caustic soda and filled the air with great blinding, billowing wads of flying, freezing droplets. It was clear that the defenders had been practicing.

The sight of the desperate struggle downstairs overwhelmed Eddy. He jumped down the stairs three at a time and flung himself into the midst of the battle. He conked a soda-covered helmet with a vicious overhead swing of his power-strip, then slipped and fell heavily on his back.

He began wrestling desperately across the soda-slick floor with a half-blinded knight. The knight clawed his visor up. Beneath the metal mask the knight was, if anything, younger than himself. He looked like a nice kid. He clearly meant well. Eddy hit the kid in the jaw as hard as he could, then began slamming his helmeted head into the floor.

Another knight kicked Eddy in the belly. Eddy fell off his victim, got up, and went for the new attacker. The two of them, wrestling clumsily, were knocked off balance by a sudden concerted rush through the doorway; a dozen Moral raiders slammed through, flinging torches and bottles of flaming gel. Eddy slapped his new opponent across the eyes with his soda-daubed hand, then lurched to his feet and jammed the loose spex back onto his face. He began coughing violently. The air was full of smoke; he was smothering.

He lurched for the door. With the panic strength of a drowning man, he clawed and jostled his way free.

Once outside the data-haven, Eddy realized that he was one of dozens of people daubed head to foot with white foam. Wheezing, coughing, collapsing against the side of the building, he and his fellow refugees resembled veterans of a monster cream-pie fight.

They didn't, and couldn't, recognize him as an enemy. The caustic soda was eating its way into Eddy's cheap jumpsuit, reducing the bubbled fabric to weeping red rags.

Wiping his lips, ribs heaving, Eddy looked around. The spex had guarded his eyes, but their filth subroutine had crashed badly. The internal screen was frozen. Eddy shook the spex with his foamy hands, finger-snapped at them, whistled aloud. Nothing.

He edged his way along the wall.

At the back of the crowd, a tall gentleman in a medieval episcopal mitre was shouting orders through a bullhorn. Eddy wandered through the crowd until he got closer to the man. He was a tall, lean man, in his late forties, in brocaded vestments, a golden cloak, and white gloves.

· This was the Moral Referee. Eddy considered jumping this distinguished gentleman and pummeling him, perhaps wrestling his bullhorn away and shouting contradictory orders through it.

But even if he dared to try this, it wouldn't do Eddy much good. The Referee with the bullhorn was shouting in German. Eddy didn't speak German. Without his spex he couldn't read German. He didn't understand Germans or their issues or their history. In point of fact he had no real reason at all to be in Germany.

The Moral Referee noticed Eddy's fixed and calculating gaze. He lowered his bullhorn, leaned down a little from the top of his portable mahogany pulpit, and said something to Eddy in German.

"Sorry," Eddy said, lifting his spex on their neck chain. "Translation program crashed."

The Referee examined him thoughtfully. "Has the acid in that foam damaged your spectacles?" he said, in excellent English.

"Yes sir," Eddy said. "I think I'll have to strip 'em and blow-dry the chips."

The Referee reached within his robe and handed Eddy a monogrammed linen kerchief. "You might try this, young man."

"Thanks a lot," Eddy said. "I appreciate that, really."

"Are you wounded?" the Referee said, with apparently genuine concern.

"No, sir. I mean, not really."

"Then you'd better return to the fight," the Referee said, straightening. "I know we have them on the run. Be of good cheer. Our cause is just." He lifted his bullhorn again and resumed shouting.

The first floor of the building had caught fire. Groups of the Referee's people were hauling linked machines into the street and smashing them to fragments on the pavement. They hadn't managed to knock the bars from the windows, but they had battered some enormous holes through the walls. Eddy watched, polishing his spex.

Well above the street, the wall of the third floor began to disintegrate.

Moral Knights had broken into the office where Eddy had last seen the Cultural Critic. They had hauled their hydraulic ram up the stairs with them. Now its blunt nose was smashing through the brick wall as if it were stale cheese.

Fist-sized chunks of rubble and mortar cascaded to the street, causing the raiders below to billow away. In seconds, the raiders on the third floor had knocked a hole in the wall the size of a manhole cover. First, they flung down an emergency ladder. Then, office furniture began tumbling out to smash to the pavement below: voice mailboxes, canisters of storage disks, red-spined European law-books, network routers, tape backup-units, color monitors....

A trenchcoat flew out the hole and pinwheeled slowly to earth. Eddy recognized it at once. It was Frederika's sandpaper coat. Even in the midst of shouting chaos, with an evil billowing of combusting plastic now belching from the library's windows, the sight of that fluttering coat hooked Eddy's awareness. There was something in that coat. In its sleeve pocket. The key to his airport locker.

Eddy dashed forward, shoved three knights aside, and grabbed up the coat for himself. He winced and skipped aside as a plummeting office chair smashed to the street, narrowly missing him. He glanced up frantically.

He was just in time to see them throw out Frederika.

▲ ▼ ▲

The tide was leaving Düsseldorf, and with it all the schooling anchovies of Europe. Eddy sat in the departure lounge balancing eighteen separate pieces of his spex on a Velcro lap-table.

"Do you need this?" Frederika asked him.

"Oh yeah," Eddy said, accepting the slim chromed tool. "I dropped my dental pick. Thanks a lot." He placed it carefully into his black travel bag. He'd just spent all his European cash on a deluxe, duty-free German electronics repair kit.

"I'm not going to Chattanooga, now or ever," Frederika told him. "So you might as well forget that. That can't be part of the bargain."

"Change your mind," Eddy suggested. "Forget this Barcelona flight, and come transatlantic with me. We'll have a fine time in Chattanooga. There's some very deep people I want you to meet."

"I don't want anybody to meet," Frederika muttered darkly. "And I don't want you to show me off to your little hackerboy friends."

Frederika had taken a hard beating in the riot, while covering the Critic's successful retreat across the rooftop. Her hair had been scorched during the battle, and it had burst from its meticulous braiding like badly overused steel wool. She had a black eye, and her cheek and jaw were scorched and shiny with medicinal gel. Although Eddy had broken her fall, her three-storey tumble to the street had sprained her ankle, wrenched her back, and barked both knees.

And she had lost her spex.

"You look just fine," Eddy told her. "You're very interesting, that's the point. You're deep! That's the appeal, you see? You're a spook, and a European, and a woman—those are all very deep entities, in my opinion." He smiled.

Eddy's left elbow felt hot and swollen inside his spare shirt; his chest, ribs, and left leg were mottled with enormous bruises. He had a bloodied lump on the back of his head where he'd smashed down into the rubble, catching her.

Altogether, they were not an entirely unusual couple among the departing Wende folk cramming the Düsseldorf airport. As a whole, the crowd seemed to be suffering a massive collective hangover—harsh enough to put many of them into slings and casts. And yet it was amazing how contented, almost

smug, many of the vast crowd seemed as they departed their pocket catastrophe. They were wan and pale, yet cheerful, like people recovering from flu.

"I don't feel well enough to be deep," Frederika said, stirring in her
beanbag. "But you did save my life, Eddy. I do owe you something." She
paused. "It has to be something reasonable."

"Don't worry about it," Eddy told her nobly, rasping at the surface of a
tiny circuit-board with a plastic spudger. "I mean, I didn't even break your
fall, strictly speaking. Mostly I just kept you from landing on your head."

"You did save my life," she repeated quietly. "That crowd would have
killed me in the street if not for you."

"You saved the Critic's life. I imagine that's a bigger deal."

"I was paid to save his life," Frederika said. "Anyway, I didn't save
the bastard. I just did my job. He was saved by his own cleverness. He's
been through a dozen of these damned things." She stretched cautiously,
shifting in her beanbag. "So have I, for that matter....I must be a real fool. I
endure a lot to live my precious life...." She took a deep breath. "Barcelona,
yo te quiero."

"I'm just glad we checked out of that clinic in time to catch our flights,"
Eddy told her, examining his work with a jeweler's loupe. "Could you believe
all those soccer kids in there? They sure were having fun....Why couldn't
they be that good-tempered before they beat the hell out of each other?
Some things are just a mystery, I guess."

"I hope you have learned a good lesson from this," Frederika said.

"Sure have," Eddy nodded. He blew dried crud from the point of his
spudger, then picked up a chrome pinch-clamp and threaded a tiny screw
through the earpiece of his spex. "I can see a lot of deep potential in the
Wende. It's true that a few dozen people got killed here, but the city must
have made an absolute fortune. That's got to look promising for the Chattanooga city council. And a Wende offers a lot of very useful exposure and
influence for a cultural networking group like CAPCLUG."

"You've learned nothing at all," she groaned. "I don't know why I hoped
it would be different."

"I admit it—in the heat of the action I got a little carried away," Eddy
said. "But my only real regret is that you won't come with me to America.
Or, if you'd really rather, take me to Barcelona. Either way, the way I see it,
you need someone to look after you for a while."

"You're going to rub my sore feet, yes?" Frederika said sourly. "How
generous you are."

"I dumped my creep girlfriend. My dad will pick up my tab. I can help
you manage better. I can improve your life. I can fix your broken appliances. I'm a nice guy."

"I don't want to be rude," she said, "but after this, the thought of being touched is repulsive." She shook her head, with finality. "I'm sorry, Eddy, but I can't give you what you want."

Eddy sighed, examined the crowd for a while, then repacked the segments of his spex and closed his tool kit. At last he spoke up again. "Do you virch?"

"What?"

"Do you do virtuality?"

She was silent for a long moment, then looked him in the eye. "You don't do anything really strange or sick on the wires, do you, Edward?"

"There's hardly any subjective time-lag if you use high-capacity transatlantic fiber," Eddy said.

"Oh. I see."

"What have you got to lose? If you don't like it, hang up."

Frederika tucked her hair back, examined the departure board for the flight to Barcelona, and looked at the toes of her shoes. "Would this make you happy?"

"No," Eddy said. "But it'd make me a whole lot more of what I already am."

Bicycle Repairman

Repeated tinny banging woke Lyle in his hammock. Lyle groaned, sat up, and slid free into the tool-crowded aisle of his bike shop.

Lyle hitched up the black elastic of his skintight shorts and plucked yesterday's grease-stained sleeveless off the workbench. He glanced blearily at his chronometer as he picked his way toward the door. It was 10:04.38 in the morning, June 27, 2037.

Lyle hopped over a stray can of primer and the floor boomed gently beneath his feet. With all the press of work, he'd collapsed into sleep without properly cleaning the shop. Doing custom enameling paid okay, but it ate up time like crazy. Working and living alone was wearing him out.

Lyle opened the shop door, revealing a long sheer drop to dusty tiling far below. Pigeons darted beneath the hull of his shop through a soot-stained hole in the broken atrium glass, and wheeled off to their rookery somewhere in the darkened guts of the high-rise.

More banging. Far below, a uniformed delivery kid stood by his cargo tricycle, yanking rhythmically at the long dangling string of Lyle's spot-welded doorknocker. Lyle waved, yawning. From his vantage point below the huge girders of the cavernous atrium, Lyle had a fine overview of three burnt-out interior levels of the old Tsatanuga Archiplat. Once-elegant handrails and battered pedestrian overlooks fronted on the great airy cavity of the atrium. Behind the handrails was a three-floor wilderness of jury-rigged lights, chicken coops, water tanks, and squatters' flags. The fire-damaged floors, walls, and ceilings were riddled with handmade descent-chutes, long coiling staircases, and rickety ladders.

Lyle took note of a crew of Chattanooga demolition workers in their yellow detox suits. The repair crew was deploying vacuum scrubbers and a high-pressure hose-off by the vandal-proofed western elevators of Floor 34. Two or three days a week, the city crew meandered into the damage zone to pretend to work, with a great hypocritical show of sawhorses and barrier tape. The lazy sons of bitches were all on the take.

Lyle thumbed the brake switches in their big metal box by the flywheel. The bike shop slithered, with a subtle hiss of cable-clamps, down three stories, to dock with a grating crunch onto four concrete-filled metal drums.

The delivery kid looked real familiar. He was in and out of the zone pretty often. Lyle had once done some custom work on the kid's cargo trike,

new shocks, and some granny-gearing as he recalled, but he couldn't remember the kid's name. Lyle was terrible with names. "What's up, zude?"

"Hard night, Lyle?"

"Just real busy."

The kid's nose wrinkled at the stench from the shop. "Doin' a lot of
paint work, huh?" He glanced at his palmtop notepad. "You still taking de-
liveries for Edward Dertouzas?"

"Yeah. I guess so." Lyle rubbed the gear tattoo on one stubbled cheek.
"If I have to."

The kid offered a stylus, reaching up. "Can you sign for him?"

Lyle folded his bare arms warily. "Naw, man, I can't sign for Deep Eddy.
Eddy's in Europe somewhere. Eddy left months ago. Haven't seen Eddy in ages."

The delivery kid scratched his sweating head below his billed fabric
cap. He turned to check for any possible sneak-ups by snatch-and-grab
artists out of the squatter warrens. The government simply refused to do
postal delivery on the Thirty-second, Thirty-third, and Thirty-fourth floors.
You never saw many cops inside the zone, either. Except for the city demolition crew, about the only official functionaries who ever showed up in the
zone were a few psychotically empathetic NAFTA social workers.

"I'll get a bonus if you sign for this thing." The kid gazed up in squint-
eyed appeal. "It's gotta be worth something, Lyle. It's a really weird kind of
routing, they paid a lot of money to send it just that way."

Lyle crouched down in the open doorway. "Let's have a look at it."

The package was a heavy shockproof rectangle in heat-sealed plastic
shrink-wrap, with a plethora of intra-European routing stickers. To judge by
all the overlays, the package had been passed from postal system to postal
system at least eight times before officially arriving in the legal custody of any
human being. The return address, if there had ever been one, was completely obscured. Someplace in France, maybe.

Lyle held the box up two-handed to his ear and shook it. Hardware.

"You gonna sign, or not?"

"Yeah." Lyle scratched illegibly at the little signature panel, then looked
at the delivery trike. "You oughta get that front wheel trued."

The kid shrugged. "Got anything to send out today?"

"Naw," Lyle grumbled, "I'm not doing mail-order repair work anymore;
it's too complicated and I get ripped off too much."

"Suit yourself." The kid clambered into the recumbent seat of his trike
and pedaled off across the heat-cracked ceramic tiles of the atrium plaza.

Lyle hung his hand-lettered OPEN FOR BUSINESS sign outside the door.
He walked to his left, stamped up the pedaled lid of a jumbo garbage can,
and dropped the package in with the rest of Dertouzas's stuff.

The can's lid wouldn't close. Deep Eddy's junk had finally reached critical mass. Deep Eddy never got much mail at the shop from other people, but he was always sending mail to himself. Big packets of encrypted diskettes were always arriving from Eddy's road jaunts in Toulouse, Marseilles, Valencia, and Nice. And especially Barcelona. Eddy had sent enough gigabyte-age out of Barcelona to outfit a pirate data-haven.

Eddy used Lyle's bike shop as his safety-deposit box. This arrangement was okay by Lyle. He owed Eddy; Eddy had installed the phones and virching in the bike shop, and had also wangled the shop's electrical hookup. A thick elastic curly-cable snaked out the access-crawlspace of Floor 35, right through the ceiling of Floor 34, and directly through a ragged punch-hole in the aluminum roof of Lyle's cable-mounted mobile home. Some unknown contact of Eddy's was paying the real bills on that electrical feed. Lyle cheerfully covered the expenses by paying cash into an anonymous post-office box. The setup was a rare and valuable contact with the world of organized authority.

During his stays in the shop, Eddy had spent much of his time buried in marathon long-distance virtuality sessions, swaddled head to foot in lumpy strap-on gear. Eddy had been painfully involved with some older woman in Germany. A virtual romance in its full-scale thumping, heaving, grappling progress, was an embarrassment to witness. Under the circumstances, Lyle wasn't too surprised that Eddy had left his parents' condo to set up in a squat.

Eddy had lived in the bicycle repair shop, off and on, for almost a year. It had been a good deal for Lyle, because Deep Eddy had enjoyed a certain clout and prestige with the local squatters. Eddy had been a major organizer of the legendary Chattanooga Wende of December '35, a monster street-party that had climaxed in a spectacular looting-and-arson rampage that had torched the three floors of the Archiplat.

Lyle had gone to school with Eddy and had known him for years; they'd grown up together in the Archiplat. Eddy Dertouzas was a deep zude for a kid his age, with political contacts and heavy-duty network connections. The squat had been a good deal for both of them, until Eddy had finally coaxed the German woman into coming through for him in real life. Then Eddy had jumped the next plane to Europe.

Since they'd parted friends, Eddy was welcome to mail his European data-junk to the bike shop. After all, the disks were heavily encrypted, so it wasn't as if anybody in authority was ever gonna be able to read them. Storing a few thousand disks was a minor challenge, compared to Eddy's complex, machine-assisted love life.

After Eddy's sudden departure, Lyle had sold Eddy's possessions, and wired the money to Eddy in Spain. Lyle had kept the screen TV, Eddy's mediator, and the cheaper virching helmet. The way Lyle figured it—the way he remembered the deal—any stray hardware of Eddy's in the shop was rightfully his, for disposal at his own discretion. By now it was pretty clear that Deep Eddy Dertouzas was never coming back to Tennessee. And Lyle had certain debts.

Lyle snicked the blade from a roadkit multitool and cut open Eddy's package. It contained, of all things, a television cable settop box. A laughable infobahn antique. You'd never see a cablebox like that in NAFTA; this was the sort of primeval junk one might find in the home of a semiliterate Basque grandmother, or maybe in the armed bunker of some backward Albanian.

Lyle tossed the archaic cablebox onto the beanbag in front of the wallscreen. No time now for irrelevant media toys; he had to get on with real life. Lyle ducked into the tiny curtained privy and urinated at length into a crockery jar. He scraped his teeth with a flossing spudger and misted some fresh water onto his face and hands. He wiped clean with a towelette, then smeared his armpits, crotch, and feet with deodorant.

Back when he'd lived with his mom up on Floor 41, Lyle had used old-fashioned antiseptic deodorants. Lyle had wised up about a lot of things once he'd escaped his mom's condo. Nowadays, Lyle used a gel roll-on of skin-friendly bacteria that greedily devoured human sweat and exuded as their metabolic by-product a pleasantly harmless reek rather like ripe bananas. Life was a lot easier when you came to proper terms with your microscopic flora.

Back at his workbench, Lyle plugged in the hot plate and boiled some Thai noodles with flaked sardines. He packed down breakfast with four hundred cc's of Dr. Breasaire's Bioactive Bowel Putty. Then he checked last night's enamel job on the clamped frame in the workstand. The frame looked good. At three in the morning, Lyle was able to get into painted detail work with just the right kind of hallucinatory clarity.

Enameling paid well, and he needed the money bad. But this wasn't real bike work. It lacked authenticity. Enameling was all about the owner's ego—that was what really stank about enameling. There were a few rich kids up in the penthouse levels who were way into "street aesthetic," and would pay good money to have some treadhead decorate their machine. But flash art didn't help the bike. What helped the bike was frame alignment and sound cable-housings and proper tension in the derailleurs.

Lyle fitted the chain of his stationary bike to the shop's flywheel, straddled up, strapped on his gloves and virching helmet, and did half an hour on the 2033 Tour de France. He stayed back in the pack for the uphill grind, and then, for three glorious minutes, he broke free from the *domestiques* in the *peloton* and came right up at the shoulder of Aldo Cipollini. The champion was a monster, posthuman. Calves like cinderblocks. Even in a cheap simulation with no full-impact bodysuit, Lyle knew better than to try to take Cipollini.

Lyle devirched, checked his heart-rate record on the chronometer, then dismounted from his stationary trainer and drained a half-liter squeezebottle of antioxidant carbo refresher. Life had been easier when he'd had a partner in crime. The shop's flywheel was slowly losing its storage of inertia power these days, with just one zude pumping it.

Lyle's disastrous second roommate had come from the biking crowd. She was a criterium racer from Kentucky named Brigitte Rohannon. Lyle himself had been a wannabe criterium racer for a while, before he'd blown out a kidney on steroids. He hadn't expected any trouble from Brigitte, because Brigitte knew about bikes, and she needed his technical help for her racer, and she wouldn't mind pumping the flywheel, and besides, Brigitte was lesbian. In the training gym and out at racing events, Brigitte came across as a quiet and disciplined little politicized treadhead person.

Life inside the zone, though, massively fertilized Brigitte's eccentricities. First, she started breaking training. Then she stopped eating right. Pretty soon the shop was creaking and rocking with all-night girl-on-girl hot-oil sessions, which degenerated into hooting pill-orgies with heavily tattooed zone chyx who played klaxonized bongo music and beat each other up, and stole Lyle's tools. It had been a big relief when Brigitte finally left the zone to shack up with some well-to-do admirer on Floor 37. The debacle had left Lyle's tenuous finances in ruin.

Lyle laid down a new tracery of scarlet enamel on the bike's chainstay, seat post and stem. He had to wait for the work to cure, so he left the workbench, picked up Eddy's set-topper and popped the shell with a hexkey. Lyle was no electrician, but the insides looked harmless enough: lots of bit-eating caterpillars and cheap Algerian silicon.

He flicked on Eddy's mediator, to boot the wallscreen. Before he could try anything with the cable box, his mother's mook pounced upon the screen. On Eddy's giant wallscreen, the mook's waxy, computer-generated face looked like a plump satin pillowcase. Its bowtie was as big as a racing shoe.

"Please hold for an incoming vidcall from Andrea Schweik of Carnac Instruments," the mook uttered unctuously.

Lyle cordially despised all low-down, phone-tagging, artificially intelligent mooks. For a while, in his teenage years, Lyle himself had owned a mook, an off-the-shelf shareware job that he'd installed in the condo's phone. Like most mooks, Lyle's mook had one primary role: dealing with unsolicited phone calls from other people's mooks. In Lyle's case these were the creepy mooks of career counselors, school psychiatrists, truancy cops, and other official hindrances. When Lyle's mook launched and ran, it appeared online as a sly warty dwarf that drooled green ichor and talked in a basso grumble.

But Lyle hadn't given his mook the properly meticulous care and debugging that such fragile little constructs demanded, and eventually his cheap mook had collapsed into artificial insanity.

Once Lyle had escaped his mom's place to the squat, he had gone for the low-tech gambit and simply left his phone unplugged most of the time. But that was no real solution. He couldn't hide from his mother's capable and well-financed corporate mook, which watched with sleepless mechanical patience for the least flicker of video dial tone off Lyle's number.

Lyle sighed and wiped the dust from the video nozzle on Eddy's mediator.

"Your mother is coming online right away," the mook assured him.

"Yeah, sure," Lyle muttered, smearing his hair into some semblance of order.

"She specifically instructed me to page her remotely at any time for an immediate response. She really wants to chat with you, Lyle."

"That's just great." Lyle couldn't remember what his mother's mook called itself. "Mr. Billy," or "Mr. Ripley," or something else really stupid....

"Did you know that Marco Cengialta has just won the Liege Summer Classic?"

Lyle blinked and sat up in the beanbag. "Yeah?"

"Mr. Cengialta used a three-spoked ceramic wheel with internal liquid weighting and buckyball hub-shocks." The mook paused, politely awaiting a possible conversational response. "He wore breathe-thru kevlar microlock cleatshoes," it added.

Lyle hated the way a mook cataloged your personal interests and then generated relevant conversation. The machine-made intercourse was completely unhuman and yet perversely interesting, like being grabbed and buttonholed by a glossy magazine ad. It had probably taken his mother's mook all of three seconds to snag and download every conceivable statistic about the summer race in Liege.

His mother came on. She'd caught him during lunch in her office. "Lyle?"

"Hi, Mom." Lyle sternly reminded himself that this was the one person in the world who might conceivably put up bail for him. "What's on your mind?"

"Oh, nothing much, just the usual." Lyle's mother shoved aside her platter of sprouts and tilapia. "I was idly wondering if you were still alive."

"Mom, it's a lot less dangerous in a squat than landlords and cops would have you believe. I'm perfectly fine. You can see that for yourself."

His mother lifted a pair of secretarial half-spex on a neck-chain, and gave Lyle the computer-assisted once-over.

Lyle pointed the mediator's lens at the shop's aluminum door. "See over there, Mom? I got myself a shock-baton in here. If I get any trouble from anybody, I'll just yank that club off the door mount and give the guy fifteen thousand volts!"

"Is that legal, Lyle?"

"Sure. The voltage won't kill you or anything, it just knocks you out a good long time. I traded a good bike for that shock-baton, it's got a lot of useful defensive features."

"That sounds really dreadful."

"The baton's harmless, Mom. You should see what the cops carry nowadays."

"Are you still taking those injections, Lyle?"

"Which injections?"

She frowned. "You know which ones."

Lyle shrugged. "The treatments are perfectly safe. They're a lot safer than a lifestyle of cruising for dates, that's for sure."

"Especially dates with the kind of girls who live down there in the riot zone, I suppose." His mother winced. "I had some hopes when you took up with that nice bike-racer girl. Brigitte, wasn't it? Whatever happened to her?"

Lyle shook his head. "Someone with your gender and background oughta understand how important the treatments are, Mom. It's a basic reproductive-freedom issue. Antilibidinals give you real freedom, freedom from the urge to reproduce. You should be glad I'm not sexually involved."

"I don't mind that you're not involved, Lyle, it's just that it seems like a real cheat that you're not even *interested*."

"But, Mom, nobody's interested in me, either. Nobody. No woman is banging at my door to have sex with a self-employed fanatical dropout bike mechanic who lives in a slum. If that ever happens, you'll be the first to know."

Lyle grinned cheerfully into the lens. "I had girlfriends back when I was in racing. I've been there, Mom. I've done that. Unless you're coked to the gills with hormones, sex is a major waste of your time and attention. Sexual Deliberation is the greatest civil-liberties movement of modern times."

"That's really weird, Lyle. It's just not natural."

"Mom, forgive me, but you're not the one to talk about natural, okay? You grew me from a zygote when you were fifty-five." He shrugged. "I'm too busy for romance now. I just want to learn about bikes."

"You were working with bikes when you lived here with me. You had a real job and a safe home where you could take regular showers."

"Sure, I was working, but I never said I wanted a *job*, Mom. I said I wanted to *learn about bikes*. There's a big difference! I can't be a loser wage-slave for some lousy bike franchise."

His mother said nothing.

"Mom, I'm not asking you for any favors. I don't need any bosses, or any teachers, or any landlords, or any cops. It's just me and my bike work down here. I know that people in authority can't stand it that a twenty-four-year-old man lives an independent life and does exactly what he wants, but I'm being very quiet and discreet about it, so nobody needs to bother about me."

His mother sighed, defeated. "Are you eating properly, Lyle? You look peaked."

Lyle lifted his calf muscle into camera range. "Look at this leg! Does that look like the gastrocnemius of a weak and sickly person?"

"Could you come up to the condo and have a decent meal with me sometime?"

Lyle blinked. "When?"

"Wednesday, maybe? We could have pork chops."

"Maybe, Mom. Probably. I'll have to check. I'll get back to you, okay? Bye." Lyle hung up.

Hooking the mediator's cable to the primitive set-top box was a problem, but Lyle was not one to be stymied by a merely mechanical challenge. The enamel job had to wait as he resorted to miniclamps and a cable cutter. It was a handy thing that working with modern brake cabling had taught him how to splice fiber optics.

When the set-top box finally came online, its array of services was a joke. Any decent modern mediator could navigate through vast information spaces, but the set-top box offered nothing but "channels." Lyle had forgotten that you could even obtain old-fashioned "channels" from the city fiber-feed in Chattanooga. But these channels were government-sponsored media, and the government was always quite a ways behind the curve in network development. Chattanooga's huge fiber-bandwidth still carried the ancient government-mandated "public access channels," spooling away in their technically fossilized obscurity, far below the usual gaudy carnival of popular virching, infobahnage, demo-splintered comboards, public-service rants, mudtrufflage, rem-snorkeling, and commercials.

The little set-top box accessed nothing but political channels. Three of them: Legislative, Judicial, and Executive. And that was the sum total, apparently. A set-top box that offered nothing but NAFTA political coverage. On the Legislative Channel there was some kind of parliamentary debate on proper land use in Manitoba. On the Judicial Channel, a lawyer was haranguing judges about the stock market for air-pollution rights. On the Executive Channel, a big crowd of hicks were idly standing around on windblown tarmac somewhere in Louisiana waiting for something to happen.

The box didn't offer any glimpse of politics in Europe or the Sphere or the South. There were no hotspots or pips or index tagging. You couldn't look stuff up or annotate it—you just had to passively watch whatever the channel's masters chose to show you, whenever they chose to show it. This media setup was so insultingly lame and halt and primitive that it was almost perversely interesting. Kind of like peering through keyholes.

Lyle left the box on the Executive Channel, because it looked conceivable that something might actually happen there. It had swiftly become clear to him that the intolerably monotonous fodder on the other two channels was about as exciting as those channels ever got. Lyle retreated to his workbench and got back to enamel work.

At length, the president of NAFTA arrived and decamped from his helicopter on the tarmac in Louisiana. A swarm of presidential bodyguards materialized out of the expectant crowd, looking simultaneously extremely busy and icily unperturbable.

Suddenly a line of text flickered up at the bottom of the screen. The text was set in a very old-fashioned computer font, chalk-white letters with little visible jagged pixel-edges. *"Look at him hunting for that camera mark,"* the subtitle read as it scrolled across the screen. *"Why wasn't he briefed properly? He looks like a stray dog!"*

The president meandered amiably across the sun-blistered tarmac, gazing from side to side, and then stopped briefly to shake the eager outstretched hand of a local politician. *"That must have hurt,"* commented the text. *"That Cajun dolt is poison in the polls."* The president chatted amiably with the local politician and an elderly harridan in a purple dress who seemed to be the man's wife. *"Get him away from those losers!"* raged the subtitle. *"Get the Man up to the podium, for the love of Mike! Where's the Chief of Staff? Doped up on so-called smart drugs as usual? Get with your jobs, people!"*

The president looked well. Lyle had noticed that the president of NAFTA always looked well, it seemed to be a professional requirement. The big political cheeses in Europe always looked somber and intellectual, and the Sphere people always looked humble and dedicated, and the South people always looked angry and fanatical, but the NAFTA prez always looked like he'd just done a few laps in a pool and had a brisk rubdown. His large, glossy, bluffly cheerful face was discreetly stenciled with tattoos: both cheeks, a chorus line of tats on his forehead above both eyebrows, plus a few extra logos on his rocklike chin. A president's face was the ultimate billboard for major backers and interest groups.

"Does he think we have all day?" the text demanded. *"What's with this dead air time? Can't anyone properly arrange a media event these days? You call this public access? You call this informing the electorate? If we'd known*

the infobahn would come to this, we'd have never built the thing!"

The president meandered amiably to a podium covered with ceremonial microphones. Lyle had noticed that politicians always used a big healthy cluster of traditional big fat microphones, even though nowadays you could build working microphones the size of a grain of rice.

"Hey, how y'all?" asked the president, grinning.

The crowd chorused back at him, with ragged enthusiasm.

"Let these fine folks up a bit closer," the president ordered suddenly, waving airily at his phalanx of bodyguards. "Y'all come on up closer, everybody! Sit right on the ground, we're all just folks here today." The president smiled benignly as the sweating, straw-hatted summer crowd hustled up to join him, scarcely believing their luck.

"Marietta and I just had a heck of a fine lunch down in Opelousas," commented the president, patting his flat, muscular belly. He deserted the fiction of his official podium to energetically press the Louisianan flesh. As he moved from hand to grasping hand, his every word was picked up infallibly by an invisible mike, probably implanted in one of his molars. "We had dirty rice, red beans—were they hot!—and crawdads big enough to body-slam a Maine lobster!" He chuckled. "What a sight them mudbugs were! Can y'all believe that?"

The president's guards were unobtrusively but methodically working the crowd with portable detectors and sophisticated spex equipment. They didn't look very concerned by the president's supposed change in routine.

"I see he's gonna run with the usual genetics malarkey," commented the subtitle.

"Y'all have got a perfect right to be mighty proud of the agriculture in this state," intoned the president. "Y'all's agro-science know-how is second to none! Sure, I know there's a few pointy-headed Luddites up in the snowbelt, who say they prefer their crawdads dinky."

Everyone laughed.

"Folks, I got nothin' against that attitude. If some jasper wants to spend his hard-earned money buyin' and peelin' and shuckin' those little dinky ones, that's all right by me and Marietta. Ain't that right, honey?"

The first lady smiled and waved one power-gloved hand.

"But folks, you and I both know that those whiners who waste our time complaining about 'natural food' have never sucked a mudbug head in their lives! 'Natural,' my left elbow! Who are they tryin' to kid? Just 'cause you're country, don't mean you can't hack DNA!"

"He's been working really hard on the regional accents," commented the text. *"Not bad for a guy from Minnesota. But look at that sloppy, incompetent camera work! Doesn't anybody care anymore? What on earth is happening to our standards?"*

By lunchtime, Lyle had the final coat down on the enameling job. He ate a bowl of triticale mush and chewed up a mineral-rich handful of iodized sponge.

Then he settled down in front of the wallscreen to work on the inertia brake. Lyle knew there was big money in the inertia brake—for somebody, somewhere, sometime. The device smelled like the future.

Lyle tucked a jeweler's loupe in one eye and toyed methodically with the brake. He loved the way the piezoplastic clamp and rim transmuted braking energy into electrical-battery storage. At last, a way to capture the energy you lost in braking and put it to solid use. It was almost, but not quite, magical.

The way Lyle figured it, there was gonna be a big market someday for an inertia brake that captured energy and then fed it back through the chain-drive in a way that just felt like human pedaling energy, in a direct and intuitive and muscular way, not chunky and buzzy like some loser battery-powered moped. If the system worked out right, it would make the rider feel completely natural and yet subtly superhuman at the same time. And it had to be simple, the kind of system a shop guy could fix with hand tools. It wouldn't work if it was too brittle and fancy, it just wouldn't feel like an authentic bike.

Lyle had a lot of ideas about the design. He was pretty sure he could get a real grip on the problem, if only he weren't being worked to death just keeping the shop going. If he could get enough capital together to assemble the prototypes and do some serious field tests.

It would have to be chip-driven, of course, but true to the biking spirit at the same time. A lot of bikes had chips in them nowadays, in the shocks or the braking or in reactive hubs, but bicycles simply weren't like computers. Computers were black boxes inside, no big visible working parts. People, by contrast, got sentimental about their bike gear. People were strangely reticent and traditional about bikes. That's why the bike market had never really gone for recumbents, even though the recumbent design had a big mechanical advantage. People didn't like their bikes too complicated. They didn't want bicycles to bitch and complain and whine for attention and constant upgrading the way that computers did. Bikes were too personal. People wanted their bikes to wear.

Someone banged at the shop door.

Lyle opened it. Down on the tiling by the barrels stood a tall brunette woman in stretch shorts, with a short-sleeve blue pull-over and a ponytail. She had a bike under one arm, an old lacquer-and-paper-framed Taiwanese job. "Are you Edward Dertouzas?" she said, gazing up at him.

"No," Lyle said patiently. "Eddy's in Europe."

She thought this over. "I'm new in the zone," she confessed. "Can you fix this bike for me? I just bought it secondhand and I think it kinda needs some work."

"Sure," Lyle said. "You came to the right guy for that job, ma'am, because Eddy Dertouzas couldn't fix a bike for hell. Eddy just used to live here. I'm the guy who actually owns this shop. Hand the bike up."

Lyle crouched down, got a grip on the handlebar stem and hauled the bike into the shop. The woman gazed up at him respectfully. "What's your name?"

"Lyle Schweik."

"I'm Kitty Casaday." She hesitated. "Could I come up inside there?"

Lyle reached down, gripped her muscular wrist, and hauled her up into the shop. She wasn't all that good-looking, but she was in really good shape—like a mountain biker or triathlon runner. She looked about thirty-five. It was hard to tell, exactly. Once people got into cosmetic surgery and serious bio-maintenance, it got pretty hard to judge their age. Unless you got a good, close medical exam of their eyelids and cuticles and internal membranes and such.

She looked around the shop with great interest, brown ponytail twitching. "Where you hail from?" Lyle asked her. He had already forgotten her name.

"Well, I'm originally from Juneau, Alaska."

"Canadian, huh? Great. Welcome to Tennessee."

"Actually, Alaska used to be part of the United States."

"You're kidding," Lyle said. "Hey, I'm no historian, but I've seen Alaska on a map before."

"You've got a whole working shop and everything built inside this old place! That's really something, Mr. Schweik. What's behind that curtain?"

"The spare room," Lyle said. "That's where my roommate used to stay."

She glanced up. "Dertouzas?"

"Yeah, him."

"Who's in there now?"

"Nobody," Lyle said sadly. "I got some storage stuff in there."

She nodded slowly, and kept looking around, apparently galvanized with curiosity. "What are you running on that screen?"

"Hard to say, really," Lyle said. He crossed the room, bent down and switched off the set-top box. "Some kind of weird political crap."

He began examining her bike. All its serial numbers had been removed. Typical zone bike.

"The first thing we got to do," he said briskly, "is fit it to you properly: set the saddle height, pedal stroke, and handlebars. Then I'll adjust the tension, true the wheels, check the brakepads and suspension valves, tune the shifting, and lubricate the drive-train. The usual. You're gonna need a better saddle than this—this saddle's for a male pelvis." He looked up. "You got a charge card?"

She nodded, then frowned. "But I don't have much credit left."

"No problem." He flipped open a dog-eared catalog. "This is what you need. Any halfway decent gel-saddle. Pick one you like, and we can have it shipped in by tomorrow morning. And then"—he flipped pages—"order me one of these."

She stepped closer and examined the page. "The 'cotterless crank-bolt ceramic wrench set,' is that it?"

"That's right. I fix your bike, you give me those tools, and we're even."

"Okay. Sure. That's cheap!" She smiled at him. "I like the way you do business, Lyle."

"You'll get used to barter, if you stay in the zone long enough."

"I've never lived in a squat before," she said thoughtfully. "I like the attitude here, but people say that squats are pretty dangerous."

"I dunno about the squats in other towns, but Chattanooga squats aren't dangerous, unless you think anarchists are dangerous, and anarchists aren't dangerous unless they're really drunk." Lyle shrugged. "People will steal your stuff all the time, that's about the worst part. There's a couple of tough guys around here who claim they have handguns. I never saw anybody actually use a handgun. Old guns aren't hard to find, but it takes a real chemist to make working ammo nowadays." He smiled back at her. "Anyway, you look to me like you can take care of yourself."

"I take dance classes."

Lyle nodded. He opened a drawer and pulled a tape measure.

"I saw all those cables and pulleys you have on top of this place. You can pull the whole building right up off the ground, huh? Kind of hang it right off the ceiling up there."

"That's right, it saves a lot of trouble with people breaking and entering." Lyle glanced at his shock-baton, in its mounting at the door. She followed his gaze to the weapon and then looked at him, impressed.

Lyle measured her arms, torso length, then knelt and measured her inseam from crotch to floor. He took notes. "Okay," he said. "Come by tomorrow afternoon."

"Lyle?"

"Yeah?" He stood up.

"Do you rent this place out? I really need a safe place to stay in the zone."

"I'm sorry," Lyle said politely, "but I hate landlords and I'd never be one. What I need is a roommate who can really get behind the whole concept of my shop. Someone who's qualified, you know, to develop my infrastructure or do bicycle work. Anyway, if I took your cash or charged you for rent, then the tax people would just have another excuse to harass me."

"Sure, okay, but..." She paused, then looked at him under lowered eyelids. "I've gotta be a lot better than having this place go empty."

Lyle stared at her, astonished.

"I'm a pretty useful woman to have around, Lyle. Nobody's ever complained before."

"Really?"

"That's right." She stared at him boldly.

"I'll think about your offer," Lyle said. "What did you say your name was?"

"I'm Kitty. Kitty Casaday."

"Kitty, I got a whole lot of work to do today, but I'll see you tomorrow, okay?"

"Okay, Lyle." She smiled. "You think about me, all right?"

Lyle helped her down out of the shop. He watched her stride away across the atrium until she vanished through the crowded doorway of the Crowbar, a squat coffeeshop. Then he called his mother.

"Did you forget something?" his mother said, looking up from her workscreen.

"Mom, I know this is really hard to believe, but a strange woman just banged on my door and offered to have sex with me."

"You're kidding, right?"

"In exchange for room and board, I think. Anyway, I said you'd be the first to know if it happened."

"Lyle—" His mother hesitated. "Lyle, I think you better come right home. Let's make that dinner date for tonight, okay? We'll have a little talk about this situation."

"Yeah, okay. I got an enameling job I gotta deliver to Floor 41, anyway."

"I don't have a positive feeling about this development, Lyle."

"That's okay, Mom. I'll see you tonight."

Lyle reassembled the newly enameled bike. Then he set the flywheel onto remote, and stepped outside the shop. He mounted the bike, and touched a password into the remote control. The shop faithfully reeled itself far out of reach and hung there in space below the fire-blackened ceiling, swaying gently.

Lyle pedaled away, back toward the elevators, back toward the neighborhood where he'd grown up.

He delivered the bike to the delighted young idiot who'd commissioned it, stuffed the cash in his shoes, and then went down to his mother's. He took a shower, shaved, and shampooed thoroughly. They had pork chops and grits and got drunk together. His mother complained about the breakup with her third husband and wept bitterly, but not as much as usual when this topic came up. Lyle got the strong impression she was thoroughly on the mend and would be angling for number four in pretty short order.

Around midnight, Lyle refused his mother's ritual offers of new clothes and fresh leftovers, and headed back down to the zone. He was still a little clubfooted from his mother's sherry, and he stood breathing beside the broken glass of the atrium wall, gazing out at the city-smeared summer stars. The cavernous darkness inside the zone at night was one of his favorite things about the place. The queasy 24-hour security lighting in the rest of the Archiplat had never been rebuilt inside the zone.

The zone always got livelier at night when all the normal people started sneaking in to cruise the zone's unlicensed dives and nightspots, but all that activity took place behind discreetly closed doors. Enticing squiggles of red and blue chemglow here and there only enhanced the blessed unnatural gloom.

Lyle pulled his remote control and ordered the shop back down.

The door of the shop had been broken open.

Lyle's latest bike-repair client lay sprawled on the floor of the shop, unconscious. She was wearing black military fatigues, a knit cap, and rappelling gear.

She had begun her break-in at Lyle's establishment by pulling his shock-baton out of its glowing security socket beside the doorframe. The booby-trapped baton had immediately put fifteen thousand volts through her, and sprayed her face with a potent mix of dye and street-legal incapacitants.

Lyle turned the baton off with the remote control, and then placed it carefully back in its socket. His surprise guest was still breathing, but was clearly in real metabolic distress. He tried clearing her nose and mouth with a tissue. The guys who'd sold him the baton hadn't been kidding about the "indelible" part. Her face and throat were drenched with green and her chest looked like a spin-painting.

Her elaborate combat spex had partially shielded her eyes. With the spex off she looked like a viridian-green raccoon.

Lyle tried stripping her gear off in conventional fashion, realized this wasn't going to work, and got a pair of metal-shears from the shop. He snipped his way through the eerily writhing power-gloves and the kevlar laces of the pneumoreactive combat boots. Her black turtleneck had an abrasive surface and a cuirass over chest and back that looked like it could stop small-arms fire.

The trousers had nineteen separate pockets and they were loaded with all kinds of eerie little items: a matte-black electrode stun-weapon, flash capsules, fingerprint dust, a utility pocket-knife, drug adhesives, plastic handcuffs, some pocket change, worry beads, a comb, and a makeup case.

Close inspection revealed a pair of tiny microphone amplifiers inserted in her ear canals. Lyle fetched the tiny devices out with needlenose pliers. Lyle was getting pretty seriously concerned by this point. He shackled her arms and legs with bike security cable, in case she regained consciousness and attempted something superhuman.

Around four in the morning she had a coughing fit and began shivering violently. Summer nights could get pretty cold in the shop. Lyle thought over the design problem for some time, and then fetched a big heat-reflective blanket out of the empty room. He cut a neat poncho-hole in the center of it, and slipped her head through it. He got the bike cables off her—she could probably slip the cables anyway—and sewed all four edges of the blanket shut from the outside, with sturdy monofilament thread from his saddle-stitcher. He sewed the poncho edges to a tough fabric belt, cinched the belt snugly around her neck, and padlocked it. When he was done, he'd made a snug bag that contained her entire body, except for her head, which had begun to drool and snore.

A fat blob of superglue on the bottom of the bag kept her anchored to the shop's floor. The blanket was cheap but tough upholstery fabric. If she could rip her way through blanket fabric with her fingernails alone, then he was probably a goner anyway. By now, Lyle was tired and stone sober. He had a squeezebottle of glucose rehydrator, three aspirins, and a canned chocolate pudding. Then he climbed in his hammock and went to sleep.

Lyle woke up around ten. His captive was sitting up inside the bag, her green face stony, eyes red-rimmed and brown hair caked with dye. Lyle got up, dressed, ate breakfast, and fixed the broken door-lock. He said nothing, partly because he thought that silence would shake her up, but mostly because he couldn't remember her name. He was almost sure it wasn't her real name anyway.

When he'd finished fixing the door, he reeled up the string of the door-knocker so that it was far out of reach. He figured the two of them needed the privacy.

Then Lyle deliberately fired up the wallscreen and turned on the settop box. As soon as the peculiar subtitles started showing up again, she grew agitated. "Who are you really?" she demanded at last.

"Ma'am, I'm a bicycle repairman."

She snorted.

"I guess I don't need to know your name," he said, "but I need to know who your people are, and why they sent you here, and what I've got to do to get out of this situation."

"You're not off to a good start, mister."

"No," he said, "maybe not, but you're the one who's blown it. I'm just a twenty-four-year-old bicycle repairman from Tennessee. But you, you've got enough specialized gear on you to buy my whole place five times over."

He flipped open the little mirror in her makeup case and showed her her own face. Her scowl grew a little stiffer below the spattering of green.

"I want you to tell me what's going on here," he said.

"Forget it."

"If you're waiting for your backup to come rescue you, I don't think they're coming," Lyle said. "I searched you very thoroughly and I've opened up every single little gadget you had, and I took all the batteries out. I'm not even sure what some of those things are or how they work, but hey, I know what a battery is. It's been hours now. So I don't think your backup people even know where you are."

She said nothing.

"See," he said, "you've really blown it bad. You got caught by a total amateur, and now you're in a hostage situation that could go on indefinitely. I got enough water and noodles and sardines to live up here for days. I dunno, maybe you can make a cellular phone call to God off some gizmo implanted in your thighbone, but it looks to me like you've got serious problems."

She shuffled around a bit inside the bag and looked away.

"It's got something to do with the cablebox over there, right?"

She said nothing.

"For what it's worth, I don't think that box has anything to do with me or Eddy Dertouzas," Lyle said. "I think it was probably meant for Eddy, but I don't think he asked anybody for it. Somebody just wanted him to have it, probably one of his weird European contacts. Eddy used to be in this political group called CAPCLUG, ever heard of them?"

It looked pretty obvious that she'd heard of them.

"I never liked 'em much either," Lyle told her. "They kind of snagged me at first with their big talk about freedom and civil liberties, but then you'd go to a CAPCLUG meeting up in the penthouse levels, and there were all these potbellied zudes in spex yapping off stuff like, 'We must follow the technological imperatives or be jettisoned into the history dump-file.' They're a bunch of useless blowhards who can't tie their own shoes."

"They're dangerous radicals subverting national sovereignty."

Lyle blinked cautiously. "Whose national sovereignty would that be?"

"Yours, mine, Mr. Schweik. I'm from NAFTA, I'm a federal agent."

"You're a fed? How come you're breaking into people's houses, then? Isn't that against the Fourth Amendment or something?"

"If you mean the Fourth Amendment to the Constitution of the United States, that document was superseded years ago."

"Yeah…okay, I guess you're right." Lyle shrugged. "I missed a lot of civics classes…. No skin off my back anyway. I'm sorry, but what did you say your name was?"

"I said my name was Kitty Casaday."

"Right. Kitty. Okay, Kitty, just you and me, person to person. We obviously have a mutual problem here. What do you think I ought to do in this situation? I mean, speaking practically."

Kitty thought it over, surprised. "Mr. Schweik, you should release me immediately, get me my gear, and give me the box and any related data, recordings, or diskettes. Then you should escort me from the Archiplat in some confidential fashion so I won't be stopped by police and questioned about the dye-stains. A new set of clothes would be very useful."

"Like that, huh?"

"That's your wisest course of action." Her eyes narrowed. "I can't make any promises, but it might affect your future treatment very favorably."

"You're not gonna tell me who you are, or where you came from, or who sent you, or what this is all about?"

"No. Under no circumstances. I'm not allowed to reveal that. You don't need to know. You're not supposed to know. And anyway, if you're really what you say you are, what should you care?"

"Plenty. I care plenty. I can't wander around the rest of my life wondering when you're going to jump me out of a dark corner."

"If I'd wanted to hurt you, I'd have hurt you when we first met, Mr. Schweik. There was no one here but you and me, and I could have easily incapacitated you and taken anything I wanted. Just give me the box and the data and stop trying to interrogate me."

"Suppose you found me breaking into your house, Kitty? What would you do to me?"

She said nothing.

"What you're telling me isn't gonna work. If you don't tell me what's really going on here," Lyle said heavily, "I'm gonna have to get tough."

Her lips thinned in contempt.

"Okay, you asked for this." Lyle opened the mediator and made a quick voice call. "Pete?"

"Nah, this is Pete's mook," the phone replied. "Can I do something for you?"

"Could you tell Pete that Lyle Schweik has some big trouble, and I need him to come over to my bike shop immediately? And bring some heavy muscle from the Spiders."

"What kind of big trouble, Lyle?"

"Authority trouble. A lot of it. I can't say any more. I think this line may be tapped."

"Right-o. I'll make that happen. Hoo-ah, zude." The mook hung up.

Lyle left the beanbag and went back to the workbench. He took Kitty's cheap bike out of the repair stand and angrily threw it aside. "You know what really bugs me?" he said at last. "You couldn't even bother to charm your way in here, set yourself up as my roommate, and then steal the damn box. You didn't even respect me that much. Heck, you didn't even have to steal anything, Kitty. You could have just smiled and asked nicely and I'd have given you the box to play with. I don't watch media, I hate all that crap."

"It was an emergency. There was no time for more extensive investigation or reconnaissance. I think you should call your gangster friends immediately and tell them you've made a mistake. Tell them not to come here."

"You're ready to talk seriously?"

"No, I won't be talking."

"Okay, we'll see."

After twenty minutes, Lyle's phone rang. He answered it cautiously, keeping the video off. It was Pete from the City Spiders. "Zude, where is your doorknocker?"

"Oh, sorry, I pulled it up, didn't want to be disturbed. I'll bring the shop right down." Lyle thumbed the brake switches.

Lyle opened the door and Pete broad-jumped into the shop. Pete was a big man but he had the skeletal, wiry build of a climber, bare dark arms and shins and big sticky-toed jumping shoes. He had a sleeveless leather bodysuit full of clips and snaps, and he carried a big fabric shoulderbag. There were six vivid tattoos on the dark skin of his left cheek, under the black stubble.

Pete looked at Kitty, lifted his spex with wiry callused fingers, looked at her again bare-eyed, and put the spex back in place. "Wow, Lyle."

"Yeah."

"I never thought you were into anything this sick and twisted."

"It's a serious matter, Pete."

Pete turned to the door, crouched down, and hauled a second person into the shop. She wore a beat-up air-conditioned jacket and long slacks and zipsided boots and wire-rimmed spex. She had short ratty hair under a green cloche hat. "Hi," she said, sticking out a hand. "I'm Mabel. We haven't met."

"I'm Lyle." Lyle gestured. "This is Kitty here in the bag."

"You said you needed somebody heavy, so I brought Mabel along," said Pete. "Mabel's a social worker."

"Looks like you pretty much got things under control here," said Mabel liltingly, scratching her neck and looking about the place. "What happened? She break into your shop?"

"Yeah."

"And," Pete said, "she grabbed the shock-baton first thing and blasted herself but good?"

"Exactly."

"I told you that thieves always go for the weaponry first," Pete said, grinning and scratching his armpit. "Didn't I tell you that? Leave a weapon in plain sight, man, a thief can't stand it, it's the very first thing they gotta grab." He laughed. "Works every time."

"Pete's from the City Spiders," Lyle told Kitty. "His people built this shop for me. One dark night, they hauled this mobile home right up thirty-four stories in total darkness, straight up the side of the Archiplat without anybody seeing, and they cut a big hole through the side of the building without making any noise, and they hauled the whole shop through it. Then they sank explosive bolts through the girders and hung it up here for me in midair. The City Spiders are into sport-climbing the way I'm into bicycles, only, like, they are very *seriously* into climbing and there are lots of them. They were some of the very first people to squat the zone, and they've lived here ever since, and they are pretty good friends of mine."

Pete sank to one knee and looked Kitty in the eye. "I love breaking into places, don't you? There's no thrill like some quick and perfectly executed break-in." He reached casually into his shoulder bag. "The thing is"—he pulled out a camera—"to be sporting, you can't steal anything. You just take trophy pictures to prove you were there." He snapped her picture several times, grinning as she flinched.

"Lady," he breathed at her, "once you've turned into a little wicked greedhead, and mixed all that evil cupidity and possessiveness into the beauty of the direct action, then you've prostituted our way of life. You've gone and spoiled our sport." Pete stood up. "We City Spiders don't like common thieves. And we especially don't like thieves who break into the places of clients of ours, like Lyle here. And we thoroughly, especially, don't like thieves who are so brickhead dumb that they get caught red-handed on the premises of friends of ours."

Pete's hairy brows knotted in thought. "What I'd like to do here, Lyle ol' buddy," he announced, "is wrap up your little friend head to foot in nice tight cabling, smuggle her out of here down to Golden Gate Archiplat—you know, the big one downtown over by MLK and Highway Twenty-seven?—and hang her head-down in the center of the cupola."

"That's not very nice," Mabel told him seriously.

Pete looked wounded. "I'm not gonna charge him for it or anything! Just imagine her, spinning up there beautifully with all those chandeliers and those hundreds of mirrors."

Mabel knelt and looked into Kitty's face. "Has she had any water since she was knocked unconscious?"

"No."

"Well, for heaven's sake, give the poor woman something to drink, Lyle."

Lyle handed Mabel a bike-tote squeeze bottle of electrolyte refresher. "You zudes don't grasp the situation yet," he said. "Look at all this stuff I took off her." He showed them the spex, and the boots, and the stun-gun, and the gloves, and the carbon-nitride climbing plectra, and the rappelling gear.

"Wow," Pete said at last, dabbing at buttons on his spex to study the finer detail, "this is no ordinary burglar! She's gotta be, like, a street samurai from the Mahogany Warbirds or something!"

"She says she's a federal agent."

Mabel stood up suddenly, angrily yanking the squeeze bottle from Kitty's lips. "You're kidding, right?"

"Ask her."

"I'm a grade-five social counselor with the Department of Urban Redevelopment," Mabel said. She presented Kitty with an official ID. "And who are you with?"

"I'm not prepared to divulge that information at this time."

"I can't believe this," Mabel marveled, tucking her dog-eared hologram ID back in her hat. "You've caught somebody from one of those nutty reactionary secret black-bag units. I mean, that's gotta be what's just happened here." She shook her head slowly. "Y'know, if you work in government, you always hear horror stories about these right-wing paramilitary wackos, but I've never actually seen one before."

"It's a very dangerous world out there, Miss Social Counselor."

"Oh, tell me about it," Mabel scoffed. "I've worked suicide hotlines! I've been a hostage negotiator! I'm a career social worker, girlfriend! I've seen more horror and suffering than you *ever* will. While you were doing push-ups in some comfy cracker training camp, I've been out here in the real world!" Mabel absently unscrewed the top from the bike bottle and had a long glug. "What on earth are you doing trying to raid the squat of a bicycle repairman?"

Kitty's stony silence lengthened. "It's got something to do with that set-top box," Lyle offered. "It showed up here in delivery yesterday, and then she showed up just a few hours later. Started flirting with me, and said she wanted to live in here. Of course I got suspicious right away."

"Naturally," Pete said. "Real bad move, Kitty. Lyle's on antilibidinals."

Kitty stared at Lyle bitterly. "I see," she said at last. "So that's what you get, when you drain all the sex out of one of them.... You get a strange malodorous creature that spends all its time working in the garage."

Mabel flushed. "Did you hear that?" She gave Kitty's bag a sharp angry yank. "What conceivable right do you have to question this citizen's sexual orientation? Especially after cruelly trying to sexually manipulate him to abet your illegal purposes? Have you lost all sense of decency? You…you should be sued."

"Do your worst," Kitty muttered.

"Maybe I will," Mabel said grimly. "Sunlight is the best disinfectant."

"Yeah, let's string her up somewhere real sunny and public and call a bunch of news crews," Pete said. "I'm way hot for this deep ninja gear! Me and the Spiders got real mojo uses for these telescopic ears, and the tracer dust, and the epoxy bugging devices. And the press-on climbing-claws. And the carbon-fiber rope. Everything, really! Everything except these big-ass military shoes of hers, which really suck."

"Hey, all that stuff's mine," Lyle said sternly. "I saw it first."

"Yeah, I guess so, but… Okay, Lyle, you make us a deal on the gear, we'll forget everything you still owe us for doing the shop."

"Come on, those combat spex are worth more than this place all by themselves."

"I'm real interested in that set-top box," Mabel said cruelly. "It doesn't look too fancy or complicated. Let's take it over to those dirty circuit zudes who hang out at the Blue Parrot, and see if they can't reverse-engineer it. We'll post all the schematics up on twenty or thirty progressive activist networks, and see what falls out of cyberspace."

Kitty glared at her. "The terrible consequences from that stupid and irresponsible action would be entirely on your head."

"I'll risk it," Mabel said airily, patting her cloche hat. "It might bump my soft little liberal head a bit, but I'm pretty sure it would crack your nasty little fascist head like a coconut."

Suddenly Kitty began thrashing and kicking her way furiously inside the bag. They watched with interest as she ripped, tore and lashed out with powerful side and front kicks. Nothing much happened.

"All right," she said at last, panting in exhaustion. "I've come from Senator Creighton's office."

"Who?" Lyle said.

"Creighton! Senator James P. Creighton, the man who's been your Senator from Tennessee for the past thirty years!"

"Oh," Lyle said. "I hadn't noticed."

"We're anarchists," Pete told her.

"I've sure heard of the nasty old geezer," Mabel said, "but I'm from British Columbia, where we change senators the way you'd change a pair of socks. If you ever changed your socks, that is. What about him?"

"Well, Senator Creighton has deep clout and seniority! He was a United States Senator even before the first NAFTA Senate was convened! He has a very large, and powerful, and very well seasoned personal staff of twenty thousand hardworking people, with a lot of pull in the Agriculture, Banking, and Telecommunications Committees!"

"Yeah? So?"

"So," Kitty said miserably, "there are twenty thousand of us on his staff. We've been in place for decades now, and naturally we've accumulated lots of power and importance. Senator Creighton's staff is basically running some quite large sections of the NAFTA government, and if the Senator loses his office, there will be a great deal of...of unnecessary political turbulence." She looked up. "You might not think that a senator's staff is all that important politically. But if people like you bothered to learn anything about the real-life way that your government functions, then you'd know that Senate staffers can be really crucial."

Mabel scratched her head. "You're telling me that even a lousy senator has his own private black-bag unit?"

Kitty looked insulted. "He's an excellent senator! You can't have a working organization of twenty thousand staffers without taking security very seriously! Anyway, the Executive wing has had black-bag units for years! It's only right that there should be a balance of powers."

"Wow," Mabel said. "The old guy's a hundred and twelve or something, isn't he?"

"A hundred and seventeen."

"Even with government health care, there can't be a lot left of him."

"He's already gone," Kitty muttered. "His frontal lobes are burned out....He can still sit up, and if he's stoked on stimulants he can repeat whatever's whispered to him. So he's got two permanent implanted hearing aids, and basically...well...he's being run by remote control by his mook."

"His mook, huh?" Pete repeated thoughtfully.

"It's a very good mook," Kitty said. "The coding's old, but it's been very well looked-after. It has firm moral values and excellent policies. The mook is really very much like the Senator was. It's just that...well, it's old. It still prefers a really old-fashioned media environment. It spends almost all its time watching old-fashioned public political coverage, and lately it's gotten cranky and started broadcasting commentary."

"Man, never trust a mook," Lyle said. "I hate those things."

"So do I," Pete offered, "but even a mook comes off pretty good compared to a politician."

"I don't really see the problem," Mabel said, puzzled. "Senator Hirschheimer from Arizona has had a direct neural link to his mook for years, and he has an excellent progressive voting record. Same goes for Senator Marmalejo from Tamaulipas; she's kind of absent-minded, and everybody knows she's on life support, but she's a real scrapper on women's issues."

Kitty looked up. "You don't think it's terrible?"

Mabel shook her head. "I'm not one to be judgmental about the intimacy of one's relationship to one's own digital alter-ego. As far as I can see it, that's a basic privacy issue."

"They told me in briefing that it was a very terrible business, and that everyone would panic if they learned that a high government official was basically a front for a rogue artificial intelligence."

Mabel, Pete, and Lyle exchanged glances. "Are you guys surprised by that news?" Mabel said.

"Heck no," said Pete.

"Big deal," Lyle added.

Something seemed to snap inside Kitty then. Her head sank. "Disaffected émigrés in Europe have been spreading boxes that can decipher the Senator's commentary. I mean, the Senator's mook's commentary...The mook speaks just like the Senator did, or the way the Senator used to speak, when he was in private and off the record. The way he spoke in his diaries. As far as we can tell, the mook *was* his diary....It used to be his personal laptop computer. But he just kept transferring the files, and upgrading the software, and teaching it new tricks like voice recognition and speech-writing, and giving it power of attorney and such.... And then, one day the mook made a break for it. We think that the mook sincerely believes that it's the Senator."

"Just tell the stupid thing to shut up for a while, then."

"We can't do that. We're not even sure where the mook is, physically. Or how it's been encoding those sarcastic comments into the video-feed. The Senator had a lot of friends in the telecom industry back in the old days. There are a lot of ways and places to hide a piece of distributed software."

"So that's all?" Lyle said. "That's it, that's your big secret? Why didn't you just come to me and ask me for the box? You didn't have to dress up in combat gear and kick my door in. That's a pretty good story, I'd have probably just given you the thing."

"I couldn't do that, Mr. Schweik."

"Why not?"

"Because," Pete said, "her people are important government functionaries, and you're a loser techie wacko who lives in a slum."

"I was told this is a very dangerous area," Kitty muttered.

"It's not dangerous," Mabel told her.

"No?"

"No. They're all too broke to be dangerous. This is just a kind of social breathing space. The whole urban infrastructure's dreadfully overplanned here in Chattanooga. There's been too much money here too long. There's been no room for spontaneity. It was choking the life out of the city. That's why everyone was secretly overjoyed when the rioters set fire to these three floors."

Mabel shrugged. "The insurance took care of the damage. First the looters came in. Then there were a few hideouts for kids and crooks and illegal aliens. Then the permanent squats got set up. Then the artist's studios, and the semilegal workshops and red-light places. Then the quaint little coffeehouses, then the bakeries. Pretty soon the offices of professionals will be filtering in, and they'll restore the water and the wiring. Once that happens, the real-estate prices will kick in big-time, and the whole zone will transmute right back into gentryville. It happens all the time."

Mabel waved her arm at the door. "If you knew anything about modern urban geography, you'd see this kind of, uh, spontaneous urban renewal happening all over the place. As long as you've got naive young people with plenty of energy who can be suckered into living inside rotten, hazardous dumps for nothing, in exchange for imagining that they're free from oversight, then it all works out just great in the long run."

"Oh."

"Yeah, zones like this turn out to be extremely handy for all concerned. For some brief span of time, a few people can think mildly unusual thoughts and behave in mildly unusual ways. All kinds of weird little vermin show up, and if they make any money then they go legal, and if they don't then they drop dead in a place really quiet where it's all their own fault. Nothing dangerous about it." Mabel laughed, then sobered. "Lyle, let this poor dumb cracker out of the bag."

"She's naked under there."

"Okay," she said impatiently, "cut a slit in the bag and throw some clothes in it. Get going, Lyle."

Lyle threw in some biking pants and a sweatshirt.

"What about my gear?" Kitty demanded, wriggling her way into the clothes by feel.

"I tell you what," said Mabel thoughtfully. "Pete here will give your gear back to you in a week or so, after his friends have photographed all the circuitry. You'll just have to let him keep all those knickknacks for a while, as his reward for our not immediately telling everybody who you are and what you're doing here."

"Great idea," Pete announced, "terrific, pragmatic solution!" He began feverishly snatching up gadgets and stuffing them into his shoulderbag. "See, Lyle? One phone-call to good ol' Spider Pete, and your problem is history, zude! Me and Mabel-the-Fed have crisis negotiation skills that are second to none! Another potentially lethal confrontation resolved without any bloodshed or loss of life." Pete zipped the bag shut. "That's about it, right, everybody?

Problem over! Write if you get work, Lyle buddy. Hang by your thumbs."
Pete leapt out the door and bounded off at top speed on the springy soles
of his reactive boots.

"Thanks a lot for placing my equipment into the hands of sociopathic
criminals," Kitty said. She reached out of the slit in the bag, grabbed a multitool off the corner of the workbench, and began swiftly slashing her
way free.

"This will help the sluggish, corrupt, and underpaid Chattanooga police
to take life a little more seriously," Mabel said, her pale eyes gleaming. "Besides, it's profoundly undemocratic to restrict specialized technical knowledge to the coercive hands of secret military elites."

Kitty thoughtfully thumbed the edge of the multi-tool's ceramic blade
and stood up to her full height, her eyes slitted. "I'm ashamed to work for
the same government as you."

Mabel smiled serenely. "Darling, your tradition of deep dark government
paranoia is far behind the times! This is the postmodern era! We're now in the
grip of a government with severe schizoid multiple-personality disorder."

"You're truly vile. I despise you more than I can say." Kitty jerked her
thumb at Lyle. "Even this nut-case eunuch anarchist kid looks pretty good,
compared to you. At least he's self-sufficient and market-driven."

"I thought he looked good the moment I met him," Mabel replied sun-
nily. "He's cute, he's got great muscle tone, and he doesn't make passes.
Plus he can fix small appliances and he's got a spare apartment. I think you
ought to move in with him, sweetheart."

"What's that supposed to mean? You don't think I could manage life
here in the zone like you do, is that it? You think you have some kind of
copyright on living outside the law?"

"No, I just mean you'd better stay indoors with your boyfriend here until
that paint falls off your face. You look like a poisoned raccoon."

Mabel turned on her heel. "Try to get a life, and stay out of my way."
She leapt outside, unlocked her bicycle and methodically pedaled off.

Kitty wiped her lips and spat out the door. "Christ, that baton packs a
wallop." She snorted. "Don't you ever ventilate this place, kid? Those paint
fumes are gonna kill you before you're thirty."

"I don't have time to clean or ventilate it. I'm real busy."

"Okay, then I'll clean it. I'll ventilate it. I gotta stay here a while, understand? Maybe quite a while."

Lyle blinked. "How long, exactly?"

Kitty stared at him. "You're not taking me seriously, are you? I don't
much like it when people don't take me seriously."

"No, no," Lyle assured her hastily. "You're very serious."

"You ever heard of a small-business grant, kid? How about venture capital, did you ever hear of that? Ever heard of federal research-and-development subsidies, Mr. Schweik?" Kitty looked at him sharply, weighing her words. "Yeah, I thought maybe you'd heard of that one, Mr. Techie Wacko. Federal R and D backing is the kind of thing that only happens to other people, right? But Lyle, when you make good friends with a senator, you become 'other people.' Get my drift, pal?"

"I guess I do," Lyle said slowly.

"We'll have ourselves some nice talks about that subject, Lyle. You wouldn't mind that, would you?"

"No. I don't mind it now that you're talking."

"There's some stuff going on down here in the zone that I didn't understand at first, but it's important." Kitty paused, then rubbed dried dye from her hair in a cascade of green dandruff. "How much did you pay those Spider gangsters to string up this place for you?"

"It was kind of a barter situation," Lyle told her.

"Think they'd do it again if I paid 'em real cash? Yeah? I thought so." She nodded thoughtfully. "They look like a heavy outfit, the City Spiders. I gotta pry 'em loose from that leftist gorgon before she finishes indoctrinating them in socialist revolution." Kitty wiped her mouth on her sleeve. "This is the Senator's own constituency! It was stupid of us to duck an ideological battle, just because this is a worthless area inhabited by reckless sociopaths who don't vote. Hell, that's exactly why it's important. This could be a vital territory in the culture war. I'm gonna call the office right away, start making arrangements. There's no way we're gonna leave this place in the hands of the self-styled Queen of Peace and Justice over there."

She snorted, then stretched a kink out of her back. "With a little self-control and discipline, I can save those Spiders from themselves and turn them into an asset to law and order! I'll get 'em to string up a couple of trailers here in the zone. We could start a dojo."

▲ ▼ ▲

Eddy called, two weeks later. He was in a beachside cabana somewhere in Catalunya, wearing a silk floral-print shirt and a new and very pricey looking set of spex. "How's life, Lyle?"

"It's okay, Eddy."

"Making out all right?" Eddy had two new tattoos on his cheekbone.

"Yeah. I got a new paying roommate. She's a martial artist."

"Girl roommate working out okay this time?"

"Yeah, she's good at pumping the flywheel and she lets me get on with my bike work. Bike business has been picking up a lot lately. Looks like I might get a legal electrical feed and some more floorspace, maybe even some genuine mail delivery. My new roomie's got a lot of useful contacts."

"Boy, the ladies sure love you, Lyle! Can't beat 'em off with a stick, can you, poor guy? That's a heck of a note."

Eddy leaned forward a little, shoving aside a silver tray full of dead gold-tipped zigarettes. "You been getting the packages?"

"Yeah. Pretty regular."

"Good deal," he said briskly, "but you can wipe 'em all now. I don't need those backups anymore. Just wipe the data and trash the disks, or sell 'em. I'm into some, well, pretty hairy opportunities right now, and I don't need all that old clutter. It's kid stuff anyway."

"Okay, man. If that's the way you want it."

Eddy leaned forward. "D'you happen to get a package lately? Some hardware? Kind of a settop box?"

"Yeah, I got the thing."

"That's great, Lyle. I want you to open the box up, and break all the chips with pliers."

"Yeah?"

"Then throw all the pieces away. Separately. It's trouble, Lyle, okay? The kind of trouble I don't need right now."

"Consider it done, man."

"Thanks! Anyway, you won't be bothered by mailouts from now on." He paused. "Not that I don't appreciate your former effort and goodwill, and all."

Lyle blinked. "How's your love life, Eddy?"

Eddy sighed. "Frederika! What a handful! I dunno, Lyle, it was okay for a while, but we couldn't stick it together. I don't know why I ever thought that private cops were sexy. I musta been totally out of my mind.… Anyway, I got a new girlfriend now."

"Yeah?"

"She's a politician, Lyle. She's a radical member of the Spanish Parliament. Can you believe that? I'm sleeping with an elected official of a European local government." He laughed. "Politicians are sexy, Lyle. Politicians are hot! They have charisma. They're glamorous. They're powerful. They can really make things happen! Politicians get around. They know things on the inside track. I'm having more fun with Violeta than I knew there was in the world."

"That's pleasant to hear, zude."

"More pleasant than you know, my man."

"Not a problem," Lyle said indulgently. "We all gotta make our own lives, Eddy."

"Ain't it the truth."

Lyle nodded. "I'm in business, zude!"

"You gonna perfect that inertial whatsit?" Eddy said.

"Maybe. It could happen. I get to work on it a lot now. I'm getting closer, really getting a grip on the concept. It feels really good. It's a good hack, man. It makes up for all the rest of it. It really does."

Eddy sipped his mimosa. "Lyle."

"What?"

"You didn't hook up that settop box and look at it, did you?"

"You know me, Eddy," Lyle said. "Just another kid with a wrench."

Taklamakan

A bone-dry frozen wind tore at the earth outside, its lethal howling cut to a muffled moan. Katrinko and Spider Pete were camped deep in a crevice in the rock, wrapped in furry darkness. Pete could hear Katrinko breathing, with a light rattle of chattering teeth. The neuter's yeasty armpits smelled like nutmeg.

Spider Pete strapped his shaven head into his spex.

Outside their puffy nest, the sticky eyes of a dozen gelcams splayed across the rock, a sky-eating web of perception. Pete touched a stud on his spex, pulled down a glowing menu, and adjusted his visual take on the outside world.

Flying powder tumbled through the yardangs like an evil fog. The crescent moon and a billion desert stars, glowing like pixelated bruises, wheeled above the eerie wind-sculpted landscape of the Taklamakan. With the exceptions of Antarctica, or maybe the deep Sahara—locales Pete had never been paid to visit—this central Asian desert was the loneliest, most desolate place on Earth.

Pete adjusted parameters, etching the landscape with a busy array of false colors. He recorded an artful series of panorama shots, and tagged a global positioning fix onto the captured stack. Then he signed the footage with a cryptographic time-stamp from a passing NAFTA spy-sat.

Pete saved the stack onto a gelbrain. This gelbrain was a walnut-sized lump of neural biotech, carefully grown to mimic the razor-sharp visual cortex of an American bald eagle. It was the best, most expensive piece of photographic hardware that Pete had ever owned. Pete kept the thing tucked in his crotch.

Pete took a deep and intimate pleasure in working with the latest federally subsidized spy gear. It was quite the privilege for Spider Pete, the kind of privilege that he might well die for. There was no tactical use in yet another spy-shot of the chill and empty Taklamakan. But the tagged picture would prove that Katrinko and Pete had been here at the appointed rendezvous. Right here, right now. Waiting for the man.

And the man was overdue.

During their brief professional acquaintance, Spider Pete had met the Lieutenant Colonel in a number of deeply unlikely locales. A parking garage in Pentagon City. An outdoor seafood restaurant in Cabo San Lucas. On the ferry to Staten Island. Pete had never known his patron to miss a rendezvous by so much as a microsecond.

The sky went dirty white. A sizzle, a sparkle, a zenith full of stink. A screaming-streaking-tumbling. A nasty thunderclap. The ground shook hard.

"Dang," Pete said.

▲ ▼ ▲

They found the Lieutenant Colonel just before eight in the morning. Pieces of his landing pod were violently scattered across half a kilometer.

Katrinko and Pete skulked expertly through a dirty yellow jumble of wind-grooved boulders. Their camou gear switched coloration moment by moment, to match the landscape and the incidental light.

Pete pried the mask from his face, inhaled the thin, pitiless, metallic air, and spoke aloud. "That's our boy all right. Never missed a date."

The neuter removed her mask and fastidiously smeared her lips and gums with silicone anti-evaporant. Her voice fluted eerily over the insistent wind. "Space-defense must have tracked him on radar."

"Nope. If they'd hit him from orbit, he'd really be spread all over.... No, something happened to him really close to the ground." Pete pointed at a violent scattering of cracked ochre rock. "See, check out how that stealth-pod hit and tumbled. It didn't catch fire till after the impact."

With the absent ease of a gecko, the neuter swarmed up a three-story-high boulder. She examined the surrounding forensic evidence at length, dabbing carefully at her spex controls. She then slithered deftly back to earth. "There was no anti-aircraft fire, right? No interceptors flyin' round last night."

"Nope. Heck, there's no people around here in a space bigger than Delaware."

The neuter looked up. "So what do you figure, Pete?"

"I figure an accident," said Pete.

"A what?"

"An accident. A lot can go wrong with a covert HALO insertion."

"Like what, for instance?"

"Well, G-loads and stuff. System malfunctions. Maybe he just blacked out."

"He was a federal military spook, and you're telling me he *passed out?*" Katrinko daintily adjusted her goggled spex with gloved and bulbous finger-tips. "Why would that matter anyway? He wouldn't fly a spacecraft with his own hands, would he?"

Pete rubbed at the gummy line of his mask, easing the prickly indentation across one dark, tattooed cheek. "I kinda figure he would, actually. The man was a pilot. Big military prestige thing. Flyin' in by hand, deep in Sphere territory, covert insertion, way behind enemy lines.... That'd really be something to brag about, back on the Potomac."

The neuter considered this sour news without apparent resentment. As one of the world's top technical climbers, Katrinko was a great connoisseur of pointless displays of dangerous physical skill. "I can get behind that." She paused. "Serious bad break, though."

They resealed their masks. Water was their greatest lack, and vapor exhalation was a problem. They were recycling body-water inside their suits, topped off with a few extra cc's they'd obtained from occasional patches of frost. They'd consumed the last of the trail-goop and candy from their glider shipment three long days ago. They hadn't eaten since. Still, Pete and Katrinko were getting along pretty well, living off big subcutaneous lumps of injected body fat.

More through habit than apparent need, Pete and Katrinko segued into evidence-removal mode. It wasn't hard to conceal a HALO stealth pod. The spycraft was radar-transparent and totally biodegradable. In the bitter wind and cold of the Taklamakan, the bigger chunks of wreckage had already gone all brown and crispy, like the shed husks of locusts. They couldn't scrape up every physical trace, but they'd surely get enough to fool aerial surveillance.

The Lieutenant Colonel was extremely dead. He'd come down from the heavens in his full NAFTA military power-armor, a leaping, brick-busting, lightning-spewing exoskeleton, all acronyms and input jacks. It was powerful, elaborate gear, of an entirely different order than the gooey and fibrous street tech of the two urban intrusion freaks.

But the high-impact crash had not been kind to the armored suit. It had been crueler still to the bone, blood, and tendon housed inside.

Pete bagged the larger pieces with a heavy heart. He knew that the Lieutenant Colonel was basically no good: deceitful, ruthlessly ambitious, probably crazy. Still, Pete sincerely regretted his employer's demise. After all, it was precisely those qualities that had led the Lieutenant Colonel to recruit Spider Pete in the first place.

Pete also felt sincere regret for the gung-ho, clear-eyed young military widow, and the two little redheaded kids in Augusta, Georgia. He'd never actually met the widow or the little kids, but the Lieutenant Colonel was always fussing about them and showing off their photos. The Lieutenant Colonel had been a full fifteen years younger than Spider Pete, a rosy-cheeked cracker kid really, never happier than when handing over wads of money, nutty orders, and expensive covert equipment to people whom no sane man would trust with a burnt-out match. And now here he was in the cold and empty heart of Asia, turned to jam within his shards of junk.

Katrinko did the last of the search-and-retrieval while Pete dug beneath a ledge with his diamond hand-pick, the razored edges slashing out clods of shale.

After she'd fetched the last blackened chunk of their employer, Katrinko perched birdlike on a nearby rock. She thoughtfully nibbled a piece of the pod's navigation console. "This gelbrain is good when it dries out, man. Like trail mix, or a fortune cookie."

Pete grunted. "You might be eating part of him, y'know."

"Lotta good carbs and protein there, too."

They stuffed a final shattered power-jackboot inside the Colonel's makeshift cairn. The piled rock was there for the ages. A few jets of webbing and thumbnail dabs of epoxy made it harder than a brick wall.

It was noon now, still well below freezing, but as warm as the Takla-makan was likely to get in January. Pete sighed, dusted sand from his knees and elbows, stretched. It was hard work, cleaning up; the hardest part of in-trusion work, because it was the stuff you had to do after the thrill was gone. He offered Katrinko the end of a fiber-optic cable, so that they could speak together without using radio or removing their masks.

Pete waited until she had linked in, then spoke into his mike. "So we head on back to the glider now, right?"

The neuter looked up, surprised. "How come?"

"Look, Trink, this guy that we just buried was the actual spy in this assignment. You and me, we were just his gophers and backup support. The mission's an abort."

"But we're searching for a giant, secret rocket base."

"Yeah, sure we are."

"We're supposed to find this monster high-tech complex, break in, and record all kinds of crazy top secrets that nobody but the mandarins have ever seen. That's a totally hot assignment, man."

Pete sighed. "I admit it's very high-concept, but I'm an old guy now, Trink. I need the kind of payoff that involves some actual money."

Katrinko laughed. "But Pete! It's a *starship*! A whole fleet of 'em, maybe! Secretly built in the desert, by Chinese spooks and Japanese engineers!"

Pete shook his head. "That was all paranoid bullshit that the flyboy made up, to get himself a grant and a field assignment. He was tired of sitting be-hind a desk in the basement, that's all."

Katrinko folded her lithe and wiry arms. "Look, Pete, you saw those briefings just like me. You saw all those satellite shots. The traffic analysis, too. The Sphere people are up to *something* way big out here."

Pete gazed around him. He found it painfully surreal to endure this dis-cussion amid a vast and threatening tableau of dust-hazed sky and sand-etched mudstone gullies. "They built something big here once, I grant you that. But I never figured the Colonel's story for being very likely."

"What's so unlikely about it? The Russians had a secret rocket base in the desert a hundred years ago. American deserts are full of secret mil-spec stuff and space-launch bases. So now the Asian Sphere people are up to the same old game. It all makes sense."

"No, it makes no sense at all. Nobody's space-racing to build any star-ships. Starships aren't a space race. It takes four hundred years to fly to the stars. Nobody's gonna finance a major military project that'll take four hundred years to pay off. Least of all a bunch of smart and thrifty Asian eco-nomic-warfare people."

"Well, they're sure building *something*. Look, all we have to do is find the complex, break in, and document some stuff. We can do that! People like us, we never needed any federal bossman to help us break into buildings and take photos. That's what we always do, that's what we live for."

Pete was touched by the kid's game spirit. She really had the City Spider way of mind. Nevertheless, Pete was fifty-two years old, so he found it necessary to at least try to be reasonable. "We should haul our sorry spook asses back to that glider right now. Let's skip on back over the Himalayas. We can fly on back to Washington, tourist class out of Delhi. They'll debrief us at the puzzle-palace. We'll give 'em the bad news about the bossman. We got plenty of evidence to prove *that*, anyhow.... The spooks will give us some walkin' money for a busted job, and tell us to keep our noses clean. Then we can go out for some pork chops."

Katrinko's thin shoulders hunched mulishly within the bubblepak warts of her insulated camou. She was not taking this at all well. "Peter, I ain't looking for pork chops. I'm looking for some professional validation, okay? I'm sick of that lowlife kid stuff, knocking around raiding network sites and mayors' offices.... This is my chance at the big-time!"

Pete stroked the muzzle of his mask with two gloved fingers.

"Pete, I know that you ain't happy. I know that already, okay? But you've *already made it* in the big-time, Mr. City Spider, Mr. Legend, Mr. Champion. Now here's my big chance come along, and you want us to hang up our cleats."

Pete raised his other hand. "Wait a minute, I never said that."

"Well, you're tellin' me you're walking. You're turning your back. You don't even want to check it out first."

"No," Pete said weightily, "I reckon you know me too well for that, Trink. I'm still a Spider. I'm still game. I'll always at least check it out."

▲ ▼ ▲

Katrinko set their pace after that. Pete was content to let her lead. It was a very stupid idea to continue the mission without the overlordship of the

Lieutenant Colonel. But it was stupid in a different and more refreshing way than the stupid idea of returning home to Chattanooga.

People in Pete's line of work weren't allowed to go home. He'd tried that once, really tried it, eight years ago, just after that badly busted caper in Brussels. He'd gotten a straight job at Lyle Schweik's pedal-powered aircraft factory. The millionaire sports tycoon had owed him a favor. Schweik had been pretty good about it, considering.

But word had swiftly gotten around that Pete had once been a champion City Spider. Dumb-ass co-workers would make significant remarks. Sometimes they asked him for so-called "favors," or tried to act street-wise. When you came down to it, straight people were a major pain in the ass.

Pete preferred the company of seriously twisted people. People who really cared about something, cared enough about it to really warp themselves for it. People who looked for more out of life than mommy-daddy, money, and the grave.

Below the edge of a ridgeline they paused for a recce. Pete whirled a tethered eye on the end of its reel and flung it. At the peak of its arc, six stories up, it recorded their surroundings in a panoramic view.

Pete and Katrinko studied the image together through their linked spex. Katrinko highlit an area downhill with a fingertip gesture. "Now there's a tipoff."

"That gully, you mean?"

"You need to get outdoors more, Pete. That's what we rockjocks technically call a road."

Pete and Katrinko approached the road with professional caution. It was a paved ribbon of macerated cinderblock, overrun with drifting sand. The road was made of the coked-out clinker left behind by big urban incinerators, a substance that Asians used for their road surfaces because all the value had been cooked out of it.

The cinder road had once seen a great deal of traffic. There were tire-shreds here and there, deep ruts in the shoulder, and post-holes that had once been traffic signs, or maybe surveillance boxes.

They followed the road from a respectful distance, cautious of monitors, tripwires, landmines, and many other possible unpleasantries. They stopped for a rest in a savage arroyo where a road bridge had been carefully removed, leaving only neat sockets in the roadbed and a kind of conceptual arc in midair.

"What creeps me out is how clean this all is," Pete said over cable. "It's a road, right? Somebody's gotta throw out a beer can, a lost shoe, something."

Katrinko nodded. "I figure construction robots."

"Really."

Katrinko spread her swollen-fingered gloves. "It's a Sphere operation, so it's bound to have lots of robots, right? I figure robots built this road. Robots used this road. Robots carried in tons and tons of whatever they were carrying. Then when they were done with the big project, the robots carried off everything that was worth any money. Gathered up the guideposts, bridges, everything. Very neat, no loose ends, very Sphere-type way to work." Katrinko set her masked chin on her bent knees, gone into reverie. "Some very weird and intense stuff can happen, when you got a lot of space in the desert, and robot labor that's too cheap to meter."

Katrinko hadn't been wasting her time in those intelligence briefings. Pete had seen a lot of City Spider wannabes, even trained quite a few of them. But Katrinko had what it took to be a genuine Spider champion: the desire, the physical talent, the ruthless dedication, and even the smarts. It was staying out of jails and morgues that was gonna be the tough part for Katrinko. "You're a big fan of the Sphere, aren't you, kid? You really like the way they operate."

"Sure, I always liked Asians. Their food's a lot better than Europe's."

Pete took this in stride. NAFTA, Sphere, and Europe: the trilateral superpowers jostled about with the uneasy regularity of sunspots, periodically brewing storms in the proxy regimes of the South. During his fifty-plus years, Pete had seen the Asian Cooperation Sphere change its public image repeatedly, in a weird political rhythm. Exotic vacation spot on Tuesdays and Thursdays. Baffling alien threat on Mondays and Wednesdays. Major trading partner each day and every day, including weekends and holidays.

At the current political moment, the Asian Cooperation Sphere was deep into its Inscrutable Menace mode, logging lots of grim media coverage as NAFTA's chief economic adversary. As far as Pete could figure it, this basically meant that a big crowd of goofy North American economists were trying to act really macho. Their major complaint was that the Sphere was selling NAFTA too many neat, cheap, well-made consumer goods. That was an extremely silly thing to get killed about. But people perished horribly for much stranger reasons than that.

▲ ▼ ▲

At sunset, Pete and Katrinko discovered the giant warning signs. They were titanic vertical plinths, all epoxy and clinker, much harder than granite. They were four stories tall, carefully rooted in bedrock, and painstakingly chiseled with menacing horned symbols and elaborate textual warnings in at least fifty different languages. English was language number three.

"Radiation waste," Pete concluded, deftly reading the text through his spex, from two kilometers away. "This is a radiation waste dump. Plus, a nuclear test site. Old Red Chinese hydrogen bombs, way out in the Takla-makan desert." He paused thoughtfully. "You gotta hand it to 'em. They sure picked the right spot for the job."

"No way!" Katrinko protested. "Giant stone warning signs, telling people not to trespass in this area? That's got to be a con job."

"Well, it would sure account for them using robots, and then destroying all the roads."

"No, man. It's like—you wanna hide something big nowadays. You don't put a safe inside the wall any more, because hey, everybody's got magnetometers and sonic imaging and heat detection. So you hide your best stuff in the garbage."

Pete scanned their surroundings on spex telephoto. They were lurking on a hillside above a playa, where the occasional gullywasher had spewed out a big alluvial fan of desert-varnished grit and cobbles. Stuff was actually growing down there—squat leathery grasses with fat waxy blades like dead men's fingers. The evil vegetation didn't look like any kind of grass that Pete had ever seen. It struck him as the kind of grass that would blithely gobble up stray plutonium. "Trink, I like my explanations simple. I figure that so-called giant starship base for a giant radwaste dump."

"Well, maybe," the neuter admitted. "But even if that's the truth, that's still news worth paying for. We might find some busted-up barrels, or some badly managed fuel rods out there. That would be a big political embarrassment, right? Proof of that would be worth something."

"Huh," said Pete, surprised. But it was true. Long experience had taught Pete that there were always useful secrets in other people's trash. "Is it worth glowin' in the dark for?"

"So what's the problem?" Katrinko said. "I ain't having kids. I fixed that a long time ago. And you've got enough kids already."

"Maybe," Pete grumbled. Four kids by three different women. It had taken him a long sad time to learn that women who fell head-over-heels for footloose, sexy tough guys would fall repeatedly for pretty much any footloose, sexy tough guy.

Katrinko was warming to the task at hand. "We can do this, man. We got our suits and our breathing masks, and we're not eating or drinking anything out here, so we're practically radiation-tight. So we camp way outside the dump tonight. Then before dawn we slip in, we check it out real quick, we take our pictures, we leave. Clean, classic intrusion job. Nobody living around here to stop us, no problem there. And then, we got something to show the spooks when we get home. Maybe something we can sell."

Pete mulled this over. The prospect didn't sound all that bad. It was dirty work, but it would complete the mission. Also—this was the part he liked best—it would keep the Lieutenant Colonel's people from sending in some other poor guy. "Then, back to the glider?"

"Then back to the glider."

"Okay, good deal."

▲ ▼ ▲

Before dawn the next morning, they stoked themselves with athletic performance enhancers, brewed in the guts of certain gene-spliced ticks that they had kept hibernating in their armpits. Then they concealed their travel gear, and swarmed like ghosts up and over the great wall.

They pierced a tiny hole through the roof of one of the dun-colored, half-buried containment hangars, and oozed a spy-eye through.

Bomb-proofed ranks of barrel-shaped sarcophagi, solid and glossy as polished granite. The big fused radwaste containers were each the size of a tanker truck. They sat there neatly ranked in hermetic darkness, mute as sphinxes. They looked to be good for the next twenty thousand years.

Pete liquefied and retrieved the gelcam, then re-sealed the tiny hole with rock putty. They skipped down the slope of the dusty roof. There were lots of lizard tracks in the sand drifts, piled at the rim of the dome. These healthy traces of lizard cheered Pete up considerably.

They swarmed silently up and over the wall. Back uphill to the grotto where they'd stashed their gear. Then they removed their masks to talk again.

Pete sat behind a boulder, enjoying the intrusion after-glow. "A cakewalk," he pronounced it. "A pleasure hike." His pulse was already normal again, and, to his joy, there were no suspicious aches under his caraco-acromial arch.

"You gotta give them credit, those robots sure work neat."

Pete nodded. "Killer application for robots, your basic lethal waste gig."

"I telephoto'ed that whole cantonment," said Katrinko, "and there's no water there. No towers, no plumbing, no wells. People can get along without a lot of stuff in the desert, but nobody lives without water. That place is stone dead. It was always dead." She paused. "It was all automated robot work from start to finish. You know what that means, Pete? It means no human being has ever seen that place before. Except for you and me."

"Hey, then it's a first! We scored a first intrusion! That's just dandy," said Pete, pleased at the professional coup. He gazed across the cobbled plain at the walled cantonment, and pressed a last set of spex shots into his gel-brain archive. Two dozen enormous domes, built block by block by giant robots, acting with the dumb persistence of termites. The sprawling domes looked as if they'd congealed on the spot, their rims settling like molten taffy into the desert's little convexities and concavities. From a satellite view, the domes probably passed for natural features. "Let's not tarry, okay? I can kinda feel those X-ray fingers kinking my DNA."

"Aw, you're not all worried about that, are you, Pete?"

Pete laughed and shrugged. "Who cares? Job's over, kid. Back to the glider."

"They do great stuff with gene damage nowadays, y'know. Kinda re-weave you, down at the spook lab."

"What, those military doctors? I don't wanna give them the excuse."

The wind picked up. A series of abrupt and brutal gusts. Dry, and freezing, and peppered with stinging sand.

Suddenly, a faint moan emanated from the cantonment. Distant lungs blowing the neck of a wine bottle.

"What's that big weird noise?" demanded Katrinko, all alert interest.

"Aw no," said Pete. "Dang."

▲ ▼ ▲

Steam was venting from a hole in the bottom of the thirteenth dome. They'd missed the hole earlier, because the rim of that dome was overgrown with big thriving thornbushes. The bushes would have been a tip-off in themselves, if the two of them had been feeling properly suspicious.

In the immediate area, Pete and Katrinko swiftly discovered three dead men. The three men had hacked and chiseled their way through the containment dome—from the inside. They had wriggled through the long, narrow crevice they had cut, leaving much blood and skin.

The first man had died just outside the dome, apparently from sheer exhaustion. After their Olympian effort, the two survivors had emerged to confront the sheer four-storey walls.

The remaining men had tried to climb the mighty wall with their handaxes, crude woven ropes, and pig-iron pitons. It was a nothing wall for a pair of City Spiders with modern handwebs and pinpression cleats. Pete and Katrinko could have camped and eaten a watermelon on that wall. But it was a very serious wall for a pair of very weary men dressed in wool, leather, and homemade shoes.

One of them had fallen from the wall, and had broken his back and leg. The last one had decided to stay to comfort his dying comrade, and it seemed he had frozen to death.

The three men had been dead for many months, maybe over a year. Ants had been at work on them, and the fine salty dust of the Taklamakan, and the freeze-drying. Three desiccated Asian mummies, black hair and crooked teeth and wrinkled dusky skin, in their funny blood-stained clothes.

Katrinko offered the cable lead, chattering through her mask. "Man, look at these *shoes*! Look at this shirt this guy's got—would you call this thing a *shirt*?"

"What I would call this is three very brave climbers," Pete said. He tossed a tethered eye into the crevice that the men had cut.

The inside of the thirteenth dome was a giant forest of monitors. Microwave antennas, mostly. The top of the dome wasn't sturdy sintered concrete like the others, it was some kind of radar-transparent plastic. Dark inside, like the other domes, and hermetically sealed—at least before the dead men had chewed and chopped their hole through the wall. No sign of any radwaste around here.

They discovered the little camp where the men had lived. Their bivouac. Three men, patiently chipping and chopping their way to freedom. Burning their last wicks and oil lamps, eating their last rations bite by bite, emptying their leather canteens and scraping for frost to drink. Surrounded all the time by a towering jungle of satellite relays and wavepipes. Pete found that scene very ugly. That was a very bad scene. That was the worst of it yet.

▲ ▼ ▲

Pete and Katrinko retrieved their full set of intrusion gear. They then broke in through the top of the dome, where the cutting was easiest. Once through, they sealed the hole behind themselves, but only lightly, in case they should need a rapid retreat. They lowered their haul bags to the stone floor, then rappelled down on their smart ropes. Once on ground level, they closed the escape tunnel with web and rubble, to stop the howling wind, and to keep contaminants at bay.

With the hole sealed, it grew warmer in the dome. Warm, and moist. Dew was collecting on walls and floor. A very strange smell, too. A smell like smoke and old socks. Mice and spice. Soup and sewage. A cozy human reek from the depths of the earth.

"The Lieutenant Colonel sure woulda have loved this," whispered Katrinko over cable, spexing out the towering machinery with her infrareds. "You put a clip of explosive ammo through here, and it sure would put a major crimp in somebody's automated gizmos."

Pete figured their present situation for an excellent chance to get killed. Automated alarm systems were the deadliest aspect of his professional existence, somewhat tempered by the fact that smart and aggressive alarm systems frequently killed their owners. There was a basic engineering principle involved. Fancy, paranoid alarm systems went false-positive all the time: squirrels, dogs, wind, hail, earth tremors, horny boyfriends who forgot the password…. They were smart, and they had their own agenda, and it made them troublesome.

But if these machines were alarms, then they hadn't noticed a rather large hole painstakingly chopped in the side of their dome. The spars and transmitters looked bad, all patchy with long-accumulated rime and ice. A junkyard look, the definite smell of dead tech. So somebody had given up on these smart, expensive, paranoid alarms. Someone had gotten sick and tired of them, and shut them off.

▲ ▼ ▲

At the foot of a microwave tower, they found a rat-sized manhole chipped out, covered with a laced-down lid of sheep's hide. Pete dropped a spy-eye down, scoping out a machine-drilled shaft. The tunnel was wide enough to swallow a car, and it dropped down as straight as a plumb bob for farther than his eye's wiring could reach.

Pete silently yanked a rusting pig-iron piton from the edge of the hole, and replaced it with a modern glue anchor. Then he whipped a smart-rope through and carefully tightened his harness.

Katrinko began shaking with eagerness. "Pete, I am way hot for this. Lemme lead point."

Pete clipped a crab into Katrinko's harness, and linked their spex through the fiber-optic embedded in the rope. Then he slapped the neuter's shoulder. "Get bold, kid."

Katrinko flared out the webbing on her gripgloves, and dropped in feetfirst.

The would-be escapees had made a lot of use of cabling already present in the tunnel. There were ceramic staples embedded periodically, to hold the cabling snug against the stone. The climbers had scrabbled their way up from staple to staple, using ladder-runged bamboo poles and iron hooks.

Katrinko stopped her descent and tied off. Pete sent their haulbags down. Then he dropped and slithered after her. He stopped at the lead chock, tied off, and let Katrinko take lead again, following her progress with the spex.

An eerie glow shone at the bottom of the tunnel. Pay day. Pete felt a familiar transcendental tension overcome him. It surged through him with mad intensity. Fear, curiosity, and desire: the raw, hot, thieving thrill of a major-league intrusion. A feeling like being insane, but so much better than craziness, because now he felt so awake. Pete was awash in primal spiderness, cravings too deep and slippery to speak about.

The light grew hotter in Pete's infrareds. Below them was a slotted expanse of metal, gleaming like a kitchen sink, louvers with hot slots of light.

Katrinko planted a foamchock in the tunnel wall, tied off, leaned back, and dropped a spy eye through the slot.

Pete's hands were too busy to reach his spex. "What do you see?" he hissed over cable.

Katrinko craned her head back, gloved palms pressing the goggles against her face. "I can see *everything*, man! Gardens of Eden, and cities of gold!"

▲ ▼ ▲

The cave had been ancient solid rock once, a continental bulk. The rock had been pierced by a Russian-made drilling rig. A dry well, in a very dry country. And then some very weary, and very sunburned, and very determined Chinese Communist weapons engineers had installed a one-hundred megaton hydrogen bomb at the bottom of their dry hole. When their beast in its nest of layered casings achieved fusion, seismographs jumped like startled fawns in distant California.

The thermonuclear explosion had left a giant gasbubble at the heart of a crazy webwork of faults and cracks. The deep and empty bubble had lurked beneath the desert in utter and terrible silence, for ninety years.

Then Asia's new masters had sent in new and more sophisticated agencies.

Pete saw that the distant sloping walls of the cavern were daubed with starlight. White constellations, whole and entire. And amid the space—that giant and sweetly damp airspace—were three great glowing lozenges, three vertical cylinders the size of urban high rises. They seemed to be suspended in midair.

"Starships," Pete muttered.

"Starships," Katrinko agreed. Menus appeared in the shared visual space of their linked spex. Katrinko's fingertip sketched out a set of tiny moving sparks against the walls. "But check that out."

"What are those?"

"Heat signatures. Little engines." The envisioned world wheeled silently. "And check out over here too—and crawlin' around deep in there, dozens of the things. And Pete, see these? Those big ones? Kinda on patrol?"

"Robots."

"Yep."

"What the hell are they up to, down here?"

"Well, I figure it this way, man. If you're inside one of those fake starships, and you look out through those windows—those *portholes*, I guess we call 'em—you can't see anything but shiny stars. Deep space. But with spex, we can see right through all that business. And Pete, that whole stone sky down there is crawling with machinery."

"Man-oh-man."

"And nobody inside those starships can see *down*, man. There is a whole lot of very major weirdness going on down at the bottom of that cave. There's a lot of hot steamy water down there, deep in those rocks and those cracks."

"Water, or a big smelly soup maybe," Pete said. "A chemical soup."

"Biochemical soup."

"Autonomous self-assembly proteinaceous biotech. Strictly forbidden by the Nonproliferation Protocols of the Manila Accords of 2037," said Pete. Pete rattled off this phrase with practiced ease, having rehearsed it any number of times during various background briefings.

"A whole big lake of way-hot, way-illegal, self-assembling goo down there."

"Yep. The very stuff that our covert-tech boys have been messing with under the Rockies for the past ten years."

"Aw, Pete, everybody cheats a little bit on the accords. The way we do it in NAFTA, it's no worse than bathtub gin. But this is *huge*! And Lord only knows what's inside those starships."

"Gotta be people, kid."

"Yep."

Pete drew a slow moist breath. "This is a big one, Trink. This is truly major-league. You and me, we got ourselves an intelligence coup here of historic proportions."

"If you're trying to say that we should go back to the glider now," Katrinko said, "don't even start with me."

"We need to go back to the glider," Pete insisted, "with the photographic proof that we got right now. That was our mission objective. It's what they pay us for."

"Whoop-tee-do."

"Besides, it's the patriotic thing. Right?"

"Maybe I'd play the patriot game, if I was in uniform," said Katrinko. "But the Army don't allow neuters. I'm a total freak and I'm a free agent, and I didn't come here to see Shangri-La and then turn around first thing."

"Yeah," Pete admitted. "I really know that feeling."

"I'm going down in there right now," Katrinko said. "You belay for me?"

"No way, kid. This time, I'm leading point."

▲ ▼ ▲

Pete eased himself through a crudely broken louver and out onto the vast rocky ceiling. Pete had never much liked climbing rock. Nasty stuff, rock—all natural, no guaranteed engineering specifications. Still, Pete had spent a great deal of his life on ceilings. Ceilings he understood.

He worked his way out on a series of congealed lava knobs, till he hit a nice solid crack. He did a rapid set of fist-jams, then set a pair of foam-clamps, and tied himself off on anchor.

Pete panned slowly in place, upside down on the ceiling, muffled in his camou gear, scanning methodically for the sake of Katrinko back on the fiber-optic spex link. Large sections of the ceiling looked weirdly worm-eaten, as if drills or acids had etched the rock away. Pete could discern in the eerie glow of infrared that the three fake starships were actually supported on columns. Huge hollow tubes, lacelike and almost entirely invisible, made of something black and impossibly strong, maybe carbon-fiber. There were water pipes inside the columns, and electrical power.

Those columns were the quickest and easiest ways to climb down or up to the starships. Those columns were also very exposed. They looked like excellent places to get killed.

Pete knew that he was safely invisible to any naked human eye, but there wasn't much he could do about his heat signature. For all he knew, at this moment he was glowing like a Christmas tree on the sensors of a thousand heavily armed robots. But you couldn't leave a thousand machines armed to a hair-trigger for years on end. And who would program them to spend their time watching ceilings?

The muscular burn had faded from his back and shoulders. Pete shook a little extra blood through his wrists, unhooked, and took off on cleats and gripwebs. He veered around one of the fake stars, a great glowing glassine bulb the size of a laundry basket. The fake star was cemented into a big rocky wart, and it radiated a cold, enchanting, and gooey firefly light. Pete was so intrigued by this bold deception that his cleat missed a smear. His left foot swung loose. His left shoulder emitted a nasty-feeling, expensive-sounding pop. Pete grunted, planted both cleats, and slapped up a glue patch, with tendons smarting and the old forearm clock ticking fast. He whipped a crab through the patchloop and sagged within his harness, breathing hard.

On the surface of his spex, Katrinko's glowing fingertip whipped across the field of Pete's vision, and pointed. Something moving out there. Pete had company.

Pete eased a string of flashbangs from his sleeve. Then he hunkered down in place, trusting to his camouflage, and watching.

A robot was moving toward him among the dark pits of the fake stars. Wobbling and jittering.

Pete had never seen any device remotely akin to this robot. It had a porous, foamy hide, like cork and plastic. It had a blind compartmented knob for a head, and fourteen long fibrous legs like a frayed mess of used rope, terminating in absurdly complicated feet, like a boxful of grip pliers. Hanging upside down from bits of rocky irregularity too small to see, it would open its big warty head and flick out a forked sensor like a snake's tongue. Sometimes it would dip itself close to the ceiling, for a lingering chemical smooch on the surface of the rock.

Pete watched with murderous patience as the device backed away, drew nearer, spun around a bit, meandered a little closer, sucked some more ceiling rock, made up its mind about something, replanted its big grippy feet, hoofed along closer yet, lost its train of thought, retreated a bit, sniffed the air at length, sucked meditatively on the end of one of its ropy tentacles.

It finally reached him, walked deftly over his legs, and dipped up to lick enthusiastically at the chemical traces left by his gripweb. The robot seemed enchanted by the taste of the glove's elastomer against the rock. It hung there on its fourteen plier feet, loudly licking and rasping.

Pete lashed out with his pick. The razored point slid with a sullen crunch right through the thing's corky head.

It went limp instantly, pinned there against the ceiling. Then with a nasty rustling it deployed a whole unsuspected set of waxy and filmy appurtenances. Complex bug-tongue things, mandible scrapers, delicate little spatulas, all reeling and trembling out of its slotted underside.

It was not going to die. It couldn't die, because it had never been alive. It was a piece of biotechnical machinery. Dying was simply not on its agenda anywhere. Pete photographed the device carefully as it struggled with obscene mechanical stupidity to come to workable terms with its new environmental parameters. Then Pete levered the pick loose from the ceiling, shook it loose, and dropped the pierced robot straight down to hell.

Pete climbed more quickly now, favoring the strained shoulder. He worked his way methodically out to the relative ease of the vertical wall, where he discovered a large mined-out vein in the constellation Sagittarius. The vein was a big snaky recess where some kind of ore had been nibbled and strained from the rock. By the look of it, the rock had been chewed away by a termite host of tiny robots with mouths like toenail clippers.

He signaled on the spex for Katrinko. The neuter followed along the clipped and anchored line, climbing like a fiend while lugging one of the haulbags. As Katrinko settled in to their new base camp, Pete returned to the louvers to fetch the second bag. When he'd finally heaved and grappled his way back, his shoulder was aching bitterly and his nerves were shot. They were done for the day.

Katrinko had put up the emission-free encystment web at the mouth of their crevice. With Pete returned to relative safety, she reeled in their smart-ropes and fed them a handful of sugar.

Pete cracked open two capsules of instant fluff, then sank back grate-fully into the wool.

Katrinko took off her mask. She was vibrating with alert enthusiasm. Youth, thought Pete—youth, and the eight percent metabolic advantage that came from lacking sex organs. "We're in so much trouble now," Katrinko whispered, with a feverish grin in the faint red glow of a single indicator light. She no longer resembled a boy or a young woman. Katrinko looked completely diabolical. This was a nonsexed creature. Pete liked to think of her as a "she," because this was somehow easier on his mind, but Katrinko was an "it." Now it was filled with glee, because finally it had placed itself in a proper and pleasing situation. Stark and feral confrontation with its own stark and feral little being.

"Yeah, this is trouble," Pete said. He placed a fat medicated tick onto the vein inside of his elbow. "And you're taking first watch."

▲ ▼ ▲

Pete woke four hours later, with a heart-fluttering rise from the stunned depths of chemically assisted delta-sleep. He felt numb, and lightly dusted with a brain-clouding amnesia, as if he'd slept for four straight days. He had been profoundly helpless in the grip of the drug, but the risk had been worth it, because now he was thoroughly rested. Pete sat up, and tried the left shoulder experimentally. It was much improved.

Pete rubbed feeling back into his stubbled face and scalp, then strapped his spex on. He discovered Katrinko squatting on her haunches, in the radi-ant glow of her own body heat, pondering over an ugly mess of spines, flakes, and goo.

Pete touched spex knobs and leaned forward. "What you got there?"

"Dead robots. They ate our foamchocks, right out of the ceiling. They eat anything. I killed the ones that tried to break into camp." Katrinko stroked at a midair menu, then handed Pete a fiber lead for his spex. "Check this footage I took."

Katrinko had been keeping watch with the gelcams, picking out pass-ing robots in the glow of their engine heat. She'd documented them on in-frared, saving and editing the clearest live-action footage. "These little ones with the ball-shaped feet, I call them 'keets,'" she narrated, as the captured frames cascaded across Pete's spex-clad gaze. "They're small, but they're really fast, and all over the place—I had to kill three of them. This one with the sharp spiral nose is a 'drillet'. Those are a pair of 'dubits'. The dubits always travel in pairs. This big thing here, that looks like a spilled dessert with big eyes and a ball on a chain, I call that one a 'lurchen'. Because of the way it moves, see? It's sure a lot faster than it looks."

Katrinko stopped the spex replay, switched back to live perception, and poked carefully at the broken litter before her booted feet. The biggest device in the heap resembled a dissected cat's head stuffed with cables and bristles. "I also killed this 'piteen'. Piteens don't die easy, man."

"There's lots of these things?"

"I figure hundreds, maybe thousands. All different kinds. And every one of 'em as stupid as dirt. Or else we'd be dead and disassembled a hundred times already."

Pete stared at the dissected robots, a cooling mass of nerve-netting, batteries, veiny armor plates, and gelatin. "Why do they look so crazy?"

"'Cause they grew all by themselves. Nobody ever designed them." Katrinko glanced up. "You remember those big virtual spaces for weapons design, that they run out in Alamagordo?"

"Yeah, sure, Alamagordo. Physics simulations on those super-size quantum gelbrains. Huge virtualities, with ultra-fast, ultra-fine detail. You bet I remember New Mexico! I love to raid a great computer lab. There's something so traditional about the hack."

"Yeah. See, for us NAFTA types, physics virtualities are a military app. We always give our tech to the military whenever it looks really dangerous. But let's say you don't share our NAFTA values. You don't wanna test new weapons systems inside giant virtualities. Let's say you want to make a can opener, instead."

During her sleepless hours huddling on watch, Katrinko had clearly been giving this matter a lot of thought. "Well, you could study other people's can openers and try to improve the design. Or else you could just set up a giant high-powered virtuality with a bunch of virtual cans inside it. Then you make some can opener simulations, that are basically blobs of goo. They're simulated goo, but they're also programs, and those programs trade data and evolve. Whenever they pierce a can, you reward them by making more copies of them. You're running, like, a million generations of a million different possible can openers, all day every day, in a simulated space."

The concept was not entirely alien to Spider Pete. "Yeah, I've heard the rumors. It was one of those stunts like Artificial Intelligence. It might look really good on paper, but you can't ever get it to work in real life."

"Yeah, and now it's illegal too. Kinda hard to police, though. But let's imagine you're into economic warfare and you figure out how to do this. Finally, you evolve this super weird, super can opener that no human being could ever have invented. Something that no human being could even *imagine*. Because it grew like a mushroom in an entire alternate physics. But you have all the specs for its shape and proportions, right there in the supercomputer. So to make one inside the real world, you just print it out like a photograph. And it works! It runs! See? Instant cheap consumer goods."

Pete thought it over. "So you're saying the Sphere people got that idea to work, and these robots here were built that way?"

"Pete, I just can't figure any other way this could have happened. These machines are just too alien. They had to come from some totally nonhuman, autonomous process. Even the best Japanese engineers can't design a jelly robot made out of fuzz and rope that can move like a caterpillar. There's not enough money in the world to pay human brains to think that out."

Pete prodded at the gooey ruins with his pick. "Well, you got that right."

"Whoever built this place, they broke a lot of rules and treaties. But they did it all *really cheap*. They did it in a way that is so cheap that it is *beyond economics*." Katrinko thought this over. "It's *way* beyond economics, and that's exactly *why* it's against all those rules and the treaties in the first place."

"Fast, cheap, and out of control."

"Exactly, man. If this stuff ever got loose in the real world, it would mean the end of everything we know."

Pete liked this last statement not at all. He had always disliked apocalyptic hype. He liked it even less now because under these extreme circumstances it sounded very plausible. The Sphere had the youngest and the biggest population of the three major trading blocs, and the youngest and the biggest ideas. People in Asia knew how to get things done. "Y'know, Lyle Schweik once told me that the weirdest bicycles in the world come out of China these days."

"Well, he's right. They do. And what about those Chinese circuitry chips they've been dumping in the NAFTA markets lately? Those chips are dirt cheap and work fine, but they're full of all this crazy leftover wiring that doubles back and gets all snarled up.... I always thought that was just shoddy workmanship. Man, 'workmanship' had nothing to do with those chips."

Pete nodded soberly. "Okay. Chips and bicycles, that much I can understand. There's a lot of money in that. But who the heck would take the trouble to create a giant hole in the ground that's full of robots and fake stars? I mean, *why?*"

Katrinko shrugged. "I guess it's just the Sphere, man. They still do stuff just because it's wonderful."

▲▼▲

The bottom of the world was boiling over. During the passing century, the nuclear test cavity had accumulated its own little desert aquifer, a pitch-black subterranean oasis. The bottom of the bubble was an unearthly drowned maze of shattered cracks and chemical deposition, all turned to simmering tidepools of mechanical self-assemblage. Oxygen-fizzing geysers of black fungus tea.

Steam rose steadily in the darkness amid the crags, rising to condense and run in chilly rivulets down the spherical star-spangled walls. Down at the bottom, all the water was eagerly collected by aberrant devices of animated sponge and string. Katrinko instantly tagged these as "smits" and "fuzzens."

The smits and fuzzens were nightmare dishrags and piston-powered spaghetti, leaping and slopping wetly from crag to crag. Katrinko took an unexpected ease and pleasure in naming and photographing the machines. Speculation boiled with sinister ease from the sexless youngster's vulpine head, a swift off-the-cuff adjustment to this alien toy world. It would seem that the kid lived rather closer to the future than Pete did.

They cranked their way from boulder to boulder, crack to liquid crack. They documented fresh robot larvae, chewing their way to the freedom of darkness through plugs of goo and muslin. It was a whole miniature creation, designed in the senseless gooey cores of a Chinese supercomputing gelbrain, and transmuted into reality in a hot broth of undead mechanized protein. This was by far the most amazing phenomenon that Pete had ever witnessed. Pete was accordingly plunged into gloom. Knowledge was power in his world. He knew with leaden certainty that he was taking on far too much voltage for his own good.

Pete was a professional. He could imagine stealing classified military secrets from a superpower, and surviving that experience. It would be very risky, but in the final analysis it was just the military. A rocket base, for instance—a secret Asian rocket base might have been a lot of fun.

But this was not military. This was an entire new means of industrial production. Pete knew with instinctive street-level certainty that tech of this level of revolutionary weirdness was not a spy thing, a sports thing, or a soldier thing. This was a big, big money thing. He might survive discovering it. He'd never get away with revealing it.

The thrilling wonder of it all really bugged him. Thrilling wonder was at best a passing thing. The sober implications for the longer term weighed on Pete's soul like a damp towel. He could imagine escaping this place in one piece, but he couldn't imagine any plausible aftermath for handing over nifty photographs of thrilling wonder to military spooks on the Potomac. He couldn't imagine what the powers-that-were would do with that knowledge. He rather dreaded what they would do to him for giving it to them.

Pete wiped a sauna cascade of sweat from his neck.

"So I figure it's either geothermal power, or a fusion generator down there," said Katrinko.

"I'd be betting thermonuclear, given the circumstances." The rocks below their busy cleats were a-skitter with bugs: gippers and ghents and kebbits, dismantlers and glue-spreaders and brain-eating carrion disassemblers. They were profoundly dumb little devices, specialized as centipedes. They didn't seem very aggressive, but it surely would be a lethal mistake to sit down among them.

A barnacle thing with an iris mouth and long whipping eyes took a careful taste of Katrinko's boot. She retreated to a crag with a yelp.

"Wear your mask," Pete chided. The damp heat was bliss after the skin-eating chill of the Taklamakan, but most of the vents and cracks were spewing thick smells of hot beef stew and burnt rubber, all varieties of eldritch mechano-metabolic byproduct. His lungs felt sore at the very thought of it.

Pete cast his foggy spex up the nearest of the carbon-fiber columns, and the golden, glowing, impossibly tempting lights of those starship portholes up above.

▲ ▼ ▲

Katrinko led point. She was pitilessly exposed against the lacelike girders. They didn't want to risk exposure during two trips, so they each carried a haul bag.

The climb went well at first. Then a machine rose up from wet darkness like a six-winged dragonfly. Its stinging tail lashed through the thready column like the kick of a mule. It connected brutally. Katrinko shot backwards from the impact, tumbled ten meters, and dangled like a ragdoll from her last backup chock.

The flying creature circled in a figure eight, attempting to make up its nonexistent mind. Then a slower but much larger creature writhed and fluttered out of the starry sky, and attacked Katrinko's dangling haulbag. The bag burst like a Christmas piñata in a churning array of taloned wings. A fabulous cascade of expensive spy gear splashed down to the hot pools below.

Katrinko twitched feebly at the end of her rope. The dragonfly, cruelly alerted, went for her movement. Pete launched a string of flashbangs.

The world erupted in flash, heat, concussion, and flying chaff. Impossibly hot and loud, a thunderstorm in a closet. The best kind of disappearance magic: total overwhelming distraction, the only real magic in the world.

Pete soared up to Katrinko like a balloon on a bungee-cord. When he reached the bottom of the starship, twenty-seven heart-pounding seconds later, he had burned out both the smart-ropes.

The silvery rain of chaff was driving the bugs to mania. The bottom of the cavern was suddenly a-crawl with leaping mechanical heat-ghosts, an instant menagerie of skippers and humpers and floppers. At the rim of perception, there were new things rising from the depths of the pools, vast and scaly, like golden carp to a rain of fish chow.

Pete's own haulbag had been abandoned at the base of the column. That bag was clearly not long for this world.

Katrinko came to with a sudden winded gasp. They began free-climbing the outside of the starship. It surface was stony, rough and uneven, something like pumice, or wasp spit.

They found the underside of a monster porthole and pressed themselves flat against the surface.

There they waited, inert and unmoving, for an hour. Katrinko caught her breath. Her ribs stopped bleeding. The two of them waited for another hour, while crawling and flying heat-ghosts nosed furiously around their little world, following the tatters of their programming. They waited a third hour.

Finally they were joined in their haven by an oblivious gang of machines with suckery skirts and wheelbarrows for heads. The robots chose a declivity and began filling it with big mandible trowels of stony mortar, slopping it on and jaw-chiseling it into place, smoothing everything over, tireless and pitiless.

Pete seized this opportunity to attempt to salvage their lost equipment. There had been such fabulous federal bounty in there: smart audio bugs, heavy-duty gelcams, sensors and detectors, pulleys, crampons and latches, priceless vials of programmed neural goo.... Pete crept back to the bottom of the spacecraft.

Everything was long gone. Even the depleted smartropes had been eaten, by a long trail of foraging keets. The little machines were still squirreling about in the black lace of the column, sniffing and scraping at the last molecular traces, with every appearance of satisfaction.

Pete rejoined Katrinko, and woke her where she clung rigid and stupefied to her hiding spot. They inched their way around the curved rim of the starship hull, hunting for a possible weakness. They were in very deep trouble now, for their best equipment was gone. It didn't matter. Their course was very obvious now, and the loss of alternatives had clarified Pete's mind. He was consumed with a burning desire to break in.

Pete slithered into the faint shelter of a large, deeply pitted hump. There he discovered a mess of braided rope. The rope was woven of dead and mashed organic fibers, something like the hair at the bottom of a sink. The rope had gone all petrified under a stony lacquer of robot spit.

These were climber's ropes. Someone had broken out here—smashed through the hull of the ship, from the inside. The robots had come to repair the damage, carefully re-sealing the exit hole, and leaving this ugly hump of stony scar tissue.

Pete pulled his gelcam drill. He had lost the sugar reserves along with the haulbags. Without sugar to metabolize, the little enzyme-driven rotor would starve and be useless soon. That fact could not be helped. Pete pressed the device against the hull, waited as it punched its way through, and squirted in a gelcam to follow.

He saw a farm. Pete could scarcely have been more astonished. It was certainly farmland, though. Cute, toy farmland, all under a stony blue ceiling, crisscrossed with hot grids of radiant light, embraced in the stony arch of the enclosing hull. There were fishponds with reeds. Ditches, and a wooden irrigation wheel. A little bridge of bamboo. There were hairy melon vines in rich black soil and neat, entirely weedless fields of dwarfed red grain. Not a soul in sight.

Katrinko crept up and linked in on cable. "So where is everybody?" Pete said.

"They're all at the portholes," said Katrinko, coughing.

"What?" said Pete, surprised. "Why?"

"Because of those flashbangs," Katrinko wheezed. Her battered ribs were still paining her. "They're all at the portholes, looking out into the darkness. Waiting for something else to happen."

"But we did that stuff hours ago."

"It was very big news, man. Nothing ever happens in there."

Pete nodded, fired with resolve. "Well then. We're breakin' in."

Katrinko was way game. "Gonna use caps?"

"Too obvious."

"Acids and fibrillators?"

"Lost 'em in the haulbags."

"Well, that leaves cheesewires," Katrinko concluded. "I got two."

"I got six."

Katrinko nodded in delight. "Six cheesewires! You're loaded for bear, man!"

"I love cheesewires," Pete grunted. He had helped to invent them.

Eight minutes and twelve seconds later they were inside the starship. They re-set the cored-out plug behind them, delicately gluing it in place and carefully obscuring the hair-thin cuts.

Katrinko sidestepped into a grove of bamboo. Her camou bloomed in green and tan and yellow, with such instant and treacherous ease that Pete lost her entirely. Then she waved, and the spex edge-detectors kicked in on her silhouette.

Pete lifted his spex for a human naked-eye take on the situation. There was simply nothing there at all. Katrinko was gone, less than a ghost, like pitchforking mercury with your eyelashes.

So they were safe now. They could glide through this bottled farm like a pair of bad dreams.

▲ ▼ ▲

They scanned the spacecraft from top to bottom, looking for dangerous and interesting phenomena. Control rooms manned by Asian space technicians maybe, or big lethal robots, or video monitors—something that might cramp their style or kill them. In the thirty-seven floors of the spacecraft, they found no such thing.

The five thousand inhabitants spent their waking hours farming. The crew of the starship were preindustrial, tribal, Asian peasants. Men, women, old folks, little kids.

The local peasants rose every single morning, as their hot networks of wiring came alive in the ceiling. They would milk their goats. They would feed their sheep, and some very odd, knee-high, dwarf Bactrian camels. They cut bamboo and netted their fishponds. They cut down tamarisks and poplar trees for firewood. They tended melon vines and grew plums and hemp. They brewed alcohol, and ground grain, and boiled millet, and squeezed cooking oil out of rapeseed. They made clothes out of hemp and raw wool and leather, and baskets out of reeds and straw. They ate a lot of carp.

And they raised a whole mess of chickens. Somebody not from around here had been fooling with the chickens. Apparently these were super space-chickens of some kind, leftover lab products from some serious long-term attempt to screw around with chicken DNA. The hens produced five or six lumpy eggs every day. The roosters were enormous, and all different colors, and very smelly, and distinctly reptilian.

It was very quiet and peaceful inside the starship. The animals made their lowing and clucking noises, and the farm workers sang to themselves in the tiny round-edged fields, and the incessant foot-driven water pumps would clack rhythmically, but there were no city noises. No engines anywhere. No screens. No media.

There was no money. There were a bunch of tribal elders who sat under the blossoming plum trees outside the big stone granaries. They messed with beads on wires, and wrote notes on slips of wood. Then the soldiers, or the cops—they were a bunch of kids in crude leather armor, with spears—would tramp in groups, up and down the dozens of stairs, on the dozens of floors. Marching like crazy, and requisitioning stuff, and carrying stuff on their backs, and handing things out to people. Basically spreading the wealth around.

Most of the weird bearded old guys were palace accountants, but there were some others, too. They sat cross-legged on mats in their homemade robes, and straw sandals, and their little spangly hats, discussing important matters at slow and extreme length. Sometimes they wrote stuff down on palm-leaves.

Pete and Katrinko spent a special effort to spy on these old men in the spangled hats, because, after close study, they had concluded that this was the local government. They pretty much had to be the government. These old men with the starry hats were the only part of the population who weren't being worked to a frazzle.

Pete and Katrinko found themselves a cozy spot on the roof of the granary, one of the few permanent structures inside the spacecraft. It never rained inside the starship, so there wasn't much call for roofs. Nobody ever trespassed up on the roof of the granary. It was clear that the very idea of doing this was beyond local imagination. So Pete and Katrinko stole some bamboo water jugs, and some lovely handmade carpets, and a lean-to tent, and set up camp there.

Katrinko studied an especially elaborate palm-leaf book that she had filched from the local temple. There were pages and pages of dense alien script. "Man, what do you suppose these yokels have to write about?"

"The way I figure it," said Pete, "they're writing down everything they can remember from the world outside."

"Yeah?"

"Yeah. Kinda building up an intelligence dossier for their little starship regime, see? Because that's all they'll ever know, because the people who put them inside here aren't giving 'em any news. And they're sure as hell never gonna let 'em out."

Katrinko leafed carefully through the stiff and brittle pages of the handmade book. The people here spoke only one language. It was no language Pete or Katrinko could even begin to recognize. "Then this is their history. Right?"

"It's their lives, kid. Their past lives, back when they were still real people, in the big real world outside. Transistor radios, and shoulder-launched rockets. Barbed-wire, pacification campaigns, ID cards. Camel caravans coming in over the border, with mortars and explosives. And very advanced Sphere mandarin bosses, who just don't have the time to put up with armed, Asian, tribal fanatics."

Katrinko looked up. "That kinda sounds like *your* version of the outside world, Pete."

Pete shrugged. "Hey, it's what happens."

"You suppose these guys really believe they're inside a real starship?"

"I guess that depends on how much they learned from the guys who broke out of here with the picks and the ropes."

Katrinko thought about it. "You know what's truly pathetic? The shabby illusion of all this. Some spook mandarin's crazy notion that ethnic separatists could be squeezed down tight, and spat out like watermelon seeds into interstellar space.... Man, what a *come-on*, what an enticement, what an empty promise!"

"I could sell that idea," Pete said thoughtfully. "You know how *far away* the stars really are, kid? About *four hundred years* away, that's how far. You seriously want to get human beings to travel to another star, you gotta put human beings inside of a sealed can for four hundred solid years. But what are people supposed to do in there, all that time? The only thing they can do is quietly run a farm. Because that's what a starship is. It's a desert oasis."

"So you want to try a dry-run starship experiment," said Katrinko. "And in the meantime, you happen to have some handy religious fanatics in the backwoods of Asia, who are shooting your ass off. Guys who refuse to change their age-old lives, even though you are very, very high-tech."

"Yep. That's about the size of it. Means, motive, and opportunity."

"I get it. But I can't believe that somebody went through with that scheme in real life. I mean, rounding up an ethnic minority, and sticking them down in some godforsaken hole, just so you'll never have to think about them again. That's just impossible!"

"Did I ever tell you that my grandfather was a Seminole?" Pete said.

Katrinko shook her head. "What's that mean?"

"They were American tribal guys who ended up stuck in a swamp. The Florida Seminoles, they called 'em. Y'know, maybe they just *called* my grandfather a Seminole. He dressed really funny.... Maybe it just *sounded good* to call him a Seminole. Otherwise, he just would have been some strange, illiterate geezer."

Katrinko's brow wrinkled. "Does it *matter* that your grandfather was a Seminole?"

"I used to think it did. That's where I got my skin color—as if that matters, nowadays. I reckon it mattered plenty to my grandfather, though.... He was always stompin' and carryin' on about a lot of weird stuff we couldn't understand. His English was pretty bad. He was never around much when we needed him."

"Pete...." Katrinko sighed. "I think it's time we got out of this place."

"How come?" Pete said, surprised. "We're safe up here. The locals are not gonna hurt us. They can't even see us. They can't touch us. Hell, they can't even *imagine* us. With our fantastic tactical advantages, we're just like gods to these people."

"I know all that, man. They're like the ultimate dumb straight people. I don't like them very much. They're not much of a challenge to us. In fact, they kind of creep me out."

"No way! They're fascinating. Those baggy clothes, the acoustic songs, all that menial labor.... These people got something that we modern people just don't have any more."

"Huh?" Katrinko said. "Like *what*, exactly?"

"I dunno," Pete admitted.

"Well, whatever it is, it can't be very important." Katrinko sighed. "We got some serious challenges on the agenda, man. We gotta sidestep our way past all those angry robots outside, then head up that shaft, then hoof it back, four days through a freezing desert, with no haulbags. All the way back to the glider."

"But Trink, there are two other starships in here that we didn't break into yet. Don't you want to see those guys?"

"What I'd like to see right now is a hot bath in a four-star hotel," said Katrinko. "And some very big international headlines, maybe. All about *me*. That would be lovely." She grinned.

"But what about the people?"

"Look, I'm not 'people,'" Katrinko said calmly. "Maybe it's because I'm a neuter, Pete, but I can tell you're way off the subject. These people are none of our business. Our business now is to return to our glider in an operational condition, so that we can complete our assigned mission, and return to base with our data. Okay?"

"Well, let's break into just one more starship first."

"We gotta move, Pete. We've lost our best equipment, and we're running low on body fat. This isn't something that we can kid about and live."

"But we'll never come back here again. Somebody will, but it sure as heck won't be *us*. See, it's a Spider thing."

Katrinko was weakening. "One more starship? Not both of 'em?"

"Just one more."

"Okay, good deal."

▲ ▼ ▲

The hole they had cut through the starship's hull had been rapidly cemented by robots. It cost them two more cheesewires to cut themselves a new exit. Then Katrinko led point, up across the stony ceiling, and down the carbon column to the second ship. To avoid annoying the lurking robot guards, they moved with hypnotic slowness and excessive stealth. This made it a grueling trip.

This second ship had seen hard use. The hull was extensively scarred with great wads of cement, entombing many lengths of dried and knotted rope. Pete and Katrinko found a weak spot and cut their way in.

This starship was crowded. It was loud inside, and it smelled. The floors were crammed with hot and sticky little bazaars, where people sold handicrafts and liquor and food. Criminals were being punished by being publicly chained to posts and pelted with offal by passers-by. Big crowds of ragged men and tattooed women gathered around brutal cockfights, featuring spurred mutant chickens half the size of dogs. All the men carried knives.

The architecture here was more elaborate, all kinds of warrens, and courtyards, and damp, sticky alleys. After exploring four floors, Katrinko suddenly declared that she recognized their surroundings. According to Katrinko, they were a physical replica of sets from a popular Japanese interactive samurai epic. Apparently the starship's designers had needed some pre-industrial Asian village settings, and they hadn't wanted to take the expense and trouble to design them from scratch. So they had programmed their construction robots with pirated game designs.

This starship had once been lavishly equipped with at least three hundred armed video camera installations. Apparently, the mandarins had come to the stunning realization that the mere fact that they were recording crime didn't mean that they could control it. Their spy cameras were all dead now. Most had been vandalized. Some had gone down fighting. They were all inert and abandoned.

The rebellious locals had been very busy. After defeating the spy cameras, they had created a set of giant hullbreakers. These were siege engines, big crossbow torsion machines, made of hemp and wood and bamboo. The hullbreakers were starship community efforts, elaborately painted and ribboned, and presided over by tough, aggressive gang bosses with batons and big leather belts.

Pete and Katrinko watched a labor gang, hard at work on one of the hullbreakers. Women braided rope ladders from hair and vegetable fiber, while smiths forged pitons over choking, hazy charcoal fires. It was clear from the evidence that these restive locals had broken out of their starship jail at least twenty times. Every time they had been corralled back in by the relentless efforts of mindless machines. Now they were busily preparing yet another breakout.

"These guys sure have got initiative," said Pete admiringly. "Let's do 'em a little favor, okay?"

"Yeah?"

"Here they are, taking all this trouble to hammer their way out. But we still have a bunch of caps. We got no more use for 'em, after we leave this place. So the way I figure it, we blow their wall out big-time, and let a whole bunch of 'em loose at once. Then you and I can escape real easy in the confusion."

Katrinko loved this idea, but had to play devil's advocate. "You really think we ought to interfere like that? That kind of shows our hand, doesn't it?"

"Nobody's watching any more," said Pete. "Some technocrat figured this for a big lab experiment. But they wrote these people off, or maybe they lost their anthropology grant. These people are totally forgotten. Let's give the poor bastards a show."

Pete and Katrinko planted their explosives, took cover on the ceiling, and cheerfully watched the wall blow out.

A violent gust of air came through as pressures equalized, carrying a hemorrhage of dust and leaves into interstellar space. The locals were totally astounded by the explosion, but when the repair robots showed up, they soon recovered their morale. A terrific battle broke out, a general vengeful frenzy of crab-bashing and sponge-skewering. Women and children tussled with the keets and bibbets. Soldiers in leather cuirasses fought with the bigger machines, deploying pikes, crossbow quarrels, and big robot-mashing mauls.

The robots were profoundly stupid, but they were indifferent to their casualties, and entirely relentless.

The locals made the most of their window of opportunity. They loaded a massive harpoon into a torsion catapult, and fired it into space. Their target was the neighboring starship, the third and last of them.

The barbed spear bounded off the hull. So they reeled it back in on a monster bamboo hand-reel, cursing and shouting like maniacs.

The starship's entire population poured into the fight. The walls and bulkheads shook with the tramp of their angry feet. The outnumbered robots fell back. Pete and Katrinko seized this golden opportunity to slip out the hole. They climbed swiftly up the hull, and out of reach of the combat.

The locals fired their big harpoon again. This time the barbed tip struck true, and it stuck there quivering.

Then a little kid was heaved into place, half-naked, with a hammer and screws, and a rope threaded through his belt. He had a crown of dripping candles set upon his head.

Katrinko glanced back, and stopped dead.

Pete urged her on, then stopped as well.

The child began reeling himself industriously along the trembling harpoon line, trailing a bigger rope. An airborne machine came to menace him. It fell back twitching, pestered by a nasty scattering of crossbow bolts.

Pete found himself mesmerized. He hadn't felt the desperation of the circumstances, until he saw this brave little boy ready to fall to his death. Pete had seen many climbers who took risks because they were crazy. He'd seen professional climbers, such as himself, who played games with risk as masters of applied technique. He'd never witnessed climbing as an act of raw, desperate sacrifice.

The heroic child arrived on the grainy hull of the alien ship, and began banging his pitons in a hammer-swinging frenzy. His crown of candles shook and flickered with his efforts. The boy could barely see. He had slung himself out into stygian darkness to fall to his doom.

Pete climbed up to Katrinko and quickly linked in on cable. "We gotta leave now, kid. It's now or never."

"Not yet," Katrinko said. "I'm taping all this."

"It's our big chance."

"We'll go later." Katrinko watched a flying vacuum cleaner batting by, to swat cruelly at the kid's legs. She turned her masked head to Pete and her whole body stiffened with rage. "You got a cheesewire left?"

"I got three."

"Gimme. I gotta go help him."

▲ ▼ ▲

Katrinko unplugged, slicked down the starship's wall in a daring controlled slide, and hit the stretched rope. To Pete's complete astonishment, Katrinko lit there in a crouch, caught herself atop the vibrating line, and simply ran for it. She ran along the humming tightrope in a thrumming blur, stunning the locals so thoroughly that they were barely able to fire their crossbows.

Flying quarrels whizzed past and around her, nearly skewering the terrified child at the far end of the rope. Then Katrinko leapt and bounded into space, her gloves and cleats outspread. She simply vanished.

It was a champion's gambit if Pete had ever seen one. It was a legendary move.

Pete could manage well enough on a tightrope. He had experience, excellent balance, and physical acumen. He was, after all, a professional. He could walk a rope if he was put to the job.

But not in full climbing gear, with cleats. And not on a slack, hand-braided, homemade rope. Not when the rope was very poorly anchored by a homemade pig-iron harpoon. Not when he outweighed Katrinko by twenty kilos. Not in the middle of a flying circus of airborne robots. And not in a cloud of arrows.

Pete was simply not that crazy any more. Instead, he would have to follow Katrinko the sensible way. He would have to climb the starship, traverse the ceiling, and climb down to the third starship onto the far side. A hard three hours' work at the very best—four hours, with any modicum of safety.

Pete weighed the odds, made up his mind, and went after the job.

Pete turned in time to see Katrinko busily cheesewiring her way through the hull of Starship Three. A gout of white light poured out as the cored plug slid aside. For a deadly moment, Katrinko was a silhouetted goblin, her camou useless as the starship's radiance framed her. Her clothing fluttered in a violent gust of escaping air.

Below her, the climbing child had anchored himself to the wall and tied off his second rope. He looked up at the sudden gout of light, and he screamed so loudly that the whole universe rang.

The child's many relatives reacted by instinct, with a ragged volley of crossbow shots. The arrows veered and scattered in the gusting wind, but there were a lot of them. Katrinko ducked, and flinched, and rolled headlong into the starship. She vanished again.

Had she been hit? Pete set an anchor, tied off, and tried the radio. But without the relays in the haulbag, the weak signal could not get through.

Pete climbed on doggedly. It was the only option left.

After half an hour, Pete began coughing. The starry cosmic cavity had filled with a terrible smell. The stench was coming from the invaded starship, pouring slowly from the cored-out hole. A long-bottled, deadly stink of burning rot.

Climbing solo, Pete gave it his best. His shoulder was bad and, worse yet, his spex began to misbehave. He finally reached the cored-out entrance that Katrinko had cut. The locals were already there in force, stringing themselves a sturdy rope bridge, and attaching it to massive screws. The locals brandished torches, spears, and crossbows. They were fighting off the incessant attacks of the robots. It was clear from their wild expressions of savage glee that they had been longing for this moment for years.

Pete slipped past them unnoticed, into Starship Three. He breathed the soured air for a moment, and quickly retreated again. He inserted a new set of mask filters, and returned.

He found Katrinko's cooling body, wedged against the ceiling. An unlucky crossbow shot had slashed through her suit and punctured Katrinko's left arm. So, with her usual presence of mind, she had deftly leapt up a nearby wall, tied off on a chock, and hidden herself well out of harm's way. She'd quickly stopped the bleeding. Despite its awkward location, she'd even managed to get her wound bandaged.

Then the foul air had silently and stealthily overcome her.

With her battered ribs and a major wound, Katrinko hadn't been able to tell her dizziness from shock. Feeling sick, she had relaxed, and tried to catch her breath. A fatal gambit. She was still hanging there, unseen and invisible, dead.

Pete discovered that Katrinko was far from alone. The crew here had all died. Died months ago, maybe years ago. Some kind of huge fire inside the spacecraft. The electric lights were still on, the internal machinery worked, but there was no one left here but mummies.

These dead tribal people had the nicest clothes Pete had yet seen. Clearly they'd spent a lot of time knitting and embroidering, during the many weary years of their imprisonment. The corpses had all kinds of layered sleeves, and tatted aprons, and braided belt-ties, and lacquered hairclips, and excessively nifty little sandals. They'd all smothered horribly during the sullen inferno, along with their cats and dogs and enormous chickens, in a sudden wave of smoke and combustion that had filled their spacecraft in minutes.

This was far too complicated to be anything as simple as mere genocide. Pete figured the mandarins for gentlemen technocrats, experts with the best of intentions. The lively possibility remained that it was mass suicide. But on mature consideration, Pete had to figure this for a very bad, and very embarrassing, social-engineering accident.

Though that certainly wasn't what they would say about this mess, in Washington. There was no political mess nastier than a nasty ethnic mess. Pete couldn't help but notice that these well-behaved locals hadn't bothered to do any harm to their spacecraft's lavish surveillance equipment. But their cameras were off and their starship was stone dead anyway.

The air began to clear inside the spacecraft. A pair of soldiers from Starship Number Two came stamping down the hall, industriously looting the local corpses. They couldn't have been happier about their opportunity. They were grinning with awestruck delight.

Pete returned to his comrade's stricken body. He stripped the camou suit—he needed the batteries. The neuter's lean and sexless corpse was puffy with subcutaneous storage pockets, big encystments of skin where Katrinko stored her last-ditch escape tools. The battered ribs were puffy and blue. Pete could not go on.

Pete returned to the break-in hole, where he found an eager crowd. The invaders had run along the rope-bridge and gathered there in force, wrinkling their noses and cheering in wild exaltation. They had beaten the robots; there simply weren't enough of the machines on duty to resist a whole enraged population. The robots just weren't clever enough to out-think armed, coordinated human resistance—not without killing people wholesale, and they hadn't been designed for that. They had suffered a flat-out defeat.

Pete frightened the cheering victors away with a string of flash-bangs.

Then he took careful aim at the lip of the drop, and hoisted Katrinko's body, and flung her far, far, tumbling down, into the boiling pools.

▲ ▼ ▲

Pete retreated to the first spacecraft. It was a very dispiriting climb, and when he had completed it, his shoulder had the serious, familiar ache of chronic injury. He hid among the unknowing population while he contemplated his options.

He could hide here indefinitely. His camou suit was slowly losing its charge, but he felt confident that he could manage very well without the suit. The starship seemed to feature most any number of taboo areas. Blocked-off no-go spots, where there might have been a scandal once, or bloodshed, or a funny noise, or a strange, bad, panicky smell.

Unlike the violent, reckless crowd in Starship Two, these locals had fallen for the cover story. They truly believed that they were in the depths of space, bound for some better, brighter pie in their starry stone sky. Their little stellar ghetto was full of superstitious kinks. Steeped in profound ignorance, the locals imagined that their every sin caused the universe to tremble.

Pete knew that he should try to take his data back to the glider. This was what Katrinko would have wanted. To die, but leave a legend—a very City Spider thing.

But it was hard to imagine battling his way past resurgent robots, climbing the walls with an injured shoulder, then making a four-day bitter trek through a freezing desert, all completely alone. Gliders didn't last forever, either. Spy gliders weren't built to last. If Pete found the glider with its batteries flat, or its cute little brain gone sour, Pete would be all over. Even if he'd enjoyed a full set of equipment, with perfect health, Pete had few illusions about a solo spring outing, alone and on foot, over the Himalayas.

Why risk all that? After all, it wasn't like this subterranean scene was breaking news. It was already many years old. Someone had conceived, planned and executed this business a long time ago. Important people with brains and big resources had known all about this for years. Somebody knew. Maybe not the Lieutenant Colonel, on the lunatic fringe of NAFTA military intelligence. But...

When Pete really thought about the basic implications.... This was a great deal of effort, and for not that big a payoff. Because there just weren't that many people cooped up down here. Maybe fifteen thousand of them, tops. The Asian Sphere must have had tens of thousands of unassimilated tribal people, maybe hundreds of thousands. Possibly millions. And why stop at that point? This wasn't just an Asian problem. It was a very general problem. Ethnic, breakaway people, who just plain couldn't, or wouldn't, play the twenty-first century's games.

How many Red Chinese atom-bomb tests had taken place deep in the Taklamakan? They'd never bothered to brief him on ancient history. But Pete had to wonder if, by now, maybe they hadn't gotten this stellar concept down to a fine art. Maybe the Sphere had franchised their plan to Europe and NAFTA. How many forgotten holes were there, relic pockets punched below the hide of the twenty-first century, in the South Pacific, and Australia, and Nevada? The deadly trash of a long-derailed Armageddon. The sullen trash-heaps where no one would ever want to look.

Sure, he could bend every nerve and muscle to force the world to face all this. But why? Wouldn't it make better sense to try to think it through first?

Pete never got around to admitting to himself that he had lost the will to leave.

▲ ▼ ▲

As despair slowly loosened his grip on him, Pete grew genuinely interested in the locals. He was intrigued by the stark limits of their lives and their universe, and in what he could do with their narrow little heads. They'd never had a supernatural being in their midst before; they just imagined them all the time. Pete started with a few poltergeist stunts, just to amuse himself. Stealing the spangled hats of the local greybeards. Shuffling the palm leaf volumes in their sacred libraries. Hijacking an abacus or two.

But that was childish.

The locals had a little temple, their special holy of holies. Naturally Pete made it his business to invade the place.

The locals kept a girl locked up in there. She was very pretty, and slightly insane, so this made her the perfect candidate to become their Sacred Temple Girl. She was the Official Temple Priestess of Starship Number One. Apparently, their modest community could only afford one, single, awe-inspiring Virgin High Priestess. But they were practical folks, so they did the best with what they had available.

The High Priestess was a pretty young woman with a stiflingly pretty life. She had her own maidservants, a wardrobe of ritual clothing, and a very time-consuming hairdo. The High Priestess spent her entire life carrying out highly complex, totally useless, ritual actions. Incense burnings, idol dustings, washings and purifications, forehead knockings, endless chanting, daubing special marks on her hands and feet. She was sacred and clearly demented, so they watched her with enormous interest, all the time. She meant everything to them. She was doing all these crazy, painful things so the rest of them wouldn't have to. Everything about her was completely and utterly foreclosed.

Pete quite admired the Sacred Temple Girl. She was very much his type, and he felt a genuine kinship with her. She was the only local that Pete could bear to spend any personal time with.

So after prolonged study of the girl and her actions, one day, Pete manifested himself to her. First, she panicked. Then she tried to kill him. Naturally that effort failed. When she grasped the fact that he was hugely powerful, totally magical, and utterly beyond her ken, she slithered around the polished temple floor, rending her garments and keening aloud, clearly in the combined hope/fear of being horribly and indescribably defiled.

Pete understood the appeal of her concept. A younger Pete would have gone for the demonic subjugation option. But Pete was all grown up now. He hardly saw how that could help matters any, or, in fact, make any tangible difference in their circumstances.

They never learned each other's languages. They never connected in any physical, mental, or emotional way. But they finally achieved a kind of status quo, where they could sit together in the same room, and quietly study one another, and fruitlessly speculate on the alien contents of one another's heads. Sometimes, they would even get together and eat something tasty.

That was every bit as good as his connection with these impossibly distant people was ever going to get.

▲ ▼ ▲

It had never occurred to Pete that the stars might go out.

He'd cut himself a sacred, demonic bolt-hole, in a taboo area of the starship. Every once in a while, he would saw his way through the robots' repair efforts and nick out for a good long look at the artificial cosmos. This reassured him, somehow. And he had other motives as well. He had a very well-founded concern that the inhabitants of Starship Two might somehow forge their way over, for an violent racist orgy of looting, slaughter, and rapine.

But Starship Two had their hands full with the robots. Any defeat of the bubbling gelbrain and its hallucinatory tools could only be temporary. Like an onrushing mudslide, the gizmos would route around obstructions, infiltrate every evolutionary possibility, and always, always keep the pressure on.

After the crushing defeat, the bubbling production vats went into biomechanical overdrive. The old regime had been overthrown. All equilibrium was gone. The machines had gone back to their cybernetic dreamtime. Anything was possible now.

The starry walls grew thick as fleas with a seething mass of new-model jailers. Starship Two was beaten back once again, in another bitter, uncounted, historical humiliation. Their persecuted homeland became a mass of grotesque cement. Even the portholes were gone now, cruelly sealed in technological spit and ooze. A living grave.

Pete had assumed that this would pretty much finish the job. After all, this clearly fit the parameters of the system's original designers.

But the system could no longer bother with the limits of human intent.

When Pete gazed through a porthole and saw that the stars were fading, he knew that all bets were off. The stars were being robbed. Something was embezzling their energy.

He left the starship. Outside, all heaven had broken loose. An unspeakable host of creatures were migrating up the rocky walls, bounding, creeping, lurching, rappelling on a web of gooey ropes. Heading for the stellar zenith.

Bound for transcendence. Bound for escape.

Pete checked his aging cleats and gloves, and joined the exodus at once.

None of the creatures bothered him. He had become one of them now. His equipment had fallen among them, been absorbed, and kicked open new doors of evolution. Anything that could breed a can-opener could breed a rock chock and a piton, a crampon, and a pulley, and a carabiner. His haul bags, Katrinko's bags, had been stuffed with generations of focused human genius, and it was all about one concept: UP. Going up. Up and *out*.

▲ ▼ ▲

The unearthly landscape of the Taklamakan was hosting a robot war. A spreading mechanical prairie of inching, crawling, biting, wrenching, hopping mutations. And pillars of fire: Sphere satellite warfare. Beams pouring down from the authentic heavens, invisible torrents of energy that threw up geysers of searing dust. A bio-engineer's final nightmare. Smart, autonomous hell. They couldn't kill a thing this big and keep it secret. They couldn't burn it up fast enough. No, not without breaking the containment domes, and spilling their own ancient trash across the face of the earth.

A beam crossed the horizon like the finger of God, smiting everything in its path. The sky and earth were thick with flying creatures, buzzing, tumbling, sculling. The beam caught a big machine, and it fell spinning like a multi-ton maple seed. It bounded from the side of a containment dome, caromed like a dying gymnast, and landed below Spider Pete. He crouched there in his camou, recording it all.

It looked back at him. This was no mere robot. It was a mechanical civilian journalist. A brightly painted, ultramodern, European network drone, with as many cameras on board as a top-flight media mogul had martinis. The machine had smashed violently against the secret wall, but it was not dead. Death was not on its agenda. It was way game. It had spotted him with no trouble at all. He was a human interest story. It was looking at him.

Glancing into the cold spring sky, Pete could see that the journalist had brought a lot of its friends.

The robot rallied its fried circuits, and centered him within a spiraling focus. Then it lifted a multipronged limb, and ceremonially spat out every marvel it had witnessed, up into the sky and out into the seething depths of the global web.

Pete adjusted his mask and his camou suit. He wouldn't look right, otherwise.

"Dang," he said.

PART V:

LATER SCIENCE FICTION AND FANTASY

The Sword of Damocles

"The Sword of Damocles" is an ancient Greek story with the deeply satisfying structure of classical legend. It's chock-full of eternal human truths, which, believe-you-me, still have plenty of meaning and relevance, even for our so-called-sophisticated, postmodern generation.

I've been looking the story over lately, and the material is great. It's just a question of filing off a few serial numbers, and bringing it up-to-date. So here we go.

Once upon a time, there was a man named Damocles, a minor courtier at the palace of Dionysius, Tyrant of Syracuse. Damocles was unhappy with his role, and he envied the splendor of the Tyrant.

Actually the term "Tyrant" is a bit misleading here, because it didn't mean at the time what it means today. All "tyrant" really meant was that Dionysius (405 BC-367 BC) had seized the government by force, rather than coming to power legitimately. It doesn't necessarily mean that Dionysius was an evil thug. After all, it's results that count, and sometimes one has to bend the rules a bit, just to get things started.

Take this "Once upon a time" business I just used, for instance. It starts the story all right, but it doesn't sound very Greek, when you come right down to it. It's more of a Grimm Brothers fairy-tale riff, kind of a kunstmarchen thing. Using it with a Greek myth is like putting a peaked Gothic spire on a Greek temple. Some people—Modernist critics—might say it's a bad move aesthetically, and kind of bastardizes the whole artistic effort!

Of course, real hifalutin Modernist critics must have a pretty hard time of it lately. They must find life a trial. I bet they don't watch much MTV. Modernists like coherent, systematic structures, but it's all hybridized by now. Especially in the places that are really moving, like Tokyo. Postmodern Japan is like a giant Shinto temple with smokestacks. Culturally speaking, the whole place is a chimera, but people don't criticize Japan's set-up much, because capitalistically speaking they're kicking everybody's ass. Whatever works, man.

You know—this is amazing, but I swear it's true—there are people nowadays who literally live in Tokyo "once upon a time." They're bankers and stockbrokers from New York and London, and they moved to Tokyo as expatriates, because they had to settle the Tokyo timezone. It's a fact! Postmodern bankers have to do twenty-four-hour trading, and the stock market closes in New York hours before it opens in London. So nowadays all the big financial operators send people out to major markets all around the world, to colonize Time. "Time" is just another postmodern commodity now.

So that kind of blows my opening sentence, but the important thing is to get the story across. Simply, directly, in an unpretentious, naturalistic fashion. So forget the Gothic fairy-tale riff. I'm just gonna tell it straight. The way I'd talk to close friends, in my own living room, here in Austin, Texas.

So y'all listen up. There was this dude named Damocles, see, and he used to hang out in this palace, in Sicily. Ancient Sicily. Damocles was Greek though, not Italian, because, y'see, way back then…This was before Rome got started, and the Greeks were really good sailors, so they got all these remote colonies started up…

Okay, never mind the historical analysis, y'all. It's kinda vital to the background, but I can't get it across in this casual hick tone of voice without making it sound really goofy. So let's stick to the drama, okay? The important plot-thing is that Damocles really envies his boss, this magnificent prince, Dionysius. So one day Damocles puts on his chiton—that's a kind of Greek tunic—and his buskins—those were tall sandals like you see in the opera, if you ever go to those, which I don't, personally. But you've probably seen them on public TV, right?

In fact, now that I mention it, since we're all here in my living room, why don't we just give this up, and watch some TV? I mean, forget this "oral storytelling tradition." When was the last time you listened to some pal of yours tell a story out loud? I don't mean lies about what he and his pals did last Friday, I mean a real myth-type story with a beginning, middle, and end. And a moral.

Let's face it, we don't really do that anymore. We postmoderns don't live in an oral storytelling culture. If we want a story we can all enjoy together, we can rent a goddamn video. *Near Dark* is pretty good. My treat.

So, yeah—if I'm gonna make this work, it's gonna have to be *literary*. It'll have to hit some kind of high archaic note. We'll have to really get into it—tell it, not like postmoderns, but just as the ancient Greeks would have told it. Simple, dignified, classical, and stately. Full of *gravitas,* and *hubris,* and similar impressive terms. We'll cast a magic net of words, something to take us across the centuries…back to the authentic, ancestral world of Western culture!

So let's envision it. We're in an olive grove together, on a hillside in ancient Athens. I'm the mythagogue, probably some blind or lame guy, kept alive for my storytelling skills. I may be a slave, like Aesop. I'm making up (or reciting from memory) these marvelous mythic tales that will last forever, but I'm no particular big deal, personally.

You, my audience, on the other hand, look really great. You're all young rambunctious aristocrats whose parents are paying for this. Your limbs are oiled, your hair is curled, and every one of you is a whiz at the discus and javelin. Some of you are naked, but nobody cares; even the snappiest dressers are essentially wearing tablecloths held together with big bronze pins.

Did I mention that you were all guys? Sorry, but yeah. Those of you who are young rambunctious women are, uhmmm…well, I'm afraid you're off weaving chitons in the darkest part of your house. You don't get to listen to mythagogues. It might give you ideas. In fact you don't get to leave the house at all. We guys will be back to see you, sometime after midnight. After we get drunk with Socrates. Then we'll have our jolly way with you.

And we'll probably get you pregnant. Decent contraception hasn't been invented yet. At least, not the nifty plastic-wrapped kinds people will use in the late twentieth century. That's one reason why Damocles has a very dear male friend called Pythias.

But wait a sec—since I'm an authentic Greek mythagogue, I have to call him "Phyntias." "Pythias" was called "Phyntias," originally. A medieval scribe made a mistake transcribing the story in the fourteenth century, and he's been "Pythias" ever since. There's even a high-minded twentieth-century club called "The Pythian Society," that's named after a misprint! What a joke on them, huh? Goes to show what can happen if a storyteller gets careless!

So anyway, Damocles and Pythias were two close friends who lived in the court of Dionysius. One day, Damocles offended the Tyrant, and was sentenced to death. Damocles begged a few days' mercy, to bid farewell to his family, who lived in another town.

But the cruel Dionysius refused him this mercy. At that point, the noble Pythias stepped forward. "I will stand in the place of my dear friend, Damocles," he declared, to the assembled court. "If he does not return in seven days, I will die in his place!"

The vindictive heart of Dionysius was touched by this strange offer. Curious to see the outcome, he granted the boon. The two friends embraced and wept, and Damocles left to carry the sad news to his family. Pythias, in his place, was clapped in a dungeon. Days passed, one by one.

Wait a minute. Damn! Did I say "Damocles"? I meant "Damon." It's "Damon and Pythias," not "Damocles." Hell, I always get those two confused.

Christ on a Harley, man! I was off to such a great start, too. I was really rolling there for a minute. Now look at me! I don't even have a character in my story. There's no real character here except *me,* the author.

I can't believe I got myself into this situation. I mean, that postmodernist lit-mag experimental stuff where authors use themselves as characters. That kind of crap really burns me up. I'm a sci-fi pop writer, myself. I write action-adventure stuff. Sure, it's weird, but it's not *structurally* weird; it's weird 'cause it's about weird *ideas,* like fractals and cranial jacks.

But now look at me. Not only am I a character in my own story, but my only real topic so far is "narrative structure." I can't stand it when postmodern critics talk about stories in terms like "narrative structure." These hard-hat deconstruction-workers harass stories as if they were gals passing by on the sidewalk. They yell out stuff that's not only obnoxious, but completely bizarre and impenetrable. It's like they yell: "Hey, check out the pelvic biomechanics on that babe! What a set of hypertrophied lactiferous tissues!"

I should have stuck to hard-SF, that's my real problem. It was clear from the beginning this was going to be one of those weird-ass historical-fantasy things. I'm not even the proper author to be a character in this story. What this story needs is a character like Tim Powers, author of *The Anubis Gates* and *On Stranger Tides*.

"Suddenly, Tim Powers appeared. He looked about himself alertly."

No, if I'm gonna do this at all, I'd better try it Powers-style.

"Suddenly, Tim Powers burst headlong into the story! His hair was on fire, and he was perched on a pair of stilts. Gnashing his teeth, he glared wildly from under layers of peeling clown-makeup and said:

"'What the heck kind of fictional set-up is this? There's nothing here but some kind of half-collapsed ancient Greek stage-set! I could do better research than this in my sleep! Anyway, I prefer Victoriana.'"

And then a voice emerged into the story from an area of narrative discourse that we can't even reach from here. It said, "-'-"Tim, what's going on in there?"-'-"

And Powers said: "I dunno, sweetheart, I was just sitting here at the word-processor, and—ow! Somebody set my hair on fire! Serena, get the shotgun!"

Aw, jeez!…uhm:

"Tim Powers quickly disappeared from the story. The makeup disappeared from his face, and he looked just like he always did. And his hair stopped burning. There was no real damage done to it. He went into the bathroom of his Santa Ana apartment, got a comb, and lent fresh meaning to his hair. Then he forgot he had even been involved in this story."

"'Don't bet on it, pal.'"

I swear it'll never happen again. Don't get mad! Lots of writers do it. Like the wife of Damocles, "Pandora." She's not the original Greek-legend Pandora, wife of Epimetheus. Pandora hasn't appeared in this story yet, but she's a really interesting character. She likes to make blunt declarations to the reader, from a really weird narrative stance. Stuff like:

"'Am I not the sister of Adolf Hitler and Anne Frank? Have I not eaten, drunk, and breathed poison all my life? Do you take me for an innocent, my colluding reader?'" That sort of thing.

"Pandora" is actually the thinly disguised author-character from Ursula K. Le Guin's experimental SF epic *Always Coming Home*! How "Pandora" got into this story I'm not really sure, I guess it's my mistake, but I'll fight any man who claims that *Always Coming Home* isn't "real SF"! Even if it's not really, exactly, a "book." For one thing, *Always Coming Home* has got an audiotape that comes with it, which puts a pretty severe dent in its narrative closure. I'd have liked to supply an audiotape with this story—maybe some Japanese pop music, or John Cage—but I was too cheap. Instead, I'll just play the *Always Coming Home* tape here in my office. I ordered it from a P.O. box in Oregon. It's got weird mellow chanting in made-up languages.

So much for Pandora. I was going to have a scene where Damocles wakes up in bed with Pandora, and she makes some biting remarks about having to weave the chitons and everything, but I guess you get the idea.

So here's Damocles quickly leaving his home and going straight to work. He's so eager to start the story that, not only does he jump right in with a Homeric "in medias res" routine, but he's willing to settle for a breathless present-tense. Damocles works as a minor palace official in the court of Dionysius. Actually he's a "flatterer," according to Cicero's *Tusculan Disputations*. He's not a bureaucrat, like a postmodern official. There's no bureaucracy in Syracuse, it's all done by a tiny group of elite families, who run everything. Syracuse is a pre-industrial city-state of maybe fifty thousand people. An independent city-state about the size of Oshkosh, Wisconsin.

Damocles earns his living by making up flattering things about people who can kill him out-of-hand. He's kind of a jackleg-poet crossed with a public-relations flack. He's done pretty well by it, considering his lowly birth. He gets to eat meat almost every week. For most other Greeks of the period, common folk, there are two kinds of dietary staple. The first is a kind of mush, and the second is a kind of mush.

Damocles, though, has pretty much reached the top of his career arc. Once the Tyrant has taken you into the palace and deigned to feed you, there's not a whole lot of room for further advancement. Everything else is pretty much determined by birth, or coup d'etat. Damocles doesn't have the birth, and if a coup d'etat came Damocles would probably get snuffed first thing for being a loudmouth intellectual.

Damocles could enlist in the army and join one of the incessant minor wars of Dionysius, but he'd probably get nicked in battle and die of infection or tetanus. There's a damn good chance he'd croak of dysentery without ever leaving the camp-tents. Homer's war-brags don't talk about sickness much, but it's there all right. There's even a killer plague of the period called "the sweats" which Thucydides talks about in his histories; it once killed off half of Athens. Nobody knows what kind of disease "the sweats" was or where it came from. We'd just better hope it never comes back.

So Damocles goes to the court, dressed in his second-best outfit, since the day doesn't augur much. Damon and Pythias are there; Damocles has known them since they were kids; he knows pretty much everybody who counts in Syracuse, since it's a small town. Ever since D&P won the favor of Dionysius, through this stunt they pulled by offering to die for each other, they've been big cheeses at the court. Damocles has had to make up a lot of flattering dithyrambs and iambics and anapests about them; he's just about run out of rhymes for "Phyntias" and wishes the guy would change his god-damn name.

Today though he finds to his surprise that there's a big celebration. Three of Dionysius's war-galleys are back from raiding the coast of Egypt, where they sank a few reed-boats and got some slaves and loot. It's a famous victory. There's lots of millet-beer and grapewine.

Damocles elbows his way through the revelers and helps himself. The wine quickly goes to his head. Nobody knows what "fermentation" is yet, so the quality of the wine varies a lot. Every once in a while it makes you puke on the spot, but sometimes it gets way up to four, five percent alcohol. This is prime stuff all the way from Greece, and it only tastes a little of the tar they use to seal the amphoras. Damocles gets totally plastered.

Dionysius is in one of his jolly moods. The kind where he thinks up in-genious psychological tortures for his hangers-on. He calls the drunken, tot-tering Damocles front-and-center to have him immortalize the glorious day in extemporaneous verse.

Damocles gives it his best shot. He picks up a goatskin tambourine and starts banging it against his hip so he can remember the proper meter. He spouts out a lot of the canned stuff from Homer, the cliched "epithets" you use when you can't think of anything original, like "So-and-so of the nod-ding plumed helmet," and "his armor rang about him as he fell," and even stuff that sounds vaguely comical nowadays, like "he bit the dust."

But he can see it's not working. He starts to get desperate. He starts babbling out whatever comes into his head. Free association, surrealism. We postmoderns are really into that kind of stuff since Max Ernst and Dada, but it doesn't cut much ice with ancient Dionysius.

So Damocles plays his last ace, and starts laying on the flattery with a trowel. What a lucky guy Dionysius is; how the Gods smile on him; how supreme the Tyrant's power is; how everybody wishes they were him.

"Oh really," interrupts Dionysius, with that awful smile of his. He gives some orders to his lithe teenage male wine-bearer and then beckons Damo-cles forward. "So you want to be the Tyrant, eh?"

"Yeah, sure, who wouldn't?" says Damocles.

"Fine," says Dionysius loudly. "You sit right here on my throne"—actually, it's a dining-couch—"and help yourself to this feast. You, the humble Damocles, can be Tyrant, just for today!" He takes the gold fillet from his head and places it on the sweating noggin of Damocles. "You can give the orders. See how much you enjoy it."

"Gosh, thanks!" says Damocles. "Hot dog!" The cup-bearer has mysteriously disappeared, but Damocles, who's somewhat partial to women, has one of the new Egyptian slave-girls do the honors for him. Soon he's eating chunks of roast boar, knocking back goblets of honey-mead, and making satirical wisecracks that have the whole court in stitches. There's a bit of nervousness in their laughter, but Damocles writes it off to the oddity of the situation.

Just to break the ice, he issues a few tentative Tyrannical orders. He forces some of the more elderly and dignified courtiers to imitate goats or donkeys. It's good clean fun.

Then Damocles spots a disquieting reflection in the polished bronze of his mead-cup. He looks up. The wine-bearer of Dionysius has shinnied high up into the palace rafters. He's got a sharp, heavy bronze sword, and he's tied it to the rafter with a single woolen thread. The sword is dangling, point-first, directly over the reclining torso of Damocles.

"What's the meaning of this?" Damocles says.

Dionysius, who has been watching and chuckling from the sidelines, steps forward. He crosses his arms, and strokes his royal beard. "This," he says, "is the true nature of political power. This is the daily terror that we Tyrants must live under, which you thoughtless subjects somehow fail to appreciate." He laughs deep in his kingly chest.

"I get it," Damocles says. "It's a metaphor. Kind of a koan."

"That's right," says Dionysius. "Now go on, Damocles, enjoy yourself. You won't be leaving that couch for some time."

"Good thing, I was just getting comfortable," says Damocles, and he pillows his head on an enormous bundle of two hundred pounds of primed TNT. He's been carrying this massive weight of explosive with him all the time, wired to his body in a kind of backpack

In fact, everybody in the palace has got a TNT bundle of their own, too. They just haven't really noticed it, until the situation was made metaphorically clear. Everybody in Syracuse has their own share of explosive. Every man, woman and child on the planet; even the innocent babes in their cradles. Everybody carries their share of the global megatonnage; they're never without it, even when they somehow manage to forget about it. They just lug it around, day in day out, because they have to; because it's the post-modern condition. The cost of it nearly bankrupts them and the weight wears calluses on their souls, but nobody dwells on the horror of it much. It's the only way to stay sane.

So, with a merry laugh, Damocles has two of the guards seize Dionysius. They demonstrate to him some of the unappreciated hazards of living like a peasant, instead of a king. They start by ripping out several of his teeth, without health insurance. Then they do some other things to him which are even funnier, and finally leave him penniless and ragged in the streets.

So much for the famous legend of "The Sword of Damocles." I hope you've enjoyed it. Damocles went on to live it up happily ever after, in his merry, pranksterish way, until he got gout, or cirrhosis, or a bad cocaine habit, or AIDS.

As for Dionysius, he retired to California, where he now lives. He often appears on talk-shows, and makes lucrative speaking-tours before Chambers of Commerce and political action committees. He is writing a set of memoirs defending his public-service record. He's looking for a movie-option, too. But it's okay—I don't think he'll get one.

Maneki Neko

"I can't go on," his brother said.

Tsuyoshi Shimizu looked thoughtfully into the screen of his pasokon. His older brother's face was shiny with sweat from a late-night drinking bout. "It's only a career," said Tsuyoshi, sitting up on his futon and adjusting his pyjamas. "You worry too much."

"All that overtime!" his brother whined. He was making the call from a bar somewhere in Shibuya. In the background, a middle-aged office lady was singing karaoke, badly. "And the examination hells. The internal proficiency tests. The manager cultivation programs.... I never have time to live!"

Tsuyoshi grunted sympathetically. He didn't like these late-night videophone calls, but he felt obliged to listen. His big brother had always been a decent sort, before he had gone through the elite courses at Waseda, joined a big corporation, and gotten professionally ambitious.

"My back hurts," his brother groused. "I have an ulcer. My hair is going gray. And I know they'll fire me. No matter how loyal you are to the big companies, they have no loyalty to their employees any more. It's no wonder that I drink."

"You should get married again," Tsuyoshi offered.

"I can't find the right girl. Women never understand me." He shuddered. "Tsuyoshi, I'm truly desperate. The market pressures and the competition are crushing me. I can't breathe. My life has got to change. I'm thinking of taking the vows. I'm serious! I want to renounce this whole modern world."

Tsuyoshi was alarmed. "You're very drunk, right?"

His brother leaned closer to the screen. "Life in a monastery sounds truly good to me. It's so quiet there. You recite the sutras. You consider your existence. There are rules to follow, and rewards that make sense. It's just the way that Japanese business used to be, back in the good old days."

Tsuyoshi grunted skeptically.

"Last week I went out to a special place in the mountains.... a monastery on Mount Aso," his brother confided. "The monks there, they know about people in trouble, people who are burned out by modern life. The monks protect you from the world. No computers, no phones, no faxes, no e-mail, no overtime, no commuting, nothing at all. It' s beautiful, and it's peaceful, and nothing ever happens there. Really, it's like paradise."

"Listen, older brother," Tsuyoshi said, "you're not a religious man by nature. You're a section chief for a big import-export company."

"Well… maybe religion won't work for me. I did think of running away to America. Nothing much ever happens there, either."

Tsuyoshi smiled. "That sounds much better! America is a good vacation spot. A long vacation is just what you need! Besides, the Americans are real friendly since they gave up their handguns."

"But I can't go through with it," his brother wailed. "I just don't dare. I can't just wander away from everything that I know, and trust to the kindness of strangers."

"That always works for me," Tsuyoshi said. "Maybe you should try it."

Tsuyoshi's wife stirred uneasily on the futon. Tsuyoshi lowered his voice. "Sorry, but I have to hang up now. Call me before you do anything rash."

"Don't tell Dad," Tsuyoshi's brother said. "He worries so."

"I won't tell Dad." Tsuyoshi cut the connection and the screen went dark.

Tsuyoshi's wife rolled over, heavily. She was seven months pregnant. She stared at the ceiling, puffing for breath. "Was that another call from your brother?" she said.

"Yeah. The company just gave him another promotion. More responsibilities. He's celebrating."

"That sounds nice," his wife said tactfully.

▲ ▼ ▲

Next morning, Tsuyoshi slept late. He was self-employed, so he kept his own hours. Tsuyoshi was a video format upgrader by trade. He transferred old videos from obsolete formats into the new high-grade storage media. Doing this properly took a craftsman's eye. Word of Tsuyoshi's skills had gotten out on the network, so he had as much work as he could handle.

At ten AM, the mailman arrived. Tsuyoshi abandoned his breakfast of raw egg and miso soup, and signed for a shipment of flaking, twentieth-century analog television tapes. The mail also brought a fresh overnight shipment of strawberries, and a homemade jar of pickles.

"Pickles!" his wife enthused. "People are so nice to you when you're pregnant."

"Any idea who sent us that?"

"Just someone on the network."

"Great."

Tsuyoshi booted his mediator, cleaned his superconducting heads and examined the old tapes. Home videos from the 1980s. Someone's grandmother as a child, presumably. There had been a lot of flaking and loss of polarity in the old recording medium.

Tsuyoshi got to work with his desktop fractal detail generator, the image stabilizer, and the interlace algorithms. When he was done, Tsuyoshi's new digital copies would look much sharper, cleaner and better composed than the original primitive videotape.

Tsuyoshi enjoyed his work. Quite often he came across bits and pieces of videotape that were of archival interest. He would pass the images on to the net. The really big network databases, with their armies of search engines, indexers, and catalogues, had some very arcane interests. The net machines would never pay for data, because the global information networks were noncommercial. But the net machines were very polite, and had excellent net etiquette. They returned a favor for a favor, and since they were machines with excellent, enormous memories, they never forgot a good deed.

Tsuyoshi and his wife had a lunch of ramen with naruto, and she left to go shopping. A shipment arrived by overseas package service. Cute baby clothes from Darwin, Australia. They were in his wife's favorite color, sunshine yellow.

Tsuyoshi finished transferring the first tape to a new crystal disk. Time for a break. He left his apartment, took the elevator and went out to the corner coffee-shop. He ordered a double iced mocha cappuccino and paid with a charge-card.

His pokkecon rang. Tsuyoshi took it from his belt and answered it. "Get one to go," the machine told him.

"Okay," said Tsuyoshi, and hung up. He bought a second coffee, put a lid on it and left the shop.

A man in a business suit was sitting on a park bench near the entrance of Tsuyoshi's building. The man's suit was good, but it looked as if he'd slept in it. He was holding his head in his hands and rocking gently back and forth. He was unshaven and his eyes were red-rimmed.

The pokkecon rang again. "The coffee's for him?" Tsuyoshi said.

"Yes," said the pokkecon. "He needs it."

Tsuyoshi walked up to the lost businessman. The man looked up, flinching warily, as if he were about to be kicked. "What is it?" he said.

"Here," Tsuyoshi said, handing him the cup. "Double iced mocha cappuccino."

The man opened the cup, and smelled it. He looked up in disbelief. "This is my favorite kind of coffee.... Who are you?"

Tsuyoshi lifted his arm and offered a hand signal, his fingers clenched like a cat's paw. The man showed no recognition of the gesture. Tsuyoshi shrugged, and smiled. "It doesn't matter. Sometimes a man really needs a coffee. Now you have a coffee. That's all."

"Well...." The man cautiously sipped his cup, and suddenly smiled. "It's really great. Thanks!"

"You're welcome." Tsuyoshi went home.

His wife arrived from shopping. She had bought new shoes. The pregnancy was making her feet swell. She sat carefully on the couch and sighed.

"Orthopedic shoes are expensive," she said, looking at the yellow pumps. "I hope you don't think they look ugly."

"On you, they look really cute," Tsuyoshi said wisely. He had first met his wife at a video store. She had just used her credit card to buy a disk of primitive black-and-white American anime of the 1950s. The pokkecon had urged him to go up and speak to her on the subject of Felix the Cat. Felix was an early television cartoon star and one of Tsuyoshi's personal favorites. Tsuyoshi would have been too shy to approach an attractive woman on his own, but no one was a stranger to the net. This fact gave him the confidence to speak to her. Tsuyoshi had soon discovered that the girl was delighted to discuss her deep fondness for cute, antique, animated cats. They had lunch together. They'd had a date the next week. They had spent Christmas Eve together in a love hotel. They had a lot in common.

She had come into his life through a little act of grace, a little gift from Felix the Cat's magic bag of tricks. Tsuyoshi had never gotten over feeling grateful for this. Now that he was married and becoming a father, Tsuyoshi Shimizu could feel himself becoming solidly fixed in life. He had a man's role to play now. He knew who he was, and he knew where he stood. Life was good to him.

"You need a haircut, dear," his wife told him.

"Sure."

His wife pulled a gift box out of her shopping bag. "Can you go to the Hotel Daruma, and get your hair cut, and deliver this box for me?"

"What is it?" Tsuyoshi said.

Tsuyoshi's wife opened the little wooden gift box. A maneki neko was nestled inside white foam padding. The smiling ceramic cat held one paw upraised, beckoning for good fortune.

"Don't you have enough of those yet?" he said. "You even have maneki neko underwear."

"It's not for my collection. It's a gift for someone at the Hotel Daruma."

"Oh."

"Some foreign woman gave me this box at the shoestore. She looked American. She couldn't speak Japanese. She had really nice shoes, though...."

"If the network gave you that little cat, then you're the one who should take care of that obligation, dear."

"But dear," she sighed, "my feet hurt so much, and you could do with a haircut anyway, and I have to cook supper, and besides, it's not really a nice maneki neko, it's just cheap tourist souvenir junk. Can't you do it?"

"Oh, all right," Tsuyoshi told her. "Just forward your pokkecon prompts on to my machine, and I'll see what I can do for us."

She smiled. "I knew you would do it. You're really so good to me."

Tsuyoshi left with the little box. He wasn't unhappy to do the errand, as it wasn't always easy to manage his pregnant wife's volatile moods in their small six-tatami apartment. The local neighborhood was good, but he was hoping to find bigger accommodations before the child was born. Maybe a place with a little studio, where he could expand the scope of his work. It was very hard to find decent housing in Tokyo, but word was out on the net. Friends he didn't even know were working every day to help him. If he kept up with the net's obligations, he had every confidence that some day something nice would turn up.

Tsuyoshi went into the local pachinko parlor, where he won half a liter of beer and a train charge-card. He drank the beer, took the new train card and wedged himself into the train. He got out at the Ebisu station, and turned on his pokkecon Tokyo street map to guide his steps. He walked past places called Chocolate Soup, and Freshness Physique, and The Aladdin Mai-Tai Panico Trattoria.

He entered the Hotel Daruma and went to the hotel barber shop, which was called the Daruma Planet Look. "May I help you?" said the receptionist.

"I'm thinking, a shave and a trim," Tsuyoshi said.

"Do you have an appointment with us?"

"Sorry, no."

Tsuyoshi offered a hand gesture.

The woman gestured back, a jerky series of cryptic finger movements. Tsuyoshi didn't recognize any of the gestures. She wasn't from his part of the network.

"Oh well, never mind," the receptionist said kindly. "I'll get Nahoko to look after you."

Nahoko was carefully shaving the fine hair from Tsuyoshi's forehead when the pokkecon rang. Tsuyoshi answered it.

"Go to the ladies' room on the fourth floor," the pokkecon told him.

"Sorry, I can't do that. This is Tsuyoshi Shimizu, not Ai Shimizu. Besides, I'm having my hair cut right now."

"Oh, I see," said the machine. "Recalibrating." It hung up.

Nahoko finished his hair. She had done a good job. He looked much better. A man who worked at home had to take special trouble to keep up appearances. The pokkecon rang again.

"Yes?" said Tsuyoshi.

"Buy bay rum aftershave. Take it outside."

"Right." He hung up. "Nahoko, do you have bay rum?"

"Odd you should ask that," said Nahoko. "Hardly anyone asks for bay rum any more, but our shop happens to keep it in stock."

Tsuyoshi bought the aftershave, then stepped outside the barbershop. Nothing happened, so he bought a manga comic and waited. Finally a hairy, blond stranger in shorts, a tropical shirt, and sandals approached him. The foreigner was carrying a camera bag and an old-fashioned pokkecon. He looked about sixty years old, and he was very tall.

The man spoke to his pokkecon in English. "Excuse me," said the pokkecon, translating the man's speech into Japanese. "Do you have a bottle of bay rum aftershave?"

"Yes I do." Tsuyoshi handed the bottle over. "Here."

"Thank goodness!" said the man, his words relayed through his machine. "I've asked everyone else in the lobby. Sorry I was late."

"No problem," said Tsuyoshi. "That's a nice pokkecon you have there."

"Well," the man said, "I know it's old and out of style. But I plan to buy a new pokkecon here in Tokyo. I'm told that they sell pokkecons by the basketfull in Akihabara electronics market."

"That's right. What kind of translator program are you running? Your translator talks like someone from Osaka."

"Does it sound funny?" the tourist asked anxiously.

"Well, I don't want to complain, but...." Tsuyoshi smiled. "Here, let's trade meishi. I can give you a copy of a brand-new freeware translator."

"That would be wonderful." They pressed buttons and squirted copies of their business cards across the network link.

Tsuyoshi examined his copy of the man's electronic card and saw than his name was Zimmerman. Mr. Zimmerman was from New Zealand. Tsuyoshi activated a transfer program. His modern pokkecon began transferring a new translator onto Zimmerman's machine.

A large American man in a padded suit entered the lobby of the Daruma. The man wore sunglasses, and was sweating visibly in the summer heat. The American looked huge, as if he lifted a lot of weights. Then a Japanese woman followed him. The woman was sharply dressed, with a dress suit, hat, sunglasses, and an attaché case. She had a haunted look.

Her escort turned and carefully watched the bellhops, who were bringing in a series of bags. The woman walked crisply to the reception desk and began making anxious demands of the clerk.

"I'm a great believer in machine translation," Tsuyoshi said to the tall man from New Zealand. "I really believe that computers help human beings to relate in a much more human way."

"I couldn't agree with you more," said Mr. Zimmerman, through his machine. "I can remember the first time I came to your country, many years ago. I had no portable translator. In fact, I had nothing but a printed phrasebook. I happened to go into a bar, and..."

Zimmerman stopped and gazed alertly at his pokkecon. "Oh dear, I'm getting a screen prompt. I have to go up to my room right away."

"Then I'll come along with you till this software transfer is done," Tsuyoshi said.

"That's very kind of you." They got into the elevator together. Zimmerman punched for the fourth floor. "Anyway, as I was saying, I went into this bar in Roppongi late at night, because I was jetlagged and hoping for something to eat..."

"Yes?"

"And this woman... well, let's just say this woman was hanging out in a foreigner's bar in Roppongi late at night, and she wasn't wearing a whole lot of clothes, and she didn't look like she was any better than she ought to be...."

"Yes, I think I understand you."

"Anyway, this menu they gave me was full of kanji, or katakana, or romanji, or whatever they call those, so I had my phrasebook out, and I was trying very hard to puzzle out these pesky ideograms..." The elevator opened and they stepped into the carpeted hall of the hotel's fourth floor. "So I opened the menu and I pointed to an entree, and I told this girl...." Zimmerman stopped suddenly, and stared at his screen. "Oh dear, something's happening. Just a moment."

Zimmerman carefully studied the instructions on his pokkecon. Then he pulled the bottle of bay rum from the baggy pocket of his shorts, and unscrewed the cap. He stood on tiptoe, stretching to his full height, and carefully poured the contents of the bottle through the iron louvers of a ventilation grate, set high in the top of the wall.

Zimmerman screwed the cap back on neatly, and slipped the empty bottle back in his pocket. Then he examined his pokkecon again. He frowned, and shook it. The screen had frozen. Apparently Tsuyoshi's new translation program had overloaded Zimmerman's old-fashioned operating system. His pokkecon had crashed.

Zimmerman spoke a few defeated sentences in English. Then he smiled, and spread his hands apologetically. He bowed, and went into his room, and shut the door.

The Japanese woman and her burly American escort entered the hall. The man gave Tsuyoshi a hard stare. The woman opened the door with a passcard. Her hands were shaking.

Tsuyoshi's pokkecon rang. "Leave the hall," it told him. "Go downstairs. Get into the elevator with the bellboy."

Tsuyoshi followed instructions.

The bellboy was just entering the elevator with a cart full of the woman's baggage. Tsuyoshi got into the elevator, stepping carefully behind the wheeled metal cart. "What floor, sir?" said the bellboy.

"Eight," Tsuyoshi said, ad-libbing. The bellboy turned and pushed the buttons. He faced forward attentively, his gloved hands folded.

The pokkecon flashed a silent line of text to the screen. "Put the gift box inside her flight bag," it read.

Tsuyoshi located the zippered blue bag at the back of the cart. It was a matter of instants to zip it open, put in the box with the maneki neko, and zip the bag shut again. The bellboy noticed nothing. He left, tugging with his cart.

Tsuyoshi got out on the eighth floor, feeling slightly foolish. He wandered down the hall, found a quiet nook by an ice machine and called his wife. "What's going on?" he said.

"Oh, nothing." She smiled. "Your haircut looks nice! Show me the back of your head."

Tsuyoshi held the pokkecon screen behind the nape of his neck. "They do good work," his wife said with satisfaction. "I hope it didn't cost too much. Are you coming home now?"

"Things are getting a little odd here at the hotel," Tsuyoshi told her. "I may be some time."

His wife frowned. "Well, don't miss supper. We're having bonito."

Tsuyoshi took the elevator back down. It stopped at the fourth floor. The woman's American companion stepped onto the elevator. His nose was running and his eyes were streaming with tears.

"Are you all right?" Tsuyoshi said.

"I don't understand Japanese," the man growled. The elevator doors shut.

The man's cellular phone crackled into life. It emitted a scream of anguish and a burst of agitated female English. The man swore and slammed his hairy fist against the elevator's emergency button. The elevator stopped with a lurch. An alarm bell began ringing.

The man pried the doors open with his large hairy fingers and clambered out into the fourth floor. He then ran headlong down the hall.

The elevator began buzzing in protest, its doors shuddering as if broken. Tsuyoshi climbed hastily from the damaged elevator, and stood there in the hallway. He hesitated a moment. Then he produced his pokkecon and loaded his Japanese-to-English translator. He walked cautiously after the American man.

The door to their suite was open. Tsuyoshi spoke aloud into his pokke-con. "Hello?" he said experimentally. "May I be of help?"

The woman was sitting on the bed. She had just discovered the maneki neko box in her flight bag. She was staring at the little cat in horror.

"Who are you?" she said, in bad Japanese. Tsuyoshi realized suddenly that she was a Japanese American. Tsuyoshi had met a few Japanese Americans before. They always troubled him. They looked fairly normal from the outside, but their behavior was always bizarre.

"I'm just a passing friend," he said. "Something I can do?"

"Grab him, Mitch!" said the woman in English. The American man rushed into the hall and grabbed Tsuyoshi by the arm. His hands were like steel bands.

Tsuyoshi pressed the distress button on his pokkecon.

"Take that computer away from him," the woman ordered in English. Mitch quickly took Tsuyoshi's pokkecon away, and threw it on the bed. He deftly patted Tsuyoshi's clothing, searching for weapons. Then he shoved Tsuyoshi into a chair.

The woman switched back to Japanese. "Sit right there, you. Don't you dare move." She began examining the contents of Tsuyoshi's wallet.

"I beg your pardon?" Tsuyoshi said. His pokkecon was lying on the bed. Lines of red text scrolled up its little screen as it silently issued a series of emergency net alerts.

The woman spoke to her companion in English. Tsuyoshi's pokkecon was still translating faithfully. "Mitch, go call the local police."

Mitch sneezed uncontrollably. Tsuyoshi noticed that the room smelled strongly of bay rum. "I can't talk to the local cops. I can't speak Japanese." Mitch sneezed again.

"Okay, then I'll call the cops. You handcuff this guy. Then go down to the infirmary and get yourself some antihistamines, for Christ's sake."

Mitch pulled a length of plastic whipcord cuff from his coat pocket, and attached Tsuyoshi's right wrist to the head of the bed. He mopped his stream-ing eyes with a tissue. "I'd better stay with you. If there's a cat in your luggage, then the criminal network already knows we're in Japan. You're in danger."

"Mitch, you may be my bodyguard, but you're breaking out in hives."

"This just isn't supposed to happen," Mitch complained, scratching his neck. "My allergies never interfered with my job before."

"Just leave me here and lock the door," the woman told him. "I'll put a chair against the knob. I'll be all right. You need to look after yourself."

Mitch left the room.

The woman barricaded the door with a chair. Then she called the front desk on the hotel's beside pasokon. "This is Louise Hashimoto in room 434.

I have a gangster in my room. He's an information criminal. Would you call the Tokyo police, please? Tell them to send the organized crime unit. Yes, that's right. Do it. And you should put your hotel security people on full alert. There may be big trouble here. You'd better hurry." She hung up.

Tsuyoshi stared at her in astonishment. "Why are you doing this? What's all this about?"

"So you call yourself Tsuyoshi Shimizu," said the woman, examining his credit cards. She sat on the foot of the bed and stared at him. "You're yakuza of some kind, right?"

"I think you've made a big mistake," Tsuyoshi said.

Louise scowled. "Look, Mr. Shimizu, you're not dealing with some Yankee tourist here. My name is Louise Hashimoto and I'm an assistant federal prosecutor from Providence, Rhode Island, USA." She showed him a magnetic ID card with a gold official seal.

"It's nice to meet someone from the American government," said Tsuyoshi, bowing a bit in his chair. "I'd shake your hand, but it's tied to the bed."

"You can stop with the innocent act right now. I spotted you out in the hall earlier, and in the lobby, too, casing the hotel. How did you know my bodyguard is violently allergic to bay rum? You must have read his medical records."

"Who, me? Never!"

"Ever since I discovered you network people, it's been one big pattern," said Louise. "It's the biggest criminal conspiracy I ever saw. I busted this software pirate in Providence. He had a massive network server and a whole bunch of AI freeware search engines. We took him in custody, we bagged all his search engines, and catalogs, and indexers…. Later that very same day, these *cats* start showing up."

"Cats?"

Louise lifted the maneki neko, handling it as if it were a live eel. "These little Japanese voodoo cats. Maneki neko, right? They started showing up everywhere I went. There's a china cat in my handbag. There's three china cats at the office. Suddenly they're on display in the windows of every antique store in Providence. My car radio starts making meowing noises at me."

"You *broke* part of the network?" Tsuyoshi said, scandalized. "You took someone's machines away? That's terrible! How could you do such an inhuman thing?"

"You've got a real nerve complaining about that. What about *my* machinery?" Louise held up her fat, eerie-looking American pokkecon. "As soon as I stepped off the airplane at Narita, my PDA was attacked. Thousands and thousands of email messages. All of them pictures of cats. A denial-of-service attack! I can't even communicate with the home office! My PDA's useless!"

"What's a PDA?"

"It's a PDA, my Personal Digital Assistant! Manufactured in Silicon Valley!"

"Well, with a goofy name like that, no wonder our pokkecons won't talk to it."

Louise frowned grimly. "That's right, wise guy. Make jokes about it. You're involved in a malicious software attack on a legal officer of the United States Government. You'll see." She paused, looking him over. "You know, Shimizu, you don't look much like the Italian mafia gangsters I have to deal with, back in Providence."

"I'm not a gangster at all. I never do anyone any harm."

"Oh no?" Louise glowered at him. "Listen pal, I know a lot more about your set-up, and your kind of people, than you think I do. I've been studying your outfit for a long time now. We computer cops have names for your kind of people. Digital panarchies. Segmented, polycephalous, integrated influence networks. What about all these *free goods and services* you're getting all this time?"

She pointed a finger at him. "Ha! Do you ever pay *taxes* on those? Do you ever *declare* that income and those benefits? All the free shipments from other countries! The little homemade cookies, and the free pens and pencils and bumper stickers, and the used bicycles, and the helpful news about fire sales…. You're a tax evader! You're living through kickbacks! And bribes! And influence peddling! And all kinds of corrupt off-the-books transactions!"

Tsuyoshi blinked. "Look, I don't know anything about all that. I'm just living my life."

"Well, your network gift economy is undermining the lawful, government approved, regulated economy!"

"Well," Tsuyoshi said gently, "maybe my economy is *better* than your economy."

"Says who?" she scoffed. "Why would anyone think that?"

"It's better because we're *happier* than you are. What's wrong with acts of kindness? Everyone likes gifts. Midsummer gifts. New Years Day gifts. Year-end presents. Wedding presents. Everybody likes those."

"Not the way you Japanese like them. You're totally crazy for gifts."

"What kind of society has no gifts? It's barbaric to have no regard for common human feelings."

Louise bristled. "You're saying I'm barbaric?"

"I don't mean to complain," Tsuyoshi said politely, "but you do have tied me up to your bed."

Louise crossed her arms. "You might as well stop complaining. You'll be in much worse trouble when the local police arrive."

"Then we'll probably be waiting here for quite a while," Tsuyoshi said. "The police move rather slowly, here in Japan. I'm sorry, but we don't have as much crime as you Americans, so our police are not very alert."

The pasokon rang at the side of the bed. Louise answered it. It was Tsuyoshi's wife.

"Could I speak to Tsuyoshi Shimizu please?"

"I'm over here, dear," Tsuyoshi called quickly. "She's kidnapped me! She tied me to the bed!"

"Tied to her *bed?*" His wife's eyes grew wide. "That does it! I'm calling the police!"

Louise quickly hung up the pasokon. "I haven't kidnapped you! I'm only detaining you here until the local authorities can come and arrest you."

"Arrest me for what, exactly?"

Louise thought quickly. "Well, for poisoning my bodyguard by pouring bay rum into the ventilator."

"But I never did that. Anyway, that's not illegal, is it?"

The pasokon rang again. A shining white cat appeared on the screen. It had large, staring, unearthly eyes.

"Let him go," the cat commanded in English.

Louise shrieked and yanked the pasokon's plug from the wall.

Suddenly the lights went out. "Infrastructure attack! "Louise squawled. She rolled quickly under the bed.

The room went gloomy and quiet. The air conditioner had shut off. "I think you can come out," Tsuyoshi said at last, his voice loud in the still room. "It's just a power failure."

"No it isn't," Louise said. She crawled slowly from beneath the bed, and sat on the mattress. Somehow, the darkness had made them more intimate. "I know very well what this is. I'm under attack. I haven't had a moment's peace since I broke that network. Stuff just happens to me now. Bad stuff. Swarms of it. It's never anything you can touch, though. Nothing you can prove in a court of law."

She sighed. "I sit in chairs, and somebody's left a piece of gum there. I get free pizzas, but they're not the kind of pizzas I like. Little kids spit on my sidewalk. Old women in walkers get in front of me whenever I need to hurry."

The shower came on, all by itself. Louise shuddered, but said nothing. Slowly, the darkened, stuffy room began to fill with hot steam.

"My toilets don't flush," Louise said. "My letters get lost in the mail.

When I walk by cars, their theft alarms go off. And strangers stare at me. It's always little things. Lots of little tiny things, but they never, ever stop. I'm up against something that is very very big, and very very patient. And it knows all about me. And its got a million arms and legs. And all those arms and legs are all people."

There was the noise of scuffling in the hall. Distant voices, confused shouting.

Suddenly the chair broke under the doorknob. The door burst open violently. Mitch tumbled through, the sunglasses flying from his head. Two hotel security guards were trying to grab him. Shouting incoherently in English, Mitch fell headlong to the floor, kicking and thrashing. The guards lost their hats in the struggle. One tackled Mitch's legs with both his arms, and the other whacked and jabbed him with a baton.

Puffing and grunting with effort, they hauled Mitch out of the room. The darkened room was so full of steam that the harried guards hadn't even noticed Tsuyoshi and Louise.

Louise stared at the broken door. "Why did they do that to him?"

Tsuyoshi scratched his head in embarrassment. "Probably a failure of communication."

"Poor Mitch! They took his gun away at the airport. He had all kinds of technical problems with his passport.... Poor guy, he's never had any luck since he met me."

There was a loud tapping at the window. Louise shrank back in fear. Finally she gathered her courage, and opened the curtains. Daylight flooded the room.

A window-washing rig had been lowered from the roof of the hotel, on cables and pulleys. There were two window-washers in crisp gray uniforms. They waved cheerfully, making little catpaw gestures.

There was a third man with them. It was Tsuyoshi's brother.

One of the washers opened the window with a utility key. Tsuyoshi's brother squirmed into the room. He stood up and carefully adjusted his coat and tie.

"This is my brother," Tsuyoshi explained.

"What are you doing here?" Louise said.

"They always bring in the relatives when there's a hostage situation," Tsuyoshi's brother said. "The police just flew me in by helicopter and landed me on the roof." He looked Louise up and down. "Miss Hashimoto, you just have time to escape."

"What?" she said.

"Look down at the streets," he told her. "See that? You hear them? Crowds are pouring in from all over the city. All kinds of people, everyone with wheels. Street noodle salesmen. Bicycle messengers. Skateboard kids. Takeout delivery guys."

Louise gazed out the window into the streets, and shrieked aloud. "Oh no! A giant swarming mob! They're surrounding me! I'm doomed!"

"You are not doomed," Tsuyoshi's brother told her intently. "Come out the window. Get onto the platform with us. You've got one chance, Louise. It's a place I know, a sacred place in the mountains. No computers there, no phones, nothing." He paused. "It's a sanctuary for people like us. And I know the way."

She gripped his suited arm. "Can I trust you?"

"Look in my eyes," he told her. "Don't you see? Yes, you can trust me. We have everything in common."

Louise stepped out the window. She clutched his arm, the wind whipping at her hair. The platform creaked rapidly up and out of sight.

Tsuyoshi stood up from the chair. When he stretched out, tugging at his handcuffed wrist, he was just able to reach his pokkecon with his fingertips. He drew it in, and clutched it to his chest. Then he sat down again, and waited patiently for someone to come and give him freedom.

In Paradise

The machines broke down so much that it was comical, but the security people never laughed about that.

Felix could endure the delay, for plumbers billed by the hour. He opened his tool kit, extracted a plastic flask and had a solid nip of Scotch.

The Moslem girl was chattering into her phone. Her dad and another bearded weirdo had passed through the big metal frame just as the scanner broke down. so these two somber, suited old men were getting the full third-degree with the hand wands, while daughter was stuck. Daughter wore a long baggy coat and a thick black headscarf and a surprisingly sexy pair of sandals. Between her and her minders stretched the no-man's land of official insecurity. She waved across the gap.

The security geeks found something metallic in the black wool jacket of the Wicked Uncle. Of course it was harmless, but they had to run their full ritual, lest they die of boredom at their posts. As the Scotch settled in, Felix felt time stretch like taffy. Little Miss Mujihadeen discovered that her phone was dying. She banged at it with the flat of her hand.

The line of hopeful shoppers, grimly waiting to stimulate the economy, shifted in their disgruntlement. It was a bad, bleak scene. It crushed Felix's heart within him. He longed to leap to his feet and harangue the lot of them. *Wake up*, he wanted to scream at them, *cheer up, act more human.* He felt the urge keenly, but it scared people when he cut loose like that. They really hated it. And so did he. He knew he couldn't look them in the eye. It would only make a lot of trouble.

The Mideastern men shouted at the girl. She waved her dead phone at them, as if another breakdown was going to help their mood. Then Felix noticed that she shared his own make of cellphone. She had a rather ahead-of-the-curve Finnish model that he'd spent a lot of money on. So Felix rose and sidled over.

"Help you out with that phone, ma'am?"

She gave him the paralyzed look of a coed stuck with a dripping tap. "No English?" he concluded. "*¿Habla espanol, senorita?*" No such luck.

He offered her his own phone. No, she didn't care to use it. Surprised and even a little hurt by this rejection, Felix took his first good look at her, and realized with a lurch that she was pretty. What eyes! They were whirlpools. The line of her lips was like the tapered edge of a rose leaf.

"It's your battery," he told her. Though she had not a word of English, she obviously got it about phone batteries. After some gestured persuasion, she was willing to trade her dead battery for his. There was a fine and delicate little moment when his fingertips extracted her power supply, and he inserted his own unit into that golden-lined copper cavity. Her display leapt to life with an eager flash of numerals. Felix pressed a button or two, smiled winningly, and handed her phone back.

She dialed in a hurry, and bearded Evil Dad lifted his phone to answer, and life became much easier on the nerves. Then, with a groaning buzz, the scanner came back on. Dad and Uncle waved a command at her, like lifers turned to trusty prison guards, and she scampered through the metal gate and never looked back.

She had taken his battery. Well, no problem. He would treasure the one she had given him.

Felix gallantly let the little crowd through before he himself cleared security. The geeks always went nuts about his plumbing tools, but then again, they had to. He found the assignment: a chi-chi place that sold fake antiques and potpourri. The manager's office had a clogged drain. As he worked, Felix recharged the phone. Then he socked them for a sum that made them wince.

On his leisurely way out—whoa, there was Miss Cellphone, that looker, that little goddess, browsing in a jewelry store over Korean gold chains and tiaras. Dad and Uncle were there, with a couple of off-duty cops.

Felix retired to a bench beside the fountain, in the potted plastic plants. He had another bracing shot of Scotch, then put his feet up on his toolbox and punched her number.

He saw her straighten at the ring, and open her purse, and place the phone to the kerchiefed side of her head. She didn't know where he was, or who he was. That was why the words came pouring out of him.

"My God you're pretty," he said. "You are wasting your time with that jewelry. Because your eyes are like two black diamonds."

She jumped a little, poked at the phone's buttons with disbelief, and put it back to her head.

Felix choked back the urge to laugh and leaned forward, his elbows on his knees. "A string of pearls around your throat would look like peanuts," he told the phone. "I am totally smitten with you. What are you like under that big baggy coat? Do I dare to wonder? I would give a million dollars just to see your knees!"

"Why are you telling me that?" said the phone.

"Because I'm looking at you right now. And after one look at you, believe me, I was a lost soul." Felix felt a chill. "Hey, wait a minute. You don't speak English, do you?"

"No, I don't speak English—but my telephone does."

"It *does*?"

"It's a very new telephone. It's from Finland," the telephone said. "I need it because I'm stuck in a foreign country. Do you really have a million dollars for my knees?"

"That was a figure of speech," said Felix, though his back account was, in point of fact, looking considerably healthier since his girlfriend Lola had dumped him. "Never mind the million dollars," he said. "I'm dying of love out here. I'd sell my blood just to buy you petunias."

"You must be a famous poet," said the phone dreamily, "for you speak such wonderful Farsi."

Felix had no idea what Farsi was—but he was way beyond such fretting now. The rusty gates of his soul were shuddering on their hinges. "I'm drunk," he realized. "I am drunk on your smile."

"In my family, the women never smile."

Felix had no idea what to say to that, so there was a hissing silence.

"Are you a spy? How did you get my phone number?"

"I'm not a spy. I got your phone number from your phone."

"Then I know you. You must be that tall foreign man who gave me your battery. Where are you?"

"Look outside the store. See me on the bench?" She turned where she stood, and he waved his fingertips. "That's right, it's me," he declared to her. "I can't believe I'm really going through with this. You just stand there, okay? I'm going to run in there and buy you a wedding ring."

"Don't do that." She glanced cautiously at Dad and Uncle, then stepped closer to the bulletproof glass. "Yes, I do see you. I remember you."

She was looking straight at him. Their eyes met. They were connecting. A hot torrent ran up his spine. "You are looking straight at me."

"You're very handsome."

▲ ▼ ▲

It wasn't hard to elope. Young women had been eloping since the dawn of time. Elopement with eager phone support was a snap. He followed her to the hotel, a posh place that swarmed with limos and videocams. He brought her a bag with a big hat, sunglasses, and a cheap Mexican wedding dress. He sneaked into the women's restroom—they never put videocams there, due to the complaints—and he left the bag in a stall. She went in, came out in new clothes with her hair loose, and walked straight out of the hotel and into his car.

They couldn't speak together without their phones, but that turned out to be surprisingly advantageous, as further discussion was not on their minds. Unlike Lola, who was always complaining that he should open up and relate—"you're a plumber," she would tell him, "how deep and mysterious is a plumber supposed to be?"—the new woman in his life had needs that were very straightforward. She liked to walk in parks without a police escort. She liked to thoughtfully peruse the goods in Mideastern ethnic groceries. And she liked to make love to him.

She was nineteen years old, and the willing sacrifice of her chastity had really burned the bridges for his little refugee. Once she got fully briefed about what went inside where, she was in a mood to tame the demon. She had big, jagged, sobbing, alarming, romantic, brink-of-the-grave things going on, with long, swoony kisses, and heel-drumming, and clutching and clawing.

When they were too weak, and too raw, and too tingling to make love any more, then she would cook, very badly. She was on her phone constantly, talking to her people. These confidantes of hers were obviously women, because she asked them for Persian cooking tips. She would sink with triumphant delight into a cheery chatter as the Basmati rice burned.

He longed to take her out to eat; to show her to everyone, to the whole world; really, besides the sex, no act could have made him happier—but she was undocumented, and sooner or later some security geek was sure to check on that. People did things like that to people nowadays. To contemplate such things threw a thorny darkness over their whole affair, so, mostly, he didn't think. He took time off work, and he spent every moment that he could in her radiant presence, and she did what a pretty girl could do to lift a man's darkened spirits, which was plenty. More than he had ever had from anyone.

▲ ▼ ▲

After ten days of golden, unsullied bliss, ten days of bread and jug wine, ten days when the nightingales sang in chorus and the reddest of roses bloomed outside the boudoir, there came a knock on his door, and it was three cops.

"Hello, Mr. Hernandez," said the smallest of the trio. "I would be Agent Portillo from Homeland Security, and these would be two of my distinguished associates. Might we come in?"

"Would there be a problem?" said Felix.

"Yes there would!" said Portillo. "There might be rather less of a problem if my associates here could search your apartment." Portillo offered up a handheld screen. "A young woman named Batool Kadivar? Would we be recognizing Miss Batool Kadivar?"

"I can't even pronounce that," Felix said. "But I guess you'd better come in," for Agent Portillo's associates were already well on their way. Men of their ilk were not prepared to take no for an answer. They shoved past him and headed at once for the bedroom.

"Who are those guys? They're not American."

"They're Iranian allies. The Iranians were totally nuts for a while, and then they were sort of okay, and then they became our new friends, and then the enemies of our friends became our friends…. Do you ever watch TV news, Mr. Hernandez? Secular uprisings, people seizing embassies? Ground war in the holy city of Qom, that sort of thing?"

"It's hard to miss," Felix admitted.

"There are a billion Moslems. If they want to turn the whole planet into Israel, we don't get a choice about that. You know something? I used to be an accountant!" Portillo sighed theatrically. "'Homeland Security.' Why'd they have to stick me with that chicken outfit? Hombre, we're twenty years old and we don't even have our own budget yet. Did you see those gorillas I've got on my hands? Do you think these guys ever listen to sense? Geneva Convention? US Constitution? Come on."

"They're not gonna find any terrorists in here."

Portillo sighed again. "Look, Mr. Hernandez. You're a young man with a clean record, so I want to do you a favor." He adjusted his handheld and it showed a new screen. "These are cellphone records. Thirty, forty calls a day, to and from your number. Then look at this screen. This is the good part. Check out *her* call records. That would be her aunt in Yerevan, and her little sister in Teheran, and five or six of her teenage girlfriends, still living back in purdah…. Who do you think is gonna *pay* that phone bill? Did that ever cross your mind?"

Felix said nothing.

"I can understand this, Mr. Hernandez. You lucked out. You're a young, red-blooded guy, and that is a very pretty girl. But she's a minor, and an illegal alien. Her father's family has got political connections like nobody's business, and I would mean nobody, and I would also mean business."

"Not my business," Felix said.

"You're being a sap, Mr. Hernandez. You may not be interested in war, but war is plenty interested in you."

There were loud crashing, sacking, and looting noises coming from his bedroom.

"You are sunk, *hermano*. There is video at the Lebanese grocery store. There is video hidden in the traffic lights. You're a free American citizen, sir. You are free to go anywhere you want, and we're free to watch all the backup tapes. That would be the big story I'm relating here. Would we be catching on yet?"

"That's some kind of story," Felix said.

"You don't know the half of it. You don't know the tenth."

The two goons reappeared. There was a brief exchange of notes. They had to use their computers.

"My friends here are disappointed," said Agent Portillo. "Because there is no girl in your residence, even though there is an extensive selection of makeup and perfume. They want me to arrest you for abduction, and obstruction of justice, and probably ten or twelve other things. But I would be asking myself: why? Why should this young taxpayer with a steady job want to have his life ruined? What I'm thinking is: there must be *another* story. A *better* story. The flighty girl ran off, and she spent the last two weeks in a convent. It was just an impulse thing for her. She got frightened and upset by America, and then she came back to her people. Everything diplomatic."

"That's diplomacy?"

"Diplomacy is the art of avoiding extensive unpleasantness for all the parties concerned. The United Coalition, as it were."

"They'll chop her hands off and beat her like a dog!"

"Well, that would depend, Mr. Hernandez. That would depend entirely on whether the girl herself tells that story. Somebody would have to get her up to speed on all that. A trusted friend. You see?"

▲ ▼ ▲

After the departure of the three security men, Felix thought through his situation. He realized there was nothing whatsoever in it for him but shame, humiliation, impotence, and a crushing and lasting unhappiness. He then fetched up the reposada tequila from beneath his sink.

Some time later he felt the dull stinging of a series of slaps to his head. When she saw that she had his attention, she poured the tequila onto the floor, accenting this gesture with an eye-opening Persian harangue.

Felix staggered into the bathroom, threw up, and returned to find a fresh cup of coffee. She had raised the volume and was still going strong. He'd never had her pick a lover's quarrel with him, though he'd always known it was in her somewhere. It was magnificent. It was washing over him in a musical torrent of absolute nonsense. It was operatic, and he found it quite beautiful. Like sitting through a rainstorm without getting wet: trees straining, leaves flying, dark, windy, torrential. Majestic.

Her idea of coffee was basically wet grounds, so it brought him around in short order. "You're right, I'm wrong, and I'm sorry," he admitted tangentially, knowing she didn't understand a word, "so come on and help me," and he opened the sink cabinet, where he had hidden all his bottles when he'd noticed the earlier disapproving glances. He then decanted them down the drain: vodka, Southern Comfort, the gin, the party jug of tequila, even the last two inches of his favorite single-malt. Moslems didn't drink, and really, how wrong could any billion people be?

He gulped a couple of aspirin and picked up the phone. "The police were here. They know about us. I got upset. I drank too much."

"Did they beat you?"

"Uh, no. They're not big fans of beating over here: they've got better methods. They'll be back. We are in big trouble."

She folded her arms. "Then we'll run away."

"You know, we have a proverb for that in America: 'you can run, but you can't hide.'"

"Darling, I love your poetry, but when the police come to the house, it's serious."

"Yes. It's very serious. It's serious as cancer. You've got no ID. You have no passport. You can't get on any plane to get away. Even the trains and lousy bus stations have facial recognition. My car is useless too. They'd read my license plate a hundred times before we hit city limits. I can't rent another car without leaving credit records. The cops have got my number."

"We'll steal a fast car and go very fast."

"You can't outrun them! That is not possible! They've all got phones like we do, so they're always ahead of us, waiting."

"I'm a rebel! I'll never surrender!" She lifted her chin. "Let's get married."

"I'd love to, but we can't. We have no license. We have no blood test."

"Then we'll marry in some place where they have all the blood they want. Beirut, that would be good." She placed her free hand against her chest. "We were married in my heart the first time we ever made love."

This artless confession blew through him like a summer breeze. "They do have rings for cash at a pawnbroker's.... But I'm a Catholic. There must be *somebody* who does this sort of thing. Maybe some heretic mullah. Maybe a Santeria guy?"

"If we're husband and wife, what can they do to us? We haven't done anything wrong. I'll get a green card. I'll beg them, I'll beg for mercy. I'll beg political asylum."

Agent Portillo conspicuously cleared his throat. "Mr. Hernandez, please! This would not be the conversation you two need to be having."

"I forgot to mention the worst part," Felix said. "They know about our phones."

"Miss Kadivar, can you also understand me?"

"Who are you? I hate you. Get off this line and let me talk to him."

"Salaam aleikum to you, too," Portillo concluded. "It's a sad commentary on federal procurement when a mullah's daughter has a fancy translator and I can't even talk live with my own fellow agents. By the way, those two gentle-men from the new regime in Teheran are staking out your apartment. How they failed to recognize your girlfriend on her way in, that I'll never know. But if you two listen to me, I think I can walk you out of this very dangerous situation."

"I don't want to leave my beloved," she said.

"Over my dead body," Felix declared. "Come and get me. Bring a gun."

"Okay, Miss Kadivar, you would seem to be the more rational of the two parties, so let me talk sense to you. You have no future with this man. What kind of wicked man seduces a decent girl with phone pranks? He's an *aayash*, he's a playboy. America has a fifty percent divorce rate. He would never ask your father honorably for your hand. What would your mother say?"

"Who is this awful man?" she said, shaken. "He knows everything!"

"He's a snake!" Felix said. "He's the devil!"

"You still don't get it, *compadre*. I'm not the Great Satan. Really, I'm not. I'm the *good guy*. I'm your guardian angel, dude. I'm trying really hard to give you back a normal life."

"Okay cop, you had your say, now listen to me. I love her body and soul, and even if you kill me dead for that, the flames from my heart will set my coffin on fire."

She burst into tears. "Oh God, my God, that's the most beautiful thing anyone has ever said to me!"

"You kids are sick, okay?" Portillo snapped. "This would be *mental ill-ness* that I'm eavesdropping on here! You two don't even *speak each other's language.* You had every fair warning. Just remember, when it happens, you *made me* do it. Now try this one on for size, Romeo and Juliet." The phones went dead.

Felix put his dead phone on the tabletop. "Okay. Situation report. We've got no phones, no passports, no ID, and two different intelligence agencies are after us. We can't fly, we can't drive, we can't take a train or a bus. My credit cards are useless now, my bank cards will just track me down, and I guess I've lost my job now. I can't even walk out my own front door.... And wow, you don't understand a single word I'm saying. I can tell from that look in your eye. You are completely thrilled."

She put her finger to her lips. Then she took him by the hand.

▲ ▼ ▲

Apparently, she had a new plan. It involved walking. She wanted to walk to Los Angeles. She knew the words "Los Angeles," and maybe there was someone there that she knew. This trek would involve crossing half the American continent on foot, but Felix was at peace with that ambition. He really thought he could do it. A lot of people had done it just for the sake of gold nuggets, back in 1849. Women had walked to California just to meet a guy with gold nuggets.

The beautiful part of this scheme was that, after creeping out the window, they really had vanished. The feds might be all over the airports, over everything that mattered, but they didn't care about what didn't matter. Nobody was looking out for dangerous interstate pedestrians.

To pass the time as they walked, she taught him elementary Farsi. The day's first lesson was body parts, because that was all they had handy for pointing. That suited Felix just fine. If anything, this expanded their passionate communion. He was perfectly willing to starve for that, fight for that and die for that. Every form of intercourse between man and woman was fraught with illusion, and the bigger, the better. Every hour that passed was an hour they had not been parted.

They had to sleep rough. Their clothes became filthy. Then, on the tenth day, they got arrested.

▲ ▼ ▲

She was, of course, an illegal alien, and he had the good sense to talk only Spanish, so of course, he became one as well. The Immigration cops piled them into the bus for the border, but they got two seats together and were able to kiss and hold hands. The other deported wretches even smiled at them.

He realized now that he was sacrificing everything for her: his identity, his citizenship, flag, church, habits, money…. Everything, and good riddance. He bit thoughtfully into his wax-papered cheese sandwich. That was the federal bounty delivered to every refugee on the bus, along with an apple, a small carton of homogenized milk, and some carrot chips.

When the protein hit his famished stomach Felix realized that he had gone delirious with joy. He was *growing* by this experience. It had broken every stifling limit within him. His dusty, savage, squalid world was widening drastically.

Giving alms, for instance—before his abject poverty, he'd never understood that alms were holy. Alms were indeed very holy. From now on—as soon as he found a place to sleep, some place that was so torn, so wrecked, so bleeding, that it never asked uncomfortable questions about a plumber— as soon as he became a plumber again, then he'd be giving some alms.

She ate her food, licked her fingers, then fell asleep against him, in the moving bus. He brushed the free hair from her dirty face. She was twenty days older now. "This a pearl," he said aloud. "This is a pearl by far too rare to be contained within the shell of time and space."

Why had those lines come to him, in such a rush? Had he read them somewhere? Or were those lines his own?

The Blemmye's Strategem

A messenger flew above the alleys of Tyre, skirting the torn green heads of the tallest palm trees. With a flutter of wings, it settled high on a stony ledge. The pigeon was quickly seized by a maiden within the tower. She gratefully kissed the bird's sleek gray head.

Sir Roger of Edessa, the maiden's lover, roamed the Holy Land on his knight errantry. Thanks to the maiden herself, Sir Roger possessed one precious cage of homing pigeons. Roger's words winged it to her, straight to her tender hands, soaring over every obstacle in a Holy Land aflame. The birds flapped over drum-pounding, horn-blaring Seljuk marauders, and evil mamelukes with faces masked in chainmail. They flitted over Ismaili fedayeen bent on murder and utterly careless of life.

An entire, busy network of messenger pigeons moved over the unknowing populace. These birds carried news through Jerusalem, Damascus, Cairo, and Beirut. They flitted over cavaliers from every cranny of Christendom, armed pilgrims who were starving, sweating, flea-bitten and consumed with poxes. Birds laden with script flew over sunburned, axe-wielding Vikings. Over fanatical Templars and cruel, black-clad Teutonic Knights, baking like armored lobsters in the blazing sun. Over a scum of Greek peltasts and a scrim of Italian condottiere.

With trembling, ink-stained fingers, the maiden untied the tidy scroll from the bird's pink leg. There was a pounding ache within her bosom. Would it be another poem? She often swooned on reading Roger's poems.

No. This bird had not come from Roger of Edessa. She had been cruelly misled by her own false hopes. The messenger bird was just another tiresome commercial bird. It carried nothing but a sordid rush of text.

Salt. Ivory. Tortoiseshell. Saffron. Rice. Frankincense. Iron. Copper. Tin. Lead. Coral. Topaz. Storax. Glass. Realgar. Antimony. Gold. Silver. Honey. Spikenard. Costus. Agate. Carnelian. Lycium. Cotton. Silk. Mallow. Pepper. Malabathrum. Pearls. Diamonds. Rubies. Sapphires.

Every good in this extensive list was followed by its price.

The girl locked the pigeon into its labeled wooden cage, along with dozens of other birds, her fellow captives within the gloomy tower. Using cuttlefish ink and a razor-trimmed feather, the girl copied the message into an enormous dusty ledger. If she ever failed in her duty to record, oh the woe she would receive at the hands of the Mother Superior. Bread and water. Endless kneeling, many rosaries.

The pigeon clerk rubbed at her watery eyes, harshly afflicted by fine print and bad lighting. She returned to lean her silken elbows on the cool, freckled stone, to contemplate the sparkling Mediterranean and a black swarm of profiteering Italian galleys. Perhaps Sir Roger of Edessa was dead. Poor Roger had been slain by a cruel Moslem champion, or else he was dead of some plague. Roger would never write a poem to her again. At the age of seventeen, she was abandoned to her desolate fate.

How likely all this seemed. Her doom was so total and utter. If Roger failed to rescue her from this miserable life tending pigeons, she would be forced to take unwelcome vows.

She would have to join the Little Sisters of the Hospitallers below the tower of birds, in that ever-swelling crowd of the Holy Land's black widows, another loveless wretch of a girl amid that pitiful host of husbandless crones and fatherless orphans, all of them bottled up behind tall, rocky walls, hopelessly trapped without any lands or dowries.

The pale brides of Christ, moody and distracted, waiting in itchy torment for some fatal pagan horde of dark-eyed Moslem fiends to conquer Tyre and ravage their fortress of chastity.

Another bird appeared in flight. The maiden's heart rose to beat in her throat. This was a strong bird, a swift one. When he arrived, his legs were clasped by two delicate bands of gold. His feathers smelled of incense.

The writing, though very tiny, was the most beautiful the girl had ever seen. The ink was blood-red, and it glittered.

DEAREST HUDEGAR
With the tip of my brush I give you the honey of good news
Our Silent Master has summoned us both
So prepare yourself quickly
For I hasten to you with a caravan of many strong men to take you to his Paradise
                    (signed) THE OLD MAN OF THE MOUNTAIN

The maiden began to weep, for her name was not Hudegar. She had never heard of any woman named Hudegar.

▲▼▲

Whether Christian or Moslem, hamlets in the Holy Land were always much the same: a huddle of dusty cottages around a well, a mill, and an oven. The Abbess Hildegart rode demurely into the plundered village, escorted by the heavily armed caravan of the Grand Assassin.

This hapless little village had been crushed with particular gusto. Vengeful marauders had hacked down the olive groves, set fire to the vineyard, and poisoned the well. Since they were still close to Tyre, the strongest city yet held by the reeling Crusader forces, Hildegart rather suspected the work of Hospitallers.

This conclusion disturbed her. Hildegart herself had founded the Hospitaller Order. She had created and financed a hospital corps in order to heal the sick, to run a chain of inns, and to give peace, comfort, and money-changing services to the endless sun-dazed hordes of holy European pilgrims.

Hildegart's idea had been a clever one, and was much appreciated by her patron, the Silent Master. However, some seventy years had passed since this invention of hers, and Hildegart had been forced to see her brilliant scheme degenerating. Somehow the Hospitaller corps, this kindly order of medical monks, had transformed itself into the most violent, fanatical soldiery in the Crusader forces. It seemed that their skills in healing injured flesh and bone also gave them a special advantage in chopping men apart. Even the Templars were scared of the Hospitallers, and the Templars frightened Assassins so badly that the Assassins often paid them for protection.

Some of the barns in the smashed village were still defensible. Sinan, the Old Man of the Mountain and the Ayatollah of Assassins, ordered his caravan to put up for the night. The caravan men made camp, buried several abandoned corpses, set up sentries, and struggled to water the horses with the tainted murk from the well.

The Abbess and the Assassin settled down behind their armed sentries, to eat and chat. Hildegart and Sinan had known each other for much longer than most people would ever live. Despite the fact that they both labored loyally for the Silent Master, their personal relations were rather strained. There had been times in her long, long life when Hildegart had felt rather safe and happy with Sinan. Sinan was an ageless Moslem wizard and therefore evil incarnate, but Sinan had once sheltered her from men even more dangerous than himself.

Those pleasant years of their history, unfortunately, were long behind both of them. At the age of one hundred seventeen, Sinan could not possibly protect Hildegart from any man more dangerous than himself, for Sinan the Assassin had become the most dangerous man in the world. The number of Crusaders who had fallen to his depredations was beyond all reckoning, though Hildegart shrewdly estimated it at somewhere over four thousand.

Underlit by red flames from his dainty iron camp stove, Sinan ate his roasted kabobs and said little. He offered her a warm, dark, gazelle-eyed look. Hildegart stirred uneasily in her dark riding cloak, hood, and wimple. Although Sinan was very intelligent and had learned a great deal about inflicting terror, Sinan's heart never changed much with the passing decades. He was always the same. Sinan was simple, direct, and devout in his habits, and he prayed five times every day, which (by Hildegart's reckoning) would likely make some two hundred thousand acts of prayer, every one of them involving a fervent hope that Crusaders would perish and burn in Hell.

Hildegart warmed one chilly hand at the iron brazier. Nearby, the homing pigeons cooed in their portable cribs. The poor pigeons were cold and unhappy, even more anxious to return to Tyre than she was. Perhaps they sensed that Sinan's mercenaries longed to pluck and eat them.

"Sinan, where did you find this horrible band of cutthroats?"

"I bought them for us, my dear," Sinan told her politely. "These men are Khwarizmian Turks from the mountains far beyond Samarkand. They are quite lost here in Palestine, without any land or loyalties. Therefore they are of use to me, and to our Silent Master, and to his purposes."

"Do you trust these bandy-legged fiends?"

"No, I don't trust them at all. But they speak only an obscure dialect, and unlike you and me, they are not People of the Book. So they cannot ever reveal what they may see of our Silent Master. Besides, the Khwarizmian Turks were cheap to purchase. They flee a great terror, you see. They flee the Great Khan of the Mongols."

Hildegart considered these gnomic remarks. Sinan wasn't lying. Sinan never lied to her; he was just grotesquely persistent in his pagan delusions. "Sinan, do I need to know more about this terrible Great Khan?"

"Better not to contemplate such things, my pearl of wisdom. Let's play a game of chess."

"Not this time, no."

"Why be coy? I'll spot you an elephant rook!"

"My markets for Chinese silk have been very disturbed these past ten years. Is this so-called Great Khan the source of my commercial difficulty?"

Sinan munched thoughtfully at his skewer of peppered mutton. Her remarks had irritated him. Brave men killed and died at Sinan's word, and yet she, Hildegart, was far richer than he was. Hildegart was the richest woman in the world. As the founder, accountant, banker, and chief moneylender of the Hospitaller order, Hildegart found her greatest joy in life managing international markets. She placed her money into goods and cities where it would create more money, and then she counted that money with great and precise care, and she placed it again. Hildegart had been doing this for decades, persistently and secretly, through a network of nameless agents in cities from Spain to India, a network linked by swift birds and entirely unsuspected by mankind.

Sinan knew how all this counting and placing of money was done, but as an Ayatollah of Assassins, he considered it boring and ignoble labor. That was why he was always sending her messenger birds and begging her for loans of cash.

"Dear, kind, sweet Hudegar," the Assassin said coaxingly.

Hildegart blushed. "No one calls me Hudegar. Except for you, they all died ages ago."

"Dear Hudegar, how could I ever forget my sweet pet name for you?"

"That was a slave girl's name."

"We're all the slaves of God, my precious! Even our Silent Master." Sinan yanked the metal skewer from his strong white teeth. "Are you too proud to obey his summons now, blessed Mother Superior? Are you tired of your long life, now that your Christian Franks are finally chased back into the sea by the warriors of righteousness?"

"I'm here with you, aren't I?" said Hildegart, avoiding his eyes. "I could be tending the wounded and doing my accounts. Why did you write to me in French? The whole convent's chattering about your mysterious bird and its message. You know how women talk when they've been cloistered."

"You never answer me when I write to you in Arabic," Sinan complained. He mopped at his fine black beard with a square of pink silk. "I write to you constantly! You know the cost of shipping these homing pigeons! Their flesh is more precious than amber!" The Assassin waved away the thickening smoke from the coals of his cookstove.

Hildegart lit the sesame oil at the spout of a small brass lamp. "I do write to you, dear Sinan, with important financial news, but in return, you write to me of nothing but your evil boasting and your military mayhem."

"I'm composing our history there!" Sinan protested. "I am putting my heart's blood into those verses, woman! You of all women should appreciate that effort!"

"Oh, very well then." Hildegart switched to Arabic, a language she knew fluently, thanks to her years as a captive concubine.

"'With the prodigies of my pen I express the marvel of the fall of Jerusalem,'" she quoted at him. "'I fill the towers of the Zodiac with stars, and the caskets with my pearls of insight. I spread the joyful news far and wide, bringing perfume to Persia and conversation to Samarkand. The sweetness of holy victory surpasses candied fruits and cane sugar.'"

"How clever you are, Hudegar! Those were my finest verses, too." Sinan's dark, arching brows knotted hopefully. "That's some pretty grand stuff there, isn't it?"

"You shouldn't try to be a poet, Sinan. Let's face it, you are an alchemist."

"But I've learned everything there is to know about chemistry and machinery," Sinan protested. "Those fields of learning are ignoble and boring. Poetry and literature, by contrast, are fields of inexhaustible knowledge!

Yes, I admit it, I do lack native talent for poesy—for when I began writing, my history was just a dry recital of factual events! But I have finally found my true voice as a poet, for I have mastered the challenge of narrating great deeds on the battlefield!"

Hildegart's temper rose. "Am I supposed to praise you for that? I had investments in Jerusalem, you silly block of wood! My best sugar presses were there... my favorite cotton dyes... and you can bet I'll tell the Blemmye all about those severe commercial losses!"

"You may quote me even further, and recite to him how Christian Jerusalem fell to the Moslems in flames and screams," said Sinan tautly. "Tell him that every tribe of Frank will be chased back into the ocean! Eighty-nine long years since these unbathed wretches staggered in from Turkey to steal our lands, looking like so many disinterred corpses! But at last, broken with righteous fire and sword, the occupiers flee the armies of Jihad like whipped dogs. Never to return! I have lived through all of that humiliation, Hudegar. I was forced to witness every sorrowful day of my people's long affliction. At last, in this glorious day of supreme justice, I will see the backs of those alien invaders. Do you know what I just heard Saladin say?"

Hildegart ate another salted olive. She had been born in Germany and had never gotten over how delicious olives were. "All right. What did Saladin say?"

"Saladin will build ships and sail after the retreating Christians to Europe." Sinan drew an amazed breath. "Can you imagine the stern qualities of that great soldier, who would trust to the perils of the open ocean to avenge our insulted faith? That's the greatest tribute to knightly bravery that I can imagine!"

"Why do you even bother with lowborn scum like Saladin? Saladin is a Kurd and a Shi'ite."

"Oh, no. Saladin is the chosen of God. He used the wealth of Egypt to conquer Syria. He used the wealth of Syria to conquer Mesopotamia. The wealth of Mesopotamia will finally liberate Palestine. Saladin will die with exhausted armies and an empty treasury. Saladin is very thin, and he suffers from bellyaches, but thanks to him, Palestine will be ours again. Those outlaw Crusader states of Christian Outremer will cease to be. That is the divine truth of history and yes, I will bear witness to divine truth. I must bear witness, you know. Such things are required of a scholar."

Hildegart sighed, at a loss for words. Hildegart knew so many words, reams and reams of words. She knew low German, French, Arabic, much Turkish, some Greek. Proper history was written in Latin, of course. Having successfully memorized the Old and New Testaments at the age of fourteen, Hildegart could manage rather well in Latin, but she had given up her own attempts to write any kind of history during the reign of Baldwin the Leper.

The Crusader King of Jerusalem had a loathsome Middle Eastern disease, and Hildegart found herself chronicling Baldwin's incessant defeats in a stale, stilted language that smelled of death. "King Baldwin the Leper suffered this crushing setback, King Baldwin the Leper failed at that diplomatic initiative…" The Leper seemed to mean well, and yet he was so stupid…. One stormy morning Hildegart had pulled years of secret records from her hidden cabinets and burned every one of them. It felt so good to destroy such weary knowledge that she had sung and danced.

Sinan gazed on her hopefully. "Can't you say just a bit more about my glamorous poetic efforts, Hudegar?"

"You are improving," she allowed. "I rather liked that line about the candied fruits. Those jongleurs of Eleanor of Aquitaine, they never write verse half so luscious as you do."

Sinan beamed on her for a moment, and returned to gnawing his mutton. However, he was quick to sense a left-handed compliment. "That Frankish queen, she prefers the love poems made by vagrants for women. All Frankish ladies enjoy such poems. I myself can write very sweetly about women and love. But I would never show those poems of mine to anyone, because they are too deeply felt."

"No doubt."

Sinan narrowed his eyes. "I can remember every woman who ever passed through my hands. By name and by face!"

"All of them? Could that be possible?"

"Oh come now, I never married more than four at a time! I can remember all of my wives very vividly. I shall prove it to you now, my doubting one! My very first wife was the widow of my older brother; she was Fatima, the eldest, with the two sons, my nephews. Fatima was dutiful and good. Then there was the Persian girl that the Sultan gave me: she was Bishar. She had crossed eyes, but such pretty legs. When my fortunes prospered, I bought the Greek girl Phoebe to cook for my other two."

Hildegart shifted uneasily.

"Then there was you, Hudegar the Frankish girl, my gift from the Silent Master. What splendid flesh you had. Hair like wheat and cheeks like apples. How you thrived in my courtyard and my library. You wanted kisses more than the other three combined. We had three daughters and the small son who died nameless." Sinan sighed from the depth of his heart. "Those are all such songs of loss and sorrow, my sweet songs of all my dear wives."

▲ ▼ ▲

Hildegart's early years had been tangled and difficult. She had left Germany as a teenaged nun in the massive train of Peter the Hermit, a tumbling migration of thousands of the wildly inspired, in the People's Crusade. They walked down the Rhine, they trudged down the Danube, they stumbled starving across Hungary, Byzantium, and the Balkans, asking at every town and village if the place might perhaps be Jerusalem.

The People' s Crusade killed most of its participants, but a crusade was the only sure way that Hildegart, who was the humble daughter of a falconer, could guarantee the remission of her sins. Hildegart marched from April to October of 1096. She was raped, starved, survived typhus, and arrived pregnant on an obscure hilltop in Turkey. There every man in her dwindling band was riddled with Seljuk arrows by the troops of Kilij Arslan.

Hildegart was purchased by a Turkish speculator, who took her infant for his own purposes, and then sold her to the aging Sultan of Mosul. The Sultan visited her once for form's sake, then left her to her own devices within his harem. The Mosul harem was a quiet, solemn place, very much like the convent she had left in Germany, except for the silks, the dancing, and the eunuchs. There Hildegart learned to speak Turkish and Arabic, to play a lute, to embroider, and to successfully manage the considerable administrative overhead involved in running the palace baths.

After the Sultan's murder, she was manumitted and conveyed to a Jewish merchant, by whom she had a son.

The Jew taught her accounting, using a new system of numeration he had learned from colleagues in India. He and the son then vanished on an overly daring business expedition into Christian-held Antioch. Hildegart was sold to meet his business debts. Given her skills and accomplishments, though, she was quickly purchased by a foreign diplomat.

This diplomat traveled extensively through Islam, together with his train of servants, in a slow pilgrimage from court to court. It was a rewarding life, in its way. Moslem courts competed in their lavish hospitality for distinguished foreigners. Foreign merchants and envoys, who lacked local clan ties, often made the most honest and efficient court officials. The Blemmye profited by this.

Literate scholars of the Islamic courts had of course heard tell of the exotic Blemmyae people. The Blemmyae were men from the land of Prester John, the men whose heads grew beneath their shoulders.

The Blemmye had no head; he was acephalous. Across his broad, barren shoulders grew a series of horny plates. Where a man might have paps, the Blemmye had two round black eyes, and he had a large, snorting nose in his chest. Where a navel might have been was his mouth. The Blemmye's mouth was a round, lipless, speechless hole, white and pink and ridged inside, and cinching tight like a bag. The Blemmye's feet, always neatly kept in soft leather Turkish boots, were quite toeless. He had beautiful hands, however, and his dangling, muscular arms were as round and solid as the trunks of trees.

The Blemmye, although he could not speak aloud, was widely known for his courteous behavior, his peaceable demeanor, and his generous gifts. In the troubled and turbulent Damascene court, the Blemmye was accepted without much demur.

The Blemmye was generally unhappy with the quality of his servants. They lacked the keen intelligence to meet his exacting requirements. Hildegart was a rare find for him, and she rose rapidly in her Silent Master's estimation.

The Blemmye wrote an excellent Arabic, but he wrote it in the same way he read books: entire pages at once, in one single comprehensive glance. So rather than beginning at the top of a page and writing from right to left, as any Arab scholar would, the Blemmye dashed and dotted his black markings across the paper, seemingly at random. Then he would wait, with unblinking eyes, to see if enough ink had arrived for his reader's comprehension.

If not, then he would dabble in more ink, but the trial annoyed him.

Hildegart had a particular gift for piecing out the Blemmye's fragmentary dabblings. For Hildegart, Arabic was also a foreign language, but she memorized long texts with ease, and she was exceedingly clever with numbers. Despite her master's tonguelessness, she also understood his moods, mostly through his snorts and his nervous, hand-wringing gestures. The Blemmye became reliant on her services, and he rewarded her well.

When his business called him far from Damascus, the Blemmye conveyed Hildegart to the care of his chief agent within the Syrian court, an Iraqi alchemist and engineer. Rashid al-din Sinan made his living from *Naphth*, a flaming war-product that oozed blackly from the reedy marshes of his native Tigris.

Like most alchemists, Sinan had extensive interests in hermetic theology, as well as civil engineering, calligraphy, rhetoric, diplomacy, and the herbarium. As a canny and gifted courtier, living on his wits, Sinan was quick to serve any diplomat who could pay for his provisions with small but perfect diamonds, as the Blemmye did. Sinan gracefully accepted Hildegart as his new concubine, and taught her the abacus and the tally-stick.

The Blemmye, being a diplomat, was deeply involved in international trade. He tirelessly sought out various rare oils, mineral salts, glasses, saltpeter, sulfur, potash, alchemical acids, and limes. He would trade in other goods to obtain the substances he prized, but his means were always subordinated to those same ends.

The Blemmye's personal needs were rather modest. However, he lavished many gifts on his mistress. The Blemmye was pitifully jealous of this female Blemmye. He kept her in such deep, secluded purdah that she was never glimpsed by anyone.

Hildegart and Sinan became the Blemmye's most trusted servants. He gave them his alchemical philters to drink, so that their flesh would not age in the mortal way of men and women. Many years of energetic action transpired, led by the pressing needs of their Silent Master. As wizard and mother abbess, Sinan and Hildegart grew in age and cunning, wealth and scholarship. Trade routes and caravans conveyed the Blemmye's goods and agents from the far reaches of Moslem Spain as far as the Spice Islands.

When Crusader ships appeared in the Holy Land, and linked the Moslem world with the distant commercial cities of the Atlantic and the Baltic, the Blemmye was greatly pleased.

Eventually, Sinan and Hildegart were forced to part, for their uncanny agelessness had aroused suspicion in Damascus. Sinan removed himself to a cult headquarters in Alamut, where he pursued the mystic doctrines and tactics of the Ismaili Assassins. Hildegart migrated to the Crusader cities of Outremer, where she married a wise and all-accepting Maronite. She had three more children by this union.

Time ended that marriage as it had all her other such relations. Eventually, Hildegart found that she had tired of men and children, of their roughness and their importunities. She resumed the veil as the female Abbess of a convent stronghold in Tyre. She became the wealthy commander of a crowd of cloistered nuns, busy women with highly lucrative skills at weaving, adorning, and marketing Eastern fabrics.

The Abbess Hildegart was the busiest person that she knew. Even in times of war, she received many informations from the farthest rims of the world, and she knew the price and location of the rarest of earthly goods. Yet there was a hollowness in her life, a roiling feeling that dark events were unfolding, events beyond any mastery.

Assuming that all her children had somehow lived... and that her children had children, and that they had lived as well... and that those grandchildren, remorseless as the calendar, had further peopled the Earth... Hildegart's abacus showed her as a silent Mother Superior to a growing horde of over three hundred people. They were Christians, Jews, Moslems, a vast and ever-ramifying human family, united in nothing but their ignorance of her own endlessly spreading life.

▲ ▼ ▲

The Dead Sea was as unpleasant as its name. Cursed Sodom was to the south, suicidal Masada to the middle, and a bloodstained River Jordan to the north. The lake gave pitch and bitumen, and mounds of gray, tainted salt. Birds that bathed in its water died and were crusted with minerals.

Arid limestone hills and caves on the Dead Sea shores had gone undisturbed for centuries.

Within this barren wilderness, the Blemmye had settled himself. Of late, the Silent Master, once so restless in his worldly quests for goods and services, moved little from his secretive Paradise, dug within the Dead Sea's barren hills. Sometimes, especially helpful merchants from Hildegart's pigeon network would be taken there, or Assassins would be briefed there on one last self-sacrificing mission. It was in the Blemmye's Paradise that Sinan and Hildegart drank the delicious elixirs that lengthened their lives.

There were gardens there, and stores of rare minerals. The Blemmye's hidden palace also held an arsenal. It concealed the many sinister weapons that Sinan had built.

No skill in military engineering was concealed from the cunning master of Assassins. Sinan knew well the mechanical secrets of the jarkh, the zanbarak, the qaws al-ziyar, and even the fearsome manjaniq, a death-machine men called "The Long-Haired Bride." With the Blemmye's aid and counsel, Sinan had built sinister crossbows with thick twisted skeins of silk and horsehair, capable of firing great iron beams, granite stones, red-hot bricks, and sealed clay bombs that splattered alchemical flames. Spewing, shrieking rockets from China were not beyond Sinan's war skills, nor was the Byzantine boiler that spewed ever-burning Greek Fire. Though difficult to move and conceal, these massive weapons of destruction were frighteningly potent. In cunning hands, they had shaped the fates of many a quarrelsome emirate. They had even hastened the fall of Jerusalem.

In his restless travels, the Blemmye had collected many rare herbs for the exquisite pergolas of his Paradise. He carefully collected the powder from within their flowers, and strained and boiled their saps for his marvelous elixirs. The Blemmye had forges and workshops full of curious instruments of metal and glass. He had struggled for years to breed superior camels for his far-ranging caravans. He had created a unique race of peculiar beasts, with hairless, scaly hides and spotted necks like cameleopards.

The choicest feature of the Blemmye's Paradise was its enormous bath. Sinan led his caravan men in a loud prayer of thanksgiving for their safe arrival. He commended their souls to his God, then he ushered the dusty, thirsting warriors within the marbled precincts.

Pure water gushed there from many great brass nozzles. The men eagerly doffed their chain-mail armor and their filthy gear. They laughed and sang, splashing their tattooed limbs in the sweet, cleansing waters. Delicate fumes of incense made their spirits soar to the heavens.

Very gently, their spirits left their bodies.

The freshly washed dead were carried away on handcarts by the Blemmye's house servants. These servants were eunuchs, and rendered tongueless.

Through her long and frugal habit, Hildegart carefully sorted through the effects of the dead men. The Moslem and Christian women who haunted the battlefields of the Holy Land, comforting the wounded and burying the slain, generally derived more wealth from dead men than they ever did from their live protectors. Female camp followers of various faiths often encountered one another in the newly strewn fields of male corpses. They would bargain by gesture and swap the dead men's clothes, trinkets, holy medals, knives, and bludgeons.

Sinan sought her out as Hildegart neatly arranged the dead men's dusty riding boots. He was unhappy. "The Silent One has written his commands for us," he told her. He frowned over his freshly inked instructions. "The eunuchs are to throw the bodies of the men into the mine shaft, as usual. But then we are to put the caravan's horses into the bath as well. All of them!" The Assassin gazed at her moodily. "There would seem to be scarcely anyone here. I see none of his gardeners, I see no secretaries.... The Master is badly understaffed. Scutwork of this kind is unworthy of the two of us. I don't understand this."

Hildegart was shocked. "It was well worth doing to rid ourselves of those evil foreign Turks, but we can't possibly stable horses in that beautiful marble bath."

"Stable them? My dear, we are to kill the horses and throw them down into the mine. That's what the Master has written for us here. See if there's not some mistake, eh? You were always so good at interpreting."

Hildegart closely examined the spattered parchment. The Blemmye's queer handwriting was unmistakable, and his Arabic had improved with the years. "These orders are just as you say, but they make no sense. Without pack-horses, how am I to return to Tyre, and you to Alamut?"

Sinan looked at her in fear. "What are you telling me? Do you dare to question the Silent Master's orders?"

"No, you're the man," she told him quickly. "*You* should question his orders."

Hildegart had not had an audience with the Blemmye in some eight years. Their only communication was through couriers, or much more commonly, through the messenger birds.

In earlier days, when his writings had been harder to interpret, Hildegart had almost been a body servant to the Blemmye. She had fetched his ink, brought him his grapes, bread, and honey, and even seen him off to his strange, shrouded bed. Then she had left him to dwell in his Paradise, and she had lived for many years many leagues away from him. As long as they were still writing to each other, however, he never complained about missing her.

The Blemmye gave her his old, knowing look. His eyes, round, black, and wise, spread in his chest a hand's span apart. The Blemmye wore baggy trousers of flowered blue silk, beautiful leather boots, and of course no head-gear. He sat cross-legged on a velvet cushion on the floor of his office, with his Indian inks, his wax seals, his accounting books, and his elaborate plans and parchments. The Blemmye's enormous arms had gone thinner with the years, and his speckled hide looked pale. His hands, once so deft and tire-less, seemed to tremble uncontrollably.

"The Master must be ill," hissed Hildegart to Sinan. The two of them whispered together, for they were almost certain that the Blemmye could not hear or understand a whispered voice. The Blemmye did have ears, or fleshy excrescences anyway, but their Silent Master never responded to speech, even in the languages that he could read and write.

"I will formally declaim the splendid rhetoric that befits our lordly Master, while you will write to him at my dictation," Sinan ordered.

Hildegart obediently seated herself on a small tasseled carpet.

Sinan bowed low, placing his hand on his heart. He touched his fingertips to lips and forehead. "A most respectful greeting, dread Lord! May Allah keep you in your customary wisdom, health and strength! The hearts of your servants overflow with joy over too long an absence from your august presence!"

"How are you doing, dear old Blemmye?" Hildegart wrote briskly. She shoved the parchment forward.

The Blemmye plucked up the parchment and eyed it. Then he bent over, and his wrist slung ink in a fury.

"My heart has been shattered / the eternal darkness between the worlds closes in / my nights burn unbroken by sleep I bleed slowly / from within / I have no strength to greet the dawn / for my endless days are spent in sighing grief and vain regrets / the Light of All My Life has perished / I will never hear from her again / never never never again / will I read her sweet words of knowledge understanding and consolation / henceforth I walk in darkness / for my days of alien exile wind to their fatal climax."

Hildegart held up the message and a smear of ink ran down it like a black tear.

▲ ▼ ▲

The two of them had never had the least idea that the Blemmye's wife had come to harm. The Blemmye guarded her so jealously that such a thing scarcely seemed possible.

But the mistress of their Silent Master, though very female, was not a Blemmye at all. She was not even a woman.

The Blemmye led them to the harem where he had hidden her.

This excavation had been the Blemmye's first great project. He had bought many slaves to bore and dig deep shafts into the soft Dead Sea limestone. The slaves often died in despair from the senseless work, perishing from the heat, the lack of fresh water, and the heavy, miasmic salt air.

But then, at Hildegart's counseling, the hapless slaves were freed and dismissed. Instead of using harsh whips and chains, the Blemmye simply tossed a few small diamonds into the rubble at the bottom of the pit.

Word soon spread of a secret diamond mine. Strong men from far and wide arrived secretly in many eager gangs. Without orders, pay, or any words of persuasion, they imported their own tools into the wasteland.

Then the miners fought recklessly and even stabbed each other for the privilege of expanding the Blemmye's diggings. Miraculous tons of limestone were quarried, enough rock to provide firm foundations for every structure in the Blemmye's Paradise. The miners wept with delight at the discovery of every precious stone.

When no more diamonds appeared, the miners soon wearied of their sport. The secret mine was abandoned and swiftly forgotten.

Within this cavernous dugout, then, was where the Blemmye had hidden his darling.

The Silent Master removed a counterweighted sheet of glass and iron. From the black gulf, an eye-watering, hellish stink of lime and sulfur wafted forth.

Strapping two panes of glass to his enormous face, the Blemmye inhaled sharply through his great trumpet of a nose. Then he rushed headlong into the stinking gloom.

Hildegart urged Sinan to retreat from the gush of foul miasma, but the Assassin resisted her urgings. "I always wondered what our Master did with all that brimstone. This is astonishing."

"The Blemmye loves a creature from Hell," said Hildegart, crossing herself.

"Well, if this is Hell, then we ourselves built it, my dear." Sinan shrouded his eyes and peered within the acid murk. "I see so many bones in there. I must go in there, you know, I must bear witness and write of all this…. Why don't you come along with me?"

"Are you joking? A mine is no place for a woman!"

"Of course it is, my dear! You simply must come down into Hell with me. You're the only aide memoire available, and besides, you know that I rely on your judgment."

When Hildegart stiffly refused him, Sinan shrugged at her womanly fears and rushed forward into the gassy murk. Hildegart wept for him, and began to pray—praying for her own sake, because Sinan's salvation was entirely beyond retrieval.

At the fifth bead of her rosary, the brave Assassin reappeared, half-leading his stricken Master. They were tugging and heaving together at a great, white, armored plate, a bone-colored thing like a gigantic shard of pottery.

This broken armor, with a few tangled limbs and bits of dry gut, that was all that was left of the Blemmye's Lady. She had been something like a great, boiled, stinking crab. Something like a barb-tailed desert scorpion, living under a rock.

In her silent life, cloistered deep within the smoking, stony earth, the Blemmye's Lady had fed well, and grown into a size so vast and bony and monstrous that she could no longer fit through the narrow cave mouth. Sinan and the Blemmye were barely able to tug her skeletal remnants into daylight.

The Blemmye pawed at a hidden trigger, and the great iron door swung shut behind him with a hollow boom. He wheezed and coughed, and snorted loudly through his dripping nose.

Sinan, who had breathed less deeply of the hellish fumes, was the first to recover. He spat, and wiped his streaming eyes, then gestured to Hildegart for pen and ink.

Then Sinan sat atop a limestone boulder. He ignored her questions with a shake of his turbaned head, and fervently scribbled his notes.

Hildegart followed the laboring Blemmye as he tugged at his bony, rattling burden. The Silent Master trembled like a dying ox as he hauled the big skidding carcass. His sturdy leather boots had been lacerated, as if chopped by picks and hatchets.

Ignoring his wounds, the Blemmye dragged the riddled corpse of his beloved, yard by painful yard, down the slope toward the Dead Sea. The empty carapace was full of broken holes. The she-demon had been pecked to pieces from within.

Hildegart had never seen the Blemmye hurt. But she had seen enough wounded men to know the look of mortal despair, even on a face as strange as his.

The Blemmye collapsed in anguish at the rim of the sullen salt lake.

Hildegart smoothed the empty sand before him with her sandaled foot. Then she wrote to him with a long brass pin from the clasp of her cloak. "Master, let us return to your Paradise. There I will tend to your wounds."

The Blemmye plucked a small table knife from his belt and scratched rapidly in the sand. "My fate is of no more consequence / I care only for my darling's children / though born in this unhappy place/ they are scions of a great and noble people."

"Master, let us write of this together in some much better place."

The Blemmye brushed away her words with the palm of his hand. "I have touched my poor beloved for the last time in my life / How pitifully rare were our meetings / We sent each other many words through the black gulfs and seas amid the stars / to understand one sentence was the patient work of years / her people and mine were mortal enemies amid the stars / And yet she trusted me / She chose to become mine / She fled with me to live in exile to this distant unknown realm / Now she has left me to face our dark fate alone / It was always her dear way to give her life for others / Alas my sweet correspondent has finally perished of her generosity."

The Blemmye tugged in fitful despair at his lacerated boots.

Resignedly, Hildegart knelt and pulled the torn boots from her Master's feet. His wounds were talon slashes, fearsome animal bites. She pulled the cotton wimple from her head and tore it into strips.

"I promised her that I would guard her children / sheltering them as I always sheltered her / That foolish vow has broken my spirit / I will fail her in my promise, for I cannot live without her / Her goodness and her greatness of spirit / She was so wise, and knew so many things / Great marvels I could never have guessed, known, or dreamed of / What a strange soul she had, and how she loved me / What wondrous things we shared together from our different worlds / Oh, how she could write!"

Sinan arrived. The Assassin's eyes were reddened with the fumes, but he had composed himself.

"What have you been doing?" Hildegart demanded, as she worked to bind the Blemmye's bleeding, toeless feet.

"Listen to this feat of verse!" Sinan declared. He lifted his parchment, cleared his throat, and began to recite. "'With my own eyes, I witnessed the corpses of the massacred! Lacerated and disjointed, with heads cracked open and throats split; spines broken, necks shattered; noses mutilated, hair colored with blood! Their tender lips were shriveled, their skulls cracked and pierced; their feet were slashed and fingers sliced away and scattered; their ribs staved in and smashed. With their life's last breath exhaled, their very ghosts were crushed, and they lay like dead stones among stones!'"

Hildegart's bloodied fingers faltered on the knot of her rough bandage. The sun beat against her bared head. Her ears roared. Her vision faded.

When she came to, Sinan was tenderly sponging her face with water from his canteen.

"You swooned," he told her.

"Yes," she said faintly, "yes, that overcame me."

"Of course it would," he agreed, eyes shining, "for those wondrous verses possessed me in one divine rush! As if my very pen had learned to speak the truth!"

"Is that what you saw in Hell?" she said.

"Oh no," he told her, "that was what I witnessed in the siege of Jerusalem. I was never able to describe that experience before, but just now, I was very inspired." Sinan shrugged. "Inside that ugly mine, there is not much to see. There is dark acrid smoke there, many chewed bones. The imps within, they screeched and rustled everywhere, like bats and lizards. And that infernal stench!" Sinan looked sidelong at the Blemmye's wounded shins. "See how the little devils attacked him, as he walked through the thick of them, to fetch out their dam."

Though the Blemmye did not understand Sinan's words, the tone of the Assassin's voice seemed to stir him. He sat up, his black eyes filmy and grievous. He took up his knife again, and carved fresh letters into the sand. "Now we will take the precious corpse of my beloved / and sink her to her last rest in this strange sea she loved so much. / This quiet lake was the kindest place to her of any in your world."

Sinan put his verses away, and pulled at one whitened limb of the Blemmye's ruined lover. The bony armor rocked and tilted like a pecked and broken Roc's egg. The wounded Blemmye stood on his bleeding feet, lifting and shoving at the wall of bone with all his failing strength. The two of them splashed waist-deep into the evil water.

As the skeleton sank into the shallows, there was a sudden stirring and skittering. From a bent corner of the shell, shaking itself like a wet bird, came a small and quite horrible young demon. It had claws, and a stinging tail, and a circlet of eyes like a spider. It hopped and chirped and screeched.

Sinan wisely froze in place, like a man confronting a leopard. But the Blemmye could not keep his composure. He snorted aloud and fled splashing toward the shore.

The small demon rushed after the Blemmye as if born to the chase. It quickly felled him to the salty shore. At once, it began to feed on him.

Sinan armed himself with the closest weapon at hand: he tore a bony flipper from the mother's corpse. He waded ashore in a rush, and swung this bone like a mace across the heaving back of the imp. Its armor was as tough as any crab's, though, and the heavy blow only enraged it.

The little demon turned on the Assassin with awful speed, and likely would have killed a fighter less experienced. Sinan, though, was wise enough to outfox the young devil. He dodged its feral lunges, striking down and cracking the vulnerable joints in its twitching, bony limbs. When the monster faltered, foaming and hissing, he closed on it with a short, curved dagger from within his robe.

Sinan rose at last from the young beast's corpse, his robes ripped and his arm bloodied. He hid his blade away again, then dragged the dead monster to the salt shore. There he heaved it with a shudder of loathing into the still water beside its mother.

Hildegart knelt beside the panting Blemmye. His wounds had multiplied.

The Blemmye blinked, faint with anguish. His strength was fading visibly, yet he still had something left to write. He scraped at the sand with a trembling fingertip. "Take me to my Paradise and bind my wounds / See to it that I live / I shall reveal to you great wonders and secrets / beyond the comprehension of your prophets."

Sinan took Hildegart by the arm.

"I'm no longer much concerned about our horses, my dear," he told her. He knelt and smoothed out their Master's writing. A spatter of his own blood fell on the sand beside the Blemmye's oozings.

"That ugly monster has hurt you, my brave hero!"

"Do you know how many times this poor old body of mine has known a wound?" Sinan's left arm had been badly scored by the creature's lashing tail. He gritted his teeth as she tied off his arm with a scarf. "What a joy that battle was, my darling. I have never killed anything that I wanted to kill so much."

The Blemmye propped his headless body on one elbow. He beckoned at them feebly.

Hildegart felt a moment of sheer hatred for him, for his weakness, for his foolish yieldings to the temptations of darkness. 'What it is that the Blemmye wants to write of now, these *great secrets* that he promises us?'

"It will be much the same as it was before," Sinan said with disgust. "That mystical raving about the Sun being only a star. He'll tell us that other stars are suns, with other worlds and other peoples."

Hildegart shivered. "I always hated that!"

"The world is very, very old, he'll insist on that nonsense, as well. Come, let us help him, my dear. We shall have to patch the Master up, for there is no one else fit to do it."

"Thousands of years," Hildegart quoted, unmoving where she stood. "Then, thousands of thousands of years. And thousands, of thousands, of thousands. Then thirteen and a half of those units. Those are the years since the birth of the universe."

"How is it you can remember all that? Your skills at numeration are beyond compare!" Sinan trembled suddenly, in an after-combat mix of rage, fear, and weariness. "My dear, please give me counsel, in your wisdom: did his huge numbers ever make any sense to you? Any kind of sense at all?"

"No," she told him.

The Assassin looked wearily at the fainting Blemmye. He lowered his voice. "Well, I can fully trust your counsel in this matter, can't I? Tell me that you are quite sure about all that."

Hildegart felt a rush of affection for him. She recognized that look of sincere, weighty puzzlement on his face; he'd often looked like that in the days when they had played chess together, whiling away pleasant evenings as lord and concubine. It was Sinan who had taught her chess; Sinan had taught Hildegart the very existence of chess. Chess was a wonderful game, with the crippled Shah, and the swift Vizier, and all their valiant knights, stern fortresses and crushing elephants. When she began to defeat him at chess, he only laughed and praised her cleverness; he seemed to enjoy their game all the more.

"My dear, brave Sinan, I can promise you: God Himself doesn't need such infinities, not even for His angels to dance on the heads of pins." Hildegart felt light-headed without her wimple, and she ran her hands self-consciously across her braids. "Why does he think that big numbers are some kind of reward for us? What's wrong with gold and diamonds?"

Sinan shrugged again, favoring his wounded arm. "I think his grief has turned his mind. We must haul him away from his darling now. We must put him to bed, if we can. No man can be trusted at the brink of his lover's grave."

Hildegart gazed with loathing at the demonic skeleton. The dense salt water still bore the she-monster up, but her porous wreck was drowning, like a boat hull riddled with holes. A dark suspicion rose within Hildegart's heart. Then a cold fear came. "Sinan, wait one moment longer. Listen to me now. What number of evil imps were bred inside that great incubus of his?"

Sinan's eyes narrowed. "I would guess at least a hundred. I knew that by the horrid noise."

"Do you remember the story of the Sultan's chessboard, Sinan? That story about the great sums."

This was one of Sinan's Arabic tales: the story of a foolish sultan's promise to a cheating courtier. Just one grain of wheat on the first square of the chessboard, but two grains of wheat on the second, and then four on the third, and then eight, sixteen, thirty-two. A granary-leveling inferno of numbers.

Sinan's face hardened. "Oh yes. I do remember that story of algebra. And now I begin to understand."

"I learned that number story from you," she said.

"My clever darling, I well remember how we shared that tale—and I also know the size of that mine within the earth! Ha-ha! So that's why he needs to feed those devils with the flesh of my precious pack horses! When those vile creatures breed in there, then how many will there be, eh? There will be hundreds, upon hundreds, multiplied upon hundreds!"

"What will they do to us?" she said.

"What else can they do? They will spill out into our sacred homeland! Breeding in their endless numbers, uncountable as the stars, they will spread as far as any bird can fly!"

She threw her arms around him. He was a man of such quick understanding.

Sinan spoke in a hoarse whisper. "So, darling, thanks to your woman's intuition, we have found out his wicked scheme! Our course is very clear now, is it not? Are we both agreed on what we must do?"

"What do you mean?"

"Well, I must assassinate him."

"What, now?"

Sinan released her, his face resolutely murderous. "Yes, of course now! To successfully kill a great lord, one must fall on him like a thunderbolt from a clear sky. The coup de grace always works best when least expected. So you will feign to help him to his feet. Then, without a word of warning, I will bury my steel blade between his ribs."

Hildegart blinked and wiped grains of salty sand from her cloak. "Does the Blemmye have ribs, Sinan?"

Sinan stroked his beard. "You're right, my dear; I hadn't quite thought that through."

But as they conspired together, the Blemmye himself rose from the bloodstained sand. He tottered and staggered into the stinging salts of the dead lake. His darling had failed to sink entirely from sight.

Half-swimming, their master shoved and heaved at the bony ridges and spars that broke the surface. The waters of the Dead Sea were very buoyant by nature, but the Blemmye had no head to keep above the water. He ignored their shouts and cries of warning.

There he sank, tangled in the heavy bones of his beloved. Minutes later, his drowned corpse bobbed to the surface like a cork.

▲ ▼ ▲

After the death of the Silent Master, life in the Holy Land took a swift turn for the worse. First, exotic goods vanished from the markets. Then trade faltered. Ordered records went unkept. Currencies gyrated in price. Crops were ravaged and villages sacked, caravans raided and ships sunk. Men no longer traded goods, or learned from one another; they were resolved upon massacre.

Defeat after wave of defeat scourged the dwindling Christian forces. Relentlessly harassed, the Crusaders lurked and starved within their stone forts, or else clung fitfully to offshore ships and islands, begging reinforcements that were loath to come.

Sinan's Moslem raiders were the first to occupy the Blemmye's Paradise. Sinan had vaguely meant to do something useful with the place. The Assassin was a fiendish wizard whose very touch meant death, and his troops feared him greatly. But armies were low on discipline when loot was near. Soon they were breaking the plumbing, burning the libraries, and scraping at semi-precious stones with the blades of their knives.

Hildegart's own Crusader forces had arrived late at the orgy, but they were making up for lost time. The Christians had flung themselves on the Blemmye's oasis like wolves. They were looting everything portable, and burning all the rest.

Six guards dragged Hildegart into Sinan's great black battle tent. They threw her to the tasseled carpet.

The pains of battlefield command had told on the alchemist. Sinan's face was lined, and he was thinner. But with Hildegart as his captive, he brightened at once. He lifted her to her feet, drew his scimitar, and gallantly sawed the hemp ropes from her wrists. "How astonishing life can be!" he said. "How did you reach me amid all this turmoil?"

"My lord, I am entirely yours; I am your hostage. Sir Roger of Edessa offers me to you as the guarantee of the good behavior of his forces." Hildegart sighed after this little set speech.

Sinan seemed skeptical. "How unseemly are these times at the end of history! Your paladin Roger offers me a Christian holy woman for a hostage? A woman is supposed to be a pleasant gift between commanders! Who is this 'Roger of Edessa'? He requires some lessons in knightly courtesy."

Hildegart rubbed her chafed wrists. Her weary heart overflowed toward the Assassin in gushing confidence. "Sinan, I had to choose Roger of Edessa to command this expedition. Roger is young, he is bold, he despises death, and he had nothing better to do with himself but to venture forth and kill demonic monsters."

Sinan nodded. "Yes, I understand such men perfectly."

"I myself forced Sir Roger to appoint me as your hostage."

"I still must wonder at his lack of gallantry."

▲ ▼ ▲

"Oh, it's all a very difficult story, very. The truth is, Roger of Edessa gave me to you as a hostage because he hates me. You see, Sir Roger dearly loves my granddaughter. This granddaughter of mine is a very foolish, empty-headed girl, who, despite her fine education, also despises me bitterly. When I saw the grip that their unchaste passion had on the two of them, I parted them at once. I kept her safe in a tower in Tyre with my message birds.... Roger is a wandering adventurer, a freelance whose family fief was lost years ago. I had a much more prosperous match in mind for this young girl. However, even bread and water could not break her of her stupid habit of loving him.... It is her hand in marriage that Roger seeks above all, and for her silly kisses he is willing to face hell itself... Do I tire you with all this prattling, Sinan?"

"Oh no, no, your words never tire me," Sinan said loyally. He sat with a weary groan, and absently patted a plump velvet cushion on the carpet. "Please do go on with your exotic Christian romance! Your personal troubles are always fascinating!"

"Sinan, I know I am just a foolish woman and also a cloistered nun, but do grant me some credit. I, a mere nun, have raised an army for you. I armed all these wicked men, I fed them, I clothed them, I brought them here for you to kill those demons with.... I did the very best I could."

"That was a very fine achievement, sweet little Hudegar."

"I am just so tired and desperate these days. Since the dark word spread of our Silent Master's death, all my agents have fallen to quarreling. The birds no longer fly, Sinan, the birds go neglected and they perish. And when the poor birds do arrive, they bear me the most awful news: theft, embezzlement, bankruptcies, every kind of corruption... All the crops are burned around Tyre and Acre, Saladin's fearsome raiders are everywhere in the Holy Land.... There is famine, there is pestilence.... The clouds take the shapes of serpents, and cows bring forth monsters.... I am at my wits' end."

Sinan clapped his hands, and demanded the customary hostage cloak and hostage hat. Hildegart donned the official garments gratefully. Then Hildegart accepted a cool lime sherbet. Her morale was improving, since her Assassin was so kindly and dependable.

"Dearest Sinan, I must further inform you about this ugly band I have recruited for your daring siege of Hell. They are all Christians fresh off the boat, and therefore very gullible. They are Englishmen... well, not English... they are Normans, for the English are their slaves. These are lion-hearted soldiers, and lion-gutted, and lion-toothed, with a lion's appetites. I promised them much loot, or rather, I made Sir Roger promise them all that."

"Good. These savages of yours sound rather promising. Do you trust them?"

"Oh no, certainly not. But the English had to leave Tyre for the holy war anyway, for the Tyrians would not suffer them to stay inside the port. These English are a strange, extremely violent people. They are drunken, foul, rampaging, their French is like no French I ever heard..." Hildegart put down her glass sherbet bowl and began to sniffle. "Sinan, you don't know what it's been like for me, dealing with these dirty brutes. The decay of courtesy today, the many gross, impious insults I have suffered lately.... They are nothing at all like yourself, a gentleman and true scholar."

Despite all difficulty, Hildegart arranged a formal parley between Sinan and Sir Roger of Edessa. Like most of the fighters dying in the Holy Land, Roger of Edessa was a native. Roger's grandfather had been French, his grandmother Turkish, his father German and his mother a Greek Orthodox native of Antioch. His home country, Edessa, had long since fallen in flames.

Sir Roger of Edessa was a Turcopole, the child of Moslem-Christian unions. Roger wore a checkered surcoat from Italy, and French plate armor, and a Persian peaked cavalry helmet with an Arabian peacock plume. Sir Roger's blue eyes were full of lucid poetic despair, for he had no land to call his own. Wherever he went in the Holy Land, some blood relation was dying. The Turcopoles, the Holy Land's only true natives, were never considered a people to be trusted by anyone; they fought for any creed with indifference, and were killed by all with similar glee. Roger, though only twenty, had been fighting and killing since the age of twelve.

With Hildegart to interpret for him, Sir Roger and his boldest Englishmen inspected their new Moslem allies. Sinan's best efforts had raised a bare two hundred warriors to combat the fiends. Somewhere over the smoldering horizon, the mighty Saladin was rousing the Moslem faithful to fight yet another final, conclusive, epic battle with the latest wave of Western invaders. Therefore, heroic Moslem warriors willing to fight and kill demons were rather thin on the ground.

Word had also spread widely of the uniformly lethal fate of Sinan's suicide martyr assassins. Nevertheless, Sinan's occult reputation had garnered together a troop of dedicated fanatics. He had a bodyguard of Ismailis from a heretical madrassa. He had a sprinkling of Fatimid Egyptian infantry and their Nubians, and some cynical Damascenes to man his siege machines. These large destructive weapons, Sinan hoped, were his keys to a quick victory.

Roger examined the uncanny siege weapons with profound respect. The copper kettle-bellies of the Greek Fire machines spoke eloquently of their sticky, flaming mayhem. Much fine cedar of Lebanon had been sacrificed for the massive beams of the catapults.

Roger had been educated by Templars. He had traveled as far as Paris in their constant efforts to raise money for the wars. He was incurably proud of his elegant French. "Your Excellency, my pious troops are naturally eager to attack and kill these wicked cave monsters. But we do wonder at the expense."

Hildegart translated for Sinan. Although the wily Assassin could read French, he had never excelled at speaking it.

"My son, you are dealing with the Old Man of the Mountain here." Sinan passed Roger a potent handful of diamonds. "You and your fine boys may keep these few baubles. Inspire your troops thus. When the very last of these foul creatures is exterminated within that diamond mine, then we shall make a full inventory of their legendary horde of jewels."

Roger displayed this booty to his two top lieutenants. The first was a sunburned English sea captain with vast mustaches, who looked rather uneasy stuck on horseback. The second was a large crop-headed Norman rascal, shorn of both his ears. The two freebooters skeptically crunched the jewels between their teeth. When the diamonds failed to burst like glass, they spat them out into their flat-topped kettle-helmets. Then they shared a grin.

Sinan's Assassin spies had been keeping close watch over the cave. The small war council rode there together to reconnoiter the battle terrain. Hildegart was alarmed by the sinister changes that had taken place on the site. The mighty door of glass and iron had been riddled with pecked holes. Fresh bones strewed the ground, along with the corpse-pale, shed outer husks of dozens of crabs. All the vegetation was gnawed and stripped, and the dusty earth itself was chewed up, as if by the hooves of stampeding cattle.

Using their pennoned lances, Roger's two lieutenants prodded at a cast-off husk of pinkish armor. Roger thoughtfully rolled a diamond through his mailed fingertips. "O Lord High Emir Commander, this place is indeed just as you told us: a very mouth of Hell! What is our battle plan?"

"We will force the evil creatures into the open with gouts of Greek fire. Then I place great confidence in your Christian knights who charge in heavy armor." Sinan was suave. "I have seen their shock tactics crush resistance in a twinkling. Especially from peasants on foot."

"My English knights will likely be sober enough to charge by tomorrow," Roger agreed. "Is our help required in moving all those heavy arbalests? I had some small acquaintance with those in Jerusalem."

"My Damascene engineers will acquit themselves to our general satisfaction," said Sinan. He turned his fine Arabian stallion. The party cantered from the cave.

"There is also the matter of our battle signals, Your Excellency," Roger persisted gamely. "Your minions prefer kettledrums, while my men use flags and trumpets…"

"Young commander, such a problem is easily resolved. Would you care to join me for this battle on the back of my elephant? With those flags, horns, drums… and our translator, of course."

Hildegart was so startled that she almost fell from her mare. "You have an elephant, Sinan?"

The Assassin caught the reins of her restive horse in his skilled hand. "My tender hostage, I brought you an elephant for the sake of your own safety. I hope you are not afraid to witness battle from atop my great beast?"

She met his eyes steadily. "Trusting in your wise care, I fear nothing, dread Prince!"

"How good you are."

Sinan's war elephant was the strangest creature to answer the call of his birds. The gray and wrinkled pachyderm had tramped some impossible distance, from the very shores of Hindustan maybe, arriving thirsty and lean at the Dead Sea, with his great padded feet wrapped in shabby, salt-worn leather. The elephant had many battle scars on the vast bulging walls of his hide, and a man-killing glare in his tiny red eyes. His ivory tusks were carefully grooved for the insertion of sharp sword blades. He wore thick quilted cotton armor, enough for a dozen tents. His towering sandalwood howdah had a brass-inlaid crossbow, pulled back by two stout whirring cranks, with forty huge barbed bolts of Delhi steel, each one fit to pierce three men clean through. His Master was a very terror of the Earth.

Hildegart gazed up at the vast beast and back to Sinan with heartfelt admiration. How had the Assassin managed such a magnificent gesture?

On the next day, Sinan made her some formal gifts: an ivory-handled dagger, a helmet with a visor and veil to hide her beardless face, padded underarmor, and a horseman's long tunic of mail. It would simply not do for the common troops to see a woman taking to the battlefield. However, Sinan required her counsel, her language skills, and a written witness to events. Clad in the armor and helmet, she would pass as his boyish esquire.

The dense links of greased mail crunched and rustled on Hildegart's arms. The armor was so heavy that she could scarcely climb the folding ladder to the elephant's gleaming howdah. Once up, she settled heavily into place amid dense red horsehair cushions, towering over the battlefield giddily, feeling less like a woman than an airborne block of oak.

The battle opened with glorious bursts of colored flames. Sinan's sweating engineers kept up a steady pace, pumping gout after gout of alchemical fire down the black throat of Hell.

A half-dozen imps appeared at once at the cave mouth. As creatures inured to sulfur, they seemed less than impressed by the spurts of Greek Fire. The beasts had grown larger now, and were at least the size of goats.

At the sight of their uncanny capering, the cavalry horses snorted and stamped below their mailed and armored masters. A few cowards fled in shock at the first sight of such unnatural monsters, but their manhood was loudly taunted by their fellows. They soon returned shamefaced to their ranks.

A drum pounded, a horn blasted, and a withering fire of crossbow bolts sleeted across the dancing crabs. In moments every one had been skewered, hopping, gushing pale ichor, and querulously plucking bolts from their pierced limbs. The men all cheered in delight. Watching through the slits in her visor, Hildegart realized that the imps had no idea that weapons could strike from a distance. They had never seen such a thing done.

Sinan's stores of Greek Fire were soon exhausted. He then ordered his catapults into action. Skilled Damascenes with great iron levers twisted the horsehide skeins until the cedar uprights groaned. Then, with concussive thuds, the machines flung great pottery jars of jellied Naphth deep into the hole. Sullen booms echoed within.

Suddenly there was a foul, crawling clot of the demons, an antlike swarm of them, vomiting forth in pain, with carapaces wreathed in dancing flames.

The creatures milled forth in an unruly burning mob. The fearless Ismaili Assassins, seeking sure reward in the afterlife, screamed the name of God and flung themselves into the midst of the enemy, blades flailing. The bold martyrs swiftly died, cruelly torn by lashing tails and pincers. At the sight of this sacrifice and its fell response, every man in the army roared with the rage for vengeance.

A queer stench wafted from the monsters' burning flesh, a reek that even the horses seemed to hate.

Trumpets blew. The English knights couched their lances, stood in their stirrups, and rode in shield to shield. The crabs billowed from the shock, with a bursting of their gore and a splintering of lances. The knights, slashing and chopping with their sabers, fell back and regrouped. Their infantry rushed forth to support them, finishing off the wounded monsters with great overhand chops of their long-handled axes.

A column of black smoke began to block the sky. Then a great, choking, roiling tide of the demons burst from their filthy hole. They had been poisoned somehow, and were spewing thin phlegm from the gills on their undersides. There were hundreds of them. They leapt over everything in their path, filled with such frantic energy that they almost seemed to fly.

In moments the little army was overrun, surrounded. The Damascenes died screaming at their siege machinery. Horses panicked and fell as lunging, stinging monsters bit through their knees. Stout lines of spear-carrying infantry buckled and collapsed.

But there was no retreat. Not one man left the battlefield. Even those who died, fell on the loathsome enemy with their last breath.

Men died in clumps, lashed, torn, shredded. At the howdah's rear deck,

Sir Roger pounded a drumskin and shouted his unheard orders. The elephant, ripped and slashed by things no taller than his knees, was stung into madness. With a shattering screech from his curling sinuous nose, he charged with great stiff-legged earthshaking strides into the thickest of the enemy. As the towering beast lurched in his fury, Sinan kept up a cool fire from the howdah's crossbow. His fatal yard-long bolts pierced demons through, pinning them to the earth.

A knot of angry demons swarmed up the elephant as if it were a moving mountain. The evil creatures seethed right up the elephant's armored sides.

Hildegart, quailing within her heavy helmet and mail, heard them crawling and scrabbling on the roof of the howdah as Roger and Sinan, hand to hand, lashed out around them with long blades.

Claws caught within the steel links of her chain mail and yanked her from the howdah.

Along with the demons seizing her, she tumbled in a kicking, scrambling mass from the plunging elephant. They crashed and tumbled through a beleaguered cluster of Egyptians on horseback.

Hildegart lay stunned and winded as more and more of the foul creatures swarmed toward the great beast, their pick-like legs scrabbling over her. Chopped almost in half by the elephant's steel-bearing tusks, a demon came flying and crashed across her. It lay on her dying, and among its many twitching legs, its broken gills wheezed forth a pale pink froth.

Hildegart lay still as death, knowing that many survived battles that way. She was utterly terrified, flat on her back amid a flowing tide of jittering, chattering monsters, men's dying screams, curses, the clash of their steel. Yet there was almost a tender peace in such stillness, for she wanted for nothing. She only wished that she were somehow still in the howdah, together with dear Sinan, to wrap her arms around him one last time, to shield his body from his fate, even at the cost of her own life.

Suddenly, as often happened in battles, there was a weird lull. She saw the blue sky and a rising billow of poisoned smoke. Then the elephant came screaming and trampling over her, blinded, bleeding, staggering to its death. Its great foot fell and rose swiftly. It stamped her flat, and broke her body.

Coldness crept around her heart. She prayed in silence.

After some vague time she opened her eyes to see Sinan's torn and bloodied face inside his dented helmet.

▲ ▼ ▲

"The day is ours," he told her. "We have killed all of them, save a very few that fled into the mine. Few of us survive… but none of them can be suffered to live. I have sworn a holy oath that they shall not trouble the next generation. My last two Assassins and I are walking into hell to settle them forever. We shall march into the very midst of them, our bodies laden with our very best bombs. That is a strategy that cannot fail."

"I must take notes for our glorious history," she murmured. "You must write the verses for me. I long to read them so!"

The Assassin eased the helmet from her braided hair, and carefully arranged her limbs. Hildegart could not feel her own numbed legs, but she felt him lift her mailcoat to probe her crushed flesh. "Your back is broken, precious." With no more word than that—for the coup de grace always worked best without warning—she felt a sharp, exciting pang through her ribs. Her Assassin had stabbed her.

He kissed her brow. "No gentleman would write one word about our history! All that sweetness was our secret; it was just for you and me."

▲ ▼ ▲

The tattered pigeon carried an urgent message:

"MY DARLING: At the evil shores of a dead sea, I have survived a siege of such blood and hellish fire that I pray that no survivor ever writes of it. My command was ravaged. All who came to this land to serve God have died for Him, and even the imps of Satan have perished, leaving nothing but cold ashes and bones. My heart now tells me: you and I will never know a moment's happiness as man and woman unless we flee this dreadful Holy Land. We must seek some shelter far beyond the Gates of Hercules, or far beyond the Spice Islands, if there is any difference. We must find a place so distant no one will ever guess our origins. There I swear that I will cleave to you, and you only, until the day I die.

"Trust me and prepare yourself at once, my beloved, for I am coming to take you from your tower and finally make you mine. I am riding to you as fast as any horse will carry me. Together we will vanish from all ken, so that no man or woman will ever know what became of us."

The laden pigeon left the stone sill of the window. She fluttered to the floor, and pecked at the useless husks of a few strewn seeds. The pigeon found no water. Every door hung broken from every empty cage. The tower was abandoned, a prey to the sighing wind.

Kiosk

The fabrikator was ugly, noisy, a fire hazard, and it smelled. Borislav got it for the kids in the neighborhood.

One snowy morning, in his work gloves, long coat, and fur hat, he loudly power-sawed through the wall of his kiosk. He duct-taped and stapled the fabrikator into place.

The neighborhood kids caught on instantly. His new venture was a big hit.

The fabrikator made little plastic toys from 3-D computer models. After a week, the fab's dirt-cheap toys literally turned into dirt. The fabbed toys just crumbled away, into a waxy, non-toxic substance that the smaller kids tended to chew.

Borislav had naturally figured that the brief lifetime of these toys might discourage the kids from buying them. This just wasn't so. This wasn't a bug: this was a feature. Every day after school, an eager gang of kids clustered around Borislav's green kiosk. They slapped down their tinny pocket change with mittened hands. Then they exulted, quarreled and sometimes even punched each other over the shining fab-cards.

The happy kid would stick the fab-card (adorned with some glossily fraudulent pic of the toy) into the fabrikator's slot. After a hot, deeply exciting moment of hissing, spraying and stinking, the fab would burp up a freshly-minted dinosaur, baby-doll or toy fireman.

Foot-traffic always brought foot-traffic. The grownups slowed as they crunched the snowy street. They cast an eye at the many temptations ranked behind Borislav's windows. Then they would impulse-buy. A football scarf, maybe. A pack of tissues for a sneezy nose.

Once again he was ahead of the game: the only kiosk in town with a fabrikator.

The fabrikator spoke to him as a veteran street-merchant. Yes, it definitely *meant something* that those rowdy kids were so eager to buy toys that fell apart and turned to dirt. Any kiosk was all about high-volume repeat business. The stick of gum. The candy bar. The cheap, last-minute bottle-of-booze. The glittery souvenir keychain that tourists would never use for any purpose whatsoever. These objects were the very stuff of a kiosk's life.

Those colored plastic cards with the 3-D models…The cards had potential. The older kids were already collecting the cards: not the toys that the cards made, but the cards themselves.

And now, this very day, from where he sat in his usual street-cockpit behind his walls of angled glass, Borislav had taken the next logical step. He offered the kids ultra-glossy, overpriced, collector cards that could not and would not make toys. And of course—there was definitely logic here—the kids were going nuts for that business model. He had sold a hundred of them.

Kids, by the nature of kids, weren't burdened with a lot of cash. Taking their money was not his real goal. What the kids brought to his kiosk was what kids had to give him—futurity. Their little churn of street energy—that was the symptom of something bigger, just over the horizon. He didn't have a word for that yet, but he could feel it, in the way he felt a coming thunderstorm inside his aching leg.

Futurity might bring a man money. Money never saved a man with no future.

II.

Dr. Grootjans had a jaw like a horse, a round blue pillbox of a hat, and a stiff winter coat that could likely stop gunfire. She carried a big European shopping-wand.

Ace was acting as her official street-guide, an unusual situation, since Ace was the local gangster. "Madame," Ace told her, "this is the finest kiosk in the city. Boots here is our philosopher of kiosks. Boots has a fabrikator! He even has a water fountain!"

Dr. Grootjans carefully photographed the water fountain's copper pipe, plastic splash basin, and disposable paper pop-out cups. "Did my guide just call you 'Boots?'" she said. "Boots as in footgear?"

"Everybody calls me that."

Dr. Grootjans patted her translation earpiece, looking pleased. "This water-fountain is the exhaust from your fuel cell."

Borislav rubbed his mustache. "When I first built my kiosk here, the people had no running water."

Dr. Grootjans waved her digital wand over his selections of panty-hose. She photographed the rusty bolts that fixed his kiosk to the broken pavement. She took particular interest in his kiosk's peaked roof. People often met their friends and lovers at Borislav's kiosk, because his towering satellite dish was so easy to spot. With its painted plywood base and showy fringes of snipped copper, the dish looked fit for a minaret.

"Please try on this pretty necklace, madame! Made by a fine artist, she lives right up the street. Very famous. Artistic. Valuable. Regional. Handmade!"

"Thank you, I will. Your shop is a fine example of the local small-to-micro regional enterprise. I must make extensive acquisitions for full study by the Parliamentary committee."

Borislav swiftly handed over a sheet of flimsy. Ace peeled off a gaping plastic bag and commenced to fill it with candy bars, placemats, hand-knitted socks, peasant dolls in vests and angular headdresses, and religious-war press-on tattoos. "He has such variety, madame! Such unusual goods!"

Borislav leaned forward through his cash window, so as to keep Dr. Grootjans engaged as Ace crammed her bags. "Madame, I don't care to boast about my modest local wares.... Because whatever I sell is due to the people! You see, dear doctor-madame, every object desired by these colorful local people has a folk-tale to tell us...."

Dr Grootjan's pillbox hat rose as she lifted her brows. "A folk-tale, did you say?"

"Yes, it's the people's poetry of commerce! Certain products appear...the products flow through my kiosk...I present them pleasingly, as best I can.... Then, the people buy them, or they just don't buy!"

Dr. Grootjans expertly flapped open a third shopping-bag. "An itemized catalog of all your goods would be of great interest to my study committee."

Borislav put his hat on.

Dr. Grootjans bored in. "I need the *complete, digital* inventory of your merchandise. The working file of the full contents of your store. Your commercial records from the past five years will be useful in spotting local consumer trends."

Borislav gazed around his thickly packed shelving. "You mean you want a list of everything I sell in here? Who would ever find the time?"

"It's simple! You must have heard of the European Unified Electronic Product Coding System." Dr. Grootjans tucked the shopping-wand into her canvas purse, which bore an imperial logo of thirty-five golden stars in a widening spiral. "I have a smart-ink brochure here which displays in your local language. Yes, here it is: 'A Partial Introduction to EU-EPCS Regulatory Adoption Procedures.'"

Borislav refused her busily flashing inkware. "Oh yes, word gets around about that electric barcoding nonsense! Those fancy radio-ID stickers of yours. Yes, yes, I'm sure those things are just fine for rich foreign people with shopping-wands!"

"Sir, if you sensibly deployed this electronic tracking system, you could keep complete, real-time records of all your merchandise. Then you would know exactly what's selling, and not. You could fully optimize your product flow, reduce waste, maximize your profit, and benefit the environment through reduced consumption."

Borislav stared at her. "You've given this speech before, haven't you?"

"Of course I have! It's a critical policy issue! The modern Internet-of-Things authenticates goods, reduces spoilage, and expedites secure cross-border shipping!"

"Listen, madame doctor: your fancy bookkeeping won't help me if I don't know the soul of the people! I have a little kiosk! I never compete with those big, faceless mall stores! If you want that sort of thing, go shop in your five-star hotel!"

Dr. Grootjans's lowered her sturdy purse and her sharp face softened into lines of piety. "I don't mean to violate your quaint local value system.... Of course we fully respect your cultural differences.... Although there will be many tangible benefits when your regime fully harmonizes with European procedures."

"'My regime,' is it? Ha!" Borislav thumped the hollow floor of his kiosk with his cane. "This stupid regime crashed all their government computers! Along with crashing our currency, I might add! Those crooks couldn't run that fancy system of yours in a thousand years!"

"A comprehensive debate on this issue would be fascinating!" Dr. Grootjans waited expectantly, but, to her disappointment, no such debate followed. "Time presses," she told him at last. "May I raise the subject of a complete acquisition?"

Borislav shrugged. "I never argue with a lady or a paying customer. Just tell what you want."

Dr Grootjans sketched the air with her starry wand. "This portable shelter would fit onto an embassy truck."

"Are you telling me that you want to *buy my entire kiosk?*"

"I'm advancing that option now, yes."

"What a scandal! Sell you my kiosk? The people would never forgive me!"

"Kiosks are just temporary structures. I can see your business is improving. Why not open a permanent retail store? Start over in a new, more stable condition. Then you'd see how simple and easy regulatory adoption can be!"

Ace swung a heavily laden shopping bag from hand to hand. "Madame, be reasonable! This street just can't be the same without this kiosk!"

"You do have severe difficulties with inventory management. So, I will put a down-payment on the contents of your store. Then," she turned to Ace, "I will hire you as the inventory consultant. We will need every object named, priced and cataloged. As soon as possible. Please."

▲▼▲

Borislav lived with his mother on the ground floor of a local apartment building. This saved him trouble with his bad leg. When he limped through the door, his mother was doing her nails at the kitchen table, with her hair in curlers and her feet in a sizzling foot-bath.

Borislav sniffed at the stew, then set his cane aside and sat in a plastic chair. "Mama dear, heaven knows we've seen our share of bad times."

"You're late tonight, poor boy! What ails you?"

"Mama, I just sold my entire stock! Everything in the kiosk! All sold, at one great swoop! For hard currency, too!" Borislav reached into the pocket of his long coat. "This is the best business day I've ever had!"

"Really?"

"Yes! It's fantastic! Ace really came through for me—he brought his useful European idiot, and she bought the whole works! Look, I've saved just one special item, just for you."

She raised her glasses on a neck-chain. "Are these new fabbing cards?"

"No, Mama. These fine souvenir playing cards feature all the stars from your favorite Mexican soap operas. These are the originals, still in their wrapper! That's authentic cellophane!"

His mother blew on her wet scarlet nails, not daring to touch her prize. "Cellophane! Your father would be so proud!"

"You're going to use those cards very soon, Mama. Your Saint's-Day is coming up. We're going to have a big bridge party for all your girlfriends. The boys at the Three Cats are going to cater it! You won't have to lift one pretty finger!"

Her mascara'ed eyes grew wide. "Can we afford that?"

"I've already arranged it! I talked to Mirko who runs the Three Cats, and I hired Mirko's weird gay brother-in-law to decorate that empty flat upstairs. You know—that flat nobody wants to rent, where that mob guy shot himself. When your old girls see how we've done that place up, word will get around. We'll have new tenants in no time!"

"You're really fixing the haunted flat, son?"

Borislav changed his winter boots for his wooly house slippers. "That's right, Mama. That haunted flat is gonna be a nice little earner."

"It's got a ghost in it."

"Not any more, it doesn't. From now on, we're gonna call that place...what was that French word he used?—we'll call it the 'atelier'!"

"The 'atelier'! Really! My heart's all a-flutter!"

Borislav poured his mother a stiff shot of her favorite digestive.

"Mama, maybe this news seems sudden, but I've been expecting this. Business has been looking up. Real life is changing, for the real people in this world. The people like us!" Borislav poured himself a brimming cup of flavored yogurt. "Those fancy foreigners, they don't even understand what the people are doing here today!"

"I don't understand all this men's political talk."

"Well, I can see it on their faces. I know what the people want. The people…They want a new life."

She rose from her chair, shaking a little. "I'll heat up your stew. It's getting so late."

"Listen to me, Mama. Don't be afraid of what I say. I promise you something. You're going to die on silk sheets. That's what this means. That's what I'm telling you. There's gonna be a handsome priest at your bedside, and the oil and the holy water, just like you always wanted. A big granite headstone for you, Mama, with big golden letters."

As he ate his stew, she began to weep with joy.

▲ ▼ ▲

After supper, Borislav ignored his mother's usual nagging about his lack of a wife. He limped down to the local sports bar for some serious drinking. Borislav didn't drink much any more, because the kiosk scanned him whenever he sat inside it. It used a cheap superconductive loop, woven through the fiberboard walls. The loop's magnetism flowed through his body, revealing his bones and tissues on his laptop screen. Then the scanner compared the state of his body to its records of past days, and it coughed up a medical report.

This machine was a cheap, pirated copy of some hospital's fancy medical scanner. There had been some trouble in spreading that technology, but with the collapse of public health systems, people had to take some matters into their own hands. Borislav's health report was not cheery. He had plaque in major arteries. He had some seed-pearl kidney-stones. His teeth needed attention. Worst of all, his right leg had been wrecked by a land-mine. The shinbone had healed with the passing years, but it had healed badly. The foot below his old wound had bad circulation.

Age was gripping his body, visible right there on the screen. Though he could witness himself growing old, there wasn't much he could do about that.

Except, that is, for his drinking. Borislav had been fueled by booze his entire adult life, but the alcohol's damage was visibly spreading through his organs. Lying to himself about that obvious fact simply made him feel like a fool. So, nowadays, he drank a liter of yogurt a day, chased with eco-correct paper cartons of multivitamin fruit juices, European-approved, licensed, and fully patented. He did that grumpily and he resented it deeply, but could see on the screen that it was improving his health.

So, no more limping, pitching and staggering, poetically numbed, down the midnight streets. Except for special occasions, that is. Occasions like this one.

Borislav had a thoughtful look around the dimly lit haunt of the old Homeland Sports Bar. So many familiar faces lurking in here—his daily customers, most of them. The men were bundled up for winter. Their faces were rugged and lined. Shaving and bathing were not big priorities for them. They were also drunk.

But the men wore new, delicately tinted glasses. They had nice haircuts. Some had capped their teeth. The people were prospering.

Ace sat at his favorite table, wearing a white cashmere scarf, a tailored jacket and a dandified beret. Five years earlier, Ace would have had his butt royally kicked for showing up at the Homeland Sports Bar dressed like an Italian. But the times were changing at the Homeland.

Bracing himself with his cane, Borislav settled into a torn chair beneath a gaudy flat-screen display, where the Polish football team were making fools of the Dutch.

"So, Ace, you got it delivered?"

Ace nodded. "Over at the embassy, they are weighing, tagging and analyzing every single thing you sell."

"That old broad's not as stupid as she acts, you know."

"I know that. But when she saw that cheese-grater that can chop glass. The floor wax that was also a dessert! " Ace half-choked on the local cognac. "And the skull adjuster! God in heaven!"

Borislav scowled. "That skull adjuster is a great product! It'll chase a hangover away—" Borislav snapped his fingers loudly—"just like that!"

The waitress hurried over. She was a foreign girl who barely spoke the language, but there were a lot of such girls in town lately. Borislav pointed at Ace's drink. "One of those, missie, and keep 'em coming."

"That skull squeezer of yours is a torture device. It's weird, it's nutty. It's not even made by human beings."

"So what? So it needs a better name and a nicer label. 'The Craniette,' some nice brand-name. Manufacture it in pink. Emboss some flowers on it."

"Women will never squeeze their skulls with that crazy thing."

"Oh yes they will. Not old women from old Europe, no. But some will. Because I've seen them do it. I sold ten of those! The people want it!"

"You're always going on about 'what the people want.'"

"Well, that's it! That's our regional competitive advantage! The people who live here, they have a very special relationship to the market economy." Borislav's drink arrived. He downed his shot.

"The people here," he said, "they're used to seeing markets wreck their lives and turn everything upside down. That's why we're finally the ones setting the hot new trends in today's world, while the Europeans are trying to catch up with us! These people here, they *love* the new commercial products with no human origin!"

"Dr. Grootjans stared at that thing like it had come from Mars."

"Ace, the free market always makes sense—once you get to know how it works. You must have heard of the 'invisible hand of the market.'"

Ace downed his cognac and looked skeptical.

"The invisible hand—that's what gives us products like the skull-squeezer. That's *easy* to understand."

"No it isn't. Why would the invisible hand squeeze people's heads?"

"Because it's a search engine! It's mining the market data for new opportunities. The bigger the market, the more it tries to break in by automatically generating new products. And that headache-pill market, that's one of the world's biggest markets!"

Ace scratched under his armpit holster. "How big is that market, the world market for headaches?"

"It's huge! Every convenience store sells painkillers. Little packets of two and three pills, with big price markups. What are those pills all about? The needs and wants of the people!"

"Miserable people?"

"Exactly! People who hate their jobs, bitter people who hate their wives and husbands. The market for misery is always huge." Borislav knocked back another drink. "I'm talking too much tonight."

"Boots, I need you to talk to me. I just made more money for less work than I have in a long time. Now I'm even on salary inside a foreign embassy. This situation's getting serious. I need to know the philosophy—how an invisible hand makes real things. I gotta figure that out before the Europeans do."

"It's a market search engine for an Internet-of-Things."

Ace lifted and splayed his fingers. "Look, tell me something I can get my hands on. You know. Something that a man can steal."

"Say you type two words at random: any two words. Type those two words into an Internet search engine. What happens?"

Ace twirled his shot-glass. "Well, a search engine always hits on something, that's for sure. Something stupid, maybe, but always something."

"That's right. Now imagine you put two *products* into a search engine for things. So let's say it tries to sort and mix together…a parachute and a pair of shoes. What do you get from that kind of search?"

Ace thought it over. "I get it. You get a shoe that blows up a plane."

Borislav shook his head. "No, no. See, that is your problem right there. You're in the racket, you're a fixer. So you just don't think commercially."

"How can I out-think a machine like that?"

"You're doing it right now, Ace. Search engines have no ideas, no philosophy. They never think at all. Only people think and create ideas. Search engines are just programmed to search through what people want. Then they just mix, and match, and spit up some results. Endless results. Those results don't matter, though, unless the people want them. And here, the people want them!"

The waitress brought a bottle, peppered sauerkraut and a leathery loaf of bread. Ace watched her hips sway as she left. "Well, as for me, I could go for some of *that*. Those Iraqi chicks have got it going on."

Borislav leaned on his elbows and ripped up a mouthful of bread. He poured another shot, downed it, then fell silent as the booze stole up on him in a rush. He was suddenly done with talk.

Talk wasn't life. He'd seen real life. He knew it well. He'd first seen real life as a young boy, when he saw a whole population turned inside out. Refugees, the unemployed, the dispossessed, people starting over with pencils in a tin cup, scraping a living out of suitcases. Then people moving into stalls and kiosks. "Transition," that's what they named that kind of life. As if it were all going somewhere in particular.

The world changed a lot in a Transition. Life changed. But the people never transitioned into any rich nation's notion of normal life. In the next big "transition," the 21st-century one, the people lost everything they had gained.

When Borislav crutched back, maimed, from the outbreak of shooting-and-looting, he threw a mat on the sidewalk. He sold people boots. The people needed his boots, even indoors, because there was no more fuel in the pipelines and the people were freezing.

Come summer, he got hold of a car. Whenever there was diesel or bio-fuel around, he sold goods straight from its trunk. He made some street connections. He got himself a booth on the sidewalk.

Even in the rich countries, the lights were out and roads were still. The sky was empty of jets. It was a hard Transition. Civilization was wounded.

Then a contagion swept the world. Economic depression was bad, but a plague was a true Horseman of the Apocalypse. Plague thundered through a city. Plague made a city a place of thawing ooze, spontaneous fires, awesome deadly silences.

Borislav moved from his booth into the freezing wreck of a warehouse, where the survivors sorted and sold the effects of the dead. Another awful winter. They burned furniture to stay warm. When they coughed, people stared in terror at their handkerchiefs. Food shortages, too, this time: the dizzy edge of famine. Crazy times.

He had nothing left of that former life but his pictures. During the mayhem, he took thousands of photographs. That was something to mark the day, to point a lens, to squeeze a button, when there was nothing else to do, except to hustle, or sit and grieve, or jump from a bridge. He still had all those pictures, every last one of them. Everyday photographs of extraordinary times. His own extraordinary self: he was young, gaunt, wounded, hungry, burning-eyed.

As long as a man could recognize his own society, then he could shape himself to fit its circumstances. He might be a decent man, dependable, a man of his word. But when the society itself was untenable, when it just could not be sustained—then 'normality' cracked like a cheap plaster mask. Beneath the mask of civilization was another face: the face of a cannibal child.

Only hope mattered then: the will to carry on through another day, another night, with the living strength of one's own heartbeat, without any regard for abstract notions of success or failure. In real life, to live was the only "real".

In the absence of routine, in the vivid presence of risk and suffering, the soul grew. Objects changed their primal nature. Their value grew as keen as tears, as keen as kisses. Hot water was a miracle. Electric light meant instant celebration. A pair of boots was the simple, immediate reason that your feet had not frozen and turned black. A man who had toilet paper, insulation, candles: he was the people's hero.

When you handed a woman a tube of lipstick, her pinched and pallid face lit up all over. She could smear that scarlet on her lips, and when she walked down the darkened street it was as if she were shouting aloud, as if she were singing.

When the plague burned out—it was a flu, and it was a killer, but it was not so deadly as the numb despair it inspired—then a profiteer's fortune beckoned to those tough enough to knock heads and give orders. Borislav made no such fortune. He knew very well how such fortunes were made, but he couldn't give the orders. He had taken orders himself, once. Those were orders he should never have obeyed.

Like a stalled train, civilization slowly rattled back into motion, with its usual burden of claptrap. The life he had now, in the civilized moving train, it was a parody of that past life. That burning, immediate life. He had even been in love then.

Today, he lived inside his kiosk. It was a pretty nice kiosk, today. Only a fool could fail to make a living in good times. He took care, he improvised, so he made a profit. He was slowly buying-up some flats in an old apartment building, an ugly, unloved place, but sturdy and well-located. When old age stole over him, when he was too weak to hustle in the market any more, then he would live on the rents.

A football team scored on the big flat screen. The regulars cheered and banged their flimsy tables. Borislav raised his heavy head, and the bar's walls reeled as he came to himself. He was such a cheap drunk now; he would really have to watch that.

▲ ▼ ▲

Morning was painful. Borislav's mother tiptoed in with muesli, yogurt, and coffee. Borislav put his bad foot into his mother's plastic foot-bath—that treatment often seemed to help him—and he paged through a crumbling yellow block of antique newspapers. The old arts district had always been a bookish place, and these often showed up in attics. Borislav never read the ancient "news" in the newspapers, which, during any local regime, consisted mostly of official lies. Instead, he searched for the strange things that the people had once desired.

Three huge, universal, dead phenomena haunted these flaking pages: petroleum cars, cinema, and cigarettes. The cars heavily dragged along their hundreds of objects and services: fuels, pistons, mufflers, makers of sparks. The cigarettes had garish paper packages, with lighters, humidors, and special trays just for their ashes. As for the movie stars, they were driving the cars and smoking the cigarettes.

The very oldest newspapers were downright phantasmagoric. All the newspapers, with their inky, frozen graphics, seemed to scream at him at him across their gulf of decades. The dead things harangued, they flattered, they shamed, they jostled each other on the paper pages. They bled margin-space, they wept ink.

These things were strange, and yet, they had been desired. At first with a sense of daring, and then with a growing boldness, Borislav chose certain dead items to be digitally copied and revived. He re-released them into the contemporary flow of goods. For instance, by changing its materials and proportions, he'd managed to transform a Soviet-era desk telephone into an lightweight plastic rain-hat. No one had ever guessed the origin of his experiments. Unlike the machine-generated new products—always slotted with such unhuman coolness into market niches—these revived goods stank of raw humanity. Raw purpose. Raw desire.

Once, there had been no Internet. And no Internet-of-Things, either, for that could only follow. There had only been the people. People wanting things, trying to make other people want their things. Capitalism, socialism, communism, those mattered little enough. Those were all period arrangements in a time that had no Internet.

The day's quiet study restored Borislav's good spirits. Next morning, his mother re-commenced her laments about her lack of a daughter-in-law. Borislav left for work.

He found his kiosk pitifully stripped and empty, with a CLOSED sign in its damp-spotted window. A raw hole loomed in the wall where the fabrikator had been torn free. This sudden loss of all his trade-goods gave him a lofty thrill of panic.

Borislav savored that for a moment, then put the fear behind him. The neighborhood still surrounded his kiosk. The people would nourish it. He had picked an excellent location, during the darkest days. Once he'd sold them dirty bags of potatoes here, they'd clamored for wilted carrots. This life was easy now. This life was like a good joke.

He limped through the biometric door and turned on the lights.

Now, standing inside, he felt the kiosk's true nature. A kiosk was a conduit. It was a temporary stall in the endless flow of goods.

His kiosk was fiberboard and glue: recycled materials, green and modern. It had air filters, insulated windows, a rugged little fuel cell, efficient lights, a heater grill in the floor. It had password-protected intrusion alarms. It had a medical scanner in the walls. It had smart-ink wallpaper with peppy graphics.

They had taken away his custom-shaped chair, and his music player, loaded with a fantastic mashed-up mulch of the complete pop hits of the 20th century. He would have to replace those. That wouldn't take him long.

He knelt on the bare floor, and taped a thick sheet of salvaged cardboard over the wintry hole in his wall. A loud rap came at his window. It was Fleka the Gypsy, one of his suppliers.

Borislav rose and stepped outside, reflexively locking his door, since this was Fleka. Fleka was the least dependable of his suppliers, because Fleka had no sense of time. Fleka could make, fetch, or filch most anything, but if you dared to depend on his word, Fleka would suddenly remember the wedding of some gypsy cousin, and vanish.

"I heard about your good luck, Boots," grinned Fleka. "Is the maestro in need of new stock?"

Borislav rapped the empty window with his cane. "It's as you see."

Fleka slid to the trunk of his rusty car and opened it.

"Whatever that is," said Borislav at once, "it's much too big."

"Give me one minute from your precious schedule, maestro," said Fleka. "You, my kind old friend, with your lovely kiosk so empty, I didn't bring you any goods. I brought you a factory! So improved! So new!"

"That thing's not new, whatever it is."

"See, it's a fabrikator! Just like the last fabrikator I got for you, only this one is bigger, fancy and much better! I got it from my cousin."

"I wasn't born yesterday, Fleka."

Fleka hustled under his back seat and brought out a sample. It was a rotund doll of the American actress, Marilyn Monroe. The doll was still unpainted. It was glossily black.

Marilyn Monroe, the ultimate retail movie-star, was always recognizable, due to her waved coif, her lip-mole, and her torpedo-like bust. The passage of a century had scarcely damaged her shelf-appeal. The woman had become an immortal cartoon, like Betty Boop.

Flecka popped a hidden seam under Marilyn's jutting bust. Inside the black Marilyn doll was a smaller Marilyn doll, also jet-black, but wearing less clothing. Then came a smaller, more risque' little Marilyn, and then a smaller one yet, and finally a crudely-modelled little Marilyn, shiny black, nude, and the size of Borislav's thumb.

"Nice celebrity branding," Borislav admitted. "So what's this material?" It seemed to be black china.

"It's not wax, like that other fabrikator. This is carbon. Little straws of carbon. It came with the machine."

Borislav ran his thumbnail across the grain of the material. The black Marilyn doll was fabricated in ridges, like the grooves in an ancient gramophone record. Fabs were always like that: they jet-sprayed their things by piling up thin layers, they stacked them up like pancakes. "'Little straws of carbon.' I never heard of that."

"I'm telling you what my cousin told me. 'Little nano tubes, little nano carbon.' That's what he said." Fleka grabbed the round Marilyn doll like a football goalie, and raised both his hands overhead. Then, with all his wiry strength, he smacked the black doll against the rust-eaten roof of his car. Chips flew.

"You've ruined her!"

"That was my car breaking," Fleka pointed out. "I made this doll this morning, out of old plans and scans from the Net. Then I gave it to my nephew, a nice big boy. I told him to break the doll. He broke a crowbar on this doll."

Borislav took the black doll again, checked the seams and detailing, and rapped it with his cane. "You sell these dolls to anyone else, Fleka?"

"Not yet."

"I could move a few of these. How much you asking?"

Fleka spread his hands. "I can make more. But I don't know how to make the little straws of carbon. There's a tutorial inside the machine. But it's in Polish. I hate tutorials."

Borislav examined the fabrikator. The machine looked simple enough: it was basic black shell, a big black hopper, a black rotating plate, a black spraying nozzle, and the black gearing of a 3-D axis. "Why is this thing so black?"

"It's nice and shiny, isn't it? The machine itself is made of little straws of carbon."

"Your cousin got you this thing? Where's the brand name? Where's the serial number?"

"I swear he didn't steal it! This fabrikator is a copy, see. It's a pirate copy of another fabrikator in Warsaw. But nobody knows it's a copy. Or if they do know, the cops won't be looking for any copies around this town, that's for sure."

Borislav's doubts overflowed into sarcasm. "You're saying it's a fabrikator that copies fabrikators? It's a fabbing fab fabber, that's what you're telling me, Fleka?"

A shrill wail of shock and alarm came from the front of the kiosk. Borislav hurried to see.

A teenage girl, in a cheap red coat and yellow winter boots, was sobbing into her cellphone. She was Jovanica, one of his best customers.

"What's the matter?" he said.

"Oh! It's you!" Jovanica snapped her phone shut and raised a skinny hand to her lips. "Are you still alive, Mr. Boots?"

"Why wouldn't I be alive?"

"Well, what happened to you? Who robbed your store?"

"I'm not robbed. Everything has been sold, that's all."

Jovanica's young face screwed up in doubt, rage, frustration and grief. "Then *where are my hair toys?*"

"What?"

"Where are my favorite barrettes? My hair clips! My scrunchies and headbands and beautiful pins! There was a whole tree of them, right here! I picked new toys from that tree every day! I finally had it giving me just what I wanted!"

"Oh. That." Borislav had sold the whirling rack of hair toys, along with its entire freight of goods.

"Your rack sold the best hair toys in town! So super and cool! What happened to it? And what happened to your store? It's broken! There's nothing left!"

"That's true, 'Neetsa. You had a very special relationship with that interactive rack, but...well..." Borislav groped for excuses, and, with a leap of genius, he found one. "I'll tell you a secret. You're growing up now, that's what."

"I want my hair toys! Go get my rack right now!"

"Hair toys are for the 9-to-15 age bracket. You're growing out of that market niche. You should be thinking seriously about earrings."

Jovanica's hands flew to her earlobes. "You mean pierce my ears?"

Borislav nodded. "High time."

"Mama won't let me do that."

"I can speak to your mama. You're getting to be a big girl now. Soon you'll have to beat the boys away with a stick."

Jovanica stared at the cracks in the pavement. "No I won't."

"Yes you will," said Borislav, hefting his cane reflexively.

Fleka the Gypsy had been an interested observer. Now he spoke up. "Don't cry about your pretty things: because Boots here is the King of Kiosks. He can get you all the pretty things in the world!"

"Don't you listen to the gypsy," said Borislav. "Listen, Jovanica: your old hair-toy tree, I'm sorry, it's gone for good. You'll have to start over with a brand-new one. It won't know anything about what you want."

"After all my shopping? That's terrible!"

"Never you mind. I'll make you a different deal. Since you're getting to be such a big girl, you're adding a lot of value by making so many highly-informed consumer choices. So, next time, there will be a new economy for you. I'll pay you to teach that toy-tree just what you want to buy."

Fleka stared at him. "What did you just say? You want to *pay this kid for shopping?*"

"That's right."

"She's a little kid!"

"I'm not a little kid!" Jovanica took swift offense. "You're a dirty old gypsy!"

"Jovanica is the early hair-toy adopter, Fleka. She's the market leader here. Whatever hair-toys Jovanica buys, all the other girls come and buy. So, yeah. I'm gonna cut her in on that action. I should have done that long ago."

Jovanica clapped her hands. "Can I have lots of extra hair toys, instead of just stupid money?"

"Absolutely. Of course. Those loyal-customer rewards will keep you coming back here, when you ought to be doing your homework."

Fleka marvelled. "It's completely gone to your head, cashing out your whole stock at once. A man of your age, too."

The arts district never lacked for busybodies. Attracted by the little drama, four of them gathered round Borislav's kiosk. When they caught him glowering at them, they all pretended to need water from his fountain. At least his fountain was still working.

"Here comes my Mama," said Jovanica. Her mother, Ivana, burst head-long from the battered doors of a nearby block of flats. Ivana wore a belted house-robe, a flung-on muffler, a heavy scarf, and brightly-knitted woolen house-slippers. She brandished a laden pillowcase.

Thank God they haven't hurt you!" said Ivana, her breath puffing in the chilly air. She opened her pillowcase. It held a steam iron, a hair dryer, an old gilt mirror, a nickeled hip-flask, a ragged fur stole, and a lidded, copper-bottomed saucepan.

"Mr Boots is all right, Mama," said Jovanica. "They didn't steal anything. He *sold* everything!"

"You sold your kiosk?" said Ivana, and the hurt and shock deepened in her eyes. "You're leaving us?"

"It was business," Borislav muttered. "Sorry for the inconvenience. It'll be a while before things settle down."

"Honestly, I don't need these things. If these things will help you in any way, you're very welcome to them."

"Mama wants you to sell these things," Jovanica offered, with a teen's oppressive helpfulness. "Then you can have the money to fix your store."

Borislav awkwardly patted the kiosk's fiberboard wall. "Ivana, this old place doesn't look like much, so empty and with this big hole...but, well, I had some luck."

"Ma'am, you must be cold in those house slippers," said Fleka the Gypsy. With an elegant swoop of his arm, he gestured at the gilt-and-glassed front counter of the Three Cats café. "May I get you a hot cappucino?"

"You're right, sir, it's cold here." Ivana tucked the neck of her pillowcase, awkwardly, over her arm. "I'm glad things worked out for you, Borislav."

"Yes, things are all right. Really."

Ivana aimed a scowl at the passersby, who watched her with a lasting interest. "We'll be going now, 'Neetsa."

"Mama, I'm not cold. The weather's clearing up!"

"We're going." They left.

Fleka picked at his discolored canine with his forefinger. "So, maestro. What just happened there?"

"She's a nice kid. She's hasty sometimes. The young are like that. That can't be helped." Borislav shrugged. "Let's talk our business inside."

He limped into his empty kiosk. Fleka wedged in behind him and managed to slam the door. Borislav could smell the man's rich, goulash-tinged breath.

"I was never inside one of these before," Fleka remarked, studying every naked seam for the possible point of a burglar's prybar. "I thought about getting a kiosk of my own, but, well, a man gets so restless."

"It's all about the product flow divided by the floor space. By that measure, a kiosk is super-efficient retailing. It's about as efficient as any sole proprietor can do. But it's a one-man enterprise. So, well, a man's just got to go it alone."

Fleka looked at him with wise, round eyes. "That girl who cried so much about her hair. That's not your girl, is she?"

"What? No."

"What happened to the father, then? The flu got him?"

"She was born long after the flu, but, yeah, you're right, her father passed away." Borislav coughed. "He was a good friend of mine. A soldier. Really good-looking guy. His kid is gorgeous."

"So you didn't do anything about that. Because you're not a soldier, and you're not rich, and you're not gorgeous."

"Do anything about what?"

"A woman like that Ivana, she isn't asking for some handsome soldier or some rich-guy boss. A woman like her, she wants maybe a pretty dress. Maybe a dab of perfume. And something in her bed that's better than a hot-water bottle."

"Well, I've got a kiosk and a broken leg."

"All us men have a broken leg. She thought you had nothing. She ran right down here, with anything she could grab for you, stuffed into her pillowcase. So you're not an ugly man. You're a stupid man." Fleka thumped his chest. "I'm the ugly man. Me. I've got three wives: the one in Bucharest, the one in Lublin, and the wife in Linz isn't even a gypsy. They're gonna bury me standing, maestro. That can't be helped, because I'm a man. But that's not what you are. You're a fool."

"Thanks for the free fortune-telling. You know all about this, do you? She and I were here during the hard times. That's what. She and I have a history."

"You're a fanatic. You're a geek. I can see through you like the windows of this kiosk. You should get a life." Fleka thumped the kiosk's wallpaper, and sighed aloud. "Look, life is sad, all right? Life is sad even when you do get a life. So. Boots. Now I'm gonna tell you about this fabrikator of mine, because you got some spare money, and you're gonna buy it from me. It's a nice machine. Very sweet. It comes from a hospital. It's supposed to make bones. So the tutorial is all about making bones, and that's bad, because nobody buys bones. If you are deaf and you want some new little black bones in your ears, that's what this machine is for. Also, these black toys I made with it, I can't paint them. The toys are much too hard, so the paint breaks right off. Whatever you make with this fabrikator, it's hard and black, and you can't paint it, and it belongs by rights inside some sick person. Also, I can't read the stupid tutorials. I hate tutorials. I hate reading."

"Does it run on standard voltage?"

"I got it running on DC off the fuel-cell in my car."

"Where's the feedstock?"

"It comes in big bags. It's a powder, it's a yellow dust. The fab sticks it together somehow, with sparks or something, it turns the powder shiny black and it knits it up real fast. That part, I don't get."

"I'll be offering one price for your machine and all your feedstock."

"There's another thing. That time when I went to Vienna. I gave you my word on that deal. We shook hands on it. That deal was really important, they really needed it, they weren't kidding about it, and, well, I screwed up. Because of Vienna."

"That's right, Fleka. You screwed up bad."

"Well, that's my price. That's part of my price. I'm gonna sell you this toy-maker. We're gonna haul it right out of the car, put it in the kiosk here nice and safe. When I get the chance, I'm gonna bring your bag of coal-straw, too. But we forget about Vienna. We just forget about it."

Borislav said nothing.

"You're gonna forgive me my bad, screwed-up past. That's what I want from you."

"I'm thinking about it."

"That's part of the deal."

"We're going to forget the past, and you're going to give me the machine, the stock, and also fifty bucks."

"Okay, sold."

▲ ▼ ▲

With the fabrikator inside his kiosk, Borislav had no room inside the kiosk for himself. He managed to transfer the tutorials out of the black, silent fab and into his laptop. The sun had come out. Though it was still damp and chilly, the boys from the Three Cats had unstacked their white café chairs. Borislav took a seat there. He ordered black coffee and began perusing awkward machine-translations from the Polish manual.

Selma arrived to bother him. Selma was married to a schoolteacher, a nice guy with a steady job. Selma called herself an artist, made jewelry, and dressed like a lunatic. The schoolteacher thought the world of Selma, although she slept around on him and never cooked him a decent meal.

"Why is your kiosk so empty? What are you doing, just sitting out here?"

Borislav adjusted the angle of his screen. "I'm seizing the means of production."

"What did you do with all my bracelets and necklaces?"

"I sold them."

"All of them?"

"Every last scrap."

Selma sat down as it hit with a mallet. "Then you should buy me glass of champagne!"

Borislav reluctantly pulled his phone and text-messaged the waiter.

It was getting blustery, but Selma preened over her glass of cheap

Italian red. "Don't expect me to replace your stock soon! My artwork's in great demand."

"There's no hurry."

"I broke the luxury market, across the river at the Intercontinental! The hotel store will take all the bone-ivory chokers I can make."

"Mmm-hmm."

"Bone-ivory chokers, they're the perennial favorite of ugly, aging tourist women with wattled necks."

Borislav glanced up from his screen. "Shouldn't you be running along to your workbench?"

"Oh, sure, sure, 'give the people what they want,' that's your sick, petit-bourgeois philosophy! Those foreign tourist women in their big hotels, they want me to make legacy kitsch!"

Borislav waved one hand at the street. "Well, we do live in the old arts district."

"Listen, stupid, when this place was the *young* arts district, it was full of avant-gardists plotting revolution. Look at me for once. Am I from the museum?" Selma yanked her skirt to mid-thigh. "Do I wear little old peasant shoes that turn up at the toes?"

"What the hell has gotten into you? Did you sit on your tack-hammer?"

Selma narrowed her kohl-lined eyes. "What do you expect me to do, with my hands and my artisan skills, when you're making all kinds of adornments with fabrikators? I just saw that stupid thing inside your kiosk there."

Borislav sighed. "Look, I don't know. You tell me what it means, Selma."

"It means revolution. That's what. It means another revolution."

Borislav laughed at her.

Selma scowled and lifted her kid-gloved fingers. "Listen to me. Transition number one. When communism collapsed. The people took to the streets. Everything privatized. There were big market shocks."

"I remember those days. I was a kid, and you weren't even born then."

"Transition Two. When globalism collapsed. There was no oil. There was war and bankruptcy. There was sickness. That when I was a kid."

Borislav said nothing about that. All things considered, his own first Transition had been a kinder time to grow up in.

"Then comes Transition Three." Selma drew a breath. "When this steadily increasing cybernetic intervention in manufacturing liberates a distinctly human creativity."

"Okay, what is that about?"

"I'm telling you what it's about. You're not listening. We're in the third great Transition. It's a revolution. Right now. Here. This isn't Communism, this isn't Globalism. This is the next thing after that. It's happening. No longer merely reacting to this influx of mindless goods, the modern artist uses human creative strength in the name of a revolutionary heterogeneity!"

Selma always talked pretentious, self-important drivel. Not quite like this, though. She'd found herself some new drivel.

"Where did you hear all that?"

"I heard it here in this café! You're just not listening, that's your problem. You never listen to anybody. Word gets around fast in the arts community."

"I live here too, you know. I'd listen to your nutty blither all day, if you ever meant business."

Selma emptied her wine glass. Then she reached inside her hand-loomed, artsy sweater. "If you laugh at this, I'm going to kill you."

Borislav took the necklace she offered him. "Where's this from? Who sent you this?"

"That's mine! I made it. With my hands."

Borislav tugged the tangled chain through his fingers. He was no jeweller, but he knew what decent jewelry looked like. This was indecent jewelry. If the weirdest efforts of search engines looked like products from Mars, then this necklace was straight from Venus. It was slivers of pot-metal, blobs of silver and chips of topaz. It was like jewelry straight out of a nightmare.

"Selma, this isn't your customary work."

"Machines can't dream. I saw this in my dreams."

"Oh. Right, of course."

"Well, it was my nightmare, really. But I woke up! Then I created my vision! I don't have to make that cheap, conventional crap, you know! I only make cheap junk because that's all you are willing to sell!"

"Well...." He had never spoken with frankness to Selma before, but the glittering light in her damp eyes made yesterday's habits seem a little slow-witted. "Well, I wouldn't know what to charge for a work of art like this."

"Somebody would want this, though? Right? Wouldn't they?" She was pleading with him. "Somebody? They would buy my new necklace, right? Even though it's...different."

"No. This isn't the sort of jewelry that the people buy. This is the sort of jewelry that the people stare at, and probably laugh at, too. But then, there would come one special person. She would really want this necklace. She would want this more than anything. She would have to have this thing at absolutely any price."

"I could make more like that," Selma told him, and she touched her heart. "Because now I know where it comes from."

III.

Borislav installed the fab inside the empty kiosk, perched on a stout wooden pedestal, where its workings could be seen by the people.

His first choices for production were, naturally, hair toys. Borislav borrowed some fancy clips from Jovanica, and copied their shapes inside his kiosk with his medical scanner.

Sure enough, the fabricator sprayed out shiny black replicas.

Jovanica amused a small crowd by jumping up and down on the toys. The black clips themselves were well-nigh indestructible, but their cheap metal springs soon snapped.

Whenever a toy broke, however, it was a simple matter to cast it right back into the fabrikator's hopper. The fab chewed away at the black object, with an ozone-like reek, until the fabbed object became the yellow dust again.

Straw, right into gold.

Borislav sketched out a quick business-plan on the back of a Three Cats beer-coaster. With hours of his labor, multiplied by price-per-gram, he soon established his point of profit. He was in a new line of work.

With the new fabrikator, he could copy the shapes of any small object he could scan. Of course, he couldn't literally "copy" everything: a puppy-dog, a nice silk dress, a cold bottle of beer, those were all totally out of the question. But he could copy most anything that was made from some single, rigid material: an empty bottle, a fork, a trash can, a kitchen knife.

The kitchen knives were an immediate hit. The knives were shiny and black, very threatening and scary, and it was clear they would never need sharpening. It was also delightful to see the fabrikator mindlessly spitting up razor-sharp knives. The kids were back in force to watch the action, and this time, even the grown-ups gathered and chattered.

To accommodate the eager crowd of gawkers, the Three Cats boys set out their chairs and tables, and even their striped, overhead canopy, as cheery as if it were summer.

The weather favored them. An impromptu block party broke out.

Mirko from the Three Cats gave him a free meal. "I'm doing very well by this," Mirko said. "You've got yourself a nine-days' wonder here. This sure reminds me of when Transition Two was ending. Remember when those city lights came back on? Brother, those were great days."

"Nine days won't last long. I need to get back inside that kiosk, like normal again."

"It's great to see you out and about, mixing it up with us, Boots. We never talk any more." Mirko spread his hands in apology, then scrubbed the table. "I run this place now...it's the pressure of business...that's all my fault."

Borislav accepted a payment from a kid who'd made himself a rock-solid black model dinosaur. "Mirko, do you have room for a big vending machine, here by your café? I need to get that black beast out of my kiosk. The people need their sticks of gum."

"You really want to build some vendorizing thing out here? Like a bank machine?"

"I guess I do, yeah. It pays."

"Boots, I love this crowd you're bringing me, but why don't you just put your machine wherever they put bank machines? There are hundreds of bank machines." Mirko took his empty plate. "There are millions of bank machines. Those machines took over the world."

IV.

Days passed. The people wouldn't let him get back to normal. It became a public sport to see what people would bring in for the fabrikator to copy. It was common to make weird things as gag gifts: a black, rock-solid spray of roses, for instance. You could hand that black bouquet to your girlfriend for a giggle, and if she got huffy, then you could just bring it back, have it weighed, and get a return-deposit for the yellow dust.

The ongoing street-drama was a tonic for the neighborhood. In no time flat, every café lounger and class-skipping college student was a self-appointed expert about fabs, fabbing, and revolutionary super-fabs that could fab their own fabbing. People brought their relatives to see. Tourists wandered in and took pictures. Naturally they all seemed to want a word with the owner and proprietor.

The people being the people, the holiday air was mixed with unease. Things took a strange turn when a young bride arrived with her wedding china. She paid to copy each piece, then loudly and publicly smashed the originals in the street. A cop showed up to dissuade her. Then the cop wanted a word, too.

Borislav was sitting with Professor Damov, an academician and pious blowhard who ran the local ethnographic museum. The professor's city-sponsored hall specialized in what Damov called "material culture," meaning dusty vitrines full of battle flags, holy medallions, distaffs, fishing nets, spinning wheels, gramophones, and such. Given these new circumstances, the professor had a lot on his mind.

"Officer," said Damov, briskly waving his wineglass, "it may well surprise you to learn this, but the word 'kiosk' is an ancient Ottoman term. In the original Ottoman kiosk, nothing was bought or sold. The kiosk was a regal gift from a prince to the people. A kiosk was a place to breathe the evening air, to meditate, to savor life and living; it was an elegant garden pergola."

"They didn't break their wedding china in the gutter, though," said the cop.

"Oh, no, on the contrary, if a bride misbehaved in those days, she'd be sewn into a leather sack and thrown into the Bosphorus!"

The cop was mollified, and he moved right along, but soon a plainclothes cop showed up and took a prominent seat inside the Three Cats café. This changed the tone of things. The police surveillance proved that something real was happening. It was a kind of salute.

Dusk fell. A group of garage mechanics came by, still in their grimy overalls, and commenced a deadly-serious professional discussion about fabbing trolley parts. A famous stage actor showed up with his entourage, to sign autographs and order drinks for all his "friends."

Some alarmingly clean-cut university students appeared. They weren't there to binge on beer. They took a table, ordered Mirko's cheapest pizza, and started talking in points-of-order.

Next day, the actor brought the whole cast of his play, and the student radicals were back in force. They took more tables, with much more pizza. Now they had a secretary, and a treasurer. Their ringleaders had shiny black political buttons on their coats.

A country bus arrived and disgorged a group of farmers. These peasants made identical copies of something they were desperate to have, yet anxious to hide from all observers.

Ace came by the bustling café. Ace was annoyed to find that he had to wait his turn for any private word with Borislav.

"Calm down, Ace. Have a slice of this pork pizza. The boss here's an old friend of mine, and he's in a generous mood."

"Well, my boss is unhappy," Ace retorted. "There's money being made here, and he wasn't told about it."

"Tell your big guy to relax. I'm not making any more money than I usually do at the kiosk. That should be obvious: consider my rate of production. That machine can only make a few copies an hour."

"Have you finally gone stupid? Look at this crowd!" Ace pulled his shades off and studied the densely clustered café. Despite the lingering chill, a gypsy band was setting up, with accordions and trombones. "Okay, this proves it: see that wise-guy sitting there with that undercover lieutenant? He's one of *them!*"

Borislav cast a sidelong glance at the rival gangster. The North River Boy looked basically identical to Ace: the same woolly hat, cheap black sunglasses, jacket and bad attitude, except for his sneakers, which were red instead of blue. "The River Boys are moving in over here?".

"They always wanted this turf. This is the lively part of town."

That River Boy had some nerve. Gangsters had been shot in the Three Cats café. And not just a few times, either. It was a major local tradition.

"I'm itching to whack that guy," Ace lied, sweating, "but, well, he's sitting over there with that cop! And a pet politician, too!"

Borislav wondered if his eyes were failing. In older days, he would never have missed those details.

There was a whole little tribe of politicians filtering into the cafe, and sitting near the mobster's table. The local politicians always travelled in parties. Small, fractious parties.

One of these local politicals was the arts districts' own national representative. Mr. Savic was a member of the Radical Liberal Democratic Party, a splinter clique of well-meaning, over-educated cranks.

"I'm gonna tell you a good joke, Ace. 'You can get three basic qualities with any politician: Smart, Honest and Effective. But you only get to pick two.'"

Ace blinked. He didn't get it.

Borislav levered himself from his café chair and limped over to provoke a gladhanding from Mr. Savic. The young lawyer was smart and honest, and therefore ineffective. However, Savic, being so smart, was quick to recognize political developments within his own district. He had already appropriated the shiny black button of the young student radicals.

With an ostentatious swoop of his camel's-hair coat-tails, Mr. Savic deigned to sit at Borislav's table. He gave Ace a chilly glare. "Is it necessary that we consort with this organized-crime figure?"

"You tried to get me fired from my job in the embassy," Ace accused him.

"Yes, I did. It's bad enough that the criminal underworld infests our ruling party. We can't have the Europeans paying you off, too."

"That's you all over, Savic: always sucking up to rich foreigners and selling-out the guy on the street!"

"Don't flatter yourself, you jumped-up little crook! You're not 'the street.' The people are the street!"

"Okay, so you got the people to elect you. You took office and you got a pretty haircut. Now you're gonna wrap yourself up in our flag, too? You're gonna steal the last thing the people have left!"

Borislav cleared his throat. "I'm glad we have this chance for a frank talk here. The way I figure it, managing this fabbing business is going to take some smarts and finesse."

The two of them stared at him. "You brought us here?" Ace said. "For our 'smarts and finesse?'"

"Of course I did. You two aren't here by accident, and neither am I. If we're not pulling the strings around here, then who is?"

The politician looked at the gangster.

"There's something to what he says, you know. After all, this is Transition Three."

"So," said Borislav, "knock it off with that tough-talk and do some fresh thinking for once! You sound like your own grandfathers!"

Borislav had surprised himself with this outburst. Savic, to his credit, looked embarrassed, while Ace scratched uneasily under his woolly hat. "Well, listen, Boots," said Ace at last, "even if you, and me, and your posh lawyer pal have us three nice Transition beers together, that's a River Boy sitting over there. What are we supposed to do about that?"

"I am entirely aware of the criminal North River Syndicate," Mr. Savic told him airily. "My investigative committee has been analyzing their gang."

"Oh, so you're analyzing, are you? They must be scared to death."

"There are racketeering laws on the books in this country," said Savic, glowering at Ace. "When we take power and finally have our purge of the criminal elements in this society, we won't stop at arresting that one little punk in his cheap red shoes. We will liquidate his entire parasite class: I mean him, his nightclub-singer girlfriend, his father, his boss, his brothers, his cousins, his entire football club...As long as there is one honest judge in this country, and there are some honest judges, there are *always* some...We will never rest! Never!"

"I've heard about your honest judges," Ace sneered. "You can spot 'em by the smoke columns when their cars blow up."

"Ace, stop talking through your hat. Let me make it crystal clear what's at stake here." Borislav reached under the table and brought up a clear plastic shopping bag. He dropped it on the table with a thud.

Ace took immediate interest. "You output a skull?"

"Ace, this is *my own* skull." The kiosk scanned him every day. So Borislav had his skull on file.

Ace juggled Borislav's skull free of the clear plastic bag, then passed it right over to the politician. "That fab is just superb! Look at the crisp detailing on those sutures!"

"I concur. A remarkable technical achievement." Mr Savic turned the skull upside down, and frowned. "What happened to your teeth?"

"Those are normal."

"You call these wisdom teeth normal?"

"Hey, let me see those," Ace pleaded. Mr Savic rolled Borislav's jet-black skull across the tabletop. Then he cast an over-shoulder look at his fellow politicians, annoyed that they enjoyed themselves so much without him.

"Listen to me, Mr. Savic. When you campaigned, I put your poster up in my kiosk. I even voted for you, and—"

Ace glanced up from the skull's hollow eye-sockets. "You vote, Boots?"

"Yes. I'm an old guy. Us old guys vote."

Savic faked some polite attention.

"Mr. Savic, you're our political leader. You're a Radical Liberal Democrat. Well, we've got ourselves a pretty radical, liberal situation here. What are we supposed to do now?"

"It's very good that you asked me that," nodded Savic. "You must be aware that there are considerable intellectual-property difficulties with your machine."

"What are those?"

"I mean patents and copyrights. Reverse-engineering laws. Trademarks. We don't observe all of those laws in this country of ours...in point of fact, practically speaking, we scarcely observe any... But the rest of the world fully depends on those regulatory structures. So if you go around publicly pirating wedding china—let's just say—well, the makers of wedding-china will surely get wind of that some day. I'd be guessing that you see a civil lawsuit. Cease-and-desist, all of that."

"I see."

"That's just how the world works. If you damage their income, they'll simply have to sue you. Follow the money, follow the lawsuits. A simple principle, really. Although you've got a very nice little sideshow here...It's really brightened up the neighborhood...."

Professor Damov arrived at the cafe. He had brought his wife, Mrs. Professor-Doctor Damova, an icy sociologist with annoying Marxist and feminist tendencies. The lady professor wore a fur coat as solid as a bank-vault, and a bristling fur hat.

Damov pointed out a black plaque on Borislav's tabletop. "I'm sorry, gentleman, but this table is reserved for us."

"Oh," Borislav blurted. He hadn't noticed the fabbed reservation, since it was so black.

"We're having a little party tonight," said Damov, "it's our anniversary."

"Congratulations, sir and madame!" said Mr. Savic. "Why not sit here with us just a moment until your guests arrive?"

A bottle of Mirko's prosecco restored general good feeling. "I'm an arts-district lawyer, after all," said Savic, suavely topping-up everyone's glasses. "So, Borislav, if I were you, I would call this fabrikator an arts installation!"

"Really? Why?"

"Because when those humorless foreigners with their lawsuits try to make a scandal of the arts scene, that never works!" Savic winked at the professor and his wife. "We really enjoyed it, eh? We enjoyed a good show while we had it!"

Ace whipped off his sunglasses. "It's an 'arts installation!' Wow! That is some smart lawyer thinking there!"

Borislav frowned. "Why do you say that?"

Ace leaned in to whisper behind his hand. "Well, because that's what we tell the River Boys! We tell them it's just an art show, then we shut it down. They stay in their old industrial district, and we keep our turf in the old arts district. Everything is cool!"

"That's your big solution?"

"Well, yeah," said Ace, leaning back with a grin. "Hooray for art!"

Borislav's temper rose from a deep well to burn the back of his neck. "That's it, huh? That's what you two sorry sons of bitches have to offer the people? You just want to get rid of the thing! You want to put it out, like spitting on a candle! Nothing *happens* with your stupid approach! You call that a Transition? Everything's just the same as it was before! Nothing changes at all!"

Damov shook his head. "History is always passing. We changed. We're all a year older."

Mrs. Damov spoke up. "I can't believe your fascist, technocratic nonsense! Do you really imagine that you will improve the lives of the people by dropping some weird machine onto their street at random? With no mature consideration of any deeper social issues? I wanted to pick up some milk tonight! Who's manning your kiosk, you goldbricker? Your store is completely empty! Are we supposed to queue?"

Mr. Savic emptied his glass. "Your fabrikator is great fun, but piracy is illegal and immoral. Fair is fair, let's face it."

"Fine," said Borislav, waving his arms, "if that's what you believe, then go tell the people. Tell the people in this cafe, right now, that you want to throw the future away! Go on, do it! Say you're scared of crime! Say they're not mature enough and they have to think it through. Tell the people that they have to vote for that!"

"Let's not be hasty," said Savic.

"Your sordid mechanical invention is useless without a social invention," said Mrs. Damova primly.

"My wife is exactly correct!" Damov beamed. "Because a social invention is much more than gears and circuits, it's...well, it's something like that kiosk. A kiosk was once a way to drink tea in a royal garden. Now it's a way to buy milk! That is social invention!" He clicked her bubbling glass with his own.

Ace mulled this over. "I never thought of it that way. Where can we steal a social invention? How do you copy one of those?"

These were exciting questions. Borislav felt a piercing ray of mental daylight. "That European woman, what's-her-face. She bought-out my kiosk. Who is she? Who does she work for?"

"You mean Dr. Grootjans? She is, uh.... she's the economic affairs liaison for a European Parliamentary investigative committee."

"Right," said Borislav at once, "that's it. Me, too! I want that. Copy me that! I'm the liaison for the investigation Parliament something stupid-or-other."

Savic laughed in delight. "This is getting good."

"You. Mr. Savic. You have a Parliament investigation committee."

"Well, yes, I certainly do."

"Then you should investigate this fabrikator. You place it under formal government investigation. You investigate it, all day and all night. Right here on the street, in public. You issue public reports. And of course you make stuff. You make all kinds of stuff. Stuff to investigate."

"Do I have your proposal clear? You are offering your fabrikator to the government?"

"Sure. Why not? That's better than losing it. I can't sell it to you. I've got no papers for it. So sure, you can look after it. That's my gift to the people."

Savic stroked his chin. "This could become quite an international issue." Suddenly, Savic had the look of a hungry man about to sit at a bonfire and cook up a whole lot of sausages.

"Man, that's even better than making it a stupid art project," Ace enthused. "A stupid government project! Hey, those last forever!"

V.

Savic's new investigation committee was an immediate success. With the political judo typical of the region, the honest politician wangled a large and generous support-grant from the Europeans—basically, in order to investigate himself.

The fab now reformed its efforts: from consumer knickknacks to the pressing needs of the state's public sector. Jet-black fire plugs appeared in the arts district. Jet-black hoods for the broken street lights, and jet-black manhole covers for the streets. Governments bought in bulk, so a primary source for the yellow dust was located. The fab churned busily away right in the public square, next to a railroad tanker full of feed-stock.

Borislav returned to his kiosk. He made a play at resuming his normal business. He was frequently called to testify in front of Savic's busy committee. This resulted in Fleka the Gypsy being briefly arrested, but the man skipped bail. No one made any particular effort to find Fleka. They certainly had never made much effort before.

Investigation soon showed that the fabrikator was stolen property from a hospital in Gdansk. Europeans had long known how to make such fabrikators: fabrikators that used carbon nanotubes. They had simply refrained from doing so.

As a matter of wise precaution, the Europeans had decided not to create devices that could so radically disrupt a well-established political and economic order. The pain of such an act was certain to be great. The benefits were doubtful.

One some grand, abstract level of poetic engineering, it obviously made sense to create super-efficient, widely-distributed, cottage-scale factories that could create as much as possible with as little as possible. If one were inventing industrial civilization from the ground up, then fabbing was a grand idea. But an argument of that kind made no sense to the installed base and the established interests. You couldn't argue a voter out of his job. So fabs had been subtly restricted to waxes, plastics, plaster, papier-mache, and certain metals.

Except, that is, for fabs with medical applications. Medicine, which dealt in agonies of life and death, was never merely a marketplace. There was always somebody whose child had smashed and shattered bones. Sooner or later this violently-interested party, researching a cure for his beloved, would find the logjam and scream: WON'T ONE OF YOU HEARTLESS, INHUMAN BASTARDS THINK OF THE CHILDREN?

Of course, those who had relinquished this technology had the children's best interests at heart. They wanted their children to grow up safe within stable, regulated societies. But one could never explain good things for vaporous, potential future children to someone whose heart and soul was twisted by the suffering of an actual, real-life child.

So a better and different kind of fab had come into being. It was watched over with care...but, as time and circumstance passed, it slipped loose.

Eager to spread the fabbing pork through his constituency, Savic commissioned renowned local artists to design a new breed of kiosk. This futuristic Transition Three ultra-kiosk would house the very fab that could make it. Working with surprising eagerness and speed (given that they were on government salary), these artisan-designers created a new, official, state-supported fabbing-kiosk, an alarmingly splendid, well-nigh monumental kiosk, half Ottoman pavilion, half Stalinist gingerbread, and almost one hundred percent black carbon nanotubes, except for a few necessary steel bolts, copper wires and brass staples.

Borislav knew better than to complain about this. He had to abandon his perfectly decent, old-fashioned, customary kiosk, which was swiftly junked and ripped into tiny recyclable shreds. Then he climbed, with pain and resignation, up the shiny black stairsteps into this eerie, oversized, grandiose rock-solid black fort, this black-paneled royal closet whose ornate, computer-calligraphic roof would make meteors bounce off it like graupel hail.

The cheap glass windows fit badly. The new black shelves confused his fingers. The slick black floor sent his chair skidding wildly. The black carbon walls would not take paint, glue or paper. He felt like an utter fool—but this kiosk hadn't been built for his convenience. This was a kiosk for the new Transition Three generation, crazily radical, liberal guys for whom a "kiosk" was no mere humble conduit, but the fortress of a new culture-war.

A kiosk like this new one could be flung from a passing jet. It could hammer the ground like a plummeting thunderbolt and bounce up completely unharmed. With its ever-brimming bags of gold-dust, a cybernetic tumbling of possessions would boil right out of it: *bottles bags knobs latches wheels pumps,* molds for making other things, tools for making other things; *saws, hammers wrenches levers,* drillbits, screws, screwdrivers, *awls pliers scissors punches,* planes, files, rasps, jacks, carts and shears; pulleys, chains and chain hoists, trolleys, cranes, buckets, bottles, barrels.... All of these items sitting within their digital files as neat as chess pieces, sitting there like the very *idea* of chess pieces, like a mental chess-set awaiting human desire to leap into being and action.

As Borislav limped back, each night, from his black battleship super-kiosk back to his mother's apartment, he could see Transition Three insinuating itself into the fabric of his city.

Transition One had once a look all its own: old socialist buildings of bad brick and substandard plaster, peeling like a secret leprosy, then exploding with the plastic branding symbols of the triumphant West: candy bars, franchised fried-food, provocative lingerie.

Transition Two was a tougher business: he remembered it mostly for its lacks and privations. Empty stores, empty roads, crowds of bicycles, the angry hum of newfangled fuel cells, the cheap glitter of solar roofing, insulation stuffed everywhere like the paper in a pauper's shoes. Crunchy, mulchy-looking new construction. Grass on the rooftops, grass in the trolley-ways. Networking masts and dishes. Those clean, cold, flat-panel lights.

This third Transition had its own native look, too. It was the same song and another verse. It was black. It was jet-black, smooth, anonymous, shiny, stainless, with an occasional rainbow shimmer off the layers and grooves whenever the light was just right, like the ghosts of long-vanished oil slicks.

Revolution was coming. The people wanted more of this game than the regime was allowing them to have. There were five of the fabs running in the city now. Because of growing foreign pressure against "the dangerous proliferation," the local government wouldn't make any more fabrikators. So the people were being denied the full scope of their desire to live differently. The people were already feeling different inside, so they were going to take it to the streets. The politicians were feebly trying to split differences between ways of life that just could not be split.

Did the laws of commerce exist for the people's sake? Or did the people exist as slaves of the so-called laws of commerce? That was populist demagoguery, but that kind of talk was popular for a reason.

Borislav knew that civilization existed through its laws. Humanity suffered and starved whenever outside the law. But those stark facts didn't weigh on the souls of the locals for ten seconds. The local people here were not that kind of people. They had never been that kind of people. Turmoil: that was what the people here had to offer the rest of the world.

The people had flown off the handle for far less than this; for a shot fired at some passing prince, for instance. Little street demonstrations were boiling up from left and right. Those demonstrations waxed and waned, but soon the apple-cart would tip hard. The people would take to the city squares, banging their jet-black kitchen pans, shaking their jet-black house keys. Borislav knew from experience that this voice from the people was a nation-shaking racket. The voice of reason from the fragile government sounded like a cartoon mouse.

Borislav looked after certain matters, for there would no time to look after them, later. He talked to a lawyer and made a new will. He made backups of his data and copies of important documents, and stashed things away in numerous caches. He hoarded canned goods, candles, medicines, tools, even boots. He kept his travel bag packed.

He bought his mother her long-promised cemetery plot. He acquired a handsome headstone for her, too. He even found silk sheets.

VI.

It didn't break in the way he had expected, but then local history could be defined as events that no rational man would expect. It came as a kiosk. It was a brand-new, European kiosk. A civilized, ultimate, decent, well-considered, pre-emptive intervention kiosk. The alien pink-and-white kiosk was beautiful and perfect and clean, and there was no one remotely human inside it.

The automatic kiosk had a kind of silver claw that unerringly picked its goods from its antiseptic shelves, and delivered them to the amazed and trembling customer. These were brilliant goods, they were shiny and gorgeous and tagged with serial numbers and radio-tracking stickers. They glowed all over with reassuring legality: health regulations, total lists of contents, cross-border shipping, tax stamps, associated websites, places to register a complaint.

The superpower kiosk was a thing of interlocking directorates, of 100,000-page regulatory codes and vast, clotted databases, a thing of true brilliance, neurosis and fine etiquette, like a glittering Hapsburg court. And it had been dropped with deliberate accuracy on his own part of Europe—that frail and volatile part—the part about to blow up.

The European kiosk was an almighty vending machine. It replaced its rapidly dwindling stocks in the Black Maria middle of the night, with un-manned cargo vehicles, flat blind anonymous cockroach-like robot things of pink plastic and pink rubber wheels, that snuffled and radared their way across the midnight city and obeyed every traffic law with a crazy punctiliousness.

There was no one to talk to inside the pink European kiosk, although, when addressed through its dozens of microphones, the kiosk could talk the local language, rather beautifully. There were no human relations to be found there. There was no such thing as society: only a crisp interaction.

Gangs of kids grafitti-tagged the pink invader right away. Someone—Ace most likely—made a serious effort to burn it down.

They found Ace dead two days later, in his fancy electric sports car, with three fabbed black bullets through him, and a fabbed black pistol aban-doned on the car's hood.

VII.

Ivana caught him before he could leave for the hills.

"You would go without a word, wouldn't you? Not one word to me, and again you just go!"

"It's the time to go."

"You'd take crazy students with you. You'd take football bullies. You'd take tough-guy gangsters. You'd take gypsies and crooks. You'd go there with anybody. And not take me?"

"We're not on a picnic. And you're not the kind of scum who goes to the hills when there's trouble."

"You're taking guns?"

"You women never understand! You don't take carbines with you when you've got a black factory that can make carbines!" Borislav rubbed his unshaven jaw. Ammo, yes, some ammo might well be needed. Grenades, mortar rounds. He knew all too well how much of that stuff had been buried out in the hills, since the last time. It was like hunting for truffles.

And the landmines. Those were what really terrified him, in an unappeasable fear he would take to his grave. Coming back toward the border, once, he and his fellow vigilantes, laden with their loot, marching in step in the deep snow, each man tramping in another's sunken boot-prints.... Then a flat, lethal thing, with a chip, a wad of explosive and a bellyful of steel bolts, counted their passing footsteps. The virgin snow went blood-red.

Borislav might have easily built such a thing himself. The shade-tree plans for such guerrilla devices were everywhere on the net. He had never built such a bomb, though the prospect gnawed him in nightmares.

Crippled for life, back then, he had raved with high fever, freezing, starving, in a hidden village in the hills. His last confidante was his nurse. Not a wife, not a lover, not anyone from any army, or any gang, or any government. His mother. His mother had the only tie to him so profound that she would leave her city, leave everything, and risk starvation to look after a wounded guerrilla. She brought him soup. He watched her cheeks sink in day by day as she starved herself to feed him.

"You don't have anyone to cook for you out there," Ivana begged.

"You'd be leaving your daughter."

"You're leaving your mother."

She had always been able to sting him that way. Once again, despite everything he knew, he surrendered. "All right, then," he told her. "Fine. Be that way, since you want it so much. If you want to risk everything, then you can be our courier. You go to the camp, and you go to the city. You carry some things for us. You never ask any questions about the things."

"I never ask questions," she lied. They she went to the camp and she just stayed with him. She never left his side, not for a day or a night. Real life started all over for them, once again. Real life was a terrible business.

VIII.

It no longer snowed much in the old ski villages; the weather was a real mess nowadays, and it was the summers you had to look out for. They set up their outlaw fab plant inside an abandoned set of horse-stables.

The zealots talked wildly about copying an "infinite number of fabs," but that was all talk. That wasn't needed. It was only necessary to make and distribute enough fabs to shatter the nerves of the authorities. That was propaganda of the deed.

Certain members of the government were already nodding and winking at their efforts. That was the only reason that they might win. Those hustlers knew that if the weathervanes spun fast enough, the Byzantine cliques that ruled the statehouse would have to break up. There would be chaos. Serious chaos. But then, after some interval, the dust would have to settle on a new arrangement of power-players. Yesterday's staunch conservative, if he survived, would become the solid backer of the new regime. That was how it worked in these parts.

In the meantime, however, some dedicated group of damned fools would have to actually carry out the campaign on the ground. Out of any ten people willing to do this, seven were idiots. These seven were dreamers, rebels by nature, unfit to run so much as a lemonade stand.

One out of the ten would be capable and serious. Another would be genuinely dangerous: a true, amoral fanatic. The last would be the traitor to the group: the police agent, the coward, the informant.

There were thirty people actively involved in the conspiracy, which naturally meant twenty-one idiots. Knowing what he did, Borislav had gone there to prevent the idiots from quarreling over nothing and blowing the effort apart before it could even start. The three capable men had to be kept focussed on building the fabs. The fanatics were best used to sway and intimidate the potential informants.

If they held the rebellion together long enough, they would wear down all the sane people. That was the victory.

The rest was all details, where the devil lived. The idea of self-copying fabs looked great on a sheet of graph paper, but it made little practical sense to make fabs entirely with fabs. Worse yet, there were two vital parts of the fab that simply couldn't be fabbed at all. One was the nozzle that integrated the yellow dust into the black stuff. The other was the big recycler-comb that chewed up the black stuff back into the yellow dust. These two crucial components obviously couldn't be made of the yellow dust or the black stuff.

Instead, they were made of precisely-machined high-voltage European metals that were now being guarded like jewels. These components were way beyond the conspiracy's ability to create.

Two dozen of the fabbing nozzles showed up anyway. They came through the courtesy of some foreign intelligence service. Rumor said the Japanese, for whatever inscrutable reason.

They still had no recycling combs. That was bad. It confounded and betrayed the whole dream of fabs to make them with the nozzles but not the recycling combs. This meant that their outlaw fabs could make things, but never recycle them. A world with fabs like that would be a nightmare: it would slowly but surely fill up with horrible, polluting fabjunk: unusable, indestructible, rock-solid lumps of black slag. Clearly this dark prospect had much affected the counsels of the original inventors.

There were also many dark claims that carbon nanotubes had dire health effects: because they were indestructible fibers, something like asbestos. And that was true: carbon nanotubes did cause cancer. However, they caused rather less cancer than several thousand other substances already in daily use.

It took all summer for the competent men to bang together the first outlaw fabs. Then it became necessary to sacrifice the idiots, in order to distribute the hardware. The idiots, shrill and eager as ever, were told to drive the fabs as far as possible from the original factory, then hand them over to sympathizers and scram.

Four of the five idiots were arrested almost at once. Then the camp was raided by helicopters.

However, Borislav had fully expected this response. He had moved the camp. In the city, riots were under way. It didn't matter who "won" these riots, because rioting melted the status quo. The police were hitting the students with indestructible black batons. The kids were slashing their paddy-wagon tires with indestructible black kitchen knives.

At this point, one of the fanatics had a major brainwave. He demanded that they send out dozens of fake black boxes that merely *looked* like fabs. There was no political need for their futuristic promises of plenty to actually work.

This cynical scheme was much less work than creating real fabs, so it was swiftly adopted. More than that: it was picked up, everywhere, by copycats. People were watching the struggle: in Bucharest, Lublin, Tbilisi; in Bratislava, Warsaw, and Prague. People were dipping ordinary objects in black lacquer to make them look fabbed. People were distributing handbooks for fabs, and files for making fabs. For every active crank who really wanted to make a fab, there were a hundred people who wanted to know how to do it. Just in case.

Some active cranks were succeeding. Those who failed became martyrs. As resistance spread like spilled ink, there were simply too many people implicated to classify it as criminal activity.

Once the military contractors realized there were very good reasons to make giant fabs the size of shipyards, the game was basically over. Transition Three was the new realpolitik. The new economy was the stuff of the everyday. The older order was over. It was something no one managed to remember, or even wanted to manage to remember.

The rest of it was quiet moves toward checkmate. And then the game just stopped. Someone tipped over the White King, in such a sweet, subtle, velvety way that one would have scarcely guessed that there had ever been a White King to fight against at all.

IX.

Borislav went to prison. It was necessary that somebody should go. The idiots were only the idiots. The competent guys had quickly found good positions in the new regime. The fanatics had despaired of the new dispensation, and run off to nurse their bitter disillusionment.

As a working rebel whose primary job had been public figurehead, Borislav was the reasonable party for public punishment.

Borislav turned himself in to a sympathetic set of cops who would look much better for catching him. They arrested him in a blaze of publicity. He was charged with "conspiracy": a rather merciful charge, given the host of genuine crimes committed by his group. Those were the necessary, everyday crimes of any revolutionary movement, crimes such as racketeering, theft of services, cross-border smuggling, subversion and sedition, product piracy, copyright infringement, money-laundering, fake identities, squatting inside stolen property, illegal possession of firearms, and so forth.

Borislav and his various allies weren't charged with those many crimes. On the contrary; since he himself had been so loudly and publicly apprehended, those crimes of the others were quietly overlooked.

While sitting inside his prison cell, which was not entirely unlike a kiosk, Borislav discovered the true meaning of the old term "penitentiary." The original intention of prisons was that people inside them should be penitent people. Penitent people were supposed to meditate and contemplate their way out of their own moral failings. That was the original idea.

Of course, any real, modern "penitentiary" consisted mostly of frantic business dealings. Nobody "owned" much of anything inside the prison, other than a steel bunk and a chance at a shower, so simple goods such as talcum powder loomed very large in the local imagination. Borislav, who fully understood street-trading, naturally did very well at this. At least, he did much better than the vengeful, mentally limited people who were doomed to inhabit most jails.

Borislav thought a lot about the people in the jails. They, too, were the people, and many of those people were getting into jail because of him. In any Transition, people lost their jobs. They were broke, they lacked prospects. So they did something desperate.

Borislav did not much regret the turmoil he had caused the world, but he often thought about what it meant and how it must feel. Somewhere, inside some prison, was some rather nice young guy, with a wife and kids, whose job was gone because the fabs took it away. This guy had a shaven head, an ugly orange jumpsuit, and appalling food, just like Borislav himself.

But that young guy was in the jail with less good reason. And with much less hope. And with much more regret.

That guy was suffering. Nobody gave a damn about him. If there was any justice, someone should mindfully suffer, and be penitent, because of the harsh wrong done that guy.

Borislav's mother came to visit him in the jail. She brought printouts from many self-appointed sympathizers. The world seemed to be full of strange foreign people who had nothing better to do with their time than to email tender, supportive screeds to political prisoners. Ivana, something of a mixed comfort to him in their days of real life, did not visit the jail or see him. Ivana knew how to cut her losses when her men deliberately left her to do something stupid, such as volunteering for a prison.

These strangers and foreigners expressed odd, truncated, malformed ideas of what he had been doing. Because they were the Voice of History.

He himself had no such voice to give to history. He came from a small place under unique circumstances. People who hadn't lived there would never understand it. Those who had lived there were too close to understand it. There was just no understanding for it. There were just...the events. Events, transitions, new things. Things like the black kiosks.

These new kiosks...No matter where they were scattered in the world, they all had the sinister, strange, overly-dignified look of his own original black kiosk. Because the people had seen those kiosks. The people knew well what a black fabbing kiosk was supposed to look like. Those frills, those fringes, that peaked top, that was just how you knew one. That was their proper look. You went there to make your kid's baby-shoes indestructible. The kiosks did what they did, and they were what they were. They were everywhere, and that was that.

After twenty-two months, a decent interval, the new regime pardoned him as part of a general amnesty. He was told to keep his nose clean and his mouth shut. Borislav did this. He didn't have much to say, anyway.

X.

Time passed. Borislav went back to the older kind of kiosk. Unlike the fancy new black fabbing kiosk, these older ones sold things that couldn't be fabbed: foodstuffs, mostly.

Now that fabs were everywhere and in public, fabbing technology was advancing by leaps and bounds. Surfaces were roughened so they shone with pastel colors. Technicians learned how to make the fibers fluffier, for bendable, flexible parts. The world was in a Transition, but no transition ended the world. A revolution just turned a layer in the compost heap of history, compressing that which now lay buried, bringing air and light to something hidden.

On a whim, Borislav went into surgery and had his shinbone fabbed. His new right shinbone was the identical, mirror-reversed copy of his left shinbone. After a boring recuperation, for he was an older man now and the flesh didn't heal as it once had, he found himself able to walk on an even keel for the first time in twenty-five years.

Now he could walk. So he walked a great deal. He didn't skip and jump for joy, but he rather enjoyed walking properly. He strolled the boulevards, he saw some sights, he wore much nicer shoes.

Then his right knee gave out, mostly from all that walking on an indestructible artificial bone. So he had to go back to the cane once again. No cure was a miracle panacea: but thanks to technology, the trouble had crept closer to his heart.

That made a difference. The shattered leg had oppressed him during most of his lifetime. That wound had squeezed his soul into its own shape. The bad knee would never have a chance to do that, because he simply wouldn't live that long. So the leg was a tragedy. The knee was an episode.

It was no great effort to walk the modest distance from his apartment block to his mother's grave. The city kept threatening to demolish his old apartments. They were ugly and increasingly old fashioned, and they frankly needed to go. But the government's threats of improvement were generally empty, and the rents would see him through. He was a landlord. That was never a popular job, but someone was always going to take it. It might as well be someone who understood the plumbing.

It gave him great satisfaction that his mother had the last true granite headstone in the local graveyard. All the rest of them were fabbed.

Dr. Grootjans was no longer working in a government. Dr. Grootjans was remarkably well-preserved. If anything, this female functionary from an alien system looked *younger* than she had looked, years before. She had two prim Nordic braids. She wore a dainty little off-pink sweater. She had high heels.

Dr. Grootjans was writing about her experiences in the transition. This was her personal, confessional text, on the net of course, accompanied by photographs, sound recordings, links to other sites, and much supportive reader commentary.

"Her gravestone has a handsome Cyrillic font," said Dr. Grootjans.

Borislav touched a handkerchief to his lips. "Tradition does not mean that the living are dead. Tradition means that the dead are living."

Dr. Grootjans happily wrote this down. This customary action of hers had irritated him at first. However, her strange habits were growing on him.

Would it kill him that this over-educated foreign woman subjected him to her academic study? Nobody else was bothering. To the neighborhood, to the people, he was a crippled, short-tempered old landlord. To her, the scholar-bureaucrat, he was a mysterious figure of international significance. Her version of events was hopelessly distorted and self-serving. But it was a version of events.

"Tell me about this grave," she said. "What are we doing here?"

"You wanted to see what I do these days. Well, this is what I do." Borislav set a pretty funeral bouquet against the headstone. Then he lit candles.

"Why do you do this?"

"Why do you ask?"

"You're a rational man. You can't believe in religious rituals."

"No," he told her, "I don't believe. I know they are just rituals."

"Why do it, then?"

He knew why, but he did not know how to give her that sermon. He did it because it was a gift. It was a liberating gift for him, because it was given with no thought of any profit or return. A deliberate gift with *no possibility* of return.

Those gifts were the stuff of history and futurity. Because gifts of that kind were also the gifts that the living received from the dead.

The gifts we received from the dead: those were the world's only genuine gifts. All the other things in the world were commodities. The dead were, by definition, those who gave to us without reward. And, especially: our dead gave to us, the living, within a dead context. Their gifts to us were not just abjectly generous, but archaic and profoundly confusing.

Whenever we disciplined ourselves, and sacrificed ourselves, in some vague hope of benefiting posterity, in some ambition to create a better future beyond our own moment in time, then we were doing something beyond a rational analysis. Those in that future could never see us with our own eyes: they would only see us with the eyes that we ourselves gave to them. Never with our own eyes: always with their own. And the future's eyes always saw the truths of the past as blinkered, backward, halting. Superstition.

"Why?" she said.

Borislav knocked the snow from his elegant shoes. "I have a big heart."